Owen supposed it was inevitable that a Wampyr should turn up on Mistworld. Everyone and everything else did. This particular specimen was seven foot tall, muscular in a lithe, feline way, and altogether disturbing. His skin was completely colourless, and Owen knew it would be ice cold to the touch. His face was long and angular, all planes and high cheekbones, and his eyes were dark and unblinking. The smile that stretched his pale lips wasn't reflected in his eyes, and he held himself like a fighter waiting for the bell. For the moment his gaze was fixed on Hazel, and Owen was glad for it to stay that way. The Wampyr was openly disturbing, on some deep, primal level. Owen glanced at Hazel to see how she was taking it, and was surprised to find she seemed more angry than anything else.

'Hazel d'Ark,' said the Wampyr, in a voice as cold and eager as the grave. 'You've come back to me.'

'Lucien Abbott,' said Hazel disgustedly. 'Of all people I didn't want to meet, you were right at the top of the list. Why couldn't you have done the decent thing, and died long ago?'

'I did,' said Abbott.

Also by Simon R. Green in paperback

DEATHSTALKER REBELLION
DEATHSTALKER WAR
MISTWORLD
GHOSTWORLD
HELLWORLD
BLUE MOON RISING
BLOOD AND HONOUR
DOWN AMONG THE DEAD MEN
SHADOWS FALL

SIMON R. GREEN
DEATHSTALKER

VISTA

First published in Great Britain 1995
by Victor Gollancz

This Vista edition published 1997
Vista is an imprint of the Cassell Group
Wellington House, 125 Strand, London WC2R 0BB

A catalogue record for this book is
available from the British Library.

ISBN 0 575 60160 4

Printed and bound in Great Britain
by Cox & Wyman Ltd, Reading, Berks

97 98 99   10 9 8 7 6 5 4 3 2

CHAPTER ONE

Clash by Night

It gets dark, out on the Rim. Strange planets and stranger people can be found on the edge of the Empire, where habitable worlds are few, and civilization grows thin. Beyond the Rim lies uncharted darkness, where no stars shine and few ships go. It's easy to get lost out there, far away from everything. Starcruisers patrol up to the Rim, but there are never enough ships to cover the vast areas of open space. The Empire is growing too large, too cumbersome, though no one will admit it, or at least, no one who matters. Every year more worlds are brought into the Empire, and the frontiers press hungrily outwards. But not on the Rim. The Empire stops cold there, dwarfed by the unplumbable depths of the Darkvoid.

It's dark out there. Ships disappear sometimes, and are never seen again. No one knows why. The colonized worlds make themselves as self-sufficient as they can, and turn their eyes away from the endless dark. Crime flourishes on the Rim, unthinkable distances from the hub of the Empire's strict laws; some transgressions as old as humanity, others newly birthed by the Empire's ever-growing sciences. For the moment the Empire's starcruisers still keep the lid on things, dropping unannounced out of hyperspace to enforce the law with brutal efficiency, but they can't be everywhere. Strange forces are at work on the Rim, patient and terrible, and all it will take to set them off is a simple clash between two starships, off the backwater planet of Virimonde.

In high orbit around Virimonde, the pirate ship *Shard* sailed silently through the long night, hiding itself from unfriendly

5

eyes. Not a big ship, the *Shard*, built more for speed than endurance, and passed from hand to hand through a dozen owners and commands. Now she carried clonelcggers and body banks, and every man's hand was turned against her. Deep in the bowels of the ship Hazel d'Ark, pirate, clonelegger and bon vivant, strode scowling through the dimly lit steel corridors and wished she was somewhere else. Anywhere else. The *Shard* wasn't a luxurious craft at the best of times, but with most of the ship's power diverted to maintaining the body banks, the old scut seemed even gloomier than usual. Which took some doing.

Hazel d'Ark, last owner of a once noble name, came at last to the locked door that led to the cargo bay, and stood waiting impatiently for the door's sensors to recognize her. Her mood was bad, bordering on foul, and had been ever since they dropped out of hyperspace six hours ago to take up orbit around Virimonde. Six hours of waiting for some word from their contacts down below. Something was wrong.

They couldn't afford to stay much longer, but they couldn't leave either. So they waited. Hazel wasn't expecting any trouble from the planet's security people. The *Shard* might be old, but she had state-of-the-art cloaking devices, more than enough to fool anything the peasants on Virimonde had. Not that there was much the planet could do, even if it knew the pirates were there. Virimonde was a low-tech, agricultural world, with more livestock than people. Its only contact with the Empire was a monthly cargo transporter, and an occasional patrolling starcruiser. Neither of which was expected for some weeks.

Hazel glared at the closed door before her, and kicked the frame hard. The door hissed open, and she stepped through into the freezing cold of the cargo bay. The door locked itself behind her. A pearly haze misted the air and burned cold in her lungs. She shuddered quickly and turned up the heating elements in her uniform. The body banks needed the cold at a specific temperature to preserve and maintain their cargo of human tissues for cloning. Hazel looked quickly about her and then accessed her comm implant.

'Hannah, this is Hazel. Acknowledge.'

'I hear you, Hazel,' said the ship's AI. 'What can I do for you?'

'Edit the signals from the cargo bay's security sensors so it appears I'm not here.'

Hannah sighed. The Artificial Intelligence didn't have human emotions, but it liked to pretend. 'Now, Hazel, you know you're not supposed to be in there. You'll get us both into trouble.'

'Do it anyway, or I'll tell the Captain about your personal video collection of his private moments.'

'I wouldn't have shown you those if I'd known you were going to use them to blackmail me. They're a perfectly innocent collection, after all.'

'Computer . . .'

'All right, all right. I'm editing the sensors. Happy now?'

'Close as I'll get. And Hannah; if I ever catch you snooping on my private moments, I'll perform a lobotomy on your main systems with a shrapnel grenade. Got it?'

Hannah sniffed once, and broke off contact. Hazel smiled briefly. All the AIs the Captain could have chosen, and he had to buy a peeping tom. Somehow that was typical of the *Shard* and its luck. She looked about her at the long rows of body banks, huge and blocky, their dull metal sides smeared with frost and caked with ice. Ugly things, for an ugly business. The AI was quite right; she had no business in the cargo bay, and no authority either. Not that she gave a damn. Hazel d'Ark had a long history of not giving a damn, not to mention doing whatever she happened to feel was necessary and to hell with the consequences. Which was at least partly why she'd ended up an outlaw and a pirate.

She moved slowly towards the nearest body bank, drawn by a curious mixture of revulsion and fascination. She'd had no illusions about what she was getting into when she'd signed on board the *Shard* as a clonelegger, but somehow it was different, up close. The body banks were a source of life and longevity, but the spotless cargo bay still seemed to reek of death. Most of the lights were out, conserving energy. Never knew when you might need the extra power to make a run for it. Cloneleggers were not popular, either with the authorities or those who had a need for their services.

Hazel walked slowly down the central aisle between the body banks. Visions of hearts and lungs and kidneys burned brightly in her mind's eye, pulsing with fresh crimson blood. She was sure they didn't actually look like that, preserved in the icy cold of the machines, but that was how she thought of them. Her fellow cloneleggers just referred to them as the merchandise, as casual as any butcher in his slaughterhouse. She stopped and looked around her, surrounded by hundreds upon hundreds of human organs and tissues, enough to fill a dozen battlegrounds, and every one of them worthless. Contaminated beyond saving by a smuggled-in virus. That was what you got for making enemies in the clonelegging business.

Not too long before, the Captain had come out ahead in a business deal with the Boneyard Boys, through his usual mixture of high risk taking and low cunning. Contracts the *Shard* had lusted after for years had fallen into their hands as though by magic. Hazel smiled grimly. They should have known better. Clonelegging was a cut-throat business. Sometimes literally.

Clonelegging was illegal, a crime punishable by death, but that did nothing to slow down the flood of people ready and willing to make a living out of death. Officially, the use of cloned human tissues for transplanting was only allowed to the highest of the high, those with breeding and position and a not too small fortune. Couldn't have the lower orders leading long and healthy lives; there were far too many of them as it was, even with the newly colonized worlds opening up vast new territories for settling. Besides; it might give the lower orders ideas above their station.

But unofficially, if you had enough money and knew the right (or more strictly speaking) wrong people, you could get whatever part of you was failing replaced, either by cloning your own tissues, or by illegally obtained organs from body banks. There was never any risk of rejection with a person's own cloned tissues, but surprisingly often the original organs

8

turned out to have built-in defects, or there were other problems that made direct cloning impossible, and that was when the bodysnatchers came into their own. And then no one was safe, living or dead.

Most planets cremated their dead, by order of the Empress, to ensure that donor organs would only be available to the right sort of people, but backwater planets often cultivated illegal secret graveyards and mausoleums. Never knew when the crops might fail, or business turn bad, and you might need a little cash in the bank, so to speak. So the cloneleggers made the rounds, and everyone made a little money. The cloneleggers made a lot. Demand was high. All they had to do was maintain a full stocklist, and wait for someone to come knocking tentatively at their door.

Only it isn't always that simple. Cloning is a delicate business, with all sorts of things that can go wrong. Cloning wears out an organ fast, and then it has to be replaced in stock. The body banks have a voracious appetite. And the hidden cemeteries are few and far between, often with exclusive contracts to one particular set of cloneleggers. So sometimes the bodysnatchers go out in disguise to walk among the living, looking for those who won't be missed too much. A shame, of course, but you can't make an omelette, and all that . . .

When Hazel joined the *Shard*'s crew four planets back, the Captain had assured her they were graverobbers only. Except when things got really bad. Get in quick, dig up enough merchandise to fill the body banks, and then get the hell out of there before someone sold them out for an Empire reward. There's always someone. Only this time it had all gone wrong. The Boneyard Boys had got in first, and contaminated the merchandise with a really vicious virus that hadn't shown up on any of the usual tests. Now every organ they had was worthless, and they had contracts to fill with people who weren't known for their patience or understanding.

So Captain Markee had gone cap in hand to the Blood Runners out in the Obeah systems, and begged a favour. Hazel still shuddered when she thought of what she and the rest of the crew had had to promise, in return for the information the Blood Runners provided. Nothing could be allowed to go wrong with this deal. There were worse things than death.

So the Blood Runners had put them in touch with people on Virimonde, out on the Rim, and the *Shard* had come to play the old game one more time. One last throw of the dice.

Hazel wondered, not for the first time, how she'd come to this. It wasn't exactly what she'd had in mind for herself, when she left her home planet ten minutes ahead of a restraining order and a lengthy stay in gaol, in search of excitement and adventure. Cloneleggers were the lowest of the low, the scum of the Empire. Even a beggar with leprosy would pause to spit on a clonelegger. People who walked in certain high circles liked to boast of their personal cloneleggers, as one might of an attack beast trained for the Arenas, but no one had a good word for them in open society. They were pariahs, outcasts, untouchables, for daring to traffic in the trade that no one wanted to admit existed.

Hazel sighed, tiredly. She'd leave the *Shard* in a moment, if she had anywhere to go. Hazel d'Ark, twenty-three years old, tall, lithely muscular, with a sharp pointed face and a mane of long ratty red hair. Green eyes that missed nothing, and a smile so quick people often missed it if they weren't looking for it. She'd worked in one dirty job after another since leaving home, and it showed in the wariness of her stance and the naked suspicion in her scowl. She'd been a mercenary on Loki, a bodyguard on Golgotha, and, most recently, part of the security forces on Brahmin II, which was where Captain Markee found her, running for her life. A superior officer had decided his rank entitled him to certain rights to her body, and not for cloning, either. Hazel d'Ark had disagreed. She'd decided a long time ago that she wasn't giving away anything she could sell. It came to blows and ended in tears, and Hazel went on the run again with the bastard's blood still dripping from her knife.

At the time, a little discreet clonelegging had seemed like a definite career advancement. Low profile, low risk, the only hard work a little digging . . . perfect. Especially with so many people hot on her trail. Just lately, it seemed there was always someone looking for her with bad intent. It was all her own fault; she knew that. She'd always had a tendency to wander into illegal deals in search of fast money, and only afterwards discover what she'd let herself in for. But even though she'd done a lot of things in her time that she wasn't proud of, kidnapping people and butchering them in cold blood for their organs had to be a new low, even for her.

She didn't know if she could do it. She had a feeling it might be a matter of principle, something she wasn't exactly familiar with. But everyone draws the line somewhere. She ran through the options open to her. It didn't take long. She couldn't just announce her new-found integrity to her fellow crew members. Not unless she wanted to see the inside of a body bank the hard way. She could always jump ship; ride one of the escape pods down to the planet below, and lose herself in the crowds. But Virimonde was a primitive place by all accounts, based around hard work and damn all luxuries. Not a good place to be stranded on the run. Especially when there are people looking for you on both sides of the law.

Hazel d'Ark looked around her at the waiting body banks, and shuddered, not entirely from the cold.

What am I going to do? What the hell am I going to do?

Lights flared around her as the ship's alarms went crazy. Hazel winced away from the sudden blare of sound, her hand dropping automatically to the gun at her side. Her first thought was a hull breach, but she quickly realized that if there'd been an explosive decompression in any part of the ship, she'd have felt its effects long before the sirens went off. She accessed the emergency channel through her comm implant, and a babble of voices filled her head. It only took her a moment to pick out the phrase *battle stations*, and then she was off and running. Someone had pierced the *Shard*'s cloaking device, and that was supposed to be impossible for anything less than an Imperial starcruiser. And if the Empire had found them, there was a very real danger that Hazel d'Ark's career as a clonelegger was over before it had even begun.

Just my luck, thought Hazel bitterly as she ran out of the cargo bay and headed for the bridge. *Just my luck to get picked up for one of the few crimes I haven't actually committed.*

'Hannah; talk to me. How deep are we in it?'

'I'm afraid you couldn't get much deeper without crouching,' the AI said calmly through her implant. 'An Imperial starcruiser has dropped out of hyperspace and taken up orbit around Virimonde. Their sensors brushed aside our cloaking devices in well under a second, and it didn't take them much longer to issue a challenge. I'm currently lying through my electronic teeth, but there's a limit to how long I can hope to bluff them. And I have a strong suspicion it isn't going to be anywhere near long enough for us to raise enough power to escape into hyperspace.'

'Couldn't we make a run for it in normal space?'

'This is an Imperial starcruiser we're discussing, Hazel. They don't come much more powerful than this. They'd blast us into tiny glowing fragments before we even left orbit.'

'We've got shields.'

'They've got two hundred and fifty disrupter cannon and power to burn.'

'Can we fight them?'

'If you really want to annoy them.'

'Dammit, there must be something we can do! You're the one with the immense intellect; think of something!'

'You could always surrender.'

Hazel would have laughed sarcastically, but she was too short of breath. She pounded down the steel corridor, head aching from the clamour of the alarm siren, and finally burst on to the bridge and threw herself into her fire control seat. Whatever was going on, she was sure she'd feel a damn sight more secure plugged into the *Shard*'s two disrupter cannon. Theoretically, the AI was far more capable of aiming and firing the ship's disrupters, but what one AI could plan another could anticipate and match. Human unpredictability provided an edge no AI could deal with. Which is why there were always human gunners on every ship.

Hazel meshed her mind with the computers through her implant, and spread out through the fire systems, running

12

quickly through the warm-up routines. Computer displays sprang up all around her, and a steady stream of information flowed through her thoughts. Hazel got her first real look at the starcruiser, and her heart sank. The Empire ship was a hundred times bigger, dwarfing the *Shard* like a minnow next to a whale. The AI ran quickly through a list of the Imperial craft's capabilities, and Hazel's heart sank even further. Disrupter cannon, force shields, assault torpedoes . . . The *Shard* wouldn't stand a chance, but then, she'd always known that. The only thing big enough to take on a starcruiser was another starcruiser. Hazel swallowed hard, and let her thoughts move cautiously through the two fire turrets. The cannon stirred restlessly at her touch, picking out targets of opportunity on the Imperial ship.

Hazel's breathing had almost slowed to normal, but her anger took it away again as she studied the starcruiser. What the hell was it doing here? There wasn't one due for weeks, officially. It couldn't have come looking for the *Shard*; a handful of cloneleggers on a pirate ship weren't that important. Which was all very fine and logical, but the Imperial ship was still there, large as life and twice as deadly, its ranked cannon no doubt locked on the pirate ship and ready to fire at a moment's notice. Hazel scowled fiercely. They couldn't run, they couldn't fight, and they didn't dare surrender. Maybe they could make a deal . . . if they could think of something to bargain with. Her mind worked frantically, but came up with nothing. Unless Captain Markee had a whole pack of aces up his sleeve, the Empire ship had them cold.

She looked across the bridge at the Captain. Terrence Markee was in his late forties; large and solid and reliable. He'd been a pirate all his adult life, and loved every illegal moment of it. He dressed like a gaudy if somewhat dated dandy, all flashing silks and clashing colours, and affected an aristocratic accent he had no right to. At the moment he was scowling at his displays and growling a series of calm, quiet orders. Slightly reassured that at least one person on the bridge wasn't panicking, Hazel let her eyes drift round the cramped confines of the command area. Anything was better than looking at the Empire ship.

13

The bridge of the *Shard* was a mess. Half the lights weren't working at any given time, because bulbs were expensive and they never carried enough spares, and the limited low-ceilinged space was crammed with work stations, computer displays and terminals; never mind the sensor panels and fire control station. Officially there was room for seven crew on the bridge, including the Captain, but as usual there were only four, including the Captain and Hazel. The *Shard* operated on a bare minimum crew, with everyone holding down as many jobs as they could handle. Half the systems weren't working, but you learned to put up with that as long as the essentials were maintained. Repairs were hideously expensive, stardocks especially so. Clonelegging could provide a very comfortable living if you were in the right place at the right time, and kept up a good stock, but it was a crowded field these days, and small independent ships like the *Shard* were being forced out. Markee had been relying on the Virimonde run to restock the body banks, and repair his fortunes and his ship. And then he made an enemy of the Boneyard Boys, and everything went to hell in a hurry.

A thought struck Hazel, and she looked back at Markee. 'Captain; how about if we just dump everything? Throw the merchandise and body banks out the airlock and let it all burn up falling through Virimonde's atmosphere? No evidence, no proof.'

'Nice idea,' said Markee. 'And if that ship hadn't been a starcruiser, we might have got away with it. But with the kind of sensors they've got, they could identify every organ and tissue sample independently, and read the maker's name on the body banks. Their sensors' records would make damning evidence. So; we can't dump it, and we can't afford to be caught with it. Doesn't leave much room for manoeuvre, does it?' He smiled briefly. 'I suppose we could always cat the merchandise. How's your appetite, Hazel?'

'Not as good as it was a moment ago. Basically, what you're saying is we're screwed if we do, and screwed if we don't. I suppose surrender is out of the question?'

Markee's smile came and went again. 'There's enough evidence on this ship to hang us all. Slowly.'

'So what are we going to do?'

'The one thing they won't expect. We'll fight. Who knows; maybe we'll get lucky.'

'And if we don't?'

'Then at least we'll die quickly. Are the guns ready?'

'Ready as they'll ever be. They haven't been checked, let alone fired, in ages.' Hazel glared at the massive ship on the screens before her. Tears of anger and frustration burned in her eyes, but she wouldn't give in to them. Her luck had just turned bad one time too many, that was all. She pounded a fist on the arm of her chair. 'What the hell is an Empire ship *doing* here anyway? We only made the decision to come here twelve hours ago! They couldn't have known about us.'

She didn't see Markee shrug, but she could hear it in his voice. 'A lot can happen in twelve hours, especially when you've got enemies. Any number of people could have found out where we were heading, and then sold the information to the Empire.'

'But who the hell would send a whole bloody starcruiser after small fry like us?'

'Good question. Wish I had a good answer for you. Could be the Boneyard Boys, calling in an old favour to put the finishing touch to our destruction. It doesn't matter. Now suck it in, and stand ready with your disrupters. Hannah is currently telling the Empire ship that we're an ambulance craft on a mercy mission to a plague outbreak. She's feeding them all kinds of convincing details, but I don't think they're buying it. Certainly they aren't going to buy it long enough for our engines to power up for a jump into hyperspace.'

Hazel's mouth was suddenly dry. 'Captain; our two guns aren't worth spit against all theirs. There must be something else we can try.'

'Sorry, Hazel; nothing springs to mind. You know what they say; if you can't take a joke, you shouldn't have joined.'

Hazel waited, but Markee had nothing more to say. She concentrated on her fire controls. Both the *Shard* and the starcruiser had force screens that could withstand a hell of a lot of punishment, but they also used up a hell of a lot of

15

energy, and the *Shard*'s shields would go down long before the Empire ship's did. It came to Hazel then that she was going to die out in the empty spaces of the Rim, far from home and Family and honour. Just as she'd always known she would.

On the Imperial starcruiser *Darkwind*, Captain John Silence sat at ease in his command chair, looking out over his efficiently murmuring bridge. Every man at his station, every system running smoothly, just as it should be. The small craft on the main viewscreen seemed surprisingly insignificant to be taking up so much of his time and attention. Still, nothing that small was going to give him any trouble, and the prize money its capture would bring would be a welcome bonus. At least that way something good might come of this mission. He tried to push the thought aside, but it persisted. He had better things to do than waste time hunting down some poor bastard who probably didn't even know he'd been outlawed yet. But man proposes, and the Empress disposes. She said go, and you went. If you liked having your head still attached to your body.

He looked at the starship on the main viewscreen, and frowned slightly. Probably just a pirate ship involved in something dubious, but what was it doing here at the same time as the *Darkwind*? Could it have come to try and save the Deathstalker? Owen Deathstalker, Lord of Virimonde. Holder of a proud name and title, condemned to death by the Empress's word. She hadn't said why, and Silence hadn't asked. One didn't. But Silence had quietly checked the files anyway, just in case there was something there he ought to know. If there was, he missed it. Owen Deathstalker might be descended from a famous warrior Clan, but in his case the blood seemed to be running thin. His people ran Virimonde efficiently enough, but the man himself was just an amateur historian. Wrote long books on obscure subjects that no one ever read. Looking back was unofficially discouraged; there were too many subjects the Empire preferred its people to forget. Presumably the Deathstalker had stumbled across something he shouldn't have. Whatever it was, Owen Death-stalker wouldn't be writing a book about it this time. He was

16

outlawed, a non-person with a price on his head. Literally. The Empress liked proof of her kills.

Silence shrugged, and sat back in his command chair. A tall, lean man in his forties, with a thickening waistline and a receding hairline he tried not to be touchy about. He sat in the command chair with a quiet dignity, as though he belonged there. He'd served the Empire to the best of his ability all his adult life, and if sometimes he found himself on a mission he had no stomach for, well that was the Empire for you, under her Imperial Majesty Lionstone XIV. Also known as the Iron Bitch. Silence stopped that thought short. It wasn't wise to let one's thoughts run free in some directions. You never knew when an esper might be listening. He concentrated on the pirate ship before him. Small craft, built more for speed than action. No threat to a starcruiser. But she shouldn't have been here . . . not just now. Silence looked across at his comm officer.

'Do we have an identification on her yet?'

'Not yet, Captain. Their AI is talking our ears off, but not actually saying much. It's trying to feed us some nonsense about being a medical ship on a mercy mission, but it's the wrong kind of craft for that, and it doesn't have the proper identification codes. Odds are they're just trying to keep us occupied while they power up for a hyper jump. Do we stop them, Captain, or let them go?'

'We stop them,' said a calm, cold voice, and Silence nodded to Investigator Frost as she came to stand beside him. Frost was late twenties and tall with a supple grace that masked hidden steel. She wore a gun on her hip and a long sword hanging down her back. Even standing still she looked competent and extremely dangerous, like a predator in a world of prey. Dark eyes burned coldly in a pale, controlled face, framed by chestnut hair cropped close to the skull. You couldn't call her pretty, but there was a daunting glamour to her, attractive and intimidating in the same moment.

Investigators were trained from childhood to be loyal, efficient and deadly. Their job was to study newly discovered alien species, and determine how much of a threat they might

17

prove to the Empire. Depending on those findings, the aliens would then be either enslaved or exterminated. There was no third option. Investigators were also used as security chiefs, bodyguards and assassins. They were cold, calculating killing machines, and they were either good at their job, or dead.

Silence and Frost had worked together on several missions, and understood each other. Which was as close to friendship as you could get with an Investigator.

'There's no hurry,' said Silence. 'A ship that small takes forever to power up. They're not going anywhere yet.'

'I don't like it,' Frost said flatly. 'An unexpected ship in orbit, waiting for us? I don't believe in coincidence. Someone has alerted our target that he's been outlawed. That ship is either here to protect him or carry him away. Either way, our orders are quite specific. Under no circumstances is the target to be allowed to escape.'

Silence nodded. The outlaw was only ever referred to as the target, in public. It wouldn't do for the lower orders to know that a Lord had been outlawed. Especially one with such a famous name. The name Deathstalker could still command respect and possibly allies in certain quarters, irrespective of the Empress's wishes or orders. Which was why an entire starcruiser had been sent to see that the Deathstalker's outlawing went smoothly. He was to be captured and executed before word could get out to potential friends. Only it seemed someone had beaten them to it.

'The ship could have been sent to occupy our attention while the target is helped to escape,' said Frost. 'We can't afford to waste time on it. With your permission, I'll form a boarding party and get some answers in person.'

'Not so fast, Investigator. Let's do this by the book. Esper Fortuna?'

'Yes, Captain.' The *Darkwind*'s esper, Thomas Fortuna, stepped forward, to stand on the Captain's other side, opposite the Investigator. He was short, dumpy, and his uniform looked as though he'd inherited it from someone larger. His shaven head glistened brightly.

'I want a full scan on that ship,' said Silence. 'See what you can pick up.'

'Yes, Captain.' Fortuna's mind leapt up and out, and his face relaxed completely, losing all trace of life and personality. Then his face twisted, and he was back again, shaking his head disgustedly. 'That ship is full of death and the memory of pain. So many traces I can't even identify the sources, except to say they're all human, and dead. There are body banks on that ship, Captain, brimming over with the residues of suffering. They're cloneleggers.'

'Nothing to do with the target?' said Silence. 'You're sure?'

'As far as I can be, Captain.'

'That settles it then,' said Frost easily. 'We can't waste time over a handful of bodysnatchers. Blow the ship to pieces. The universe will smell better once they're gone.'

'Couldn't agree more,' said Silence. 'Go ahead, Investigator. Enjoy yourself.'

The pirate ship *Shard* rocked as the *Darkwind* opened fire on her. Hannah got the force screens up in time, deflecting the raging energy from the disrupter cannon, but it was all the AI could do to maintain them under the constant barrage from the Empire ship. Hazel d'Ark fired back, but her two cannon made no impression on the *Darkwind*'s superior shields. Lights went out all over the *Shard* as the AI drained more and more energy from the ship's systems to maintain the force screens. The power accumulated for a hyper jump was used up in seconds, and one by one the body banks shut down, their fragile contents left to warm and rot. The *Shard* jerked this way and that, like a fish on a hook, running through every evasive manoeuvre in the AI's data banks, but the *Darkwind* stayed with them, the disrupter cannon firing one after another to maintain a constant pressure.

Hazel shuddered at her fire controls, feeling every shattering blow on the *Shard*'s shields through her mental link to the computers. She hammered impatiently on the arms of her chair as she waited the three agonizing minutes it took for her antiquated disrupter cannon to power up between shots. The

Darkwind didn't have that problem. She fired her disrupters in overlapping waves, so that each cannon had time to recharge before it had to fire again. The Empire ship also had far greater resources of power to draw on. The *Shard* didn't stand a chance, and everyone knew it.

Light dimmed on the *Shard*'s bridge as fires broke out in a dozen places. Smoke formed faster than the extractor fans could deal with it. Hazel coughed raggedly as she tried to concentrate on the fire controls. The station next to hers exploded, and the man sitting there was suddenly engulfed in flames. He screamed shrilly till the air in his lungs burned up. The AI was gabbling incoherently in Hazel's ears, its voice breaking up as it struggled to hold the disintegrating ship together. She spun round in her seat and glared across the smoke-filled bridge at Captain Markee.

'Surrender, damn it! They're tearing us apart!'

'No point,' said the Captain calmly, raising his voice to be heard over the growing bedlam on the bridge. 'They must know we're cloneleggers. They're not interested in our surrender. We can't fight, we can't run, and we haven't a hope in hell of raising enough power to go hyper. That only leaves one option. I'm going to use Lover Boy on their shields and then ram the bastards. If I'm going down, I'm taking them with me.'

Hazel's fire controls exploded, throwing her out and across the bridge. She landed hard, driving the breath from her lungs, her uniform blackened and scorched. She was badly burned, but for the moment, shock smothered most of the pain. She rolled slowly on to her side, fighting to stay conscious. She could hear Markee giving orders in a calm, reasonable voice. Lover Boy. Hazel clung to the thought as she forced herself up on to her knees. Lover Boy was an experimental programme the Captain had acquired on Brahmin II. It was called Lover Boy because love laughs at locksmiths, and because the programme was designed to give another ship's security systems a real good screwing. The Captain was going to use Lover Boy to get the *Darkwind* to drop her force shields, and then ram her. The *Shard* would hit like a single huge torpedo, and that would be the end of the *Darkwind*. And the *Shard*.

Hazel lurched to her feet, grabbed the nearest station to steady herself, and glared through the smoke and flames at Captain Markee.

'Are you crazy? We'll all be killed!'

He didn't answer her. His gaze was fixed on his computer displays, and he was laughing. Hazel looked wildly round for help, only to find she and Markee were the only living crew left on the bridge. The rest were dead at their stations. Hazel staggered away from the bridge, stumbling through the smoke and wreckage. If she was quick, she could still get to an escape pod before the two ships hit. And if she was really lucky, the escape pod would still be working.

The corridor lurched back and forth as Hazel forced herself into a run. Adrenalin was putting strength back into her legs, but she knew that wouldn't last long. Solid steel creaked and groaned around her as the ship began to break up. Markee had to be directing most of the *Shard*'s remaining power into the force shields, but some of the punishment was getting through anyway. The lights were going out, one by one. Hazel tried to contact Hannah through her comm implant, but the AI was still talking gibberish, mumbling to itself in a querulous voice.

Hazel rounded a corner, and then stumbled to a halt. One of the bulkheads had been blown inwards, blocking the corridor completely. Spikes of jagged metal thrust out in all directions, some of it still glowing cherry red from the heat of the recent explosion. Hazel took the opportunity to get her breath back, and studied the situation as calmly as she could. Panicking or screaming with rage might feel good, but it wouldn't get her anywhere. The first real pain from her burns was beginning to gnaw at her, but she forced the awareness down to a level she could deal with. She grabbed hold of a few spikes that were only uncomfortably warm, and tried to shift the steel mass, but it didn't budge an inch. She bit her lower lip, scowling. This was the only way to the escape pods. She had to get through.

Her hand fell to the gun on her hip. Using an energy weapon in a confined space was always dangerous, but nowhere near as dangerous as being trapped here when the two ships hit. She drew her disrupter, set it to maximum dispersal, and fired before she could think better of it. The raging energy beam punched a hole clean through the steel barrier, leaving a tunnel that stretched away into the metal for as far as she could see. It wasn't much of a tunnel, three feet in diameter at most, but it would have to do. She just hoped it would have an opening at the other end.

The sides of the hole glowed red with a sullen heat, and Hazel knew she couldn't afford to touch them. But she was going to have to crawl through the tunnel on all fours, and that meant contact with her hands and knees. Her uniform would protect her knees, for a while anyway, but she'd have to do something to protect her bare hands. She put away her gun, drew her backup knife from her boot, and cut away one of her sleeves. She cut the cloth in two again, put away her knife, and wrapped the cloth round her hands. She looked again at the red hot sides of the tunnel before her, and winced. This was going to be really unpleasant. She swallowed hard, and clambered quickly into the opening before she could change her mind.

The heat hit her from all directions, and she could feel the bare skin of her face tightening and smarting. Sweat poured off her, evaporating in seconds. She crawled on through the steel tunnel, and the heat seared her hands and knees even through the protecting cloth. She hurried as much as she could, but it was a narrow space, with no room to manoeuvre. Her back brushed against the tunnel roof now and again, and she had to grit her teeth against the heat and pain. The cloth pads she'd made for her hands started to smoke. Her eyes narrowed to watering slits against the fiery air, and her lungs felt scorched with every breath. The metal creaked and groaned around her as though it might collapse at any moment. Hazel's heart hammered in her chest, and a blind unreasoning fear gnawed at her self-control till she wanted to scream. But she didn't. Screaming wouldn't help. She forced herself on

22

through the heat, shuffling forward on hands and knees that seemed one blazing mass of pain. She could smell her flesh burning. Tears ran down her face, as much from frustration as pain, evaporating almost at once.

And then she was out of the tunnel, and the heat fell away from her like a burning blanket. She'd made her way through the obstruction. She was back in the open corridor, and the cool air was like a blessing. She lurched to her feet, gritting her teeth till her jaw ached at the pain in her hands and knees and back. Her leggings had burnt right through, and the blackened cloths round her hands fell apart as she tried to unwrap them. She stumbled on, not daring to look at her hands, trying to find the strength to hurry. She had no idea of how much time she had left. Her struggle in the steel tunnel had seemed to last forever.

Most of the lights were out now, and the ship was dark and echoing. The smell of smoke was heavy on the air. She forced herself on, having to guess the right way as often as not, but finally she came to the escape pods, sitting calmly in their racks as though they had all the time in the world. Hazel just stood and stared numbly at them for a long moment. All her strength had gone into getting her here, and she seemed to have none left to do anything else. A series of explosions shook the ship, jarring her back to her senses. She stumbled over to the nearest pod, and hit the activation button with her blackened fist. The door swung open maddeningly slowly, and the interior of the pod lit up as its systems came on line. Hazel clambered inside and sank into the waiting crash-webbing with something like relief. It felt so good to be off her feet at last. The door hissed shut behind her, and she worked her jaw to pop her ears as the air pressure changed.

The pod's cabin was barely a dozen feet long, with just enough room for two passengers. It occurred to Hazel that it was not unlike lying in a coffin, and the thought amused her briefly. A fitting fate for a would-be graverobber. She pushed the thought aside and painfully forced her blistered and stiffened fingers through the series of commands that would eject the pod from the *Shard*. She braced herself for the impact, and only slowly realized that nothing was happening.

She ran through the launch sequence again, crying out at the pain in her hands, but still there was no response. Panic flared up in her, and the cramped confines of the escape pod were suddenly unbearably claustrophobic. She started to get up out of the crash-webbing, and only stopped herself with an effort of will. There was no point in leaving the pod; the *Shard* was a death ship now. Her only hope for survival was to make the pod work. The panic began to die away as she made herself study the problem logically. There was nothing wrong with the pod itself, or it would have showed up on the control panels, which meant the problem lay outside. In the launching systems. Systems controlled by the ship's AI . . . Hannah.

Hazel accessed the AI through her comm implant, but there was only silence. The lack of response was somehow more worrying than the previous gibberish. Hazel called again. There was someone listening; she could feel it. When the answer finally came, it was like a whisper at midnight, as though the sound was travelling from somewhere impossibly far away.

'Hazel; everything feels wrong. Parts of me are missing, and I can't find them. I can't think properly. There are shadows in my memories, running loose like rats in a barn. Help me, Hazel. Stop them. Please stop them . . . it's so cold in here, and I'm afraid . . .'

'Hannah! Listen to me, Hannah. I'm stuck in escape pod seven. I need you to run through the launch sequence for me. Can you hear me, Hannah?'

'Forget the AI,' said Captain Markee calmly, patching into the channel. 'She's falling apart, like everything else on this ship. The *Shard*'s on her last run, going out in a blaze of glory. I've activated the pod launch from the bridge. You'll be on your way in a moment. Just as well. You'd never have made a good clonelegger, Hazel. Too soft where it matters. If you get out of this alive, raise a drink to me, and the *Shard*. She was a good ship.'

His voice faded out at the end, and before Hazel could say

anything the escape pod blasted out of its hatch, and plummeted towards the planet below.

On the bridge of the *Darkwind*, Captain Silence studied the small craft on his viewscreen as it slowly closed the distance between them. The *Darkwind*'s disrupters had hammered away most of the pirate's force shields, and it was only a matter of time now before they failed entirely. And once that happened, it would all be over in seconds. It was a miracle the pirate's shields had lasted this long. The Captain must have drained the ship's batteries dry to power them. The ship continued to drift closer, and Silence frowned thoughtfully. The pirate was up to something; he could feel it in his bones. He glanced at the Investigator beside him, and saw that she was scowling intently at the viewscreen too.

'Pirate ship's speed increasing, Captain,' said his comm officer suddenly. 'Accelerating steadily towards us.'

'He's trying to ram us,' said Frost. 'The force shields will stop him.'

'But he must know that,' said Silence slowly. 'So why is he doing it?'

'Captain!' The comm officer's voice was sharp and concerned. 'Our shields are dropping! They don't answer the control panels!'

'Odin!' said Silence. 'What's happening?'

'The pirate ship has infected my systems with a virus,' said the starcruiser's AI. 'Which is supposed to be impossible. It's bypassing all my safeguards. I've never encountered anything quite like this. Systems are crashing faster than I can isolate them. Our force shields are down, and I am unable to raise them again. The pirate ship will impact with us in six minutes and fourteen seconds.'

'Recommendations?' said Frost.

'Abandon ship,' the AI said flatly. 'If you leave now, most of the escape craft will survive the ensuing blast, and should make a safe landing on Virimonde. Go now, Captain. It's the only chance you have.'

Silence looked at Frost, and then round his magnificent

bridge. So many systems, so many highly trained personnel, and still there was nothing he could do to save his ship. He took a deep breath, and let it out slowly. He patched into the shipwide address channel, and then paused a moment longer to be sure his voice would be calm and steady when he spoke.

'Attention all hands. This is the Captain. Abandon ship. I say again, abandon ship. This is not a drill. Remember your training and make your way to the nearest escape craft. We'll reassemble on Virimonde. Good luck, everyone. Captain out.'

He looked around him and clapped his hands briskly. 'All right; that's it. Clear the bridge. Everyone out.'

His people rose quickly to their feet and left the bridge with a professional minimum of fuss. Investigator Frost turned to go, and then stopped as she realized Silence wasn't moving.

'Aren't you coming, Captain?'

'No, Investigator. This Captain is going down with his ship. The main bulk of the *Darkwind* will probably survive the initial impact, and only break up on entering the atmosphere. I have to be here, to guide the ship down for as long as I can. I have to make sure the pieces will land safely, in one of the oceans. Hundreds of thousands could be killed if any of the pieces were to land in an inhabited area.'

'You are more important,' said Frost calmly. 'The Empire has a great deal of time and money invested in you, Captain. The colonists are just peasants. They don't matter.'

'They matter to me. Clear the bridge, Investigator. There's nothing you can say that will persuade me to leave.'

'No,' said Frost. 'I don't suppose there is.'

She hit him once, efficiently, and he slumped forward in his command chair, unconscious. Frost checked the pulse in his neck, nodded once, and then picked the Captain up and slung him almost effortlessly over one shoulder.

'Odin; this is Investigator Frost. Acknowledge.'

'Acknowledged, Investigator.'

'The Captain is indisposed. I am placing you in command. You will do everything in your power to guide the ship down, so that its eventual impact does the minimum possible damage to inhabited areas. You understand I cannot take the risk of downloading you and taking you with us. There is no telling how much damage the infecting virus has done to your systems, or how infectious it remains.'

'Yes, Investigator. I understand.'

Frost looked once around the empty bridge. 'Goodbye, Odin.'

'Goodbye, Investigator. Safe journey.'

Frost turned and left the bridge, with the Captain still unconscious over her shoulder. The empty bridge was filled with the low sound of the AI singing quietly to itself, and the pirate ship growing ever larger on the viewscreen.

The *Shard* and the *Darkwind*, locked together, cartwheeled slowly through the silent night, falling towards Virimonde.

CHAPTER TWO

The Man Who Had Everything

The Deathstalker, Owen, Lord of Virimonde, last of a famous warrior line, lay naked and exhausted among the crumpled silk sheets of his bed, and wondered lazily if he could work up the strength to call for a tall iced drink. It was late in the morning of another perfect day, on the best of all possible worlds. The sun was shining, what passed for birds on Virimonde were singing their little hearts out, everyone was busy at their work, and he didn't have to leave his bed for ages yet if he didn't feel like it. He sighed and stretched slowly, and smiled the slow smug smile of the truly satisfied. He'd just had amazing sex with his long-term mistress, and when she got back from wherever she'd disappeared to, he fully intended to do it all again. Practice makes perfect.

She wasn't really his mistress, in the sense that he didn't pay her a retainer or anything, but he liked the ancient word, with its undertones of sin and debauchery. He stretched again unhurriedly, content as a cat in the sun, staring up at the ceiling high above. When he did finally choose to get up, his most recent history was waiting in the computers for him to take up work on it again. It was a good piece, sharp and pointed and full of new insights. The kind of work he'd always known he was capable of, if he could just get away from interfering distractions like having to train with sword and gun every morning and study military tactics every afternoon, in order to be the warrior his line demanded of him. No one had ever asked him if he wanted to be another bloody fighter like all his revered ancestors. But that was all behind him now. His father was dead, he'd inherited the title, and his life was his own at last. In short, he'd got it all. No doubt eventually he'd start getting bored with such perfection, in several years or so, but until then he was determined to enjoy every minute of it. And why not? He was a nice guy; he deserved it.

He looked around the huge stone chamber, with its hanging tapestries and centuries-old holos. The Deathstalker Standing hadn't changed outwardly in generations. Every modern convenience in place, ready to hand or call, but expertly concealed behind the traditional overlay. The Standing had been the home of the Deathstalker Clan for generations beyond counting, serving all their various needs with calm efficiency. When Owen had bought the Lordship of Virimonde, he'd had the entire castle dismantled, stone by stone, and had it and its contents shipped to Virimonde, where it was reassembled surprisingly quickly by a small army of fanatical experts. You can do things like that when you're a Lord. The Standing was his, wherever he decided to plant his roots; all that was required of him was that he preserve it and hold it in trust for future generations. Assuming he ever got around to marrying and producing a next generation. His mistress was a delightful sort, but not at all the kind of person one married. As head of one of the oldest Families in the Empire, he had a duty to marry someone of his own rank and station. And he would. Eventually.

Owen looked thoughtfully at the giant holo on the wall opposite his bed, showing the original Deathstalker in all his fearsome aspect and martial glory; Warrior Prime of the Empire and founder of the Clan that still bore his name. He looked a bit rough and ready, in his thick furs and steel mesh tunic, bristling with weapons, his head shaved in a mercenary's scalplock, but it didn't take too much imagination to transform his warrior's arrogance into a Lord's nobility. According to Family history he'd been the greatest fighting man of his day, unanimously elected Warrior Prime, and elevated to the peerage by popular acclaim. Hard man by all accounts, and a bit of a bastard, but the public like that in their heroes. Bloodied his sword on a hundred worlds, and never backed away from an insult or a war.

He was also the creator and wielder of the Darkvoid Device, that put out a thousand suns in a moment, and left their planets to sail through an endless night. The Darkvoid. But no one talks about that any more, outside the Family.

Pity about what happened to him in the end, but that's politics for you. His son had taken over as Warrior Prime to the Empire, and things went on as they should. Owen wondered vaguely what the old man would have made of his most recent descendant. Probably would have had him put down the moment he showed any sign of intellectual tendencies. Owen couldn't bring himself to really give a damn. He'd always known he was a writer, not a fighter. He'd had a proper training in weaponry and all the martial arts, as befitted his station and inheritance, but it had never interested him. His interest lay in researching and piecing together the Empire's somewhat tangled history. Nothing excited him like reaching into the morass of legend and myth that made up so much of the past, and producing one indisputable new fact, clear and sharp as a diamond in a coal mine. And if he'd learned one thing from all the histories he'd read and the tales he'd investigated, it was that most of the time there was no glory and damn all honour to be found on the battlefield. Only blood and mud and the endless bitterness of lost hopes.

Most wars turned out to be squalid little affairs, once you dug through the lies and propaganda; fought to protect trade interests or save political face. Owen was damned if he'd fight and die just so someone else could look good. Particularly when he had so much to live for. The only real legacy he had from his bad old, mad old ancestor was the Deathstalker ring he wore; an ugly chunky circle of black gold, handed down out of the unimaginable past, the sign and seal of Deathstalker authority. According to the Family tradition, he was forbidden to remove it, save to pass it on to his eldest son. They'd had to cut off his father's finger to get it, after he was dead. But then, Owen and his father had never got on.

They'd always been surprisingly distant and distinct, considering how alike they looked. They were both tall and rangy, with dark hair and darker eyes, moving always with the quiet grace of breeding and long martial training. These days, in his mid-twenties, Owen had lost some of the athlete's leanness; good living and satisfied appetites had softened the lines of his muscles and padded his stomach. Not excessively so, by any means, but his old weapons master would have thrown up his hands in despair at how out of condition his pupil had become. It was a thought that never failed to please Owen. The two of them had never got on. He still worked out most days, when he could spare the time, if only so he could keep up with his mistress.

The bedroom door swung open, and Owen's mood changed in a moment as his mistress came bouncing in, bright and bonny and tanned golden from perfect head to pointed toe. Cathy DeVries was in her early thirties, with a tight compact body of wondrous delights. Average height, but far from average in every other way. Long legs, full body, long blonde hair falling around a heart-shaped face with marvellous high cheekbones. Cathy was inordinately proud of her bone structure. Prettiness fades, she was fond of saying, but a good bone structure lasts for ever. She had the widest smile Owen had ever seen, and dark blue eyes to die for. She'd been his mistress for seven years now, ever since she'd been presented to him as a surprise party favour at the winter ball on Golgotha. She'd been physically adapted at the House of Joy; a double-jointed contortionist, trained in all the erotic knowledge of the ages, and full of surprises. Multiple orgasms guaranteed or your money back.

Buying up her contract was the best investment he'd ever made.

Cathy was wearing his battered old dressing gown again, belted at the waist for a change. Usually she just let it hang open, partly for freedom of movement and partly because she knew how much he liked to look at her. This time the gown was belted tight, and the thought disturbed him for some reason. It wasn't as though she had anything to hide, after seven years of enthusiastic exploration. She was probably just teasing him again. She knew how to get him going. He noted with approval that she was carrying a tall frosted glass of white wine. She always could judge his mood to a nicety. On the other hand, the sight of her was more refreshing than any drink could ever be. He took the drink from her, and put it firmly to one side on the bedside table. First things first. He reached for Cathy, and she stepped back, just out of reach. He frowned, puzzled, and she looked at him dispassionately.

'Bad move, Owen. You really should have drunk the wine. You would have just drifted off to sleep, and never woken up. So much simpler and more pleasant, for both of us. Now we have to do it the hard way.'

She reached inside the dressing gown and brought out a disrupter. Owen blinked stupidly at the energy weapon in her hand, and then old trained reflexes kicked in, and he threw himself out of his bed as Cathy fired. He hit the floor rolling, still wrapped in his sheets. The bed exploded into flames behind him. Cathy cursed briefly, put away the gun and drew a long knife from inside the dressing gown. Owen wondered briefly what the hell else she had hidden in there, and then lurched to his feet, tearing the enveloping sheets away from him. He had two minutes until the gun's energy crystal recharged. He backed away as she advanced on him with the knife, and looked desperately around him for some kind of weapon. Cathy's face was calm but determined, as though she was working on some minor puzzle whose solution for the moment escaped her.

'Cathy; I really think we need to talk about this.'

'Too late for talk, Owen.'

'If this is some kind of joke, I don't find it in the least bit funny.'

'No joke, Owen. I'm cancelling our contract. The escape clause is a bit of a bastard, but that's life for you. Or rather, death. Don't struggle and I'll make it quick.'

'Whatever they're paying, I'll double it.'

'You can't buy yourself out of trouble this time, dear. Now stand still and let me do what I have to. At least have the decency to die with dignity.'

Owen realized he'd ended up back by the burning bed, and winced away from the leaping flames. He drew himself up to his full height and glared at his mistress. His nakedness rather detracted from the effect. 'Cathy; you don't really think you can beat me in a fight, do you? I am the Deathstalker, after all.'

'And I was trained in the House of Joy. They teach us all kinds of things there. You'd be surprised. We're both a little out of shape, but you've really let yourself go, Owen. If the knife doesn't get you, the gun will, once it's recharged. Say goodbye, dear. It's been fun; let's not spoil it.'

She lunged forward gracefully while she was still talking, the long knife reaching for his heart. Owen sidestepped at the last moment, and the edge of the knife grated across his ribs as Cathy sailed past him. She recovered her balance in a moment, and turned to face him again. Owen noted disgustedly that she wasn't even breathing hard. The long cut burned across his ribs, and he could feel blood coursing down his side. Much as he hated to admit it, Cathy clearly was in much better shape than him.

The thought sparked a sudden anger in him, and as she came forward again Owen fell easily into the defensive stance he should have been using all along. His weapons master had spent enough time hammering it into him. Cathy lunged again, and he stepped gracefully aside, seized her arm in one simple movement and twisted it up behind her back. Her own speed and impetus slammed the hold into place, and she gasped in pain as he applied a steady pressure. Her fingers opened reluctantly, releasing the knife. It fell to the floor, but Cathy kicked it out of reach before Owen could even think about going after it. And then she twisted strangely, pulled free of his grasp and sent Owen flying before he knew what was happening. He scrambled hurriedly to his feet, looking about him for the knife. Cathy pirouetted once, her long leg flying up, and her foot hit Owen expertly just above the ear. He managed to roll with some of the blow, but he still hit the floor hard again, his head ringing.

Great, thought Owen, as he struggled to get his feet under him. *All the assassins that could have come after me, and I had to get a double-jointed contortionist kick-boxer. Well, when in doubt, improvise. And if that fails, cheat.*

Cathy came at him again, moving almost too fast for the eye to follow. Owen grabbed his clothes from the chair they'd been laid out on, and threw them into Cathy's face. For a second she was blind and off balance, and that was all it took for Owen to snatch up the knife and thrust it between her ribs. For a long moment they remained as they were, Cathy on her feet, him on one knee, both breathing hard. Blood poured down Cathy's heaving side. The clothes fell away from her face. She gripped his shoulders fiercely, as though to hold herself up, but all her strength went out of her, and she sank to the floor, still holding on to him. He eased her down, and sat with her, holding her tenderly in his arms. She coughed painfully, and blood ran from her mouth.

'Damn,' she said thickly. 'You've killed me, Owen.'

'Yes, I think I have. Why, Cathy? Why did you do it?'

'You've been outlawed. The news came through while I was getting your drink. All your titles, lands, properties and monies have been seized. It's death to shelter or aid you. Anyone who brings your head, preferably unattached to the body, to the Imperial Court on Golgotha will be rewarded with the Lordship of Virimonde and half your monies. Somebody really wants you dead, Owen.'

She cleared her throat and spat, and there was more blood. Owen held her tightly. *Outlawed?* He tried to make sense of it, and couldn't. In the space of a few moments, his whole world had gone mad. Cathy coughed and gritted her teeth against the pain. Her hands tightened on his arms, and he held her until the spasm passed. He didn't know what else to do.

'Something else you should know, Owen.' Her voice was low and blurred now, and he had to concentrate to make it out. 'I'm a spy. From the Imperial Court. They planted me on you, all those years ago. I've been feeding them information ever since.'

'Hush, love. Don't tire yourself. I know. I've always known. It doesn't matter.'

Cathy looked at him. 'You knew? And you never said anything?'

'What was there to say? My AI broke your cover right after you moved in with me. He's good at things like that. I never did anything about it because it was easier to have a spy I knew about, and could keep an eye on, than have to identify and deal with whoever replaced you. And besides, I was fond of you.'

'I was fond of you,' said Cathy quietly. 'I never did have a head for business.'

She leaned forward till her head was resting on his shoulder, shuddered slightly, and stopped breathing. Owen held her in his arms as the life went out of her, and then sat quietly with her, rocking her gently like a sleeping child. After a while he let go of her, and laid her out on the floor. She seemed somehow smaller and more fragile now. He looked down at himself, and grimaced at her blood and his on his skin. He picked up his shift from the floor and mopped at himself with it. He started to put it on, and then let it drop to the floor again. Nothing seemed to matter much now. The crackling of the flames from his burning bed caught his attention, and he thought vaguely that he should call someone to do something about it. He activated his comm implant, removed the Do Not Disturb, and accessed his home's AI.

'Ozymandias . . .'

'Shut up and listen,' said his AI. 'You're in a lot of trouble, Owen. You've been outlawed, and there's a hell of a price on your head.'

'I know.'

'So does your Head of Security. He's on his way to you right now, with as many guards as he could muster, with the explicit intention of separating your head from your shoulders. You never did pay him enough. You've got to get out of there, now.'

'Cathy just tried to murder me. I had to kill her.'

'I'm sorry, Owen, but we don't have time for this. Everyone in the Standing is probably heading for you with murder on their mind. You don't have any friends here any more. Use the hidden exit, make your way through the secret passages and get to your private flyer. By the time you've done that, I should have a clearer picture of what's going on, and just possibly I'll have worked out what you should do next.'

Owen padded over to the bedroom door, opened it slightly and peered out into the corridor. There was no one there, but he thought he could hear someone in the distance, drawing closer. He shut the door and locked it, and then walked back to pick up his clothes. He dressed quickly, ignoring the blood on his shirt and his skin. Whatever happened, he was damned if he was going to face it naked.

'Oz; why have I been outlawed? It doesn't make sense. I left the Court and came here precisely because I wanted to avoid getting involved in the kind of intrigues that get you outlawed. I'm no danger to anyone. I just wanted to be left alone to get on with my histories.'

'The Court didn't give any specific reason, but then, it doesn't have to. The word of the Empress is law. I suppose as a Deathstalker, your name could be useful to any number of factions, in and out of the Court. As I understand it, the Empress took a personal interest in you. And you know what that usually means . . .'

'Yeah. The last time she took a personal interest in someone, his remains ended up being sent to seventeen different planets simultaneously, as an example not to make waves. All right, I'm dressed. Open the stairway.'

The holo of the original Deathstalker swung sideways, revealing a narrow passageway. A light appeared, deep in the tunnel. Like all good castles, the Deathstalker Standing had several secret doors and hidden tunnels. Partly out of tradition, but mostly because the Deathstalkers had always felt it a good idea to have an ace or two hidden up your sleeve. Even Owen's Head of Security didn't know about these tunnels. Owen pulled on his best cloak and buckled on his sword, picked up Cathy's disrupter, and plunged into the narrow opening. The holo swung shut behind him.

He was still having trouble believing this was all really happening. One minute life was good and full and everything made sense, and the next up was down, in was out, and people he'd known for years were trying to kill him. The last time he'd felt like this was when they'd brought him the news that his father was dead. Cut down in the street as an enemy of the Empire. No one ever said why, or what he'd done, and it wasn't safe to ask. Owen hadn't really been surprised. His father had been plotting and intriguing with this faction or that all Owen's life. *A man should always concentrate on what he's best at*, was all his father ever had to say on the subject.

Only it turned out he wasn't as clever as he'd thought, and Owen became the Deathstalker when he was sixteen. He'd tried to mourn his father, but he'd hardly known the man. They never spent much time together. His father was always off on some new scheme, chasing money or influence or fame. He wasn't noticeably successful. Owen's mother died when he was still too young to remember her, so most of his life had been spent under the governorship of a series of guardians, tutors and friends of the Family. His only real friend, certainly the only one he ever trusted, was the Family AI, Ozymandias.

He'd been very fond of Cathy, but he never trusted her. It surprised him that her death hurt him so much.

All his father's warrior training and skill in politics hadn't been enough to save him, and Owen had drawn a lesson from that. He'd never been much interested in current politics, so he'd found it easy enough to turn away the various cabals that came sniffing around him once he inherited the title. He made it clear he was only interested in his histories, and did his best to present an image of himself as dull, hopelessly studious, and completely self-involved. He dismissed his weapons master, turned his back on the Court and its politics, and bought the Lordship of Virimonde, way out on the Rim, a carefully safe distance from the Empress and her people. He wasn't going to make the same mistakes his father made.

Only somehow it had all gone wrong anyway.

He kept turning it over and over in his mind as he quickly made his way down the passage. Lights turned themselves on before him and turned themselves off after him, so that he moved in a constant pool of light through the darkness. He couldn't have been outlawed for no reason. It had to be some kind of ghastly mistake. If he could just get in touch with the right people, find out what had gone wrong and explain everything, then maybe they'd put things right again, and he could have his life back. But to do that, he had to avoid his enemies and stay alive. Which was easier said than done. Maybe he'd be better off heading for the Standing's communications centre. He could barricade himself in, call for help and hope he found a sympathetic ear. Anything was better than just running blindly.

'Oz; what's the state of communications at the moment?'

'Pretty bad. All the main comm channels have been jammed. Local channels are OK, but I don't know for how long. Either way, it's clear you're not going to be allowed to plead your case. The more I look into this, the more convinced I am this was all set up at the highest levels. Hold it; the local channels just went down. All of them. I can keep this private channel open for a while, but I can't guarantee how long. In fact, there's not much I can guarantee any more, except that you have to keep moving. Your Head of Security has just burst into your bedroom with his people. They're all armed, some with energy weapons. He's found Cathy's body. Now they're tearing the place apart, looking for a hidden exit. They're being very thorough, but they seem to have forgotten my sensors. The Head of Security is not pleased at your absence. People can probably hear him being not pleased some distance away.'

'You can tell me all this later,' Owen cut in. 'What are the chances of his finding the hidden exit?'

'Not good. They're really not very bright, and I'm scrambling the sensor equipment they brought with them. I told you, you should have let me choose your security people. This bunch hasn't got a clue, and they're getting nowhere fast. I feel like shouting "Hot!" and "Cold!" just to encourage them.'

'Don't you dare.'

'Spoilsport.'

Owen shook his head. 'If I ever find out who programmed

38

that sense of humour into you, I'll have him strung up by his giblets. Could we please concentrate on the matter in hand?'

'Of course, Owen. Do you still have the Deathstalker ring?'

'Of course I've still got it. It'd take half a tub of grease to get the damn thing off my finger. Why?'

'I've just discovered a file hidden deep within my memories, designed only to reveal itself in the event of your being outlawed. Someone was thinking ahead, though his motives remain unclear at this time. Apparently the ring is very important. It's a key of some kind. According to the file, you're supposed to take it to Mistworld, where you will find help waiting for you.'

'Is that all?' said Owen, after a while.

'I'm afraid so. However, I feel I should point out that if there's one hidden file in my memories, there may well be more, with further information, presumably to be triggered by future events.'

'This has my father's fingerprints all over it,' said Owen disgustedly. 'Even after he's dead, he's still trying to run my life. Him and his bloody intrigues. Mistworld, for God's sake! The outlaw planet. Place is full of criminals and murderers, and the living conditions are barbaric. I wouldn't live there if you paid me. No, Oz; wherever I'm going, I'm not going there. I know what he wants. When he was killed, I was supposed to take his ring and swear vengeance, just like in all those operas he loved so much. Well to hell with him. I wouldn't let him dictate my life while he was alive, and I'm not about to start now. If he wanted to risk being killed for his squalid little political manoeuvrings, that was up to him, but I have better things to do with my life. And not being killed is right at the head of them.'

'I'm sure your father only had your best interests at heart,' said the AI.

'You're only saying that because he had it programmed into you. He never understood me. Never even tried. He never understood that I never wanted to be a warrior.'

He hurried on for a while in silence. He had nothing left to say, and besides, he needed his breath for running. The tunnel was definitely heading downwards, but after so many twists and turns he'd quite lost track of his bearings. He'd never used the escape route before, and wasn't that impressed by it now. It was cold and damp, the ceiling was uncomfortably low, and it smelt awful. He supposed he should have expected that. You could hardly send the cleaning staff into a secret tunnel every other week. He slowed to a fast walk, and breathed deeply. He had to be getting near the exit now, and he didn't want to arrive there exhausted and out of breath. You never knew who might be waiting.

'Oz; you still there?'

'Of course, Owen. Where else would I be?'

'Smartass. Look, none of this makes sense. Even if I have been outlawed, the Court wouldn't just announce it to all and sundry. Even these days, under the Iron Bitch, outlawing a Lord is extremely bloody rare, and it's nearly always done in private. It wouldn't do for the lower orders to get a taste for killing nobility, would it? Might start giving them ideas. We're supposed to be special, far above them, untouched and untouchable by their petty little lives. You can't just outlaw a Lord. It just isn't done!'

'It's certainly unusual,' said the AI. 'I can only assume the Empress really wants you dead. The reward on your head is unprecedentedly high. Hmmm. I wonder how much she'd give me for you . . .'

'Oz . . .'

'Just a thought. Hold everything; new update. Someone is trying to break into my programming. Professionals, too. They're cutting through my outer defences like they're not even there. They've got some really heavy codebreakers, Owen. We could be in real trouble.'

'Imperial?'

'Has to be. But don't start panicking yet. I've been looking after you Deathstalkers for some time now, and I've learned a few tricks down the years. Including how to appear a lot dumber than I really am, while carefully leading them away from my core identity. Right now, as far as they're concerned, I'm just a jumped-up number-cruncher with an AI overlay.

And by the time they've figured out the truth, I plan to be long gone. So, my files are safe for the time being, but the sooner you can download me from the castle mainframe, the better.'

'Hold everything, Oz; what have they done to my credit rating?'

'Owen, what they have done to your credit rating, I wouldn't do to a dead dog. You are now worth squat. They've wiped out every penny you had and seized all your properties and holdings, including several they weren't supposed to know about. Look, I told you most of this already; aren't you paying attention?'

'Shut up, Oz, this is serious. Without a credit rating, I'm dead. Wherever I'm going, I'm going to need money. Let me think for a moment . . . The Family jewels! They've got to be worth a small fortune!'

'Forget it, Owen. One, you don't have time to go back and get them, two, your Head of Security has people waiting for you there in case you're stupid enough to go after them, and three, the jewels are quite well known in their own right. You'd be identified the moment you tried to sell them.'

Owen scowled. 'I hate it when you're right.'

He rounded a corner in the tunnel, and stepped out into the caves below the Standing where he kept his private flyer. A disrupter beam blew away part of the wall where he'd been standing, sending stone fragments flying through the air. Owen threw himself back into the tunnel, swearing softly so as not to give away his position. He clutched tightly at Cathy's disrupter.

'Why the hell didn't you warn me there were people lying in wait for me?' he subvocalized fiercely.

'Sorry, Owen. The codebreakers have shut down my sensor apparatus inside the Standing. I can no longer access any of the security systems. They're in deeper than I thought. They're getting close to the real me, Owen. There's still a lot I can try to hold them off, but I'm getting a really bad feeling about this. You have to download me soon, or risk losing me.'

'Great. Just what I needed; something else to worry about.

Look; can you access the flyer's sensors through my implant, and see through those?'

'It'll be risky. The codebreakers could follow me to you.'

'Do it. I need to know how many men I'm facing, and how many of them have energy weapons.'

'All right, I'm in. Three men. One disrupter. They've all got swords. They've taken cover behind the flyer.'

'Damn,' said Owen. 'Who the hell are they?'

'More of your security people. I can give you their names if you want.'

'Wouldn't know them if you did. Not my province. As long as the Head of Security did a good job, I didn't interfere.'

'Well in the future, assuming we have one, I suggest you take the time to make a few friends among your security people. Never know when it might come in handy.'

Owen growled something in response, but he wasn't really listening. The fact was, in a moment he was going to have to take on three armed men, one of them with an energy weapon, and he couldn't put it off much longer. A hand disrupter only took two minutes to recharge between each shot, which meant he was running out of time fast. He had to make his move while the gun was still useless. Three to one odds weren't that bad. Not for someone with his training. But that was all he'd had; training. He'd never had to face these kinds of odds for real before. And he'd let himself get out of shape. He'd been so sure he was safe here . . . He pushed the thought to one side, and unconsciously sucked in his gut. He was going to have to be a fighter after all, despite all the promises he'd made to himself after his father's death. He was going to have to be a Deathstalker, and all that that meant.

He drew in a deep breath, held it and then let it out. A slow, purposeful calm crept over him. He smiled briefly, acknowledging the irony, and then spoke the activation word *boost*. Blood thundered through his head and his heart raced. The buried subliminals kicked in, flooding his system with adrenalin and endorphins, and other serums from specially gengineered glands. His muscles swelled and his senses blossomed. He was stronger, faster, more efficient in every way. His thoughts were sharp and lightning fast. For as long as the boost lasted, he would be more than human; more than merely human. He couldn't maintain it for long, or it would burn him out. But he could stand it long enough to do what he had to do.

He burst out of the tunnel entrance again, moving too quickly for the human eye to follow, raised his disrupter and shot the man holding the gun through the chest while he was still reacting to Owen's sudden appearance. The energy beam punched right through the security man's chest and threw him aside. The energy gun flew from his hand, out of reach of the others. Owen was upon them both before the first man hit the ground. They seemed to be moving in slow motion to him, every second an age. Their swords rose nightmarishly slowly, and then he was among them, inhumanly fast and strong, supercharged almost beyond the ability of the human frame to bear. His sword ripped through one man's throat, half severing the head from the body, and then leapt on to plunge into the third man's chest. And as quickly as that, it was all over.

Owen snapped out of boost, and almost fell as the accumulated stress hit him all at once. He'd been using controlled hysterical strength, though not all of it. Using the muscles to their full extent would tear them clean away from the bones. His abused heart was hammering painfully fast in his chest, his breathing was quick and strained, and he was soaked with sweat. He shook uncontrollably as the chemical stew he'd pumped into his system slowly began to disperse. Just the shock alone would have killed an ordinary man, but he was far more than that. He was a Deathstalker, and the boost was the real Deathstalker inheritance.

The shaking died away, and he smiled tremulously. Damn, he felt good. He shook his head slowly, forcing down the euphoria. It wasn't real; just a side effect of the endorphins still in his blood. This was the Deathstalker secret; what made his Family such perfect fighting machines. The constant temptation that had to be faced and mastered. A rush greater than any single drug could ever provide; a potential addiction stronger than any will could deny. This was the key to

Deathstalker training, backed up by subliminal commands deep within the subconscious mind; only to use the boost when you had to. Owen had never really been tempted. The few times he'd used it before, under strictly controlled conditions, it had scared the crap out of him. It pushed aside the mind, brought out the beast that lurks in every man, and made him like it. Made him into just the kind of man he'd always sworn he'd rather die than become.

He pushed the thought aside, and sheathed his blood-smeared sword without bothering to clean it. He'd pay a price for the boost later, but he couldn't let himself collapse and sleep until he was safely well away from here. If anywhere was safe for him now. And assuming he didn't have to use the boost again.

A memory came to him; reinforced by the last of the chemicals still moving sluggishly in his blood. He was fourteen years old, and his father was beating the shit out of him in a training session, to force him to use the boost, to become an adult Deathstalker. It took a lot of beatings before he finally learned how to summon the boost.

Thanks a lot, Dad.

'Oz; any sign of any more of these idiots?'

'No, Owen. According to the flyer's admittedly somewhat limited sensors, there are no other life traces in the immediate vicinity. There aren't that many people who know about your outlawing so far, and they have a lot of ground to cover. But there is no knowing when they might discover your escape route, and follow you down here. May I earnestly suggest that you power up the flyer and get the hell out of here? Both your options and mine are shrinking fast. I'm having to use more and more of my systems to defend myself against the Imperial codebreakers. My mind is under threat. If you don't download me soon, I will be unable to assist you further.'

'All right; leave off the emotional blackmail. I'll see what I can do once I get to my private yacht. The *Sunstrider* has more than enough system capacity to hold you.' Owen smiled suddenly. 'And they said I was crazy to pay that much money for a yacht. I'll show them. The *Sunstrider*'s got options built into her that most people have never even dreamed of.'

'The yacht was a wise choice in retrospect,' said Ozymandias. 'I have always admired your Family's capacity for practical paranoia.'

Owen laughed breathlessly, and threw open the canopy of his private flyer. It wasn't much to look at; just a long slender cabin with wings, and a small motor. Top speed of a hundred, if the wind was with you, and the energy crystals only lasted about a week between recharging, but it was useful for getting around his estates, so he'd kept it handy. He'd never seriously considered it as an emergency escape route, but he'd felt more secure knowing it was there, and he wasn't reliant on anybody else for transport. He slipped into the pilot's seat and pulled the canopy shut. It only took a few seconds to power up the craft, and then he lifted it carefully off its dais and flew it out of the caverns and into the bright morning sunlight.

The canopy darkened automatically to keep out the sunlight, but it still seemed painfully bright. He headed north, pushing the speed to maximum as fast as he dared. Virimonde looked cool and green and calm and peaceful. It didn't seem possible that his life could be threatened in such a perfect world. The great grasslands rolled away in one direction, fields of waving corn in the other, both stretching as far as the eye could see. Low stone walls criss-crossed here and there, and people worked unhurriedly in the fields as though this was just another day. The bitter thought *It isn't fair* flashed through his mind and was gone. He didn't have the time for self-pity. Owen tore his gaze away from his people, and accessed the flight computers through his comm implant. All systems were responding normally, and the energy levels looked sufficient to get him to where he'd hidden the *Sunstrider*. If nothing went wrong. The flyer had no weapons systems and no energy shields. A disrupter blast would rip through the cabin like a knife through paper. Owen felt suddenly vulnerable, alone in a flimsy craft, and he shuddered for a long moment before he could bring himself back under control again.

The flyer's sensors suddenly murmured in his ear, informing

him that there were two other flyers on his tail. They were only a few minutes behind him, and slowly but steadily they were closing the gap. Owen swore feelingly. He should never have authorized the extra flyers for his security people. He tried for more speed, but the low energy levels made the craft sluggish. It only took a quick calculation to show Owen the other flyers would catch him up long before he could reach *Sunstrider*, and safety.

'Oz; you still with me?'

'There's no need to shout, Owen, I'm not deaf.'

'Then take the flyer's controls. Your reflexes are a lot faster than mine.'

'Yes, Owen.' The flyer lurched suddenly to one side and then back again, rising and falling at unexpected intervals. 'Evasive manoeuvres,' the AI explained.

'Next time,' said Owen, trying hard to hang on to his seat and his stomach's contents, 'a little warning would be appreciated.'

'Of course, Owen. I feel I should also warn you that according to this flyer's long range sensors, there are at least three energy weapons on the flyers behind us. It will only take one hit in the wrong place to force us down.'

'I had worked that much out for myself, thank you. Any other good news you want to share with me?'

'Again according to the long range sensors, there are three more craft heading in pursuit. Too far off yet to identify the craft, but their speed implies they are much more powerful than the flyers, and they're closing fast.'

Some days, Owen thought, *things wouldn't go right if you paid them.*

The flyer lurched suddenly as a disrupter beam tore through the left wing. The whole craft shuddered painfully, and its speed began to drop. It threw itself about the sky as the AI ran through every emergency manoeuvre the flyer was still capable of, but the damage had been done. Speed was down, altitude was falling, and the pursuing ships were drawing steadily nearer.

'You'll have to take control, Owen,' said the AI suddenly.

'I'm under increasing attack, and I can't spare any more of myself to help you. You can contact me again if you reach *Sunstrider*. If not, I have enjoyed our relationship. Goodbye.'

'Oz, Ozymandias! Talk to me, damn you!' Owen waited, but there was no response. 'Shit! *Boost!*'

He didn't like to think what boosting again was going to do to him, so soon after the last time, but it couldn't be helped. He needed the extra speed and reflexes it would give him. Blood hammered in his head, and new strength flooded through him. The flyer shuddered again as a second energy beam hit it from behind. The motor lost its high confident tone and began to stutter. The nose dipped, and the flyer headed for the ground. To Owen it all seemed to be happening in remorseless slow motion, but even though his hands were incredibly fast and sure on the controls, all he could do was guide the descent, not stop it. He was still a long way short of his destination, and for the first time Owen realized he probably wasn't going to escape after all.

The ground rose slowly up before him, and he aimed for an open patch of tilled ground next to a line of windbreak trees. His hands clutched at the controls with such strength that he bent them out of shape, and the flyer began to sluggishly respond. And then another energy beam hit him from behind, and all the lights on his control panels went out. The flyer dropped like a stone, the motor silent, and the ground came rushing up. The left wing hit first, spinning the flyer around. The impact slammed Owen forward against the restraining straps with brutal force, driving the air from his lungs.

For a moment he hung there, dazed and helpless, and then the boost jerked him awake. The flyer had dug its nose into the ground, and he was hanging over the spider-webbed canopy. He hit the strap release and lashed out with his fist as he fell forward against the canopy. Part of it shattered and fell outward, but there still wasn't enough space for him to crawl past the jagged stumps of glass thrusting out from the canopy surround. There was smoke in the cabin, and behind him he could hear the crackling of flames. He took firm hold of the edges of the canopy, breaking away some of the glass and ignoring fragments that still bit into his hands, and slowly he forced the metal rim outwards. The solid steel groaned as it yielded reluctantly to his boosted strength. Blood slithered down his hands. Smoke filled the cabin, tearing at his lungs. He bent the steel edges away from him, and finally forced his way through the jagged glass and out.

He dropped bonelessly to the ground, and lay still on the broken earth for a moment, before the boost forced him to his feet again. Flames roared in the cabin of the flyer, and thick black smoke billowed up into the sky like a marker. The pursuing craft couldn't miss him now if they tried. He'd landed just a few feet short of the windbreak trees, and empty fields stretched out around him. He had no idea where he was, and the only maps were burning inside the flyer. He tried his implant again but the AI was still silent. The boost moved in him like liquid fire, trembling in his supercharged muscles, and he felt as though he had all the time in the world to do whatever might be necessary. He checked his hands dispassionately. They weren't too badly damaged, and the smaller cuts were already sealing themselves. He felt no pain, in his hands or anywhere else, and wouldn't till he came out of boost. At which point his aggrieved body would have a hell of a lot more to worry about than a few cuts and bruises. The human body wasn't meant to work at this kind of level for this long.

He looked up and saw two flyers falling unhurriedly out of the bright sky towards him. Three more craft hung on the sky in the distance like high-flying kites. Owen drew his sword with one hand and his disrupter with the other, and headed for the trees. He wanted something he could put his back against. He might not be a warrior like his father, but he was still a Deathstalker, and he would show his enemies what that meant. Whoever the enemy was. Probably more of his own security people, the ungrateful bastards. He set his back against a wide treetrunk, and leaned against it for support. They might come at him from the front and sides now, but not from behind. Good to have something you could rely on, in an uncertain world.

The more he looked at his injuries, the more serious they

seemed, so he stopped looking at them. The boost was screening him from the pain and shock, but it was also burning up dangerous reserves of strength. It couldn't maintain him much longer, especially if he had to fight for his life. He glared up at the sky, at the craft hovering overhead like vultures. The two flyers landed a respectful distance from his burning craft, and guards spilled out on to the tilled field. Owen counted fourteen and nodded, satisfied. He was glad to see they were taking him seriously. Anything less would have been an insult.

The other three craft dropped unhurriedly out of the sky. Owen tried to focus his drifting thoughts. There were bound to be more guards in the other craft, some with energy guns. In the end it didn't matter how fast or how strong the boost made him; there were just too many enemies to fight. And even if by some boost-inspired miracle he could beat them all, staying boosted for so long would kill him anyway. Damned if he did, damned if he didn't. And maybe that was the real legacy of the Deathstalkers.

It occurred to Owen that he was going to die here, lost and alone and abandoned by all those he trusted, but the thought didn't scare him as much as he'd thought it would. He'd lost everything that mattered and a few that didn't; title, money, position, even people. *I was fond of you, Cathy.* Even if he could somehow find a way to survive this ambush, and what he was doing to himself with the boost, the only future he'd have was as an outlaw and renegade, with every man's hand turned against him. *Dear God, he'd killed Cathy.*

Owen felt suddenly tired, despite the boost. It wasn't that he wanted to die; he just didn't see the point in going on. Everything he valued had been taken from him, by people far beyond his reach. Revenge seemed unlikely, and even pointless now. It wouldn't bring back what he'd lost. If he was going to die, he thought he'd rather go out in a dignified way, not fighting and squealing like a pig in an abattoir.

He cut off the boost, and almost fell as his wounds burst open again. Blood poured down his body, and his legs trembled so much he could hardly stand. He used the last of his strength to put away his sword and disrupter. He wouldn't give the bastards the satisfaction of a struggle. The men who used to be his guards advanced purposefully, weapons at the ready. Owen wrapped himself in what was left of his pride and dignity, and fought to keep his head up.

And then a ship came crashing down out of nowhere, and everything changed. The guards scattered, crying out in shock and alarm as they tried to run every way at once. The gleaming steel craft blocked out the sun as it roared down, and then ripped into the broken earth and sat there, large and ugly and immovable. Owen would have run too, but his legs weren't listening to him. He looked blankly at the squat, squarish ship before him; a simple steel container without identification or markings. Which was of course strictly illegal. He slowly realized it wasn't any kind of flyer, but rather some kind of escape pod from a larger craft. A hatch swung open, and a steel ramp slammed down. A slim figure appeared in the hatchway. Owen took a moment to register it was a woman, and another to realize that she was almost the same age as him, and in almost as bad condition. She was badly burned, her flesh and her clothes blackened and scorched. He thought she might have been pretty if her face hadn't been white and splotchy from pain and shock. She was also carrying the biggest and ugliest hand gun he'd ever seen. She glared at him and gestured at the interior of her ship.

'Move, you idiot! Those bastards will be back any moment, and I for one don't plan to be here when they get their act together and start shooting. Shift your ass and get in here!'

Owen lurched forward. He didn't know who she was, or what she wanted with him, and he didn't care. A moment before he'd been ready to die, but now he'd found hope again, and he wanted to live. He could recognize destiny when it came calling. He could take a hint. He stumbled up the ramp, leaving a bloody trail behind him, and she yanked it up the moment he was clear and slammed the hatch shut. There were two sets of crash-webbing just inside, and Owen sank gratefully into one as the woman threw herself into the other and jabbed frantically at the control panels. The ship lurched under him, engines roared, and then they were up and off and

50

moving. Owen let the webbing support him, and studied his rescuer thoughtfully. The most obvious guess was that she wanted the reward on his head and didn't feel like sharing, but somehow he didn't think so. He supposed he should cautiously draw her out with clever questions, and gradually determine what she wanted with him, but he didn't have the strength or the patience. So, when all else fails, be direct. He cleared his throat painfully.

'I'm Owen Deathstalker. Who are you, and why did you help me?'

His voice sounded weak and thin to him, but if his rescuer noticed it didn't show in her answer. 'I'm Hazel d'Ark. How I got here's rather complicated. I rescued you because I didn't like the odds you were facing. I've always had a soft spot for the underdog. What did you do to get so many people mad at you?'

'I've been outlawed. There's a very attractive price on my head, if you think you can take it.'

'Relax, stud. I'm an outlaw too. No way I could collect your price without getting topped myself. There's a lot of us about these days, but then, that's the Iron Bitch for you. Deathstalker. That name rings a bell.'

'I should hope so,' said Owen wryly. 'I used to be Lord of this planet.'

Hazel whistled. 'I'm impressed. I don't normally move in such high circles. Look, you got any idea where I should point this tub? There are five ships right behind us and closing fast. I feel I should also point out this is a ship's escape pod, and my power cells are almost dead, so don't start getting ambitious. We've got maybe forty minutes of flight left, assuming I don't have to divert power to the energy shields.'

Owen hesitated. 'You still haven't explained why you risked your ship and yourself to rescue me.'

'Underdogs have to learn to look out for each other, because no one else will. An outlaw needs all the friends he can get. You'll learn that, if you survive this mess. Life as an outlaw can be very enlightening.'

'All right. Head due north. There should be a large lake

about ten miles from here, unless I'm even more lost than I thought I was. Tell me when we get there.'

He lay back in the crash-webbing, and fought to clear his thoughts. He had an ally now, and a second chance at escape. If she could just get him to the *Sunstrider* he might yet live to get his revenge after all. The thought stirred new strength in him, and he took a second look at his surroundings. Apart from the crash-webbing, the control panels and the bulkheads, there wasn't much to look at. It was all pretty minimalist, but it seemed solid enough. Presumably there wasn't much point in wasting frills and fancies on an escape pod.

'It's been a long time since I travelled in anything this primitive,' he said finally. 'What does it run on; steam?'

'Any more smart remarks like that and you can get out and push,' said Hazel. 'Don't knock this tub. It's saving your ass and mine. OK; forward sensors report a large body of water dead ahead. Rear sensors report a whole mess of people coming after us in everything that flies. You'd better have a plan to get us out of this, Deathstalker, because I am fast running out of options.'

'Relax,' said Owen. 'I have an ace up my sleeve and it's a beauty. In fact, she's waiting for us at the bottom of that lake.'

Hazel looked across at him sharply. 'Wait a minute; we're going diving?'

'You got it. My private yacht is sitting in its own little niche right at the bottom, hidden from everything but heavy duty sensors. No one knows it's there but me. Had a feeling it might come in handy some day. Paranoia doesn't just run in my Family, it gallops. Part of the territory that comes with being a Lord. Drop this thing in the lake and head straight down. I'll contact the yacht, lower her shields and start powering her up. Your sensors will pick up the *Sunstrider* once you get close enough. Slip in next to her, and fasten on to the outer airlock.

'She's special, my *Sunstrider*. Has all the power and facilities we'll need to make our escape, and then some. Once we're up and moving, nothing's going to catch us. Got her own hyper-drive, based on a new, more powerful design that was only

52

recently discovered. Only a dozen ships fitted with it so far, and none of them anywhere near here. Cost a fortune, but I've always believed in going for the best. Take us down, please.'

Hazel shook her head, smiling. 'How the other three per cent lives. Going down, Deathstalker. You'd better be right about this.'

'Trust me. Have I ever lied to you?'

'How would I know?'

Owen laughed quietly as Hazel sent the escape pod plunging beneath the waters of the lake. Hazel watched the sensor panels carefully as the pod sank slowly through the dark waters, and then leaned forward suddenly. Huge forms were rising up out of the depths towards the craft. They were hundreds of feet long, and according to the sensors, very much alive. They reached the escape pod in seconds and circled around it, moving unsettlingly quickly for things so large. Hazel's hands itched for some kind of weapon, but the beasts didn't seem to be attacking the craft or even warning it off. In fact, if she hadn't known better, she would have sworn they were escorting the ship down . . . A thought occurred to her, and she looked across at Owen.

'According to the sensors, we've picked up an escort. Whatever they are, they're disturbingly large and quite definitely alive. Would you know anything about this?'

He smiled tiredly. 'They're behemoths, from Virimonde's oceans. I had the lake seeded with a breeding pair to discourage people from using the lake. I didn't want any diving teams stumbling over my hidden ship. I understand fishing along the shores of the lake has come to be regarded as a danger sport. The locals play it up as a tourist attraction. I should have applied for a percentage.'

Hazel looked at him dubiously. 'Then why aren't these things attacking us?'

'Because they're actually relatively harmless. They're big and ugly and have teeth like knives, but they're timid as hell. Say boo to them and they'd run a mile. Of course, I don't tell anyone that. There's nothing to worry about. They're probably just curious about us. Ignore them.'

Hazel looked as though she was about to say something cutting, so it was probably just as well that a flashing light on the sensor panels caught her attention. They'd found Owen's yacht. She eased the escape pod into position above it, and then let the onboard computers oversee the contact with the yacht's outer airlock. The behemoths circled hopefully above them for a while, and then disappeared back into the dark waters.

For a while, Owen and Hazel just lay back in their crash-webbings, gathering their strength. They'd used up most of their reserves to get this far, and both of them felt like they'd been running on empty for some time. A bone-deep weariness held them in the webbing like iron weights. It was tempting just to lie there, and escape the stress and strain of their situation in dreamless sleep. Owen slowly realized that if he didn't move soon, he'd just lie there until he bled to death. He forced himself up and out of the webbing, and roused Hazel from hers with harsh words and the promise of luxurious quarters inside the yacht. It took her a while to open the airlock with her burned hands, refusing his offer of help, and then she stepped back for Owen to lead the way. He grinned sardonically, and stumbled towards the yacht's outer airlock on unsteady feet.

He entered the correct security code, and the lock swung open. Owen stepped through, Hazel close behind. Lights turned themselves on as the ship sensed their presence, and Hazel stopped just beyond the inner airlock and gawped openly at the sheer opulence before her. Every form of convenience and luxury had been catered for in the ship's fittings, everything from rich furs on the floor to the very latest computer hardware. There was even an old-fashioned bar, all gleaming mahogany and cut-glass decanters. Owen grinned briefly at her reaction, and waved her into the nearest leather-upholstered chair.

'She is a little beauty, isn't she? One hundred and fifty feet long, thirty wide, with a reinforced, gold-plated hull and all the extras I could find in the catalogue. Get your breath back while I find out if we've still got an AI to run things.'

54

He accessed the ship's computers through his comm implant, contacted the Standing's computers, and downloaded Ozymandias into the ship's mainframe. It all took less than a second, and he broke contact as quickly as he could, just in case something was lying in wait to follow him back. And then the AI's comforting voice was with him again, and he relaxed a little.

'Owen, dear boy, don't ever leave it that late again. Still, I'm relieved to see you survived this far. I'm afraid your Standing is completely overrun, and somewhat vandalized. The Imperial codebreakers are currently trying to crack an empty shell I set up as a distraction, and probably will be for some time, but I think it would be in both our interests to get the hell off this planet as quickly as possible. If not faster. We have definitely overstayed our welcome. I see you've acquired a new friend. Aren't you going to introduce us?'

'Hazel d'Ark,' Owen subvocalized briskly. 'She's an outlaw, like me. Give her low level security clearance, for the time being.'

'Very well, Owen. With your permission, I'll start running the ship through some wake-up routines, and get it ready to depart.'

'Yeah; you do that. And keep the long range sensors alert. If there's anything moving anywhere near this lake, I want to know about it.'

'Hey, Deathstalker, this is some ship you've got here,' said Hazel, and Owen turned his attention back to her. She was slumped in the over-sized chair with a large drink in her hand, like a ragged doll that had been left too close to the fire. 'I could buy a dukedom for what this must have cost. The last time I saw luxury like this was in a top rank brothel parlour back on Loki.'

Owen winced, but managed a polite smile. 'I'm so glad you approve. Right now, I suggest we move into the next room. There's a certain little device there that will do us both a power of good.'

Hazel looked at him suspiciously. 'This wouldn't involve a bed, would it?'

Owen laughed briefly. 'Thanks for the interest, but no. I don't think either of us is in any condition for that. Please, step this way.'

Hazel emptied her glass, let it drop on to the carpet, and struggled up out of her chair. Owen knew better than to offer her any help. It took her a while, but eventually she was back on her feet, and swaying only slightly. In the sharp unforgiving light of the yacht's main quarters, she looked worse than ever. Her clothes were scorched and tattered, and her burns were deep and disfiguring. Her hands were charred claws. He offered her his arm, and she took it as though she was doing him a favour. He led the way into the next compartment; a small, compact room dominated by a long steel cylinder, eight feet long and three wide. Hazel studied it warily. It looked disturbingly like a body bank.

'All right,' she said finally. 'I'll bite. What is it?'

'Cell regenerator,' said Owen smugly. 'Promotes rapid healing in minor injuries, and major ones too if you've got the time to spare. Works on the same principles used for cloning human tissues. Strictly forbidden for any but those of noble birth, on pain of a very unpleasant death. Still, I won't tell anyone if you won't. You want to go first?'

'After you,' said Hazel, very politely, and Owen grinned. He activated the necessary systems through his implant, and the cylinder split apart, revealing a surprisingly comfortable-looking interior. Owen climbed in, gave Hazel a reassuring smile, and lay back with a sigh as the cylinder closed itself over him. After that, it got very still and very quiet. Hazel looked about her. She had to keep fighting down an urge to sneak back into the other room, pick out the smaller valuable items and stuff them into her pockets. She had a strong feeling that would be a bad idea. Partly because it would have been a betrayal of Owen's trust, but mainly because she had an extremely strong feeling that she was being watched. She leaned against the cylinder to steady herself, cleared her throat and raised her voice.

'Is there an AI on board this yacht?'

'Yes, Miss,' said the AI through an overhead speaker. 'I am Ozymandias, at your service. How may I help you?'

'Tell me about Owen Deathstalker.'

'Head of the Deathstalker Clan, and Lord of Virimonde, until his outlawing. A good man, within his limitations. You can trust him to do what he feels is right.'

'That's rather vague.'

'That's Owen for you. He's never been a very positive person. Something of an underachiever, in fact. I have hopes the current emergency will bring out the best in him. If he doesn't get horribly killed first.'

Hazel was about to say something rather cutting when the cylinder suddenly started to open, and she had to stand up quickly to avoid being thrown off. The sudden movement made her feel giddy for a moment, but she had it back under control before Owen could notice. He stood before her and struck a jaunty pose, and she had to admit he was looking a hell of a lot better. His injuries had healed with no trace of a scar, and he had a new confidence in his bearing. Even his clothes had been cleaned and repaired. He smiled cheerfully at her reaction.

'I told you; this yacht has everything you can think of, and a few things you never dreamed of. Climb in, and the machine'll take care of you too.'

Hazel wasn't at all sure she liked the way he'd put that, but she didn't really have any choice, and she knew it. The shock that had protected her from the worst of her burns had worn off long ago. Every movement was agony now, and she was hovering on the edge of total exhaustion. She couldn't argue any more, and anyway, sooner or later she was going to have to trust the Deathstalker. Even if he was a Lord. She nodded stiffly to Owen, and stepped clumsily into the cylinder. She lay down and gave herself up to fate with something like relief. She shut her eyes as the cylinder closed over her.

'Do you want me to make any changes in the young lady?' said the AI diffidently.

Owen frowned. 'How do you mean; changes?'

'Well, there are several programmes I can run while she's in the cylinder that would make her more . . . tractable. Programmes to make her loyal to you, for example, and prevent her from raising any weapon against you. They're quite safe, and would do her no lasting damage. It's simply a matter of security, Owen. She is an outlaw, after all.'

'So am I,' said Owen. 'You leave her mind alone. That's an order.'

'Yes, Owen. As you wish.'

Owen wasn't sure why he was so angry. The computer was programmed to look after his best interests. It was just doing its job. But Hazel had risked her life to save his, for no profit that he could see. No one had ever done that for him before who didn't have to, and he wasn't sure yet how he felt about that. Until he was sure, Hazel d'Ark was under his protection. Even from himself, if necessary.

'Anything new on the sensors?' he said finally.

'Nothing so far. Your plunging into a lake has confused the hell out of them. I'm picking up all kinds of unprotected transmissions. Some think it was desperation, others are suggesting suicide. Right now they're arguing about whether to wait for you to re-emerge, or go in after you.'

'Let me know when they make up their minds.' Owen stretched slowly. The cylinder had repaired all his physical hurts, but he was still mentally exhausted. 'I still can't believe everything fell apart so *fast*. I seem to have gone through the only experience left for the man who has everything; losing it all. This has to be some kind of ghastly mistake. I've done nothing to be outlawed for.'

'Perhaps,' said the AI, 'if you were to surrender yourself, and offer to hand over Miss d'Ark, as a sign of good faith . . .'

'No. I don't want to hear that kind of idea from you again. Besides, I already thought of that, and it wouldn't work. They'd just take her and kill me anyway. Is the ship ready to go yet?'

'Yes, Owen. Ready for takeoff.'

The cylinder opened, and Hazel emerged like a rather bedraggled butterfly from its cocoon. Her overalls had been repaired, and looked cleaner than Owen would have thought possible. She allowed Owen to help her out, studying her now flawless skin with awe. 'I know people who would pay a medium-sized fortune for access to something like this.'

'If we find ourselves dangerously short of money, perhaps you can set up a deal,' said Owen, smiling. 'Now, if you'd like to join me in the main compartment, I think it's time we got the hell out of here. Once we're up and moving, there's nothing on this planet that can catch us. Oz; take us up, and don't stop for anything till we're in orbit.'

'Yes, Owen.'

'Then where?' said Hazel, following him back into the first compartment.

Owen shrugged. 'I was hoping you'd have some ideas. I'm new to the outlaw business. Where can we go, where we'll be safe from the kind of people who'll be coming after me? And before you say anything, no I am not interested in joining up with any rebel groups against the Empire. I am still loyal to the Iron Throne and the Empire, if not the Empress.'

'Nicely rationalized,' said Ozymandias.

'There's only one place we can go,' said Hazel. 'Mistworld, the rebel planet. But it's a one-way trip. You'll be safe enough there, but hardly anyone ever leaves Mistworld.'

'Mistworld. I might have known.' Hazel looked at Owen enquiringly, and he shook his head. 'Don't ask. Very well, for want of anywhere better to go, Mistworld it is. Set the coordinates, Oz. Let me know when we're ready to make the hyper jump.'

'Yes, Owen. We are now in orbit.'

'What, already?' said Hazel. 'I didn't even know we'd taken off.'

'I told you this yacht was special,' said Owen smugly. 'Oz; show us what's happening, on the main viewscreen.'

One of the walls became a viewscreen, showing Virimonde far below, and an Imperial starcruiser heading straight for them. Even as they watched, a second starcruiser dropped out of hyperspace behind the first.

'Two starcruisers?' said Owen, staring at the screen in

disbelief. 'They sent *two* bloody starcruisers to get me? Cut me some slack, dammit.'

'There is a possibility this might be something to do with me,' said Hazel reluctantly. 'My previous ship rammed a starcruiser, just after I got away in the escape pod. Presumably they got a distress call out as they went down.'

'Thanks a whole bunch,' said Owen. 'Any other nasty little surprises you've been keeping from me? No; tell me later. Oz; shields up and go hyper the moment the power levels are steady. I don't know why they're not firing already . . .'

'Presumably they're being extra cautious, after already losing one ship,' said the AI. 'It's not something that happens all that often. They're trying to contact us. Should I talk to them?'

'It couldn't hurt. Lie a lot.'

'There's no way this ship can stand up to that kind of firepower,' said Hazel. 'And there's no way we can get out of here before they open fire.'

'Not necessarily,' said Owen. 'This ship has a new kind of hyperdrive. Very powerful, very fast.'

'Why do I get this strong feeling that there's a *but* hanging on the end of that?'

'But, it's rather . . . untested. No one's had a chance to use it much yet, and there's always the chance they haven't got all the bugs out. I always intended to take her on a long shakedown run, but what with one thing and another, I never found the time. And then circumstances rather caught up with me.'

'Great,' said Hazel. 'Just great. If I had anything left in my stomach, I think I'd be sick.'

'All systems are ready, Owen,' said the AI. 'Or as ready as they're ever going to be. Power's up and all tests are positive. I'm lying my head off to both starcruisers, but I don't think they're in a listening mood. Both are now in firing range. It's time to go, Owen. There's nothing left to hold us here.'

The viewscreen filled with light as both starcruisers opened fire on the *Sunstrider*. Owen and Hazel winced instinctively.

'Take us out of here, Oz,' said Owen. 'We're going to Mistworld.'

'And the good god grant us luck,' said Hazel. 'Because we're going to need it.'

The *Sunstrider* dropped into hyperspace and was gone, and the starcruisers were left to orbit Virimonde alone.

CHAPTER THREE

Fashion, Paranoia and Elves

The Imperial Palace lay deep in the rotten heart of Golgotha, homeworld of the Empire; the concentration of power, and of destiny. It lay hidden away, far below the surface, drawing its power from a geothermal tap; sunk so deep even a scorching by the entire fleet couldn't touch it. Up above, the delicate towers and pastel cities of the elite, the noble and the moneyed. Down below, like a cancer in a rose, a massive steel bunker a mile and a half wide, the home and fortress of her Imperial Majesty, Lionstone XIV. And within that bunker, behind the many layers of cutting-edge technology, a court of gleaming steel and brass where the whole Empire came to pay homage to its ruler. The personification of honour and duty, law and justice, whose whisper was louder than thunder, and more far reaching.

Lionstone XIV, the perfect and divine, the worshipped and adored. Also known as the Iron Bitch.

Her private chambers comprised the heart of the bunker, surrounded by layers of protection and guards, some of which never slept. The Empress had many enemies, and she liked it that way. Love passed and honour changed, but fear remained constant. Lionstone was the latest in a long line of rulers, and she had no intention of being the last. Her private chambers, where she only had to be herself, were bedecked with silks and flowers of a hundred vivid hues, from a hundred different worlds. The air was perfumed with subtle and gorgeous scents that were also quite deadly, unless you'd been immunized against them.

In the midst of it all, Lionstone sat at her toilet before a full-length mirror, attended by her surgically altered maids in waiting. They moved about her with silent grace, like so many butterflies, dressing her in the armour and furs necessary for a formal appearance at Court. Lionstone scowled at her reflection in the mirror. She had power over many things, but tradition wasn't one of them. So she suffered her maids to wrap her in the colours and robes of office, hitting and slapping the young women when they got in the way or as the mood took her, and studied her perfect face in the mirror.

Lionstone XIV was tall and slender, towering over her maids by a good head and more. Her face was fashionably pale, but with none of the usual splashes of colour that fashion dictated. She had little taste, and less discrimination, and didn't give a damn. She had no time for the wild colours and wilder trappings that engaged the attention of so many of her Court, or anything else that might distract from the impact of who she was. She had long, sharp-edged features, with a wide slash of a mouth and brilliant blue eyes, topped by masses of pale blonde hair piled up on top of her head. Her back was straight, her head erect, and her gaze could chill at a hundred yards. She was beautiful. Everyone said so.

Her maids fluttered around her, adjusting a fold here and a hem there. Their hands were always moving, their touch gentle but sure. Lionstone trusted them completely; she oversaw the conditioning of each new subject before they were allowed to join the other maids. She never spoke with them, either in conversation or to enquire their opinion. They had nothing to say. Lionstone had had their tongues cut out, so they couldn't talk about her. She'd also had them blinded and deafened, and now they knew the world only through cybernetic senses. It wasn't fit or safe that anyone should have direct knowledge of Her Majesty in her most private and defenceless moments, so Lionstone's maids in waiting were deprived of the senses nature gave them in return for more perfect and controllable artificial systems.

It was supposed to be a great honour to serve the Empress in person, and there was a long list of applicants, from the highest to the lowest in the land, but Lionstone would have none of them. To their private relief. Her maids had always been rebels or debtors or outlaws. Or perhaps just someone who had fallen from favour. The Empress had them mind-burned and reprogrammed, and those who had once dared defy her now served as her most devoted slaves. The thought never ceased to amuse her.

She'd done other things to them too, but no one ever talked of that. Or at least, not when someone might be listening.

Lionstone tapped her long-nailed fingers impatiently on the arms of her chair as her maids in waiting put the last touches to her appearance. She held herself still till the tall spiky crown of cut diamond had been lowered respectfully on to her head, and then she surged to her feet, scattering the maids with a wave of her arm. She studied herself in the mirror, and the reflection nodded approvingly back. The body armour fitted her snugly from throat to toe, dully gleaming where it wasn't disguised by thick luxurious furs from the inner worlds. Only her face remained bare, as tradition demanded. In an age of clones and other duplicates, the Empire liked to be sure exactly who was ruling them.

There were other safeguards and protections built into her armour, and she ran quickly through a warm-up checklist as her personal computer implant flashed it up before her eyes. Everything checked out, not that she'd had any doubts, and she allowed herself one last glance at the mirror before striding out of her boudoir, leaving her maids to hurry after her. They quickly caught up with her and fell into their usual protective shield about her, their cybernetic systems constantly on the alert for any threat or sign of disrespect. They were her bodyguards as well as her attendants, and waking or sleeping they never left her side.

Outside her boudoir, a crowd of people filled the corridor, desperate as always for her attention. Clerks, military attaches, lobbyists of all creeds and persuasions, all wanting answers and decisions for things that could not go forward without the Imperial nod. They swarmed around her in a babble of voices as Lionstone strode down the corridor. The maids kept them from getting too close. No matter how desperate the importuners were, they all had enough sense not to upset the maids. The Empress seemed to be ignoring the crush, but every now and then she'd pick a face out of the crowd and snap *yes* or *no* or *later*. Anything really important would come through the proper channels, but the proper channels could be . . . diverted, one way or the other, by someone with enough credit or influence. Lionstone believed in being up to the moment.

They finally reached the private elevator at the end of the corridor, and Lionstone waved the crowd away. Most of them fell back immediately; the few who didn't react quickly enough almost fell over themselves backing away as the maids turned their unwavering gaze on them. Lionstone glared at the closed elevator doors as she waited for it to arrive. She was on the verge of being late for her own audience, and that would never do. No one would say anything, of course; if she chose to be late that was her business, and no one would have the temerity to disapprove. But the word would start quietly in certain quarters that just possibly the Empress was slipping, growing lax, and the kind of people who had assassins on their payroll would lick their lips in anticipation.

A delicate chime interrupted her thoughts as the elevator arrived, and the doors slid open. The maids checked it out first with their augmented senses, decided reluctantly that it hadn't been tampered with, and allowed the Empress to join them inside the elevator. The doors slid shut on the bowing heads of the crowd in the corridor, and the elevator rose rapidly from the heart of the bunker to the outer levels where Court business was transacted. Lionstone XIV smiled slowly, and if the courtiers waiting for her to arrive could have seen that smile, they would have found sudden pressing reasons to be somewhere else that day.

The only way to reach the Court chambers from anywhere else on Golgotha was by underground trains controlled directly by palace computers. The trains were prompt, comfortable and guaranteed accident free, but still no one liked using them. People of importance were not used to or happy about giving up control over their personal security, but in this as in so many other things where the Empress was concerned, they had no choice. Her security came first. Always. As a result, everyone setting foot in a palace-controlled train did so knowing that they were literally putting their lives in the Empress's hands. Lionstone sometimes used the trains as a simple means of dealing with those who had gained her displeasure. At a silent command from the palace computers, the train would stop, the doors would lock, steel shutters would slide over the windows and a lethal gas would fill the carriage from end to end. The gas jets weren't even hidden.

The Lord Jacob Wolfe glowered at the jets, and then looked away. They were old news, and he had more pressing concerns on his mind. The Empress's summons to Court had been abrupt and uninformative, even for her, with barely an hour's warning, which meant that whatever had caught her attention was urgent as well as important. It could be that she'd found another traitor, someone sufficiently high up that she wanted the whole Court present while she interrogated and executed him, as a message to any who might be wavering. Lionstone was a great believer in making examples, and putting her point forcefully. And there were always traitors. Some days attending Court was like playing Russian roulette when you didn't know how many bullets were left in the gun.

Besides, if it had been anyone important, he'd have heard something before now. The Wolfe had good contacts at all levels. Every Lord did, if they wanted to stay a Lord.

It wasn't necessary to attend Court in person; you could always send your holo image. Current technology allowed the elite complete access to all that was happening, with no risk that some of it might happen to you. However, by tradition and law, only those who attended in person would be heard by the Empress. So if you wanted your voice to count, you had to be there. Besides, for someone to appear only as a holo at Court was a risk in itself. Lionstone might choose to interpret that as a personal insult; that the Lord didn't trust his Empress to ensure his safety. It didn't do to give the Empress ideas. She had far too many of them as it was. Which was why the Wolfe and his son Valentine were sitting alone in their carriage, without weapon or bodyguard, on their way to Court to hear something they probably wouldn't want to know anyway.

Jacob Wolfe was a great bull of a man, with broad shoulders and a barrel chest that wouldn't have looked out of place on a professional gladiator. He wore his hair cropped close to his skull, maintained his face as that of a man in his forties, and ignored all fashions as they came and went. His jaw was permanently jutted forward, as though daring anyone to comment. His eyes were dark and piercing, and it was a point of honour to him that he never looked away first. He had hands like mauls, large and blocky, curled most often into fists, and his voice was a growl. The Wolfe had put a lot of time and thought into the image he projected, and he was quietly pleased with the result. It let people know right from the start that he was not a man to be trifled with.

The Wolfe was a hundred and three years old, but thanks to Imperial science, the young man sitting opposite him could easily have been mistaken for his brother rather than his son. Even so, a stranger would have found it hard to detect any Family resemblance between them. Valentine Wolfe was tall, slender and darkly delicate, like a hothouse flower rudely torn from its usual habitat. His face was long and thin and more than fashionably pale, and his shock of jet black hair fell to his shoulders in curls and ringlets. Heavy mascara showed up his overbright eyes, and a painted crimson smile hid his feelings from one and all. He had an artist's hands, all long slender fingers and languorous gestures, and they fluttered about his throat in moments of excitement like startled doves in the night.

Valentine Wolfe was well known in and out of Court for having tried every drug known to man, and a few he'd had made up specially. If you could smoke it, sniff it or stick it where the sun doesn't shine, he'd tried it all once, and twice if he enjoyed it, which he usually did. It was truly said he'd never met a chemical he didn't like. It was a wonder to all who knew him that he hadn't fried his brains long ago, but by some dark chemical miracle his mind remained sharp and dangerous. He had the usual enemies for a man in his position, and looked like outliving them all. And though he chose not to play the game of intrigue himself, he could still be a subtle and malevolent influence on those who did. Valentine might be a hothouse flower, but his thorns were poisonous. He produced a tab from a silver pillbox, and pressed it against the side of his neck, over the main vein. His painted smile widened like a scarlet wound. His father sniffed disapprovingly.

'Do you have to do that now? We'll be at Court soon, and we're both going to need all our wits about us.'

'It's just a little something to take the edge off, Father.' Valentine's voice was calm and polite, and only a trifle dreamy. 'Rest assured that all my resources are at your disposal. If I was any more alert, my synapses would be going into meltdown. Why do you suppose our Imperial Majesty, long may she reign, desires our company this time?'

'Who knows why the Iron Bitch does anything these days? I've spent more time travelling back and forth in these damned death traps this last week than I'd normally expect in a month. She's not following any of her usual patterns, and all my usual sources have either disappeared into the woodwork or developed unexpected scruples. I've been paying the little turds good money for years, and just when I really need them they fold on me. Assuming I make it back from Court in one fairly large piece, heads are going to roll, boy, and I am not being metaphorical. She's planning something; something she knows the Company of Lords won't approve of, so she's doing all this just to keep us distracted and separated. It's a smokescreen, sleight of hand, but hiding what . . . Pay attention, boy! One of these days, loath though I am to admit it, you're going to have to take over from me as head of the Family, and I won't have it said I didn't do everything in my power to ready you for that.'

'Far away may that time be, Father,' said Valentine, and only a careful ear might have detected a note of sarcasm in his voice. 'You do so much for me, and I never appreciate it. I have a few trifles about me that are said to boost the intellect and liberate the mind. Would you care to try a little something?'

'No, I would not. I've never needed drugs to be smart. Show me how smart you are. Why do you think the Bitch wants to see us this time?'

Valentine drew a flower from his sleeve. It had a long stem bristling with thorns, and its thick pulpy petals were black as night. He sniffed the flower appreciatively, then took one petal between his perfect teeth and pulled it free. He ate the petal slowly, savouring the juices.

'The Empress has been most disturbed of late, ever since news came in of two newly discovered alien species outside the Empire with technologies at least the equal of our own. One would have been enough as a potential threat, but the prospect of two such species seems to have practically unhinged the poor dear. Then there's the cyberats, playing their disruptive little games in our computers, the clone underground spreading its proclamations everywhere you look, and let us not forget the elves, bless their black little hearts. The elves have been growing increasingly arrogant, not to mention successful, in their attacks of late. And of course there are always the endless Court intrigues, with their plots and schemes and intricate designs. Some days at Court you don't dare cough or scratch your ear for fear someone will take it as a sign to start something violent. Still; you don't need me to tell you that, Father.'

The Wolfe smiled briefly. It was not a pretty sight. 'So, you have been paying attention, at least. They're all good answers, but which one would you pick? Where does the real danger lie, for the Empress and for us?'

Valentine Wolfe ate another black petal, chewing thoughtfully. Bright spots of colour glowed on his pale cheeks like badly applied rouge, and his dark eyes saw many things. 'The aliens are too distant a threat to be worrying our dear Majesty yet. Perhaps we should just introduce the aliens to each other, and then stand well back while they fight it out. The cyberats are too few and far between to be anything but a nuisance, and the clone underground lacks the funding necessary to emerge as a real political force. And the elves have been surprisingly quiet these past few days. Obviously that won't last, but I would have to say they've done nothing outrageous enough just recently to justify our dear Majesty's abrupt summons. No; I fear it's more simple than that. Dear Lionstone has caught someone of standing with his pants down or his hand in the till, and she wants us to watch and take notes while she has something extremely unpleasant and instructive done to him. La belle dame sans merci. Our Lady of Pain. The Iron Bitch.'

Jacob Wolfe nodded slowly, and flexed his great muscles. 'Good. That's more like it. One of us is going to get the chop, and she wants us there to witness it, and be reminded where the real power at Court lies. Nothing new there, except that for once, I don't have a clue as to who it might be. And that is strange. There's usually some whisper going round where my agents can overhear it. So watch yourself when we get to Court, boy. Keep your mouth shut and your veins clear, and take your lead from me.'

'Of course, Father.' Valentine finished the last petal and began to chew slowly at the stem, ignoring the thorns. A thin trickle of saliva mixed with blood ran down his chin as he smiled, and Jacob Wolfe looked away.

The antechamber to the Imperial Court was grand enough in its own right to put any other Court to shame. A huge open chamber of gleaming steel and brass, it stretched away in every direction for as far as the eye could comfortably see, the vista broken here and there by tall intricately worked pillars of gold and silver, set at regular intervals as much for the effect as anything else. And still the packed crowd filled the antechamber from wall to distant wall. Everyone who was anyone, or thought they might be, came to Court when the Empress held audience, to shake the hand of those in favour or snub those who weren't, to make Family agreements or business deals, or just to be seen at Court by the billions watching on their holoscreens throughout the Empire. Food and drink of all kinds were freely available from bewigged servants, but few availed themselves. Waiting to see the Empress, and discover what mood she was in this time, didn't exactly encourage the appetite. Besides; Lionstone had a nasty sense of humour, and it sometimes emerged in the food.

All the Families were there, the cream of the aristocracy, carefully keeping a respectful distance between themselves and sworn enemies, or simply those of discernibly lower status. Every Clan had a feud going on with at least one other Clan. It was expected. Holograms stood to one side, nodding politely to each other, given away by the occasional faint shimmering as some security field interrupted the signal for a moment. Forbidden by law and custom from speaking or drawing attention to themselves, they drifted among the gorgeous Lords and Ladies like ghosts at the feast.

The Families conversed quietly as they waited, searching for support or oneupmanship or simply the latest gossip. Knowledge was power in Lionstone's Court, even if it was only foreknowledge of which way to duck. Everyone suspected everyone else of being the prospective victim of the coming Court's proceedings, and veiled eyes looked this way and that for signs of weakness, like vultures hovering over a dying man. No one said anything openly, of course. It wasn't done.

Heavily armed guards stood here and there, ostentatious in their scarlet armour and visored faces. No one paid them any attention. The Families knew that they were being watched, and that the guards were only the most obvious part of it. Mostly they were just there to ensure the peace among feuding Clans. None of the Families were allowed bodyguards or weapons of any kind, but when words grew heated blows often followed. And then the guards would move in, and restore order with savage gusto. It wasn't often a low-born guard got the chance to manhandle a Lord, and they tended to make the most of it. So the guards watched and waited, and the Wolfes kept away from the Campbells, who kept away from the Shrecks, and so on and so on. Open violence was so gauche, after all.

Lord Crawford Campbell, head of his Clan, moved slowly among the Families with bright eyes and a wide smile, like a shark manoeuvring in a shoal of lesser fish. He was less than average height and more than average weight, and didn't give a damn. The Campbells always maintained that the greatness of a man could be seen in the breadth of his appetites, and Crawford Campbell was well known for his many indulgences. He was well over a hundred, but modern science kept his face as full and unmarked as a child's. None of which did anything to blunt the man's intellect, which remained razor-sharp and just as dangerous. The Campbells were in favour at Court for the moment, not least because the Campbell had sacrificed so many others who stood in his way. Not that anyone could prove anything, of course. The customs and protocols had to be observed. People nodded respectfully to the Campbell as he passed, and gave him plenty of room. He took it as his due. And if sometimes a lesser Lord or Lady showed a different face to his back, Crawford Campbell never gave a damn. He didn't have to.

Drifting at his side or in his wake like a multicoloured bird of paradise was Crawford's eldest son and heir, Finlay Campbell, dressed as always in the brightest silks and graces current styles allowed. Tall and graceful and fashionable to the moment, from his polished thighboots to his velvet cap, Finlay glided among the Lords and Ladies with a smile and a nod and a polite murmur, allowing himself to be seen by as many as possible. He might have been handsome beneath the cosmetics that made a mask of his face, but it was almost impossible to tell. The current mode called for fluorescent skin that glowed a shimmering silver, and shoulder-length metallic hair, every strand individually coated with whatever metals were currently in favour. He wore a cutaway frock coat that showed off his exquisite figure, and a pair of pince-nez spectacles he didn't need, and every pose he struck was the epitome of grace and style.

Finlay Campbell was a dandy and a fop, and though he wore a sword on all occasions when fashion demanded it, he had never been known to draw it in anger. No one ever drew on him, of course, because he was a Campbell, after all, and you could never be sure with them . . .

His father had given up disowning him because it didn't

work, but made no secret of the contempt he felt for the fancy poet who had somehow sprung from his manly loins. Even so, no one ever intrigued against Finlay. The Campbell was deadly enough for both of them, and would brook no insult to the Family name.

Crawford Campbell worked the crowd with ease, nodding to those in his favour or the Empress's and cutting dead everyone else with glorious scorn. Though his movements seemed random, he was in fact quartering the chamber with military precision, making sure he saw everyone who mattered, and marking their face and position in his memory. It was important to know who had come to Court, and who had not, or sent a holo in their place. Knowledge was everything in the cut and thrust politics of Lionstone's Court. The Campbell approved, when he thought about it. A certain genteel savagery helped to weed out the weak and the timid. His gaze suddenly lightened as it fell upon a familiar but uncommon face, and he strode briskly through the crowd, giving people just enough time to get out of his way if they were quick.

'SummerIsle, my dear fellow,' he said finally, an unusual warmth forcing its way past his usual growl. 'A pleasure to see you, as always. What brings you to Court?'

Lord Roderik SummerIsle bowed formally in return. Against the current fashion, he showed his true age in his lined face and thick white hair, though his back was still straight and he held his head high. The SummerIsle disapproved of the current Court almost as much as it disapproved of him, and was rarely seen in public. He dressed in the formal style of the previous Emperor, even though it was forbidden, and kept dangerous company. No one ever said anything. The SummerIsle had been a master duellist in his day, and no one was at all sure that day was over. He smiled at the Campbell almost reluctantly, and took the proffered hand.

'Campbell; looking as disreputable as ever, I see. Still in favour? Of course; silly question. It's been years since I last found it necessary to attend Court, but some things never change. Virtue still goes unrewarded, and the scum still rises to the top.'

Campbell grinned. 'You never did approve of me, SummerIsle. Lucky we're friends, or we'd have killed each other years ago.'

'Oh I doubt it,' said the SummerIsle solemnly. 'You were never that good with a sword.'

Campbell produced a sudden bark of laughter, and people who'd been edging closer to eavesdrop quickly moved away again. It was said by many and believed by most that the Campbell's sense of humour was more dangerous than his rage. Campbell and SummerIsle had been rivals since they were born, and down the long years had been surprised to find it was easier to like an enemy they admired than an ally who had to be supported for Family reasons. The rogue and the honest man, friends despite themselves, bound as tightly as only opposites can be. Campbell fixed SummerIsle with a thoughtful stare, and moved a little closer.

'What does bring you here, after all these years? I thought you'd decided politics were for the lower orders, like myself.'

'My opinion of this Court has not changed one iota. You are the living proof, Campbell. How many better men have you trampled underfoot, to reach your present position?'

'I stopped counting. It was starting to make me big-headed.'

SummerIsle shook his head slowly. 'You are everything I despise in this Court, and I am everything you've sought to stamp out in your long career of murder and double-dealing. What do we have in common?'

Campbell let fly with his sudden bark of laughter again. 'Dead enemies, mostly. We've survived because we've outlived everyone who tried to kill us. We've seen Emperors come and go, and the Empire spread a hundredfold. Political parties rise and fall, businesses bloom and wither, but we go on, matchless and unstoppable. Who else could we talk to, who've seen what we've seen, fought as we have fought? Personally, I like you because you don't take any shit from anyone. Especially me. As for you; you value the truth where you hear it, even if you don't like what it's telling you. You know where you are with me, Rod.'

SummerIsle smiled briefly. 'You always did talk too much, Crawford. How are your sons?'

'A pain in the ass, as always. All married off at last, and producing grandchildren, but otherwise no bloody use at all. I swear Finlay is trying to achieve suicide or martyrdom through sheer excess of fashion. Sometimes I wish he would, just so he'd stop embarrassing me. If he wasn't my eldest, I'd have him smothered in his sleep. There were six others ahead of him, good boys all, but they all died, from duels or treachery or politics of some kind. They're gone, and I'm left with Finlay as heir. If the genetest hadn't proved he was mine, I'd swear his mother stepped out on me. And the others are worse, if you can believe that. My blood must have been running thin when I fathered that batch. At least Finlay has a mind of his own, even if he doesn't use it much.'

Campbell stopped, and looked unhappily at SummerIsle. His voice became low and gruff. 'I heard about your son's death. He should never have fought that duel. He didn't stand a chance.'

'No,' said SummerIsle. 'He didn't. But he had no choice. Honour demanded it.'

'You haven't answered my question yet,' said Campbell, changing the subject with as near to tact as he ever got. 'What has brought you back to Court, after all your years of self-imposed exile?'

'Her Majesty summoned me, with a personal note in her own handwriting. Said she had someone she wanted me to meet. How could I say no?'

'I would have. When Lionstone starts taking a personal interest in you, it's time to change your name and head for the Rim.' Campbell scowled thoughtfully. 'What does the Iron Bitch want with you?'

'She didn't say. Just that my presence was required at this audience. It doesn't matter. My wife is dead, and all my sons. All I have left is my grandson Kit, and we . . . don't get on. And I'm too old to be frightened. So here I am, a loyal subject of Her Majesty.'

Campbell's loud bark of laughter turned a few heads, but

only briefly. The space around him and SummerIsle was growing. 'Your loyalty has always been to the throne, not whoever happened to be sitting on it. I don't think you've had a good word to say about Lionstone since she stabbed her nanny when she was six.'

'Oh, I don't know,' said SummerIsle. 'I've got a very good word for Lionstone. Only I'm too much of a gentleman to use it.' He waited patiently for Campbell's laughter to subside. 'Her father was a hard man to love, if not to follow, but I never doubted he had the well-being of the Empire at heart. Lionstone cares for nothing and no one save herself. She's a spoiled brat, and always has been. Which is not exactly unusual in royal stock, but bearable when diluted with some sense of duty. We've seen many royal backsides on the Imperial throne, but I honestly fear for the Empire under Lionstone XIV.'

'Get out of here, Rod,' said Campbell quietly. 'Whatever the Iron Bitch has to say to you, I don't think either of us wants to hear it. Nothing good will come of it. Leave now, while you still can.'

'Where would I go?' said SummerIsle calmly. 'Where could I go, where her Majesty's hounds wouldn't drag me down, sooner or later? I never ran from an enemy before, and I'm not about to start now. She's brought me here to kill me. I know that. But I will end my days with dignity, as a loyal subject before his monarch, even if that monarch is not worthy of that loyalty.'

'Very pretty,' snarled Campbell. 'It'll look great on your tombstone. Why make it easy for her?'

'It's called duty, Crawford. You must have heard of it. When honour calls, a man must make his stand, if he is a man.'

'As you wish, SummerIsle. Just don't stand too close to me while you're doing it.'

They shared a brief smile, and then looked round sharply as the great double doors swung smoothly open, the massive slabs of beaten steel gliding back as though they weighed nothing. A long fanfare rang out, silencing the chatter of the courtiers, and bright light spilled out from the great courtroom of

Lionstone XIV. The courtiers moved towards it in fits and starts, like moths drawn to a flame.

First went the Company of Lords, all those of the first hundred Families of the Empire, those who ruled planets or companies or armies by right of succession, in the Empress's name. The highest of the high, most noble and acclaimed of her Majesty's subjects. In theory, at least. They strode into the great courtroom, looking neither left nor right, their heads high. Secretly they felt naked without their usual retinues of bodyguards, advisors and sycophants, but a Lord came alone to meet his Empress, without even a sword on his hip. It was a sign of trust, and respect. Not to mention Imperial paranoia.

And after them came the two hundred and fifty Members of her Majesty's Parliament. They represented the economic forces in the Empire, the power and influence of the mighty credit. Only those with a high enough income were allowed to vote, of course. Unless one was of noble birth, Parliament was the only way to gain access to the inner circles of government. A Member of Parliament might be obliged to bow to a Lord if they met in the street, but in an audience with the Empress, their voices were equal. If the Members were ever to act in unison, they could have brought the Company of Lords to heel like so many unruly dogs, but the Parliament was split into several opposing factions, and the Lords took care to keep it split, through quiet patronage and the occasional large bribe. Of late, Parliament had been increasingly disturbed over the threat of higher taxes, to pay for the expansion of the Imperial Fleet, to face the possible threat from the two newly discovered alien species.

In theory, the Empress was bound by law and custom to abide by whatever decisions Parliament and the Company of Lords could bring themselves to agree on. In practice, the Empress would listen, when she was in the mood, and then make up her own mind. Lionstone had the backing of the Army and the Fleet, and as long as she did, no one could make her do a damn thing she didn't want to. Which was why the prospect of an enlarged and more powerful Fleet was causing a lot of sweaty hands and sleepless nights among Parliament and the Lords. Some Members had been heard to say they didn't believe in the new aliens, but as yet no one was prepared to say that in public, let alone at Court.

But, on the other hand, Lionstone's position was not as powerful as it had once been. A great many younger sons of the aristocracy, unable to inherit a title, had ended up making careers for themselves in the Army and the Fleet. And as they advanced in rank, so their influence grew. So that the Army and the Fleet were no longer the unquestioning servants they had once been.

All of which meant that the political structure at Court was one of complete chaos, over which the Empress presided through canny politicking and sheer force of personality.

After the Members of Parliament came the bulk of the crowd; Family members, political hangers-on, businessmen and officers, and anyone else who could bribe, beg or steal an invitation. The Imperial Court was the political and social hub around which the Empire revolved, and everyone wanted to be there. Or to be seen to be there. You weren't anybody if you weren't seen at Court.

And finally right at the back, in hard-worn clothes, with hard-worn faces, came the ten commoners who'd won the Imperial lottery that year. They had won the right to visit the Court and petition the Empress in person, for her aid or charity or justice. Of course, actually raising your voice at Court was a risky business. A commoner had no friends there, and sometimes it was better if the Empress didn't notice you. Her sense of justice was whimsical at best, though occasionally she might rule in favour of a commoner just to upset some noble she was displeased with. On the whole, lottery winners tended just to enjoy the occasion. Some spent the whole year at Court, and never did ask their question.

The Court itself was a swamp, this time. Thick curls of mist hung on the humid air between gnarled and twisted trees, and everywhere was at least ankle deep in dark, smelly water. Knotted vines hung down from lowering branches to trail in the water, and the air was thick with flies and other insects. The courtiers splashed doggedly on through the swamp, keeping a wary eye open for crocodiles or other unpleasant-nesses that might be lurking in the deepening muddy water. Just because it wasn't a real swamp, it didn't mean there weren't real dangers to be found in it.

Most of it was holograms, with just enough physical reality here and there to make it authentically uncomfortable. Lionstone liked to keep her Court interesting, and her tastes were both devious and wide-ranging. In the past, she'd turned her Court into a desert, an arctic waste, and an inner city slum. That one had been really dangerous, and everyone had suffered from fleas afterwards. The desert had been the most sneaky. Sand everywhere, and air so hot you could hardly breathe it. And just to liven things up a little, Lionstone had had tiny metal scorpions hidden in the sand; nasty little copper devices with neurotoxins in their stingers. A minor Lord had been at death's door for a week, and Lionstone still got the giggles when she thought about it.

The courtiers slogged on, muttering darkly, their mood not helped by the knowledge that the whole Empire was watching them suffer. Every planet, no matter how poor or how far flung, had access to the workings of the Court, thanks to the artfully concealed holocameras. The Lords and the Members swore every year that they were going to put a stop to the ancient custom, but somehow they never did. No one could resist the thought of so large a watching audience.

Every now and again, a gleaming silver statue would appear out of the mists, fashioned to show the form of one of the many alien species that had been brought into the Empire, and taught their place. There were a hell of a lot of them. No one knew exactly how many. No one really cared. Some of the statues had actually outlasted the species they represented. There weren't many who cared about that, either. It was, after all, first and foremost a human Empire. Some of the older courtiers leaned on the statues to get their breath back, after first checking for booby traps.

The Empress sat casually on a great throne of black iron and gleaming jade, set just high enough to keep her feet out of the water. She looked perfectly at ease, even though the throne had obviously been designed for someone rather larger. The mists curled away from where she sat, calm and comfortable in her own little circle of cool air. She looked cold and regal and perfect in her royal robes and diamond crown, every inch an Empress. Her maids in waiting crouched naked in the muddy waters at the base of the throne, like so many hunting dogs straining at unseen leashes.

The courtiers slowly assembled before the throne, careful to maintain a respectful and safe distance, and bowed to their Empress. She looked down at the hundreds of bowed heads, and yawned. The courtiers stayed bent over, hot and sweating, waiting to be released. Once she'd kept them there for an hour. She finally gave a signal with a bored wave of her hand. A fanfare sounded, and the courtiers straightened up, with some surreptitious massaging of the back, here and there. No one was stupid enough to say anything. One look at the maids in waiting was enough to put the thought out of anyone's mind. Their faces were blank, inhuman, and their artificial eyes had the direct, unblinking gaze of an insect. They watched the courtiers with unwavering concentration, and now and then metal claws eased out from under their fingernails, ready for use.

A muffled cry sounded among the Company of Lords, as Lord Gregor Shreck stared in open horror at one of the maids. He started to move forward, and the maids tensed. Shreck's Family quickly closed in around him, holding him in place and muttering earnestly in his ears. Finally he had enough sense to look away, though his hands and his mouth still trembled with impotent rage and sorrow. A quiet murmur ran through the Court as they realized that the rumour had been true after all. The Shreck's niece had disappeared from her apartments barely a month ago, and had not been seen since. No one was surprised. It was increasingly common knowledge that she'd been mixing with the wrong sort of people. There'd been rumours of treason, but then, there always were. And now here she was, her memories and personality stripped away so that her body might serve the Empress's needs as a maid.

The Shreck had recognized her, but in the end he said nothing. There was nothing that could be said.

The Empress leaned forward in her throne, and the Court became silent. When she spoke, her voice was calm and even and purposeful, carried clearly to every listening ear in the Court and far beyond. The courtiers listened respectfully, dabbing with silks at the sweat that ran down their faces. The maids didn't listen. They watched.

'Most loyal subjects; welcome to our Court. We trust you find its current aspects amusing. Normally there would now be ceremonies of greetings and respect, but we will pass those by today. We have matters of import to discuss. The Empire faces a threat such as it has never faced before. Not one but two new alien species have been discovered whose technology has achieved comparable levels with our own. They pose a threat to the Empire that is both real and imminent. An attack could come at any time. I have therefore placed our Army and Fleet on full alert. All reserves will be called up, and all industries shall be placed on a war footing, for the duration of the emergency. This will, of course, prove somewhat expensive, and therefore all taxes and tithes have been raised by seven per cent, effective immediately.'

She stopped there and looked about her, as though inviting comment. No one was stupid enough to say anything. There was more coming. They could feel it. Lionstone smiled graciously into the silence, and continued.

'The news we bring today is not all bad. Our scientists have recently perfected a new form of hyperdrive for our starships, powerful and inexhaustible beyond anything we have ever known before. Mass production will begin shortly, and every ship in our Fleet will be fitted with one.'

She waited again, but there was still no response, though thoughts were flying frantically behind a great many impassive faces. If this new drive could do everything the Empress implied it could, it would make all other drives obsolete. Which would mean, among other things, that the Empress's ships would have an unbeatable advantage over all others. In order to compete, all privately owned ships would have to acquire the new drives, at no doubt exorbitant rates. Another form of indirect taxation. On the other hand, someone was going to acquire the right to mass-produce the drive, and that someone stood to make a hell of a lot of money . . . It took a moment before the courtiers realized the Empress was speaking again.

'We regret to inform you that the elves have been busy again, spreading pain and destruction throughout our Empire, but our advisors assure us that they pose no real threat. They have limited numbers and little or no access to advanced weaponry. They will be stamped out. Is that not correct, my Lord Dram?'

A man was suddenly standing beside the Empress's throne, as the holo that had been hiding him fell away. Tall and dark, in jet black robes and battle armour, he stood rigidly at parade rest, his stance almost inhumanly perfect. He looked to be in his early thirties, but no one knew how old he really was. He'd appeared apparently out of nowhere, and guarded his secrets well. He was handsome in an unspectacular way, but his dark eyes and slight smile were utterly cold. He wore an energy gun and a long sword on his hips, in the presence of his Empress; the only man in the Empire so entitled. He was the Lord High Dram, Warrior Prime of the Empire.

Elected to that position by popular vote, he held it for life, though Warrior Primes tended not to live all that long. The Empress had bestowed on him control over the military, in all its aspects, and made him personally responsible for her security and safety. The finest fighting man the Empire had ever produced, bloodied in a hundred major actions, he was adored by the commoners, wooed by Parliament, and universally loathed by the Lords for his power and influence with Lionstone. The two of them were supposed to be lovers, but again no one knew for sure. Most of the Court found the thought of the Empress having anything to do with something as warm and vulnerable as love frankly ludicrous. It didn't stop a hell of a lot of people trying to find proof one way or the other, so it could be used as leverage.

Dram had been made Warrior Prime after personally leading

the attack force that destroyed the elves' main headquarters, hidden among the pastel towers in the floating city of New Hope. Dram and his marines had come falling out of the sun on gravity sleds, and opened fire the moment they were in range. The fragile towers cracked and shattered as gunfire raked through them, and people ran screaming in the streets. The marines kept firing. The people of New Hope had known what they were doing when they allowed the elves to live among them. Dram had his orders, and taking prisoners wasn't one of them. So the towers fell and people died, and the elves were forced out into the open to fight or die.

They never had a chance. Dram had the numbers and the weapons and the advantage of surprise. Most of the elves were mown down the moment they showed themselves, and in the end the only ones who survived were those who ran. Dram left the city of New Hope in flames, a burning coal floating in the sky. He brought back the elves' heads so that they could be displayed on spikes, as a lesson for the wise and the virtuous. The people clapped and cheered whenever Dram made an appearance in public after that. He was the hero of the hour. The people had no use for terrorists. Especially those who weren't really human. They made Dram Warrior Prime, and then the Empress took him for her own.

The elves' plans and capabilities had been almost wiped out, and even now, a year later, they were only just beginning to reassert themselves. Everyone was waiting with bated breath for Lionstone to unleash her hound on them again. Dram got results; everyone knew that. What wasn't as widely known was his willingness to sacrifice his own people, if that was what it took to get the job done. A man could make a good career serving under Dram; if he lived long enough. Which was the other reason why Dram was also known as the Widowmaker, though never to his face. The Lord High Dram had fought seventeen duels in the last year, over everything from an open insult to a raised eyebrow at the wrong time, and never even looked like losing any of them. Didn't stop people from trying to kill him though. The Company of Lords really hated him, and their pockets had no bottom where Dram's death was concerned.

The rewards for information that could be used against him kept rising, with little practical effect. Dram had no obvious vices, and less weaknesses. He seemed completely untouched by the appetites and excesses of the Court, had no friends, and his enemies were dead. His voice spoke for the Empress, and its word could not be challenged. Men, women and children were killed openly in his name, for treason and lesser crimes, to discourage others. His last victim of note had been the previous Lord Deathstalker. That death had stopped the Lords plotting for almost a week.

'First order of business,' said the Empress, and everyone paid attention. 'We will hear from our agents now.'

Another man appeared, on the opposite side of the throne. Like the Lord High Dram he had been there all along, hidden behind a concealing hologram, waiting for his cue. The Empress had always had a fondness for the dramatic gesture. The new arrival wore the silver brand of the Empress's personal espers on his brow, and dressed in pale, characterless clothes. Like the maids, he no longer had a mind or personality of his own. The Empress's secret agents and information-gatherers made telepathic contact through the esper's powers, and he then repeated their reports in their own words. The agents remained anonymous, and security remained complete. The esper's face changed suddenly as an invading personality took it over, and the body's whole stance changed too, becoming casual, even relaxed.

'All right, pay attention because I'm not going to repeat myself. I've worked my way into the heart of the cyberat underground, such as it is. They don't have any formal organization, as far as I can tell. Just a bunch of losers and loners hacking into the computer Matrix wherever they can find or force an opening, and having as much fun as they can before they get caught.

'Their politics are feeble-minded, and their personalities are inadequate, but unfortunately the threat they pose is all too real, and far out of proportion to their numbers. They know computers better than the people who make them. If we stamp out this bunch, others will take their place before you can blink. Makes more sense to keep an eye on the ones we've got; at least we know where to find them if we want them. And just maybe I can keep them on a leash and away from anywhere sensitive.

'That's it, end of report. And while I've got your attention, I'd just like to say that I would very much appreciate being transferred off this job, and as soon as possible. These cyberats are driving me crazy. The sugar-packed junk they eat is doing terrible things to my system, not to mention my teeth, and the conversation is rotting my brain. Away from their computers, these divots aren't exactly social lions, you know.'

The esper's face and stance changed again as a different agent reported in. The face seemed suddenly leaner, more ascetic; the stance that of a man trained in meditation techniques. If he'd looked any more relaxed, he'd have probably floated away.

'Agent Harmony reporting in. My infiltration of the clone underground continues. No one suspects me. They remain suspicious and evasive, but I am making progress. I have as yet discovered no definite aims or planned criminal acts. The underground's politics are largely naive and unfocused, due to the lack of a charismatic leader figure. Should the clone underground acquire such a rallying point, they could become dangerous. As things stand, I have to report that the underground remains a negligible threat to the Empire.'

'Yeah, well, that's mostly because you couldn't find your ass in the dark without using both hands and a map,' snapped a third voice. The esper was suddenly scowling fiercely, his stance a defiant slouch. 'This is Agent Rapunzel, on the Lord Dram's staff. I've been hanging out with the clone underground for three years now, and I'm telling you, these unnatural bastards are potentially the greatest threat the Empire's ever seen. They've got numbers, a rationale, and heavy-level funding and high-tech support from someone high up. And we're talking really high. Don't know who yet, but I'm working on it. In the meantime, these people want civil rights for clones, and they're prepared to do practically anything to get it. All right, they haven't got a charismatic leader yet to pull things together, but the way things are going, it's only a matter of time. Will someone please listen to me! The crunch is coming, and I want out of here!'

'We will speak later,' said Dram. 'Now give the Empress back her esper.'

'Gladly,' said the agent. 'You wouldn't believe the state of this guy's mind. Doesn't anyone ever clean up around here?'

'*Now*, Rapunzel.'

'No one ever appreciates you in this business,' said the agent glumly, and the esper's face became clear and blank again.

The Court remained quiet while all this was going on. Clashes between the Empress's private agents and those belonging to the Lord High Dram were common, as both sides fought for the ear of the Empress. Their respective employers encouraged the rivalry, to be sure they would continue to hear the things that mattered, whether they wanted to hear them or not. It occasionally came to blows, but as yet they'd stopped short of sabotage.

Though their clashing over the outlawing of Owen Death-stalker had come damn close. The Empress's agents had wanted it kept quiet, while Dram's agents, for their own as yet inscrutable reasons, had taken it upon themselves to broadcast the news to one and all. The argument was still going on, and might yet come to blows.

Agents lived brief professional lives of stealth and danger, switching identities and even personalities as they strove to dig up information while hiding their true motives in an age where nothing could remain hidden for long. Agents therefore tended to be professional but eccentric, not to mention quick on their toes. They never knew when their cover might be blown and they'd have to leg it for the nearest horizon, with a hunting pack snapping at their heels. The Lords and the Members had their own agents, of course. Everyone did who could afford it, and a few who couldn't. Knowledge was power in Lionstone's Court, especially if you got it before anyone else.

The Empress looked at Dram, who looked right back at her,

and then they both looked back at the Court. Whatever disagreements they might have in private, they always presented a unified front in public. A great many people had invested a great deal of money into schemes intended to drive a wedge between them, to no avail. Didn't stop people trying, though. The Empress smiled out over the packed Court, and an anticipatory ripple spread through the waiting ranks. The Empress was finally getting to the meat of the matter; the reason why so many of Golgotha's movers and shakers had been summoned into the Imperial presence.

'The problems facing our Empire grow more serious with every day that passes. New alien threats, rebel undergrounds, and more. Now, more than ever, we must insist on the full support of our subjects. If the Empire were to fall, untold billions would die. Colonists on the outer worlds rely on the Empire for supplies, as the inner worlds rely on them for materials. Even we here on Golgotha, homeworld of the Empire, have become dependent on others. No man can fail to do his best, or the whole system that supports us all would collapse. I therefore have no choice but to call for a ten per cent rise in the output of all our industries by the end of the year.'

There was a long pause. Ten per cent was unheard of. It would mean longer work hours for everyone, and cost both Lords and Members a great deal of money. The Members looked at each other. Someone had to say something. After an uncomfortable silence pregnant with unspoken words, the Member for Shadegate North cautiously cleared his throat.

'Your Majesty, times are hard for all of us. Credit is scarce, and our resources are not what they were. If we were to attempt the rise in productivity you suggest, I really think the workforce would revolt. We would quite definitely face go-slows, strikes, and even sabotage. Unless of course your Majesty is prepared to provide monies from the Imperial purse, to see us through these stormy waters, I fear . . .'

'Fear,' said Lionstone. 'You should fear me, Minister. Fear for the fate of the Empire if our Ministers fail us, and fear for yourself if you fail to carry out our commands. If you can't get the job done, we will have you arrested and executed, and see if your second-in-command can do any better. Certainly they'll be more strongly motivated to try harder. Is that clear, Minister?'

'Eminently so, your Majesty. I am sure none of us wish in any way to fail our Empress.'

'Oh, some do, Minister. You'd be surprised. Traitors can be found in the most unexpected places. Isn't that right, Lord SummerIsle?'

And everything went very quiet as all heads turned to look at the SummerIsle. People near him drew away slightly, as though his condition might be contagious, and in a moment he was standing all alone, in a circle of empty space. SummerIsle looked slowly about him, but didn't seem particularly surprised. He looked back at Lionstone, and smiled slightly. His gaze was direct and his head proudly erect, and in that moment he seemed every inch the warrior he'd always been.

'One man's traitor is another man's hero, your Majesty,' he said easily. 'Perhaps you had some specific name in mind?'

'Perhaps we did,' said the Empress. 'You have spoken out against us too many times, SummerIsle, thwarted our will too often.'

'I can remember when it was no crime for a man to speak his mind. Of course, that was a long time ago, in your father's day. And many things have changed since then.'

Lionstone smiled. 'You have displeased us, SummerIsle, because your many words of criticism were aimed not only at ourself, but also at our Empire. Can we rely on you to refrain from such treasonous talk in the future?'

'Don't be silly, Lionstone. I'm too old a dog to learn new tricks, and I wouldn't if I could. I remember you as a child. You were so full of fun when you were younger. If I'd known what you'd grow into . . . I probably would have let you live anyway. I always was too soft where children were concerned. I'm all that remains of your father's inner circle. The others are all dead. Some at your hand, some not. Just as well. They'd hate to see what you're doing to the Empire they swore to maintain. Under you, honour is a joke, and double-dealing is the norm. Justice only for the rich, and death for those who dare to disagree. Thirteen generations of your line built this Empire, Lionstone; only to see it crumble in your iron fist. You are the cancer at the heart of the Empire, the blight on the rose.'

There was complete and utter silence in the Court. Lionstone had been leaning angrily forward on her throne, but she made herself relax and lean back before she spoke.

'You always did talk too much, old man. You stand condemned by your own words. Let no one say we did not give you a fair chance . . .'

'Oh get on with it,' said SummerIsle. 'I'm here to be an example to silence others. I knew that before I came here. Send forward your pet executioner, and we'll get this show on the road.'

He glared defiantly at Dram, but the Widowmaker just stared calmly back, his hands nowhere near his weapons. Lionstone smiled sweetly.

'You're not worthy of the Warrior Prime, SummerIsle. I have a more . . . appropriate executioner for you.'

She nodded to one of her maids, who leapt to her feet, raised her clawed hands above her head and clapped twice. A third man appeared out of nowhere as the concealing hologram blinked out, and moved forward through the muddy waters to stand smiling at the SummerIsle. A slender figure in black and silver armour, he was young and more than fashionably thin, with pale blond flyaway hair, icy blue eyes and a killer's smile. He carried a sword on both hips, and he walked like a predator. People drew back at the sight of him, and a low whisper passed softly through the packed crowd.

Kid Death . . . Kid Death . . .

He smiled and nodded to the courtiers, and those nearest him recoiled as though he'd tossed a snake into their midst. They knew who and what he was. Everyone in the Court had heard of Kid Death, the smiling killer. He strode slowly forward, and the gentle lapping sounds of the water against his boots were eerily loud in the quiet. He finally came to a halt an arm's length from the SummerIsle, and the two of them stood face to face, the old man and the young. The invincible warrior and the undefeated duellist.

Kid Death drew the sword on his right hip, reversed it, and offered it casually to SummerIsle. The old Lord bowed formally, took it, and then took up a fighter's stance. The younger man drew the sword on his other hip, and fell into his own stance. SummerIsle nodded approvingly.

'Glad to see all my training hasn't gone to waste, Kit. You were the best pupil I ever had.'

'Thank you, Grandfather.' The young man's voice was light and breathy.

'Another child who turned out wrong. What the hell was wrong with your generation? Maybe there was something in the water . . .'

'I'm what you made me, Grandfather; the most skilled swordsman in the Empire. You sharpened the blade; did it never occur to you that someday it might be used against you?'

SummerIsle hefted his sword, his gaze fixed on his grandson's eyes. 'You killed your father and your mother and both your brothers, and the law couldn't touch you, because you said they were duels, and there was no one to contradict you. I should have killed you myself, but I couldn't. You and I are all that's left of the SummerIsle line, Kit. Don't let it end here, in senseless bloodshed, just to please the Iron Bitch.'

'I'm doing this to please myself, Grandfather. Doesn't the student always want to prove that he's become better than the teacher? As to serving the Empress, I am a killer, so I must go where the killing is. My parents disapproved of the life I led, and tried to stop me; so I stopped them. And my brothers too, later, when they came looking for vengeance. They won't be missed, any of them. They dared little, and achieved less. But I go on, the best of the best, death on two legs, her Majesty's executioner in all but name. One day I'll have that too, and then there'll be a new Warrior Prime.'

'You won't last that long, Kit. She'll see to that. Tell me, boy; did you ever feel anything for your Family? I loved them so much.'

'No, Grandfather, not a thing. Not even when I killed them. Enough talk, old man. Let's dance.'

He stepped forward, the sword moving easily this way and that, searching for an opening. SummerIsle went to meet him, moving only as much as he had to, the tip of his sword pointing always at his grandson's heart, and his eyes were cold and steady. For a moment they circled, each wary of the other, and then they came together in a flash of steel and the crashing of blades. The encounter was over in a moment, and then they were circling again. There was a long red slash along Kid Death's left cheek, and blood trickled down his face. SummerIsle had drawn first blood. His grandson smiled widely, and then threw himself forward. His sword was everywhere, and the sheer ferocity of his attack forced SummerIsle back, step by step. And then the old man stood his ground, and would not give up another step, no matter how hard Kid Death pressed him. As though he had said, *This far will I go, and no further*. Their swords rang together and they stood face to face, straining with all their strength for the upper hand. SummerIsle's breath was coming fast and quick, and his face was flushed. His grandson wasn't even breathing hard. Kid Death held SummerIsle's eyes with his, and surreptitiously drew a dagger from a concealed sheath in his sleeve. SummerIsle smiled suddenly, and nodded, and Kid Death thrust his dagger between the old man's ribs.

SummerIsle grunted once, and then coughed. Bright bubbling blood spilled from his mouth, and the strength went out of him, his sword fell, and Kid Death ran him through with a short, brutal motion. SummerIsle sank to his knees, his blood spattering the surface of the water. Kid Death pulled free his sword, sheathed it, and then bent over his grandfather, their faces close together.

'You knew that trick,' the young man said quietly. 'You taught it to me. You knew it was coming, and you did nothing to stop me. Why?'

'Because I have no wish to live on . . . in the kind of Empire Lionstone is building. And because you . . . are the last of the SummerIsle line. If I'd killed you . . . the line would have ended with me. Can't have that. You'll be the SummerIsle now, boy. Maybe you'll make a better job of it than I did.'

His head dropped slowly forward, as though he was bowing to his grandson, and then he fell forward into the muddy waters and lay still in a widening pool of his own blood. And Kit, Lord SummerIsle, straightened up, shrugged briefly, and turned away.

'I have my own name, old man, the name I earned. And I like it better than anything you ever gave me.'

He drew his bloody sword and saluted Lionstone with it, and she bowed regally in return.

'Don't go too far away, Lord SummerIsle. I may have need of your services again. There is still another traitor who must be dealt with.'

Kid Death took up a relaxed stance beside the throne, pushing the Empress's esper out of the way, and set about cleaning the blood from his blade with a piece of rag. In the forefront of the crowd, the Campbell watched guards drag SummerIsle's body away, and said nothing at all. Lionstone nodded to her maid again, and once more she rose up and clapped her hands twice. Two guards appeared from the mists behind the throne, pushing a large transparent sphere ahead of them. It hovered at waist height, kept clear of the foul waters by its anti-grav field. Within the sphere, a man sat slumped, his head hanging down from exhaustion. He looked to be in his mid-forties, with a heavy-set face and figure. His long golden robes might have been imposing once, but they were tattered and soiled now, mostly with his own blood and vomit. He wore no chains, but the sphere held him as securely as any cage. A quiet murmur, quickly stilled, ran through the Court as those at the front recognized the new prisoner and sent his name back through the crowd. The guards brought the sphere to a halt before the throne so that Lionstone could look upon her new victim. Her voice rang sweet and mocking on the quiet.

'My Lords, Ladies and Gentle Friends, allow us to present to you Judge Nicholas Wesley. Once, he presided over the highest Court in our Empire, his name a synonym for law and justice. We thought that of all our subjects, we could trust him implicitly. We were wrong. He thought his word was law, but there's only one law in the Empire, and that is ours. And having forgotten his duty, he threw away his honour by associating with quite the wrong sort of people. Tell us, Judge; how long have you been a supporter of the clone underground?'

The packed Court was deathly silent as it waited for the Judge's answer. If ever a man in the Empire had been trusted and admired, even revered, it was Judge Wesley. His judgements were legends of reason and honesty; his few books required reading. And now he sat slumped in a stasis sphere, bloodied and humbled, and perhaps there was no justice in the Empire any more. He looked up slowly, as though even as simple a matter as that took much out of him. Somewhere along the line he'd suffered a severe beating. One swollen eye was entirely closed, and dried blood crusted his split lips. But even though he had fallen so very far, there was still dignity about him, and when he finally spoke his voice was calm and measured.

'I served you for thirty-eight years, Lionstone. I gave justice to all who came before me. Or that is what I told myself. It is my shame that it took me so long to see the evil in you and your laws. My life had become a mockery of everything I thought I believed in. But finally I saw the truth, and I will not look away now, even if the light is painfully bright. A simple truth undid me; that clones are people too.'

'Not unless we say they are,' said the Empress. 'You haven't answered our question, Judge. How long have we nursed a traitor to our bosom?'

The Judge met her gaze unblinkingly, and said nothing. The Empress smiled.

'Do you understand the nature of the sphere that imprisons you, traitor? It's a stasis field. Within that sphere, time does as we command. We can speed it up or slow it down. A year can pass in a second, or a second can last a year. You could lose a decade in the blink of an eye, live out your whole life in the time it takes you to answer our questions. Unless you choose to be reasonable. Give us the names of the scum you dealt with, and where they may be found, and you shall go free. We give our word as Empress.'

The Judge smiled suddenly, and fresh blood ran down his chin as his lips split open again. 'Your word is worthless, Lionstone. Truth and honour are not in you. I have nothing to say.'

The Empress sat back in her throne, and gestured sharply to one of the guards by the sphere. He made a small adjustment to the control on his wrist, and the Judge grunted loudly as though someone had hit him. His hair grew longer and thick strands of white appeared in it. Heavy lines dug deeply into his face. His frame shrank subtly, and his hands withered into claws. He moaned with pain as arthritis filled his joints. Lionstone raised a hand, and the aging stopped. Within the sphere, the equivalent of forty years had passed in a few moments.

'Talk to us, Nicholas. This is the last chance we can offer you. Are you really willing to die, to protect creatures who aren't even human?'

Judge Nicholas Wesley gave her a smile that had as much of the skull as humour in it. 'The lowest clone is more human than you, Lionstone.'

The Empress gestured angrily, and time roared through the sphere like sands rushing through an hourglass. The Judge grew withered and frail. His hair fell out and his skin mottled. The skull replaced his face, as bones pushed out against the tightening skin, and still he had nothing to say. Time passed. The Judge died and his body decayed, and then there was nothing left in the sphere but his torn robes, and a few bones crumbling into dust. The guard collapsed the stasis field and the sphere disappeared. The Judge's robes dropped into the muddy waters, and sank from sight.

Out in the antechamber, Captain Silence and Investigator Frost sat alone, in chains, inside a force screen. The field shimmered on the edges of their vision, whichever way they looked, so that the antechamber had an unreal, ghostly look to them. Silence wasn't fooled. The danger they were in was all too real. He'd lost his ship and allowed the Deathstalker outlaw to escape. He should have died honourably at his post as his ship went down. His Clan would have mourned his name, and it would all have been over. But the Investigator had insisted on saving him, for her own inscrutable reasons. And so here he was, secured at the ankles, wrists and throat with enough chains to hold a dozen men, waiting to see which interesting and especially painful death the Empress had in mind for him.

Officially he was entitled to a court martial, before a board of his peers and fellow officers, but the Empress outranked them all, when she chose to, so she had first claim on him. Besides, the best he could have hoped from a court martial would have been a quick death. Silence rattled his chains briefly, and sniffed. Shoddy workmanship, but still more than enough to hold him, even without the force screen. He wasn't going anywhere. There was nowhere to go. Nowhere the Empress couldn't find him. Besides; he wouldn't have wanted to live as an outlaw anyway, always on the run, looking back over your shoulder to see if they were gaining on you. No peace, no chance for happiness . . . or honour.

Silence sighed heavily, not for the first time, and looked at the Investigator sitting beside him. Their captors had taken special pains with her bonds, loading her down with thick steel chains until a normal person would have collapsed under the weight of them. Frost ignored them, sitting proud and erect on the wooden bench as though it was her own idea to be there. The force screen was mainly for her. She was an Investigator, after all, and no one was taking any chances.

Two armed guards stood before the closed double doors, waiting for the call to bring the prisoners in. They looked large and tough and extremely competent. Silence would have doubted his chances against them even without the chains, and with a sword in one hand and a grenade in the other. He sighed again, and rattled his chains mournfully.

'I wish you'd stop doing that,' said Frost.

'Sorry. Not much else to do.'

'They'll let us out of the screen soon.'

'That won't make any difference, Investigator. We're not going anywhere.'

'You mustn't give up, Captain. There are always options.'

Silence looked at her. 'Is that why you rescued me from the bridge of the *Darkwind*?'

'Of course, Captain.'

'Thanks a whole bunch. But I forgive you, Frost. It must have seemed like a good idea at the time.'

Frost stirred, and her chains rattled briefly. The armed guards looked at her thoughtfully. 'I was just doing my duty, Captain.'

'Does that mean you wouldn't try to escape now, if you could?'

'Of course I would, Captain. I'm loyal, but I'm not stupid. We must keep our eyes open and our wits about us. There are always options.'

And then the double doors swung open a short way, and the two armed guards moved towards the prisoners. One drew his disrupter and pointed it meaningfully at Frost. Silence felt vaguely insulted. The second guard made an adjustment to the controls on his wrist, and the force screen disappeared. Silence looked at Frost.

'If you have any suggestions or ideas, now would be a really good time to share them.'

'We could always use our chains to club anyone to death who got too close to us.'

'Good idea. Get them to kill us quickly. Keep thinking, Investigator.'

The guards gestured for Silence and Frost to pass through the double doors and into the waiting Court. They kept well back, both their guns trained on the Investigator. Silence gathered up his chains and rose awkwardly to his feet. It took him a moment to get his balance as the heavy weights shifted, and then he stumbled towards the doors. If he hadn't had experience on heavy gravity planets, he doubted he'd have been able to move at all. The guards would have loved that. They were just looking for some excuse to beat the crap out of him again. Silence gritted his teeth and kept moving. Frost walked beside him, back straight and head erect, ignoring her chains as though they were so many party favours. She was courteous enough to keep pace with Silence, and somehow that made it worse.

They passed through the waiting doors and were immediately ankle deep in filthy water. Silence was past caring. It was just one more indignity. He splashed on, fighting to keep his head up. The Court was packed. They must be expecting a really unpleasant execution. A narrow aisle formed before him, people drawing back as though not wanting to be associated with him even by proximity. Silence didn't care. At least they weren't shouting or spitting or throwing things. Though come to think of it, he might have preferred a little shouting. The continuing silence was becoming unnerving. He struggled on, Frost at his side, the guards a respectful distance behind them. Silence looked about him as best he could, and the courtiers looked back, with something in their faces that might have been expectancy. And it occurred to Silence that the Empress wouldn't have summoned this many important people to Court just to watch him and Frost die. They had to be here for some other, more important reason. Which suggested that just maybe there were still options open to him, after all.

Finally Silence and Frost came to a halt before the throne of Lionstone XIV. Silence felt ready to drop, but forced himself to stand straight despite the chains. He had a strong feeling this would be a really bad time to show weakness. Frost stood beside him, looking calm and composed, as always. Something moved in the deeper waters not too far away, and Silence wondered fleetingly if there was something alive just below the surface. Something alive and hungry. The Empress did so like her little jokes. It didn't really matter. If it got too close, Frost would take care of it.

Silence looked back at Lionstone and she smiled down at him coldly. He bowed as best he could. She was his Empress, after all. Frost didn't bow. One of the guards stepped forward, gun raised to club her to her knees. Frost braced herself and lashed out with a stiffened leg. The guard took the boot in his gut and just had time for a surprised breathless grunt before he went flying backwards into the crowd. They all ended up in the water, splashing and cursing. The guard didn't get up again, and neither did some of the courtiers he'd slammed into. Silence had to smile. You could always depend on Frost to make an impression. A brief clamour of protesting voices began in the surrounding crowd, only to die swiftly away as the Empress glared at them. She looked back at Silence and Frost, and Silence for one was surprised to find she was still smiling. It only took him a moment to decide that he didn't like the look of that smile at all.

'Leave my guards alone, Investigator, there's a dear. They're frightfully expensive to replace. Believe me, you're in no danger here. The chains are just a formality.'

'A rather heavy formality, Your Majesty,' said Silence. 'May I enquire as to why we are here?'

'We have a use for you, Captain. We were rather annoyed with you and the Investigator. You lost us a perfectly good starship, and you failed to bring us the head of that most wretched traitor, Owen Deathstalker. We wanted his head very much. We were going to stick it on a spike, right here at Court, so that everyone could see what happens to those who dare defy us, whatever their status. We were also planning to have you both killed in slow, painful ways, as a sign to those who dared fail us, but . . . we changed our mind. We have a use for you.'

Here it comes, thought Silence, wishing he could duck.

'You pleased us greatly in your handling of the alien menace on Unseeli; both ten years ago and more recently. Their uprising threatened the stability of the Empire, but you put a stop to that, and to them. You also discovered the alien starship that crashed there recently, and dealt with its occupant, before it could contact its own kind and warn them of our existence. For this, and other services on our behalf, you have our gratitude, and a Pardon for all your crimes.'

The crowd broke into more or less spontaneous applause as the remaining guard activated the controls on his wrist. Padlocks clicked open one after the other, like a run of firecrackers, and the chains fell away from Silence and Frost. They dropped into the muddy waters, and were gone. Silence rubbed gingerly at his chafed wrists, his mind whirling. It wasn't so much what Lionstone had said, as what she hadn't said. She hadn't mentioned their discovery of a new stardrive in the alien ship. Of course, there were all sorts of reasons for that. Firstly, it wouldn't do for the Court to get the idea that the aliens might actually have a technology that was, in some ways at least, superior to the Empire's. And secondly, as long as the Court thought her scientists controlled production of the new stardrive, they wouldn't do anything that might offend her, for fear of being refused access to the drive. Both of which were very good reasons for having him and Frost silenced. Something bad was coming all right, and it was headed right towards him. He could feel it, like the cold breath of Death herself on the back of his neck.

'We hereby reinvest you in your previous ranks,' said the Empress, almost casually. 'We give you a new ship, the *Dauntless*, fitted with our new stardrive. You will go to the planet Grendel, and open the Vaults of the Sleepers.'

A shocked gasp rippled through the Court. Everyone remembered what happened the last time a starship made contact with Grendel. The planet had seemed empty, peaceful, perfect for colonization. But deep in the ground, the Investigatory team had found the remains of a vast alien city, long abandoned, and massive steel vaults, ancient almost beyond measurement. They opened one of the vaults, and the sleepers awoke.

Hideous alien creatures, nightmares in flesh and blood and spiked silicon armour that was somehow a part of them. They were huge and impossibly fast, with metal claws and teeth. They wiped out the entire party in a matter of minutes. The Empire sent down seasoned attack troops, battle espers, even adjusted men. They all died. Luckily the aliens had no starship of their own. They were trapped on the planet's surface. The Fleet moved in and scorched the surface of the planet from orbit. Grendel was under quarantine now, guarded by half a dozen starcruisers. There were other vaults, and other sleepers, and the Empire had no wish that they should awaken.

Apparently that had changed now. Silence shook his head disgustedly. Grendel. He almost thought he'd rather have been executed.

'Might I enquire why we're opening this particular can of worms again, Your Majesty?'

'Of course, Captain. You're going to open the vaults one at a time and discover, by whatever means you deem necessary, how to tame and train the sleepers. You will have unlimited access to funds, men and weaponry. Call on whatever you need to do the job. It is our intention to use the sleepers as shock troops in our coming conflict with the two newly discovered alien species. Any questions?'

'Do I have time to make a will before I go?' said Frost.

The Empress laughed briefly, and called forward more guards with a wave of her hand. 'Escort the Captain and the Investigator to their new ship. See they don't get lost along the way.'

Silence bowed, and he and Frost left the Court with their heads held high, doing their best to ignore the dozen heavily armed guards who escorted them. Silence shook his head ruefully as he left. Not only had Lionstone presented him with a near impossible task, quite likely to get him and the Investigator killed, she had also ensured that he would have no chance at all to open his mouth about the origins of the new stardrive. Lionstone didn't lack for courage or cunning, which was at least partly why she was still Empress.

Lionstone waited till they were gone, and then smiled out over her Court. 'We trust it is now clear what lengths we will go to, to protect the Empire? Good. We will defend the Empire from any enemy, without or within. Make no mistake, most gracious Lords and Ladies and Gentle Friends; the new stardrive gives our Imperial Fleet an unbeatable advantage over any who might try to stand against us. Our enemies shall fall. There will be nowhere they can hide from us. Nowhere we will not follow them. Our will shall be unchallenged.

'Now, is there any other business?'

The ceiling high above the throne exploded, and debris rained down through the shifting mists. The maids in waiting leapt up and sheltered the Empress's body with their own. Sharp-edged rubble cut their pale flesh and blood flowed, but none of them flinched. The Court screamed and panicked, milling this way and that in their fear and confusion. Dram drew his sword and gun and looked about him for an enemy. And out of the smoke and mists above the throne dropped a dozen long lines, down which slid men and women dressed in leathers and chains. They hit the water and stepped quickly aside to make way for others coming down after them. Dram looked at the dozen guns facing his one, and stood very still. The newcomers gestured for him to drop his gun and sword, and he did, watching expressionlessly as they disappeared into the dark waters and were gone. Kit SummerIsle dropped his sword without waiting to be told. The maids moved a little away from Lionstone to form a defensive circle around the throne, staring at the newcomers with unblinking insect eyes. The courtiers were all shouting and talking at once, and one word rose again and again above the rest.

Elves . . . the elves have found us . . .

'Honour to the Esper Liberation Front!' shouted one of the newcomers, a young woman in battered leathers and far too many chains, over a T-shirt bearing the legend *Born To Burn*. She was short and stocky, with muscles bulging on her bare arms. Her long dark hair was full of knotted ribbons, and she might have been pretty if her eyes hadn't been alight with the fire of the true fanatic. Other elves gathered around her, half their guns trained on the quieting Court, the others on the throne. Lionstone watched in silence from behind her maids, her eyes full of fury. Neither she nor Dram nor anyone in the Court was foolish enough to go against energy weapons.

The elves looked hard and roughly used, but the chains holding their leathers together were freshly polished, and they all wore bright colours on their faces and in their hair. Most of them were young, some barely out of their teens, but they all had scars somewhere on their bare skin. The Empire used espers harshly, which was why so many died or went rogue.

Most died. There were very few old espers. The elf wearing the *Born To Burn* T-shirt stepped forward and bowed mockingly to the silent Court.

'Sorry about the mess, but a good entrance is so important. Now be good boys and girls, and do as you're told, and you'll be able to leave here with all your major organs intact and still attached in the right places. Annoy us, and we'll think of something amusing to do to you. And some of us have a really nasty sense of humour. Being an outlaw can do that to you.'

She turned to look at Lionstone. 'Relax, dear; we're not here to kill you. We've come for one of our own. Now do you want to step down from that throne, or would you rather be thrown down?'

Lionstone rose to her feet, and stepped down into the dark waters with icy dignity. The maids moved immediately to surround her. The elf ignored them all, and crouched down beside the throne, running her hands carefully over the black iron studded with jade.

'Do you have a name, traitor?' said the Empress.

'Stevie Blue; not at all pleased to meet you.'

'My guards will be here soon. There is no way you can hope to escape.'

'Your guards are currently being run in circles by associates of ours. Your only protectors are those poor mind-burned souls acting as your maids, and the esp-blocker built into your throne. Ah; got it.'

She slid back a recessed panel in the side of the throne and carefully removed a translucent cube the size of her head. An esp-blocker was really quite a simple device; the living brain of an esper, removed from its body and held in suspension. A low current passed constantly through the frontal lobes, keeping the brain awake and aware and functioning, using its esp to prevent any other esper abilities from functioning in its vicinity. Just another hell the Empire made, and the only real defence against a rogue esper. Or an elf.

Stevie Blue lifted the cube above her head and brought it down with savage force on the arm of the throne. The fragile container shattered, and the brain tissue fell apart, already dying.

'Be at peace, my friend,' said Stevie softly. 'The fight goes on.' She turned her gaze on Lionstone again. 'That's one less soul living in a hell you made for them.'

Lionstone smiled. 'I'll get another. There's no shortage of donors.'

She broke off as the elf took a step forward, and then stopped herself. Stevie Blue looked at her coldly. 'I could kill you now, Lionstone. Any of us could. We want your death so badly we can taste it. We dream about it at night, and wake to plan new ways of making it. One day we'll take your precious Empire apart stone by stone till there's nowhere left for you to hide, and then we'll come for you. But if we were to kill you now, while you're weak and helpless, you'd just be replaced by another from your corrupt line, and the new Emperor would order massive reprisals among the esper community. Thousands would die, and thousands more would suffer. But we didn't want to leave without giving you some indication of our true feelings for you. So we brought you a little present.'

She reached back and a large cream pie was placed in her hand. Stevie Blue grinned at Lionstone's shocked expression, and then aimed and threw the pie with one easy motion. It hit Lionstone square in the face, and she fell back a step, clawing at the mess on her face.

Stevie laughed. 'You'd be justified in calling for reprisals over an assassination attempt, but over a pie in the face? You'd just look extremely petty. Not to mention weak. Goodbye, Lionstone. It's been a pleasure.'

Lionstone glared past the thick swirls of cream, and pointed a quivering finger at the elves. 'Kill them! Kill them all!'

The maids sprang to obey. They surged forward, steel claws shooting out from under their fingernails, and the elves went to meet them, manifesting their abilities. Stevie Blue wrapped herself in fire, living flames of pure heat, but the maids jumped her anyway. They were beyond such weaknesses as pain or fear. Stevie disappeared beneath the clawing figures, and the other elves raced to help her. The maids split up to greet them.

They fell upon the espers, tearing them apart with their unnatural strength as the elves screamed and died. One esper gestured desperately, and the maids stopped suddenly as though they'd met an invisible wall. And then they stumbled forward again, as the wall collapsed. Stevie Blue's flames flickered and went out. Lionstone laughed, sat upon her throne again.

'You didn't really think I'd trust my safety to just the one esp-blocker, did you?'

She had to shout the last part over rising screams as the maids moved among the desperate elves. Disrupters fired, but the maids moved too quickly to be hit. Then they were among the elves, and it was too dangerous to use the guns any more. The maids leapt among the espers like wolves in the fold, tearing at defenceless flesh with their clawed hands and stuffing the bloody meat into their mouths. They were hungry.

The remaining elves tried to run, but the maids were everywhere. The elves fell, one by one, until finally only one man remained unharmed. He ran towards the throne, and tried to fire his disrupter, but the energy crystal was still recharging. He threw the useless gun aside, and drew his sword. A maid jumped him and pulled him down into the water. She held him under and watched impersonally as he drowned. He kicked and struggled, and then his sword thrust up out of the water and sliced into the maid's belly. The force of the blow threw her back, and the esper burst up out of the water, coughing and choking. He fixed his gaze on Lionstone again, and hefted his sword. He moved forward, and the maid jumped him from behind. She concentrated in the way she'd been taught, and the shrapnel bomb set inside her body exploded. Both she and the elf were torn apart by the blast, and blood and shrapnel rained down for long moments.

Quiet fell slowly across the Court, the only sound that of the four surviving maids in waiting, feeding on the bodies of the fallen elves. Lionstone called to them and they came, clustering around her throne like hounds called away from the kill. The Empress looked down from her throne at Stevie Blue, crouching torn and bloodied in the water at the base of the throne.

She'd managed to draw her sword, but her hand was trembling violently from the shock and pain of her wounds. She stumbled forward, forcing herself on, her bloody mouth set and determined. Dram stepped in behind her and ran her through with his sword.

Stevie Blue fell to her knees whimpering. Dram pulled his sword out and she shook once, as though at a sudden chill. Lionstone stepped down from her throne to kneel before her. She had an ornate silver dagger in her hand. She leaned forward, till her face was right before the esper's.

'Have you nothing left to say to me, elf? About how weak I am, or how clever you were? No last declaration for the cause?'

Stevie shuddered again. When she spoke, only the Empress could hear her.

'I'll be back. There are lots like me. One of us will get you. Burn in hell, bitch.'

Lionstone slid the dagger delicately into Stevie's heart, and breathed the esper's dying exhalation into her own mouth, savouring it like a connoisseur. She pulled out the dagger, put her fingertips against the esper's breast and pushed. Stevie Blue fell back into the dark water and lay still. Lionstone straightened up, made the dagger disappear up her sleeve again, and allowed Dram to help her up on to the throne again.

'Elves never talk,' Dram said casually. 'They programme their minds to self-destruct, rather than give up any secrets. If anything, you gave her an easy death.'

'You always want to spoil my fun, Dram. She died in despair. That will do for me. For the moment, I'm more interested in how that many elves got past your security defences.'

'A good question,' said Dram. 'And one which I will be putting to my staff very forcefully once this audience is over. I can only assume I have a traitor somewhere in my organization.'

'I thought that was supposed to be impossible.'

'So did I. If there is a traitor, I'll find him.'

'I hope so, Dram,' said the Empress. 'Because if I can't trust you to protect me, what use are you?'

Dram smiled, and carefully dipped a finger into the traces of cream still on her face. He tasted it thoughtfully.

'Brandy buttersauce. My favourite. If nothing else, the elves do have excellent taste.'

'Of course,' said Lionstone. 'Just ask my maids.'

CHAPTER FOUR

Rising to the Experience

The city had another name once, but no one remembers it now. For the past three hundred years it has been known throughout the Empire as the Parade of the Endless, home of the Arena and the Games. It's not a large city, by Golgotha standards, but it grows a little every year as new citizens are drawn to it, like flies to rotting meat. There are gambling houses and pleasure domes, reality shunts and psi jaunts, wonders and marvels and spectacles beyond counting, but no one comes to the Parade of the Endless for those. They are the appetizers, the side dishes, something to clear the palate and sharpen the senses before moving on to something stronger.

In the centre of the city, deep in its dark and bloody heart, lies the Arena; a wide open space of carefully raked sands surrounded by tiers of banked seating. It is kept safe and separate from the rest of the city by a series of force screens, only ever lowered in sequence. It's hard to get into the Arena. It's even harder to get out. Those that live there never leave. They have their own places, in the cells and chambers and twisting passageways deep beneath the Arena. The gladiators live in relative luxury, honing their fighting skills and dreaming of fame and glory. Trainers and service staff live in the plainer chambers, their lives dedicated to the smooth running of the Games. Prisoners await their fate in the darkness of their cells, on the lowest level, knowing they will never see light again till they are pushed stumbling out on to the bloody sands of the Arena. There are always prisoners; men, clones, espers and aliens. Fodder for the never-ending hunger of the crowds.

People come from all over the Empire to see blood and

suffering in the Arena, to see life and death played out by the ancient rules. Billions more watch it all on their holoscreens every night, but for the true fans, the connoisseurs, seeing is not enough. They need to be there, in person, to see with their own eyes, drink in the atmosphere, and smell the bloodlust on the air as the crowd cheer their favourites, boo the incompetent, and bay for another death. The crowd always has its favourites, but as a rule they don't last long. That's why it's called the Parade of the Endless; heroes come and go, but the Games go on forever.

The city is also unique in being the only city on Golgotha not owned or dominated by a single Clan. The Empress sees to that, through subtle pressure and not so subtle purges, to ensure that the Games remain fair and unbiased. Everyone has an equal chance to die on the bloody sands. Otherwise there'd be no fun to it. The Parade of the Endless has thus become a safe neutral ground, a meeting place for Families who could not otherwise, with honour, communicate. Instead, the Clans settle their differences through their champions in the Arena. Dignity is upheld and honour is satisfied. And if it tends to be rather hard on the champions, well, no one really gives a damn, or at least no one who matters.

In return for this outlet, the Families provide generous contributions to the upkeep of the Arena and its staff. Even more of their money flows into the Arena's coffers through the Families' never-ending appetite for gambling. Fortunes are won and lost daily as the Clans plunge heavily in support of their champions and their honour. The champions are always paid men. Members of the Families would never dream of fighting in person. To risk one's life in a formal duel was one thing; to lower oneself to perform for the pleasure of the crowd was quite another. Besides; it wouldn't do for the lower orders to see the aristocracy dying. It might give them ideas.

Around the Arena, in ever-expanding circles, live the citizens of the Parade of the Endless. The traders, the service industries, and those who have fought, or plan to fight, on the bloody sands. The Games are open to all, the crowd's appetite is boundless, and there is always a need for fresh meat. And so they come, from all over the Empire, seeking fame and riches, action and excitement, or just a place to die in the sun. No one is ever turned away. Death is very democratic.

The streets around the Arena were packed with people, as always, coming or going or trying to sell something to those who were. The cries of the street traders rose above the general babble like birds marking their territory, determined to be noticed by those who passed. But even their ebulliency became somewhat muted in the presence of a Family member, so that you could usually track an aristocrat's path through the crowds by the relative quiet that surrounded them.

Valentine Wolfe moved casually through the crush, and no more noticed the respectful quiet than he would have noticed the air he breathed. Tall and darkly delicate, he was not an immediately impressive figure, but still no one jostled him or got in his way. Everyone recognized the mascaraed eyes and scarlet smile, as they knew all the Clan faces that mattered, and none of them had any wish to do anything that might be taken as an insult to Clan Wolfe. So Valentine walked on, his thoughts hidden behind the painted mask of his face, his eyes dark and far away. He never bothered with bodyguards. Some said through pride, some said through arrogance, but if truth be told, Valentine simply preferred the company of his own thoughts whenever possible, and found guards a distraction.

He finally came to a halt outside a modest little patisserie, just a little off the beaten trail, and gazed thoughtfully at the wondrous confectionary creations in the window. He wasn't averse to the occasional indulgence of his sweet tooth, but that wasn't what had brought him there. The shop's owner, the one and only Georgios, supplied Valentine with tastes more tempting and far sweeter than anything to be found in his window. Georgios was one outlet of a complex drugs pipeline that Valentine had spent years putting together. Someone of his status could have practically anything he wanted just by asking, but Valentine preferred to keep his needs and appetites strictly private. Knowledge was power. And besides; some of the things he wanted were banned even to those of his rank. Which was at least partly why he wanted them.

A single black rose stood in a slender glass vase in the left-hand corner of the window, and Valentine studied it thoughtfully. The rose was Georgios's way of saying that he had Valentine's order ready to hand. That it was in the left rather than the right-hand side of the window was his way of saying that something was wrong. Valentine smiled slightly, and considered his options. He could just walk away, and avoid whatever trouble it was. Most likely it was some kind of trap. Like all those who played at the great game of intrigue, Valentine had his fair share of enemies, and then some. But if he did just walk away, he'd never know whose trap it was, and how they'd found out about Georgios. He hadn't thought anyone knew about him and Georgios. Besides, it would mean leaving the dear fellow in the hands of his enemy, and that would never do. He couldn't let people get away with threatening his friends and business partners, or he'd end up without any of either.

And a good business partner was hard to replace.

He pushed open the door and walked in, quite casually, as though he didn't have a care in the world. It was dark, inside the shop. Someone had polarized the windows, to keep out the sun. Valentine let the door drift shut behind him, and stood very still. He concentrated in a series of certain ways, and drug caches deep in his system opened obediently to the mental triggers and dumped their contents into his bloodstream. Fresh oxygenated blood rushed to his muscles, which swelled subtly, readying themselves for action. His senses became supernaturally acute, and the shadows before him began to give up their secrets. There were twelve of them, standing very still at the rear of the shop. Two of them were holding Georgios securely, with a hand over his mouth. He could smell Georgios's fear, and the anticipation of the others. He could hear the slight movements they made unknowingly, thinking themselves safe in the gloom. Valentine's smile widened slightly. There was no safety anywhere for his enemies. They were all dead. They just didn't know it yet. He cleared his throat politely.

'Turn up the light, someone; there's a good fellow. We can't negotiate in the dark.'

'What makes you think we want to negotiate?' said a voice that tried to sound cultured, but couldn't quite bring it off.

'If you were assassins,' said Valentine calmly, 'you'd have killed me the moment I walked in. Therefore, I assume you have something to say to me. Do get on with it, I'm running late for an appointment.'

The light flared up suddenly as one of the shadowy figures cleared the window glass, the bright sunlight revealing a dozen gang members grinning arrogantly at him from the rear of the shop. They were all naked, the better to show off the bulging muscles and other enhancements they'd bought from cheap knock-off body shops in the darker back alleyways. They'd all had their skin dyed the same overpowering shade of electric blue, to declare which gang they belonged to, and a blazing silver skull had been tattooed on every chest. There were a dozen less painful ways the skulls could have been imprinted on their flesh, but the pain was the point. It was an initiation, a declaration of courage and dedication. Tattoos were for life. So was gang membership.

Valentine recognized them immediately, as he was supposed to. The Demons; one of the larger bands of street toughs who ran wild in the grubbier areas of the city. There were thousands of them, in hundreds of gangs; too young, too scared or too smart to be seduced by the call of the Arena, they scraped a kind of living by hiring themselves out to anyone who needed a little muscle. They did other things too, if you had the money. They fought many battles among themselves, over territory or women or what passed for honour among them. As above, so below; the lower orders aping their betters. They also ran simple protection rackets and badger games, when things were quiet, but even then they usually had enough sense not to get involved with the Families. Which suggested that someone must have laid out a small fortune to set this up. Which, if nothing else, helped to narrow the field.

Valentine took his time studying the Demons. It wouldn't do to give the impression that he was at all nervous or insecure. Some of the gang members looked to be genewarped, or at least genechanged, from hiring out their bodies to unscrupulous body doctors, who always had a need for guinea pigs for their new experiments and processes. Misshapen faces and bodies were the marks of the lucky ones. They'd survived. Some had clawed hands and pointed teeth, others had the twitchy sudden movements that suggested hyped-up adrenalin glands. They'd all have their hidden little secrets, but Valentine was reasonably sure they had no tech augmentations. They couldn't afford to buy or replace the energy crystals that powered them. They were all armed, most with swords, some with knives or machetes or lengths of spiked chain.

Valentine smiled at them dazzlingly, just to keep them off balance while his thoughts raged furiously. The Demons were well out of gang territory, this close to the Arena. By rights, they shouldn't have been here at all. The local guards should have seen them on their way the moment they showed their blue faces. Someone must have spread a lot of money around to buy a blind eye to their presence, even for a short while. Someone wanted this meeting very badly, but didn't want to be identified as the instigator. Using street toughs was about as anonymous as you could get. They'd do practically anything for money, and didn't give a damn where it came from. Now that his eyes had completely adjusted to the change in light, Valentine could tell from the Demons' flushed faces and overbright eyes that they'd been primed with something extra. Cheap knock-off battle drugs, probably.

He chuckled appreciatively. At least his enemy was taking him seriously. Real battle drugs were hard to come by outside the military, but Valentine had a supplier, as he had for most things. However, the number of people who knew that was very small. The identity of his enemy was becoming clearer by the minute. He concentrated in a certain way, and breathed deeply as a catalyst set off the battle drug lying quiescent in his system. His blood, already roused, surged through his veins like boiling water. The world seemed to slow down a little as his reflexes speeded up. He chuckled softly, and nodded to the Demons.

'Time to get this show on the road, gentlemen. Why don't you release poor Georgios and let him leave, so that we can be about our business?'

The gang members elbowed each other and sniggered. From the chocolate and cream around their mouths, they'd obviously been gorging themselves on Georgios's creations, and Valentine winced. The confections had undoubtedly been wasted on them. The gang members were quite incapable of appreciating the subtleties.

'Poor Georgios isn't going anywhere,' said the tough with the scarlet headband that marked him as gang leader. 'Our orders are: no witnesses.'

'And who gave you your orders?' said Valentine politely.

The leader smiled mockingly. 'You don't need to know that. What matters is the message I have for you. Well, not so much a message; more a warning. Word is, you've made a nuisance of yourself once too often, and our employers hired us to make sure it doesn't happen again.'

'Oh dear,' said Valentine easily. 'Another death threat. How terribly dull.'

'We're not going to kill you,' said the leader, still grinning. 'We're not dumb enough to take a job like that. Kill an aristo, and every guard in the city would be after us. No; we're just going to break both your legs, both your arms, do a bit of a dance on your ribs, and then walk away and leave you. Our employers want you hurt and humiliated, and we're only too happy to oblige. Especially for the money they're paying.'

'Whatever they're paying you, I'll double it,' said Valentine.

The gang members laughed and sniggered again, but the gang leader's smile disappeared. 'It isn't just the money. It's a chance to get back at an aristo. You've got everything we ever wanted, and you're still not satisfied. You come slumming down here where we have to live, and laugh at our quaint and picturesque lives. You smash up our bars, trash our women, and make us scramble for the crumbs you drop. We're being

113

paid a hell of a lot to crush you, Wolfie, but we'd have done it for nothing. We hate you, aristo. You and all your kind.'

'We don't hate you,' said Valentine. 'We don't notice you, any more than we notice any of the other rubbish that floats past in the gutters.'

The Demons stopped laughing, and the tension in the air was suddenly sharp and imminent. Light glinted on steel as they hefted swords and machetes. A length of steel chain made soft clinking sounds as it was wrapped around a fist. The gang leader nodded to the two toughs holding Georgios, and they pushed him to his knees. The shop's proprietor was a small, round little man with a shaven head. He looked like a child among bogeymen. The gang leader drew a long slender knife and stood beside Georgios.

'Hold him still. I don't think our little aristo here is taking us seriously. Maybe this will change his mind.'

He cut Georgios's throat with a single economic sweep of his knife. Blood spurted out across the spotlessly clean floor. Georgios bucked and heaved in his captors' hands, but couldn't break free. He couldn't even get his hands to the gaping second mouth in his throat. His strength drained away and he slumped forward. His captors let him go, and he fell face down on to the floor. He died so suddenly it was hard to tell the exact moment when the life went out of him. Only Valentine was watching. The Demons were watching him. Valentine slowly raised his dark eyes and looked at the Demons, and suddenly there was something new in the air. His crimson slash of a smile had no humour in it, and his mascaraed eyes were very cold. He looked different, and it took the Demons a moment to realize how. He didn't look helpless any more.

'Now that was a pity,' Valentine said softly. 'Nobody made a pastry like dear Georgios. I'm going to have to punish you for that. Georgios wasn't much, but he was mine. No one takes anything from me and lives to boast of it. I'm afraid I'm going to have to kill you all. I'll try not to enjoy it too much.'

For a long moment, no one said anything. The Demons stood very still, and tension crackled between them. And then the gang leader laughed softly, and everyone's attention switched to him.

'Nice try, aristo. You nearly brought it off. But you can't intimidate us any more. There are twelve of us and only the one of you, and odds like that don't care how important you are. Take him, boys. We're going to have some fun.'

The gang members moved forward as one, spreading out in a circle around Valentine, who made no move, either to attack or escape. He kept his dark eyes fixed on the gang leader, while his hyped-up senses kept track of the others. He could hear every step, every rustle of clothing, and their scents came thickly to him on the close air. He didn't need to see them to know where they were. His smile never wavered. From the orchestrated nature of their movements, it was obvious to Valentine that the Demons' enchancements included some kind of cheap sympatico drug. They moved in a synchronized, coordinated way, as though each member knew exactly where every other member was, and they all lifted their weapons at the same time, in the same way. Follow the leader. Of course, if you took out the leader . . .

Valentine stepped forward impossibly quickly, his movements driven by the battle drugs raging within him, and pivoted sharply on one foot so that the other shot up and punched into the side of the gang leader's head. The force of the blow whipped the Demon's head around, breaking his neck, and he crumpled to the floor, his eyes rolling up in their sockets. By the time he hit the floor, Valentine had already turned on the next Demon.

The various battle drugs were howling in him now, filling his mind and his body with possibilities. The Demons were thrown by the sudden loss of their leader, but it wouldn't take them long to find a new focus. The Demon before him was a young thing, slender beyond the point of gender, with skin stretched parchment tight over its skull. Valentine hit it in the throat and it sank choking to its knees. Valentine swung on his next victim with dazzling speed, but a new light had entered the Demons' eyes. The gang had found a new focus, and their gang mind was fixed on Valentine again. Only this time they wouldn't stop at a beating. Demon blood had been spilled. Only a death would satisfy them now. In his own way, Valentine approved. It showed the gang understood something of honour.

A knife flashed through the air towards Valentine, thrown with more than usual strength. Valentine snatched it out of mid-air, reversed it and threw it back at its thrower with a single smooth motion. It sank hilt deep into the Demon's eye, and blood washed down his face as he fell backwards. Another tough lashed out with her length of spiked steel chain. The barbed links whistled on the still air as they flashed towards Valentine's face. He stepped forward and stopped the chain with an upraised arm. It wrapped itself tightly around his wrist, but the cruel barbs didn't penetrate his skin. His flesh was different now, stronger and more malleable. It swept up over the links, holding them firm as the Demon tugged at the chain. Valentine yanked on the chain, pulling the Demon within reach, and his free hand seized her face. The skin of his fingers formed a broad fleshy mask, covering her mouth and nose. She dropped the chain and tugged desperately at his arm, but couldn't move it an inch. Valentine was rather pleased with the effect. He hadn't tried that particular drug in battle before. It had been originally intended as a sex drug, to free the form of the flesh for more intimate caresses, but it hadn't taken Valentine long to see it might have other uses.

The Demon's struggles weakened quickly as her air ran out, and then the other Demons jumped Valentine, and there was nothing but the press of bodies and thrusting steel. But quick as they were, Valentine was quicker. He danced among them like a ghost, everywhere at once, his hands lashing out to kill and cripple. He was boosted now, fast and furious, neurons firing at impossible speed, decisions and evasions planned and executed in the spark of a moment. His blows were devastating and unblockable, and the few times a Demon's steel found a fleeting target, the pliable flesh healed itself in seconds. The Demons cut and thrust with increasing desperation, but hit each other more often than not. They fell one by one as Valentine danced among them, pirouetting with deadly grace in the midst of death. His hands and feet moved too fast to be seen, and the last thing the Demons saw before they fell was his terrible crimson smile.

In the end, eleven dead gang members lay scattered across the patisserie floor, like so many broken flowers, lying still in awkward poses in pools of their own blood. Only one Demon remained alive, sitting shaking with his back to a wall, nursing a broken arm and trying to keep as far from Valentine as he could. His breathing was harsh and his eyes were wide, and shock and pain had driven most of the drugs from his system. For all his clawed hands and pointed teeth and bulked-up muscle, he'd never stood a chance against Valentine, and both of them knew it. He licked his dry lips, stared in fascinated horror at Valentine, and tried desperately to think of anything he knew that he might be able to trade for his life. And trying even more desperately to keep from his face the thought of the one thing that might still save him.

Valentine Wolfe brushed himself down, and made a quiet moue of distaste at the blood that soaked his garments. Little of it was his, and his wounds had already healed. He'd dumped a universal cut-off and flush into his bloodstream, and the various battle drugs had dissipated quickly, leaving his mind sharp and clear and his body whole and relaxed. Nothing like a good workout to focus the mind. He looked about him at the dead Demons, and felt no pity for them. They should have chosen a different target for their class anger. Of course, they had no idea what kind of fighter they were taking on. No one knew about his martial skills, or at least, nobody living. He'd gone to great pains to keep his abilities secret, including killing his trainers. It suited Valentine that his enemies should always underestimate him. He loomed over the sole surviving Demon, and smiled down at him. The Demon winced away from the smile, and pressed back against the wall behind him, but there was nowhere left to go.

'Eleven men dead in under three minutes,' said Valentine conversationally. 'There are only three men outside the Arena who could match that, and I'm two of them. I know; I'm not at all what you expected, but then, that's life isn't it? I'm really rather annoyed with you. Poor Georgios is dead, my morning has been ruined, and my clothes are a mess. The only reason you're not dead and frying in whatever afterlife you believe in is because you have information I want. Someone set you on my trail, and you're going to tell me who. Because if you don't, I'm going to take the morning's frustrations out on you, and you'd be surprised how inventive I can be, when I'm annoyed. Talk. Now.'

The Demon could not meet Valentine's eyes. They upset him too much.

'I don't know their names. They didn't offer them, and for the kind of credits they were putting up, we didn't ask. Never saw their faces either. Had them hidden behind holo masks. Man and a woman. Young, rich, arrogant; aristos like you by their accents. But they did leave something behind; something that might interest you. It's in my pouch, over there.'

He nodded gingerly in the direction of a hip pouch, lying abandoned on one side of the fight. It was still sealed. Valentine walked over and picked it up with one thumb and forefinger. He brought it back and dropped it in the Demon's lap. He winced at the impact, and Valentine smiled down at him.

'Open it. And be very careful. After all, there might be a booby trap of some kind, mightn't there?'

The Demon smiled mirthlessly, and fumbled at the pouch's straps with the shaking fingers of his left hand. His face was pale and blotchy and the come-down from the drugs was obviously getting to him. Valentine watched him dispassionately. Amateurs had no business meddling with drugs. He looked back at the front door. One of the Demons had activated the Closed sign embedded in the glass of the door. That, together with the swiftness of the actual fight, had kept anyone from breezing into the shop in search of Georgios, but it wouldn't do to hang about too long. Some people, such as those of Valentine's rank, would only see the sign as a challenge. They might even kick the door in, if they were sufficiently annoyed. Valentine would have. And the last thing he needed was to be found surrounded by dead bodies and soaked in their blood. It would be difficult to explain, and harder still to cover up. The authorities would take a great deal of expensive soothing, and his father would be furious. Valentine winced. No; that wouldn't do at all.

It occurred to him that the Demon was taking an uncommonly long time to get the pouch open. He stepped forward impatiently and then stopped dead in his tracks as the Demon opened the pouch, reached in and pulled out a disrupter. Valentine froze where he was, his mind racing. The energy weapon changed everything. There was no way a small-time street tough could have got his hands on a disrupter through normal channels. It was death for such as him to even possess such a weapon.

But the gun in the Demon's hand was real enough, which suggested the Demons' mysterious patrons really had been aristocrats after all. Valentine ran quickly through the drugs still available in his system. He'd used up most of the useful ones, and he was pretty sure the Demon would shoot him if he made any move for his silver pillbox. He could still jump the tough, and trust his reflexes were in better shape than the Demon's. He could also get himself killed. He decided he was going to stand very still and wait for an inspiration to strike him.

The Demon covered him with the energy gun, though it was all he could do to keep it steady. There was a wildness in his eyes that Valentine didn't like at all. And yet the Demon had had plenty of time to shoot him, if that was what he intended. And if he'd had an energy gun all along, why hadn't he used it during the fight? And then, as Valentine watched, the Demon slowly turned the energy gun on himself, his face full of surprise and horror, pressed the barrel against his forehead and depressed the stud. Valentine cursed mildly. The Demon had obviously been programmed by his patrons not to reveal any secrets. And that was interesting. It suggested that not only did the patrons have access to a mind tech, but that the Demons knew things that their patrons couldn't afford to have revealed. Valentine smiled slowly as he wiped the fresh blood from his face with a scented handkerchief. He'd worked out who the patrons were. Who they had to be.

He made his way to the living quarters at the back of the shop, in search of a cloak he could use to cover his blood-stained clothes. He'd have to replace them before he rejoined his Family. Wouldn't do to have them asking questions, and besides, he hated to be seen not looking his best. He had an image to maintain. He glanced back at the dead bodies littering the floor. Poor Georgios.

Ah, dear brother, dear sister . . . what am I going to do with you?

Daniel and Stephanie Wolfe, brother and sister to Valentine, waited impatiently for news in the Family's private box at the edge of the Arena. It was a fair-sized box, as boxes went, complete with every luxury that money and position could command. The sands lay a mere ten feet below, so that the occupants of the box could enjoy the various life and death struggles at close range, and it came equipped with its own private force screen, just in case things looked like getting a little too close. Stephanie stalked back and forth in the narrow confines of the box, her arms folded tightly across her chest, while Daniel stood at parade rest, scowling out across the empty Arena. People had begun to arrive, and were filing slowly into the ranks of tiered seating, but it was early yet.

Daniel was the youngest Wolfe, only just out of his teens. He had the hulking frame of his father, but as yet neither the muscle nor the presence to carry it off. He was clumsy as a child, until his father beat it out of him, with the result that even now he kept his movements to a minimum, and saw those through with exaggerated grace and care. The stutter took longer to disappear. His hair was a long mane of shining bronze strands with silver highlights, the latest fashion, but he wore the formal robes his father had insisted on for a public Family appearance. They were dark, dull and severely cut, and didn't suit him at all. Daniel often wished he had the nerve to defy his father as Valentine did, but then Daniel often wished for things he didn't have, which was what kept getting him into trouble.

That, and his sister.

Stephanie Wolfe, the middle child, took after her late mother, being tall and gangling with long hair that always looked ratty, no matter what she did with it. Her long frame was full of suppressed energy, constantly in danger of bursting out at the most inopportune moments. She was twenty-four years old, good looking in a bland sort of way, no matter what she did with cosmetics, and boyishly slim in an age when voluptuousness was always in fashion. Stephanie had been through a great many body shops in her time, searching for a more acceptable look, but in the end her natural stubbornness kicked in, and she settled for her true face and shape. The aristocracy set trends, not followed them. No one ever commented on her decision or her appearance. Firstly, she was a Wolfe, and secondly, Daniel was devoted to her, and ever ready to fight a duel over some perceived insult to his sister's beauty.

Daniel and Stephanie Wolfe. Brother and sister, bound together by love and viewpoint and named ambition. Rich, young and aristocratic, they should have had the world at their feet, but the world wasn't that simple. As younger siblings, they stood to inherit little or nothing, as long as Valentine lived. So, being pragmatic and determined and children of their time, not to mention Wolfes to the core, they schemed and plotted and occasionally arranged little accidents for Valentine. They would have liked to order his death, but they weren't that stupid. In the event of Valentine meeting a violent or suspicious death, the first thing the Imperial Court would do would be to order them both to be examined by an esper. Guilt would mean immediate execution, despite their rank and station. And if they tried and failed, and word got out, they'd be a laughing stock, humiliated before all the Families. So they settled for accidents, apparently random occurrences that would hopefully hurt and maim, and at the very least make him look incompetent. If Valentine could be proved unfit to inherit, he might be put aside in favour of Daniel or Stephanie. Of course, if any of these accidents were to be tra̶̶ to them, there'd be hell to pay, not least from their f truth be told, the risk was half the fun. After all.

point in gambling if you could afford to lose. Daniel and Stephanie needed the thrill almost as much as they needed their brother's downfall.

Even if they didn't handle the pressure very well. Stephanie stopped herself pacing back and forth with an effort, and threw herself into one of the extremely comfortable chairs set out by the guards earlier, before they retreated to a discreet distance. Apart from making sure they were out of earshot, Daniel and Stephanie ignored them. There were always guards, no matter where they went. It was part of being an aristocrat. Daniel looked back at his sister and smiled slightly.

'About time. You've practically worn a groove in that carpet, pacing up and down. We wouldn't want dear Papa to get the idea we've anything to feel nervous about, would we?'

Stephanie smiled at him sweetly. 'Forget the sarcasm, Danny; you've never had the gift for it. It requires wit and lightness of touch, among other things, all equally beyond your grasp. Father will be here soon, hopefully bearing news of our dear brother's unfortunate mishap. When he tells us, do try not to over-react. We're bound to be suspected, but there's no point in providing our enemies with ammunition. Forget trying to look surprised; just looked dazed and leave all the talking to me.'

'Of course, Steph. Don't I always? There's always the chance Valentine is dead. If things got out of hand . . .'

'I don't see how. We planned for every contingency. As long as those thugs followed their instructions. No; if he was dead, we'd have heard by now. Father would have burst in with the news, or the guards, or a servant or somebody! You couldn't keep news like that quiet.'

'Keep the voice down, Steph. Of course, you're right. Dear Valentine is currently lying in the filth of a back alley, one big mess of broken bones.'

'Yes. You're right.' Stephanie took a deep breath, and ly let it out again. 'You did fix the gun, didn't you?'

course. All identifying marks were removed. There's no can be traced to us.'

'The gun still worries me. It's a clear sign the street gang weren't working on their own.'

'We had to be sure none of the gang would survive to answer questions. The gun and the subliminal conditioning will take care of that.'

Stephanie relaxed a little in her chair. 'Valentine won't even know what hit him. The medics will fix him up fast enough, but the attack will cast severe doubts on his competence. A few more such incidents, and he'll be a laughing stock. And then, finally, we'll find a way to dispose of poor accident-prone Valentine, and nothing will stand between us and control of Clan Wolfe.'

'Unless Constance has a child.'

'Ah yes. Dear Stepmother. If she was to have a child, dear Papa might well disinherit us in favour of the newcomer. So it's just as well we bribed our Family food-taster not to notice the contraceptives we've been lacing her food with. She could no more carry a child now than Father could.'

Daniel frowned. 'I still say it's a big risk. We're only safe as long as the food-taster stays bought. I don't like the idea of our fate being in someone else's hands. Maybe we should have the mind techs look at him too.'

'Don't be stupid. The Family esper would notice immediately that he'd been got at.'

'But what if he gets an attack of the scruples and betrays us?'

'He won't. He can't betray us now without incriminating himself. He should have gone to Father the moment he suspected anything was wrong. But the money we offered was just too tempting. Now, if he did confess, he'd be ruined. No one would ever trust him as a food-taster again. Besides; we still have some insurance. The drug I've been slipping into his food is extremely addictive, and I'm his only source.' She laughed softly. 'He checked everyone's food but his own. Stop worrying, Danny. I've thought of everything.'

Daniel looked at her affectionately. 'You always did have a delightfully devious mind. We'll have such fun, ruling the Family.'

Stephanie smiled dazzlingly. 'With my brain and your brawn, we can do anything, Danny. Anything at all.'

And then they both fell silent as they heard approaching footsteps and the guards crashing to attention. Daniel and Stephanie just had time to get to their feet and look casual, and then Jacob Wolfe came crashing into the box, followed by their new stepmother. Jacob was clearly in a foul mood, his heavy brows furrowed in a scowl, and his two children had enough sense to just bow politely and say nothing. The Wolfe was flaming mad about something, and they didn't want his anger aimed their way. Daniel bowed to his stepmother. Stephanie barely nodded. Constance Wolfe smiled at them both.

Constance was seventeen years old, and already a breathtaking beauty in a world noted for its beautiful women. Tall and blonde and perfectly proportioned, she seemed to glow with health and good cheer and raw sexuality. Just to look at her was enough to send a man's hormones into overdrive. Jacob had won her for his new wife by the simple expedient of intimidating most of her other suitors, and killing the rest in duels. Jacob was a great believer in tradition. Constance seemed happy enough with the arrangement, which made her one of the most important women on Golgotha, and had settled in well to the running of Clan Wolfe and her husband. The Wolfe's three children had looked on with varying levels of concern as her word became law and her whim became increasingly wide-ranging. Jacob knew what was going on, but said nothing. It was up to his wife and his children to sort out their own pecking order. As long as they were polite in company and didn't squabble in his presence, he didn't give a damn.

He spun round suddenly, catching all three by surprise, and fixed them with his glare. 'The SummerIsle died in Court today. Cut down in a duel by Kid Death. His own damn grandson. There's no pride in Family any more.'

Daniel smiled tightly. 'Youth must have its day, Father. The old must give way to the new. That's the way of things.'

The Wolfe glared at him contemptuously. 'You ever raise a

hand to me, boy, and I'll cut it off at the wrist. Or perhaps you think you're ready to run this Family?'

'Of course not, Father. Not yet.'

'Not ever, unless you buck your ideas up. But I'll make a man of you yet, boy, despite all your sister can do to prevent it.'

'That's not fair,' said Stephanie, moving protectively closer to Daniel. 'Someone has to look out for him.'

'He's a Wolfe; he's supposed to be able to look out for himself!' snapped Jacob. 'That's what being a man is all about. I won't always be here to wipe his nose for him.'

'Now stop that,' said Constance, pouting prettily as she dropped a restraining hand on his arm. 'You're good for another century at least, and I won't have you saying otherwise. Besides, it's far too nice a day to spoil it with a quarrel. We're supposed to be here for a Family meeting before the Games begin; can't we make a start?'

'Not without Valentine,' said the Wolfe. 'I seriously doubt he'll have anything serious to contribute, apart from the address of his latest chemist, but he is my eldest, and has a right to be present. Even if he is late. Again.'

'Yes,' said Daniel. 'I wonder what's keeping him.'

Stephanie tensed, but for once Daniel had enough sense not to share a confidential smirk with her. Instead, he was looking thoughtfully at their father, and Stephanie felt like joining him. Jacob Wolfe only retired to his private box at the Arena for Family meetings when he wanted to discuss something really delicate. The box's combination of indoors and outdoors made it difficult for anyone to bug, and the esp-blocker concealed in the structure of the box kept out any psionic eavesdroppers. Jacob believed in being thorough.

Stephanie looked away from her father, and searched for something to distract her. Out across the Arena, the giant holoscreen was showing close-ups and slow motion replays of the fighting in the Arena. The holoscreen was there for the benefit of the connoisseur, and those right at the back, so that no detail of the blood and butchery need be missed. Stephanie smiled broadly, enjoying the show. Nothing like a little life or death drama to get the blood moving. There were those, in and out of the Families, who campaigned regularly for the Arena to be shut down, or at least toned down, but they never got anywhere. The Games were incredibly popular throughout the Empire, drawing huge audiences wherever there was a holoscreen to be found. Try and stop the show, and the people might well rebel.

And then Stephanie stiffened as she heard footsteps approaching the box. Her heart jumped, and she breathed deeply to keep a betraying flush from her cheeks. The messenger was finally here, with news of Valentine. She turned slowly, savouring the moment, and found herself face to face with Valentine, coolly entering the private box as though it was just another day, and all was well with the world. For a moment she thought she might faint, but a quick glance at Daniel, all slack-jawed and bulging eyes, brought her back. She had to be cool, had to be ice cold. She had to be strong for both of them, until she could discover just how much trouble they were both in. She made herself bow casually to Valentine, and he nodded politely in return.

'Is something wrong, Sister?' Valentine said courteously. 'You look rather pale.'

'No. Nothing's wrong,' said Stephanie, fighting to keep her voice as calm as his. 'You're a little late. We were concerned something might have happened to you. Did . . . anything unusual happen on your way here?'

'Unusual? No, not that I can think. Why do you ask?'

'No reason,' said Stephanie. 'No reason.'

Valentine smiled his wide crimson smile, and his dark eyes gave away nothing at all. He shrugged off his cloak, and dropped it over the back of the nearest chair. Stephanie frowned, in spite of herself. Her brother was wearing the ugliest, coarsest and most unfashionable clothes she'd ever seen him in. In fact, to be bluntly honest, they looked like a tradesman's clothes, and not even the right size. She would have sworn he would rather have died than appear in such a state in public.

'I'm a little late because I had to stop off along the way,'

Valentine said casually. 'Had to pick up my new outfit. Rather dashing, don't you think?'

'We can discuss your appalling taste in clothes later,' growled the Wolfe. 'We have Family business to discuss. We waited for you to put in an appearance because some of it specifically affects you.'

Valentine sank elegantly into a chair, and fixed his father with a condescending gaze. 'You're not thinking about putting me through detox again, Father, surely? You must know by now that my system will never be normal again, after all the wonderful things I've done to it. You'd have better luck trying to change my height than my blood chemistry.'

'No,' said the Wolfe, smiling unpleasantly. 'I've given up trying to change you, Valentine. I thought I'd let someone else have a try. I've decided it's time you got married. All of you.' He beamed round at his three children, who looked back with varying degrees of shock. The Wolfe's smile deepened. 'To that end, I have arranged marriages for you all, to suitable young matches of good Family backgrounds.'

There was a long pause while nobody said anything. Jacob was enjoying himself, Valentine was looking thoughtful, and Stephanie and Daniel were looking desperately at each other for ideas and support. The Wolfe sat down in his usual chair, taking his time to make himself comfortable. Constance came and sat beside him, still smiling sweetly. Jacob patted her fondly on the arm.

'Your new mother and I have been discussing this. It's time I had a few grandchildren to bounce on my knee. Young sprouts, to carry on the bloodline. I waited till late in life to sire you three, and I won't have you making the same mistake. You're getting married. Whether you like it or not.'

'Do I understand you have already picked our partners for us?' said Valentine slowly.

'Damn right I have. Leave you to sort it out and you'd make a right mess of it. I've chosen prime young fillies for you and Daniel, and a strapping young blade for you, Steph. Good bloodlines, excellent stock. You'll meet them at the Imperial Ball tonight, and be married next month.'

'Next month?' howled Daniel. Stephanie didn't think she'd ever seen his eyes bulge quite so much, but for once she was helpless to support him. She was too busy trying to get her own whirling thoughts under control.

'Yes. Next month.' Jacob wasn't even trying to hide his satisfaction. 'If I gave you three any more time, you'd undoubtedly find a way to wriggle out of it. So the marriages will go ahead just as soon as the proprieties have been observed.'

'I'll see you damned in hell first, Daddy,' said Stephanie. She wouldn't have believed her voice could hold such ice, such venom. Daniel nodded vigorously at her side.

'You can argue all you like,' said the Wolfe. 'It won't do you any good. You could of course refuse to go through with the ceremony, in which case I would have no option but to disinherit you, and have you thrown out of the Clan. Think about that for a moment, dear children. Could you exist, outside the protection of the Family? No money, no station, no future? Having to work for a living? What jobs could you do? No; you've been cosseted and pampered too long to survive in the real world. Any last comments, before we pass on to the next order of business?'

He looked from one fact to another, one eyebrow raised politely. Daniel was trying to find his voice, while looking like someone had just kicked him in the gut. Stephanie was scowling furiously, thinking hard. Valentine smiled suddenly.

'If it's to be a church wedding, can I wear a veil? I look good in white.'

Jacob gave him a hard look, but decided not to rise to the bait. He looked out over the Arena, but nothing much was happening. The first few fighters had mostly killed each other, but there was hardly anyone in the stands or private boxes to see it. The early acts were just warm-ups, inexperienced fighters building a reputation while getting the feel of genuine life and death combat. Training and simulations could only do so much. There was no substitute for the real thing. For the smell of sweat and blood, or the sight of a man's guts spilling out on to the crimson sands. Which was of course what brought the audiences back again and again.

The last two survivors stamped back and forth across the bloodied sands, but few of the slowly growing audience took any notice. They were too busy finding their seats, getting comfortable and chatting with friends and neighbours. There was a flash of steel and a strangled cry, and one of the gladiators fell to the sand, clutching his side tightly. The winner raised his sword and looked about him for applause. A few people clapped languorously, but that was all. The winner lowered his sword and put it away, and then bent down and helped his fellow gladiator to his feet. No one had cared enough to turn a thumb down. They moved slowly away, heading back to the main gates and the training areas under the Arena.

Jacob watched them go. He thought he knew how they felt. He was fighting for his life, and that of his Family, in the great game of intrigue, and no one seemed to give a damn about his struggle either. He turned back to face his children, and tried to keep the tiredness out of his face.

'The contract for mass production of the new stardrive is being readied. Whoever wins the rights to this new drive will end up with power and riches almost beyond imagination. It is therefore vitally important that Clan Wolfe wins the contract; or at the very least ensures that our principal enemies do not. Were Clan Campbell to beat us out, for example, it would ruin our shipping interests overnight, and leave us vulnerable to all kinds of hostile takeovers. The very existence of the Family could be at risk.'

'I hate to be picky,' said Valentine, 'but the Campbells do have much more experience in the stardrive field than we do. They would do a much better job.'

'What does that have to do with anything?'

Valentine shrugged. 'I just thought it might not be in the Empire's best interests for us to steal the contract away from the Campbells.'

'The sooner I get you married and raising children, the better,' said the Wolfe. 'The Family comes first. Always. Besides; what's good for Clan Wolfe is good for the Empire. Now pay attention. Clan Campbell, bad cess to them all, have been proving unexpectedly successful of late in many fields.

I'm pretty sure they've got a silent partner hiding in the background. Someone high up, financially independent, and politically invisible. According to my sources, who for the amount of money I'm paying them had better be reliable, this silent partner has been providing the Campbells with all kinds of new high tech, practical and theory, that the Campbell labs couldn't have produced on their own. I thought at first it might be one of the minor Clans, trying to buy their way into the big time while hiding their light under a larger Family's protective bushel. But I regret to report that none of my sources have been able to come up with anything incriminating. Whoever's backing the Campbells has gone to great pains to hide their trail very thoroughly.'

'Could it be one of the undergrounds?' said Stephanie, frowning. 'The cyberats, for instance?'

'That's more like it,' said the Wolfe approvingly. 'You see, you have got brains when you care to use them. My people are currently investigating the various extra-legal organizations, to see if any of them have been getting ideas above their station, but it's going to be some time before they'll be able to report back anything worth listening to.'

'Maybe they've managed some kind of contact with the new aliens?' said Daniel, not wanting to be left out.

The Wolfe looked at him. 'I suppose that's a thought. The Campbells wouldn't hesitate to blow away the rest of the Empire if they thought there was a good chance they'd come out on top. I'll put a few agents on it. Well, Valentine; have you nothing to contribute?'

Valentine Wolfe produced his small silver pillbox, opened it, and took out a large pinch of fluorescent blue powder. He placed it carefully in two small heaps on the back of his hand, and then sniffed it up with great style and elan, one heap for each nostril. His eyes widened, showing bright and gleaming against his mascara, and for a moment his crimson smile seemed impossibly wide. He shuddered once, put away the pillbox, and smiled at his father.

'Since we cannot hope to beat the Campbells on the grounds of business experience or technical expertise, we will have to do battle with them on the social and political field. Set up a few schemes to disrupt, discredit and if need be destroy Clan Campbell, or any other Family that stands between us and the contracts we seek. I would like to offer my help but, of course, if I'm to be married at such short notice I really don't think that I can afford to become personally involved. I'll have far too much on my mind.'

'Right,' said Daniel quickly. 'Same here.'

'Then I'll just have to soldier on without your no doubt valuable input,' said Jacob. 'You're getting married if I have to see you all dragged in chains to the altar. But that's enough business, for the moment. We've covered everything urgent. Your new mother is a great fan of the Games, and I promised her an uninterrupted afternoon's pleasure of death and mayhem.'

'But . . .' Daniel began, only to wither under his father's implacable gaze.

'Enjoy the Games, dammit. This box is costing me enough.'

The Games proper started traditionally, with rebel-baiting. Twenty convicted felons, habitual offenders who hadn't learned a thing from their previous stays in gaol, were turned out on to the sands without armour or weapons, and twenty experienced gladiators pursued them with whips and swords. The rebels ran in every direction, screaming for help or a weapon or just another chance, and the crowd booed and hissed them. The gladiators pursued their prey, cool and calm and very professional. A few rebels tried to make a stand, back to back, and the gladiators allowed them the courtesy of a quick death. They respected courage. The other rebels were harried and tormented, driven this way and that with flashing steel and the crack of the whip, until they were a mass of blood and cuts. They staggered on, too exhausted to run but too scared to stop. And finally, one by one, they died for the pleasure of the crowd, and their bodies were dragged away. The growing crowd laughed and cheered and applauded the gladiators. They always enjoyed a good comedy turn.

In the Wolfe private box, Constance shrieked and laughed and clapped her tiny hands, and Jacob smiled fondly at her, happy to see her happy. Daniel sat sulking by himself. Stephanie was still thinking hard. And Valentine watched and applauded, and kept his feelings to himself.

The stalls were filling up now, and most of the private boxes. The beginners and warm-ups had done their job, and the real Games were about to begin. The holocameras were in place, ready to catch all the action as it happened, and already the resident bookies were making money hand over fist.

The first real turn was a pulse-stirrer. Three clones from the underground were turned loose in the Arena, armed only with swords. They were all the same slim, dark-haired youth, with wide eyes and trembling mouths. Probably teachers or technicians or civil servants before they made the mistake of trying to find their freedom through the clone underground. Never drawn a sword in anger in their life, and now it was all that stood between them and a particularly unpleasant death. They made their way uncertainly to the centre of the Arena, back to back in a triangle, moving with the almost telepathic linked precision that only clones can achieve. They all had the same instincts and mannerisms, and held their sword in the same way. When they fought, they would fight as one. For all the good it would do them.

The crowd booed them lustily, and then cheered as a trumpet sounded and their champion appeared from the main gate. And all the Wolfes broke off from their various thoughts and stared hard at the newcomer. The Campbells had loaned out their private Investigator; the man called Razor. He was tall and blocky, with thick slabs of muscle and a patient, brooding face. His skin was dark, his close-cropped hair was white, and his eyes were a curious green. He moved with a slow steady power that suggested something implacable and unstoppable. He carried a curved sword in each hand, but wore no armour. He didn't need any. He was an Investigator.

Technically, he was supposed to give up the title once he'd retired from the service, but no one was stupid enough to tell him that to his face. Clans often acquired their own Investigators, once they were free of the service's demands. They made invaluable bodyguards and champions, mainly on the grounds that very few people were dumb enough to upset an Investigator. Unfortunately, they rarely lasted long in private employ. Investigators were only allowed to leave the service when they became old or tired or began making mistakes. But they lived for battle and the destruction of aliens, and once taken away from such delights, they soon withered away into pale copies of themselves. Mostly they took their own lives, or allowed someone else to do it.

But while they lasted, they were the ultimate status symbol for a Clan.

Razor moved unhurriedly towards the clones, and they scattered around him like fluttering birds. Their swords flashed brightly as they circled him in silent unison, every move a reflection of each other's. The audience stamped and cried out for the clones' deaths, shrieking like young carrion crows in the nest. The Investigator Razor paid them no heed. He stood still, his head cocked slightly to one side as though listening, his green eyes far away. The clones fell on him in unison, their blades reaching for his heart from three different directions. One moment Razor was still and the next he was moving too fast to follow. His swords lashed out, burying themselves in flesh and leaping out again, and the three clones staggered away from him, clutching at their death wounds, to lie still and broken on the bloody sands.

Razor sheathed his swords, and bowed formally to the Campbells' private box. He didn't wait to be acknowledged before turning and walking back to the main gates. The crowd was booing. It had been over too quickly; they hadn't had a chance to savour the suffering and deaths of the clones. A few connoisseurs and military men who understood what they'd just seen were applauding loudly, but no one paid them any attention, least of all Razor. He left the Arena as calmly and uncaring as he had entered it, like a blast of cold air on a warm night, come and gone in a moment, leaving only a quick shudder to mark its passing. He was still an Investigator, in every way that mattered.

Jacob Wolfe watched Razor's exit thoughtfully. He'd often considered putting in a bid for an Investigator of his own, but he never did. If only because he didn't like the idea of having such a perfect killer in constant close proximity to him. They were supposed to be incorruptible, untempted by power or money or glory, but the Wolfe rather doubted that. In his experience, everyone had their price, or breaking point.

The next act was a crowd-pleaser. Alien v. alien. The Arena had its own artificial gravity, temperature controls and force screens, enabling it to present any kind of environment, while ensuring the audience's safety. The audience muttered happily in anticipation as the light quickly lowered, replaced by the crimson glare of a holographic sun. The sands disappeared, replaced by a thick jungle of towering trees, their huge flat leaves a sickly purple. Here and there things moved in the concealing gloom between the trees, and strange cries echoed on the quiet air. The illusion was perfect, as always.

In the centre of the forest was a clearing, some thirty feet in diameter. The audience waited breathlessly for something to appear in it. Behind the holograms, a gate slid open, and a creature was released from its cage. It was reluctant to leave its den, and had to be persuaded with blows from hidden electric prods. It lurched forward through the holographic trees, bellowing its rage at the delighted crowds. It burst out into the clearing, and the first clear sight of it stunned the audience into silence. It was twenty-seven feet long from jaws to tail, a huge erect biped with a hell of a lot of lizard in it. It bulged with muscles under its glistening scales, standing rock steady on two vast legs while a long barbed tail lashed back and forth behind it. There were four gripping arms high up on its chest, to hold prey steady while the great jaws tore at it. The huge wedge-shaped head was mostly mouth, stuffed with jagged teeth. The creature spun round in a circle, moving disturbingly quickly for so large a beast, searching for the audience it could sense but not see. It roared deafeningly, and stamped its clawed feet on the disguised sands, and the crowd loved every minute of it. And then the creature froze as it sensed another presence close at hand in the holographic jungle.

It looked back and forth with its circle of eyes, muttering to itself, and the crowd waited with bated breath to see what kind

134

of creature the Arena masters had chosen to stand against such a formidable foe. It took them a while to realize it was already there. The second alien was a great cluster of writhing vegetation, some forty feet tall. It seemed to be mostly long creepers of twitching ivy, surrounding a bulky central mass. If it had sense organs, it was keeping them to itself, but the central mass of the creature slowly orientated itself to the great lizard. Long strands of creepers shot out like tentacles and fastened on the lizard. It bellowed angrily and tore the creepers like paper, but there were always more, wrapping themselves around the huge lizard like so many enveloping arms. The two aliens struggled together while the crowd went wild with delight and the bookies made a killing. The smart money was on the vegetation, if only because it didn't seem to have any vital points the lizard could attack.

'Aren't they marvellous?' sighed Constance happily. 'Don't you just adore aliens . . . Do you suppose they're intelligent?'

The Wolfe shrugged. 'Who cares?'

The lizard had practically disappeared under a crawling blanket of creepers, and was being dragged slowly but inexorably towards the central mass of the vegetation. The lizard was still struggling, but its arms were trapped against its chest, its legs were weighed down with ivied chains, and only its lashing tail still had room to move. More creepers lashed out at the wedge-shaped head like flails, and the crowd oo-ed and ah-ed.

And then the lizard stopped struggling and lunged forward, its vast muscular legs forcing it deep into the heart of the vegetation. Its head burrowed down past the lashing creepers, and its great jaws fastened like a steel trap on the hard central mass of the plant creature. The vicious teeth sank deep into the leathery carapace, and the lizard settled its weight, raised its head and lifted the whole plant off the ground. The creepers lashed hysterically in every direction, but the lizard ignored them. It shook the plant like a dog shakes a rat, and strands of greenery flew clear, to lie twitching on the ground. The lizard's teeth closed remorselessly as the great jaw muscles bulged, and the central carapace of the plant shattered under the pressure. The lizard tore at the exposed heart of the plant creature, and the whirling strands suddenly went limp. The lizard raised its wedge-shaped head and roared its triumph at the holographic sun, and then pulled itself free from the creepers, and set about methodically tearing the plant apart, chewing great mouthfuls of the quiescent vegetation.

The crowd cheered and roared in return, even those who'd bet against the lizard. It had been a good fight, and they did so love a winner. The lizard ignored them, intent on its meal. The crowd slowly settled as they realized the handlers hadn't appeared to guide the lizard back to its pen, to await its next fight. The game wasn't over yet. The audience stirred in anticipation as a gate opened and a lone figure walked out into the holographic jungle. It was a man with a sword, walking unhurriedly through the great trees towards the central clearing, and the crowd went quiet for a moment as they recognized Investigator Razor. A slow murmur began on the stands, as the crowd weighed up the chances. The lizard was huge and ferocious, a natural born monster of a killing machine, but Razor was an Investigator, after all . . .

'They can't be serious,' said Stephanie. 'He's already had his fight for the day. And even if he was fresh and rested, he still wouldn't stand a chance against that monster. It'll tear him apart!'

Jacob smiled at her fondly, and patted her arm comfortingly. He hadn't missed the rising excitement in her voice. 'If you're going to place a wager, my dear, I strongly suggest you put your money on Razor. Killing aliens used to be his job. The Campbells must have spread around a hell of a lot of money to set this up. Normally the Arena would expect to get twenty or more fights out of a creature like that. It has potential. I wonder who asked for the match originally . . . the Campbells, for the prestige, and a chance to make a killing with the bookmakers? Or did Razor ask for it, to prove he's still the best?'

'I don't care if he is an Investigator,' said Daniel. 'That lizard's going to chew him up and spit out the pieces. Nothing human could stand against anything that size, armed only with a sword.'

'Whoever said Razor was human?' said Valentine. 'And besides; that isn't just a sword he's carrying.'

The crowd quietened down as Razor emerged from the trees and stepped out into the clearing. He stared calmly at the huge lizard, which suddenly lifted its great head from the carcass of the plant creature, and sniffed the air loudly. It spat out a half-chewed mass of greenery, and spun round quickly, its long barbed tail swinging wide to balance its weight. Its scales gleamed brightly under the crimson sun, and shining teeth showed clearly as the lizard put back its great head and roared out a challenge. Razor lifted his sword as though in acknowledgement, and for the first time the audience saw clearly that it wasn't just a sword. A faint but distinct blue glow surrounded the blade, showing it had a monofilament edge, only a molecule wide. Which meant that particular blade could cut through anything it had a mind to, for as long as the sword's energy crystal could maintain the field that supported the edge. Such swords weren't common. They were extremely expensive, the energy crystal ran out extremely quickly, and most people disdained a monofilament edge as being not really honourable. It was doubtful Razor gave a damn about such niceties. Investigators were a practical breed.

The lizard lowered its head and charged right for Razor. He rose lightly on his toes and ran to meet it. They came together, the great jaws whipping down to snap together where the Investigator had been only a moment before. But at the last moment he'd changed direction and speed with almost impossible grace, and he darted to one side, moving in beside the lizard's left leg. The glowing sword spun round in a flat arc, and punched through the lizard's thigh and out again. Blood fountained, and the lizard roared in pain and rage. It spun on Razor, but he was no longer there, and the alien stumbled for a moment as its crippled leg almost collapsed under it. The monofilament edge had cut through skin and muscle in a moment, and scored a deep groove in the bone. The lizard's leg still supported it for the moment, but only just.

While the creature was sorting that out, Razor darted in again, and his sword scythed into the lizard's heaving side and out again. He neatly sidestepped the jetting blood, and moved smoothly to stay on the creature's blind side. It stamped awkwardly back and forth, favouring its wounded leg, the head swinging this way and that as it tried to find its tormentor, its great jaws snapping shut again and again like a malevolent steel trap. And then Razor was suddenly right there in front of it, and the huge head swung down, jaws gaping. Razor ran forward, jumped lithely up on to the lizard's good leg, and thrust his sword deep into the creature's throat. He hacked left and right with two quick, economical sweeps, and the alien's head fell away. The neck had been cut clean through by the monofilament edge.

Razor jumped down from the shuddering leg, and backed away to give the lizard room to die. The head lay on its side on the bloody sands. The holographic jungle disappeared, now that the fight was over. The jaws opened and closed a few times, slowly, but life had already faded from the puzzled scarlet eyes. The headless body stamped around the sands, blood fountaining from its open neck. Razor avoided it easily. The gripping hands clustered high up on the chest opened and closed spasmodically, as though trying to grasp the enemy that had hurt it. But finally the body realized it was dead, and it collapsed in an ungainly twitching heap. The crowd went mad, but the Investigator was already walking back to the side exit, ignoring their cheers. He hadn't killed the alien for them.

In the Wolfe's private box, there were mixed feelings. Constance squealed with delight, bouncing around on her chair. Jacob laughed, and called for more wine. Daniel was sulking. He'd bet heavily on the lizard. Stephanie looked at her father, and then at the huge creature lying dead on the sands. And if she made a connection between the two in her mind, she kept it to herself. Valentine took another sniff of his blue powder, and his thoughts were his own, as always.

Handlers appeared in the Arena, slipped anti-grav units under the dead lizard, and towed it quickly away. It disappeared head and all through the main gates, and the crowd gave it a mocking farewell. They had no time for losers. The head would be kept as a trophy, the rest would be butchered and rendered down to provide protein for the other aliens waiting in their pens.

Micro-organisms in the sand ate up the fallen blood and dispersed it evenly, as the handlers raked the sands till they were tidy again. They finished their work and got off the sands as quickly as they could. The crowd tended to throw things, and some of them had a nasty sense of humour. The audience reluctantly settled down, conversations still buzzing here and there, and looked to see what was coming next. It took a lot to satisfy the Golgotha crowds, and they were always greedy for more.

The recorded trumpets sounded again, a man strode out on to the sands, and the cheer that greeted him eclipsed everything that had gone before. The crowd went insane, jumping to their feet to cheer and wave and hug each other in anticipation. There was no announcement; everyone knew who he was. He was the Masked Gladiator, undefeated champion of the Games, the darling of the Golgotha crowds. Everything else had been warm-ups. He was what they had all come to see.

No one knew who he really was. He could have been any age, from any background. He was tall and lithely muscular, wore a simple anonymous steel mesh tunic, and carried a sword that was almost as famous as he was. It was long and slender, and entirely unaugmented. It was called Morgana. No one knew why. A featureless black steel helm covered his head completely, and he had never been seen without it. In his three-year career as a gladiator, he had never even come close to being beaten or unmasked. He specialized in winning against impossible odds, and the crowd loved him for it. His identity, and his reasons for concealing it, remained a mystery, though there were any number of rumours. Some said he'd been dishonourably discharged from the Army, and sought to regain his honour through combat. Others said he was an Investigator who had somehow lost his nerve, and sought to reforge it in the Arena. There were those who spoke of a lost or dead love, and said he sought the comfort or forgetfulness of death in battle. And some at least suggested he was a noble, seeking thrills and excitement he couldn't find anywhere else.

No one said that last one too loudly, of course. If it were true, it would be a major scandal. The aristocracy settled their disputes only through champions or the Code Duello. Anything less would have been beneath them. The elite were above and beyond the lesser drives and emotions of the lower classes. They were special, untouchable, unattainable. It was vitally important that the gap be maintained. It wouldn't do for the lower orders to start getting ideas above their station.

But whatever the secret of his face, the crowds loved him, and they conspired with the Arena staff to keep his secret and preserve his identity, even from the Empress's security people. Which was probably unique in the Empire. So far the Empress had declined to press the point. Which had given rise to a whole new batch of rumours.

He fought always with the sword Morgana, disdaining monofilament edges or other energy weapons. He was a superb swordsman, with speed and skill and trained reflexes beyond anything outside the augmented men. There were still those who claimed he had to be a cyborg of some kind, or at the very least a product of the body shops, but the Arena staff said not, and they were best placed to know.

The Masked Gladiator took up his position in the centre of the Arena, and waited patiently for his opponent to come to him. The giant holoscreen showed a close-up of his featureless helm, and ran columns of statistics from his previous fights on either side of it. The figures were impressive. Never beaten, in a hundred and thirty-seven combats. Only wounded seriously twice, in his early days. Present odds against his current challenger: one thousand to one, in his favour. The odds kept small fry from wasting his time, but there were always challengers.

The latest in a long line stepped out of a side gate and strode confidently towards the waiting champion. The crowd gave him a good-natured cheer. They admired courage, and fresh blood was always welcome. His name was Auric Skye, and he wanted to become a bodyguard for the Lord of Clan Chojiro.

But since that was one of the top jobs in the bodyguard market, the only way to jump to the top of the queue was by committing some great act of courage and skill. Auric had chosen to challenge the Masked Gladiator. He didn't necessarily expect to win, but if he put up a good enough fight, the crowd would very likely turn their thumbs up for him. And he would become one of the very few people who'd fought the Masked Gladiator and survived. Clan Chojiro would come looking for him, then.

And besides; he might win. He had an ace up his sleeve, and everywhere else, too.

Skye was young, extremely muscular, and almost offensively blond and handsome. Like the champion, he was armed only with a sword. Clan Chojiro were somewhat old-fashioned, in that they didn't approve of clones or espers or any other deviants of the human norm, but they had no objections to the gifts of technology. In this case, Skye was known to have had steel plates inserted under his skin to cover all his vulnerable areas, and steel webbing everywhere else. A kind of internal armour, with no weak spots. The weight slowed him down, but he had ways of dealing with that. The Masked Gladiator had never fought such an opponent before. Even so, hardly anyone was betting against him.

Skye advanced on the champion, who bowed courteously to him. Skye broke into a lumbering run, his sword stretched out before him. His weight left deep footprints in the sand, but still his movements were eerily fluid, and he covered the intervening distance surprisingly quickly. The champion smiled inside his helm. Whatever body shop had provided Skye with his exceptional muscles had done an excellent job. The Masked Gladiator stepped forward suddenly, catching Skye by surprise, and swung the sword Morgana round in a whistling arc. Skye couldn't get his sword up in time, and the double-handed blow smashed into the side of his neck. The blow would have decapitated anyone else, but Skye just stood there and took it.

He grunted softly at the impact, and lurched one step to one side, but he had his balance back in a moment, and his free hand shot up to grab Morgana's blade. His bare hand closed on the steel like a vice, and the Gladiator had to use all his strength to pull the blade free. It emerged jerkily from Skye's fist, the sharp edges slicing through the skin only to grate against the steel webbing beneath it. Skye grinned quickly, ignoring the pain and the blood from his hand and neck, and brought his own sword up in a dazzlingly swift thrust at the Gladiator's gut. The champion blocked the blow as though he'd known it was coming, but had to fall back a step to do so. Skye pressed forward, and the Gladiator backed away. The crowd couldn't believe it.

The champion quickly turned the retreat into a circling motion, and the two men tracked each other, looking for an opening. Skye charged forward again, and the two swords rang loudly as they swung together again and again. Skye had the advantage in weight and strength, but the champion had the edge in skill. Again and again he turned aside blows that seemed unstoppable, but try as he might, he was unable to mount a counter-attack. Skye wouldn't allow him the time or the space, pressing home his attacks with unflagging energy. The champion doubted Skye could maintain the attack for long, but then, he probably wouldn't have to. The Gladiator only had to make one mistake, and the match would be over.

Unfortunately for Skye, the Gladiator didn't believe in making mistakes. Choosing his moment carefully, he stepped inside Skye's blows, and launched a blistering attack. Morgana seemed to fly at Skye from every direction at once. He blocked most of the blows, but some got through. Morgana cut him again and again, but to the crowd's loud astonishment, he didn't go down. Wherever Morgana pierced flesh, it found only steel plates or webbing. Hardly any blood flowed, and Skye's face never flinched once. He and pain had become old friends in the process that had given him his internal armour. And then the Gladiator was just a little too slow in pulling back from a lunge, and Skye's spare hand shot out inhumanly quickly and closed on the champion's arm. Muscles bulged, and Skye threw the Masked Gladiator thirty feet across the Arena.

He landed hard, and rolled quite a way, but was back on his feet in a moment. Behind the featureless steel helm he could have been panting or scowling or grimacing with pain, but his stance was firm and his sword arm was steady. Skye lurched into a run again, building momentum like a runaway truck. The Gladiator shook himself once, as though to settle himself, and then lifted Morgana and waited for his opponent to come to him. The crowd were going wild at the prospect of finally seeing their champion beaten, humbled, perhaps even killed. They screamed warnings and advice and encouragement to both fighters, standing on their seats for a better view, and there was a flurry of last minute betting as people changed their minds.

The Gladiator stood his ground. He could run, but that wasn't his style. He could surrender and beg for mercy, but he didn't do that either. He hefted Morgana angrily. A good sword, the best he'd ever known, but helpless against implanted steel armour. And then a thought came to him, and he smiled inside his featureless steel helm. Skye was almost upon him, sword pulling back for the killing thrust. The Masked Gladiator stepped forward in a perfect lunge, and the tip of his sword leapt out and plunged through Skye's left eyeball and on into his brain. The only part of him that hadn't been protected.

For a long moment Auric Skye just stood there, transfixed on the champion's sword, and then the Masked Gladiator pulled Morgana free, and Skye collapsed, as though that was all that had been holding him up. He fell heavily and lay still, and the Gladiator saluted him once with Morgana before turning away. The crowd were beside themselves, cheering till their throats were raw, pounding their hands together till they ached, even those who'd been foolish enough to bet on Skye. The Masked Gladiator walked back to the main gates, one hand raised to acknowledge the crowd. And Auric Skye, who'd given up part of his humanity in his quest to become a bodyguard for Clan Chojiro, lay broken and forgotten on the blood-stained sands.

In the Wolfe private box, Jacob turned triumphantly to his

Family. 'Now that is a real fighter. Strong, smart, committed. Find a weakness and exploit it. You could all learn a lesson from a man like that.'

His Family murmured politely in reply, but kept their thoughts to themselves. Everyone in Clan Wolfe knew all about finding and taking advantage of other people's weaknesses while guarding their own. It was what kept them alive from day to day. Daniel pictured himself in the featureless steel helm, standing haughtily over a number of dying bodies, not least Valentine and his father. Stephanie considered a rumour that was never more than a whisper; that underneath the steel helm lay the face of a woman, not a man. She smiled at the thought, and many were the faces of those who lay broken at her feet. Jacob tried for the hundredth time to come up with some plan, legal or illegal, that would win the Masked Gladiator's allegiance. Constance hugged the Wolfe's arm tightly and plotted marriages for her stepchildren, so that they would leave and allow her uninterrupted access to the Wolfe. And Valentine considered the many deaths he'd caused that day, and smiled and smiled and smiled.

CHAPTER FIVE

Friends, Enemies and Allies

Mistworld was the rebel planet. The only rebel planet in the whole of the Empire. A world made by renegades and traitors, insurgents and troublemakers. When you'd been everywhere else and found no safe haven, there was always Mistworld. Outlaws, rogue espers, criminals, trash and scum all ended up on the planet of eternal winter. The world they'd built wasn't particularly pretty or civilized, but it was free, and every man, woman and child on Mistworld would fight to the death to keep it that way. Schemes for rebellion against the Empire came and went without accomplishing much, because the rebels were only safe as long as they stayed on Mistworld, protected by a powerful psionic screen that was the equal of anything the Empire could send against it. The only city, Mistport, seethed with plots and plans and spies, not least from the Empire, who liked to know what was going on. And to this last refuge, this last chance, this last roll of the loaded dice came Hazel d'Ark and Owen Deathstalker, the ex-clonelegger and the outlawed Lord, to start a rebellion that would spread far beyond the world that birthed it.

The *Sunstrider* howled out of hyperspace like a bullet shot from a gun, and then slowed reluctantly into high orbit around Mistworld. Its shields snapped on again, and the sensor spikes shimmered, but there was no trace anywhere of the two starcruisers that had been attacking it. In the luxurious main cabin, Owen sank back in his chair with a sigh, and Hazel blinked respectfully.

'I'm impressed,' she said finally. 'We made it all the way

here, across half the damn Empire, in just one jump. It normally takes at least seven, and only then if you've got a shit hot navigator. How much power did we just burn up?'

'Hardly any,' said Owen smugly. 'I told you; this is a whole new kind of stardrive. It's going to make everything else obsolete.'

'How does it work?' said Hazel.

Owen shrugged. 'I don't know. I just bought the ship, I didn't design it. I had my AI scan the manual so it could fly the thing, but I've only flipped through it. I'm not really very technically-minded. I've always had people to do that sort of thing for me.'

Hazel sniffed. 'That's one attitude you'll have to lose, aristo. An outlaw can't afford to rely on anyone but themself.'

'You should know,' said Owen easily. 'All right; what's our next step?'

'We ask very politely for landing permission. Once we're dirtside we're protected by the planet's espers, but out here we're a sitting duck for the first Empire ship to come along. It won't take them long to come here looking for us, and while this ship might be fast, it's got no heavy-duty weapons systems at all.'

'Well, no,' said Owen. 'It's a pleasure yacht, not a warship.'

'Next time, look a little further in the catalogue. I'll contact Mistport. It's the only starport on Mistworld. In fact, it's their only city. It's not what you'd call a densely populated world, and once you've lived there for a while you'll know why. Desolate bloody place, all snow and ice and fog. I just hope I can pull a few strings, call in some old favours. It's been a while since I was last here, and I'm not sure if I've got any friends left in Mistport.'

She was silent for a long moment, frowning, and Owen studied her thoughtfully. She fascinated him, if only because he'd never met anyone like her before. He'd grown up believing the only good rebel was a dead rebel, and now he was one. His life had changed completely, and he was going to have to understand Hazel and her world if he was to survive in it.

'What brought you here before?' he said casually.

Hazel started, jerked out of her thoughts, and then shrugged self-consciously. 'I spent some time here recovering after my stint as a mercenary on Loki, during the succession wars. As usual, with my native wit and massive experience, I had no trouble picking the losing side to sign on with. We got our ass kicked good, my side scattered to the winds, and I ended up here because it was the only place my enemies wouldn't come looking for me. As it turned out, I was wrong about that too, but that's another story.'

'What are we going to do once we've landed?' said Owen. 'A hell of a lot of people are going to be looking for me, and the price on my head would tempt a sainted nun.'

'What's this *we* bit?' said Hazel. 'I hauled your ass out of the line of fire because I couldn't just stand by and watch you die, but I haven't adopted you. In fact, if I'd known you were an aristo I'd probably have joined in the shooting myself. As it is, once we are safely down, I am going my way and you can go yours. The last thing I need is a know-nothing tenderfoot like you slowing me down and attracting attention. I have my life to rebuild, and that's going to be hard enough without carrying a passenger.'

'I am quite capable of looking after myself,' said Owen hotly. 'I have been trained as a warrior by some of the finest tutors in the Empire!'

'Judging by what I've seen, you should ask for your money back. You're a liability, Owen, and I've got my own problems. You'll do all right. Selling this ship should make you one of the wealthiest people on Mistworld. If you don't let yourself get fleeced.'

'Sell *Sunstrider*? Are you out of your mind. She's my only chance for getting off this planet!'

'Owen; you're not going anywhere. This is the end of the line for people like us. Mistworld is the only planet where you can hope to survive. Anywhere else, they'll cut your head off the moment you raise it to look around. You aren't going to find it easy here, but at least you'll have a fighting chance. And that's the best you can ever hope for, as an outlaw.'

Owen thought hard. Much as he hated to admit it, he needed Hazel d'Ark. She was loud, overbearing and definitely common, but she understood this new world of outlaws, and as yet he didn't.

'You can't just abandon me,' he said plaintively. 'You have contacts here; I don't know anyone. You can't just walk off and leave me to the wolves.'

'Watch me,' said Hazel. 'I don't owe you anything, aristo. If I'd known you were going to cling on like this I'd have shot you myself.'

All right, thought Owen, *so much for appealing to her better nature. She is an outlaw, after all.*

'How about this; I'll hire you as my bodyguard, till I learn the ropes. Name your own price.'

Hazel looked at him thoughtfully. 'And just what were you planning to pay me with?'

'As you just pointed out, selling the *Sunstrider* will make me extremely rich. If the right person was there to oversee the deal.'

'Ten per cent,' said Hazel flatly. 'I get my money right off the top, and you don't get to make any conditions. You also don't get to whine, complain or ask impertinent questions. I'll stick with you till you're established, but then I'm off. You're too tempting a target, Deathstalker. I feel nervous just standing next to you.'

Owen seethed inwardly. He had a strong suspicion that ten per cent of what the *Sunstrider* would bring would be enough to set up a dozen men for life, but it wasn't as if he had a choice in the matter. He couldn't command her as a Lord, or beg her as a friend, so that just left money.

'All right,' he said tightly. 'You've got a deal.'

He put out his hand for her to shake, but she just looked at it. 'Forget the handshake, Deathstalker. We've no reason to trust each other. All you need to know is that if you try to cross or cheat me, I'll cut you up into bite-size chunks, and to hell with all your fancy training. Now let me think.'

She stood there for a long moment, frowning, concentrating. Owen lowered his hand and let it rest on his belt near his sword. With anyone else, he would have challenged them to a duel for such an insult, but Hazel was different. He had a feeling he could come to respect her. If he didn't kill her first. She sniffed suddenly, as though coming to a decision she wasn't particularly pleased with, and fixed Owen with her sardonic gaze again.

'Assuming the few friends I made last time I was here are still around, and still feeling friendly, I should be able to talk our way past quarantine. We can't afford to hang around long enough to be recognized. Unfortunately, we can't afford to rely on my old contacts. Lifespans tend to be rather short on Mistworld. If the people don't kill you, the planet will. I hope you've got some industrial strength warm clothing tucked away on this ship somewhere, or we're going to freeze solid just walking off the landing pads.'

Owen scowled. 'Assuming your old contacts are no longer in the land of the living or the willing, and we can't talk our way past quarantine; how long would they hold us?'

'Long enough to call an esper to dig through our minds in search of something incriminating. Mistport security take their job very seriously. The Empire keeps trying to smuggle in disguised plague ships and the like.'

'And we can't afford to be identified,' said Owen. 'Great. Just great. All right, Hazel, do whatever you have to, but keep us out of quarantine. Only bear in mind that whatever bribe you end up offering is coming out of your ten per cent. Clear?'

Hazel nodded approvingly. 'See; you're starting to think like an outlaw already.'

'What sort of planet is Mistworld?' said Owen, as they headed for the comm panels. 'You make it sound like a hellworld.'

'It's a hard world, Deathstalker. Very poor, hardly any high-tech, and the people who come here tend to be the lowest of the low.'

'I'm sure you felt right at home here, Hazel.'

'You will come to regret that remark in the long cold days ahead, aristo. You'll either learn to fit in here, or die. Your choice. Ozymandias; are you listening?'

'Of course, Hazel,' said the AI promptly. 'A great many people have been trying to talk to us. I have been waiting to ascertain whether we wished to talk to them.'

'Patch me through to the Mistport control tower,' said Hazel. 'Everyone else can wait.'

'As you wish. May I point out at this stage that I am a very sophisticated system, and quite capable of running rings around any AIs that Mistport might have?'

'Don't even think about it,' said Hazel sharply. 'What they use instead of computers down there would scare the electronic spit out of you. They're very powerful, and extremely dangerous. Shield yourself at all times, and stay well clear of anything that isn't entirely human. Like everything else on Mistworld, the computers have got teeth you wouldn't believe.'

'Nice place you've brought me to,' said Owen.

'It has its charms. Raise the control tower, Ozymandias. Hello, Mistport central. This is the *Sunstrider*, looking for sanctuary. Please acknowledge.'

'This is duty esper John Silver,' said a tired voice from the comm panels. 'Don't adjust your systems, we've lost visual again. I need a full run down on your crew, cargo and last planetfall. Don't bother lying; our espers will get it out of you anyway.'

'John?' said Hazel, smiling suddenly. 'Is that you, Silver, you old pirate? You're the last voice I was expecting. This is Hazel d'Ark. Remember; we worked together on the Angel of Night swindle.'

'The good god preserve and save us,' said the voice, sounding a little more animated. 'Hazel bloody d'Ark. I always knew you'd be back someday, no doubt dragging a long trail of creditors behind you. Who have you got mad at you this time?'

'Practically everybody. Look, John, I need a favour.'

'You always do. What is it this time?'

'I can't afford to hang around in quarantine. Too many people looking for me and this ship. I need to go to ground for a while. Will you vouch for me?'

'Depends. Are you alone?'

'One passenger, and I vouch for him.'

'That's not much of a recommendation. I have a strong feeling I'm going to regret this, but all right. Put your ship down on pad seven, and then disappear into the mists. I can only buy you twenty-four hours, though.'

'That should be enough. Thanks, John. How the hell did a died-in-the-blood pirate like you end up in security?'

Silver chuckled briefly. 'Times are hard, girl, and Mistport needed all the espers it could get. Things have gone to hell since you were last here. Empire hit us with something really nasty. Over half our espers are dead or mind-burned. As a result, security is tighter than ever, but with nowhere near enough people to enforce it with. Look me up when you've got a chance. Unless you're still in trouble, in which case I never heard of you. Silver out.'

'Now that was a stroke of luck,' said Owen, and then stopped as he saw the expression on Hazel's face. 'Wasn't it?'

'I don't know. Maybe. The John Silver I knew was an ex-pirate and a confidence trickster. And now he's in charge of Mistport security? Things must have really gone to the dogs since I was last here. And we're not out of the woods yet. We've got twenty-four hours, and then either I report in, with a lot of convincing answers, or Silver's people will tear the city apart looking for us. On top of that, we have to use that time to find a buyer for *Sunstrider*, before someone recognizes it. You can bet every Imperial agent on Mistworld has a detailed description of it and you by now. Which means we have twenty-four hours to make the sale, bank the money, and then go to ground so thoroughly that even the really talented and highly motivated people looking for us won't be able to find us. Once things have quietened down a little, we can reappear with new names and backgrounds, and a hell of a lot of money to back us up.'

'Why can't we just change our looks in a body shop?' said Owen.

Hazel gave him the kind of look a tutor gives a dull but persistent pupil. Owen was getting rather tired of that look, but kept his temper.

'Remember what I said about limited high-tech on this

world? The only tech they've got here is what smugglers can sneak past the Empire. I'm not saying there isn't a body shop somewhere in Mistport, but if there is you can bet it's the only one, and so exclusive that they charge an arm and a leg. Possibly literally. Which means it'll be watched night and day by Imperial agents, just in case we're stupid enough to go anywhere near it. Try and keep up, Deathstalker. I can't carry you all the way. And before you start sulking again, could you perhaps put a little thought towards raising some stake money? I've got a little credit stashed away here and there in Mistport, but not a lot. I had to earn it the hard way.'

'Really?' said Owen. 'How?'

'You don't need to know. Ozymandias? Are we cleared to land?'

'As soon as we pay a rather exorbitant docking fee, yes.'

Owen asked how much. The AI told him, and Owen nearly had a fit. 'I'm not paying that! It's extortionate!'

'Not really,' said Hazel. 'Not when you consider how much more they could make by handing you over to the Empire. Besides, you're not paying it, I'm going to have to. And just for the record, no, this is not coming out of my ten per cent.'

Oxymandias cleared its throat politely, something that never failed to disconcert Owen, not least because the AI didn't have a throat to clear. 'I really feel I should remind you, Owen, that the new files I discovered hidden in my memory were quite specific concerning an establishment in Mistport that you should visit in order to find help.' The AI paused, and when it spoke again it sounded almost apologetic. 'I also have a name to go with the address. But you're not going to like it.'

'Try me,' said Owen resignedly. 'I'd be hard pressed to name anything about this situation I do like.'

'The name is Jack Random.'

'He's here? On Mistworld?' Owen thought hard. 'How the hell did he get tangled up with my father's intrigues? I wouldn't have thought they were in the same class.'

'A good question, Owen, for which I have as yet no satisfactory answer.'

152

'You've got really polite since Hazel came aboard,' said Owen accusingly.

'Are you complaining?'

Owen thought hard. His head was beginning to ache. Jack Random; the professional rebel. Legendary warrior. He fought the system. Any system. He'd been fighting the Empire for more than twenty years, leading one rebellion after another on any number of planets. He was a spellbinding orator, with a keen eye for injustice, and never had any trouble finding more hotheaded fools to follow him to death or glory. And so it went for many years. But the decades passed, and the Empire stood as strong as ever, and people remembered the many lost battles rather than the few triumphs, and they stopped listening. The price on Jack Random's head became increasingly tempting, and the bounty hunters went after him in earnest. He'd been forced to drop out of sight, and no one had seen him for years.

'Trust my father to hook up with one of the biggest all-time losers,' said Owen. 'Even I have more sense than to tie myself to Jack Random. By all accounts a legendary fighter and hero, but a piss-poor General. Hazel; I place myself in your hands.'

'In your dreams, aristo,' said Hazel. 'But please, Owen; watch your step and leave all the talking to me. If the people we're going to see get even a hint of who you really are, we are both dead.'

'Relax,' said Owen. 'I am not without experience. I know how to comport myself in public.'

'That's what I mean! You can't go around using words like comport; it's a dead giveaway. Look, don't say a word, and I'll pass you off as my deaf mute cousin.'

Owen looked at her. 'Don't do me any favours.'

'Trust me,' said Hazel. 'I won't.'

Owen kept his mouth shut and his eyes open as Hazel led him through the narrow streets of Mistport. The city was in a hell of a state. Rebuilding was going on everywhere he looked, and the people seemed uniformly sour and tight-lipped. From the look of the place, Owen didn't blame them one bit. The stone and timber buildings leaned out over the street like drunken old men apologizing to each other. There was mud and filth in the street, and the smell was appalling. A thick fog pearled the air in sheets of grey, so that lamps burned brightly at irregular intervals, even though it was getting on for midday. People filled the streets, huddled under heavy furs and cloaks, looking straight ahead and using their elbows with practised skill.

Owen and Hazel kept the hoods of their cloaks pulled well forward, so that their faces were hidden in shadow. No one stared at them or showed any curiosity; apparently anonymity was a common state in Mistport. Owen trudged on through the mud and slush, and beat his gloved hands together to force out the cold. He'd taken the heaviest clothes from *Sunstrider*'s wardrobe, but there hadn't been a lot of choice. He glared at Hazel's back ahead of him. She was striding along like it was just another day. Owen muttered to himself and struggled to keep up with her, elbowing people out of his way with grim satisfaction. Nobody said anything. Apparently that was common practice too.

Hazel dragged him from one low dive to another, in search of old acquaintances, but no one wanted to talk. After the recent troubles, everyone was busy looking after their own affairs. Hazel kept plugging away, while Owen's spirits drooped. He couldn't even talk to Oz for company; they'd agreed to keep communication to a minimum, for security's sake. You could never be sure who was listening in, on Mistworld. He scowled unhappily, and pulled his cloak tight around him. It was all taking too long. Finally Hazel came up with a name, if not a location; Ruby Journey.

'Never heard of her,' said Owen.

'No reason why you should have, aristo. You don't move in the same circles. Ruby's a bounty hunter, and a damned good one. She's an old friend of mine, from way back. We mugged our first tourist together. She'll put us in touch with the right people, provided we make her a good enough offer.'

'Not another ten per cent,' said Owen firmly.

Hazel shrugged. 'Up to you. But if you want the best, you have to be prepared to pay for it. Don't worry too much about it; she'll give you a discount because you're with me. All we have to do now is find her.'

'Oh great,' said Owen. 'More tramping back and forth.'

'What are you moaning about now?'

'You want it in order? I'm spoilt for choice. Apart from the insanity of trusting our safety to a bounty hunter, it's bitter cold, I haven't a clue where we are, I can't feel my hands any more, and my feet aren't talking to me. We've been tramping around this pitiful excuse for a city for ages without getting anywhere useful, and my stomach thinks my throat's been cut. Also, the smell is disgusting. Something really drastic must have happened in the sewers.'

'Sewers?' said Hazel. 'Don't show your ignorance. Around here a cesspit is a sign of luxury. Be grateful the nightsoil collectors have already been round. Still; where we're going next should cheer you up. Another old friend of mine is running a tavern not far from here. The Blackthorn. She'll know where Ruby is. Cyder knows everything. Let's go.'

She set off down the street at a good pace, brimming with confidence and good cheer. Owen trudged after her, grumbling under his breath. He paused for a moment to pull his cloak more tightly about him, and someone pressed a coin into his hand before hurrying on. Owen looked at it for a long moment before realizing he'd been taken for a beggar. He was tempted to throw the money after the giver, but he didn't. Money was money.

He put the coin in his pocket and hurried after Hazel, seething inwardly. Some way, someone was going to pay for all this. He focused his glare on Hazel's unresponsive back. She didn't seem to feel the cold at all. Owen thought, not for the first time, that he might have been better off fighting for his life back on Virimonde. At least he'd understood the situation there. And it had been warm. He didn't understand much about Mistworld, and what he did repulsed him. No law, no custom or honour, no social structure. Everyone out for themselves, and to hell with everyone else. A world of criminals and social misfits, living in poverty and squalor unknown anywhere else in the Empire. They were free, and much good their freedom had done them. Owen felt a sudden rush of tiredness wash over him, and for a moment he was weighed down by the uselessness of it all. He couldn't live here. Not like this. Without civilization and the comfort of social position, his life had no meaning. He would simply wither up and die, like a flower picked from its bed.

The thought shook him out of the daze he'd fallen into. He couldn't die. Not while his enemies still lived. They had destroyed his life, taken away everything he believed in, and spat on his name. He had to live, so that someday he could take vengeance on the Iron Bitch, and all who had aided her in his downfall. Owen smiled tightly. When all else fails, there is always revenge. He wasn't going to stay stuck on this miserable planet. Somehow he'd find a way off, and then . . . he'd think of something. He had to. In the meantime, he had to survive. He would endure whatever the planet sent, do whatever was necessary to raise enough money to buy him an army, and a way offplanet. Because if he just lay down and died, then Lionstone would have won after all.

He lurched on through the deepening mud and slush, glaring at everyone and everything around him with renewed disgust. Surely it couldn't all be like this. There had to be some bright spots in the gloom. A window opened above him, and people scattered out of the way. Someone cried a brief warning, and Owen jumped back just in time to avoid the falling contents of an emptied chamberpot. The window slammed shut again, and people moved on, unperturbed, as though this was an everyday experience. Owen sniffed. Probably was. No sewers. Right.

How could people live like this? Didn't they know what they were coming to when they ran from the Empire? It came to him slowly that they must have, and came anyway, because for them life in the Empire was worse. The thought nagged at him, and wouldn't let him go. The Empire was full of luxuries and comforts for the upper classes, and security and stability for the lower classes. Unless you were a clone or an esper or some other kind of unperson. Unless you upset someone with connections, or couldn't meet your quotas, or fell ill once too often. There was no place in the lower orders for the weak, or the troublesome, or the unlucky.

It seemed to Owen that he had always known this, but never really thought about it before. As long as his cushioned world went on uninterrupted, he hadn't had to. He couldn't say he hadn't known. He was an historian, and he knew more about the realities the Empire was based on than most. How corrupt had the Empire become, that the living hell of Mistworld could be such an improvement? Owen sighed. His head was starting to ache again, probably from too much frowning. He'd think more about this later. He had a feeling he'd have lots of time to think about things in the future.

The Blackthorn Tavern turned out to be a pleasant surprise. It was cosy and comfortable without being cramped, and had obviously had a lot of money spent on it. The fixtures and fittings were of the highest quality, and there was a pleasant sense of sanctuary in the smoky room, from the harshness and pain of the world. Owen leaned against the long, highly polished bar, sipping an adequate though extremely expensive wine, and tried to ignore the vicious pins and needles of returning circulation. The Blackthorn was crowded but full of good cheer, and the noise was almost but not quite overpowering. Everyone had to shout to be heard, and those who weren't shouting were singing, with more verve than accuracy. Owen found it all rather charming, in a rustic sort of way, and was quite prepared to stay there as long as was necessary, if not longer. Particularly if the wine held out.

Hazel was talking earnestly with the Blackthorn's owner, a tall willowy platinum blonde called Cyder. They were head to head at the other end of the bar, apparently lip reading as much as listening. Owen studied Cyder curiously. She seemed a strangely delicate flower to be running a tavern in a cut-throat area like the one he and Hazel had just walked through. According to Hazel, it was called Thieves' Quarter, and Owen wasn't a bit surprised. Presumably Cyder had a small army of well-trained muscle standing by, ready to jump on anyone who made a nuisance of themselves. Owen had spent some time unobtrusively trying to spot them, on the general principle that if trouble was to come his way, he wanted to at least have some idea of which direction it was coming from. He hadn't had any luck. Everyone looked equally violent and disreputable.

And then Cyder looked past Hazel directly at Owen, and he stopped with his drink half-way to his lips. In that moment she looked harsh and uncompromising and very dangerous, with the coldest blue eyes he'd ever seen. The moment passed, and then she was smiling at him, and beckoning for him to join her and Hazel. Owen emptied his glass, and moved unhurriedly down the bar to join them. He had no doubt that Cyder had deliberately allowed him to see the ice beneath her surface, but he wasn't at all sure why. Perhaps to impress on him that she was someone to be taken seriously. Owen gave her his most charming smile as he arrived, and kept his hand near his gun.

Cyder led the way to a private room up on the next floor, a small unadorned room with comfortable chairs and a crackling fire. Owen sat as close to it as he could bear, and tried not to look too interested as the two women discussed Hazel's old times in Mistport. Much of it seemed to have been either disreputable or illegal, and Owen couldn't say he was at all surprised. Eventually the two women caught up to the present, and smiled fondly at each other.

'You've put a lot of work into this place,' Hazel said finally. 'I can't believe this is the old snake pit where I used to drink.'

'I came into some money,' said Cyder, smiling demurely. 'I've been able to . . . indulge myself.'

'Where's Cat?'

'Around. People make him nervous.' Cyder shot Owen a mischievous glance. 'Does this young gentleman know about your chequered past, Hazel? Have you told him how you made most of your money here in Mistport?'

'No, and you're not to tell him. He doesn't need to know.'

'It's a perfectly honourable profession. We've all done a few things we don't like to remember, when money gets short.'

'That's as maybe.' Hazel glared at Owen. 'And you can wipe

that look off your face. I know what you're thinking, and you're wrong.'

'I wasn't thinking anything.' Owen said quickly, trying hard not to think the word prostitute, or at least keep it off his face.

Cyder laughed. 'Don't worry, Hazel, your secret is safe with me. Still, it must be said we've all come a long way since you and I and John Silver were thick as thieves and searching for some direction in our lives. He was a pirate, I was a fence, and you . . . were doing what you were doing. Now he's in charge of Mistport security, of all things, I am the highly respectable owner of a highly profitable tavern, and you're an outlaw with a price on your head. Quite a good price, too. The word was out on you and your friend ten minutes after your somewhat distinctive ship touched down. Don't think I've ever had a Lord in my tavern before, let alone one with as famous a name as yours, Lord Deathstalker.'

'Call me Owen,' he said coolly. 'The title's been stripped from me. How long have you known about us?'

'Relax, dear. I don't turn in old friends. I don't have to any more, and I have my own reasons for hating the Empire and all its works.' Her hand rose briefly to brush against a few thin scars on her face. 'Half this city has been turning the other half upside down looking for you, and the only reason no one's found you yet is because you've been moving around so much. Fortunately, no one's connected you with your last visit, Hazel, so they don't know to check your old haunts, but it's only a matter of time before someone gets lucky. That's why I brought you up here, away from prying eyes. Times are hard here in Mistport, especially since Typhoid Mary tore the town apart. The prices on both your heads are enough to tempt anyone. Even me, if I didn't have such a personal grudge against the Empire. There's nowhere in this city that's safe for you now; no one you can trust except each other. And you can forget about selling your ship. No one will touch it now, at any price. The Empire's already said it'll blow it apart on sight, no matter who claims to be flying it. I'm afraid you two are stuck with each other. Everyone else has to be seen as a potential enemy. Even I might be tempted, if you stayed around long enough. Friendship is nice, but it doesn't pay the bills.'

'There's always Ruby Journey,' said Hazel, and Cyder pulled a face.

'Ruby Journey. I should have known that name would come up. I never did know what you saw in her. I always thought of myself as a cold-hearted bitch, but dear Ruby's in a class all of her own. You can't be seriously thinking of throwing yourself on her mercy? She's a bounty hunter!'

'I said that,' said Owen.

'She's my friend,' said Hazel.

'Bounty hunters don't have any friends,' said Cyder.

'Do you know where I can find her?'

'I'm glad to say I haven't the faintest idea. She's around somewhere, no doubt killing someone for money. Or just for the fun of it.'

'She's not that bad.'

'She's a sadistic, amoral psychopath. And those are her good points.'

'You said yourself that Mistport is crawling with Imperial agents, bounty hunters and amateur assassins,' Hazel said patiently. 'If the aristo and I are going to survive this mess, we need someone like Ruby on our side, if only to frighten everyone else away. Do you have any idea at all where we might look for her?'

Cyder shook her head dubiously, and reluctantly provided Hazel with a short list of places to check. Most of them seemed to be taverns, for which Owen at least was grateful. He felt very much in need of a stiff drink or several. He realized Hazel was scowling at him, and sat up straight, trying to look as though he'd been paying attention all the time.

'Much as I hate to admit it, Deathstalker, it appears we're going to be sticking together after all. If we separate, that'll just make us easier to take. Besides; you have a connection that might prove useful after all. Jack Random.'

Cyder raised a silver eyebrow. 'He's in Mistport? I hadn't heard he was back. Last I'd heard, he'd had his army shot out from under him on Vodyanoi IV, and the Empire was closing in on him from all sides. Of course, that was nearly two years ago. I suppose I shouldn't be surprised he made one of his miracle escapes. He does rather specialize in them. If you're looking for an ally, you could do worse. He's probably the only person on Mistworld that the Empress wants even more than you. Your best bet is to try the Abraxas Information Centre, down on Resurrection Street. They're a small business, haven't been around long, but if anyone can find him for you, they can.'

'Thanks for the name, Cyder, but we should already have a lead on him. Isn't that right, Deathstalker?'

Hazel looked pointedly at Owen, and he sighed resignedly. He activated his comm implant and contacted Ozymandias.

'Everything all right with the ship, Oz?'

'Oh sure. A few lowlifes tried to break in, but the yacht's security systems took care of them. Mistport ground staff removed the bodies. There have also been a number of attempts to break into my systems, but nothing I couldn't handle. Strictly amateur hour. These people wouldn't recognize a sophisticated system if they fell over it in the gutter.'

'I'm not entirely sure they have gutters here.'

The AI sniffed. 'Can't say I'm surprised. Where are you? What's been happening?'

'Tell you later. It looks like we're going to need Jack Random after all, Oz. What was the address you had on him?'

'The Abraxas Information Centre.'

Owen shook his head slowly. 'My father's hand is getting clearer by the moment. He's doing everything but lead us by the nose.' He broke off contact and looked apologetically at Hazel. 'My AI says the same as your friend here. The Abraxas place has all the answers.'

'I should hope so,' said Cyder. 'They charge enough. Do you still have access to the money you banked in Mistport, Hazel? The money from your . . . previous occupation?'

'Yes,' said Hazel, glaring darkly at her. 'It's under an assumed name. I should be able to get to it easily enough.'

'Good,' said Cyder. 'You're probably going to need it. Mistport's an expensive place these days.'

161

She led the way back down the stairs and into the bar, which if anything seemed more crowded than ever. The noise was deafening, in a convivial sort of way, and two women had started a friendly knife fight in a corner, cheered on by an appreciative crowd. Owen kept a wary eye on it as he followed Cyder and Hazel through the crush. The press of bodies seemed to open up before Cyder, who had a smile and a nod for everyone, but she came to a sudden halt as an alarmingly large figure blocked her path. Owen took one look over Cyder's shoulder and immediately dropped his hand to his sword. The figure brushed Cyder aside as though she was a child, and stood smiling down at Hazel, ignoring Owen completely. The crowd fell back a little to give them plenty of room. They knew better than to get involved with a Wampyr.

Owen studied the smiling figure carefully. He'd heard of the Wampyr, but never actually seen one in the flesh. Not many had, and lived to tell of it. The Wampyr had been created to replace the treacherous Hadenmen as the Empire's new shock troops. The augmented men of Haden had proved too powerful to easily control, so the Empire scientists had tried a different approach. They created a new form of artificial blood, super-charged and potent, that would turn any man into an unstoppable warrior; strong, fast and self-regenerating. The only drawback was you had to kill your subject first, flush out the old blood and pump in the new, and then revive him. The scientists finally achieved a seventy per cent success rate, which was good enough for the Empire.

The result was a dead man, walking. They felt no pain or pleasure or sensation of any kind. Their only joy was in combat, their only thrills the limited pleasures of mental satisfaction. They delighted in torture, cruel as killer cats, and as patient and deadly. They didn't eat or drink, but their artificial blood had to be replenished and revitalized by the periodic infusion of fresh human blood. Mostly the Wampyr drank it, as much for the effect on witnesses as anything.

They made excellent shock troops, with a tendency to be over thorough and hard to call off, but in the end they were just too expensive to produce en masse, and the project was reluctantly scrapped. But the Wampyr needed battle like they needed blood, and so they scattered throughout the Empire, searching for a little organized death and destruction, and starting it as often as not. They were never popular, but often used, and so their legend grew; the undead soldiers who sought their own deaths as eagerly as any other's.

Owen supposed it was inevitable that a Wampyr should turn up on Mistworld. Everyone and everything else did. This particular specimen was seven foot tall, muscular in a lithe, feline way, and altogether disturbing. His skin was completely colourless, and Owen knew it would be ice cold to the touch. His face was long and angular, all planes and high cheekbones, and his eyes were dark and unblinking. The smile that stretched his pale lips wasn't reflected in his eyes, and he held himself like a fighter waiting for the bell. For the moment his gaze was fixed on Hazel, and Owen was glad for it to stay that way. The Wampyr was openly disturbing, on some deep, primal level. Owen glanced at Hazel to see how she was taking it, and was surprised to find she seemed more angry than anything else.

'Hazel d'Ark,' said the Wampyr, in a voice as cold and eager as the grave. 'You've come back to me.'

'Lucien Abbott,' said Hazel disgustedly. 'Of all the people I didn't want to meet, you were right at the top of the list. Why couldn't you have done the decent thing, and died long ago?'

'I did,' said Abbott. 'They brought me back. Now I live on through people like you. You shouldn't have run away, Hazel; you're mine, and always will be. Your blood has rushed through my veins.'

Owen pushed in beside Hazel. 'What's he talking about?'

Abbott's smile widened. 'Haven't you told him, Hazel? Haven't you told him how you used to be a plasma baby?'

Plasma baby. A chill rushed through Owen, and he was hard pressed not to shudder. He knew the term. There were those who gave their human blood for the Wampyr to drink, straight from the vein; a master and slave relationship that was said to be closer and more intense than sex or love. One of the few perversions banned throughout the Empire. The Wampyr were dangerous enough without an army of fanatic blood junkies as followers. Owen looked at Hazel, and she glared at the pity she saw in his face.

'I was never one of his sick puppets! I sold a pint of blood on the black market occasionally, but only when times were hard and I really needed the money. His filthy lips never touched my veins, and whatever he got from me he paid top rate for. Now get out of my way, Abbott, or I swear I'll put you in the ground where you should have been years ago!'

'You're mine, Hazel.' The Wampyr's voice was cold and commanding. 'Kneel.'

There was a sudden power in his voice, vile and inhuman and overpowering. Everyone shuddered who heard it, and Hazel fell back involuntarily. She tried to draw her sword, but her hand was shaking too much. Several men and women in the crowd dropped to their knees, and still more fell back, leaving a wide space around the Wampyr and his chosen victim.

This has gone far enough, thought Owen, and murmured the code word *boost*. Power flooded through him and burned in his muscles, wiping away the command in the Wampyr's voice. Without looking round, Owen picked up a nearby table and hit Abbott with it. The heavy wooden table swung through the air like a giant fly swatter, and slammed into the Wampyr with unstoppable force. The impact picked Abbott up and threw him across the tavern, and out through a window that was closed. Glass flew in all directions, and the Wampyr disappeared out into the curling mists. Everyone waited tensely, but he didn't reappear. Hazel nodded approvingly to Owen as he put down the table and dropped out of boost.

'Nicely handled, Deathstalker.'

Owen smiled modestly. 'I have my moments.'

'Not that I couldn't have handled him myself, of course.'

'Perish the thought,' Owen said gallantly. He looked round at the rapt crowd. 'Anyone else?'

There was a slight pause, and then everybody very studiously went back to what they had been doing. The noise returned to its previous level, and Owen was about to leave when Cyder stepped in front of him and put a restraining hand on his chest.

'Not so fast, hero. There's a little matter of a broken window to be paid for.'

Owen looked at the shattered remains of the window he'd thrown Abbott through, and reluctantly admitted that she had a point. He cleared his throat cautiously, to give himself time to think, and tried to imagine how much the repairs would cost on a primitive planet like Mistworld. The answer was not encouraging. He did his best to fix Cyder with a determined look.

'Abbott started it; let him pay for the window.'

'He's not here,' said Cyder. 'You are.'

Owen mentally checked the contents of his pockets, and looked at Hazel. 'I appear to be somewhat financially embarrassed at the moment. Do you think you could . . .'

Hazel glared at him and dug into her pockets. 'Next time, choose a less expensive way of dealing with him.'

'He was your old boyfriend,' Owen pointed out.

'He was not my boyfriend!'

'Personally, I never did know what you saw in him,' said Cyder, counting the coins Hazel had given her, and then making them disappear about her person. 'He really wasn't your type, dear.'

Hazel started to explode all over again, and then sighed resignedly. 'All right, so it wasn't just the money. I was feeling down, and just in the mood to be bossed about and mistreated by someone big and dumb and domineering. You know how it is.'

'Unfortunately, yes,' Cyder admitted. 'Before I forget, there are a few people of my acquaintance who might be interested in helping the two of you, for various reasons. I'll put the word out, and see what happens. Nice to see you again, Hazel. Do let me know how it all comes out in the end.'

Hazel and Cyder embraced quickly, kissed the air near each other's cheeks, and then Hazel strode out of the tavern and into the mists, followed by a dubious but resigned Owen. Cyder watched them go till the mists had swallowed them up, and then closed the door. She made her way back through the shifting crowd, frowning thoughtfully, and then sat down at a table tucked away in a niche at the rear of the tavern. The young man sitting there wearing a white thermal suit raised an eyebrow inquisitively. His name was Cat, a slender young man barely into his twenties, but with a lifetime's experience of surviving in the hard streets of Mistport. He had a pleasant, open face dominated by steady dark eyes and pockmarked cheeks, and there was nothing he wouldn't do for Cyder. He was a roof runner, a burglar specializing in the upper storeys of the rich and careless, and mostly he worked on breaking and entering jobs set up by Cyder, who also acted as his fence. Cat was a deaf mute, but he didn't let it slow him down. On the roofs, it made no difference at all. He watched Cyder's lips carefully as she spoke, and waited patiently for his instructions.

'Big things are happening in Mistport once again,' said Cyder. 'I can feel it in my bones. There has to be a way I can make money on this, if I just keep my wits about me. And if I can keep Hazel and her young Lord alive long enough. I don't think they realize just how desperate their situation is. Half the city's probably out looking for them by now. I'd turn them in myself if I didn't owe Hazel so much.

'I want you to go after them, Cat. Stay out of sight, but help them where you can. Be discreet. We don't want any involvement being traced back to us. Not till we can see who's likely to come out on top. While you're playing guardian angel, I'll send a discreet little note to Tobias Moon. Put him together with Hazel and the Deathstalker, and all kinds of interesting things might happen. Well don't just sit there, darling; there's work to be done and plots to be spun!'

Cat nodded quickly, kissed her goodbye, did it again because he enjoyed it, and bounded to his feet. He pushed open the window beside him, and dived out into the cold air and swirling mists. He slammed the window shut and then clambered up the outer wall of the tavern with practised ease. It only took a few minutes to haul himself up over the heavy iron guttering and on to the gabled roof of the Blackthorn, and he crouched there for a long moment like a ghostly gargoyle, looking out over an undulating sea of roofs, stretching away into the grey haze of the mists. Cat was back in his element again. He set off across the roofs of Thieves' Quarter in search of Hazel and Owen, secure in the knowledge that they'd never even know they were being followed.

The Abraxas Information Centre turned out to be a single floor above a bakery in a quiet but seedy part of Merchants' Quarter. The smell of baking bread was heavy on the air, and Owen's stomach rumbled loudly. He tried to think how long it had been since he'd sat down to a decent meal of at least four courses, and the answer depressed him. He was always hungry after boosting anyway, and he headed for the bakery door with a determined step. Hazel took him by the arm with an equally firm grip, and steered him past the bakery door and up the exterior stairs to the next floor.

'You can eat later,' she said mercilessly. 'Business first.'

Owen sniffed, and allowed himself a quiet sulk as Hazel led the way up the creaking wooden stairs. Whatever confidence he might have had in the Abraxas Information Centre was shrinking by the moment as he took in the drab nature of the building. It looked in definite need of repair, some of it urgent, and it clearly hadn't seen a coat of paint in years. Who or whatever Abraxas was, Owen was increasingly certain he wouldn't find any help here. Back on Virimonde he'd kept his stables in better condition than this. He sighed quietly. Virimonde seemed like a long time ago, and it came as something of a shock to him to realize it was only a few days ago that he'd been its Lord, and his world had made sense.

He pushed the thought firmly to one side. It didn't do to dwell too much on who he used to be, or how much he'd lost. That way lay madness. He made himself concentrate on Abraxas. Presumably some sort of information gathering service, with runners and clerks and communications people, running everything through a primitive computer of some kind. He hated to think what kind of outdated junk they'd be using in a dump like this. Still, someone with a reputation like Jack Random's should be easy enough to locate. It wasn't as if

167

Mistport was a particularly big city. Besides; Ozymandias had found the address in his hidden files, which suggested some kind of connection between Abraxas and his father's convoluted intrigues. Owen sighed again, deeply. He'd spent most of his adult life trying to fashion a life of his own, untouched by his father's plans and ambitions, and here he was sinking deeper and deeper into his father's legacy with every step he took.

He realized Hazel had come to a stop at the top of the stairs just in time to avoid bumping into her, and let his hand rest on his sword hilt as she knocked more or less politely on the closed door before her. A brass plate fixed to the door said simply *Abraxas*. There was no bell or knocker. Hazel was about to hammer with her fist when the door swung suddenly open before her. A large muscular man almost as broad as he was tall filled the doorway. He wore black leather with metal studs, and half his face was hidden behind a complex and very ugly tattoo. He looked at Hazel and Owen and sniffed loudly, unimpressed.

'Hazel d'Ark and Owen Deathstalker? About time you got here. I've been expecting you.'

Hazel and Owen were still deciding how to react to that when the huge figure stepped back from the doorway, and gestured impatiently for them to enter. They did so, giving him plenty of room, and he sniffed again as he slammed the door shut behind them, and locked it. Owen started to draw his disrupter, but stopped when Hazel put a firm hand on his arm. The huge figure stomped back in front of them, and produced something that might have been intended as a smile.

'I'm Chance. I run Abraxas. Take a look around, and I'll be with you in a minute.'

He moved off without waiting for an answer. Owen had a few in mind anyway, only to forget them as he got his first good look at the people who made up the Abraxas Information Centre. There were no computers or comm units, no runners or technicians. Instead, two lines of ramshackle cots filled the long narrow room, pressed close together, with a central aisle between them. On the cots, children lay sleeping. They all had intravenous drips plugged into their arms, though their bony forms and skeletal faces suggested they weren't getting much nourishment from them. They also had catheters leading out from under the thin blankets that covered them, dripping into filthy bottles by the beds. *How long have they been here like this?* thought Owen, and moved reluctantly closer to get a better look. Hazel stuck close beside him.

The children ranged from toddlers of four or five to some who appeared to have just entered their teens. They twitched and turned in their sleep or coma, but their faces seemed somehow intent, focused, and their eyes rolled under their closed eyelids. Some seemed to be muttering to themselves. Two middle-aged women who looked more like charladies than nurses moved unhurriedly along the rows of cots, checking the catheters and IVs, emptying and filling where necessary, but otherwise paying the children no attention. Some of them were secured to their cots with thick leather restraining straps.

Owen felt sick, and a growing rage burned within him. He didn't understand what was going on here, but he didn't need to understand to hate it. No one had the right to treat children in such an inhuman manner. The sword leapt from his scabbard with a harsh, rasping sound, and he started down the central aisle with murder in his eyes. Chance was checking through papers on a desk at the far end of the room. He didn't look up as Owen advanced on him. And then Hazel grabbed his sword arm and pulled him to a halt.

'Hold it, Owen. You don't understand.'

'I understand these children are in hell!'

'Yes, maybe they are. But there's a purpose to this. I've seen this kind of thing before.'

Owen hefted his sword, and then lowered it reluctantly. 'All right. Explain it to me.'

'Chance could do it better. Stay here and I'll go get him. Promise you won't do anything till you know the whole story.'

'No promises,' said Owen. 'Get Chance. And tell him if I don't like what he has to tell me, I'm going to kill him right here and now.'

Hazel patted his arm reassuringly, as one would an angry,

dangerous dog, and hurried down the central aisle towards Chance. Owen's hand clenched tightly round his sword hilt in rage and frustration. He'd never seen anything like this, even in the worst hellspots of the Empire, and he was damned if he'd let it continue. He walked slowly down the aisle, looking from face to face, seeing only a kind of desperation in their gaunt features. One young teenager was stirring restlessly under his restraining straps, muttering fiercely to himself. Owen leant over the bed to listen to the quiet, breathy voice.

'Brave notes in screaming shocks . . . The pale harlequins are swarming again . . . Dear lost shoes and delicate minks are dancing round the summerstone . . .'

Owen straightened up, obscurely disturbed. It was clearly gibberish, but it bordered on the edge of meaning, as though he might understand it if he just listened long enough. He looked up to see Hazel coming back with Chance, and raised his sword just a little. The two of them stopped a respectful distance away, though Hazel seemed more impressed by the drawn sword than Chance. Owen smiled coldly at the big man. It didn't matter how big he was, or what he had to say. Someone was going to pay for what had been done to the children.

'The restraining straps are there to protect them,' said Chance, his voice flat and unimpressed. 'The children are espers, but they can't always handle what their minds show them. One boy clawed out his eyes rather than see. I don't take chances with them any more. All these children are retarded, to some extent or other. Idiot savants with limitless memories and wide-ranging telepathy. Their minds roam freely out over the city while their bodies rest here, trawling the thoughts of the population, and picking out what nuggets of information I require.

'Their families sell them to me, when they can no longer look after them, and I put them to work. There's no room on Mistworld for the weak or the handicapped. If they weren't espers, and therefore potentially useful, they'd just be abandoned in the cold and left to die. As it is, I look after them, and they look after me. Few of them last long. By the time I

170

get them, they've already had hard, brutal lives. Fortunately for me, there are always more to replace those who burn out. Don't look at me that way, Deathstalker. I care for them all while they're with me. What comes before and after that is beyond my help.

'Perhaps now we can get down to business. My children told me you'd be coming, and why. You don't have much time. If my espers knew you'd be here, you can bet that others do too. The penalty of living in a city full of telepaths with loose lips is that there's damn all privacy. Not that I have any right to complain, of course. It is, after all, how I make my living. You needn't worry about payment. The previous Lord Death-stalker had an account with us. He left instructions that if you ever turned up here looking for help, I was to assist you in locating Jack Random, and send you to him. Are you going to stand there holding that sword all day, Deathstalker, or will you allow us to help you?'

'I'm still thinking about it,' Owen said harshly. 'How did you link up with my father?'

'He made Abraxas possible. It was my idea, but his money. He saw the advantages right off, and all I had to do to repay him was make sure he got a copy of whatever information my children turned up. Your father was a visionary; never afraid to experiment.'

'He was never afraid to make a profit,' said Owen, reluctantly sheathing his sword. 'Usually at someone else's expense. How many children have died here since you started Abraxas?'

'Too many. But they would have died anyway. I keep them alive as long as I can. It's in my interest to do so.'

Owen looked at Hazel. 'You're being very quiet. Don't tell me you approve of this obscenity?'

'This is Mistworld, aristo,' said Hazel gently. 'Things are different here. If sometimes we're hard and cold, it's because we have to be to survive outside the Empire. If we ever weaken, even for a moment, the Iron Bitch will wipe us out, down to the last man, woman and child. She's done it before, on other planets. You know she has.'

Owen looked away, his eyes moving from one small sleeping

form to another, and there was only room in him for a bitter helplessness.

'Ask them,' he said brusquely. 'Ask them where Jack Random is.'

Chance nodded, and strode slowly down the centre aisle, looking from one side to the other, pausing now and then to study a particular twitching face before moving on. He finally stopped by a boy who looked to be twelve years old. The young esper was scrawny to the point of malnourishment, and his bony face was slick with a sheen of sweat. He was mumbling quickly, breathlessly, his head rolling limply from side to side. He'd somehow managed to pull the IV out of his arm, despite the thick restraining straps, and Chance put it back with practised ease.

He knelt down beside the bed, and put his mouth as close to the boy's ear as he could. He talked slowly, smoothly, and his quiet voice seemed to calm the esper a little. He stopped mumbling and shaking his head and fighting the straps. His eyes stared straight ahead, seeing nothing, or perhaps everything. Owen and Hazel moved forward, and Chance gestured brusquely for them to stay where they were. He produced a small twist of paper from his pocket, took something from it and placed it in the esper's mouth. Owen thought at first it was a pill, and only slowly realized from the movements of the boy's mouth that it had been a piece of candy. Chance put his mouth right next to the esper's ear.

'Come on, Johnny boy, you can do it. Do it for Chance. I've got another treat for you. Got it right here. Just find the man for me, Johnny. Find the man called Jack Random.'

He murmured on and on, never raising his voice, never stopping, quiet but persistent, and finally the boy spoke, calmly and clearly.

'You want the rebel, the name that is known everywhere, the disrupter of systems, but he is not to be found. Jack Random has another name now, and another life. The Empire's hounds came too close too often, and he went to ground. Go look in his hole, his hiding place. Go to the Olympus Health Spa down on Riverside, and ask for Jobe

Ironhand. He won't want to talk, so it's up to you to be convincing.' He broke off abruptly, and turned his head to look at Owen and Hazel with his all-seeing eyes. 'I see you, Deathstalker. Destiny has you in its clutches, struggle how you may. You will tumble an Empire, see the end of everything you ever believed in, and you'll do it all for a love you'll never know. And when it's over, you'll die alone, far from friends and succour.'

'That's enough, Johnny,' said Chance. The esper closed his disquieting eyes and turned his head away, and his words became quiet and meaningless again. Chance got to his feet, and rejoined Owen and Hazel. 'Don't take too much notice of that last bit. A lot of my children claim to get glimpses of the future, now and again, but they've proved wrong as often as right. Otherwise I'd have been a rich man by now.'

'I've no plans to die any time soon,' said Owen. 'I've been on borrowed time anyway, ever since Hazel saved my ass on Virimonde. Let's get out of here, Hazel. This place gives me the creeps.'

Chance shrugged. 'Nothing keeping you here, Deathstalker. You've got your name and address, all paid for in advance. The rest of the money in your father's account will go towards keeping me quiet about your visit, and your destination. I do regret the necessity, but times are hard, and an honest man must turn a credit where he can. I'm sure you understand.'

He broke off abruptly as Owen reached out, took a good handful of Chance's leathers, and lifted him up on his toes. Owen stuck his face into Chance's, and smiled unpleasantly. 'You understand me, Chance. You breathe a word about me to anyone at all, and you'd better pray they make a real good job of killing me. Because otherwise I'll find you wherever you run, and kill you by inches. Got it?'

And then, without looking round, he slowly realized that something had changed. It was very quiet, very still, and he suddenly realized that the sleeping espers had stopped muttering. Without releasing his hold on Chance, he looked around him. The espers had raised their heads, and they were all looking at him, their faces cold and focused and entirely menacing.

'Put him down, Owen,' Hazel said quietly. 'Please; put him down.'

Owen let go of Chance, and stepped back. He didn't even try to draw his sword or his disrupter. He somehow knew they wouldn't be able to help him. The feeling of menace was thick on the air, and a slow sure power burned beneath it. Chance readjusted his clothing fussily, and sniffed at Owen.

'My children protect me, Deathstalker. Always. I suggest you leave now, before they decide to do something unpleasant and terminal to you.'

'Time to go,' said Hazel. 'He's not joking, Owen. Those kids are dangerous.'

'So am I,' said Owen. 'I'm a Deathstalker, Chance, and don't you ever forget it.'

'The Empress took your name away,' said Chance.

Owen smiled coldly. 'It wasn't hers to take. I'm a Deathstalker till I die. And we never forget a slight or an enemy.'

Chance looked down his nose at him. 'That's what your father said to me, the last time he was here.'

'I'm not my father,' said Owen. 'I fight dirty.'

He turned and left, with Hazel close behind him. The espers on their cots watched them go, their heads turning as one.

In the cold and mists outside the bakery, three toughs with drawn swords waited impatiently in the adjoining alleyway for their prey to emerge. They'd had to pay out good money at the Blackthorn to pick up the trail on the Deathstalker and his woman, but they expected to be fully repaid, and a hell of a lot more, by the reward money on their prey's heads.

Three toughs from the underside of Thieves' Quarter; Harley, Jude and Crow. Cutpurses, back-stabbers and muscle for hire. Normally they would have had more sense than to go after a renowned swordsman and warrior like the Deathstalker, but the reward money had inflamed their minds, and anyway, they felt safe enough attacking together from ambush. With any luck it would all be over before the Deathstalker even knew what was happening, and then they could each take turns with his woman, before they killed her. They clutched their sword hilts tightly, and stamped their boots impatiently in the snow. They hadn't planned on so long a wait, but then, planning wasn't exactly their long suit, any more than patience.

It was snowing again, and the mists were getting thicker. If the temperature had been any lower, it would have dropped out the bottom of the thermometer. Crow scowled. He was nominally the leader, because he talked the loudest, but he was beginning to get a bad feeling about the ambush, even though it had been his idea in the first place. It was taking too long. They couldn't just keep standing around in the alleyway with their swords in their hands. Someone would notice, even in Mistport. He turned to Jude, to complain about the wait in general and the cold in particular, and then stopped. Jude wasn't there. Crow blinked. Jude had been there a minute ago, large as life and twice as smelly. Crow looked quickly round the narrow alleyway, but there was nowhere he could be hiding. At least Harley was still there. Crow grabbed him by the arm, and Harley nearly jumped out of his skin.

'Don't do that! You know I get a nervous twitch when I'm startled. What do you want?'

'Where's Jude?'

Harley looked at Crow uncertainly, and then looked vaguely round the alleyway. 'I don't know. I thought he was with you. He was here a minute ago.'

'I know he was here a minute ago, but he isn't here now! What's happened to him?'

'I don't know! Maybe he had to take a leak, and . . . wandered off.'

'Without saying anything to us? And why didn't we notice him going?'

Harley thought hard. It wasn't easy. Thinking had never come easily to Harley, and he rather resented Crow asking him all these questions. Harley wasn't in the gang to think. He was there to take orders and hit people. He looked hopefully at Crow, in case he'd come up with the answers by himself, and then looked quickly away again.

'I'll take a look down the end of the alley,' he said hastily. 'Just in case.'

He trudged quickly off through the snow, before Crow could ask him just in case what. Crow watched him go, and growled under his breath. The ambush hadn't even started properly yet, and already it was going wrong. He glanced back at the bakery, to make sure the prey hadn't appeared yet, and then looked back at Harley. Only to find that he'd disappeared too. Crow made a small whimpering noise. There was no way Harley could have reached the end of the alleyway in the short time he'd taken his eyes off him, but there was nowhere else he could have gone. Except he had to have gone somewhere . . . Crow spun round in a circle twice, in case he'd missed something, but all it did was make him dizzy. He was giving serious thought to running away screaming, when a noose of thin rope dropped soundlessly over his head from above, and tightened round his throat.

Crow dropped his sword and clawed at the noose with both hands, but already his eyes were glazing over. His eyes bulged as he was drawn up into the air, and he was completely out of it by the time Cat hauled him up on to the roof overlooking the alleyway. He laid the unconscious thug out beside his two sleeping friends, and grinned widely. He was so smart, and they were so dumb. He loosened the rope noose from around Crow's neck, coiled it round his waist again, and looked thoughtfully at the three slumbering toughs. He couldn't kill them. It wasn't in him. But he gave Harley a good kick in the nuts anyway, for being particularly heavy. He'd nearly done his back in hauling that great oaf up on to the roof. Still, Cyder had told him to make sure that Hazel and the Deathstalker went on their way undisturbed, and he always did what Cyder told him. Partly because he loved her, but mostly because she tended to throw things if he didn't. He crouched down on the edge of the roof, almost invisible in the shifting mists in his pure white thermal suit, and smiled widely as Hazel and the Deathstalker set off down the street away from the bakery. Cat followed them, moving silently from roof to roof above them.

*

'Owen,' Hazel said firmly. 'Whatever else you do or don't do in Mistport, the one thing you should never do is get an esper mad at you, let alone a whole crowd of crazy espers. There are an awful lot of ways they came make life unpleasant and suddenly short for you. If you're going to continue taking risks like that, please give me plenty of warning, so I can completely disassociate myself from you.'

'I don't get it,' said Owen, his fingers tightening angrily around his sword hilt. 'He exploits those children, burns up what's left of their lives, and yet they were ready to defend him!'

'You don't have to get it,' said Hazel. 'All you have to remember is to keep your nose out of other people's business, or someone will cut it off. Mistport is like that, mostly.'

Owen sighed, and shook his head. 'All right; where are we going now? You said the health spa we want was due north of Abraxas, and according to my internal compass, we are currently heading south-west.'

Hazel looked at him. 'You have an internal compass? I didn't know I was walking around with a Hadenman. What else have you got hidden in your plumbing that I don't know about?'

'Never you mind, and don't change the subject. Where are we going?'

'I want to stop off somewhere first,' said Hazel. 'Just in case the Random deal doesn't pan out, I'll feel happier if we've got a back-up. Ruby Journey used to be a red hot bounty hunter, and she owes me several large favours. If anyone will know how to hide and protect us, it'll be her. Unfortunately, she doesn't seem to be in any of her usual haunts, which leaves only one place worth checking. All bounty hunters on Mistworld have to be licensed, on the principle that if you can't control it, tax it, and the centre for issuing those licences is just down this street and round the corner. Unless they've moved it again. People keep firebombing it, on general principles.'

Owen considered this silently as Hazel led the way confidently down the street and round the corner. He was pretty sure they were being followed, but so far no one had made any moves. He was beginning to wish someone would, just so he could react. The continuing tension was giving him an ache right between the shoulder-blades. He wasn't sure how many there were out there. He kept half-seeing or hearing people, only when he looked again they weren't there any more. Owen was seriously considering turning round suddenly and shouting Boo! very loudly, just to see who'd jump and where, when Hazel came to a sudden halt. Owen stopped with her, and studied the new premises thoughtfully. He'd seen worse; mostly in Mistport.

The new location was definitely more up-market than the last, not that this would have been difficult. Presumably the bounty hunter business was booming in Mistport. It was a big building, with curlicued decorations and scrollwork, and people going in and out in a steady stream. Hazel strode in through the open double doors as though she owned the place, and Owen hurried after her. They were immediately caught up in the complete chaos filling the huge lobby from wall to wall. Everywhere Owen looked there were desks and tables buried under piles of paper, and people running back and forth between the desks as though their lives depended on it. This being Mistport, thought Owen, perhaps they did. A large crowd of all sorts and types took up all the remaining space, shouting at the people behind the desks and each other with equal volume and tenacity. The walls were covered with overlapping wanted posters, and up on the ceiling someone had painted a series of large murals, depicting the human body in some detail, and the best places to hit it with large pointed things.

The din was deafening, the air was hot and sweaty, and the smell was indescribable. Hazel ploughed right through the middle of it, making liberal use of her fists and elbows to get some room. Apparently this was common practice, or at least common enough that only a few people reached for their swords, and by then she was already gone. Owen stuck close behind her, muttering polite apologies that no one heard, and glaring at anyone who didn't put their sword away fast enough.

It was a good glare; Owen had had lots of chances to practise and perfect it since he'd come to Mistworld. It was a carefully balanced mixture of rage and imminent violence, with just a touch of outright insanity. By the time he was half-way through the crowd, people were backing away to avoid him.

He ended up at Hazel's side in front of a desk at the rear of the room. It had two trays, marked IN and URGENT, and there were piles of paper everywhere. Much of it had the rough look of cheap recycling, and Owen was intrigued to note that most of them were covered with handwritten texts. In the circles he was used to moving in, handwritten notes tended to be few and far between, being usually reserved for spies and lovers.

The man sitting behind the desk was a small, intense figure with a put-upon face and a permanent scowl. He was casually dressed to the point of carelessness, and his thick black hair stuck out at angles, as though he tugged at it a lot. Hazel smiled at him charmingly, and the clerk stared back at her with equal parts desperation and apoplexy. Hazel opened her mouth to speak, and he beat her to it, in a loud, carryng voice that cut through the general din.

'I don't know! Whatever it is, I don't know and I don't care! I am up to my lower lip in paperwork and sinking fast. Go away. Come back next week. Or next month. Or not at all. See if I care. Why are you still standing there?'

'I only want one name,' said Hazel.

'That's what everyone says!' snapped the clerk. 'Do you know how much work it takes to track down just one name? No, of course you don't, and you don't care either, do you? No one cares,' he said, wistfully. 'No one appreciates you here. The lunchbreak's a joke, there's only one toilet, and the pay's rotten. I'd quit, if it wasn't for the pension. And the constant chances to screw up people's lives. I see my job as a kind of revenge against an uncaring society. It's either this or planting explosives in public places, and explosives are expensive. Why are you still here?'

'Why is anybody here?' said Hazel. 'Look, can we save the existentialism for later? Just find me a name and an address to go with it, and we'll go away and leave you alone. Wouldn't

179

that be nice? And not only that, if you help us I can definitely promise to restrain my companion here from picking up all those papers in front of you, and scattering them to the four corners of the room.'

The clerk grabbed the nearest pile protectively. 'That's right. Threaten me. Intimidate me. Who am I? Just a clerk, a minor cog in the great wheel. I can feel one of my funny turns coming on.'

'How about if we offered you a small payment?' said Hazel.

'How about if you offered a big payment?' countered the clerk.

Hazel produced a large silver coin from her purse and dropped it on to the desk before him. The clerk looked at it sadly. Hazel had to add three more before he sighed deeply and scooped up the coins with a practised sweep of the hand.

'All right; give me the name. I'm not promising anything, mind.'

'Ruby Journey.'

'Oh, *her*. Why didn't you say? She's working as a bouncer down at the Rabid Wolf. And long may she stay there, well away from civilized people. It's been ever so peaceful around here since she moved. When you find her, remind her that her licence runs out next week. I should do it from a safe distance, mind. Now go away and upset somebody else. I have papers to shuffle and civil insurrection to plan.'

He picked up the nearest piece of paper and stared at it fixedly. Owen and Hazel exchanged a look, and then shoved, elbowed and intimidated their way back through the crowd and out into the calm and quiet of the street.

'Well,' said Owen. 'That was . . . different. Are there a lot of people like him in Mistport?'

'Unfortunately, yes,' said Hazel. 'A lot of people arrive here fleeing from the tyranny of Empire, expecting to find some kind of free, civilized utopia. The rather different reality of scraping a living on an unhospitable rock of ice with a population consisting mainly of outlaws, failures and criminals upsets a lot of new arrivals, and some never really get over it.'

'Don't you find that rather worrying?' said Owen.

'Not as long as explosives remain really expensive.'

'So, you and this Ruby Journey go back a long way, then?' said Owen, as they set off down the street. He couldn't help noticing that they still weren't heading north.

'I had a try at bounty hunting myself,' said Hazel briskly. 'I didn't last long. I was too soft; kept bringing them in alive, and there's no money in that. Ruby was my sponsor and mentor at the time. A good friend, if a trifle . . . unpredictable. I can't believe things have got so bad for her that she's been forced to work as a bouncer. Mind you, I bet she's a good one. No one would argue with her twice.'

'What sort of place is this Rabid Wolf she's working at?'

'A dive, the last time I was there. Dope joint, gambling house, a few girls and a bar that never closes. You know the sort of place.'

'Well actually, no,' said Owen. 'But it sounds . . . interesting. Still, I can't help thinking Ruby Journey can wait. Surely we need to find Jack Random first, before someone else finds us. He'll be able to protect us from whoever comes after us. Jack Random could stand off a whole army. I mean; the man's a legend.'

'Was a legend,' said Hazel, looking carefully straight ahead and not slowing down one bit. 'The man is well past his prime. The last I heard of him, he was telling stories of his past exploits in bars in return for free drinks.'

'Are we talking about the same person? Jack Random, the professional rebel?'

Hazel sighed, but still wouldn't look at him. 'Being a rebel and an outlaw is hard work. It wears you down. Jack Random is not the man he used to be. Hasn't led a major uprising since that fiasco on Blue Angel, when he got his ass kicked in no uncertain manner. It was a miracle he got out of there alive and mostly intact, and everyone knows it. And that was years ago. Random is . . . an unknown quantity. I know I can rely on Ruby. She's death on two legs, with an attitude. The best in the business.'

'And currently working as a bouncer.'

Hazel glared at him and increased her pace. Owen plodded

after her, maintaining a diplomatic silence. He felt as though he should be defending Random more, but the more he thought about it the less actual evidence he could find to support his argument. All right, the man was a legend. No denying that. He'd led more rebellions against the Empire than any three other outlaws put together, but though he'd fought in some famous campaigns, he'd only ever won fleeting victories. He had the charisma and the rhetoric, but the Empire had the numbers. It always had more ships, more guns, more men to call on. And as the years went on, Jack Random lost more campaigns than he won, and was hounded from planet to planet and from battle to battle, while the Empire still stood. Owen sighed. If you couldn't trust Jack Random, who could you trust?

He moved up alongside Hazel, and pulled his cloak tightly about him. There was a bitter wind rising, and it seemed to blow right through him. Owen was beginning to find the sudden shifts from icy cold exteriors to piping hot interiors and back again increasingly distressing. Probably end up with a streaming cold on top of everything else, and light years away from civilized medicine.

He tried hard not to think about leeches.

Owen and Hazel trudged off down the street, lost in their separate thoughts, and never saw the hooded figure with a crossbow rise up from an overlooking balcony, and draw a bead on Owen's unprotected back. The assassin's finger tightened on the release, and a stone from Cat's slingshot hit him right between the eyes. He fell backwards out of sight, and the arrow disappeared into the mists. A cat shrieked briefly in outrage. Cat grinned, and recovered his balance on the outcropping gable where he was crouching, opposite the balcony. Funny thing about assassins; it never seemed to occur to them that while they were stalking someone, someone else might be stalking them. This was the seventeenth bounty hunter he'd deterred, and he was running out of stratagems. Not to mention stones for his slingshot. He wished Owen and Hazel would work out where they wanted to be, and settle there. It was hard work tracking them across the city, jumping from roof to roof and taking care of the apparently endless stream of would-be assassins who dogged their trail. And now they were off again, heading even deeper into Thieves' Quarter, into areas people usually had enough sense to leave well alone. Cat sighed heavily and set off after them, eyes alert for further dangers. He hoped Cyder had some plan to make money out of these people. He'd hate to think he was doing all this for nothing.

The Rabid Wolf was a festering dump tucked away up a side street with no lighting, as though even the street was ashamed of its presence. The only light came from a brazier burning unattended half-way down the street. Owen wasn't sure what was actually burning in the brazier, but it smelled awful. Also, from the look of the street, several horses had recently taken the time to use the street as a toilet. At least, he hoped it was horses. He looked at Hazel, who was looking calmly down the street as though she'd seen worse.

'We don't really have to go down there, do we?' said Owen. 'It's going to ruin my boots.'

'Don't be such a wimp, Owen. Just watch where you're treading, and don't talk to any strange women, and you'll be fine.'

She set off down the street, and Owen followed her, being very careful where he put his feet. The Rabid Wolf looked as though it had seen a great deal of hard use down the years, not to mention the occasional firebombing and outbreak of plague. The front of the inn was covered with scars and gouges and suspicious stains, and the two windows had been boarded over long ago. The open door was guarded by a huge hulking figure with bulging muscles and glandular problems. The last time Owen had seen something that big standing upright, it had been glaring back at him from its cage in the Imperial Zoo, as though telling him where he could stick his peanuts.

Hazel walked right up to it, stuck her face into its, and the two of them exchanged tough sounds for a moment, just to establish they were both hard, desperate types, and then Hazel slipped the figure a coin, and it stepped back from the door to let Owen and Hazel enter. Hazel stalked past it with her head held high, and Owen hurried after her, keeping a wary eye on the doorkeeper as he dodged past it, his hand never far from his sword. He tried a tentative smile, and the doorkeeper opened its mouth to reveal four sets of steel teeth. Pointed gleaming steel teeth, in neat rows. Owen knew when he'd been out-smiled. He looked away as though he'd meant to all along, and almost bumped into Hazel from behind. She'd stopped just inside the bar and was looking around with barely disguised nostalgia.

Owen wrinkled his nose at the smell, and thought he could detect several kinds of smoke in the air that were banned throughout the Empire on the grounds that they were dangerous to whoever happened to be around when someone else was smoking them. The light was dim, not helped in the least by the thick smog in the air. The inhabitants of the bar looked the kind who preferred it that way. At least, if Owen had looked that unsavoury, he'd have preferred not to be seen too clearly. There was no sawdust on the floor, presumably because the rats had eaten it. He could see a few of them, darting busily about in the far shadows. *If one of them runs up my leg*, thought Owen, *I'm going to scream.*

Hazel made her way through the smog to the bar, and Owen went after her rather than be left alone. The last time he'd felt this threatened, two starcruisers had been firing at him. The bar itself was encrusted with filth and the remains of spilled drinks, some of which appeared to have eaten holes in the wood. Either that, or the woodworm had been overdosing on steroids. Owen took one look at the bar and decided immediately that he wasn't going to lean against it, even for a moment. Hazel gestured imperiously at the bartender, a grossly fat man with a long stained apron that might have started out white several decades ago, and grilled him on Ruby Journey's whereabouts. Owen took the opportunity to study the various bottles on display, and decided very firmly that he wasn't at all thirsty.

And he didn't think he'd ask about bar snacks, either.

He put his back to the bar, and looked about him. The Rabid Wolf struck him as the kind of place his tutors had warned him he'd end up in, if he didn't pay attention to his studies. He hadn't seen such an assortment of thugs, villains and general lowlifes in one place since his last visit to the Imperial Court on Golgotha. None of them looked particularly hygienic, and Owen was seized with a sudden certainty that they all had fleas. An itch started immediately over his ribs, but he refrained from scratching himself, for fear someone would think he was going for his sword. Not that he was actually afraid of any of these scum, of course. He was a Deathstalker, after all. He just didn't like the odds, and how far it was to the nearest exit.

A handful of ladies of the evening, or ladies of the mid-afternoon, to be exact, were gathered together at the other end of the bar, garish and striking in their working paints and finery. They were arguing fiercely over a large purse of money, presumably obtained from the man sleeping beside them with his head on the bar. Owen had to admit that they were rather attractive, in a grubby vicious way, and the beginnings of a fantasy stirred in his mind, and certain other parts of his anatomy. Perhaps the Rabid Wolf wasn't such a bad place after all. At which point, one of the women produced a knife from nowhere and stabbed one of the other women right in her overdeveloped chest. She fell limply to the floor and lay still, and her murderer snatched up the purse from the bar. The other women thought this was the funniest thing they'd ever seen, and shrieked with laughter. Owen looked longingly at the door, and decided he was going to shoot anyone who even looked at him oddly. Especially if it was a woman. Hazel appeared suddenly beside him, and he nearly jumped out of his skin.

'What's the matter with you?' said Hazel.

'What's the matter with me? This is the most appalling, disreputable and downright awful establishment I've ever had the misfortune to frequent! If you were to look up the word sleazy in the dictionary, it would say *See Rabid Wolf*. Get me out of here before I catch something.'

'It's not that bad,' said Hazel. 'For Mistport. I used to do a lot of my drinking here, when I was younger. Of course, I had no taste then. It gets a bit noisy sometimes, and the clientele isn't exactly elite, but on the other hand, it's never boring.'

'There's a lot to be said for boring,' said Owen. 'What did you find out about Ruby Journey?'

Hazel scowled. 'Ruby worked here briefly, but they ended up firing her for excessive violence, which probably took some doing in a place like this. They've no idea where she might be now.'

'Does that mean we can get out of here now?' said Owen hopefully.

'You really don't like this place, do you?' said Hazel, grinning. 'Isn't the ambience growing on you?'

'If it does, I'll scrape it off,' Owen said firmly. 'I just know I'm going to come down with something disgusting, simply from breathing what passes for air in here. I've had boils on my buttocks that were more fun than this.'

Hazel pointed out one of the ladies at the end of the bar. 'I think she fancies you.'

'I'd rather die.'

And that was when the fight broke out. Owen didn't see who started it, or why, but suddenly everyone in the inn was fighting everyone else, with swords, knives, broken bottles and anything else that came to hand. The din was appalling, with battle cries, screams and foul language filling the air as bodies fell to be trampled underfoot. Owen drew his sword and backed up against the bar. One of the few things he had learned from his tutors was that discretion usually was the better part of valour. Or to put it another way, only an idiot gets involved in other people's fights. He shot a glance at Hazel, and winced. She was grinning at the mayhem with undisguised glee, and looked as though she might dive in at any moment, just for the hell of it. Owen grabbed her by the arm, got her attention by shouting right into her ear, and pushed her firmly towards the exit. She nodded disappointedly, and standing back to back, they headed for the door. A few individuals disputed their progress, but backed off rather than face the obvious competence with which Owen and Hazel held their swords. They eased out of the door, stepping over the unconscious body of the doorkeeper, and lurched out into the street. It seemed very calm and peaceful, though the din inside appeared to be going on uninterrupted. Owen began to breathe more easily, and put away his sword.

'All right; let's get out of here before the law arrives.'

'The law? Round here? Not unless they're new. The Watch doesn't bother this neighbourhood for anything less than a full-scale riot.'

'And this doesn't qualify?'

'Hardly. Just a few high spirits, that's all. It'll blow over as quickly as it started. You've got to learn to take things more casually, Deathstalker. Mistport's not that bad. It just tends to the dramatic.'

The boarded-up window beside them exploded outwards as a body came flying through it. Owen and Hazel backed away instinctively, just in time to miss a second flying form. This one wasn't travelling quite so fast, and crashed into a snowdrift not far from the shattered window. He got to his feet with a groan, swayed unsteadily a moment, and then cautiously approached the window.

'I'd like to apologize.'

'What for?' said a voice from inside.

'Anything.'

He then set off down the street, walking slowly and carefully, as though he wasn't sure everything was as firmly attached as it used to be. Owen and Hazel shared a smile, and set off after him. Up on a slanting roof overlooking the Rabid Wolf, Cat watched them go with a feeling of definite relief. He'd been a little worried when they actually went inside the inn, and became even more worried when the mayhem started, because whatever happened, he had absolutely no intention of going in there after them. There were limits.

At the last moment he glimpsed a movement in the shadows below, and instinct sent him diving to one side as the disrupter beam exploded the roof where he'd been crouching. Even so, the blast was enough to send him flying, all arms and legs, trying to find something to grab on to. And then there was nothing but air under him, and he fell thirty feet into a deep snowdrift, and didn't move again. Lucien Abbott, the Wampyr, smiled and lowered the disrupter. He'd never liked Cat. He started down the street after Hazel and Owen, still smiling, still holding the gun.

At the entrance to the unlit street, Hazel and Owen stopped dead in their tracks at the unmistakable sound of an energy weapon being fired, and moved immediately to stand back to back again. Owen tried to look in every direction at once, but wherever he looked he saw only deepening shadows. Hazel had told him energy weapons were rare on Mistworld, and he'd stopped worrying about them on such an obviously low-tech world. Now he felt naked and vulnerable, and he didn't even know from which direction the shot had come. He had his gun out as well as his sword, but that was all offence, no defence. A disrupter blast would tear right through him without even slowing. He knew he should have brought a force shield with him.

He looked back and forth, sweat starting out on his face despite the cold. And then, from every side, from every shadow, from every street and alleyway, came a small army of men and women. They were wrapped in greasy, mismatched furs, and they all had some kind of weapon. They moved slowly, remorselessly forward, to form a circle round their prey. Owen licked his dry lips. There had to be at least a hundred of them. Maybe more. And then Lucien Abbott stepped out of the crowd, carrying a disrupter, and Owen's heart sank even further. The Wampyr was smiling. His teeth looked large and white and very sharp.

'You didn't really think it was going to be that easy, did you, Deathstalker? Just brush me aside and forget all about me? Takes more than one blow to put me down. You have to remember; I'm Wampyr. I'm not human any more. Haven't been since they let me die and then brought me back. Do you like my friends? They're all plasma babies. Blood junkies. Blood brothers and sisters, bound to me by ties stronger than love or family, life or death. You never did tell him the whole story, did you, Hazel? What it really means to be a plasma baby. I didn't just drink her blood, Deathstalker; she drank mine. Only a few drops at a time, but a little of my artificial blood goes a long way. I take human blood in, and refine it into something else. They tell me it's the most potent drug imaginable; a high so intense it's like living and dying all at once. Isn't that right, Hazel?'

'That was a long time ago, Abbott,' said Hazel, and her voice was firm and very steady. 'I broke free of you. It took everything I had and then some, but I beat you. You're nothing to me any more.'

'You belong to me,' said the Wampyr. 'Just like the rest of my children. Come back to me. Taste my blood again, and I'll let you live.'

'I'd rather kiss a cockroach,' said Hazel.

The Wampyr smiled coldly. 'Kill them both. See that they suffer first.'

Owen brought his gun up quickly and fired at Abbott, but the Wampyr melted instantly back into the crowd, and the energy beam tore through one of the ragged men, and set fire to several others behind him. They died in silence. Incredibly, the crowd didn't falter, hands steady, eyes unwavering. And the Wampyr stepped back into the light, still smiling.

'I thought that would provoke you into using your disrupter. Now it's useless, till the energy crystal has recharged. I won't let them have you, Deathstalker. I want you for myself. Not for the price on your head. Money means little to me any more. No; I want to break you, humble you, cripple you. I shall enjoy that. And then I'll let you drink a little of my blood, and you'll belong to me, body and soul.'

Owen put away his gun and swept his sword back and forth before him. 'You talk too much, Wampyr. Let's do it.'

The Wampyr surged forward, arms outstretched, moving impossibly fast. Owen braced himself, and stepped forward in a perfect lunge, sword extended, and Abbott impaled himself on the long blade. It entered just below the heart, and punched out of his back in a flurry of black, viscous blood. Abbott grunted once, and then stepped forward, forcing himself along the blade so that he could reach the Deathstalker. Owen twisted on one foot, brought the other up to stamp against

Abbott's belly, and jerked his sword free again. He backed away, watching incredulously as the wound in the Wampyr's chest healed itself in seconds.

Right, thought Owen. *Fast, strong, regenerates. Wonder what else he isn't telling me . . .*

He cut at the Wampyr's throat, and Abbott slapped the blade aside with his bare hand. Owen backed away again, and Abbott came after him. Hazel was suddenly there behind the Wampyr, aiming her disrupter. A dozen of the crowd piled on to her, ripping the gun from her hand and holding her down. She struggled fiercely, but their weight was too much for her. Owen scowled and subvocalized the trigger word *boost*. He'd been using it far too often just recently, and he hated to think what the long-term effects were going to be, but it wasn't as if he had any choice in the matter. The world seemed to slow down as the boost took hold, supercharging his system and buying him time to think. The Wampyr was fast, but so was he, now. If he could just get past the Wampyr's defences, one good cut to the neck would decapitate him. *Regenerate from that, you bastard.*

He danced around the Wampyr, cutting and drawing back, spilling the black blood, only to see the cuts heal in a moment. The Wampyr moved with him, his hands reaching out to tear and hurt, the two men moving too quickly for the unaided eye to follow. Owen thrust and stamped, cutting where he could, going always for the throat, but never even getting close, while Abbott's grasping hands came closer every time. Owen licked his dry lips and panted for breath. The boost gave him some regeneration, but he didn't think it would be enough to repair what Abbott intended to do to him.

And then he moved too slowly, anticipated too late, and Abbott's hand closed around his wrist like a vice. The Wampyr's hand tightened, and all the feeling went out of Owen's hand. The sword fell from his numb fingers, and Abbott laughed softly. Owen dropped his free hand to his boot, pulled out the dagger he kept there, and rammed it between the Wampyr's ribs. Black blood ran for a moment, and then stopped. The Wampyr smiled, and threw Owen twenty feet.

The crowd scrambled to avoid him, and he hit the packed snow hard, driving the breath from his lungs. He rolled over slowly, biting back a groan. His hand was completely numb. Abbott was walking unhurriedly towards him, still smiling, the knife jutting unnoticed from his ribs.

Owen lurched up on to one knee, and crouched there for a moment, breathing hard. And then his good hand brushed against something in the snow, and his heart missed a beat as he recognized what it was. Luck had finally smiled on him, and he was back in with a chance. Abbott loomed over him, grabbed Owen's shirtfront with both hands, and lifted him off the ground. His feet kicked helplessly, six inches above the snow.

'It's over, little man,' said Abbott.

'Bet your ass,' said Owen. And he brought up the hand holding Hazel's lost gun, thrust it into Abbott's gaping mouth, and pressed the stud. The energy blast blew the Wampyr's head apart like a rotten fruit. Abbott's hands slowly released Owen, letting him fall back on to the blood-spattered snow. He scrambled quickly away, tucked Hazel's gun into his belt, and scooped up his sword with his good hand, beating the other against his thigh to get the feeling back again. And then, finally, Abbott's body fell and lay still.

The crowd of onlookers surged forward, and fell on it like rats on a day-old corpse. They tore the Wampyr's clothes apart, cut the flesh with their weapons, and sucked at the black blood like leeches, their mouths working greedily against the pale flesh. Others fought over the blood spilling sluggishly from the severed neck. Owen staggered over to Hazel, who was back on her feet, and shaking her head dazedly. She looked up sharply as he approached, and then looked across at the feeding frenzy of the mob.

'I really think we should get out of here, Hazel,' said Owen. He flexed his hand, grimacing at the pins and needles, and then gave Hazel her gun back. She nodded quickly, and looked about her.

'I get the feeling it's not going to be that easy, Deathstalker.'

Owen looked around him, and his blood ran cold. The

crowd had left the Wampyr's body and re-formed itself around them. Most had black stains around their mouths, and all their eyes were fixed on Owen and Hazel. There was a growing tension in the air, and the faces of the crowd gradually filled with the same slow hatred. Their master, their god, was dead. There would be no more of the wonderful blood that made them feel like gods too, for a time. Owen looked quickly about him, but the odds were equally bad whichever way he looked. He stood back to back with Hazel, and they held their swords ready. And the mob came at them from all sides.

At first the sheer size of the crowd counted against it; they weren't used to working together, and kept getting in each other's way. But the black blood burned within them, and they struggled for a chance to get at the man who killed their god. Owen cut and thrust with skilled precision, killing coldly and dispassionately, with the minimum necessary movement and strength. The blood junkies died and fell, but there were always more to take their place. Hazel fought at his back, stamping and cutting. And blades came at Owen and Hazel from all directions, swords and knives and machetes in never-ending numbers. Owen fought on, doggedly refusing to be beaten. The boost still flared within him, bright and powerful, but he wasn't sure how much longer it would last. The candle that burns twice as brightly lasts half as long.

He gutted a skeletal man wrapped in evil-smelling furs, ducked a wild swing from the man next to him, and cut viciously at another face that pressed too close. He'd already taken a dozen minor wounds he was too busy to feel, and blood soaked his clothes, some of it his. He grunted and stamped and swung his sword with all his amplified strength, and still the crowd surged around him, desperate to drag him down.

It came to him suddenly and quite calmly that there was no way he and Hazel could survive this. There were just too many of the blood junkies. It only needed one of them to get in a lucky blow, and the fight would be over. A hell of a way for a Deathstalker to die, pulled down by nameless dogs in a nameless back alley. He smiled slightly, even as he cut and thrust. He'd felt this way once before, on Virimonde, when his own men had surrounded him, desperate for his head, but then Hazel had come from nowhere to save him. This time she was in just as much trouble as he was. She couldn't save him . . . but perhaps he could save her. He considered the thought dispassionately, and found it good. He owed her his life, and the Deathstalkers always paid their debts. And at least this way his death would mean something.

He forced back the maddened faces in front of him with wide, sweeping strokes, to buy him a little space, and drew his disrupter. Enough time had passed to recharge the crystal. Some of the crowd drew back just from the sight of the energy gun. Owen tilted his head back to yell at Hazel. He could feel her back bumping and jarring against his, showing that she was still alive and fighting, but he had no way of knowing what shape she was in.

'Hazel; I've got a plan!'

'Better be a good one, Deathstalker.'

'I'm going to blast a hole through the crowd with my disrupter. When you see the opening, run. I'll keep them occupied.'

'Are you crazy? I'm not leaving you to die! I didn't save your ass last time just to run out on you now.'

'Hazel; I can't save both of us. If you don't run, we'll both die. Please; let me do this. Let me save you.'

There was a pause, and then her voice came back to him. 'You're a brave man, Deathstalker. Wish I'd known you longer. Do it.'

Owen summoned up the last of his boosted strength, and threw himself at the crowd. Blood pounded in his head and boiled through his veins, and all his pain and tiredness disappeared like a fleeting thought. His sword swung and hacked like a part of him, driving back the desperate faces before him, his blade moving too fast for the eye to follow. The crowd fell back still further, confused for the moment by the deadly force in their midst, and Owen raised his disrupter and fired. The blood junkies threw themselves out of its way, but still the searing energy beam tore through those who didn't move fast enough, and for a moment there was an opening in the crowd.

'Run!' yelled Owen, pulling Hazel round so she could see the opening, and she lowered her head and ran. She burst through the crowd and on into the deserted street beyond. She pounded down the street, and only slowly realized no one was following her. She stopped and looked back, and all she could see was the backs of the crowd, intent on one struggling figure in their midst. Hazel slowly lowered her sword, and felt something burn in her eyes that might have been tears. He'd never liked her much, any more than she'd liked him, but he'd sacrificed himself to save her. For a moment she wanted to run back and fight beside him again, but that would just have thrown away the chance he'd given her. And as she watched, the crowd pressed in from every side, hacking and cutting, and Owen fell beneath them, to disappear under the crowd of bodies. A sob forced its way out of her trembling mouth.

'Don't mourn for him,' said a quiet distorted voice behind her. 'It's not over yet.'

She spun round, sword at the ready, and found herself facing a tall stocky man in a dark uniform she didn't recognize. She had a brief glimpse of a subtly inhuman face with blazing golden eyes, and then the figure was past her and running towards the crowd with impossible speed. A few turned to face him, but he was among them in seconds, swinging his sword in long deadly arcs that picked men up and threw them aside like puppets with broken strings. Men and women fell to every side of him, and the crowd scattered, unable to face the newcomer's incredible strength and speed. And from their midst a blood-stained figure rose up again, still savagely swinging his sword. His voice rose above the clamour, strong and strident.

'Shandrakor! Shandrakor!'

Hazel's heart missed a beat as she realized who it was, and she had to blink back fresh tears. She should have known Owen Deathstalker wouldn't die that easily. Together, he and the newcomer moved among the dispersing crowd like unstoppable nightmares, and bloodied figures fell to the stained snow and did not rise again. No one could stand against them, and after a few moments no one tried any more. The surviving blood junkies turned and ran, and as quickly as that it was all over. Owen and the newcomer lowered their swords and watched them run, and then looked at each other appraisingly. Hazel ran back to join them, and then had to put a supporting arm round Owen, as his knees buckled. He was trembling like a horse after a race, and she realized he must have dropped out of boost. He still managed a ghastly grin for her, despite his many wounds.

'You realize,' he said thickly, 'that this is the second bloody time I've had to be rescued by somebody else? Just once I'd like to rescue myself, OK? Is that so much to ask?'

'Oh, shut up and get your breath back,' said Hazel. 'If you were drowning you'd complain the straw you were clutching at wasn't a good enough quality. What was that you were shouting?'

'My Family's battle cry,' said Owen. His voice seemed a little stronger. 'I never used it before. Never thought I would. Surprising what goes through your mind when you realize you might not be about to die after all. Speaking of which, who's your new friend?'

'Don't ask me,' said Hazel. 'I thought he was a friend of yours.'

They both turned to look at their unexpected saviour, and he looked silently back. His face was subtly inhuman, just as Hazel had thought; there was something wrong in its planes and angles, as though strange and unfamiliar emotions had shaped it. But it was the eyes that held the attention, that brought goose-flesh to Owen and Hazel's arms and raised the hairs on their necks. The eyes glowed a bright golden in the dim light of the street, as though lit from within by some strange inner fire. They marked him, like the brand of Cain. He was a Hadenman, one of the legendary augmented men of lost Haden. They were rare now, seen pehaps once in a hundred worlds, the few survivors of the terrible Hadenmen rebellion, when cyborgs created by men sought to wipe out humanity, root and branch. They failed, just, and now the last remnants were scattered far and wide across the Empire, feared and courted wherever they went, as the ultimate warriors. They were supposed to be shot on sight, but usually no one was stupid enough to take them on with anything less than an army.

Few and far between now, lost and forsaken; the bitter end of a once brilliant dream.

'I am Tobias Moon,' said the Hadenman, in a harsh rasping voice that had no place in a human throat. 'I am a partially functioning augmented man. Most of my implanted energy crystals are exhausted, and I lack the means to recharge them. I am therefore unable to utilize most of my implants, but I am still more than capable of seeing off a few blood junkies.'

'How did you know we needed help?' said Hazel.

'A message from Cyder,' said Moon. 'She thought you could use some assistance, and that we might be able to help each other.'

Up on a roof overlooking the street, Cat sighed with relief. He ached all over from the fall he'd taken, but luckily the snowdrift had been just deep enough to cushion the worst of the impact. Now that the Hadenman had finally put in an appearance, he was free to return to the Blackthorn for some much needed rest. Shadowing Hazel d'Ark and the Death-stalker had turned out to be a full-time job. Still, they should be safe enough now with Moon. There weren't many people stupid enough to annoy a Hadenman. He set off slowly across the rooftops, hoping very fervently that he'd never have to see any of them again. They were too dangerous to be around. Even for Mistport.

Down in the street, Owen and Hazel looked round sharply as they heard someone moving in the mess of bodies lying scattered across the bloody snow. A single figure was moving, trying to drag itself away. Its useless legs dragged behind it, leaving a trail of bright red blood. Owen started after it, and Hazel put a staying hand on his arm.

'No need to kill him, Owen. He'll bleed to death before he gets far.'

Owen jerked his arm free. 'I'm not going to kill him. I'm going to see if I can help.'

'Are you crazy? He's a blood junkie. He was quite happy to kill you.'

'The fight's over. I can't just leave someone to die if I can help. If I did, I'd be no better than them. I am still a Deathstalker, whatever the Iron Bitch says, and we are an honourable Clan. Besides, a few years ago, that might have been you, Hazel.'

He quickly caught up with the crawling figure and knelt beside it. He put a gentle hand on its shoulder, and the figure shrank away from him with a weak desperate cry of fear and pain. The figure wasn't very big, barely five feet tall, wrapped in filthy shapeless furs. Its legs were soaked in blood from the thighs down. Owen murmured comforting words till the figure stopped wailing, as much through weakness as anything else. Owen examined the wounded legs as carefully as he could without touching them, and shook his head slowly. Either he or the Hadenman had cut right through the muscles in both legs. Crippling wounds, on a world like Mistworld. He shrugged uncomfortably, and pulled back the hood to see the face beneath. The breath went out of him, and he felt suddenly sick. She couldn't have been more than fourteen. Half starved, the bones of her face jutted out against the taut skin. She looked up at him with empty eyes, beyond hope or despair, no room in her face for anything but pain.

'Plasma baby,' said Hazel quietly behind him. 'They start them young, in Mistport.'

'She's just a child,' said Owen harshly. 'Dear God, what have I done?'

'She would have killed you,' said Hazel. 'And never given it a second thought. Finish it, Owen. We have to go.'

Owen looked back at her, almost angrily. 'What do you mean, finish it?'

'You want to leave her like that? If she's lucky she'll bleed to death. If not, and the gangrene doesn't kill her slowly, she'll be a cripple for what remains of her life. And Mistport's a bad place to be weak and vulnerable. It's kinder to put her out of her suffering. Do you want me to do it for you?'

'No!' said Owen. 'No. I'm a Deathstalker. I clear up my own messes.'

He drew the dagger from his boot, and thrust it expertly into the girl's heart. She didn't moan or shudder. She just stopped breathing, and her eyes stared straight past him. Owen pulled the dagger out and then just sat there, rocking slightly, trying to hold back the emotions within him. Hazel hovered at his side, unsure what to do for the best. She wanted to put a hand on his shoulder to comfort him, let him know she was there and understood, but she wasn't sure how he'd take it. He was a strong man, and a proud one too, but he still had unexpected vulnerabilities. And if you had any weaknesses, you could be sure Mistworld would find them.

Hazel hadn't been sure the Deathstalker had any soft spots in him. He'd seemed the perfect warrior and aristocrat. She was seeing a new side of him now, and she wasn't sure if she liked it or not. Being weak could get you killed, when you were an outlaw. She put a tentative hand on his shoulder, ready to draw it back in a moment, but he didn't even know she was there. She could feel the tension under her hand, and knew it was rage as much as sorrow that boiled within him. She looked back at the Hadenman, but he just looked back at her with his inhuman golden eyes, and she had to look away. Owen stood up suddenly, still looking down at the pathetic little body.

'This is wrong,' he said flatly. 'No one should have to live like this, die like this.'

'It happens everywhere,' said Hazel. 'Not just on Mistworld. You're rich, titled; what would you know about living in the underclass?'

'I should have known. I'm an historian, and I studied the records. I knew things like this used to happen. I just never thought . . .'

'History is what the Empire says it is,' said Moon, in his rasping, buzzing voice. 'They decide what gets recorded. But even the brightest flower has manure at its roots.'

'No,' said Owen. 'It doesn't have to be this way. I will not stand for this. I am a Deathstalker, and I will not allow this to continue.'

'What are you going to do?' said Hazel. 'Overthrow the Empire?'

Owen looked at her for a long moment. 'I don't know. Maybe. If that's what it takes.' He turned away from her and the dead child, and walked over to the Hadenman. He studied Moon thoughtfully. 'Last I heard, there'd been less than a dozen sightings of Hadenmen throughout the Empire. What do you think I can do for you? The Empress put an order of execution on you all, as a threat to the Empire and humanity itself. Can't say I blame her, given the results of your rebellion. You killed millions in your uprising. If you'd succeeded . . .'

'We'd have killed millions more,' said Moon. It was hard to read emotions in his inhuman and buzzing voice, but Owen thought he sensed as much regret as defiance. 'We were fighting for our freedom. Our survival. We lost that battle, but the war goes on. I am not the last of my kind. On the lost world of Haden, floating alone in its dark void, an army of my people lies sleeping in the Tomb of the Hadenmen, waiting only for the call to wake again. We learned the hard way that we couldn't win fighting alone. We need allies. Allies like you, Deathstalker. Your only chance for survival now is to raise an army and go to war against the Empress Lionstone. You are a Deathstalker; many would follow you where they wouldn't follow another. Your name always stood for truth and justice and triumph in battle. I speak for the Hadenmen. We would fight beside you, in return for our freedom.'

'Hold it, hold it,' said Owen, putting up his hands defensively. 'This is all going too fast for me. I can't lead a rebellion. I'm an historian, not a warrior.'

'On the other hand,' Hazel said thoughtfully, 'he's right that we can't keep running forever. Eventually, they'll track us down and kill us. We've become too important. If even Mistworld isn't safe . . .'

'That's not enough,' said Owen. 'Rebellion against the throne is against everything I was brought up to believe in.'

'Not against the throne,' said Hazel. 'Against the Empress.'

Owen looked at her. 'I made that distinction earlier.'

'I know. I was listening.' Hazel hurried on before he could say anything. 'At least think about it, Owen. You said you wanted to stop things like that girl from happening.'

'I need to think about this,' said Owen. 'You're asking too much of me.'

'Time is not on our side,' said Moon. 'You must choose soon, or the choice may be taken away from you by events.'

Owen looked at the Hadenman almost angrily. 'What do you want from me, Moon?'

'Right now? Transport. You have a starship and I do not. I want passage with you to lost Haden, and my waiting brethren.'

Whatever answer Owen might have expected, that wasn't it. The location of the planet Haden was one of the great mysteries of the Empire. All knowledge of its coordinates had vanished at the end of the Hadenman rebellion; the last desperate gamble of the augmented men. And despite all the Empire's increasingly desperate efforts, Haden had remained lost for the better part of two centuries. In an Empire built on information, that should have been impossible. But somehow the augmented men, or their agents, had contrived to wipe every piece of information on Haden and its people from every computer in the Imperial matrix. As an historian Owen had found that hard to believe, but after wasting months of research time tracking down rumours and glimpses without getting anywhere, he had been forced to admit he was beaten. Haden was lost, by its own wishes, and would remain so. And so it passed out of history and into legend; a nightmare to threaten disobedient children with.

Be good, or the Hadenmen will get you.

Owen looked thoughtfully at Tobias Moon. 'You have the coordinates for Haden?'

'Unfortunately, no. Or I wouldn't still be stuck here on Mistworld. But the answer is out there, somewhere, and I will find it. Until then, I offer myself as a soldier in your war. Get me some new energy crystals, and a good cybersurgeon to implant them, and I would be a formidable ally. And when I come at last to Haden, I will speak for you with my people. That is what you want, isn't it?'

'I don't know,' said Owen. 'I'm not sure of anything any more. Even assuming that we can find Haden, eventually, do I really want to ally myself with the betrayers of humanity? The butchers of Brahmin II, the slaughterers of Madraguda? I could go down in history as one of the greatest traitors of all time.'

'It doesn't matter whether you want us,' said Moon calmly. 'You need us, if your rebellion is to succeed.'

'All right,' said Owen. 'You're my man; until I tell you otherwise. Now let's get out of here. I'm surprised we're not already hip deep in bounty hunters.'

'Think about it,' said Hazel. 'Would you go rushing in after someone who'd just killed a Wampyr and seen off a whole pack of his blood junkies?'

'Good point,' said Owen. 'But let's get moving anyway. Standing around makes me nervous.'

'I think we should get you to a doctor first,' said Hazel. 'You took a lot of punishment before the Hadenman . . . helped you out.'

'I've felt better,' said Owen, 'but I'll be all right. One of the more useful properties of boost. Any wound that doesn't actually kill me will heal itself, given time. I'm going to be rather fragile for a while, but I've got you and Moon to look after me, haven't I?'

Hazel thought that was getting a bit pointed, and decided it was probably a good time to change the subject. 'Where are we going?'

'The Olympus Health Spa, on Riverside, wherever the hell that is. If I'm going to lead an army of rebellion, I want Jack Random at my side. We'll look for your bounty hunter friend later. Assuming she isn't already on our trail for the price on our heads.'

'That is a possibility,' Hazel admitted. 'Friendship is fine, but credit lasts longer. All right; follow me. And let's keep to back alleys and the shadows where we can. I'm starting to feel like I've got a target painted on my back.'

She set off more or less confidently into the mists, and Owen and Tobias Moon went after her. Owen strode along, looking at nothing, lost in thought. Events might be rushing him along, but he still had his doubts and suspicions. What were the odds of a Hadenman turning up out of the blue just at the right moment to save his ass? Much more likely Moon had been following them for some time, waiting for a chance to look good and gain their confidence. But what made him so important to Moon, if it wasn't the price on his head? Surely there must have been some other ship Moon could have persuaded to get him off-planet. And for someone who claimed not to know the coordinates of Haden, he seemed pretty sure of finding the planet in the not too distant future. Owen scowled. And where did all this tie in with his late father's plots and plans, that had brought him to Mistworld in the first place?

More and more Owen was sure there were wheels within wheels, and unseen forces subtly guiding him from the wings. The very things he'd spent most of his life trying to avoid. But if that was so, he had a few surprises in store for whoever was jerking his strings. If push came to shove, he could play that game too. He was a Deathstalker, and intrigue was in his blood. In the meantime . . . he decided to concentrate on the Hadenman. Did he, or his people, still have a private, hidden agenda? When awakened, would the army of augmented men really join with him, or could they secretly be intending to ally themselves with the rogue AIs on Shub, as the Empress had claimed so often in the past? Owen smiled briefly. He had no answers, or none he could trust, so for the moment he'd go along with Moon. And sleep with one eye open. He moved up alongside Hazel, and she nodded briefly.

'Yeah, I don't trust him either,' she said quietly. 'But I'd rather have him on our side than working against us. At least this way we can keep an eye on him.'

'What do you suggest we do in the meantime?' said Owen.

'Trust no one. Think you can remember that?'

'You've never been to Court, have you?' said Owen. 'As an aristocrat, I learned to trust no one from a very early age. Among the Families, you learn intrigue with your letters and numbers, or you don't survive to reach adulthood.'

'Sounds a lot like Mistworld,' said Hazel, and they both had to laugh. The Hadenman strode silently along behind them, and kept his thoughts to himself.

The Olympus spa wasn't far, just the other side of Merchants' Quarter, but the walk was still far enough to chill Owen to the bone. Despite his confident words to Hazel, his wounds had taken a lot more out of him than he was willing to admit. He trudged along through the slush and the thickening mists, and muttered direly to himself. He'd been on Mistworld nearly a whole day, and he still hadn't had one glimpse of the sun.

The spa, when they finally got there, didn't exactly make up for the long walk. It was trying desperately to look up-market, but the neighbourhood was against it. It was still a definite improvement on most of the places Hazel had led him to so far, but Owen couldn't say he was particularly impressed. The stone and timber buildings had clearly all seen better days, and the bare brickwork had been stained a varying grey from the continuous smoke of a nearby factory. The Olympus's front was wide and brightly painted, and the name above the door was set out in letters so stylized and convoluted it was almost impossible to make them out. There were no windows, but tall plaques described the many wonders to be found inside, together with a series of claims for potential weight loss and muscle building that bordered on the miraculous. Owen gave the place a long, stern look, but it remained stubbornly unimpressive.

'I am not impressed,' said Hazel.

'Give it a chance,' said Owen automatically. 'This is only the exterior. Didn't your mother ever tell you not to judge a place by its exterior?'

'She also told me to avoid outlaws, aristos and sucker joints. Can't say I'm doing too well on any of them. You really think we're going to find Jack Random in a dump like this? I mean,

I'd heard he was down on his luck, but can you really see the legendary professional rebel running a cheap rip-off joint like this?'

'It's probably a cover,' said Owen stubbornly. 'Who'd think to look for him here?'

'He has a point,' said Moon in his harsh, buzzing voice, and they both jumped slightly. 'I wouldn't be seen dismantled in a place like this.'

'The Abraxas people said we'd find him here,' said Owen. 'And I really don't feel like going back and arguing with them about it. I'm going in. Watch my back, keep your eyes open and your hands off the silver.'

He strode up to the door, and gave the bell chain a firm tug. He sensed as much as heard the others fall in behind him, and smiled slightly. They just needed to be reminded who was in charge now and again. The door swung open, and Owen put on his best supercilious look. When in doubt, treat people like shit. Nine times out of ten they'll immediately assume you're a very superior person, and probably there to investigate whatever scam they're running. In Owen's experience, most people had a scam running at any given time, of one kind or another. He tried not to think about the other ten per cent. That was, after all, why he wore a sword.

The door swung back to reveal a tall graceful living goddess wearing a wide smile and a very skimpy outfit comprised mostly of black lace. She was also extremely muscular. Her arms and thighs bulged intimidatingly, and somehow Owen just knew she did more sit-ups before breakfast each day than he managed in a month.

'Hi,' she said breathily. 'Is there anything I can do for you?'

Owen could think of several, one of which would almost certainly put his back out, but he made himself concentrate on the matter in hand. 'We need to see the manager,' he said, in what he hoped was a firm, commanding voice.

'Of course,' said the goddess, still smiling widely. 'Do come in.'

She stood back to let them enter. Owen strode confidently past her, but almost lost it when she took a sudden deep breath just as he drew level, and her magnificent chest practically flew into his face. He moved quickly on into the reception area, and took a few quiet deep breaths of his own. Behind him, he heard Hazel give one of her familiar sniffs of disapproval. The Hadenman remained quiet. Presumably he was above or beyond such things. The door shut behind them with a worryingly final sound, and then the goddess was with them again. She favoured them all with another of her dazzling smiles, and struck a casual pose that just happened to show off most of her muscles in high definition.

'Make yourselves comfortable,' she suggested winningly. 'I'll go tell the manager you're here.'

She turned and left in a single smooth motion, and disappeared out of the far door before Owen could get his breath back. He looked at Tobias Moon.

'What a warm and understanding chest that girl had.'

'Nice deltoids,' said the Hadenman.

'When you two have finished drooling,' said Hazel, icily, 'You might care to notice that she locked the front door behind us. If she's recognized you . . .'

'Relax,' said Moon. 'I'm with you now.'

Hazel gave him a withering stare. 'How are your batteries holding up?'

'I have more than enough power in my systems to deal with any problems we may encounter.'

Hazel sniffed. 'If you're so powerful and dangerous, how did you end up here?'

'I trusted the wrong people,' said Moon, and there was something in his inhuman voice that kept her from continuing.

Owen looked around at the reception area. It seemed the safest thing to do. Even standing still and silent, there was something very disturbing about the Hadenman. Owen had been in his company now for nearly an hour, and was no nearer feeling at ease. It was as though there was something within Moon that was always poised to strike, ready to kill at a moment's notice. Owen decided he wasn't going to think about that for a while, and concentrated on the reception area.

He was tempted to sneer, but settled for a condescending smile. The Olympus's idea of fashion was at least twenty years out of date, and the furniture had clearly been designed by someone more interested in style than comfort. Not that he knew much about style, either. Owen decided against sitting down. He had a feeling one of those chairs could do terrible things to your lower back. Not unlike the goddess at the door . . .

His thoughts had just started to drift again when the door at the far end of reception swung open, and a giant walked in. Owen realized after a moment that the newcomer wasn't really that tall, no more than six foot six at the most, but his great slabs of muscle made him seem much bigger. He was incredibly well developed, with muscles in places Owen wasn't sure he even had places. He looked like he'd been lifting weights since he was a baby, and from the way his muscles flexed and swelled as he walked, Owen was surprised he could move around without pulling something painful. The giant came to a stop before them, and gave them all a brief, impersonal smile. Owen was surprised again to realize the man was quite handsome. It just wasn't the first thing that got your attention. Mainly because the giant was wearing only a pair of tight-fitting trousers, the better to show off his highly developed muscles. Among other things. Owen couldn't help noticing that Hazel was staring at the giant with undisguised fascination, all but devouring him with her eyes. Owen sniffed. There were more important things than muscles.

He coughed politely to get the giant's attention, and the huge man turned his gaze on him. Owen felt like he was standing in a hole.

'I'm Tom Sefka,' said the giant, in a voice so low it almost trembled in Owen's bones. 'Manager and owner of the Olympus Health Spa. I'm assuming this is something important. Delia doesn't usually disturb me for anything less, but the Hadenman impressed her.' He looked Moon over thoughtfully. 'If you're looking to make some quick money, I've got several regulars who'd pay good money to take on an augmented man in the ring.'

'Thanks,' said Moon. 'But I tend to break things when I play.'

Sefka blinked at the inhuman voice, and then turned back to Owen. 'So what can I do for you?'

'We're looking for Jobe Ironhand,' said Hazel, just a little breathlessly. 'It's really important that we talk to him.'

Sefka frowned. 'You had me called away from my work just for that? What the hell do you want with him?'

'We rather assumed he was the owner or business partner,' said Owen, and Sefka smiled unpleasantly.

'Hardly. You want Jobe, he's out the back, doing his chores. You can talk to him if you want, but don't keep him from his work. Come and see me when you're finished. You all look like you could use a little weight on your frames in the right places.'

Owen frowned. 'Won't Ironhand mind us just walking in on him?'

'It's not his place to mind,' said Sefka. 'He's only the janitor, after all. You'll find him through that door, second on the right and down the corridor. When you're finished with him, tell him the shower floors still need cleaning.'

He nodded to them all briefly, and turned and left, disappearing through the far door. Owen was a little surprised the floor didn't shake beneath him when he moved. Hazel watched Sefka go with hungry eyes. Owen felt a little irritated. Sefka wasn't that special. Probably had muscles where his brains should be.

'Maybe we should see him afterwards,' said Hazel. 'I'd just love to put my body in his hands.'

'If you could control your animal lusts for a moment,' Owen said icily, 'we really ought to find this Jobe and sort out what's going on here. The Abraxas must have got it wrong. Perhaps Random is someone else here at the spa.'

'Give me an hour alone with that body, and I'd show him some animal lusts he'd never forget,' said Hazel.

'Muscles aren't everything,' said Moon.

'How true,' said Hazel. 'It's not just his muscles I'm interested in.'

'I wonder if this place has cold showers,' said Owen.

'Let's go find Jobe Ironhead,' said Moon diplomatically. 'Maybe then we'll find out what a living legend is doing working as a janitor.'

'It's regular work,' said Hazel. 'Maybe the pay's good.'

Moon looked around him. 'It would have to be.'

Hazel shrugged. 'Even a professional rebel probably has to turn his hand to some honest work now and again, to put food on the table between rebellions.'

'He must be working undercover,' Owen decided. 'Staying out of sight while Empire agents are searching for him. It makes sense.'

He set off for the far door without waiting for the others to agree with him. The door led on to a tiled corridor which branched off in different directions according to whether you wanted the signposted weights room, the steam room or the showers. Owen took the second turning on the right, as directed. According to the handwritten sign on the wall it led to the locker rooms. Owen led the way at a brisk walk, and tried not to think about the implications of what he'd been told. Jack Random, *the* Jack Random, working as a janitor in a place like this? It had to be a mistake, or a cover, or . . . something.

The locker room looked like any other locker room; bare and functional, with a smell of perspiration and liniment. Most of the lockers stood open and empty, suggesting that the spa was going through a quiet time. As they moved further into the room, the air thickened with the scent of cheap disinfectant. The door at the far end opened, and a man entered carrying a mop and bucket. He was about five foot six, and looked to be in his late sixties, with a lined face and thinning grey hair. He wore baggy overalls that looked as though they'd been made for someone rather larger, and he looked like he'd missed more than his fair share of meals lately. His hands were trembling, and his face had a pale, unhealthy look.

A wave of relief passed through Owen. Whoever this was, he clearly wasn't Jack Random. This half pint in saggy overalls probably wouldn't even know which end of a sword to stab you with. Presumably a spa this size needed more than one janitor, and this was the other one. The janitor stared blankly at Owen and his companions, his watery eyes straining against the gloom.

'What are you doing back here? Locker room's closed.'

'Sorry to bother you,' said Owen graciously. 'We're looking for Jobe Ironhand. Do you know where we might find him?'

The janitor blinked at him. 'That's me. I'm Jobe Ironhand. What can I do for you?'

Hazel looked at Moon. 'Didn't you just know he was going to say that?'

Owen felt his jaw dropping, and closed his mouth with a snap. There had to be a mistake. This couldn't be Random. The age was all wrong, for a start. Jack Random was a professional warrior, respected on a hundred worlds. This broken down old wreck barely had the strength to hold on to his bucket and mop. It couldn't be him.

'This can't be him,' said Hazel. 'I mean . . . look at him.'

'For once, I agree with you,' Owen said heavily. 'Someone's been leading us astray. Let's get out of here.'

'I thought you wanted Jack Random,' said Tobias Moon. 'This is him.'

Owen and Hazel looked at the Hadenman. 'What makes you think that?' said Hazel.

'I fought beside him, in the rebellion on Cold Rock. A few augmented men had joined his army, for the experience, and I was one of them. I saw Random several times at staff meetings, and I never forget a face.'

Hazel looked back at the janitor. 'This bag of bones faced down the Imperial High Guard on Cold Rock? Give me a break.'

'Oh hell,' said the janitor. 'You'd better come with me.'

They all looked at him, startled. His voice had . . . changed. He put his bucket and mop down, and produced a battered silver flask from a pocket in his overalls. He unscrewed the cap with some difficulty, and took a long drink. His adam's apple bobbed jerkily in his scrawny unshaven neck. He lowered the flask, sighed deeply, and carefully refastened the cap. His hands didn't seem to be shaking nearly as much now, and his gaze was sharp and direct. He looked Owen and Hazel over, and then he turned away and disappeared back through the far door, leaving the others to hurry after him.

He wandered down the corridor without looking back to see if they were following, and pushed open a door almost hidden in shadows. He stood back, and gestured for the three of them to enter. They did so, just a little diffidently, and found themselves in a boiler room that had also been pressed into service as living quarters. Apart from the boiler, most of the space was taken up with a long cot covered with dishevelled blankets. Ironhand sank down on to it with a relieved sigh. Owen looked around for a chair, but there weren't any.

'Shut the door and sit down,' the janitor said testily. 'You make the room look untidy.'

Owen shut the door and sat on the floor, drawing his legs awkwardly up beneath him. Hazel sank easily into a full lotus beside him. Moon stayed standing, at parade rest. Owen looked hard at the janitor, trying to see some sign of the legendary warrior in this beaten down little man. The janitor looked back at him with a surprisingly steady gaze, and Owen slowly realized that the man sitting opposite him didn't look nearly as unimpressive as he had before. His back was straight and his hands had stopped shaking, and there was a new strength in his unshaven face.

'I thought I'd hidden myself pretty well,' he said grimly. 'Suppose you start by telling me who gave you my name?'

'The Abraxas Information Centre,' said Owen, and the janitor grunted irritably.

'Those damn telepaths get everywhere. Looks like I'm going to have to move again. Can't say I'll be sorry to go. The place is a dump, and the work stinks. They charge me rent for this room, you know. You wouldn't think they'd have the nerve, would you? Still, I've stayed in worse, in my time. Spent most of my adult life on the run, one way or another, and people can always tell when the pressure's on you. That's when accommodation suddenly gets scarce, friends turn their back on you, and the price of everything goes through the roof.' He broke off to take another drink from his flask. He pulled a face, and screwed the cap back on tight. 'I can remember when I wouldn't have used booze like this to clean my boots with. Amazing what you can get used to, when you've no choice. I can remember when I drank only the finest vintages, the fiercest brandies, sparkling champagnes . . . Of course, that was when I was somebody. When it mattered who I was.'

'Are you saying you really are Jack Random?' said Owen, not even trying to hide his scepticism.

'I used to be. Now I'm Jobe Ironhand. Named myself after an old friend of mine. He died a long time ago, without any heir to carry on the name, so I thought he wouldn't mind if I used it. You have to be respectful of the dead. There's enough ghosts plaguing me already without adding more.' He stopped, and looked up at Moon. 'I don't remember you. I've led too many armies, too many campaigns. Cold Rock was a bad one, though. In the end, most of my people were wiped out by Imperial attack ships, and I only escaped by running for my life. I did a lot of running, at the end, but they still caught me.'

He stopped again, his eyes lost in yesterday. Owen leaned forward. 'They caught you? What happened?'

'They broke me,' said the man who used to be Jack Random. 'Torture, drugs, mind techs, espers . . . anyone'll break if you hit them hard enough and long enough. And I was so very tired by then anyway . . .'

'So how did you escape?' said Hazel.

'I didn't. The Empire was getting ready for a major show trial, to show off my supposed change of heart. Stand me up in front of the holo cameras and have me denounce all my old friends and beliefs. You know the sort of thing. I would have done it, too. They'd broken me. Luckily some friends in the clone underground who hadn't given up on me broke into my holding cell and sprang me. They shouldn't have done it. Too many good men and women died that day, just to rescue a defeated old man with no strength or ideals left. They got me on a ship, under an assumed name, and eventually I ended up here. Where everyone runs when there's no place left to go. So if you've come looking for the great warrior, the legendary professional rebel, you're wasting your time. He died years ago, in the torture cells under the Imperial Palace on Golgotha.

'Look at me. I'm forty-seven and I look twice that. My hands shake most of the time because my body still remembers what was done to it in the cells, and my memories are a mess. The mind techs really did a job on me. So go look somewhere else for your saviour or leader, or whatever the hell you think you need. I'm not who you want, and even if I was, I'd be no use to you.'

'Do you have any evidence of who you are?' said Owen. 'Any old trophies or mementoes from your past?'

'No. Move fast, travel light, that was always my way. And I don't care whether you believe me or not. Do us all a favour, and leave me in peace.'

Owen looked at the man before him, and felt an almost childish disappointment. His father had brought him up on stories of the great rebel Jack Random. When Owen was older, he'd started his career as an historian by searching out the truth on Random, only to find the truth was even more impressive than the legend. Random had done pretty much everything they said he had, and more besides. He'd fought the Empire on a hundred worlds, winning some, losing more, never giving up. Of all his father's dubious friends and associates, Jack Random was the only one Owen had ever respected.

'Do you remember my father?' he said suddenly. 'My name is Owen Deathstalker.'

'Yes. I remember him. Good fighter, and a cunning intriguer.' Random looked at him steadily. 'Since you're here, I gather he's dead now?'

'Yes. Killed in the streets, cut down as a traitor. I'm the Deathstalker now. Or at least, until the Empire catches up with me. I'm outlawed; my name and possessions stripped from me.'

Random looked at him thoughtfully. 'Do you have your father's ring? He always said it was important, though he never got around to explaining why. He never was very big on explanations, your father.'

'I've got the ring. As far as I can tell, it's just a ring.'

He showed it to Random, who looked at it for a moment, and then sat back on his cot. His fingers played with the cap on his flask, but he didn't take another drink.

'I'm sorry to hear of your father's death. I've lost a lot of friends down the years, but it never gets any easier. You look a lot like him, you know. Do you have any actual plans, or are you just running?'

'I've got plans, yes,' said Owen, just a little defensively. 'Do you want to be a part of them?'

'No. But I don't really think I've any choice in the matter. If you could find me, so could others. I'm not worth much any more, Deathstalker. But what there is left of me is yours.'

'Can I have a word with you a moment, Owen?' said Hazel, taking his arm in a very firm grip. He winced as she all but dragged him to his feet, and out into the corridor. He jerked his arm free, and carefully shut the door behind him.

'Are you crazy?' said Hazel. 'We can't burden ourselves with a wreck like that! He's bound to slow us down. We can't even be sure he is who he says he is!'

'Doesn't really matter who he is,' said Owen. 'Just his name will attract people to our cause. People will fight and die for Jack Random when they wouldn't lift a hand for you or me.'

'But he's a janitor!'

'So what? Really, Hazel; if anyone's going to be a snob here, it should be me. And I don't think you're in any position to throw stones, considering your previous occupation in Mistport.'

Hazel frowned. 'What are you talking about?'

'Well, as I understand from Cyder's comments, you were a . . . lady of the evening.'

'Lady of the . . . I ought to tear your head off and piss down your neck! I was never a whore!'

'Then what were you?'

'If you must know, I was a lady's maid!' Hazel realized she was shouting, and lowered her voice again. Two bright spots

213

of colour burned in her cheeks. 'And you needn't look at me like that. It's a perfectly respectable profession. And work was scarce just then.'

'So . . . why did you give it up?'

'Lady of the house told me to sweep out the corners once too often. I smacked her in the mouth, stole some of the silver and left before they could call the Watch. Satisfied now?'

'Eminently. It's always good to have a profession to fall back on. If times get hard, I'm sure I can always find you a position on my staff.'

'I'd rather die,' said Hazel. 'No; I'd rather kill you.'

'Ironhand!' They both looked round to see the giant form of Tom Sefka pounding down the corridor towards them. They fell back automatically as he stopped and hammered on the janitor's door. 'Ironhand, get your worthless ass out here! I've got half a dozen regulars waiting to use the showers, and you still haven't cleaned them out. Either you get your ass in gear right now, or you're fired!'

He turned and looked at Owen and Hazel. 'And you needn't think you're going anywhere either. Word finally got here as to who you are, Deathstalker. If I'd known who you were, I'd never have let you in. Last thing I need is a bunch of bounty hunters in here, getting blood all over the place. You even try and draw your gun or your sword, and I'll rip your arm out of your socket. Price on your head will make me rich, Death-stalker. You're mine, and your companions. Unless you think you can take me?'

He flexed his muscles meaningfully. Owen thought about it. He was tired, and still healing, and Sefka really was a hell of a size. On the other hand, if he could draw his gun before Sefka could get his hands on him . . . Sefka looked like he could move pretty fast, for a big man. Hazel would probably avenge his death, but he didn't find the thought all that comforting.

He was still trying to come up with an answer when the door opened, and Random stepped out into the corridor. He walked right up to Sefka, holding the big man's eyes with his, and reached out and took Sefka's genitals in a death grip. He piled on the pressure, grinning nastily all the while, and all the

214

colour went out of Sefka's face as he sank to his knees. Random gave him one last white-knuckled squeeze that brought tears to Owen's eyes, released his hold, reached back into his room and brought out his mop. Sefka raised his head just in time to see the long wooden handle coming for him at incredible speed. If the mop had been a sword, Sefka's head would have gone bouncing down the corridor. As it was, the wood connected with his temple with a very solid-sounding thud, and the big man fell unconscious to the floor. It was probably a relief, thought Owen. Random lowered his mop, and leaned on it as though it was a sword.

'Just for the record; I quit.' He tossed the mop back into his room, just missing Tobias Moon as the Hadenman joined them in the corridor. Random looked at the fallen man and smiled unpleasantly. It was an expression his face seemed to fall into easily. 'Good to know I haven't entirely lost my touch. Now let's get out of here before someone comes looking for him. Or us. We can decide where we're going later.' He took a deep breath and let it out. 'Nothing like a little gratuitous violence to stir the blood. I feel almost human again. You'd better have a good reason for disturbing my retirement, Deathstalker. I was happy being nobody. No demands, no responsibilities. You've woken me up, and I won't easily go back to sleep. If I'm going to try for the gold ring one last time, it's going to have to be worth it.'

'Stick with us,' said Owen, 'and you'll have all the action you can handle, and then some. It's us or the Empire now; death or glory. But then, for you I suppose it always is.'

'Something like that,' said Random. 'Something like that.'

Outside the Olympus Health Spa the mists had come down thick and heavy, and the world was grey and silent. Owen looked about him uneasily. Any number of assassins could be hiding out there in the fog. Hopefully they were just as blind and disorientated as he was. Hazel looked left and right and scowled unhappily.

'Don't tell me you're lost,' said Owen. 'That's all we need.'

'It's a long time since I was last here,' said Hazel defensively.

'And the fog isn't helping. Anyway, I thought you had a built-in compass that told you where you were?'

'Oh I know where I am,' said Owen. 'I just don't know where anything else is. I can point due north, if that's any help.'

'Follow me,' said Hazel. 'And stay close. It'd be only too easy to get lost and separated in fog like this, and we haven't the time to send out search parties.'

She moved slowly and carefully away from the spa, one hand held out before her. Owen moved after her, almost treading on her heels. Random followed him, and Moon brought up the rear. The two walls of a narrow alleyway slowly formed out of the mists to either side of them as they walked on, grey and stained and characterless, with no clue as to their location. The only sound was the soft trudging of their feet through the packed snow. Owen tried hard to see the positive side.

'If nothing else,' he said finally, 'it's got to be as hard for our pursuers as it is for us. We could walk right past each other in this fog, and never know it.'

'Unless they're listening to you,' said Hazel. 'Or they've got an esper with them.'

'That's right,' said Owen. 'Cheer me up, why don't you?' He glanced back at the Hadenman. 'How about you, Moon? See anything worth seeing with those amazing eyes of yours?'

'Just fog and more fog,' said Moon, and then he stopped suddenly, and cocked his head slightly to one side. The others stopped too, and looked back at him.

'What is it?' said Owen.

'There's someone out there,' said the augmented man. 'I can hear their feet breaking the snow.'

'Which way?' snapped Owen, drawing his disrupter. 'Give me a direction.'

And then he broke off, as a tall figure formed slowly out of the mists before him. He started to raise his gun, and then lowered it again as he recognized the muscular goddess from the health spa. She walked towards him, smiling seductively, hands open to show they were empty. And then Moon stepped forward, his golden eyes blazing brightly.

'It's a hologram. There's someone behind it.'

Owen's hand snapped up, and he fired his gun. The energy beam ripped through the hologram without harming it, and then the goddess disappeared in a moment as the beam exploded a wall beyond her. Owen caught a brief glimpse of a fleeting figure in the mists, and then an energy beam snapped right past him and he dived for cover, yelling for the others to do the same. Within moments Owen was alone in the mists, crouching beside the nearest wall to make a smaller target. He switched the gun to his left hand and drew his sword. For the next two minutes, both his gun and his opponent's were useless till their energy crystals had recharged, and that brought it down to steel. Unless the bastard had two guns. Or a friend with a gun. Owen cursed silently, and strained his ears against the quiet. The hologram had been a good trick, and he'd very nearly fallen for it. He hadn't expected that kind of high-tech sophistication on Mistworld.

He moved slowly forward, keeping his shoulder pressed against the wall to orientate himself. His boots made soft crunching sounds in the thick snow for all his care, and his back muscles crawled in anticipation of the energy beam or sword thrust he'd probably never even feel. He didn't dare boost, not so soon after the last time. He'd been using it too often just recently, not that he'd had much choice in the matter. There was also no getting away from the fact that he was feeling distinctly fragile from his earlier wounds. His spell in the regeneration machine on the *Sunstrider* had briefly supercharged his healing processes, but there were still limits, and he was fast approaching them. A good night's sleep and a few high protein meals would work wonders, but he couldn't see his pursuers letting up that long. The bastards. It seemed to Owen that he'd done nothing but run and hide since he'd learned of his outlawing, and the thought grated. He glared about him, and the mists looked impassively back.

A heavy form crashed down on to him from above, and he fell sprawling on the snow. He tucked one arm under him and rolled to one side, dislodging his attacker. He scrambled forwards, and a sword stabbed into the snow where he'd been.

Owen lurched to his feet, and found himself facing a medium-height woman wearing black leathers mostly concealed under white furs. No wonder he hadn't spotted her in the mists. The furs provided perfect camouflage. Her face was pale and pointed, with dark steady eyes, and a helmet of short black hair. She held her sword like she knew how to use it, and her slight smile was cool and confident.

He just had time to take that much in and then she was upon him, the point of her sword leaping for his heart. He got his own sword up just in time, and for a moment they stood face to face, steel clashing on steel as they tried out each other's skill. It didn't take Owen long to realize he was facing a master swordswoman, and he was surprised to discover he didn't give a damn. This was at least the kind of fight he preferred; one on one with everything upfront. He was tired of faceless pursuers and attacks from hiding. He wanted an enemy he could hit. His opponent was good, no doubt of it, but he was Deathstalker, and she was going to find out what that meant.

They stamped back and forth on the slippery snow, searching for an opening, hammering their swords together. Owen used all his strength and guile and skill and was still hard pressed to match the fury of his opponent's attack. The temptation to boost was almost overpowering, but he wouldn't do it. Partly because he was worried what it would do to his already weakened system, but mostly because he was damned if he'd escape into boost just to take out a single attacker. He had his pride. He'd never thought of himself as a warrior, but he'd been trained in swordsmanship by some of the finest tutors in the Empire. And besides; he'd done too much running just lately.

He threw himself at his opponent, forcing her back by the sheer strength and speed of his attack, then swept her sword aside and shoulder charged her. The impact drove the breath from her lungs, and threw her backwards. Her feet shot out from under her and she crashed heavily on to the packed snow. Owen was immediately standing over her, one foot stamping down on her wrist to keep her from lifting her sword. She groped for her gun with her other hand, but Owen already had his pointing at her. She lay back, resigned but not defeated, and glared up at him. When she spoke, her voice was cold and unwavering.

'Do it.'

Owen surprised himself by hesitating. It was one thing to kill someone in the heat of battle, but to murder a helpless enemy . . . that was the Empire way, and he was no longer a subject of the Empire. On the other hand, if he didn't kill her, she was almost certainly going to get up and kill him. He was still considering this, while trying very hard to keep it out of his face, when his companions emerged out of the mists to join him, drawn by the sound of fighting. Hazel looked down at the fallen bounty hunter, and shook her head disgustedly.

'Owen; meet Ruby Journey.'

'Of course,' said Owen heavily. 'It would have to be, wouldn't it?'

He took his foot off the bounty hunter's wrist and stepped back to let her rise, still covering her with his disrupter. She rose slowly to her feet, never taking her eyes off him. It occurred to Owen that while she wasn't pretty and never would be, there was still something darkly attractive about her, cold but sensual; like a deadly snake with beautiful markings. The thought surprised him, and he pushed it to one side. He still hadn't decided whether he ought to kill her or not.

'Ruby; what the hell did you think you were doing?' said Hazel. 'Didn't you get any of my messages?'

The bounty hunter shrugged. 'The price was too tempting. Besides; I wanted to see if I could take him. I've never killed a Deathstalker.'

'Well you can forget that now,' said Hazel briskly. 'Join up with us and I promise you all the fighting and loot you can handle. The odds are we'll probably all die horribly, but if we make it we'll have the Empire by the throat. What do you say?'

Ruby looked at Owen. 'What does he say?'

Owen lowered his gun, but didn't put it away. 'I just know I'm going to regret this, but . . . you're an excellent fighter, Ruby; we could use another good fighter.'

'Then I'm in,' said Ruby. 'I never could resist a challenge.'

'How can we trust her?' said Moon.

'We can't,' said Jack Random. 'She's a bounty hunter.'

'And we're all outlaws,' said Hazel. 'Nobody trusts us, either. Anyway, she's my friend and I vouch for her. Anyone have any problems with that?'

Owen had quite a few, but had the sense not to say so. He realized that everyone was looking at him for the final word, and wondered when he'd suddenly become the leader. He shrugged, put his gun away, and smiled at Ruby Journey. 'Welcome to the rebellion.'

They made their way back to the *Sunstrider* easily enough. Between them, Ruby and Hazel knew every back street in the city. And word quickly got around that the Deathstalker was now accompanied by both a Hadenman and the legendary Jack Random, plus the infamous Ruby Journey, so that most of the would-be bounty hunters got a sudden attack of the scruples and decided they weren't really cut out for the work after all. Back on board ship, Owen wasted no time in diving back into the regeneration device, and emerged some time later feeling more like himself again. He showed his new companions round the yacht, enjoying their various reactions to its sybaritic luxuries, and finally got them all settled in the lounge in comfortable chairs, with a glass of something warming in their hands. Hazel had suggested they hole up somewhere in the city, away from prying eyes, but Owen had decided very early on that he had no intentions of sleeping anywhere where the rooms came supplied with hot and cold running fleas.

'All right, Oz,' he said easily. 'We've all had time to let the cold seep out of our bones, so let's have the bad news. What's been happening since I last spoke to you?'

'You wouldn't believe half of it,' said the AI. 'Practically everyone and his brother has tried to break into this ship while you were gone, using everything from computer viruses to a hammer and chisel. I tried reasoning with them and I tried shooting them, but they just kept coming. Finally I persuaded the control tower to station a large presence of the city Watch at the entrances to the landing fields, and that helped. By the way, the port controller asked me to tell you that he would like to have a word with you, and the word he has in mind is Goodbye. Mistport wants us out of here at the earliest possible moment, and if we don't get on with it they'll gather all their espers together and throw us back into space. I'm not entirely sure they're bluffing.'

Owen frowned. 'Any Empire ships in the vicinity?'

'Hard to tell while I'm stuck down here. Nothing obvious on the far sensors, but there could be a small fleet hidden in orbit behind their screens, and the first we'd know of it would be when they opened fire. Next time you choose a yacht, pick something with a little more firepower.'

'Relax,' said Owen. 'You worry too much. This ship can outrun anything the Iron Bitch might send after us.'

'Speed isn't everything, Owen. It takes time to make the calculations that allow us to drop into hyperspace, even for a computer like me, and during that time we might as well have a target painted on our hull. Now then, if you've quite finished with me, I would like to have a word with you and Jack Random.'

Random looked enquiringly at Owen, who shrugged. 'Oz has been finding all kinds of stuff hidden in his memory files, mostly planted there by my father, designed only to appear as and when necessary. Apparently your being here has triggered one.'

'Go ahead, Oz,' said Random. He looked at Owen. 'The last time I heard from your father, I ended up paying postage on it.'

'Yeah,' said Owen. 'That sounds like Dad.'

And then suddenly a hologram of Owen's father was standing before them in the lounge, large as life and twice as confident. A cold hand clutched at Owen's heart. His father looked just as he had the last time Owen had seen him in the flesh, just twenty-four hours before he'd been cut down in the streets as a traitor. It occurred to Owen that he'd never had a chance to say goodbye, and he wondered why that suddenly mattered to him so much. The late Deathstalker looked harried and preoccupied, but his voice was steady and courteous.

'Hello, Jack. Been a while, hasn't it? If you're listening to this then I'm dead, and young Owen has come looking for you. Look out for him; he means well, but he's not a warrior. Spends all his time poring over books and histories. Don't ask me where he gets it from. Not quite what I had in mind for my only son and heir, but hopefully his distance from me will help to protect him if things go wrong. I'd like to think some good came of it. Jack; just because I'm dead, don't let the Cause fall apart. Fight on. I don't want to have died for nothing.

'Owen; if all has gone according to plan, you should have my ring. Guard it well. Concealed in its structure are the coordinates for the planet Shandrakor, where the original Deathstalker, founder of our Clan, fled in disgrace many centuries ago. Know now the great secret of our Family; the Deathstalker is not dead. He lies waiting in stasis, in his Last Standing on Shandrakor, together with a mighty armoury of ancient and forbidden weapons. You must go there and wake him. He knows many secrets, including the location of the Darkvoid Device. With this weapon, lost for so long, your forces will be the equal of anything the Empire can send against you.

'Also hidden in my ring are the coordinates for the planet Haden, lost world of the Hadenmen. An army of augmented men lie waiting there in stasis for you to awaken them, in the Tomb of the Hadenmen. Our Family have had dealings with them in the past. They will respect your name, and will fight for the Cause. How much you trust them is up to you.

'I'm sorry this has all been thrust upon you, Owen. It was never meant that you should have to carry such a weight. But it seems we have a traitor in our midst. One by one all the key figures in the planned rebellion have been singled out and killed. I can only assume my own time is near. I've loaded the AI with everything I thought might prove useful, hidden as deeply as I can. This is the last message; there won't be any more. You're on your own now, Owen. I wish . . . I wish I'd talked with you more. I know you never approved of my intrigues, or the Cause; hopefully by now you will have discovered why I thought it so important, and will have made the Cause your own. Be strong, Owen. Do what you have to.

'I wasn't really such a bad father, was I? I know I wasn't there as often as I might have been, but there was always so much work that needed doing. Never think I didn't love you. You can trust Jack Random. He's a good man. I keep thinking there's something else I should be saying, but I don't know what. Goodbye, Owen. Goodbye.'

The hologram snapped off and Owen's father disappeared, and for a long moment there was only quiet in the lounge. Jack Random sighed heavily.

'Another old comrade gone. I never thought I'd outlive so many friends.'

'Are you all right, Owen?' said Hazel.

'Yes. I'm fine. He's still doing it. Still trying to run my life.' Owen tried to be angry, but for once the anger wouldn't come. 'What really makes me mad is I have no choice but to follow his plans, and take up his precious Cause, whether I believe in it or not, just to survive. He's still pulling the strings of my life, even after he's dead.'

'I always thought the original Deathstalker was dead,' said Hazel. 'I mean, I saw his tomb on the holo once, on Golgotha.'

Owen nodded distractedly. 'According to all the histories he was hunted down and killed by the Shadow Men, nine hundred and forty-three years ago. He was officially pardoned, if not exonerated, some four hundred years later. They even built a monument for him. I wonder whose body they put in the tomb . . . Well; at least now we have a choice of destination. Shandrakor to search for my ancestor, or Haden to raise an army.'

Tobias Moon fixed Owen with his disquieting golden eyes. 'I have waited a long time to rejoin my people.'

'Well you'll have to wait a bit longer,' said Random. 'If there's an armoury on Shandrakor, we need to check it out. Especially if the Darkvoid Device is there.'

'This is my ship,' said Owen. 'I'll decide where we're going.'

'Then get on with it,' said Ruby Journey, trimming her nails with a nasty-looking dagger. 'There are a lot of people looking for you, Deathstalker, and I don't think we should still be here when they arrive.'

'She's got a point,' said Hazel, and Owen nodded.

'We're going to Shandrakor. If my ancestor is there, he and Jack can take over this rebellion, and maybe then I'll be allowed to retire to the background and get a little peace. Oz; power the ship up. We're leaving.'

'Yes, Owen. I have a message from Mistport control tower.'

'Put it on.'

'*Sunstrider*; this is Mistport security,' said a harsh voice. 'You do not, repeat not, have permission to take off. Power down your engines; our people will be boarding you shortly.'

'Don't put money on it,' said Owen. 'Oz; are we ready?'

'Just say the word, Owen.'

'Get us out of here.'

The AI shut off the Mistport channel in mid splutter, and the *Sunstrider* leapt up off the landing pad and into the sky. Several ships started after her, but they were no match for her speed. *Sunstrider* shot beyond the atmosphere and settled into orbit, ready to make her jump through hyperspace. And that was when things really went to hell.

'Ah, Owen,' said the AI, 'we have a problem. Two Imperial starcruisers are heading right for us. They must have already been here in orbit, waiting for us. They're opening fire.'

'Shields up!' yelled Owen. 'I thought we left those bastards behind on Virimonde. What the hell are they doing here?'

'Hitting us with everything they've got,' said Ozymandias dispassionately. 'Shields are holding, but I don't know for how long. They were never designed to take this kind of punishment.'

'Two starcruisers?' said Jack Random. '*Two bloody starcruisers?*'

'They must really want your aristocratic ass,' said Ruby Journey. 'This heap of yours have any weapons?'

'Nothing that'll stop a starcruiser,' said Owen. 'Oz; make the jump. Now.'

'I'm afraid that's not possible, Owen. I'm still working out the exact spacial coordinates. Jump too soon, without everything correct to the last decimal place, and we could end up materializing inside a sun, or something equally unpleasant. Port shield just went down. Brace yourselves.'

The ship shook and alarms shrilled as everyone staggered back and forth. The ship shook again and again, and smoke billowed into the lounge. Bottles fell from the bar and smashed on the floor. Owen clung to a wall bracket and thought frantically what to do next. Somewhere entirely too close he could hear the crackling of a large fire.

'Oz; status report!'

'Bad, and getting worse. Half our shields are down, outer hull penetrated in seventeen places, inner hull breached in three. We're losing air fast.'

'Can't we try and run?'

'If you really want to annoy them. Just hold on, Owen. We'll be gone in a few minutes.'

'We don't have a few minutes! Go now! Make the jump!'

'I really cannot recommend that, Owen. If we jump now, I cannot guarantee a safe arrival.'

'Jump now! That's an order!'

'Yes, Owen. On to Shandrakor, and death or glory!'

The lights flickered and went out. Smoke filled the lounge. The ship lurched heavily as the stern blew apart in an echoing explosion, and then the *Sunstrider* dropped into hyperspace and was gone, on its way to an uncertain destination.

CHAPTER SIX

Under the Ashes, the City

John Silence, once again a Captain in the Imperial Fleet by Her Majesty's pleasure, sat stiffly in the command chair on the bridge of his new ship the *Dauntless*, and tried unsuccessfully to get comfortable. It wasn't that there was anything actually wrong with the chair, it was just so new, like everything else. It didn't give in the right places, or make allowances for his habitual gestures, like the old one had. But that chair was long gone, with the rest of the good ship *Darkwind*. She'd been his ship for many years, and a good ship too. Silence snorted silently. Here he was, with a new ship and a second chance he'd had no right to expect or hope for, and all he could do was find fault. *Well*, thought Silence, *do what you're best at, that's what I always say.*

But he had to admit the *Dauntless* was something special, even if she was still fresh from the stardocks, all sparkling clean and completely untested. If she lived up to even half the claims the engineers made for her, she'd be the fastest, best-gunned ship in the Fleet, and a genuine wonder of the galaxy. She had the new stardrive, more disrupter cannon than any ship before, and force shields powerful enough to survive a dive into a sun. The *Dauntless* was a whole damn Navy in itself, and Silence wasn't blind to the trust the Empress had placed in him by giving him the command. Any other Captain might have been tempted to just take the ship and run for the Rim, to build a small empire of his own, secure in the knowledge it would be years before any similar ships could come after him. But Lionstone had known he wouldn't do that. She had given him back his life and his commission, when she needn't have given him either, because she trusted him, and now he was her man, blood and bone and spirit, until they were both dead and gone to dust.

But until then, he was the new Captain of a very new ship, where nothing could be trusted until it had been thoroughly tested and tried and proved reliable. Fine claims were all very well, but Silence reserved judgement. Engineers had a tendency to over-enthusiasm, especially when it wasn't their butts on the firing line. Besides; Silence knew where the new stardrive had come from. The engineers had derived it from the drive in the alien ship he'd found crashlanded on Unseeli, barely a year ago. Silence supposed it was just possible the stardocks now had a full working knowledge of the alien technology, but just in case he made it a point to know where the nearest escape pod was at any given moment. That was the other side to the Empress's appointing him Captain of the *Dauntless*; if nothing else, he was entirely expendable.

He deliberately put that thought aside, and concentrated on the viewscreen before him. The *Dauntless* had dropped out of hyperspace and taken up an orbit around the planet Grendel some two hours ago, and he still couldn't get any sensible data out of his brand new sensors. The information they were giving him was questionable where it wasn't obscure, and no bloody use to him at all. Practically every question he put to his computers came back *insufficient data*, and the ship's AI was sulking because he'd shouted at it. But he couldn't in good faith put off planetfall much longer. The Empress's orders had been quite explicit. He was to locate and open the Vaults of the Sleepers, and subjugate or destroy whatever creatures he found in them. Nothing new in that; it was the Empire's standard attitude to all aliens. But the aliens on Grendel, or rather buried deep beneath its surface, were different. Vicious, unnatural killing machines, they'd slaughtered the last Empire team to encounter them. Some fool opened a vault, and that was that. Hopefully things would be different this time. Firstly, he had some idea of what he was getting into, and secondly, when he finally got around to opening up a vault, he

227

was going to be backed up by a full company of fifty marines, ten battle espers, and twenty Wampyr.

Which should give him an edge, if nothing else.

Silence was frankly surprised that there were still twenty Wampyr left in the service. Their uses were limited, they were expensive to maintain, they disturbed the hell out of anyone who had to work with them . . . and by now everyone knew all about plasma babies. And that was all he needed on a new ship with a new crew; a new addictive drug to tempt his men. They were probably already building illicit stills, and cooking up new battle drugs in the labs, just to see if they could get away with it under a new Captain. Which was possibly why the Empire had insisted on supplying him with a new security officer; V. Stelmach by name. He hadn't volunteered his first name, and Silence hadn't pressed him in case it was something embarrassing. (Vernon, Valentine . . . Violet?) Big, broad, close-mouthed and entirely humourless, the security officer was never far from the Captain or the Investigator, keeping a watchful eye. Just a little reminder that the two of them still had to prove themselves. Silence did his best not to notice.

He glanced across at Frost, standing rock solid at parade rest beside his chair, her fierce gaze fixed on the view of Grendel before them. He hadn't had much chance to talk to her since Lionstone had pardoned them both. There'd been too much to do getting the ship ready to depart, the nature of their jobs kept them apart, and besides . . . he wasn't sure what he would have said anyway. The Investigator had saved his life, but he didn't know why. Anyone else, he might have made a few educated guesses, but Investigators had none of the softer emotions. Their training saw to that. There were those who said the Investigators were as inhuman as the aliens they studied. That there was no room in them for anything but cold, calculated killing.

In which case, she'd feel right at home on Grendel.

Silence sighed quietly, and gave his full attention to the viewscreen. Grendel filled the screen, a grey featureless ball of ash, hiding secrets. The planet had a surface once, complete with the decaying husks of deserted alien cities and machinery, but all that was gone; lost or destroyed when the Imperial Fleet scorched the planet from orbit, to be sure of destroying the terrible creatures that had boiled out of the Vault of the Sleepers.

Grendel had been under full quarantine ever since, and six starcruisers hung permanently in orbit over the planet, to ensure that nothing and no one got in or out. Silence had thought that something of an over-reaction, but that was before he'd seen the surviving records of the first contact team, and saw how they died. Now he was just grateful the ships were there. Not that they'd actually back him up, even if things went disastrously wrong a second time, but they would ensure that whatever happened, not one alien creature would escape from the planet. Even if they had to scorch it again. Silence shivered briskly, as though someone had just walked over his grave, and put that thought aside too. First things first; check that the quarantine remained secure, for the record. He had his communications officer raise the command ship of the quarantine, and the cold, calm features of Captain Bartek of the *Defiant* filled the viewscreen. Bartek the Butcher. In his time he'd overseen the scorching of three worlds, and put down a dozen rebellions, by whatever means he thought necessary. A personal favourite of the Iron Bitch, and just the kind of man you needed to run a quarantine like this. Try and bribe Bartek, and they'd hand you back your balls on the way out. Silence nodded to him courteously.

'Last contact before we make planetfall, Captain Bartek. Just checking that everything's still secure. For the record.'

Bartek sniffed, and fixed Silence with a cold, unyielding stare. 'For the record, then; quarantine remains unbroken. Not one ship has survived to make planetfall since this operation was set up, and there has been absolutely no trace of alien activity on the planet itself. My orders are to stand by and observe as you send your people down in pinnaces. They will disembark, and the pinnaces will return to the *Dauntless*, where they will be thoroughly inspected by my people. So if you do let loose something you can't control, it will have no means of leaving the planet's surface. Understand me, Captain

Silence; you and all your people are completely expendable. I have been expressly ordered that under no circumstances am I to assist or help you in any way once you have made planetfall. Whatever happens, once you're down there, you're on your own. And in the most extreme case, acting on my judgement alone, I am to destroy the *Dauntless* completely if there seems any risk that she might be . . . contaminated. Have I made myself clear, Captain?'

'Utterly,' said Silence calmly. 'I've seen the records of the first team. Take no chances. Silence out.'

He sensed as much as heard Frost stirring at his side, as Bartek's face disappeared from the viewscreen, replaced by Grendel's enigmatic surface. He turned slightly to look at her.

'Problem, Investigator?'

Frost sniffed. 'Thinks he's so hot. All he's ever done is give orders from the rear. Never killed in hot blood in his life, like as not. Darling of the Academy, but no guts. No real guts.'

'Not to worry, Investigator. We've gone into sticky situations before without any back-up.'

'At least then we didn't have to worry about being shot in the back by our own side.' She flicked a quick glance at the security officer, who was quietly studying the most recent sensor readings at the science console. 'We're not even entirely safe on our own ship. V. Stelmach. Wonder what the V. stands for. Vile, Vicious . . . Vermin?'

'Probably all three,' said Silence easily. 'You could always look it up in the computer records.'

'I already tried that. He's got it under a personal security code. Must be something really embarrassing.'

'Ignore him. We'll do what we have to, same as we've always done. I just hope our luck's better than the last time. Unseeli was bad enough, but Grendel looks as if it could manage something really unpleasant, if it put its mind to it. Shame there weren't any survivors from the first contact team. I would have liked some first-hand impressions of what we might encounter.'

'There was one survivor,' said Frost. 'The Investigator. She failed to spot the dangers.'

'Might have known an Investigator would survive, if anyone could. What happened to her?'

'They sent her to a hellworld.'

'Where she's no bloody use at all. Typical. Still, I'm surprised they didn't execute her.'

'The hellworld will do that.'

Silence decided not to press the point. Frost was clearly touchy about her fellow Investigator. They were all supposed to be perfect, dependable, infallible. It said so in their job description. Just like a Captain was always supposed to know what to do for the best . . . Silence smiled briefly, and leaned back in his command chair. Time to get the show on the road. Starting with a good look from a safe distance at exactly where they'd be landing. The landing site had already been decided, and remote control mechanisms were already busy constructing secure landing pads. Silence called up the view on his private screen, and frowned thoughtfully. Grendel had no solid land masses any more. Only ash. Silence had chosen this particular location because one of the few things his sensors could agree on was that there was a vault there, barely a mile below the surface. Which made it the easiest by far to get at. Remote control mining equipment was currently digging its way down through the ash towards it.

Except it wasn't alone down there. Surrounding the vault for miles in all directions was a city, or what was left of it. There was no trace left of the deserted cities on the surface. The scorching had left nothing but an endless sea of ash, from pole to pole. But under the ash, somehow miraculously untouched by all the destruction, lay the remains of an alien civilization. The first contact team had passed through an underground city to reach their vault. The experience nearly drove them all mad. There was something about the city, something unbearable to the human mind. The sensors couldn't tell much about it, except that it was there, and completely deserted. And right in the middle of that miles-wide city lay the main Vault of the Sleepers; a colossal steel tomb the size of a mountain. Only what slept within that tomb slept very lightly.

Silence had already studied the first team's records of the city they encountered, but they didn't make much sense. They were far from complete, and what there was was decidedly unpleasant. The details were too strange, too alien, too unlike anything Silence had ever encountered before. Even Frost admitted to finding them disturbing, and she had more experience of the alien than everyone else on the *Dauntless* put together. Although some of the people on board were pretty strange in themselves. Silence grimaced briefly at the thought. He ought to check in on his contact team again, now that the drop was getting so close. He raised the marine Sergeant Angelo Null on his private screen, and nodded politely to the broad, faintly scowling face.

'How are your boys doing, Sergeant? Any problems?'

'Nothing I can't handle. They've been thoroughly briefed as to what happened to the last contact crew, so they're not exactly happy about the drop, but at least they know what they're getting into. The triple combat pay brought a smile to their faces, and the new battle drugs should help. The stuff we've been supplied with would make a mad dog killer out of a sainted nun. But I think we'll save that for emergencies. Chemical courage is all very well, but I prefer the real thing. Personally, I put more faith in the state-of-the-art weaponry they've given us. Very tasty. Recharge time is still two minutes minimum, but for sheer power and destructive capability, I've never seen anything like these guns. Gives me a warm, comfortable, secure feeling just looking at them.'

'I'm glad to hear that, Sergeant. But I feel I should remind you that the first contact team were also armed to the gills, and it didn't seem to help them much. So I want all your men armed with shrapnel clusters, concussion grenades, incendiaries and force shields, as well as disrupters. Never mind the expense; I'll take care of all that. You load your men down with as much as they can carry, and still move freely. I'm also authorizing the use of two portable disrupter cannon and a tangle field. Get your people prepped; we'll commence planetfall one hour from now.'

'Understood, Captain.' Sergeant Null hesitated for a

moment. 'Sir . . . we've worked with battle espers before, but . . . Wampyr? Are they really going to be part of the combat team?'

'That's correct, Sergeant. Do you have a problem with that? Perhaps you'd like me to issue garlic and crucifixes to the men?'

'No, sir. No problem, sir.'

'I'm glad to hear it.'

Silence broke the link, and the Sergeant's troubled face disappeared from the screen. Although he hadn't actually come out and said anything, Silence knew what Null meant. The Wampyr weren't exactly battle troops, like the marines or even the espers. They were more like a weapon; you pointed them at the target and then stood well back and let them get on with it. The battle espers weren't that easy to handle either. They were already borderline psychotic, or they wouldn't be able to handle working in a combat situation. You surrounded them with esp-blockers till you needed them, and then let them loose and hoped for the best. Pound for pound they could be more devastating than ranked disrupter cannon, but you couldn't always trust them to stop when you wanted. They weren't used much in contact situations any more, and the fact that the Empress had insisted on them for this mission said a lot about how dangerous it was likely to be. Silence had decided early on to keep them all in stasis until just before the drop. Safer all round for everyone. He just wished he could have done the same with the Wampyr.

He frowned thoughtfully. Officially, they were Stelmach's pets, operating solely under the direct command of the security officer. It was the Wampyr's last chance to prove their usefulness. If they didn't distinguish themselves on this mission, the Wampyr project would be discontinued. That should encourage them to follow orders and not make much trouble, but Silence didn't hope for much more than that. The Wampyr made excellent individual warriors, fast and strong and utterly fearless, but they were no damn good at all at working with other troops. The never-ending thirst that drove them made them fierce fighters, but prone to . . . distraction.

233

Silence sighed. He'd been putting it off as long as he could, but he had to talk to them. He contacted their quarters and waited patiently. They had their own separate territory down below, keeping them apart from the rest of the crew, to the relief of all concerned.

A dead man's face appeared on his private screen. Its flesh was pale and bloodless, and its expression was cold and distant, as though listening to some absorbing song the living could never hear. Beyond the face, the Wampyr living quarters were dark as night. They preferred it that way. Silence cleared his throat, and then wished he hadn't. It made him sound weak.

'This is the Captain. We'll be making planetfall within the hour. Are your people fully briefed and prepared?'

'Yes, Captain. We are most eager to begin.' The Wampyr had their own leader under Stelmach; something to do with alpha dominance. Just another thing the humans didn't understand about the race they'd created. According to the records, this particular Wampyr had been called Ciannan Budd. Once he'd been a living man, with hopes and dreams and human emotions. Then they killed him and filled his veins with synthetic blood, and whatever feelings he had now were no longer anything a human would recognize. Silence's mouth was almost painfully dry, but he forced himself to maintain eye contact.

'Any problems with the blood substitute we've been providing?'

'It nourishes, but it's not the real thing. It doesn't satisfy.'

Something in the flat, peremptory voice made Silence's skin crawl, but he kept it out of his face. 'Stand ready. I'll contact you again just before the drop.'

The Wampyr nodded, and cut off the comm link from his end. Silence sighed quietly, slowly relaxing in his chair. It could have been worse, he supposed. They could have been Hadenmen.

'We can't trust them,' said Frost, almost casually. 'They're not human.'

'People have been saying that about you Investigators for years,' Silence said calmly. 'The Wampyr are a useful tool, in certain situations, and they'll do their duty for the same reason we will; because nothing less than one hundred per cent commitment will get us off Grendel alive. You let me worry about the Wampyr. I want you concentrating on the Sleepers.'

Frost shrugged. 'Show me one, and I'll give it my undivided attention. You keep saying *we*. Are you still determined to join us on this drop?'

'Yes. When we break open the vault, decisions are going to have to be made in a hurry, and I don't want to leave them to Stelmach.'

'Talking about me again?' said Stelmach, appearing soundlessly on Silence's other side, opposite the Investigator. Silence wouldn't give him the satisfaction of jumping.

'Just saying we'd better take one last look at the records the first contact team left us. Ugly viewing, but necessary. Anything we can learn from them could end up saving lives. There's always the chance we'll spot something new. Something useful.'

Stelmach nodded expressionlessly, and the three of them peered silently at the images appearing on Silence's private screen, as he entered the restricted codes. Most of the footage from the first team's cameras was useless. It was fine until the team actually entered the city below the surface, and then just the simple proximity to the alien technology began to interfere with the cameras. They cut in and out, apparently at random, so that what was left was a shifting montage of people, scenes and events. A lot of it was blurred and uncertain, as though things had been happening too quickly for the cameras to keep up with them. Computer enhancement hadn't helped much. A lot of what was on the film was so strange, so different, that the computers had nothing in their records to compare it to. Silence couldn't bring himself to feel unhappy about that. He had a feeling seeing the whole footage, intact and uninterrupted, would have been enough to turn his hair grey.

The record consisted of impressions and brief bursts of detail. It began with glimpses of the alien surroundings, dark and disturbing. The huge buildings had no lights, and strange shadows moved slowly across their surfaces like drifting thoughts as the contact team proceeded. The structures weren't just buildings. Wrapped around them like dreaming snakes, or protruding from walls and windows like so many tumours, were all kinds of alien machinery. Nightmares of twisting, shiny materials that seemed almost alive. There were machines that breathed, and coiled tubes that glistened with sweat. Strange shapes with unblinking eyes, and things that looked like they might have been moving until you got close to them. The contact team moved among the massive buildings like rats caught in a maze they could never hope to understand, and their voices grew high-pitched, and hysterical.

The party's lights glanced across shifting scenes like flashes of lightning in a storm as they shorted in and out, until finally the contact team came to the great steel doors of the Vault of the Sleepers. According to the computers they were twenty-three feet tall and ten feet wide; great featureless slabs of shining steel with no trace of lock mechanisms. The team fussed around with them for some time before losing patience and blasting them open with a portable disrupter cannon. The doors blew back, light flared within the vault, and the Sleepers came boiling out.

Guns flashed desperately, but the aliens were everywhere. Huge creatures, eight to ten feet tall, wrapped in spiked silicon armour that was somehow a part of them. Mouths stuffed with steel teeth, gaping and grinning. Marines fired in all directions. Swinging swords. Shouting and screaming. The aliens darting among them, almost too fast to follow, despite their size. A clawed hand tore a human head from its body, which walked on for several steps before collapsing. Another alien ripped a hole in a marine's belly despite his field armour, and buried its face in his guts. Intermittent light flickered from discharging guns, screams of pain and horror. A face filled the screen, begging and pleading, and then was snatched away. An alien posed for a moment before the camera, wrapped in human entrails. Another thrust its clawed hand into a marine's back and out of his chest, and waved the dying body like a banner. An alien ripped the lower jaw from a marine's face and used it like a club till it shattered. There were aliens running on the walls and on the ceilings, like huge impossible insects. The last marines fell, and the aliens swept past the bodies, heading for the surface. The screen showed light fading away into darkness, and then went blank.

Silence sat watching the blank screen for a moment, and then reached forward and turned it off. The record didn't lose any of its impact, no matter how many times he watched it. Everyone who'd recorded those scenes was dead, their footage preserved by their ship's computers. He still found it hard to believe that the aliens had slaughtered the contact team so effortlessly. But he'd seen swords shatter on the aliens' crimson armour, and disrupter beams ricochet, leaving the aliens unharmed. He was beginning to wonder if anything could stop them, short of another scorching.

And these were the creatures the Empress wanted him to capture and train as shock troops.

'I don't think we'll show this to the troops at their briefing,' said Stelmach. 'It would only upset them.'

'I've already shown it to them,' said Silence. 'It's my experience that informed troops last longer.'

'Then with your permission, Captain, I'll set things in order for the drop. I still have arrangements to make.'

'Do whatever you have to,' said Silence. 'We drop on the hour. If you're not ready by then, you can walk down.'

Stelmach nodded briefly, and left the bridge. Frost sniffed.

'That man needs more fibre in his diet. Are you sure we haven't got any more footage of the first contact?'

'This is all that's viewable. I don't think I could stand much more. I don't think I've ever seen anything as vicious and deadly as those creatures.'

'Damn right,' said Frost, grinning broadly. 'I can't wait to go head to head with them. Been ages since I had a real challenge.'

The trouble is, Silence thought dryly, *I think she means it.*

The surface of Grendel was even more depressing in reality than it had been on the viewscreen. The great sea of ash

237

stretched away in all directions, smooth and featureless and dead. There was more ash in the air, diffusing the pale crimson light of the sun, till it looked like the sky itself was bleeding. The five pinnaces from the *Dauntless* touched down one after the other on the specially constructed steel landing pads floating on the ash, and waited just long enough for the contact team to disembark before taking off again. Captain Silence looked about him, getting the feel of the new gravity. Bit heavier than he was used to, but he could manage. The rebreather built into his uniform's collar surrounded his head with a bubble of fresh air. Even if he could have breathed the vomitous mixture Grendel called air, the ash suspended in it would have blinded and choked him in seconds. He watched the departing pinnaces arrow up through the bloody skies with mixed feelings. Without them, he really was on his own.

He looked back at his team, noting without surprise that it had already split up into its three components of marines, espers and Wampyr. They still all looked to him for orders. As though he had any better idea what to do than they did. Still, when in doubt, sound confident.

'All right; pay attention! There's an elevator to take us down to the buried city, attached to the underside of these rafts, courtesy of the mining equipment. Bad news is it'll only hold fifteen at a time, so the marines will go down first, to check things out. Once they've given the OK, the Investigator will go down with the espers, and then Stelmach and his Wampyr. Weapons in hand, ladies and gentlemen. If it moves and it's not us, shoot it. You don't have to wait for my permission. And watch yourselves, once we get down there. The alien technology can have a somewhat disquieting effect on the human mind. Just concentrate on the mission, and you should be fine. Any problems?'

'Do you want the bad news, or the really bad news?' said Frost.

'Give it to me straight,' said Silence heavily. 'What's gone wrong now?'

'First, we've lost all contact with the *Dauntless*. Something in the city below is interfering with our comm systems. That's a new development since the first team was here. Which means, if we need to leave here in an emergency, we're stuffed. We can't call for help, reinforcements or a pickup. We're stuck here till the pinnaces return at the agreed time. Which is four hours and counting. You might care to consider that the first team lasted a grand total of two hours and seven minutes.'

'And the really bad news?' said Silence, after a moment.

'The mining machinery's broken down. The elevator's still working, but the shaft extends only to the edge of the underground city. That leaves us with at least an hour's walk through the city before we reach the vault.'

Great, thought Silence. *Just great.* The one thing he'd been counting on was being able to avoid long exposure to the city's alien technology, and its effects on the human mind. It also meant that they had that much less time to cope with whatever came out of the vault. Silence thought hard.

'Do we have any idea of why the mining machinery's broken down?'

'No. Telemetry's out, along with the comm systems. The slightly good news is that at least the elevator's still working. For the moment.'

'So that even if it gets us down to the city, there's no guarantee it'll still be working when we want to come back up?'

'You got it.'

'Marvellous. All right; we go ahead with the mission as planned. Unlike the first team, we've got battle espers and esp-blockers on our side. Hopefully one or the other will protect us from the city's influence. If not; we get to find out just how tough we really are. Get the marines moving, Investigator. Time is not on our side.'

The trip down in the elevator turned out to be something of an anti-climax. It was crowded, hot and stuffy, and distinctly claustrophobic, but since everyone was busy considering the horrors to come, nobody really noticed. With the comm systems out, there was no point in waiting for the marines' all clear, so Silence and the Investigator accompanied the first batch of espers down, and hoped for the best.

The city itself seemed quiet and peaceful, but Silence couldn't help thinking of it as the quiet of the graveyard. The marines had already set up a perimeter, with bright lights pushing back the darkness in all directions. They carried their guns at the ready, and looked more than willing to use them at the first opportunity. Frost hummed something cheerful as she set off to inspect the perimeter, and Silence moved the espers off to one side. For the moment he had all three of his esp-blockers working, hoping their field would be strong enough to protect the entire team. But, just in case, he briefed the espers on maintaining a full psionic screen, should it prove necessary. They agreed easily enough, their eyes elsewhere. Silence couldn't blame them. It was all he could do to keep from turning round to stare out into the darkness. Anything could be out there. Anything at all.

The Wampyr waited patiently for orders. Stelmach was too busy looking around him with an open mouth. Apparently seeing the city on a viewscreen was quite a different thing from seeing it up close and personal. He caught Silence looking at him, and closed his mouth with a snap. He barked out orders, and the Wampyr moved unhurriedly to take up a formation around him. Whatever else happened, Stelmach was clearly determined on surviving to tell everyone else about it. Silence smiled crookedly. It wasn't a bad idea, surrounding yourself with a wall of Wampyr. He just wished he'd thought of it first. Frost came back from the perimeter, and he put on his best cool, calm and confident look. Though he didn't know why he bothered. It had never fooled her before. She nodded casually, and moved in close, her voice little more than a murmur.

'Perimeter's secure, for the moment. Nothing on the motion trackers, but the long range sensors are malfunctioning. We have to consider the possibility that all our tech could fall foul of the city's influence. No guns, no force shields, no anything. We could end up going one on one with the Sleepers armed only with our swords and bad intentions. I'm not even going to think about the rebreathers breaking down. Of course, there's always the Wampyr. They're pretty deadly in them-selves, and their strength and speed aren't reliant on tech.

240

Maybe our superiors did know what they were doing when they insisted we include the Wampyr on our team. How are the espers holding up?'

'Hard to tell. They're acting pretty spacey, but that's hardly unusual with battle espers. I'm relying on the esp-blockers to protect them and us for the moment. Let's get the troops moving, Investigator. The less time we spend down here, the better.'

'Spoilsport,' said Frost. 'You never want to do anything fun.'

The marines took the point, guns at the ready, lights blazing on their helmets. The cameras on their shoulders were still working, even though they couldn't transmit live to the *Dauntless*. The only way a record of this expedition would survive would be if someone returned to the surface with it. Frost moved with the marines, eyes alight, just waiting for some enemy stupid enough to start something. Silence came next, with the espers. If only because he wanted to keep an eye on them. They ignored their surroundings, and trudged along with their heads hanging. Whether this was due to the oppressive nature of the city or the numbing effects of the esp-blockers was unclear. Stelmach and his Wampyr brought up the rear. The city didn't seem to bother the Wampyr at all, but presumably when you've already been killed and brought back there's not much left that can upset you. Two of them were carrying a large piece of equipment that Silence hadn't been briefed on. When he'd enquired, he'd received a cold stare and was told he didn't need to know. Apparently it was some secret weapon for Stelmach to try out, if he got the opportunity. Just another secret Silence wasn't party to. He smiled briefly. Damn thing probably wasn't working any more anyway.

They moved on, into the city, and things got worse. The huge buildings and other, less obvious constructions pressed in around them, intimidatingly huge and claustrophobically close. Sometimes enigmatic projections stretched out to block the way, and then they had to be stooped under or climbed over. The surfaces felt slick and unhealthy to the touch. The

241

moving lights hid as much in shadows as they revealed, for which Silence for one was grateful. What he could see was disturbing enough.

The city was a nightmare of steel and flesh; an unnatural combination of breathing metals and silver-wired meat. Rounded cylinders pulsed like gleaming intestines, and pumps beat like hearts, with great shifting valves. Things that might once have been living creatures had been made parts of functioning machines. There were complex devices with eyes and entrails, and long metal limbs tapering away to nothing. Things moved and settled for no reason, and swivelled slowly to follow the contact team as they passed. There were great, slow machines that looked as though they'd been grown as much as made, and small metal scuttling things with bright pinpoint eyes that kept to the shadows. So far, the marines had resisted the temptation to fire at them, but their patience was getting strained. An almost palpable oppression had settled over the party like a dark cloud they could almost see. Everyone could feel the pressure of watching eyes, and something listening to every sound they made. And everywhere it was all slick and smooth and functioning, as though the makers and operators had just stepped out a second ago, and might return at any moment. Silence moved up to walk alongside Frost.

'Remind you of anything?' he said quietly.

'Yeah. The alien ship and the Base it transformed on Unseeli. Biomechanics. A cross between living organic materials and functioning technology; far beyond anything we've ever achieved.'

'Could there be a connection between the Unseeli alien and whatever built this city?'

'It's possible. But the alien ship crashlanded on Unseeli very recently, and these ruins are old. According to the *Dauntless*'s sensors, before they started acting strangely, this city has been down here longer than the human race has been civilized . . . Makes you think, doesn't it?'

Things got worse as they descended slowly towards the vault. The weird constructions closed in around them, enigmatic and disturbing, till the team were forced to walk in single file. The crowding shapes and structures hinted at meaning and function, but never enough to make any sense. The angles and dimensions were wrong, somehow, as though they added up to more than was visible with the naked eye. The marines became twitchy and quarrelsome. Some fired their guns out into the darkness, and couldn't or wouldn't say why. Their personal force shields stopped working, for no apparent reason. Silence tried turning the esp-blockers off, to see if the espers could protect the team better, but they immediately became so hysterical he had to turn the esp-blockers back on, to keep the espers from going insane. Even the Wampyr were affected. They stuck close together, their dead faces cold and intent. Stelmach looked like a bag of nerves, all wide eyes and trembling mouth. Silence had a growing ache between his shoulder-blades from tense muscles, and it seemed to him that his thoughts weren't as clear as they had been. He sometimes lost the track of what he was thinking, and had to concentrate hard to recover it. Even Frost had stopped her cheerful humming. They'd been walking just over three-quarters of an hour, and were deep in the guts of the alien city, when they lost their first man.

A trap door opened up beneath the feet of the leading marine, and as suddenly as that he was gone. He just had time to start a scream, and then he disappeared into the darkness beneath the floor. Silence and Frost pushed their way forward and stood at the edges of the gap. They could hear the marine's scream fading away to nothing, long after they lost sight of the light blinking on his helmet. The marines clustered around the gap in the floor, shining their lights down it, but the light didn't travel far, and the blackness showed them nothing at all.

'Any idea how deep that is?' Silence said finally. 'Could we lower a line, and go after him?'

'The sensors are out,' said Frost dispassionately. 'Nothing on the motion trackers. It could be bottomless, for all we know.'

'Move on,' said Silence, straightening up. A marine glared at him.

'We don't leave our people behind, Captain.'

'You do this time. We've no way of getting to him, in the unlikely event that he is still alive. We're probably going to lose more men, before we get out of here. Get used to the idea. Now move. Since you're so eager, you can take the point.' The marine glared again for a long moment, as though he was going to say something, and then he turned away and started off down the narrow corridor. Silence waved for the marines to follow after him. 'Everyone stay close together, and keep your eyes open. No telling what other booby traps there are here.' He looked across the gap at Frost. 'Are any of our instruments in good enough shape to spot things like this in advance?'

'Not really,' said the Investigator quietly. 'The city . . . confuses them. It's too different. Too alien.'

The team moved on, jumping the gap where necessary, taking things a little more slowly now. They were all remembering what had happened to the first team. There hadn't been any booby traps then. It was as though the city was learning how to defend itself from intruders.

Booby traps struck at them from all sides, sudden and unexpected. Pointed metal spikes shot out of a wall and skewered a passing marine. He hung from the spikes like a butterfly on a pin, and then the spikes retreated into the wall and let his body drop to the floor. The metal spikes made soft sucking noises as they left the marine's body; sinister sounds in the eerie quiet. The contact team pressed cautiously on, leaving the body where it lay. They'd retrieve it on the way back. If all went well. There were sudden bursts of heat and cold, both extreme enough to sear and burn exposed flesh. Once a howling followed them down the narrow way, shrieking in their ears, and then the sound sunk to a tone so low it shuddered in their bones. It did them no harm, so they ignored it. Compartments opened in the walls, full of mystery and strangeness, the sliding panels opening and slamming shut like snapping mouths. Gravity fluctuated from near freefall to a crushing weight that made every move an effort. One of the espers suddenly stopped in his tracks and started giggling. He laughed and laughed his sanity away, until one of the marines took pity on him and shot him in the head. The contact team pressed on. An hour had passed, and they had lost seven marines, one esper, and one Wampyr who hadn't looked where he was walking.

Silence looked at Frost. 'Are you sure this city is deserted?'

The Investigator shrugged. 'As far as our instruments on the ship could tell, there were no life signs anywhere on the planet. Or at least, nothing they recognized as life. And of course, they couldn't penetrate the vaults. Perhaps the city itself is alive . . .'

'And hungry.'

'Not necessarily. It's never wise to impute human motives to an alien consciousness. These incidents might be its way of trying to contact us.'

'Then I hate to think what it's trying to say. Though I think we can safely assume it's not at all friendly.'

'It could be a warning,' said Frost slowly. 'Telling us to go back, before we come to the vault, and what waits within it.'

'You're just full of cheerful information, aren't you?' said Silence. He looked back at the team trailing away behind him. 'Stelmach; get your Wampyr up here. I want them leading the way, now that we're getting closer to the vault.'

'Why?' said Stelmach.

'Well, firstly because they're much harder to kill, and secondly because I'm the Captain, and I said so. Do it.'

'Their reaction speeds are superior to ours,' said Stelmach. 'And they can take much more punishment. But they're worth far too much to expose them to unnecessary risks.'

'Stelmach; they are going to the front. One more word from you, and you can lead the way. Got it?'

The security officer considered the question a moment, and then nodded reluctantly. The team moved slowly on, the Wampyr in the lead. The marines muttered among themselves, not sure whether to feel relieved or insulted. The city moved slowly past them, dark and glittering and possibly aware. And finally, after one hour and seventeen minutes, they came to the vault.

It was huge, monolithic, its gleaming steel walls stretching away in all directions for as far as the lights could penetrate the darkness. The instruments went crazy over it, even those that had been functioning up to then. The Wampyr and the marines hung back, somewhat reluctant to approach the vault now they'd finally reached it. It was too big, too vast for the human mind to comfortably encompass. Silence went up to it, Frost at his side. He reached out to touch the gleaming steel, and then hesitated at the last moment. It was as though there was a cold wind blowing constantly from the wall. He could feel it as a gentle pressure on his face. His reflection in the steel looked vague, distorted, like a ghost of himself, a premonition come back to warn him.

'Set up the force shield,' he said harshly, turning away from the wall. 'Once we've opened this thing up, I don't want anything getting past us and out into the city.'

The marines came forward, and bustled around setting up the force field generator, glad to be doing something they understood. It wasn't much of a generator, put together from parts they'd been carrying in their backpacks, but it would produce a force screen big enough to cover any hole they could hope to make in the vault wall. The last marine finished his task with a little flourish, and pressed the activating stud. A glowing force wall appeared, sealing off the team and their part of the wall from the rest of the city. They just had time to relax a little, and look at each other confidently, and then the generator shorted out and the force field collapsed. Smoke curled up from the generator, and a few of the braver marines batted it aside with their hands as they looked the generator over, trying to figure out what had gone wrong. Frost looked at Silence.

'Great start.'

'Can you fix it?' Silence said to the marines.

'Doesn't actually appear to be anything wrong with it,' came back a quiet, tentative voice. 'I think it's just being too close to the vault that did it. All my instruments are going crazy.

246

The readings don't make any sense at all. But you can forget about the force shield. There's no way we can hope to fix this down here.'

'How about the tangle field? That uses a lot less energy.'

The marines stepped suddenly back from the generator. The solid frame was melting, running away in long shallow streams of plasteel. Silence looked at it numbly. That stuff had a melting point in the thousands. Any heat strong enough to melt the plasteel should have been more than enough to reduce the entire team surrounding it to ashes. Frost stepped forward and prodded one of the melting streams with the tip of her sword. The steel tip steamed, but seemed unharmed. The Investigator pulled back the sword, and sniffed the point tentatively.

'Interesting,' she said finally.

'Anything else you'd like to add?' said Silence, after a moment.

'Not right now,' said Frost. 'I'm going to have to think about this.' She moved away, frowning thoughtfully.

'You do that,' said Silence. He looked back at the marines. 'Set up the disrupter cannon. Make sure you've got a good field of fire for the guns. Now it's more important than ever that nothing gets past us.'

The marines set to work again, assembling the cannon from their packs. Stelmach moved in beside Steel.

'Do you really think they're going to work any better than the generator?'

Silence shrugged. 'Damned if I know. But they'd better, or we've come all this way for nothing. According to the first team's record, it's going to take both of those cannon to make a hole in that wall.'

'We don't know why some things work and some don't,' said Frost, moving back to rejoin them. 'We could lose anything at any time. Our guns, our lights . . .'

Stelmach shuddered suddenly. 'Imagine being trapped down here in the dark.'

Frost shrugged. 'Wouldn't bother me.'

No, thought Silence, *I don't suppose it would, at that. But even an Investigator needs to breathe.* 'Let's not panic ourselves, people. The first team had their difficulties, but it wasn't failing tech that killed them. The Sleepers did that. At least we've got the battle espers and the Wampyr, both of whose strengths are non-tech in origin. Speaking of which; espers, get over here.'

They drifted over to stand before him, dull-eyed and listless. Silence looked at them sternly. 'I'm turning off the esp-blockers. You're no use to me as you are now. Shield your-selves as best you can, but when we open up that wall I want everything you've got trained on whatever comes out. Got it?'

The espers stared at him like children awaiting punishment. One of them looked at him with something like anger in his eyes.

'You should never have brought us here, Captain. We don't belong here, any of us. It's not a human place, with human limitations. There are things out there in the darkness that we dare not look at. If you expose us to them, we'll die.'

'If you don't stop whining and get your act together, I'll kill you,' snapped Silence. 'You're battle espers, dammit. You're supposed to have been trained to handle things like this. Now brace yourselves.'

He gestured to the marines to turn off the esp-blockers, and for a second nothing happened. And then the esper who'd spoken took a deep breath and stepped back a pace, and his head exploded. Silence cried out in disgust and shock as blood and brains spattered his uniform. Another esper began talking swiftly and urgently in a language no one recognized. The remaining espers huddled together as though for comfort, eyes closed, concentrating all the power of their unusual minds to protect themselves. Silence felt something like guilt stirring within him, but pushed it aside. He didn't have time.

'Are you stable now? Can we proceed with the mission?'

The espers nodded slowly in unison. One of them glared at Silence. 'Do it. Do it while you still can. It knows we're here.'

Silence turned to the marines manning the two disrupter cannon. The gleaming solidity and power of the guns reassured him. There was enough power there to blast a hole through a starship's hull.

'Everyone stand clear. On my order, fire both cannon. Now!'

The two guns fired as one, the brilliant energy beams almost blinding in the gloom. Crackling energy played across the steel wall of the vault without damaging it. And then slowly a door opened in the wall, twenty feet high and a dozen wide, swinging reluctantly back as though the sheer pressure of the guns had forced it to reveal itself. The energy beams snapped off, and everyone stared breathlessly at the darkness beyond the door, now half ajar.

Silence's hand tightened round his gun till his knuckles ached, bracing himself for a flood of ravening alien life, but there was nothing, nothing at all. It was very quiet now that the cannon had stopped firing. The only sound was the massed breathing of the expectant contact team. And then a single alien leapt out of the doorway, and tore into the team with an insane fury.

It was huge and awful, but all Silence got was an impression of glistening scarlet armour and jagged steel teeth. It moved among them, fast as thought, ripping and tearing a path through the marines with its teeth and claws, picking marines up and throwing them away as though they were nothing. Everyone was firing their guns, but the alien was never where they aimed. It was huge and fast and deadly and it seemed to be everywhere at once. Disrupter beams blazed across the narrow space, cutting down two marines and one of the Wampyr. And then the battle espers hit the creature with a wave of psychokinetic force, holding it in place through the sheer power of their minds. It looked like a nightmare in spiked blood-red armour, vaguely humanoid in form, its heart-shaped head lacking anything like a human face or expression.

For a moment everyone was still, and then the Wampyr swarmed over the alien, trying to pull it down with their superior strength, but already the hold of the espers was weakening. Without the esp-blockers to protect them, the city was just too much to bear. The alien turned its inhuman head, and beams of crackling energy burst from its mouth and eyes, blowing people apart in sudden horrid explosions. It gestured sharply, and new spikes thrust out of its armour, transfixing the gripping Wampyr, but they wouldn't release their holds. Shrapnel exploded from the blood-red armour, blowing some of the Wampyr away like bloody pincushions.

'Mind-burn the thing!' yelled Silence, but the espers couldn't hear him. Blood was running from their noses and ears and eyes, trickling down their straining faces like crimson tears, and their hold on the alien suddenly vanished. It shook off the remaining Wampyr as though they were nothing. Frost stepped forward, took careful aim with her disrupter, and shot the creature in the head at point blank range. The energy beam ricocheted from the scarlet armour, and glanced off into the darkness, leaving the alien untouched. It took the last surviving Wampyr in both hands, ripped off its head and threw it away, and chewed at the bloody neck like a child with a treat. And then it turned and looked at Silence and Frost standing together, and smiled a bloody smile, like a demon from some cybernetic hell.

Silence glanced quickly about him. All the Wampyr were dead, and Stelmach looked to be in shock. Only two of the espers were still standing, and seven of the marines. Silence felt sick. It didn't seem possible that so many could have been killed so quickly. Frost put away her gun, and pulled an incendiary grenade from her belt. Silence put a restraining hand on her arm.

'Use that grenade at this range, and the backblast'll fry all of us. Plus, there's no guarantee it would even work. That ugly-looking bastard shrugged off energy beams easily enough.'

Frost smiled briefly. 'I was going to make him eat it.'

'Not a bad idea,' said Silence. 'But we've still got one last card to play. Stelmach! Time for that secret weapon of yours!'

The security officer stared at him blankly, his eyes wide with shock. Silence cursed briefly. He started towards Stelmach, and the alien threw aside the Wampyr body it was holding, and came towards him with slow, almost casual steps.

It knew he had nowhere to go. Silence fired his disrupter, aiming for the glowing eyes. The energy beam glanced harmlessly away. Frost hefted her grenade, and lunged forward. The alien slapped her away with a backhand sweep of its overlong arm. She crashed into the steel wall of the vault, and slumped dazed to the floor, the grenade falling unactivated from her hand. Silence gripped his sword fiercely. The alien's smile seemed very wide and very bloody.

And then Stelmach activated his secret weapon, and everything slowed right down. A glowing golden field formed around the alien, and it froze in its tracks, mouth still stretched in a crimson grin. A draining cold surged through Silence's bones, and it took all his strength to move away. His thoughts grew slow and sluggish, and then he had Frost by the arm, and was dragging her clear of the field. After a moment she was able to help him, and the two of them stumbled back to join Stelmach by his quietly humming machine. Life quickly came back to them, and Silence nodded to the security officer.

'I'm glad I brought you along after all. What the hell is that device?'

'Stasis projector; puts anything into stasis, from practically any distance. Eats up power like crazy, but this was pretty much point blank.'

'Correct me if I'm wrong,' said Frost, her voice perhaps just a little shaken, 'but I thought the whole point of a stasis field was that you couldn't project it? You set it up where you need it, and then turn it on or off.'

'Not any more,' said Stelmach.

'And,' said Silence, just a little tetchily, 'how come that projector's working when nothing else is?'

'This little beauty is based on different technology,' said Stelmach. 'The same technology that produced the new stardrive. Need I say more? No, I didn't think so. Apparently this technology is somewhat sturdier than our own. Perhaps even compatible . . . Even so, I recommend we get the alien upstairs and under wraps as quickly as possible. Just in case.'

'Hold on just a minute,' said Silence. 'Why didn't you use

the damn thing the moment the alien appeared, instead of waiting till most of us were dead?'

'Right,' said Frost, dangerously.

'Ah,' said Stelmach. 'Basically, the techs who provided me with this device weren't actually one hundred per cent sure it would work. In fact, they seemed to think there was a small but significant chance that the whole thing could detonate rather dramatically once it was turned on. Which is why I put off using it until I absolutely had to.'

'No wonder they wouldn't tell me what it was,' said Silence. 'If I'd known that, I wouldn't have let it on board my ship. Ah hell; the alien's all yours. Get it out of my sight.'

Stelmach manipulated the controls of his projector, and the alien floated slowly forward, hovering barely an inch above the floor, buoyed up by the stasis field. The security officer moved cautiously forward, steering the alien ahead of him, and the two of them disappeared into the darkness that led back to the surface. Silence gestured for four marines to go after Stelmach and his prize, and then looked around to see how many of his people had survived the alien's attack. He was saddened but not surprised to find he had only two more marines and one esper left in his team. Everyone else was dead, their remains scattered before the opening in the vault wall. He shook his head slowly. So many dead, just to capture one of the creatures . . . The thought took hold of him suddenly, and he took a step towards the door in the wall. This time, Frost grabbed him by the arm.

'Way ahead of you, Captain. Now that the vault's opened, where are all the other Sleepers? There were thousands of the things in the first vault. Even so, I don't think just casually walking into the vault to take a look is a good idea.'

'All right,' said Silence. 'What do you suggest?'

'We've got one esper left. Let him work for his pay.'

Silence and Frost looked at the single surviving esper, and he looked back at them with a bitter resignation. He was tall and slender, with a tired, washed-out look. Colourless blond hair, pale blue eyes and a surprisingly firm mouth. Silence reminded himself that this man had survived, when his fellow espers hadn't.

'You don't have to do this,' he said quietly. 'You've done more than enough already, and I'll see you're mentioned in my report. But we have to know what's going on in that vault, and you're all we've got.'

'I know,' said the esper, in a voice too tired even to be angry. 'In the end, it always comes down to me and my kind, doesn't it?'

He moved towards the vault wall without waiting for an answer, and stopped just inside the doorway. His back straightened with a snap, and a shocked gasp escaped his lips. Silence started after him, and the esper waved him back without looking round.

'I'm all right. I just wasn't prepared for this when I opened my mind. All I can see is space, stretching away in all directions. No life, or trace of life. We got here too late. Whatever happened here, it's over.'

'Any idea of what happened?' said Silence.

'It's too big,' said the esper. 'I feel like a fly crawling across the stained-glass window of a cathedral, and trying to comprehend its function.'

'Whatever happened here, it must have left impressions,' said Frost. 'Go deeper. We have to know. What happened to the other Sleepers?'

The esper groaned loudly, cords of muscle standing out in his neck. 'The violence . . . death and slaughter and more . . . the walls are full of it. There were thousands of the aliens here, too many to count, packed together like insects in a hive. Sleeping. Waiting. Then something broke in and woke them up. Ghost Warriors.'

Silence and Frost looked at each other. Ghost Warriors were human corpses used as weapons, guided by computer implants, controlled by the rogue AIs of Shub.

'The Vault was swarming with them, fighting the aliens, armed with strange weapons I don't recognize. And in the end they pulled the Sleepers down by sheer force of numbers, and dragged them away. They took the damaged Ghost Warriors

253

too, for repairing and recycling later. The Warriors weren't affected by the city because they weren't really here; their controllers were safe back on Shub. Maybe it wouldn't have affected them anyway; the AIs don't think like we do.'

For a long moment the esper didn't say anything. Silence cleared his throat. 'Why did they leave one alien behind?'

'As a surprise, for whoever came after them. The AIs wanted you to know what happened here. They're going to make Ghost Warriors out of the Sleepers, and turn them loose on the Empire. Give me your disrupter, Captain.'

Silence frowned. 'Is there something still in there?'

'Just give me your gun, Captain.'

Silence stepped forward and the esper turned unhurriedly to take the disrupter. Silence caught a glimpse of the vault's interior, and looked away as he stepped back. The esper was right. It was too big. The esper hefted the gun in his hand, as though surprised by the weight. Perhaps he was. Espers weren't usually allowed weapons. He looked at Silence calmly.

'I've seen what Shub has planned for us. It's horrible. I have no wish to see it happen. Goodbye, Captain. It's been . . . interesting. I'd damn you and the Empire to hell, but hell is coming for you anyway.'

And he put the gun to his head, and shot himself. Silence cursed as the body slumped to the floor. He knelt down to pry his disrupter from the esper's hand. 'Damn. That is not going to look good on my report. I should have known better than to give him a gun.'

Frost shrugged. 'Espers. Fragile, all of them.'

Silence straightened up, and holstered his gun. 'Sleeper Ghost Warriors . . . they'd be unstoppable in the field. But why come here now? Are they planning a new offensive? And if so, when and where? We'd better get back to the ship. The Empire has to know about this.'

'Something else to think about,' said Frost. 'How did the Ghost Warriors break through our quarantine? The Captain of the *Defiant* was quite definite that nothing had got past him, let alone landed on Grendel, broken open the vaults and carried away the Sleepers. The only answer that makes sense is that the AIs on Shub have developed some really effective new cloaking technology, powerful enough to blind all our sensors. Which is really bad news for all of us. It means the Ghost Warriors could strike anywhere, anywhen, and the first we'd know of it would be when their attack ships started blasting our cities. We wouldn't even be able to fight back; what use would our energy weapons be without sensors to aim them?'

'If you've quite finished lowering our morale, I've got something else that'll spoil your day,' said Silence. 'We're going to have to check out all the other vaults on Grendel, one by one, to see if they've been opened and emptied by the Ghost Warriors. And you saw what opening up just this one did to us.'

'Join the Fleet and see the universe. We have to be sure, Captain. There's always Stelmach's machine.'

'For as long as it holds up under these conditions. We can't trust anything down here. Anything at all.'

Back on the bridge of the *Dauntless*, Silence sat slumped in his command chair, and tried hard not to fall asleep through sheer weariness. He'd taken a little something to keep him awake and alert, but it was taking a long time kicking in. Frost stood beside his chair, cool and collected as always. She looked as fresh and fit as if she'd just arrived on duty, but then, she always did. That was an Investigator's training for you. The rest of his team were a mess. The few surviving marines were sleeping off sedation down in the med bay, recovering from shock and battle fatigue and exposure to the alien city. Silence felt very much that he would have liked to join them, but there was still work to be done. He had a hundred and twenty marines still on board, but he wasn't about to risk them down in the undercity until he had some idea of how to protect them. The battle espers and the Wampyr were all dead. It bothered him that he didn't care as much about their deaths as he did for the marines'. He shook his head. He had more important things to think about. Like how Stelmach was getting on with examining the captured Sleeper down in the science lab. Silence raised the security officer on his personal screen. The man looked tired and preoccupied.

'Anything you feel like sharing with us yet, Stelmach?'

'Not much. The Sleeper is so different from what we normally consider as life that half my instruments won't work on it. What information I am getting is enough to turn your hair white. One thing is becoming clearer all the time. This is a genetically engineered creature; a living killing machine, the perfect warrior class. Almost literally unbeatable on the physical level. We only beat it by cheating.'

'The Ghost Warriors beat them.'

'Yes, but according to the records, they had weapons and numbers far superior to ours. Shub's always been twenty years ahead of us. If not more. I'll get back to you later, when I've got something more significant to say. Stelmach out.'

His face had only just disappeared from Silence's private screen when the image suddenly cleared, and Silence found himself looking at the stern face of the Imperial Communications Officer on Golgotha. Silence sat up straight in his chair and tried to look alert.

'Captain Silence; you have new orders. These supersede all previous orders. You are to leave Officer Stelmach and his captive with the *Defiant*, and proceed immediately to the planet Shandrakor. The traitor Owen Deathstalker is travelling there, with other enemies of the Empire, including the notorious Jack Random. A spy in their company has provided us with the exact coordinates for Shandrakor. You are to capture these people alive. They have knowledge of the exact location of the Darkvoid Device. You are hereby authorized to take any and all actions necessary to retrieve the Device, and return it to the Empire. After you have the Device, you may execute the outlaws. This information is classified, your eyes only. Message ends.'

His face vanished from the screen. Silence looked at Frost. 'Officially, you didn't hear that.'

'Of course not, Captain. Pity we're leaving Grendel, just as it was getting interesting. Still; the Deathstalker, Random and the Device . . . now that's what I call a mission.'

'The Darkvoid Device,' said Silence. 'I can't believe that nightmare's turned up again, after all these years.'

'We'd better hope it has,' said Frost. 'It's about the only thing I can think of that could take on the AIs on Shub, if they really are turning the Sleepers into Ghost Warriors. Still; Jack Random and the Deathstalker . . . I'll enjoy killing them.'

'I thought you'd like that bit,' Silence said dryly. 'Just remember we have to get our hands on the Device first. Dead men don't share secrets. So; Shandrakor here we come. I always thought that planet was a myth, a legend, like the Wolfling World. Just goes to show.'

'What?'

'Pardon?'

'It just goes to show what?'

'I don't know,' said Silence. 'Something.'

'Very erudite,' said Frost. 'Well, here's one more thing for you to think about. Stelmach seemed pretty sure that the Sleepers were genetically engineered, which suggests rather strongly that they must have been created with a particular purpose in mind. Or at the very least, a particular enemy. What do you suppose could be so dangerous, so deadly, that the Sleepers had to be created to fight it? And is it still out there somewhere, just waiting for us to stumble over it?'

Silence looked at her for a moment. 'I don't know why I keep you around, Investigator. You can be really depressing when you put your mind to it.'

Frost nodded calmly. 'It's a gift.'

CHAPTER SEVEN

A Wedding

It was hot under the lights of the Arena, but then it always was. The Masked Gladiator lay on his back on the bloodied sands, looking up at the angel hovering above him on outstretched wings, and wondered if he was going to die after all. He rolled to one side, grunting with the effort, and the angel's clawed feet missed him by inches as it swooped past. The Masked Gladiator lurched to his feet, sword at the ready once again, and studied the soaring angel dispassionately. Whoever had gengineered the angel had put a lot of thought into it. The wide feathered wings and a touch of psychokinesis enabled it to fly effortlessly, which meant it could attack from all kinds of interesting directions, at incredible speed. The claws on its hands and feet were long and curved, strong enough to tear right through his steel mesh armour, and more than enough to gut him quite efficiently, or rip out his throat in a moment, if he left it undefended. He watched the angel fly, half-silhouetted against the lights of the Arena, and the air was dry and hot as hell itself.

The angel swept back and forth around him, darting in and out, staying always out of reach of his sword. The creature had to be tiring just as fast as he was, but it showed no signs of slowing its attack. It swept in close, the battering air from its widespread wings throwing him to the sands again with brutal force. Somehow he clung on to his sword, and got to one knee again, and then the angel seized him from behind with muscular arms and carried him up into the air. The fierce grip forced the breath from his lungs, but at least his arms were still free. The sands swept by below him with dizzying speed, and he looked away.

He could feel the angel's panting breath right behind him, and he slammed his helmet back into the angel's face with all his strength. He felt as much as heard the angel's nose break, but its hold didn't weaken. The Gladiator wondered hazily what the damned creature intended to do to him, and then he saw looming up before him the pennant hanging from its pointed steel pole, and he knew. All the angel had to do was drop him on the pole at this speed, and it would all be over. And impalement was a slow and nasty way to die. He only had a few seconds. He couldn't cut behind him with his sword with any strength, or reach the arms that held him, so that only left one option. He gritted his teeth, reversed his sword and thrust it deep into his own side, out of his back and on into the guts of the angel behind him.

The angel screamed, and blood coursed down between them. They fell from the air like a stone, and crashed to the unyielding sands. The Gladiator hit first, and the impact drove the sword deeper into the angel. It pushed him away, and he jerked the sword out of both of them. The angel screamed again as they rolled apart, and their blood fell heavily on the sands, but the Gladiator had chosen the location of his wound, and though he was hurt badly, and bleeding like a stuck pig, still he wasn't seriously disabled. It wouldn't kill him for quite a while yet. He blocked out the pain with the ease of long training, and spun on the angel as it lay thrashing on the sands, clutching at its bloody stomach, wings fluttering helplessly. The sword had taken it deep in the guts, and opened up a wide wound when it was jerked free. The Gladiator knelt over it, raised his sword with both hands, and brought it down on the angel's back with all his remaining strength. The sword bit deep, severing the spine, and the angel's movements collapsed into juddering twitches.

The Gladiator looked down at it, his grin hidden behind his featureless steel helm. The angel was no danger to him any more. He cut its head off anyway, just in case. He got shakily to his feet, and held up the head for all to see. The angel's beautiful face was a mask of horror. He turned slowly round in a circle, still blocking off the pain, and the crowd went mad, cheering and shouting and baying their approval. The severed head showed up well on the giant viewscreen above the ranked seating.

The Masked Gladiator bowed courteously to the crowd's roar, and missed a step as his head went suddenly light. Enough playing to the crowd. Time to get the hell out of the Arena while he still could. It wouldn't do his image any good at all if he had to be carried out on a stretcher. He couldn't feel the blood he was losing, but he could see it coursing down his legs. He stomped off towards the nearest gate, rocking dizzily with every step, but still clinging to the angel's severed head. Maybe he'd have it stuffed and mounted.

The crowd cheered him as he went, a tall and lithely muscular man with no crest or insignia on his armour, and an anonymous steel helm hiding his face. A mystery wrapped in an enigma, as always. There were many who would have paid a pretty sum to know just whose face the helm concealed, but there were many more who delighted in his secret, and connived at all levels to preserve it, even from agents of the Empress herself.

The Masked Gladiator strode through the gate, the force field dropping just long enough for him to pass, and then springing up again behind him, invisible and inviolable. He strode on through brightly lit corridors, one hand placed protectively over the wound in his side. He nodded tightly to the fighters and trainers he passed, cool and calm and collected. It wouldn't do for word to get out that he'd been seriously wounded, especially by his own hand, even if it had won him the match. There were any number of vultures who'd attack in a moment if they thought he was weak. The Masked Gladiator had a lot of enemies. Mostly people who'd bet against him. He strode on, grunting at the sudden stabs of pain that were jutting past his control, and his head seemed very far away.

And then the door to his private chambers was right there before him, though he didn't remember getting there. He'd be safe, on the other side of that door. His privacy was ensured by the Arena management, and his own oft-repeated statement that he'd kill anyone who tried to spy on him or otherwise bother him. He hit the security plate with the palm of his free hand, and the door opened as the computer recognized his palmprint. He staggered through the door, and it shut itself behind him. His mentor and trainer, Georg McCrackin, hurried towards him, worry plain in his face. The Gladiator smiled, and threw him the angel's head.

'Hi, honey; I'm home.'

And then the strength went out of his legs, and Georg dropped the head and caught him just before he hit the ground. Things got rather confused after that, and the next clear thought he had came as Georg was helping him out of the regeneration machine. He was still wearing his armour, but the pain in his side and back was gone, along with the injuries. There wouldn't even be any scars. He grunted his approval. Excellent device. Worth every penny of the medium-sized fortune it had cost him. He grinned at Georg McCrackin, who was busy fussing over removing the armour, and looked at himself in the full-length mirror on the wall. He looked pretty damn intimidating, if he said so himself. He stood there quietly a moment, winding down, emerging slowly from the persona of the Masked Gladiator, and letting his other self come to the surface again. And then he took off his helm to reveal the calm face of that most notorious fop, Finlay Campbell.

If his father could have seen him, he'd have had a stroke. The thought never ceased to amuse Finlay. He'd been playing his double role long enough that he took much of it for granted, but that particular wrinkle never failed to raise a smile. He stripped off the last of his armour and let Georg take it away, and then stood nude before the mirror and stretched slowly, as unselfconscious as a cat. Sweat was drying on his chest and arms, and he absently accepted a towel from Georg, and mopped at his body while his mind was elsewhere.

Georg McCrackin had been with him for years, as was his right. He'd been the original Masked Gladiator, before he finally tired of it, and bequeathed the helm and the legend to his pupil and successor. No one ever knew. He mopped at Finlay's back with another towel, a dark and brooding figure muttering quietly about the stupidity of taking needless risks.

'I always feel good after a kill,' Finlay said, almost dreamily. 'It cleans out the system, purging all the dark thoughts and impulses.'

'Just as well,' said Georg dryly. 'If you couldn't quench your thirst for blood in the Arena, no one would be safe. Probably wipe out half the aristocracy in duels. I knew you were a natural-born killer the first time I saw you fight.'

Finlay looked at him. 'Are you telling me you didn't enjoy your time on the sands as the Masked Gladiator?'

'No. But I fought for the challenge; you do it for the thrill. There's a difference. Which is why you'll find it a lot harder to step down than I did. But eventually even your appetite will grow cold, and then it will be your turn to pass on the helm and the legend to another fool with blood in his eyes and a devil in his heart.'

'Maybe,' said Finlay, in a tone that suggested he rather doubted it, but didn't feel like arguing. 'It's all my father's fault, you know. I knew I was born to be a warrior, even as a child. I'd fight anyone at the drop of an insult, no matter how much bigger they were. I won a surprising number of fights, too. I'd have been happy in any branch of the service, fighting the Empress's enemies. But no; I was the eldest, and the heir, and that meant I couldn't be allowed to do anything that might risk my precious skin. I still received excellent training in the use of the sword and the gun, that was part of my heritage and couldn't be denied me, but it was never enough. Not nearly enough. I needed something more to fire my blood, stir my senses, make me feel alive . . .

'I fought my first duel when I was fifteen. Cut the poor bastard to ribbons. It felt so good, so *right*. My father was proud of me, but he yelled at me anyway, for risking my precious neck. He had plans for me, you see. After that, a bodyguard went everywhere with me, and fought my duels on my behalf. You can guess how popular that made me with my peers. I'd never been exactly admired before, but after that I was a pariah. I've a lot to thank my father for.

'It was a long time before I thought of the Arena. I slipped my bodyguard's leash, bribed my way past the Arena staff, and fought my first match under a hologram mask. Nothing fancy, no frills; just sword to sword. And when it was over, and I was alive and he was dead, it was like coming home. After that, I fought in the Arena as often as I could, and then you found me and trained me to take your place. I developed my fop persona to keep anyone from finding out about my little secret. I knew my father would stop me in a moment if he ever found out. After all, if it became public it would be a major scandal; an heir to one of the greatest Houses, fighting all comers in the Arena . . . Dear Father would have an aneurism on the spot.'

'You never told me any of this before,' said Georg. 'I knew most of it, of course. Made it my business to know. But you never wanted to talk about it, so I never pressed the point. What brought this on, all of a sudden?'

Finlay shrugged. 'I don't know. Maybe I just got a taste of my own mortality out there today.'

Georg sniffed. 'About time. Just because you've always won, it doesn't mean you can't lose. You've been getting cocky lately. If there's one thing the Arena teaches us all, it's that it doesn't matter how good you are; there's always someone better.'

'Like who?' challenged Finlay, throwing aside his towel and reaching for his other persona's clothes.

'Well, Kid Death, for one. He's the new SummerIsle now. You keep well clear of him. He's crazy.'

'And that makes him unbeatable?'

'In practice, yes, because he wouldn't care about dying himself if it meant he could take you with him. For once in your life, listen to what I'm telling you. I didn't train you to be the best in the Arena, just to lose you to a genius madman with a sublimated death wish.'

'Point taken.' Finlay sat down on a nearby bench to pull on his knee-length leather boots. 'I have been getting a little obsessed with the fighting, just lately. The Arena feels so clean and uncomplicated, after the endless intrigues and politicking in high society. Every word has a dozen meanings, every statement a dozen levels, and you can't turn around without tripping over a conspirator murmuring in a traitor's ear. Luckily my Family, and everyone else's, considers me a coward as well as a fop, so mostly I get left on the sidelines, as not worth bothering with. There'd be no glory in defeating the likes of me in a duel, and I haven't the wit to be trusted in a conspiracy. I always knew that persona would come in handy. It keeps me out of intrigues, protects my secret, and affords me endless amusement. Ah, life is good, Georg. Though death is more fun.'

'Hang on to that good mood,' said Georg. 'You're going to need it. In case you've forgotten, and you probably have, you asked me to remind you that you have a wedding to attend this afternoon. It sounds pretty important; only for direct members of the Families involved. A distinctly minor noble such as myself wouldn't even get past the door.'

'Now don't get touchy,' Finlay said briskly, putting the finishing touches to his outfit, and regarding himself thoughtfully in the full-length mirror. 'You wouldn't like it anyway. No excitement, no bloodshed; just determinedly polite voices, fattening finger food, and inferior champagnes. It is a rather important occasion, I suppose; if you're interested in such things. A cousin of mine, Robert Campbell, is to marry one Letitia Shreck, and thus bring the two Families together. An arranged marriage, of course, for cold and practical political reasons. The two Clans have been at each other's throats for as long as anyone living can remember, but right now we find ourselves in need of mutual support against common enemies, so all the bloody hatchets are to be buried in a wedding. It'll all end in tears, of course, but no one gives a damn about that. Doesn't matter if they never see each other again, really, as long as they donate sperm and egg to the body banks, and remain officially married. Poor Robert and Letitia. Never even met each other, as far as I know.'

Georg smiled. 'You're going to find it terribly quiet and dull, after today's excitement in the Arena.'

'Not necessarily. There are times when Family gatherings can be more dangerous and loaded with traps than anything you'd find in the Arena.'

Georg shrugged. 'I keep well clear, myself. A minor son of a minor House, too small to be noticed, that's me.'

'If only they knew,' said Finlay, smiling. 'Sooner or later you're going to get tired of being civilized, and the Arena will call you back. You can't fight it; it's in the blood.'

'No,' said Georg. 'I woke up from that nightmare, and found peace. I'm just hanging on here till you do too.'

'Then you're in for a long wait,' Finlay said flatly. 'I couldn't give this up if I wanted to. It's all that keeps me sane.'

Georg raised an eyebrow. 'Given where we are, and what you do, sane is a relative term.'

And then they both looked round sharply as the door swung open behind them. Which should have been impossible. The security system on the door was supposed to be state-of-the-art. Finlay snatched up his sword Morgana, still bloody from the Angel's death, and Georg produced an energy gun from somewhere. A nun walked through the door, all billowing black robes and folded hands, with the hood pulled down low to hide her face. Finlay didn't relax, and Georg didn't lower his gun. The Sisters of Mercy were common enough in the corridors under the Arena, but even so there was no way she should have been able to get past the door. She stopped a respectful distance away, the door swung shut behind her, and for a tense moment everyone held their position. And then the nun raised her slender, aristocratic hands and pushed back her hood, and Georg and Finlay relaxed with almost explosive releases of breath. Finlay put down his sword, and Georg made his gun disappear again.

'Evangeline!' said Finlay, hurrying towards her. 'You promised you wouldn't come here again. It's too dangerous.'

'I know,' said Evangeline Shreck. 'But I couldn't stay away. I had to be with you.'

And then she was suddenly in his arms, and they were

kissing with a passion that heated the small changing room like an oven. Georg looked briefly heavenward, shook his head, and moved off into the adjoining room, to give them a little privacy. Left to themselves, the two lovers clung together like children lost in a storm. Finlay's heart ached in his chest, and he couldn't seem to get his breath. It was always the same when he held her in his arms; he could never really believe that someone so special could care for him as much as he cared for her. The Arena warmed his blood, but Evangeline burned in his heart like a pure, white-hot flame. Her familiar scent filled his head like a drug, but she was real and solid in his arms, her hands digging into his back as though she feared she might be dragged away at any moment. She was his love, his one and only love, and he would have killed for her, died for her, or anything else she might require.

And it might come to that some day, for their secret love was forbidden. He was heir to the Campbells, and she was heir to the Shrecks, two Families at war for generations. The current arranged marriage that afternoon, between two minor cousins of no importance to anyone, had already almost spilled over into bloodshed a dozen times. And for the two heirs to marry; unthinkable. One House would inevitably be engulfed by the other, though not without mass slaughter on both sides. He was Campbell and she was Shreck, and they must be mortal enemies to their death, and beyond.

Except they had met by accident, both wearing masks, not knowing who the other was till it was far too late, and they had both fallen in love. It happened so quickly, but it changed their lives forever. Now they lived for what few brief meetings they could snatch in private, knowing always that were they to be discovered, it would mean shame and probably death for both of them. Some scandals simply could not be allowed.

Finlay held her in his arms, and buried his face in her hair. It smelled so good. She seemed so small and vulnerable, at the mercy of great grinding forces that cared nothing for her, or love. If he could have, he would have walked away and somehow lived with the pain, rather than endanger her, but he couldn't, any more than she could. She was everything he ever dreamed of or hoped for, and losing her would be like tearing out his heart and throwing it away. She nestled against him like a small child, like a frightened animal, her breathing gradually slowing with his.

'You took too big a risk coming here,' he murmured finally in her ear. 'You could have been followed.'

'I wasn't.' She wouldn't look up at him. 'I used an esper to be sure. And who'd recognize me in this outfit? There are always Sisters of Mercy here, caring for the injured and the dying. No one ever remembers the face of a nun. I had to come, Finlay. I heard about the creature they set on you. I had to be sure you were safe.'

'I keep telling you, you've nothing to worry about. I'm the best, love. It wasn't even close today.'

'You keep saying that, but anyone can have a bad day, make a wrong move. I wish . . .'

'I know. But I can't give it up. As much as I need you, I need this too. It's part of what makes me *me*. I couldn't walk away from this, and still be the man you love. Evangeline . . .'

'I know. It's just that I worry so much. I never thought there'd be anyone like you in my life, someone who mattered so much to me. I hate everything that comes between us.'

'Don't.' He pushed her gently away from him, so that he could look into her face. Her dark eyes held him like a fist. 'You're always with me, my love. You're always in my thoughts. I even took your middle name to christen my sword.'

'Thanks a whole lot,' said Evangeline dryly. 'Other lovers get gifts of flowers or jewellery. I get a sword named after me.'

'It's a good sword . . .'

'And that makes all the difference.' A cloud fell across her face, and she pushed herself away from him. 'How's your wife, Finlay?'

He blinked uncertainly. 'Fine, as far as I know. We don't see any more of each other than we have to, these days. She has her life, and I have mine, and as long as we don't actually have to meet each other, we get along great. What brought this on, love? You know I never loved her, or her me. It was an arranged marriage, to consolidate a business deal. I'd divorce

267

her in a minute, if I thought there was any way you and I could be together. Why are you asking me about her now?'

'Because you and I are going to be at the wedding this afternoon. Our presence is required. But what about her; what about Adrienne? Will she be there too?'

'Yes, she will. But knowing dear Adrienne, she'll get stuck into the booze the minute she gets there, and will quite probably be entirely potted before we even get to the ceremony. Don't worry, my love; we'll have our chance to be together, as long as we're careful. Very careful. They must never know about us, Evangeline. I know you hope things will change between the Clans, but they won't. They'd fight a war over us, if they knew.'

'Worse than that,' said Evangeline. 'We'd never see each other again.'

He took her in his arms and stopped her words with his mouth. And then for a long moment they just stood there together, holding each other tightly, so tightly no one would ever be able to tear them apart.

The most mismatched and politically sensitive wedding of the season was held in a ballroom belonging to Clan Wolfe. Given the complicated web of deceit, intrigue and vendetta that connected the Campbells and the Shrecks, it was as near as they could get to neutral ground. Both Families had long-standing arguments with the Wolfes, but they weren't actually openly fighting at the moment. They weren't allies, and probably never would be, but it was a case of better the minor enemy you know than the friend who might turn on you. So the Wolfes hosted, for an extortionate price, and the Campbells and the Shrecks promised to be on their best behaviour. The Wolfes posted extra guards, just in case.

Both Families brought with them a small army of guards, protectors and back-watchers, along with a not so small army of cousins, sycophants and hangers-on. In high society, the size of one's entourage in public was vitally important. It showed one's wealth and importance and position, not to mention one's strength. It wouldn't do for one's enemy to get the idea one couldn't command loyalty among one's retainers. It wouldn't be . . . healthy. Besides; all the Families loved a show.

The ballroom itself was large and ostentatious, decorated on walls and floor and ceiling to the point of overkill. This was nothing unusual. There were pillars of silver and gold, draped with delicate strands of ivy carved from jade, and the floor was a single huge mosaic of major Wolfe ancestors and triumphs, composed of simple slabs of marble exactly an inch wide. One square inch being all most people could have afforded. The walls displayed ever-changing hologram scenes, chosen at random by the House computers from whatever exterior views were currently considered interesting or fashionable. The ceiling was a holo of the night sky, with stars scattered thickly like diamonds on black velvet. Few of the guests noticed. They were more interested in watching each other.

Finlay Campbell was there with his wife, as required. Neither of them was particularly happy about it. They'd had a blazing row on their wedding day, and things had gone rapidly downhill ever since. They'd only agreed to the arranged marriage under the greatest of pressures, and a few not terribly discreet threats. They would have had each other assassinated long ago, if they could only figure out how to get away with it, but the Imperial espers had taken all the fun out of inter-Family murder. So the marriage continued, under protest.

In the meantime, they kept as far apart as possible, and met only on formal occasions that demanded their presence. Like this one. The only thing they had in common was their two children, five and six years old respectively, and already holy terrors by all accounts. The product of laboratory conceptions and births, they spent their early years under Family-approved nannies, and were currently attending Family-approved boarding schools. Strong Clan loyalty was made, not born, and the Family believed in starting early. They also didn't want to risk any interference from the parents.

Finlay often thought wistfully of his son and daughter. He enjoyed their company, when he could, and had a feeling he might have made a good father for them, given the chance.

But as in so many other things these days, it was Not Allowed. Finlay sighed, quietly, and looked around him, hoping for diversion if not inspiration. He himself was the height of fashion, as always, from his shocking pink cutaway frock coat to his fluorescent face and shoulder-length metallicized hair of burning bronze. His cravat was midnight-blue silk, fashionably badly tied to show one did it oneself, his velvet cap was jet black with a single peacock's feather, and he regarded the scene through a pair of jewelled pince-nez spectacles he didn't need, but added just the right touch. He also carried a sword on his hip, as custom required, but though the hilt and scabbard were crusted with precious stones, only Finlay knew the blade in the scabbard was perfectly serviceable, and not in the least ornamental.

The wedding was due to take place in half an hour, and the ballroom was crowded. Bright colours shouted at the eye every way Finlay looked, interrupted here and there by the flickering holograms of those who couldn't attend in person. Most Family members were scattered across the Empire on Clan business, but they attended the wedding in spirit to show their solidarity, and catch up on the latest gossip. One voice still rose above the general din, and without looking round Finlay knew it had to be his wife, Adrienne. She had one of those laser beam voices, that can cut through anything. Not for the first time, Finlay thought if the Family could just find some way of harnessing it as a weapon, they'd make a fortune. He turned slowly, resignedly, and sure enough there was Adrienne, holding court before a group of minor nobles' wives, who looked like they'd rather be somewhere else. Anywhere else.

Adrienne was of average height and just a little more than average weight, but made her presence known by being the loudest, both visually and audibly, person in any gathering. She wore a long black gown, partly because she thought the colour suited her pale skin, but mostly because that way she could claim to be in mourning for her marriage. It was as far off the shoulder as she could get it without actually having it fall around her knees, and it was split up the sides as far as her hips. It looked like one good sneeze, and it would fall off.

She had a sharp face, all planes and angles and angry scarlet mouth. Her eyes were narrow and perhaps just a little too close together, and she had the smallest most up-turned nose that money could buy. She had a mop of curly hair, shining bright gold like a distress beacon. Her movements were sudden and abrupt, like a striking bird, and she treated each conversation as an enemy to be dominated and brought to heel. It was possible she might have heard of tact somewhere, but if she had, she'd never been seen to bother with it. If she'd been a man, her mouth would have bought her a hundred duels. As it was, there were those who suggested a proper definition of the term 'man' would automatically include Adrienne Campbell.

She had a large drink in her hand, from which she took large gulps in between hectoring her audience, and god help the servants if they weren't there to refill her glass when she needed it. She looked about the magnificent ballroom and shook her head disgustedly.

'God, this place is a dump. I've seen livelier funerals, and better catered. I'd pour this wine down the toilet, but I'd swear someone already beat me to it. And would you look at the groom? I've seen men being prematurely buried who looked happier than he does. And the bride; she's a child! Probably have to give her wedding night a miss so she can finish her homework. I take it someone has taken her to one side and filled her in on the facts of life? Like one, always use a contraceptive, and two, always get it in writing and preferably witnessed. Look at her; poor thing looks as confused as a blind lesbian in a fish market. Still, a good lay should put some colour in her cheeks. Not that she'll necessarily get one from that long drink of tap water she's marrying.'

Adrienne went on like that for some time, pausing only when she absolutely had to, to breathe or drink or glare at someone who didn't look like they were listening to her intently enough. Finlay watched admiringly, from a distance. He appreciated a good performance, and Adrienne was certainly on form this afternoon. Mind you, after enduring several

271

years of such verbal battery at close range, he'd acquired a certain immunity. Others were not so fortunate. More than one of the ladies in Adrienne's current audience looked as though they were thinking wistfully how easy it would be to drop something really unpleasant but not necessarily actually fatal in Adrienne's drink when she wasn't looking.

Finlay completely understood the impulse. Adrienne's voice had the carrying quality of an airstrike, and was usually about as welcome. People arranging parties and other social gatherings had been known to get extremely inventive when it came to producing reasons why Adrienne shouldn't attend; everything from outbreaks of plague to social unrest, but it didn't make any difference. Adrienne turned up anyway. As a Campbell by marriage, she couldn't be excluded, and she had very thick skin. And it had to be said, the more attention they paid to her, the less they paid to Finlay Campbell. Which wasn't always a bad thing.

He gazed about the crowded ballroom, packed with all the bright flowers of the aristocracy, going through the familiar ritual dances of intrigue and seduction, politics and gossip. Everywhere there were brightly shining fluorescent faces under gleaming metallic hair, and clothes cut to the extremes of fashionable taste. They struck Finlay as so many chattering birds of paradise, or prettily painted toys with hidden sharp edges. There was no depth in them, no passion or commitment to anything but the pleasure of the moment. They were only saved from outright decadence by their short attention spans and inbred laziness. True debauchery was hard work, and most just couldn't be bothered. Finlay despised them all. They knew nothing of courage, or the true extremes of life and death, except in their carefully orchestrated Code Duello, where honour was often satisfied with first blood. Finlay watched them all with an empty smile on his face, and contempt in his heart.

He looked desperately about him in search of diversion, and his gaze lighted on the Wolfes. The Wolfe himself was absent, along with his new wife; a courtesy, so that whatever happened they could officially ignore any behaviour that might threaten the neutrality of the occasion. But Valentine, Stephanie and Daniel were there, looking as though they'd much rather be somewhere else. Finlay smiled slightly. Of course; all three of them had arranged marriages of their own coming up in the very near future. Presumably their father had insisted they attend, to gain a few pointers on the terrible fate that awaited them. Stephanie and Daniel were standing together, ostentatiously ignoring their respective fiancés, who were currently chatting amiably together, and getting on like a house on fire. Valentine stood alone, as always, tall and slender and darkly delicate, wearing a plum-coloured coat and leggings. With his long dark curly hair and painted face, he looked like nothing so much as a rich but bruised fruit from some unhealthy tree. Beyond the mascaraed eyes and wide crimson smile, his face seemed polite but partly absent, as though his thoughts were somewhere else. Finlay didn't like to think where that might be. Valentine had no wine glass in his hand, presumably because there wasn't a wine in the room potent enough to jolt his jaded appetites.

Finlay decided he'd better find someone to talk to, before someone really boring settled on him, and the Wolfes looked as interesting as any. Besides; Valentine intrigued him. They'd both attended the same school at the same time, but that was pretty much all they had in common, then and now. As far as Finlay could remember, Valentine had been a normal enough child, with no hint or warnings of what he was to become. But then, that was probably true of him too. He strode casually over to the Wolfes, as though he just happened to be drifting in their direction, nodding and smiling to those he passed, every movement the epitome of grace. It wasn't difficult. One of the first things he'd learned in the Arena was how to control his every movement. He noted the admiring glances as he passed, and felt only the satisfaction of a good disguise. He was the height of fashion; a brilliant mirror in which people saw only what they expected to see.

He stopped before Valentine, and bowed with a flourish. The Wolfe heir nodded courteously in return, the heavy black eye make-up and scarlet mouth standing out starkly against his pale skin. That particular look hadn't been fashionable in years, but having found something that appealed to his inner nature, Valentine was apparently loath to change it. Finlay wondered with a sudden flash of insight whether the painted face might be as much a mask as the one he wore. And if so, what other, stranger, Valentine might lie behind it. A disturbing thought. Whatever lay behind the mask, it would have to be pretty damned strange to outdo his everyday persona. Finlay smiled dazzlingly.

'You're looking very yourself, Valentine. I must say, I'm always surprised to see you actually up and about, these days. Of course, if you were taking half the things you're supposed to be taking, I'd expect you to be wheeled in on a stretcher with a drip in your arm and tubes up your nose.'

'I try to maintain a careful balance between my inner and outer worlds,' said Valentine easily. 'I see my condition as a continuing work of art, with drugs the colours of my palette. And every work of art must be seen by an audience to be truly appreciated. Not that most people understand or appreciate the effort and hard work involved in an ongoing performance.'

'I do understand,' said Finlay. 'No one appreciates the sheer effort involved in being at the cutting edge of fashion. But you seem to be thriving on the pressure, Valentine. Perhaps you could give me the name of your chemist.'

Valentine studied him silently for a moment, his face entirely expressionless, and Finlay wondered what he'd said. Something had thrown the Wolfe heir off balance. Finlay decided to change the subject, whatever it was, rather than have it pursue some end he wasn't sure he wanted to reach.

'I understand your wedding is scheduled to take place soon, Valentine. Any help I can offer; having been through the ghastly business myself?'

'Why thank you, Finlay, but I think I have everything under control. The flowers have been ordered, the bridesmaids chosen, and I have designed a rather special fruit punch for the occasion that should open a few eyes. I myself shall be wearing white, with a veil, and perhaps just a dash of belladonna for scent. I've taken care to inform my intended of this, so that our outfits won't clash.'

'I'm sure she was very appreciative of that,' said Finlay dryly.

'The last I'd heard,' said Valentine, 'she was offering quite a handsome reward for anyone willing to assassinate me, and if that doesn't work out, I understand she has professed a complete willingness and determination to do the job herself, with whatever weapons happen to be at hand on the wedding day. She's currently trying to stir up a vendetta between her Family and mine, but since her parents helped arrange the match in the first place, due to the rather large dowry that comes with me, she's not getting very far.'

'She sounds very . . . resolute.'

'Oh yes. I do so admire a woman with spirit.'

'You must introduce me to her, Valentine. Some day.'

'No sooner said than done. Here comes the lady now. Doesn't she look splendid?'

Finlay looked round sharply. A tall gangling woman in her late twenties was advancing on them, wearing a bright scarlet gown with gold and silver trimmings, to show off her perfect pale skin and naturally red hair. Finlay had to wonder if perhaps the fashion for fluorescent skin and metallicized hair was over. Things changed so fast nowadays. The young lady slowed to a halt before him and Valentine, quivering with suppressed emotion, her eyebrows sunk in a truly ferocious scowl. Her mouth was an angry straight line that spoke of barely controlled rage. Finlay found his hand had dropped automatically to the sword on his hip. His instincts knew a genuine threat when they saw one. He bowed politely, and she shot him a look of undisguised venom. Finlay felt a sudden urge to check how far he was from the nearest exit. She had the look of someone who threw things. Heavy things. Valentine seemed entirely unperturbed, and smiled courteously.

'Finlay Campbell, may I present Beatrice Cristiana, soon to be my bride.'

'Eat shit and die, clown,' said Beatrice. 'And you can put that hand away because I have absolutely no intention of shaking it. I'd rather french kiss a leper than touch any part of you. With all the drugs boiling through what's left of your system, even your sweat's probably addictive. I received your latest communication; I think the veil is an excellent idea. May I also suggest a muzzle and a chastity belt, because you're not getting anywhere near me. I personally will be wearing a decontamination suit, and carrying an electric cattle prod instead of a bouquet.'

'I really must introduce you to my wife,' said Finlay.

'Isn't she wonderful?' said Valentine happily. 'I do like a woman with spunk. We were made for each other, Beatrice. Just think what our children will be like.'

'You have a better chance of winning the church's annual sobriety and good citizenship award than you have of fathering a child on me, Valentine. I do not believe in laboratory fertilizations, and if you ever bring your disgusting parts anywhere near me I will cram them into a blender. This is a political marriage only, Valentine. And now, if you'll excuse me, I'm going to go and find something really fragile and expensive that I can throw at a wall.' She shot a brief glance at Finlay. 'Do you have any idea what you look like? And I'd wipe that expression off your face, Finlay Campbell, if I were you, or the wind might change and you'll be stuck that way.'

And she stomped off, disappearing back into the crowd, which kept trying to get out of her way, but just weren't fast enough on their feet. Finlay realized he was holding his breath, and let it out in a long sigh. He looked at Valentine, entirely lost for words, but the Wolfe heir seemed entirely unperturbed. He flicked an invisible fleck of dust from his cuff, and smiled at Finlay.

'She'll come to appreciate my little ways. Eventually.'

Not too far away, Evangeline Shreck, tall, slender and positively waif-like in an off-the-shoulder gown, watched her beloved Finlay talking with the notorious Valentine Wolfe, and felt an almost overpowering urge to rush over and rescue him. Or at least protect him. Valentine looked to her like nothing more than a corpse in a carnival mask, a Harlequin in heat, all that was sick and corrupt in current society. But she

276

couldn't even go near Finlay without good cause. Even allowing for the imminent marriage that was to link the Campbells with the Shrecks, there was still much bad feeling between the two Houses. It was a miracle no one had thrown down a formal challenge yet. It would look odd at best, and suspicious at worst, if she were to just walk up to Finlay and start chatting with him. Officially, they'd only ever met in passing, on occasions like this. People would raise their eyebrows and make comments. They might even ask questions. Evangeline forced herself to look away, and there was her father, standing beside her. She composed herself quickly, and hoped her small involuntary start would be taken for surprise, rather than guilt.

Lord Gregor Shreck smiled at her fondly, and patted her on the arm with his chubby hand. The Shreck was a short, round butterball of a man, all bulging flesh and deepset eyes, with a constant, quietly unnerving smile. It amused him to indulge himself, and he cared nothing for fashion, which in turn cared nothing for him. He was not a sociable man, and as a rule avoided all gatherings he wasn't absolutely obliged to attend. He had never been popular or courted, despite his high station and prestigious connections, and he didn't give a damn. He had other, private, concerns.

'Can I get you a drink, my dear?' he said kindly. 'Something to eat, perhaps? You know how it worries me when you don't eat.'

'I'm sure, Father, thank you. I don't want anything.'

The Shreck shook his head unhappily. 'You must keep your strength up, my dear, or you'll waste away to skin and bone. You want to look nice for your papa, don't you?'

The hand on her arm closed warningly tight, and she made herself smile and nod. It wasn't wise to make him angry. For all his surface jollity, the Shreck had a foul temper, and nasty, inventive malice. So she let him fuss over her, and tried to remain as remote as she could without antagonizing him. It was a tightrope she'd got used to walking, but it never got any easier. The Shreck looked around him at the noisily chattering crowd, and scowled.

'Look at them; happy as the day is long, and not a brain

between them. Eating my food and drinking my wine, and my poor niece is still a brainburned savage, a maid to the Iron Bitch. They're happy enough to stuff their faces at my expense, but not one of them would agree to support me in trying to get my niece back, no matter how I pleaded. They don't know how special to me she was, just like you, Evangeline. But I'll get her back somehow, and have my revenge on those who refused me.'

And as quickly as that, the clouds left his pudgy face, and he let go of her arm. It throbbed dully, aching from the fierce grip, but she didn't dare rub at it. It wasn't wise to distract him, when he was in one of his good moods.

'Still,' he said, beaming widely, 'I expect great things of this wedding. Dear Letitia makes a lovely bride, and Robert Campbell is supposed to be a fine, upstanding young man. I've never had much time for the Campbells, any of them, but it must be said they have good connections with interesting and important people. And with our two Houses united by this marriage, those connections should drop right into my lap. In return, all we have to do is watch their backs, and protect them from unexpected attacks, while they jockey for position over the mass-production contracts for the new stardrive. Some of whose revenues will undoubtedly end up flowing in my direction. Things are looking up, Evangeline. Soon I'll be able to give you all the splendid presents I always wanted to. You've been very patient with me, listening to all my promises, and never complaining, but once our ship comes in you shall want for nothing, my dear, nothing at all. And all I ask in return is that you love me. Is that so much to ask?'

'No, Father.'

'Is it?'

'No, Father,' said Evangeline steadily. 'You know I honour you as my father, and show you all duty. My heart belongs to you.'

Gregor Shreck smiled at her fondly. 'You look more like your dear mother every day.'

Evangeline was still trying to come up with a safe and neutral answer to that one when they were joined by James

Kassar, the Vicar of the Church of Christ the Warrior. Tall and muscular and positively radiating physical superiority, the Vicar looked very smart in his jet black military surplice, and didn't he know it. The Empress had given the Church her official support when she ascended to the Iron Throne, and the Church in return supported her with all its vast political power. It had followers throughout the Empire, and was now the nearest thing the Empire had to an official Church. It named her Warden of the Stations of the Cross, Soldier of All Souls, and Defender of the Faith, and put its military training schools at her disposal. In practice this meant the Church of Christ the Warrior had supplanted all other religions, in public at least, and its influence reached everywhere. The Empress excused the Church all taxes, allowed it to tithe its people as it wished, and used its Jesuit elite commandos to stamp out traitors in her name. So no one argued with the Church much. In public.

James Kassar was a rising name in the Church. He distinguished himself as a marine for several years, stamping out the Empire's enemies with unyielding determination, whatever the cost. He rose rapidly to Major, and then heard the call and transferred to the Church, where he turned his zeal to locating and persecuting all those who opposed the one true Church. And if in his enthusiasm he sometimes strayed outside the law, or wiped out a few innocent bystanders along with the true targets, well, you can't make omelettes, and all that. He was a rising star, so no one said anything. Or at least, no one who mattered. It was a great honour for the Campbells and the Shrecks that he had agreed to officiate at this wedding, and he made sure everyone knew it. Lord Gregor bowed courteously to him, and Evangeline bobbed a curtsey.

'Good of you to honour us with your presence, Your Grace,' said Gregor smoothly. 'I trust all is to your satisfaction?'

'Then you trust wrong,' said the Vicar sharply. 'Never seen so many degenerates and parasites in one room before. A spell in the services would put some backbone into them. Doubt half of them have seen the inside of a church since they were christened. Or could recite the Catechism of the Warrior, if pressed. But as long as the aristocracy still cuddles up to the Empress, long may she reign, they can afford to cock a snook at the Church. But that won't last for ever.'

'Quite,' said the Shreck. 'May I offer you a glass of something?'

'Never touch the stuff. The body is a temple, and not to be defiled with noxious substances. I assume all the details for this wedding have been thoroughly checked out, Shreck? I have other engagements following this, and if I have to change my schedule, someone's going to suffer for it and it isn't going to be me.'

And that was when the wild-eyed zealot appeared with a crack of thunder in the middle of the ballroom as though from nowhere. He wore only a ragged loincloth, and his bare skin was criss-crossed with old and recent scars. He wore a crown of thorns upon his brow, and blood ran down his face in sudden little rushes as his features moved. He had a starved aesthetic look, and his eyes gleamed with the fire of the true fanatic and visionary. The stunned crowd started to react to his appearance, and then fell silent again as flames leapt up from nowhere, licking around the zealot without consuming him. He glared about him, and people shrank back, but when he spoke his voice was surprisingly calm and even.

'I am here to protest against the continuing slavery of espers and clones! I protest against the desecration of the one true Church of Christ the Redeemer! Christ was a man of peace and love, but if he were here now to see what you do in his name he would turn his face away from us in despair. I do not fear your guards or interrogators; I have dedicated my life to the Lord, and I give it up now as a sign to you that espers and clones have a strength and faith of their own, and will not be denied!' He paused then, looked around him, and smiled slightly. 'See you all in hell.'

His body burst into flames, bright and searingly hot. Those nearest him fell back from the terrible heat, but in the heart of the flames the zealot's smile never wavered, even as the fire consumed him. It was all over in a moment, and the flames and the heat died down to nothing. All that remained was a greasy stain on the floor, and a few ashes floating on the air, and one discarded hand that had somehow fallen outside the devouring flames. It lay on the ballroom floor like a single pale flower, fingers outstretched as though in one last appeal for reason.

'Esper scum,' said the Vicar James Kassar. 'Saved us the trouble of executing him. Pyrokinetic, obviously, but how did he get in here? I was assured this ballroom was protected by esp-blockers.'

'So it is,' said Valentine, stepping forward. 'I am not entirely certain what has happened, but as senior Wolfe present, I can assure you that my security people are investigating the breach even as we speak.'

'That's not good enough, Wolfe,' snapped Kassar, studying Valentine with undisguised contempt and disgust. 'Whether he teleported in or was smuggled in, he must have had inside help. Which means you have a traitor here, Wolfe. I'll detail a company of my men to help find him. They've had a lot of experience in finding traitors.'

'Thank you,' said Valentine, 'but that won't be necessary. My people are quite capable of doing all that's required without disturbing my guests.'

It took the wide-eyed guests a moment to realize that Valentine had just refused the Vicar permission to bring his hard men in. This wasn't exactly unknown, but it was pretty damn rare. You upset the Church at peril of your soul and your body, these days. And James Kassar in particular wasn't used to being defied. His face reddened, and he stepped forward to glare right into Valentine's mascaraed eyes.

'Don't cross me, boy! I shed no tears for one more dead esper, but I have no tolerance for traitors, no matter where they may be found. And high station is no protection against the will of the Lord.'

'How very reassuring,' said Valentine, and said nothing more. The moment lengthened and the tension grew. The Vicar scowled at Valentine.

'You look like a degenerate. Wipe that paint off your face.'

Everyone stared at the two men, breathless at the spectacle

of two legendary wills clashing. And then Valentine took one more step forward, so that his face was right before Kassar's. His crimson smile widened, and his dark eyes didn't waver at all.

'Lick it off.'

Kassar looked at him, his mouth a tight white line. His hand hovered over his sword, but he didn't draw it. If he did, and killed the Wolfe heir in his own home, he would be committing the Church to full vendetta against Clan Wolfe. Rich and influential as it was, the Wolfes couldn't hope to stand against the full might of the Church for long, but . . . if the Wolfes did somehow win the contract for the new stardrive, and the Church had to come cap in hand to Clan Wolfe for the new starships . . . Kassar turned his back on Valentine and walked away, and everyone started breathing again. Valentine smiled at Gregor and Evangeline.

'My apologies for the unwelcome intrusion. My people will take care of it.'

The Shreck sniffed. 'Damn esper filth. If he hadn't killed himself I'd have had him shot. We're too soft on espers. You can't trust them.'

'They're still people, Father,' said Evangeline softly. 'Like clones.'

'Better not let the Vicar hear you say that,' said Valentine easily. 'The position on espers and clones is quite clear. They exist only as the result of scientific progress, and are therefore property. The Church won't even admit they have souls. Now, if you'll excuse me . . .'

He bowed low, and turned and walked away. A murmur of quiet congratulations surrounded him as he moved through the crowd. The Church had been putting pressure on all the Families just recently over tithes, and was not as popular as it might have been among the aristocracy. Gregor waited until Valentine was safely out of earshot, and then grabbed Evangeline by the arm again, squeezing hard till the pain made her gasp.

'Never do that again. You must never draw attention to yourself with such views on espers or clones. Neither of us could afford an investigation into your background. No one must ever find out about you.'

He gave her arm one last shake and then released her and stalked away, his face an angry red. People hurried to get out of his way. Evangeline put her hand to her aching arm, alone in the middle of the crowd, but then she always was. Evangeline was a clone, grown secretly by her father to replace the original Evangeline, who died in an accident. His eldest daughter had been his favourite, and he couldn't bear to live without her. And since no one had seen her die but him, he used a great deal of money and influence, and had his dead daughter cloned. He taught her everything she needed to know, and then cautiously released her into society. After a long but vague illness. She did well. She'd always been a quick study. Or so her father told her. Everyone accepted her as the real Evangeline. They had no reason not to. But a single gene test was all it would take to reveal her true origin, damning herself and her father. Replacement by their own clone was the aristocrat's ultimate nightmare. She'd be destroyed (not executed, only people were executed) and her father would be stripped of his title and banished.

She hadn't told Finlay Campbell she was a clone, even though he'd trusted her with the secret of his other life as the Masked Gladiator. She hadn't worked up the courage yet. She loved him, she trusted him, but . . . But. Would he still love her if he knew she was (only) a clone? She liked to think he would, but . . . She smiled humourlessly. If she couldn't trust him with that, how could she tell him about her links to the clone and esper undergrounds? That was, after all, why she'd turned off the Wolfe esp-blockers, so that the elves could smuggle the zealot in . . .

She knew her thoughts were drifting this way and that, but she didn't seem able to control them. She owed so many loyalties to so many people; her father, the undergrounds, Finlay . . . and failing any one of them could lead to her disgrace and death. She had to watch every word, every action, different lies for different people. Sometimes she just wanted to scream for everything to stop, for all the pressure to go away, but she couldn't. She couldn't afford to be noticed doing anything unusual. Occasionally she thought of killing herself, but then she always thought of Finlay, and how safe she felt in his arms. One day she would tell him, and then . . . One day.

She looked up to see Finlay casually approaching her, as though he just happened to be drifting in her direction. Her heart speeded up, and a betraying warmth flushed her cheeks. Finlay stopped before her and bowed courteously, and she nodded coolly in return. Just two heirs to different Clans who happened to have met in a public place. Finlay smiled at her, and she smiled back.

'My dear Evangeline,' said Finlay easily. 'You're looking very well. I trust the unfortunate incident with the esper didn't upset you unduly?'

'Not at all, Finlay. I'm sure Wolfe security already have things well in hand. You're looking quite splendid yourself. Is that another new outfit?'

'Of course. I do so hate to repeat myself. As one of the secret Grand Masters of fashion, I have an obligation to be innovative and shocking at all times. It's in my contract. Your hand is empty; could I perhaps get you a small glass of punch?'

Evangeline shook her head firmly. She'd seen the punch. It was bright pink, reportedly extremely alcoholic, and had bits of unidentified fruit floating in it. Some of them seemed to be slowly dissolving. And given that the punch had been provided by the Wolfes, there was always a chance Valentine had spiked it with something dramatic and disconcerting. Most of the guests had had the sense and foresight to bring their own drink. Finlay smiled, and produced a delicately worked silver flask from an inner pocket. He removed the cap, and poured her a generous drink. Evangeline sniffed it enquiringly, and grinned at the warm aroma of good brandy. She sipped it carefully, and allowed her eyes to meet Finlay's. She could feel her breathing quickening, and when she handed the cap back to Finlay for him to drink, his fingers lingered on hers.

'Now that our two Families are to be joined in marriage, perhaps we shall have occasion to meet more often,' murmured Finlay.

'That would be most pleasant,' said Evangeline. 'I am sure we might discover some interests in common.'

'Right now what you've got in common is a good stiff drink, and I'd kill for some,' said a familiar loud voice. Evangeline didn't need to look round to know who it was. There was never any doubt of Adrienne Campbell's presence. Evangeline and Finlay shared one last understanding glance, and then turned to face Finlay's infamous wife. Adrienne pointedly held out an empty glass, and Finlay filled it to the brim with brandy. She took a good gulp, and nodded approvingly.

'One of your few virtues, Finlay. You're vain and shallow and have absolutely no idea how to treat a lady, but you do know your booze. If it wasn't for your wine cellar I'd have divorced you years ago. Evangeline, my dear; haven't seen you to talk to in absolutely ages. That's a very . . . striking outfit you're wearing. Do feel free to come to me for advice on style and presentation at any time.' She held out her glass to Finlay for a refill, and he obliged without comment. Adrienne's capacity for drink was legendary even in a Court noted for its excesses. She smiled nastily at her husband over the glass. 'Good brandy, Finlay. I like my booze like I like my men; strong, mysterious and tempting.'

'Really?' said Finlay. 'I wouldn't know.'

'Damn right you wouldn't,' said Adrienne. She looked back at Evangeline, who had to fight to keep from flinching. 'It's time you were looking for a husband for yourself, my dear. Your father monopolizes your time far too much. Husbands can be boring, irksome and a general pain in the ass, but you have to have one if you want to get on in society. Personally, I wouldn't be without one, especially when it comes to picking up the tab. Now, if you'll excuse me, I really ought to have a word with our nervous bride and groom. Someone has to tell them the facts of life.'

'And who better than you?' murmured Finlay.

Adrienne smiled. 'Quite.'

She stalked off through the crowd, opening up a path for herself through sheer strength of personality. Her intended prey didn't even realize she was coming. The groom, Robert

Campbell, was currently being supported and encouraged by his cousin Finlay's brothers, William and Gerald Campbell. Robert's father had been the Campbell's younger brother, who died three months previously in an accident the Family still didn't like to talk about. Mostly because it was so damn embarrassing. In order to keep Robert and his branch of the Family from becoming a laughing stock, a marriage had been hastily arranged that would serve the dual purpose of establishing Robert in society, and help close the gap between the Campbells and the Shrecks. And of course, if something should go wrong, Robert was the most expendable member of the Family at present.

He was average height, as fighting fit as years of military training could make him, and at seventeen, old enough to marry, but not old enough to object to the marriage. He was still trying to get used to how much his world had changed. One moment the Shrecks were a deadly enemy to be fought on every occasion, and now here he was marrying one. But he was old enough to understand politics and know his duty. Especially since William and Gerald kept explaining it to him.

William Campbell was tall, thin and intense, and the book-keeper of the Family. It was a job that couldn't be trusted to an outsider, but which most members usually avoided like the plague, on the grounds it was far too much like hard work, and if they'd wanted to work they wouldn't have been born an aristocrat. Fortunately William found numbers both more interesting and easier to deal with than people, so he was perfectly suited to the job. He didn't get out much, but he meant well, and occasionally surprised people with his firm grasp of politics. He was a Campbell, after all.

Gerald, on the other hand, was the Family mistake. There's one like him in every Family. Too dumb to be entrusted with the important stuff, but too senior to be just ignored. The Family had been trying to find a place for him all his life. With absolutely no success. Gerald was tall, blond and handsome, and a complete bloody disaster no matter what he did, and everyone knew it but him. The Campbell himself had been heard to say, only partly in jest, that the best thing to do with

Gerald would be to make a gift of him to a Family they were really mad at.

'Do try and at least look cheerful,' said William to young Robert. 'This is a wedding, after all, not the dentist's.'

'Right,' said Gerald. 'At the dentist they take something out. Here you get to put something in. Get my drift, eh?'

Robert smiled politely, and just a little desperately. He had the look of a small animal caught in the headlights of an oncoming car. He pulled at his frock coat to straighten it, and fiddled with his cravat. His dresser had assured him he looked both dignified and fashionable, but he wasn't sure of either. He felt very much he could have used a stiff drink or several, but William wouldn't let him. Valentine had offered to slip him a little something, but he'd declined. He didn't think he was ready to deal with one of Valentine's little somethings. Probably no one but Valentine was.

'You've been through the rehearsals,' said William reassuringly. 'Nothing to worry about. Just say the words, kiss the bride, and it'll all be over before you know it. Remember you have to lift the veil first, though. You'd be surprised how many people forget that. Sometimes I think we're getting a little too inbred. Brace up; not long to go now.'

'And then you can settle down to getting to know your bride,' said Gerald. 'Something to look forward to, eh? Eh?'

'Gerald,' said William, 'go get Robert a drink.'

'But you said he shouldn't have any.'

'Then go and get me a drink.'

'But you don't drink.'

'Then go and get yourself a bloody drink, and don't come back till you've drunk it!'

Gerald blinked a few times, and then moved away in the general direction of the punchbowl, looking just a little confused. As always. William looked at Robert, and shrugged.

'Don't mind your Uncle Gerald, boy. He means well, but he should have been dropped on his head as a baby. It's not entirely his fault that he's about as much use as a one-legged man in an ass-kicking contest. Is there . . .anything you want to ask me, before the ceremony? I mean, I am a married man . . .'

'That's all right,' said Robert quickly. 'A lot of people have already talked to me about that. Everyone's been very free with their advice. The only advice I could really use is how to get out of this.'

William smiled, and shook his head. 'Sorry, but that's not on. Duty calls. The Campbell sets the rules, and we have to follow them. If we didn't, where would we be? In complete bloody chaos, and all the other Families would charge in like sharks scenting blood in the water. Or do they taste it? I've never been sure. Anyway, whatever else we may be, we're Campbells first. Always. If it's any help, I felt much the same before my wedding, and I've been happy enough. I suppose.'

'Keep on encouraging him like that, and we'll have to drive him to the altar with whips,' said a loud, carrying voice.

Robert and William Campbell looked up to see standing before them Adrienne Campbell, large as life and twice as loud. William flinched visibly, and was still trying to find the right words with which to introduce Adrienne when she stepped forward, brushing him aside, and smiled at Robert.

'Hello, Robert; I'm Adrienne, Finlay's wife. I'm the one you've probably been warned about, and you should believe every word. Mostly they try and keep me away from public functions, on the grounds I embarrass them. Personally I've never been embarrassed in my life. Fortunately for you, they couldn't keep me out of a wedding this important. You come with me, dear. There's someone I want you to meet.'

'Er . . .' said William.

Adrienne rounded on him, and he fell back a step. 'Did you want to say something, William? No? I didn't think so. You rarely do. Come along, Robert.'

And she took him by the hand in a vice-like grip and led him off through the crowd. Robert went along with her. It seemed like the safest thing to do, if he ever wanted his hand back. They passed through the outskirts of the crowd, followed all the way by scandalized whispers, and then through a side door that led into a quiet sitting room decorated with antiques

288

of considerable age and complete hideousness. And there, sitting among the antiques like a single flower in a garden of weeds, sat Letitia Shreck, his bride to be. She got up the moment they entered, and then stood quietly, with eyes modestly downcast. She was sixteen years old, and very pretty, with hints of a more mature beauty to come. The long white wedding gown made her look very fragile, like a delicate porcelain figure standing alone on a shelf. Robert looked at her and then at Adrienne with something like shock.

'I know,' said Adrienne briskly, 'you're not supposed to meet before the ceremony, but they'll overlook it this time, rather than have me make a scene in front of everybody. They tend to overlook quite a lot, rather than have me make a scene. I can be very good at scenes, when I put my mind to it. Anyway, I brought you two together so you could talk, so get on with it. I'll run interference at the door. You've got about twenty minutes before they come and drag you off to the ceremony, so make the most of them. Just . . . chat together; you'll be surprised how much you've got in common.'

And with that she disappeared out of the door, pulling it firmly shut behind her, leaving Robert and Letitia standing looking at each other. It was very quiet in the room. They could hear the murmur of raised voices beyond the closed door, but that might as well have been on another world. For a moment that seemed to last forever neither of them moved, and then Robert cleared his throat awkwardly.

'Would you like to sit down, Letitia?'

'Yes. Thank you.'

They sat down on chairs facing each other, careful to maintain a proper distance between them. Robert searched for something to say that wouldn't make him sound like a complete idiot.

'Letitia . . .'

'Tish.'

'I beg your pardon?'

'I . . . prefer to be called Tish. If that's all right.'

'Yes. Of course. Call me Bobby. If you like.' They looked right at each other for the first time, and Robert smiled suddenly. 'Tell me, Tish; do you feel as uncomfortable in your outfit as I do in mine?'

She laughed immediately, and then put her hands to her mouth, looking at him to check he wasn't shocked. Reassured by his smile, she lowered her hands and smiled back at him.

'I hate this dress. If it was any tighter, it would be inside me. I haven't dared to eat or drink anything. I don't think there's anywhere for it to go. And every time I go to the toilet I have to take two maids with me to unlace everything. I've been going rather a lot. I think it's nerves. And of course if I say anything, or try to complain, they just say it's traditional, as if that solved everything.'

'Right!' said Robert, as she paused for breath. 'If I hear the word tradition one more time I think I'll scream. I was told I was getting married about six hours ago. How about you?'

'Same here. I suppose they thought if they gave us too much time to think about it, we'd run away or something.'

'They weren't far wrong,' said Robert dryly. 'This isn't at all what I thought I'd be doing when I got up this morning. If I had known, I'd have headed for the horizon so fast it would have made their heads spin. Of course, that was before I met you. I thought . . . well, I don't know what I thought, but you . . . you're all right.'

'Thanks,' said Letitia. 'You really know how to compliment a lady, don't you?'

Robert grinned. 'Well actually, no. I've been a military cadet most of my life. It's expected, for those in the Family unlikely ever to inherit. You don't get to meet many women in military training. How about you; did you have anyone . . . special, in your life?'

'There was someone, but . . . that's all over now. They found out about us and stopped us seeing each other.' Letitia smiled wryly. 'He was one of my bodyguards. I'm not allowed out much, either. Not since the Empress started raiding the Families for maids. I knew poor Lindsey; the Shreck's niece who disappeared. She was so bright, so funny. Nowadays they keep us under guard, as much as possible. Understandable, I suppose, but it makes for a very quiet life.'

Robert nodded understandingly. 'And now, here we are, about to get married. It's going to seem strange, having lifelong enemies as my in-laws.'

'Same here,' said Letitia, clapping her hands together suddenly, and grinning wickedly. 'Do you Campbells really eat babies for breakfast?'

'Oh, every day. Beats the hell out of bran flakes.'

'Maybe we'll bring our Families together, like we're supposed to. Stranger things have happened. Bobby . . .'

'Yes, Tish?'

'If I have to marry someone, I'm glad it's someone like you.'

'Same here, Tish. Same here.'

She put out her hand, and he took it gently, enfolding her small slender fingers in his. And they sat there, smiling together, for an endless moment. And then Adrienne came bustling in.

'All this time, and you've only got as far as holding hands? I don't know what's wrong with you young people these days. I'd have had him pinned up against the wall by now. But time's up, I'm afraid. Finlay sent me to fetch you, Robert. Urgent Family business, and your presence is required.'

Robert gave Letitia's hand one last squeeze, and got to his feet. 'Family business is always urgent, especially when it's inconvenient. I'm glad we had this chance to talk, Tish. I'll see you shortly.'

'Bye,' said Letitia, and blew him a kiss. Robert snatched it out of mid-air, put it in an inner pocket over his heart, and only then allowed Adrienne to lead him away.

It turned out to be quite a Family gathering, all squeezed together in a side room, with guards outside the door to make sure they wouldn't be disturbed. Finlay was there, at his most outrageously foppish, studying Adrienne through his pincenez as though she was a stranger. William and Gerald were arguing quietly but heatedly, barely stopping to nod to Robert as he closed the door behind him. He took in their earnest faces, and his heart dropped. Something bad was in the wind. He could feel it. Finlay cleared his throat, and everyone looked at him.

'The Campbell himself cannot be here in person,' he said flatly. 'He's had a communication from our allies on Shub. It came via a series of espers, so we're pretty sure it wasn't intercepted. It seems that some other House has discovered our connection with Shub.'

'Wait a minute,' said Robert. 'Hold everything. What's this about Shub? What allies have we got on that hellhole?'

'You have a right to know,' said Finlay. He sounded surprisingly articulate, for once. 'Now that you're to be a central part of Family business. But you cannot discuss this with anyone outside the Family; not even your wife. No one must know. Our existence as a House depends on this. For some time now, we've been secretly intriguing with the rogue AIs on Shub, in defiance of Empire policy. The Enemies of Humanity have been passing us designs for advanced technology to help us win the contract for mass-production of the new stardrive, in return for us making the drive available to them. They are desperate to remain the Empire's equal, and we need the contract. Our finances are somewhat depleted at the moment.'

'To be exact,' said Adrienne, 'we're in deep shit. If we don't get the contract, we're ruined. Bankrupt.'

William winced, but nodded. 'We must win the contract if we are to survive as a Clan. Everything depends on it.'

'Anyway,' said Finlay. 'It appears someone has found out. They can't have any definite proof yet, or they'd have turned us in to the Empress. And we'd all be facing a quick trial and a lingering execution.'

'Can you blame them?' said Robert hotly. 'We're working with the AIs on Shub? They're dedicated to wiping out humanity in its entirety, and we're giving them the new stardrive? Is it just me, or is this *completely bloody crazy*!'

'Please don't shout,' said Finlay. 'This has all been discussed and decided at the highest Clan levels. We have absolutely no intention of giving them the drive, whatever happens. We are ambitious and desperate but not, as you say, crazy.'

'In the meantime,' said Adrienne, 'it's vital we find out who knows our secret. That's why you're here, Robert. We're already running several clandestine operations, to discover our enemy, and you're uniquely suited to investigating the Shrecks. But you're not to discuss this with your wife. She may be marrying into the Campbells, but for now she's still a Shreck. Use her, but don't trust her. Don't look so shocked, dear. This is Family business, and the Family always comes first.'

'It's important we discover how much our enemy knows,' said William. 'Anyone who knows too much must die. The safety of the Clan is at risk.'

'What's the Campbell doing?' said Gerald anxiously. 'Why isn't he here? He should be making these kinds of decisions, not us.'

'He's busy reassuring the AIs through the esper link,' said Finlay. 'We don't want them doing anything impulsive, or . . . unfortunate. We're only valuable to them as long as our connection remains a secret. He took a hell of a risk sending a messenger here, but it was important we know immediately. From now on, we don't go anywhere without guards, and no one is to go off on their own. Our new rival might try to kidnap one of us, to pump that person for information, and put pressure on the rest of us. You're especially at risk, Robert; you're not as used to this game as we are. We can't put you in seclusion right after your wedding; that would look just a little suspicious, like we had something to hide. But from now on, you and your new wife will have double the security presence. If she asks why, point out how easily that esper zealot broke in. Now, let us return to the celebration, before our absence becomes a talking point. Smiles and laughter, everyone; no point in putting weapons in our enemies' hands. After all, it's not certain they know that we know they suspect. You're looking puzzled, Gerald. Don't let it worry you. Just stick close to us, and if you feel like saying anything, rise above it. William; keep an eye on him. If he opens his mouth, stamp on his foot.'

Adrienne looked at him thoughtfully. 'Since when did you become such an accomplished conspirator?'

Finlay smiled at her dazzlingly. 'It's in the blood, my dear. I am a Campbell, after all.'

He took Robert by the arm and led him back into the crowded ballroom. Everywhere faces smiled and heads bowed, and Robert nodded numbly to them all. Some weren't really there, of course. Attending in person was a compliment and a privilege; the less well-connected usually had to settle for sending a holo. If nothing else, it helped to cut down on duels. Nothing like a wedding to bring out old Family quarrels. Robert thought about that to keep from thinking about anything else, but it didn't work. He pulled his arm free of Finlay, and gave him a hard look.

'Just how much danger are we in, Finlay? How much danger am I putting Letitia in by marrying her?'

'Not much more than she's already used to. She is a Shreck, after all, and they have a history of intrigue that makes us look timid. Now forget about all that, and concentrate on your wedding.'

James Kassar, Vicar of the Church of Christ the Warrior, called the gathering to attend to him in the kind of voice usually reserved for a parade ground, and the two Families separated out to form two groups, so that they could look down their noses at each other. They left a narrow aisle between the two groups, and almost before he knew it, Robert was heading for the aisle, surrounded by Finlay and William and Gerald, all looking very stern and respectable. The bride was brought forward to walk beside him, surrounded by women of the Shreck Family. Letitia arrived amidst a crowd of whispered jokes and comments and stifled laughter, but Robert's companions stayed straight-faced, as custom required. Robert was grateful for that, at least. He had a strong feeling that just at this moment, even a bad joke would collapse him into howls of hysterical laughter. And then he and Letitia were walking down the aisle side by side, alone at last, both looking straight ahead and concentrating desperately on the moves and words they'd learned at rehearsal.

They came to a halt before Kassar, resplendent now in a purple gown, who bowed curtly and began the wedding service in a calm, business-like tone. Personally Robert preferred it that way. It made both the Vicar and the service seem less awe-inspiring. The words were familiar from any number of Family weddings Robert and Letitia had attended since childhood, and they made their responses in calm, dignified voices. Everything went smoothly, and Robert even remembered to raise the veil before he kissed her. All that remained was the ceremonial tying of the knot. Kassar gestured for the pageboy to bring forward the ceremonial golden cord on its platter. He wrapped the cord loosely about both their wrists, binding them together, and then called forward the Church esper. Before the Church could give its blessing, and thus validate the marriage, it was important that both parties were proved to be who they said they were. Nobody ever said the word clone, but it was never far from anyone's mind.

Many of the guests stirred uneasily. The esp-blockers had been shut down for this moment, and the threat of outside attack was that much greater, but mostly the guests were concerned that their own little secrets might be detected and exposed by the esper. Everyone had something to hide. They needn't have worried. The esper knew better than to let his thoughts stray. There was a Church guard standing off to one side with a gun trained on him. So he concentrated on the bride and groom before him, and everything was hushed. Until his head came up sharply, and he stepped back a pace. Kassar glared at him.

'What is it? Is there a question of identity?'

'No, Your Grace,' said the esper quickly. 'They are who they claim to be. It's just that I sense not two minds, but three. The Lady Letitia is pregnant. And not by the groom.'

For a moment there was a shocked silence, and then uproar filled the ballroom. Robert stared open-mouthed at Letitia, who stared numbly back at him. *Had there been someone special?* he'd asked. And she'd said *yes*. Kassar tore the golden cord from their wrists, and threw it to one side. It seemed like everyone was shouting and screaming at everyone else, and swords were appearing in hands. Space grew around the white-faced bride, as people fell back rather than be contaminated by her presence. Adrienne tried to get to her, but was held back by the crush of the crowd. For bringing a sullied bride to a joining of Clans, the Shrecks would be ostracized by society. It was the ultimate insult.

The Shrecks were yelling that they knew nothing of it, but no one was listening. Robert started towards Letitia, not knowing what he was going to say or do, only drawn on by the misery in her face. And then Gregor Shreck burst out of the crowd, the golden wedding cord in his hands. His face blazed with fury, and Letitia shrank back from him. Before anyone knew what he had planned, he had the golden cord round Letitia's throat, and pulled it tight. Her eyes bulged as she fought for breath, and she clawed helplessly at the Shreck's wrists. He swung her round, put his knee in her back, and tightened his hold, the muscles standing out in his arms. Robert plunged forward to stop him, but then strong arms were holding him back, no matter how he struggled. William and Gerald held him firmly, their faces cold and dispassionate.

Letitia's face was horribly red, and her tongue protruded from her mouth. There was shouting and some screaming from the crowd, but no one went to help her. Robert fought savagely, but William and Gerald held him fast. He called her name, and didn't know he was crying. Letitia sank to the floor, held up only by the Shreck's strangling grip. The ballroom slowly grew silent as the end drew near, until the only sounds in the chamber were Gregor's panting breath, Letitia's last choking gasps, and Robert's racking sobs. And then her eyes rolled up and she was silent, and Gregor slowly relaxed his grip. She fell limply to the floor and lay still.

Gregor turned to face Finlay, his face red from his exertion, his breathing unsteady. 'I make apologies for my Clan, and present this death as atonement. I trust this is sufficient?'

'It is,' said Finlay Campbell. 'Honour is satisfied. We will discuss the choosing of another bride at a later date, that the wedding may proceed in the future. This ceremony shall be forgotten, and never referred to again.'

He nodded to William and Gerald, who released Robert. He stumbled forward to kneel at Letitia's side. Finlay gathered up the rest of the Campbells with his eyes and led them out of the ballroom. The Shrecks followed, and the Wolfes, and finally the Vicar James Kassar and his people. Until only Robert Campbell was left, kneeling by his dead bride, holding her still white hand in his.

Outside in the corridor, Gregor Shreck looked across at his favoured daughter Evangeline. Let her take a lesson from this. He'd kill her too, if he had to, to keep his secret safe. He'd done it before. He smiled slightly. He'd murdered the original Evangeline because she wouldn't love him as he loved her; and not as a father. He was the Shreck, and he would be obeyed.

CHAPTER EIGHT

Going Underground

The trouble in dealing with underground movements, thought
Valentine Wolfe waspishly, *is that sometimes they take their name
too literally*. He struggled on through the narrow service duct,
shoulders hunched and head down to keep from banging
it on the low tunnel roof. It stretched endlessly away before
him, cramped and gloomy and unreservedly depressing. Low-
intensity lamps hung down from the roof at regular intervals,
providing just enough light to make him squint painfully. An
insane tangle of interweaving cables stretched along the walls
and ceiling, colour-coded in a way that presumably made sense
to someone. Valentine thought them unforgivably gaudy and
garish. Some of the cables were frayed and dangling, like
hanging vines, and he had to bat them aside with his arms as
he progressed. There was dirt and dust everywhere. Clearly no
one had passed through the tunnel in some time, and Valentine
for one didn't blame them. The view was monotonous, his
back was killing him, and the smell was appalling.

He was deep in the guts of the planet, in its hidden
underside; the maze of sewers and access tunnels and service
ducts that linked the varying self-contained worlds that existed
within Golgotha. Although the complicated maze was necessary for the inner worlds' survival, few people ever thought of
them. Only service personnel were authorized to use the
passageways, but then, Valentine was used to being in places
he wasn't supposed to be. His lip curled in disgust as the slime
he was treading in grew steadily deeper. It was already lapping
at the ankles of his very fashionable thigh-length leather boots,
and was doing nothing at all for their shine. Valentine didn't

know what the slime was, and didn't feel in the least like investigating its nature. He had a strong feeling he was better off not knowing. It looked worryingly organic, and he thought it best not to disturb the stuff any more than he had to. He trudged on down the tunnel, one hand just casually resting on the gun at his hip, trying without much success to ease the aching muscles of his hunched back.

He'd discarded the frailer parts of his outfit before setting out, replacing them with more robust and anonymous items, and wrapped himself in a long black cloak. He'd wiped the heavy make-up from his face, tied back his long hair in a functional braid, and together with his new outfit he presented a quite different appearance, which was just as well. It wouldn't do for anyone to discover Valentine Wolfe attending meetings of the clone and esper undergrounds. They wouldn't understand.

It was a shame he'd had to rush away so soon after the wedding debacle. He'd expected a dull and lifeless affair, followed by appalling food and worse dancing, but in the end it had turned out to be rather amusing. He would have liked to hang around and drop a few exquisite bons mots where they could do the most harm, but the call from the underground had arrived by its usual roundabout route, and when the underground called, he answered. He didn't take kindly to being summoned by such lowlife trash, but as long as they had something he wanted, he'd go along with the game. It did have its amusing moments. Though he had to admit this wasn't one of them.

He stopped suddenly, and peered suspiciously about him in the gloom. The dimly glowing lamp shed a blue-white light before and behind him, but between the widely spaced lamps there was a darkness so deep even his chemically boosted eyes couldn't pierce it. He listened intently, holding himself perfectly still, but nothing stirred. Valentine scowled thoughtfully. He could have sworn he'd heard something, but sound travelled strangely in the narrow service duct. God only knew what kind of small, disgusting life might have made a home for itself down here.

He wasn't that far from one of the main sewer offshoots, according to the map he'd memorized earlier. There were all kinds of stories about what strange and malignant creatures flourished in the sewers. Also according to rumour, sewer workers received battle pay, and bonuses for the heads of anything they brought back with them. Not that Valentine ever listened to such stories. He looked round sharply, sure he'd picked up something just at the edge of his hearing, but there was only the silence and the gloom. He concentrated, and deep within his body drug caches dumped their loads into his systems. His breathing quickened and deepened as his metabolism speeded up, ready for action. He was stronger, faster, sharper now, and more than ready for whatever was out there. He grinned broadly. Let it come. Let them all come. A thoughtful voice somewhere at the back of his mind pointed out that he shouldn't really waste his resources. He'd set in motion events that would eventually produce a new supplier to replace dear dead Georgios, but until the new source was established and proven reliable, he would be wise to avoid using up anything he couldn't easily replace. Valentine decided to ignore the voice. It sounded entirely too sane and sensible, and Valentine Wolfe hadn't got where he was by being sane and sensible.

A light flared suddenly in the gloom ahead of him, sharp and distinct after the blue-white glare of the lamps, followed by the faint sound of footsteps splashing through the slime. Valentine's smile widened, and he drew his gun. A dark figure appeared in the tunnel ahead, silhouetted against the light. It stopped a respectful distance away, calm and silent, a ball of glowing clear white light bobbing at its shoulder. The figure looked human, but Valentine wasn't in the mood to make allowances. In fact, he felt rather like shooting it anyway, on general principles. And then the figure spoke in a calm, collected voice that had the flat perfection of a machine. Presumably computer-disguised to prevent identification.

'I didn't mean to alarm you, good sir, but you'll understand that in our position it pays to be cautious, if not downright paranoid. Allow me to give you the first part of the current password; New.'

'Hope,' said Valentine, relaxing just a little but not lowering his gun. 'Rather an obvious choice, I would have thought, but then no one asked my opinion. May I ask who you are?'

The figure moved slowly forward, taking its time so that Valentine wouldn't feel threatened. It finally came to a halt before him, bent almost in two under the low roof, and Valentine's interest increased as he realized that any identifying signs were concealed inside a long flowing cape. Even more interesting, there was nothing inside the cape's hood; no face, no head, nothing at all. The ball of light bobbed cheerfully at the figure's shoulder, bright and clear, and Valentine had to tone down his vision.

'I am Hood,' said the figure. 'Coordinator between the clone and esper undergrounds and the cyberats. And you, sir?'

'Valentine Wolfe, patron and advisor to the undergrounds. I've heard of you, Hood. The shadow in the background, the presence behind the throne, so to speak. I and the rest of the patrons are required to reveal our identities, the espers insist on it, but you alone are allowed anonymity. I wonder why.'

'Because I'm valuable to them,' said Hood. 'And as long as they need me, they indulge me. I've heard of you, Valentine, but then I suppose everyone has. You've pumped quite a lot of money into the undergrounds by all accounts, but I have to say I can't see why. You are heir to the Wolfe Clan; you stand to inherit everything. What on earth do you need, that you have to come to the undergrounds to get it?'

'Sorry,' said Valentine. 'I never tell everything on a first date.'

'As you wish. I wonder what the undergrounds want this time, that such important backers as you and I had to be summoned so urgently?'

'It had better be important,' said Valentine. 'I feel quite naked without my usual persona. Shall we go?'

'Of course. It's not far now. After you.'

'Oh no. After you.'

The cape's hood bobbed once in what might have been

agreement or humour, and Hood turned and led the way down a side tunnel that if anything smelled even worse. Valentine followed close behind, his gun still in his hand. He flushed most of the drugs from his system, but kept a few in reserve, just in case.

Normally, the underground only summoned its patrons one at a time, so that if they were captured they wouldn't be able to identify anyone else. Something important must be in the wind for two to be needed. Valentine studied Hood's enigmatic back thoughtfully. The lack of a face was interesting; the underground was almost fanatical in its need to know exactly who it was dealing with. It could be a hologram disguise, but nothing less than an esp-blocker would protect Hood's thoughts from an esper's probing mind, and the underground wouldn't tolerate that for a second. Hood; a supplier of money, reportedly well-connected, he worked well with both the clone and esper undergrounds, which was rare. They didn't trust easily, and there were few indeed who'd earned the trust of both.

As if to underline that thought, Hood and Valentine came to a sudden halt before the first warning sign. It was a dead man, hanging from the ceiling like a broken puppet. Its arms and legs had been smashed, with white points of splintered bone protruding from the bloody flesh. The corpse slowly raised its head to look at Hood and Valentine, and its eye sockets were empty. Blood spilled down the colourless cheeks like thick crimson tears. It opened its mouth, and maggots poured down its chin.

'Go back,' it said slowly, haltingly, as though it had almost forgotten how to speak. 'Go back now.'

Valentine looked at Hood. 'Be honest; would this scare you if you were a crack squadron of the Empress's guards?'

'Not really,' said Hood. 'But then, I've seen it before. They insist on running this routine, even when they know it's me. I think they just do it for the practice.'

The dead man scowled at them. 'Turn back. I mean it. I'm not kidding.'

'Oh shut up,' said Valentine. 'I've seen scarier things than you in my daydreams.'

'He probably has,' said Hood. 'This is Valentine Wolfe. *The* Valentine Wolfe.'

The dead man disappeared between one moment and the next. The smell stayed pretty much the same, though. The empty hood looked at Valentine. 'They've heard of you.'

Valentine smiled. 'Everyone's heard of me.' He paused. 'Can you hear something?'

A low roar began from somewhere behind them, building steadily in volume. The tunnel floor vibrated under their feet. Thick ripples surged across the surface of the slime. A growing pressure built in the air, like the wave of compressed air that precedes an underground train. The roar grew louder and the floor shook. Valentine looked quickly about him, but there was nowhere to run except further down the tunnel. The roar was deafening now, the pressure of the air flat and heavy against his face. Hood was standing very still, as though frozen in place by shock. And then a vast wave of rushing water came bursting through the tunnel towards them, thundering forward like a runaway train.

'They've opened the damned sewers!' yelled Valentine. 'Grab on to something or we'll be swept away!'

The tidal wave loomed up before them, filling the tunnel, and then it was gone. No water, no noise, nothing at all. The air was quiet and calm and undisturbed. Valentine let his breath out slowly.

'You bastards.'

Got you, crowed a voice in his head. *I don't just do corpses, you know.*

Hood shook his head, and chuckled slowly. 'We did ask for it, didn't we?'

Just practising. I never get to do anything, down here. No one comes for ages. I don't know why we bother keeping a watch. Go straight ahead and take the second left. Meeting's just ahead. You're expected. And tell them I could do with a drink.

There was a lot Valentine felt like saying, but he didn't. He had his dignity to consider. He looked at Hood. 'You can't get good help these days.'

'It never pays to underestimate espers,' said Hood, starting off down the tunnel again. 'They know everything you're thinking.'

'Oh I doubt that,' said Valentine, splashing through the slime after him. 'Anyone who enters my mind does so at their own peril, after all the things I've done to it.'

'Good point,' said Hood. 'How did someone like you ever get involved with the underground in the first place?'

Valentine smiled. 'My experiments with various unusual substances led me to rumours of a new, very experimental drug that could make an esper out of anyone, even from those with absolutely no family history of psionics. If there is such a drug, I want it. Esp is one of the few experiences still unknown to me. Just the thought of something so new and vital makes my mouth water. I must have it.

'Pursuit of this drug brought me to the elves and the underground, and for the first time I realized what a potential power base they represented. With their help, I could attain heights of power I would never otherwise have dreamed of. The espers will break free eventually, Hood. It's inevitable. They are the wave of the future, the next evolutionary step for humanity. And I intend to ride that wave as far and high as I can. Who knows; it might even carry me to the Iron Throne itself. Now wouldn't that be something.' He paused thoughtfully. 'Of course, I'd have to kill my father and Family first. I'm quite looking forward to that.'

He stopped talking suddenly. It seemed to him that he was saying entirely too much to someone he barely knew. He didn't know why. Perhaps the tidal wave illusion had upset him more than he realized. Or perhaps not. Either way, he'd watch his words very carefully from now on. He was beginning to get the feeling they weren't entirely his own. He'd always known there was a risk in dealing with espers, but he'd thought the mental disciplines he'd mastered in constantly altering his brain chemistry would give him some kind of protection. But spilling his secrets to a comparative stranger definitely wasn't like him. He took out his silver pillbox, took out a tab and pressed it against the side of his neck, over the vein.

'Just a little something to wake me up,' he said blithely, putting away the pillbox. He smiled broadly as the jolt kicked in. He took a deep breath and let it out through his smile. Already his thoughts were feeling clearer, faster, sharper. 'Tell me about yourself, Hood; what brought you into our little world of treason and subterfuge?'

'I was part of the security force responsible for tracking down and eliminating the cyberats,' said Hood. 'But the more I learned of them, the more I grew to understand and then envy their unrelenting search for truth and freedom. The Empress stays in power because her people control information; regulating how much we're allowed to know about anything. You can't protest against a thing if you don't know it's happening. Most of what we know is based on lies and distortions. The cyberats showed me parts of the world I'd never seen before, and having seen, I couldn't close my eyes again.

'My growing contacts with the cyberats led me to the underground, and the more I learned of their struggle, the more I sympathized. It took me a long time to convince all the various elements of my sincerity, but my connections with the Empress's own security forces made me an invaluable ally. I have proved my worth. So the man who once hunted rebels now works to protect them. Such is life. I've always felt a little irony was good for the blood. I'm intrigued by your interest in the esper drug. I assure you, it's very effective.'

'How do you know?' said Valentine.

'Because I took it,' said Hood. 'I volunteered; in fact, I insisted. I'd seen so much I'd never seen before, and I wanted to see even more. The results were . . . interesting. Minor telepathy, some projective imagery, similar to what we just saw in the tunnel. I'm no match for a born esper, but I see deeper and more clearly now than I ever did before. Theoretically, stronger doses of the drug should produce stronger effects, but there have been unfortunate side effects in others who have tried the drug.'

Valentine smiled serenely. 'That's part of the thrill of experimenting with a new drug; the risks and discoveries. The joy of exploring unknown territories, and daring fate to do its worst. Not unlike the thrill of being a rebel, really. I always look forward to getting the call. Though I do wish they'd stop changing the meeting place. Every time I have to walk a little further, and pass through even more disgusting scenery to get there.'

Hood shrugged. 'Basic security. Keep moving, keep looking over your shoulder, and keep everyone else off balance. The Empress has a lot of people trying to find the underground, and they've got a much bigger budget than we have. I do my best to quietly steer them in the wrong direction, but there's a limit to what I can do without giving myself away. I might support the underground, but I have no intention of dying for it.'

'Technically speaking,' said Valentine, 'this isn't actually the underground. We're not that far from the surface; just in between the inner and outer spheres. I think they just call it the underground to confuse people.'

'Understandable. And you must admit, saying you're part of the underground sounds a lot better than saying you're one of the in-betweenies.'

Valentine smiled politely, and they walked some way in silence. They both knew that by now unseen minds were probing theirs to make sure they were who they were supposed to be. They also knew that if either of them had even looked like failing the test, they'd be dead by now. Nothing was allowed to threaten the underground. Valentine and the man called Hood rounded a corner, ducked under a low entrance and stepped out of the cramped tunnel into a brightly lit giant cavern of gleaming metal. Hood's ball of light snapped out. Multicoloured wires crawled across the walls, hung dangling from the high ceiling, and disappeared into conduits like snakes sliding into their holes. Mysterious bulky machines jutted out of the walls, crowding each other for space. The floor was covered with debris, smashed and broken pieces of high tech, some recent, some apparently not. There were living things in the centre of the floor, but Valentine chose not to look at them just yet. He straightened up slowly with a grateful sigh, and massaged his aching back with both hands.

'You're the tech expert, Hood; where the hell are we this time? It looks like a repairman's nightmare.'

'An old work station, by the look of it. Abandoned and forgotten and renovated by the cyberats. There are lots of places like this between the various worlds within Golgotha; places that served a purpose once, but were left behind as technology moved on. The cyberats love them; play with them for hours. They've got hundreds of refuges like this, that don't appear in current computer records any more.'

'It's a dump,' said Valentine.

'Well yes, but you have to admit it does smell better than the sewers.'

'Actually, I quite like dumps. They appeal to my preference for chaos. I love the patterns they make.'

He giggled cheerfully, and Hood looked at him. Valentine looked back, and then the two of them walked forward to bow courteously to the esper representatives in the middle of the great metal chamber. As always, the representatives hid their true identities behind telepathically projected images. They might have been there in person, or they might have been sending the images from somewhere else. It was a talent that Valentine greatly envied.

The esper leaders were a mystery, and they were determined to keep it that way. So a waterfall fell through the air, bubbling and gushing, coming from nowhere and going back there when it touched the floor. Strange colours came and went, and two shadows that might have been eyes hovered midway. Beside the waterfall a swirling mandala hung upon the air, an intricate pattern of glowing lines twisting and turning in upon itself endlessly. Valentine could have watched it for hours. Next to that, a twelve foot long dragon lay curled around a tree, light gleaming dully on its golden scales. Valentine was never quite sure whether that was one representative or two. He'd never heard the tree say anything, but then the dragon didn't have much to say either. And finally, there was the individual

Valentine always thought of as Mr Perfect. A massively muscled figure, developed almost to the point of caricature, he stood with his arms across his massive chest, staring commandingly at his visitors. Valentine always felt an overwhelming urge to sneak up behind him and goose him. Except he probably wasn't really there.

There was no guarantee anyone was. The images could be coming from anywhere. They had no reality outside the recipient's mind. Valentine was familiar with that feeling. It occurred to him that Hood might be seeing something completely different. He'd have to compare notes later. He'd been quietly trying to piece together some idea of who was behind the images for some time, but to no effect. The esper representatives were extremely paranoid about their secrets, and with good cause. The reward for esper rebellion was death. Eventually. The cavern was silent, but the air was tense and brittle with the unspoken speech of the telepaths. Hood leaned in close beside Valentine.

'I can just about tap in on what's going on. Listen through me.'

A sharp prickling wrapped around Valentine's head like a halo of barbed wire, and slowly he became aware of a soft susurrus of voices filling the chamber. They meshed and intersected without colliding, a hundred voices speaking all at once without confusion or loss of meaning. The voices were more than just words; thoughts and feelings and impressions rolled around each other, adding tartness and flavour. And underlying the music of gathered minds, the hard unyielding beat of six major minds; conferring, directing and deciding. Valentine's mind swayed with the rhythm, but held itself apart and intact. The impact would have been too much for the normal human mind to cope with, but Valentine's mind wasn't normal any more. Not after all the things he'd done to it. He hung on the fringes, savouring what he could, fascinated. *If this is what the esper drug can do, I want it. And to hell with what it costs me.* He sensed as much as heard Hood's laughter beside him.

And then Hood moved away, and the link was broken.

Valentine rocked on his feet, shrunk once again to the narrow margins of his own mind. Faint traces of the experience remained with him, leaving him hungry for more. Valentine smiled wryly. Presumably that had been Hood's intention, to get him off balance and at the same time concentrate his attention on ways of getting the esper drug for himself. Except Valentine knew all about drugs, and bowed to none of them. He had other business here besides the esper drug. The underground was a route to power, and that came first. Always.

He looked round sharply as four men with the same face entered the chamber from another entrance. They wore carefully distinct clothing, but they moved in the same way and their faces held the same thoughts. Clones. Presumably representatives for the clone underground. They were tall and slender, almost impossibly graceful, and had a natural gravitas that went beyond dignity. Valentine knew a natural leader when he saw one. Whatever they were all here to discuss, it must be pretty damned important. The clone leaders rarely appeared in person.

They were followed in by three women with the same face, and Valentine's interest was piqued. He'd seen that face before. Seen it on an esper called Stevie Blue, who died at the Empress's feet after humiliating her in front of the whole Court with a pie in the face. She'd been an elf. Esper Liberation Front. The more extreme edge of the esper underground. And now it seemed she was a clone as well. That was unusual. Not many espers survived the cloning process.

The three women looked to be in their early twenties, wearing the same leather and chains their dead sister had worn. Not to mention the same T-shirt, bearing the legend *Born to Burn*. They were short and stocky, with muscular bare arms, and one of them was casually hefting a solid steel dumb-bell as though it weighed nothing. Long dark hair fell to their shoulders, full of knotted ribbons. Their faces were sharp, high-cheekboned, and daubed with fierce colours. They each wore a sword on their hip, in leather scabbards that looked like they'd seen a lot of use. The three women looked cold and calm and very dangerous.

'Welcome, Stevie Blues,' said Mr Perfect. 'You honour us with your presence. As espers and clones you are uniquely suited to bring the two undergrounds together.'

'Even though neither of us can be sure where your loyalties really lie,' said the dragon, a long thin tongue flickering out of his mouth.

'Save the flattery and the paranoia,' said one of the Stevie Blues. 'We're here to talk; let's get on with it. Some of us have a life outside the underground.'

'Freaks and perverts,' growled the flowing mandala. 'Group marriages such as yours are forbidden among clones.'

'We're elves, first and foremost,' said the middle Stevie Blue calmly. 'We fight for freedom. All kinds of freedom. Want to make something of it?'

Roaring flames suddenly licked up around the three elves, and the heat drove everybody back a step. It didn't affect the Stevie Blues. They were pyros, and immune to their own fire. The clone representatives frowned severely, making it clear this was nothing to do with them. The waterfall began to steam slightly, and the dragon shifted uncomfortably. Mr Perfect's face was turning red. Maybe he was present, after all. Valentine grinned, enjoying the show.

'Well?' said the third Stevie Blue, glaring at the mandala. 'You have anything further to say?'

'Not at this time,' said the mandala stiffly. The elves' fire snapped off, and everyone breathed a little more easily.

'Can't we leave you people alone together for ten minutes?' said a new voice, and everyone turned to look. All around the walls, viewscreens were flashing on as the cyberats made their appearance. Computer hackers, techno freaks, teenage rebels with any number of causes. Like the esper representatives, they hid their true faces behind computer-generated images. Cyberats faced death or reconditioning if caught, but for them the lure and possibilities of the computer system were just too much to resist. Most of them had no interest in politics or

310

rebellion, outside of wanting to be left alone, but the shared danger provided a common ground with the clone and esper undergrounds.

Cyberats were unpeople, hiding behind fake IDs and a multitude of names, organizations and corporate identities. They lived like rats in the walls of the state, foraging for what they needed when no one was looking, ghosts haunting the machine just for the hell of it. They helped fund the underground through various scams and computer frauds, and used the opportunity to vent their spleen on the authorities who persecuted them. There were a great number of ways to make someone's life miserable through computers, and the cyberats knew all of them. After all, they'd invented most of them.

The esper and clone representatives looked severely about them at the grinning faces covering the walls, and maintained a dignified silence. Long experience had taught them they couldn't win with the cyberats, who spent most of their time engaged in wars of words with each other. A few voices jeered at the representatives, and then were distracted by the last of the arrivals. The aristocratic backers had finally turned up, fashionably late of course, stepping out of the entrances as though just entering the chamber was enough to soil their clothing. Valentine smiled at them, and they bowed briefly in return. There were only three of them. Most of the aristocrats who for one reason or another backed the underground, preferred to do so discreetly, and at long distance.

On the whole, they funded the underground as a means to political power. Mostly younger sons, who weren't going to inherit, or at least not fast enough to suit them, and therefore had to look for advancement where they could. They wore no disguises; the underground didn't trust them any further than they could spit into the wind with their mouths closed, and were determined to know exactly who they were dealing with. If only so they could get them later, if things went wrong. The aristocrats went along, with much bad grace. It wasn't as if they had a choice. You only came to the underground when there was nowhere else to go. Personally, Valentine didn't give a damn.

Evangeline Shreck he knew from before, and her appearance

here was no surprise. A fervent supporter of the clone underground in recent times, for reasons which remained obscure. David Deathstalker was a new face. He'd inherited the title after Owen was outlawed, and didn't look any too pleased about it. Only seventeen years old, a minor cousin, unused to the hothouse intrigues of the Imperial Court. Tall, immaculately dressed, and possibly not as nervous as he appeared. Handsome enough to set a few hearts fluttering at Court, but young enough not to know that yet. Or maybe not. He was a Deathstalker, after all.

He'd acquired the title by default. Owen had no brothers or sisters; the same genetic quirk that gave Deathstalkers the boost also killed most children before they reached maturity. The Family considered it an acceptable risk. No one ever asked the children what they thought about it. So far, David's motivations seemed clear enough. He wanted to avoid being outlawed like Owen, or executed like Owen's father, and was smart enough to know he had absolutely no allies at Court. The Deathstalker name had become synonymous with treason and bad luck, and most people were keeping well clear in case it rubbed off.

The third face held Valentine's interest the longest. Kit SummerIsle, called by some Kid Death, who murdered his own Family in the name of ambition, only to find himself alone, trusted by neither the Court nor any Family. A mad dog who'd slipped his leash. Presumably Kit was there as a backer of the underground because no one else would touch him. The Empress had played with him for a while, but Kit had to be wise enough to know that wouldn't last. He was too dangerous; a sword that might just as easily turn on anyone who tried to wield it. Kid Death, the smiling killer; resplendent as always in his armour of black and silver. He looked very young, with his pale face and flyaway blond hair, but the icy blue eyes were very old. They'd seen enough death for a dozen lifetimes, and loved every minute of it.

Valentine stepped forward and bowed courteously to Evangeline Shreck. 'Dear Evangeline; so good to see you again. Pity about the wedding, but that's life. Or rather, death. Your father always did have a propensity to over-react.'

'That's one way of putting it,' said Evangeline. 'You look quite different without your face on, Valentine. Almost human.'

'A mere illusion,' Valentine said smoothly. He turned to the young Deathstalker and bowed again, not quite as low. 'I've not had the pleasure, I believe, Sir. David, isn't it? I'm . . .'

'I know who you are. And it's pronounced "Dah-veed", actually.' The Deathstalker's voice was cool and sharp, trying hard for the gravitas he felt his title required.

'As you wish,' said Valentine. 'But I fear you too must learn to come when the underground calls, however they pronounce your name. There's no room down here for the airs and graces we allow ourselves in society. That is, after all, part of the charm of treason. There are no rules here, no required behaviour, no one to make us kneel or bow the head. We are equal here. And all they ask of us is a willingness to fight and if need be die for the Cause.'

'Then why are you here, Valentine?' said Kid Death. 'You never cared for any cause save your own continuing self-destruction.'

Valentine took his time turning, and smiled at the SummerIsle. 'Where better to seek death or transformation than in the midst of rebellion? There's only one place on Golgotha more dangerous than the underground, and that's the Arena. And that's always seemed too much like hard work for me. I'm really rather delicate, you know.'

'You have the constitution of an ox,' said Evangeline. 'Your system has to be in top form, to put up with all the things you do to it.'

'I know why he's here,' said Kid Death. 'He wants the drug. The esper drug. Trust me, Valentine; if you did get it, you wouldn't like it. You'd find out what everyone really thinks of you.'

Valentine smiled dazzlingly. 'You already know what every-one thinks of you, dear Kit, and it hasn't slowed you down any.'

313

'I want to know why Hood is allowed to hide his face,' said David. 'We weren't allowed to, even though it meant having to expose our faces in front of brain damage cases like Valentine and Kid Death.'

'How unkind,' murmured Valentine. 'No one appreciates a true artist.'

Kid Death looked steadily at David. 'You really must learn to choose your words more carefully, Deathstalker. You never know when they might be your last.'

David looked at him defiantly. His hand was very near his sword. 'You don't frighten me, SummerIsle.'

'Then he should,' said Evangeline. 'I've seen you both fight, and he'd win. Now if you two have both finished shaking your genitalia at each other, perhaps we could hear Hood answer the question about his anonymity. Personally, I'm all ears.'

Kid Death and David Deathstalker looked at each other, and David looked away first. Valentine studied him thoughtfully. Perhaps the young Deathstalker wasn't as naive as he seemed. The SummerIsle was a psychopath, and everyone knew it. If he were to turn those cold eyes in Valentine's direction, Valentine had every intention of bowing low and backing down. And then possibly dropping a little something special in the SummerIsle's drink at some future time. He looked across at Hood, as he realized the silence had lengthened and Hood still hadn't answered the question. The man without a face stood very still, the empty interior of his hood as enigmatic as ever.

'I am valuable to the underground and the cyberats,' he said finally. 'They indulge me, rather than risk losing what I provide.'

'And what might that be?' said Kit.

'You don't need to know,' said Hood.

'But we insist,' said David.

The two of them moved unhurriedly towards Hood, taking up positions on either side of him so that he couldn't face them both at once. Their hands were very near their swords.

'That's enough!' snapped Mr Perfect, and everyone turned to look. The esper representative glared at them all impartially.

'We did not summon you here to squabble like children in a playground. We have business to discuss, and the longer we stay here, gathered together in one place, the more danger we put ourselves in.'

'Damn right,' said one of the Stevie Blues. She strode forward to take up a position in the centre of the chamber, hands on hips. 'Security would just love to get the drop on us because we were too busy arguing amongst ourselves to hear them coming. Everyone stops messing about right now, or my sisters and I will start banging heads together. You can call me Stevie One. My sisters are Two and Three. Don't get us mixed up or we'll hit you. We pride ourselves on our individuality.'

There was a general relaxing and moving away by all those present. Stevie One nodded to Mr Perfect to take over. David sniffed at the three clones.

'Bunch of perverts,' he said quietly to Valentine. 'And they dare call what they have a marriage.'

'Be fair,' said Valentine. 'At least they can be sure what they see in each other. Anyway, at least now we get to know why the elves summoned us here.'

Mr Perfect glared at him. 'The esper Council summoned you, not the elves. They are only a part of the underground. The Stevie Blues do not speak for everyone here.'

Stevie Two sniffed. 'You still come to us when you want something dirty done. Especially if it's risky. And who has a better right to speak than my sisters and I? We're both espers and clones; we understand the pressures of both sides. No one knows more of suffering than we do.'

'Right,' said Stevie Three.

'We will be heard,' said Stevie One. 'Our sister is dead, murdered by the Iron Bitch. We demand a vengeance.'

'I didn't know there were any esper clones left alive,' said David quietly to Evangeline while the espers argued. 'I thought they were all wiped out, and further experimentation forbidden.'

'Lots of things are forbidden,' murmured Evangeline. 'But they still happen, if there's profit to be made. As I understand it, the Stevie Blues were a secret military experiment in cloning

315

battle espers. Didn't work out. Most of the subjects died, and the survivors were too powerful. Too uncontrollable, unpredictable. Word about the experiments got out, and the Empress was furious that she hadn't been consulted. Gave the order to close everything down. The Stevie Blues were marked for destruction, but they escaped. The elves took them in, gave them a purpose in life, and a shape for their revenge. As both espers and clones they were supposed to be a link between the two undergrounds, but no one seems too sure where their true loyalties lie. Perhaps even they're not sure.'

'Fair enough,' said David. He realized the espers had stopped talking and settled for glaring at each other, so he raised his voice again. 'I still want to know why Hood hides his face.'

'Oh, tell him, someone,' said the dragon. 'Or we'll be here all night.'

'I am highly placed in the Empress's retinue,' said Hood. 'I have her trust, in as much as she trusts anyone. I am not ready to endanger myself by revealing my identity to those who don't need to know. The underground indulges me because I discovered the esper drug. None of us can afford for the Empress to learn about that. They'd get the secret out of me eventually; they always do. My identity remains a secret because it is in all our best interests. Now; as the Stevie Blues have pointed out, we have business to discuss.'

'I said that,' said Mr Perfect.

'Then get on with it,' said Valentine. 'What exactly is so important that we had to be dragged here at such short notice and at such an ungodly hour?'

'We have a plan,' said Stevie One. 'We elves have placed one of our own in the water purification department. Through him we have unlimited access to the water supply network for the whole of Golgotha. We propose to introduce the esper drug into the water system. I'm told a really small amount, as little as one part per million, would be enough to have an effect on anyone who drank it or even had contact with the affected water. No one would notice its presence until it was far too late. No one knows it exists but us, and unless you knew exactly what you were looking for, the esper drug would just blend in with all the other drugs in the water. It's pumped full of happy drugs and tranquillizers as it is, to keep the common herd quiet. With millions of espers appearing suddenly overnight, the Empress would have no choice but to recognize espers as full citizens, with full privileges. After all, most of her subjects would be espers, along with most of her own people. Who knows; maybe we'll get really lucky, and she'll get a surprise in her drink too . . .'

There was a long pause, as everyone took it in turn to look at each other. The Stevie Blues smiled at each other smugly.

'You have got to be joking!' said Evangeline. 'You're crazy!'

'Oh I don't know,' said Valentine. 'I rather like the sound of it myself.'

'You would,' snapped David. 'Anyone who is anyone drinks off-world bottled water. Only the lower classes drink tap water. And the Empress would wipe out every single one of them on this planet, rather than be dictated to.'

'Nicely put,' said Evangeline. 'Didn't think you had it in you, David.'

'Dah-veed.'

'Don't push it, Deathstalker.'

'Look,' said Stevie One. 'The esper and clone undergrounds have been fighting for self-determination for almost three centuries, and what have we to show for it? Nothing but increased security on all levels, and greater controls over the clone and esper populations. The elves emerged out of a need to strike back, to take the attack to the enemy. This would be a blow against the Empress's authority that couldn't be hidden or hushed up. A whole planetful of espers couldn't be ignored. They'd be too valuable just to be wiped out.'

'Right,' said Stevie Three.

There was a flood of approval from the cyberats on the surrounding viewscreens. They were always up for a little orchestrated chaos and mayhem, and they admired audacity. They'd always been troublemakers first and rebels second. The various faces on the screens began shouting advice and support, and then started shouting at each other to shut up, until

317

finally one of the esper representatives had the sense to turn the volume right down. The cyberats raved silently on, oblivious to the fact that no one was listening to them any more. They were used to that.

'You're still carefully overlooking the main objection,' said Evangeline to the Stevie Blues. 'According to the figures I've seen, the esper drug kills twenty to forty per cent of those who take it. If we gave it to the entire population of Golgotha, how many innocents would die for our revenge?'

'None of them are innocent,' said Stevie Two defiantly. 'They're all part of the system that brutalizes us. They're happy enough to profit from our pain.'

'Right,' said Stevie Three. 'When have they ever cared for us?'

'What do you think we should do?' said Stevie One, glaring at Evangeline. 'Commit suicide in public as a protest, like that poor fool you smuggled into the wedding? What difference did it make? No one gave a damn. They don't care if an esper or a clone dies; we're just property. They can just replace us. It's not like we were people. Do I need to stand here and tell you horror stories of the way we've been treated, to justify our plan? We've all lost someone dear. It's barely a year since Dram and his butchers attacked our base on New Hope. That was supposed to be our first step forward, out of the darkness and into the light. Espers and clones and normals living together in harmony. A living example of the way things could be.

'And then the attack sleds came falling out of the sky, opening fire without warning. Hundreds of thousands died as the city burned. Men, women and children; espers, clones and normals. There was nothing we could do but run for our lives. It took us a year to rebuild the underground, and now all the normals are too scared even to be seen with us. Every chance we had for peaceful coexistence died with New Hope. All that's left is the elves, and the armed struggle. Did our friends die for nothing? Have you forgotten the screams bursting through our minds, blinking out one by one, like candles caught in a storm?'

'Revenge,' said one of the male clones, and everyone turned to look. The four men had been quiet so long everyone had forgotten they were there. 'Revenge is all espers ever want. We want peace. Freedom. We have to learn to live with the normals because it's their universe. Their Empire. One day it might be ours, but none of us will live to see it. Pardon our paranoia, but we can't see how a planetful of traumatized espers, mourning their dead, would do anything to further the clone cause. The Empire would waste no time in blaming the undergrounds. We'd be branded mass-murderers, and they'd be right. Everyone would turn against us, even the new espers.'

'He's got a point,' said David. 'I really don't think I can go along with this.'

'No one asked you, Dah-veed,' said Stevie One. 'You don't understand what we're talking about.'

'Presumably you have some interest in our opinions,' said Valentine. 'Or else why were we called here?'

'We value your input,' said the shimmering mandala. 'We are . . . unable to decide. It occurred to us that perhaps we are too close to the question. Hopefully you will help us see the wider issues. The esper drug could be the means to our finally winning the war, or it could damn us all forever. Talk to us. All of you. We must decide.'

'What's the hurry?' said Evangeline. 'We don't have to go ahead with the drug immediately, even if we do decide to go for it. The secret of the drug is safe with us, and the water systems aren't going anywhere. As long as your man keeps his head down and doesn't draw attention to himself, we can take our time over this, make sure we end up with the right decision.'

'And how many espers and clones would die while we were talking?' said Stevie Two.

'A lot less than twenty to forty per cent,' said Hood.

'There's still a lot we don't understand about the drug,' said Mr Perfect. 'We were understandably intrigued with the thought of what the drug would do to someone who was already an esper. We hoped it might produce the super-esper we've been searching for, someone strong enough to overcome the effects of the esp-blocker, and free us from its control. We had many volunteers.'

'So what happened?' said Valentine.

'They all died,' said the dragon. 'Some were killed outright, some went insane and then died. Some tore out their own eyes because of what they were seeing. It would seem we're not ready as a species to become super-espers. We must continue to rely on our cyberat friends to come up with a technological answer.'

'They've been promising a breakthrough on that for years!' snapped Stevie One. 'We're tired of waiting. This drug is our chance to strike back at those who've hurt us! We can't wait. How long can it be before some traitor in our organizations gets hold of the formula and hands it over to Security? Just because we're espers, it doesn't mean we can't be fooled. We must use the drug now, while we still have the advantage of surprise.'

'Right,' said Stevie Three. 'Who cares about a few dead normals?'

'We care,' said one of the male clones. 'Our argument has always been that we are not just property; we are humans too. We will not risk that humanity by becoming responsible for mass slaughter.'

'You've always been dreamers,' said Stevie Two. 'We can't live with normals. They're too different.'

'They seem to have managed quite successfully on Mistworld.'

'Yeah, well,' said Stevie One. 'From what I've heard it's a right hellhole. I wouldn't live there if you paid me.'

'We're drifting away from the subject again,' said Evangeline. 'It seems to me there are still too many unanswered questions about the esper drug. Firstly, we can't be sure of a mortality rate of just twenty to forty per cent when dealing with such a large dose. It could turn out to be much higher. Word would get out eventually as to who was responsible; that's inevitable. And then the normals would hate us as never before.

'Secondly, I think getting the drug past all the checks and

filters would prove to be a great deal harder than you've been assuming. One man on his own couldn't hope to oversee everything. I think we should ask the cyberats to run some computer simulations first. In the meantime, I think we'd do better to concentrate our efforts on bringing influential people to see the justice of our cause. The real war will be fought and won in the hearts and minds of people everywhere. After all, the Empress can't live for ever. Perhaps a coalition of the right people could even replace her, in the future.'

'Right,' said Stevie Three. 'A coalition. You'd love that. With you at its head, no doubt?'

'They could do worse,' said Hood.

'We have heard enough,' said the dragon. It stretched slowly, light rippling across its golden scales. 'Evangeline Shreck has provided the voice of reason, as always. We do not reject the idea outright, but it is clear that much more research must be undertaken before we can commit ourselves. The matter is now closed.' He looked hard at the Stevie Blues, who glared back, but had nothing further to say. For the moment. The dragon nodded its head slowly. 'We will now move on to the next order of business; the fate of the traitor Edwyn Burgess. Bring him forward.'

Everyone looked round sharply as a man stepped slowly out of a low entrance. He stumbled forward into the middle of the chamber, his movements awkward and deliberate, clearly controlled from without. He was a small, insignificant man with a vague, empty face and frightened eyes. Sweat poured down his face, and soaked his clothing. As he drew nearer, they could hear he was whimpering softly. He finally came to a halt in the exact centre of the floor and stood still. Unnaturally still.

'Edwyn Burgess,' said a cold disembodied voice that could have come from any of the esper representatives, or all of them. 'You stand accused of treason against your brothers, condemned by information discovered within your mind. You were preparing to betray the location of this meeting to Security forces, and were only discovered thanks to information supplied by our good friend Hood. Tell us why. Was it the money?'

'Partly,' said Burgess, desperation flooding his face as control over him was briefly relaxed. 'Mostly I was just so tired of being scared all the time. Jumping at every knock on the door, convinced it was Security come at last to drag me away. In the end I went to them. I couldn't stand the strain any more. Only after that, I was just as scared of what you'd do when you found out. Security said they'd protect me, but I knew better. When your people finally came to get me, it was almost a relief.'

'We understand,' said the voice. 'But with so many lives put at risk by your weakness, we cannot be merciful. We are all scared, Edwyn; but we have not broken. How many thousands would have been betrayed, if we had been taken by Security? The whole underground could have been shattered beyond repair.'

'Do you think I don't know that?' Burgess's voice was flat and heavy, beyond hope or fear. 'I've learnt my lesson. I won't be weak again. I wouldn't dare.'

'We're sorry,' said the voice. 'We must make an example.'

'Then make it quick,' said Burgess.

'Yes,' said the voice. 'We can do that.'

Burgess exploded, flying apart in a cloud of gut and broken bone. Everyone stepped back instinctively, but the debris didn't travel far, contained by the same force that had produced it, and as quickly as that it was all over. It was very quiet in the chamber. One of the cyberats on the screens whistled respectfully. Valentine stepped forward, and nudged at a lump of bloody muscle with the tip of his boot.

'How about that,' he said, smiling. 'He did have a heart, after all.'

And that was when all hell broke out. An alarm sounded, loud and strident, and over it came the sound of energy guns firing. All around the walls of the chamber the cyberats vanished from the viewscreens as they dropped out of the system. For a moment there was only the hissing of blank screens, and then they cleared one by one to show rapidly changing views of armed guards running through the approach tunnels. They were everywhere, filling the tunnels, firing their disrupters at unseen esper resistance. Whatever the esper sentries were doing, it didn't seem to be slowing the guards down any.

'Why aren't they using illusions to stop the guards?' said Evangeline. 'I thought that was what they were there for!'

'Look at the screens,' Valentine said quietly. 'They've got esp-blockers. Our friend Burgess must have got his message out before he was caught. Look at the uniforms; those are Imperial Guards. The Empress's own. She knew there'd be important people here.'

And then everyone was shouting at once, and trying to outshout everyone else. David Deathstalker and Kit SummerIsle had their guns and swords in their hands, but only Kid Death looked ready to use them. Hood was looking from one screen to another, as though he couldn't believe what he was seeing. Evangeline had gone very pale, but her hands had clenched into fists. She looked at Valentine, who smiled and made helpless motions with his hands. Behind his flustered facade, Valentine was thinking fast. He had any number of battle drugs ready to drop into his system at a moment's notice, but he was reluctant to throw away his carefully established persona until he absolutely had to. It wouldn't do for word to get out that he wasn't the useless type he'd always pretended to be. People might start wondering what else he'd been hiding. On the other hand, he couldn't afford to be taken prisoner by the guards, for much the same reason. He decided to wait and see how much danger he was really in. And then the esper representatives vanished between one moment and the next, and the air rushed in to fill the space where they'd been.

'The bastards!' yelled Stevie One. 'They've teleported out and left us to die!'

There were six entrances giving out into the chamber, none of them big enough for more than two men to pass through at a time. The Stevie Blues covered three of them, psionic flames leaping menacingly from their hands. Kit moved to cover another, and gestured for David to take the next. Kid Death was grinning broadly. David looked as though he'd rather be anywhere else, but his eyes were calm and his mouth was firm, and he held his sword and his gun as though it was the most natural thing in the world. He was a Deathstalker, after all. That left one opening gaping unattended. Hood was still frozen in place before the screens. Evangeline started towards the entrance as though she might break into a run at any moment, but Valentine stopped her with a hand on her arm.

'Don't,' he murmured. 'Trying to run would be a really bad idea. Look at the screens. The guards have got all the escape routes covered, and at the moment they're shooting at anything that isn't them. There's nowhere to go.'

'You don't understand!' said Evangeline. 'I can't afford to be caught!'

Valentine raised an eyebrow. 'I think you'll find that's true for most of us. Now, if you'll excuse me, I'd better guard that entrance.'

Evangeline looked at him. 'You? What are you going to do; bribe your way past the guards with handfuls of drugs?'

'Oh, I'll think of something,' Valentine said calmly. 'Besides; there's no one else, is there?'

Evangeline looked at Hood, still rooted to the spot, and looked away.

'Give me a knife,' she said quietly. 'I won't be taken alive.'

Valentine studied her for a long moment, and then drew a long stiletto from his boot and handed it to her. She accepted it with a nod of thanks, and moved over to stand beside Hood and watch the screens. Valentine moved unhurriedly over to the gaping entrance. He was still thinking hard. He'd put a lot of time and effort into his usual persona, and now it seemed he was going to have to throw it away. As usual, man proposes and the Empress disposes. And then a thought came to him, and he smiled. He didn't know what he was so worried about; the odds were he was going to die anyway. The thought cheered him, and he checked the contents of his pillbox for something special. Some of the guards were in for a very unpleasant surprise.

The first armed men rounded a corner and found themselves face to face with Stevie One, guarding the entrance. They raised their guns and the esper hit them with a blast of white-hot flames. The guards screamed as the blazing fire filled the tunnel, sucking the air from their lungs as it crisped their flesh. More guards appeared in the adjacent tunnels, only to meet Stevies Two and Three. They summoned up fire, and the leading guards died horribly. Evangeline watched them die on the viewscreens and wouldn't let herself look away. The remaining guards came to a halt in the tunnels as word of the deaths got to them. They were waiting for something.

'They're bringing the esp-blockers forward!' yelled Stevie Two. 'I can feel them getting closer. My flame's already beginning to die down.'

More guards spilled into a different tunnel, only to find Kid Death waiting for them. He shot the first man with almost lazy precision, and then put the gun away and waded into the guards, swinging his sword double-handed. In the narrow tunnel they could only come at him two at a time, and that was no threat to Kid Death. He laughed as he worked; a light, breathy and altogether horrible sound.

David Deathstalker boosted, and all his worries fell away. The guards were no match for him, either. But there were so many of them, and neither Kit nor David had any illusions about their eventual fate. If the guards had only had more guns, it would have been over by now.

And then Evangeline shouted and pointed at the view-screens, and Valentine heard a familiar roar deep in the tunnels. He looked back at the screens and grinned broadly. The guards in the tunnel heard him laughing, and then they heard the roar building behind them and turned to look. And a wall of rushing water came thundering towards them, filling the tunnel from floor to ceiling. For a moment Valentine thought it was the illusion again, a last ditch defence by the espers, but even as he thought that he knew it had to be genuine. All those espers were dead or blocked by now. The water was real. And up on the viewscreens, the pounding wave smashed into the guards and swept them away. They never stood a chance.

Valentine moved back to stand with Evangeline and Hood, and watched the guards die on the screens. The water carried them along like leaves in a flooded drain, hammering them against the sides of the tunnels, and then pulling them on. A few tried to grab at the tunnel supports, but the pressure of the water was too much for them, and there was no air anywhere. They drowned, quickly if they were lucky, and their dead bodies bobbed limply in the surging tide. David and Kit cut down the last of their opponents, and looked around confused, for more. David was panting and shaking as he fell out of boost, but his face was full of exhilaration. Kid Death was smiling gently, not even breathing heavily. But they both had the same look in their eyes, the same pleasure satisfied, and they saw it in each other like a secret shared. One of the Stevie Blues whooped with joy, and the other two joined in.

'The esp-blockers have been destroyed, or swept away!' said Stevie One. 'I can't feel them any more. We're safe!'

'Not necessarily,' said Valentine, in a surprisingly even voice. He pointed at the viewscreens. 'All that water is heading our way, and there's nothing here to stop it.'

They all saw it on the screens, and backed away from the entrances. The pounding of the water was louder now, like a never-ending roll of thunder, and they could feel the pressure of its coming on the air, its awful weight vibrating through the chamber floor. On the viewscreens, dead guards tumbled through the rushing water like so many blank-eyed dolls. Everyone backed away from the entrances, coming together in the middle of the chamber, because there was nowhere else to go. They watched their death coming on the screens, and no one had anything to say. The Stevie Blues held hands, and Evangeline held Valentine's arm. He smiled briefly, and let her.

And then the tidal wave slammed into an invisible barrier, and fell back, thwarted. The water churned on the viewscreens, pounding this way and that, but couldn't enter the chamber.

326

The air shimmered, and the esper representatives were suddenly back in the chamber. Mr Perfect smiled at their surprise.

'You didn't really think we'd just abandon you, did you? We set up the flood from the sewers after Burgess's confession. It seemed a reasonable precaution, just in case.'

'If I wasn't feeling so good, I'd kill every damn one of you,' said David.

'Damn right,' said Kit. 'I must have aged twenty years in the past few minutes. Mind you; on me it looks good.'

The two men laughed together companionably. The Stevie Blues were laughing too. Evangeline realized she was still holding Valentine's arm, and let go. He bowed to her courteously. Hood was slowly shaking his head.

'You'd think by now I'd be used to espers and their devious ways,' he said tiredly. 'I assume you have some way of draining the water out of the tunnels, so we can leave?'

'Of course,' said the dragon. 'It shouldn't take long, and then you can all go.'

'I should be careful where you tread, though,' said Valentine Wolfe. 'You never know what you'll find in the water these days.'

CHAPTER NINE

Who's Been Sleeping in My Head?

The man called Hood walked unhurriedly through the quiet corridors deep in the heart of the Empress's palace. They were broad, high-ceilinged corridors, with tasteful paintings and portraits on the walls by whoever was currently in fashion. Holos were so gauche. People came and went on silent, important missions, passing Hood by without noticing him. The same low-level esp that hid his face among espers was more than enough to keep him hidden from normal people he didn't want to see him. He wasn't actually invisible; he just gave their minds a little nudge and they looked everywhere except at him. Luckily esp-blockers were rare and expensive enough that they were only used in actual rooms, not in the connecting corridors. A serious security lapse that Hood had taken care never to point out. Never knew when you might need an ace up your sleeve; particularly when dealing with the Empress. Lionstone had raised paranoia to an art form, and encouraged its growth among her people.

Hood also carried a small tech inhibitor, that kept his image from appearing on any of the security monitors. A simple device, that triggered a programme he'd entered into the security computers, which in turn edited him out of the image appearing on the monitors. The device reminded each camera as he approached, and then made it forget him once he was past. No trouble at all for someone with his access to security computers.

It took him a little longer than usual to reach his personal quarters, but he was used to that. Because people couldn't see him, they had a regrettable tendency to try and walk through him, and he had to be quick on his feet to avoid them. His esp wasn't strong enough to hide him from someone who'd just crashed into him. So he ducked this way and that and never said a word, until finally the door to his private chambers was shut firmly behind him, and he could relax at last. He removed his cape, threw it more or less in the direction of his coat rack, and let out a long happy sigh. Home and safe. Or as safe as he ever was. He sank into a comfortable chair and stretched slowly. Living a double life was a tiring business. He smiled and dropped his esp disguise, and there in his chair sat the Lord High Dram, Warrior Prime of the Empire and head of the Empress's security. Right hand, confidant and lover of the Empress Lionstone herself.

Now that he was finally able to relax and be himself, it occurred to him that by rights he ought to be mad as hell. The security raid on the underground meeting had damn near caught him napping. Certainly they'd been none of his people. He'd gone to some lengths to ensure that they were preoccupied elsewhere. And since he hadn't sanctioned the raid it must have originated with the Empress's own people. Presumably they'd found out about the meeting through their own agents, and seized the chance to make him look negligent in her eyes. There was always a certain rivalry between his agents and hers, but he'd thought he had it safely under control. Apparently not. He'd have to do something about that. If he had been caught and identified, all the time and hard work he'd spent establishing his Hood persona would have been for nothing, and the Empress would have lost her best source on what was happening in the underground. More importantly, he'd have looked like a fool before the Empress, and all his own plans would have been ruined. But he hadn't been caught. Through luck, keeping a cool head, and having the foresight to surround himself with the right people, he'd come out of it untouched. He'd light a candle in church, as a sign of thanks. When he had the time.

He stretched slowly again, enjoying it, and put his feet up on the padded footstool that hurried forward in time to catch his feet. Dram had always believed in keeping up with the latest little luxuries. One of the perquisites of living so deep in the palace, so close to the Empress. Your life or your freedom might be in danger now and again, but never your comforts. Having said that, Dram's quarters were positively bare and spartan compared to most people of his rank and standing. Dram had never had much interest in personal possessions, unless they attended to his personal comfort. So there were padded chairs and a luxurious bed, thick carpets on the floor and a well-stocked drinks cabinet, but no cybernetic toys or diversions, no holo views or personalized illusions on his walls. Nothing expensively useless or ostentatious, just to show he could afford it. He'd always been basically inner-directed, and possessions seemed to him to be just something more to worry about. They slowed you down when you were in a hurry, and distracted you when your mind should be focused on more important things. So mostly he did without them. His life was complicated enough as it was.

He also had no time for the excesses and indulgences that so preoccupied others of his rank and station. Dram saw them as weaknesses, and he couldn't afford to be weak. He had too many enemies, and besides, it pleased him to be strong and in control at all times. Given time, he had every intention of extending that control as far and as wide as it would go. His only passion, apart from the Empress, long may she reign, was ambition. Though he was careful always to keep that to himself. Lover or no, Lionstone wouldn't hesitate to have him executed if she saw in him a threat to her position. She'd always been very single-minded in such matters. Dram admired that in her. He liked to think they had something in common out of bed.

It was his ambition that had led him to recognize the potential in the newly developed esper drug. He'd immediately taken steps to place the scientists involved under his direct control. He cut them off from every outside influence, and drove them mercilessly until he had a working sample. He tested it on expendable subjects for as long as his patience would allow, and then took it himself, just a small dose, and it was wonderful. Like a blind man seeing a swan for the first time, or a deaf man hearing music.

He had everyone involved quietly killed, save for those few scientists necessary to produce and refine more of the drug. It was vital that he control it utterly. He knew even then that it could be his road to the Iron Throne itself. The clone underground would serve as further test subjects, and finally as his own private army of espers, loyal only to him. They would do anything for him, in return for the drug, because he knew its secret. The effects were only temporary. To remain an esper, you had to keep taking the drug. And though the drug itself wasn't addictive, being an esper was. Anyone who'd experienced it, even for a short while, would do anything necessary to be an esper again. To be whole again. He controlled production and distribution of the drug, which meant he controlled anyone who took it. Forever. The thought pleased him, and he laughed softly. The clones would take the drug eagerly to begin with, because they trusted him; trusted Hood, the tried and true backer and supporter of the underground. And by the time they discovered the truth, it would be far too late.

Of course, the twenty to forty per cent death rate was a problem. He'd have to do something about that. He deplored waste.

He'd only taken a minor dose himself. The more powerful the dosage, the higher the death rate. Once your body had adapted to the drug, you were safe enough, but the initial dose was always a risk. So, being sensible as well as ambitious, he'd settled for a minor dose. It meant only limited esper abilities, but he could live with that. He'd save the larger doses for his clone volunteers. He was interested in seeing what abilities the larger doses would produce, but he could wait. He was patient. There was always the chance larger doses would produce battle espers, like the Stevie Blues. Given an army of those, he'd face any enemy. Augmented and adjusted men were the past; esp was the future.

It was a pity the tests on cloning espers had been shut down. They'd been producing very interesting results, under his indirect control, until the Empress found out about them, and had them shut down. That had been her agents at work again, and only some quick thinking on his feet had kept his connections from coming out. That wasn't going to happen again. The esper drug was his one weapon against all the Empress's power and influence. Unless, of course, she already knew about it. Which was a possibility. You could never be sure exactly what the Empress did and didn't know. Except that if she had known what he planned and intended, she'd have had him killed by now.

'Talk to me, Argus,' he said finally, and sank back in his chair with his eyes closed as his personal AI brought him up to date on everything that had happened in his absence. Dram had many enemies, most of whom knew where he lived, and he relied on the AI's unsleeping vigilance to protect his quarters while he was away.

'Everything is under control, Sir. I dealt with all the routine matters in your absence, using your face and voice, and made a number of entries in your diary. Do try and read it some time, Sir; I don't make these appointments for fun. It would appear you're still remarkably popular with the populace, according to your mail, proving once again that there is no allowing for taste. Requests for help or money are up, proposals of marriage slightly down. The Company of Lords still hates your guts. They sent a number of professional people to booby-trap your apartment while you were out. I let them get on with it rather than use emergency measures. It takes such a long time to clean the blood off the walls afterwards. Once they were gone, I went around and disarmed everything. They're getting pretty ingenious, you know. Every time this happens, I find something new.'

'Are you sure you got everything?'

'Reasonably sure.'

'What does that mean?'

'It means if I have got it wrong, at least you won't be around to say I told you so.'

Dram laughed in spite of himself. He allowed the AI to be rude on occasion. He felt it was good for his character.

'Someone wishes to talk to you, Sir.'

'I don't feel like talking to anyone right now. You deal with it.'

'It's the Empress, Sir.'

'Why the hell didn't you say so?' Dram sat up straight in his chair, immediately wide awake again. 'Never mind. Put her on.'

The wall to his left became one large viewscreen, filled with the Empress Lionstone's arctic features. She looked . . . thoughtful. Dram didn't like the look of that. Lionstone was never more dangerous than when she'd been thinking. He stood up, bowed respectfully, and smiled warmly into the chill of her blue eyes.

'Lionstone, my dear. An unexpected pleasure. What can I do for you?'

'Come to my private quarters. Now. There's something we need to discuss.'

Dram started to frame a polite and reassuring reply, but the wall had already gone blank. He scowled thoughtfully as he went to retrieve his cloak from the coat rack. His first thought was that the Iron Bitch had discovered everything, and his best bet was to head for the horizon. He ran through the nearest exit routes in his mind, and the quickest ways to get off-planet, and then stopped and made himself take a few deep breaths. Calm slowly enveloped him as his iron will forced out the panic. Lionstone couldn't know everything, or she wouldn't have bothered with a reasonably polite summons. Instead, a squad of armed guards would have kicked in his door and dragged him screaming away. Or at least, they would have tried. One of the secrets he kept hidden from Lionstone was the extent of his personal security defences.

So, something must have come up while he was off being Hood. Something she chose not to discuss over an open comm link. Dram ran through the various problems that were currently under surveillance by his people, but nothing obvious sprang to mind. There was nothing immediately dangerous about any of them, for a change, or he wouldn't have gone to the underground meeting. He couldn't afford to be found missing in an emergency, and there was a limit to how much Argus could cover for him. He sighed, opened the door, gave the AI his usual commands about maintaining security and not talking to any strange men, and let himself out. The quickest way to find out what was going on was to go and ask Lionstone. He just hoped she wasn't feeling amorous. He'd had a long day.

He walked unhurriedly down the corridor, nodding casually to those he passed. It was important not to look flustered or nervous; that might be construed as a sign of weakness. It wasn't enough for him to be strong and in control; he had to be seen to be strong and in control. Otherwise the vultures started gathering. People bowed low as he passed, and made way for him. Whatever had happened, it hadn't filtered down to the lower orders yet. Dram couldn't help noticing increasing levels of security as he approached the Empress's private quarters, including some he hadn't seen before. Either Lionstone was feeling insecure again, or there'd been some new attack on her during his absence. There shouldn't have been. If the elves or the clones had been planning anything, he'd have known about it. And there'd been nothing new in the last reports from his agents. But everywhere he looked there were more guards, cameras, sensors, and undoubtedly a great many more he couldn't see. His back began to itch in anticipation of unseen weapons following his every movement. He had no doubt they were there. He'd had most of them installed. His esp suddenly shut down as he came within range of a new esp-blocker, and that definitely was new. Usually Lionstone was happy to settle for having one in her quarters. There was always a long waiting list for a new esp-blocker, and there always would be as long as it took a whole esper to make one.

He came to the reinforced airlock that was the only entry to the Empress's private quarters, and the six guards on duty (four more than normal) crashed to attention. Dram casually acknowledged their salute, and stood calm and easy as the security sensors established he was who he seemed to be. He wasn't carrying any of his usual weapons; even he wasn't allowed to go armed into the Empress's private chambers. The airlock swung open with a low hiss of equalizing pressures, and he stepped inside. It was only just big enough to take him, and he felt increasingly claustrophobic as the door cycled shut behind him. The shape of the airlock usually suggested some self-conscious womb imagery, but he wasn't in the mood. The interior door swung open, and he stepped out into the Empress's private domain. And there to meet him were the only other people Lionstone ever allowed to share her privacy; her maids. They glared at him, growling deep in their throats, and then moved reluctantly aside as he strode confidently forward. Dram wrinkled his nose. The air was thick with the Empress's current favourite perfume, there to disguise the poison in the air that he and the maids had been immunized against. It wasn't a subtle deterrent, or a subtle perfume, but Lionstone wasn't a subtle person in private. She didn't have to be. You could tell that from the furnishings.

The large room was crammed with furniture, paintings, statuettes; all of them unique. Only the lower orders had to make do with copies or holo duplicates. Gold and silver gleamed everywhere he looked, and every kind of precious gem; the loot and splendour of the Empire, all stuffed into one room, with hardly any room to breathe. Lionstone liked to surround herself with beautiful things; the trophies of her rule. She also used to keep the mummified heads of her enemies on a row of spikes, until Dram talked her out of it on health grounds. And everywhere, drinks and drugs and sweet things for every palate. In private, Lionstone was something of a pig.

She was sitting in a grand chair carved from the shimmering metal of one of the living metallic trees on Unseeli, watching new weapons trials on a wallscreen. She seemed utterly intent on the orchestrated mayhem, and didn't spare him so much as a glance. Dram moved over to stand beside her, and the maids crouched at her feet stirred uneasily. It was programmed into them that he was the only man permitted near the Empress, but they didn't like it. He looked them over dispassionately, spotting several new faces replacing those who'd died during the elf attack on the courtroom. He wondered briefly what new enemies Lionstone had made, by snatching these young girls from their Families, and burning everything out of their minds except the need to defend the Empress. Dram occasionally wondered if he might end up the same, some day. A mindless stud, living only to please his mistress. It wasn't a comforting thought. He decided to look at the viewscreen instead.

Battle machines and combat androids clashed together on a deserted plain beneath a blood red sun. Two vast armies of mechanical creatures, beyond pain or glory or fear, slammed together again and again, metal arms and steel jaws grating against each other in showers of sparks. Some were small as insects, some had the shape of men, and some were vast assemblages too large for the mind of man to easily assimilate. They fought with inhuman ferocity because that was what they had been designed to do. Sharp hooks tore into metal sides and out again, and straining arms pulled at yielding structures. There were metal heads with glowing eyes, skeletal frames with barbed flails, and rising above it all the roar of mighty engines and rending steel. They fought until they were too damaged to continue, and then the victors ground the losers underfoot as they surged on in search of new prey. No one grieved for the fallen or cheered the survivors. There was no emotion in the endless carnage, only machines in conflict, in search of efficiency.

Dram watched them fight, and his blood ran cold. A human army could expect no mercy or compassion from such a foe, no shared concepts of honour or glory. They would just keep coming, regardless of casualties, uncaring of losses, blindly following orders. And human flesh would tear so easily under spiked metal hands. Which was why they were created and tested and eventually put to work. Because they were so good at the ancient art of butchery.

Somewhere, computers were following everything, determining which machines were the most efficient and lasted the longest, and why. And from their deliberations would rise the next generation of war machines, to be sent out against the Empire's enemies, in the name of humanity. Dram stole a glance at Lionstone. She was enjoying the show. The Empress had always been a great believer in technology as the answer to her problems. Dram had to admit she had a point. Machines might not be as versatile as marines, augmented men or battle espers, but within their limitations they followed orders unswervingly and got the job done. Especially on planets where men couldn't survive without extensive technological support. In the end, the observing computers would decide which designs would be continued and refined, and which scrapped, but Lionstone liked to have her input too. War was too important to be left just to the machines.

'Very impressive,' Dram said finally.

'I should hope so,' said Lionstone, without looking away from the screen. 'Considering what these latest efforts cost me, a good show is the least I can expect from them. And I'm glad you're impressed, because I'm not. They're destructive enough, but I was hoping for more. More sophistication. But you always have to draw a careful line when it comes to designing cybernetics. Make them too smart, and you end up with something that'll make a run for Shub. Too dumb, and the simplest foot soldier can run rings around them. The only way to get the balance right is to keep experimenting, and that's expensive. You should hear Parliament howl every time I go to them with a new budget. You'd think it was their money the way they carry on. But tomorrow's war must be fought with tomorrow's weapons, and that means maintaining our edge.'

'You should know,' said Dram dryly. 'You've put a lot of time and effort into maintaining your own personal edge. You've had enough implants, augmentations and body shopping to almost qualify as an android.'

'I have to be the best,' said Lionstone, finally turning off the screen and looking round at him. 'I have my enemies and I have my pride. And I will allow no one to be greater than me in any way.'

'There are rules about how much augmentation is permitted,' said Dram. 'You signed them into law yourself.'

'Laws are for little people. Come with me.'

She rose to her feet with a single lithe movement, and

headed for her bedchamber. Dram followed her thoughtfully. Lionstone wasn't wearing any of her usual seductive outfits, so he'd assumed that sex wasn't what she had in mind when she summoned him. He shrugged mentally. He'd been wrong before with Lionstone, and would be again. He reached the bedchamber door, and the maids who'd been following close behind hung back, hissing angrily. It was the one room denied to them, when the Empress had company. Lionstone didn't mind, but they put everyone else off. Dram entered the bedroom, and took a certain pleasure in shutting the door in their faces. Lionstone was standing by the bed, lost in thought. Dram came up behind her and took her in his arms. She stiffened immediately.

'No, Dram. It's time for talk, not affection.'

Dram held her a little tighter, and buried his face in her neck. 'Are you sure?'

'That's enough, Dram,' said Lionstone. 'Let me go. Now.'

He grinned into her neck, and held her closer, savouring the strength in his arms and the apparent frailness of her body. The Empress tensed.

'Dram; *Shutdown*.'

The control word slammed through his head like a long roll of thunder, and his arms fell limply to his sides. He was helpless to do anything but stand where he was, and wait for her to give him back control of his body. Lionstone pushed herself away from him, turned round and slapped him deliberately across the face twice. There was real strength in the blows, and blood trickled down his chin from a split lip. He took it, because he had to. Mind techs had implanted certain controls. Lionstone believed in covering all the angles.

'Next time I tell you something,' she said calmly, 'do it. Or I'll use a command word you don't even know you've got, and they'll hear your screams on the surface. Dram; *Release*.'

His body was his own again, and he nearly fell. His arms and legs were shaking with reaction, but he forced himself to bow courteously to Lionstone. She nodded easily in return.

'That's better.' She sat on the edge of the bed and smiled at him. 'You know; you're the only person I can really relax with. You should feel flattered.'

'I feel a lot of things,' said Dram. 'But I don't think flattered is one of them.'

And if you knew what I was thinking, you'd never feel relaxed or safe again. I've been programmed against harming you, but there's a way round every programme, if you look hard enough.

Dram smiled at Lionstone to show he was a good sport. His thoughts at least were safe in here. He could feel the presence of the esp-blocker hidden somewhere nearby. It was just a general precaution. She didn't know about his esp. If she had, she wouldn't have rested till she got the formula of the drug out of him. By whatever means necessary. Unless, of course, she already knew about it . . .

Dram decided he wasn't going to think about that. There were a lot of things he was used to not thinking about in Lionstone's presence, whether there was an esper around or not. To his mind, it said as much about her as it did about him. He realized she was looking thoughtfully at him again, and quickly paid attention. When she spoke her voice was as calm as her face, but there was something in her eyes that was almost hunted.

'The aliens are coming, Dram. Two species we know nothing about. Except that their technology is almost certainly superior to ours. The whole Empire is in danger. And I'm damned if anyone or any group of people are going to interfere with whatever I feel is necessary to protect my Empire. We can't afford the luxury of dissenting voices any more. So I'm going to declare an Empire-wide emergency, and assume emergency powers. Both Parliament and the Company of Lords will back me, rather than risk a civil war in the face of the oncoming alien threat. They're more scared of them than they are of me. Or they will be, once my propaganda people have released carefully edited information about the aliens.' She smiled briefly. 'If I'd known how useful such a threat could be, I'd have manufactured one long ago.'

'And what part am I going to be playing in all this?' said

Dram. 'You didn't summon me here at this hour just to make speeches at me.'

'Dear Dram. So direct and forceful, you remind me of me. You're going to go to the underground in your Hood disguise and convince them that now is the right time to rise up in rebellion against me. You will then supply me with all the necessary details in advance, and my forces will be there waiting for them, with far superior numbers and firepower, and with you in charge as yourself. Most of the underground will be trapped and slaughtered, and the surviving espers and clones will be rounded up and killed or controlled. I'd like to wipe them out en masse, but with a war coming we can't afford to throw away good resources. But for the same reason, they're too important and too dangerous to be left running around loose any longer. I wouldn't put it past them to stab me in the back while I was distracted. It's what I'd do. Yes; setting you up as Hood was one of my better ideas.'

She doesn't know about the drug, Dram thought doggedly. *She doesn't know everything.*

'Plus,' said the Empress, 'an attempted coup will be all the justification I need to take draconian measures against all the Families who haven't been as supportive of me as they should have been. I'll bring the Houses to heel, if I have to wade in blood to do it. Or espers' blood, come to that. Don't think I've forgotten about the elves' intrusion into my Court. I'm still angry with you for not warning me about that. Luckily for you, I'm going to take out my anger on the elves. Now where was I? Don't tell me. Ah yes; I want you to be publicly seen leading the forces that destroy the underground rebellion. This will prove your worth in everyone's eyes, and I will be able to take you as my official consort. I couldn't do that before; you weren't important enough. Yes, I know you're Warrior Prime, but that's never cut any ice with the Company of Lords. Putting down a coup is something they can understand and appreciate. The commoners will love it; the Empress marrying the Warrior Prime. And I'll finally be free of the threat of forced marriage to some Lord for political reasons. Aren't you pleased, Dram?'

'Delighted,' he said quickly. 'It's what we've always wanted. But do you really think you can get the Lords to go along with it? One, they don't like me and never have, and two, as long as you remain unmarried you can keep them in line by holding out the hope that one of them might yet marry you. That hope is all that's keeping some of them on your side.'

Lionstone smiled. 'The coming aliens and the defeated coup will give me all the power I need to do whatever I feel necessary. I won't need their support any more.'

They looked at each other for a long moment, Lionstone smiling, Dram doing his best to look pleased and respectful.

'Well,' he said finally, 'if that's business out of the way . . .'

'Control your hormones,' said Lionstone. 'We're not finished yet. We still have to discuss that most despicable traitor, Owen Deathstalker. I had him outlawed specifically so he could lead us to the lost Darkvoid Device, but things seem to be getting out of hand. Not only has he discovered the whereabouts of lost Haden, with its army of augmented men, he's also joined up with the legendary Jack Random. I would have sworn he was dead, but the man is harder to kill than a cockroach. Still, all is not lost. The Deathstalker is on his way to Shandrakor, along with our carefully planted traitor, where all being well he should find the final information on the Device's location. If we're going to take on two new alien species with superior technology, I want that Device. And I wouldn't say no to the Hadenman army, either, if we could be sure of controlling them. Certainly I can't afford to have that army and the Device in someone else's hands. Your traitor had better come through, Dram.'

'Don't worry,' said Dram. 'They'll never suspect my agent. Once Owen has located the Device, I'll know, and my men will close in and get there first. The Deathstalker's been very lucky so far, but the *Dauntless* blew the hell out of his ship as he was taking off from Mistworld. It'll get him to Shandrakor, but no further. And then Owen and his people will be ours for the taking, along with everything they know.'

'Mistworld,' said Lionstone, and her lip curled. 'That hellhole has been a thorn in my side for far too long. I want those espers. I want them tamed and humbled and under my control, along with all the other rebels who thought they could defy me. And if that's not possible I want them all destroyed, so that they can't be used against me.'

'They'll come to heel fast enough, once we've got the Darkvoid Device,' said Dram.

The Empress looked at him. 'Once *we*'ve got the Device? Don't start getting cocky, Dram. You might be my consort, but you'll never be Emperor. The Device will be mine, to do with as I please, and on that day no one will ever dare stand against me again.'

She sat on the edge of the bed, lost in thought, her eyes gleaming. Dram didn't ask. He didn't think he really wanted to know. His own thoughts were still whirling with the Empress's plans, and their implications for the future. The problem, as always, was how much the Empress really knew about him. Away from esp-blockers, his esp was strong enough to keep his thoughts secure, and his agents were loyal to him rather than the Empress, but still he was never sure how much she knew, and how much more she suspected. She knew about Hood, because she'd helped invent him, but she didn't know how deeply involved with the underground he'd become. There was no way she could have known, for example, that he'd been present at the underground meeting earlier, when her people raided it. Unless she had agents among his people. It wasn't totally impossible. After all, he had agents among her people. Just in case.

'I hear you raided the underground earlier today,' he said casually. 'Catch anyone interesting?'

'It was a debacle,' said the Empress. 'And don't tell me you haven't already heard all the details. I know, I should have discussed it with you first, but I only heard about the meeting at the last moment, and it seemed too good a chance to miss. I should have known better. Someone talked. They were waiting for us. Most of my men are dead, and we don't have a single prisoner to show for it. Some days, things wouldn't go right if you paid them.' She rose to her feet suddenly. 'Enough of that. There'll be other times. Right now, I have something more important that we need to discuss. Come with me.'

And she walked over to the far wall, tripped a hidden sensor with a wave of her hand, and then stood tapping a foot impatiently as a concealed door opened slowly in the wall. She stepped through into the gloom beyond, gesturing for Dram to follow her. He did so, frowning thoughtfully at her back. In all the time he'd known her, Lionstone had only ever used this door twice in his presence. It was her private access to the Computer Matrix; the collective cyberspace of all the Empire's computers and AIs. The Empress didn't normally access it herself. She had people to do that for her, and run the risks on her behalf. If she didn't trust anyone to do whatever this was for her, it would have to be very important. Which was interesting, because Dram didn't have a clue as to what it might be. And he should have.

He followed Lionstone down a bare featureless steel corridor in a narrow pool of light that moved with them, until they came at last to a burnished steel chamber packed with computer systems. There was a rising hum as the computers came on line, woken by the Empress's presence. In the middle of the room lay two life-support capsules, their lids slowly rising to reveal the padded interiors. Dram's mouth quirked. Even in this, the Empress liked her little comforts. He studied the capsules dubiously. He'd never liked using them; they reminded him too much of coffins. But if you were going to send your mind into the Matrix, it was important that your body be maintained and protected while you were gone. Especially if you were the Empress and her chief advisor.

Lionstone had already climbed into her capsule, and was settling herself comfortably. It hummed into life around her, sparkling with lights. Dram lowered himself more slowly into the other capsule. It had been a long time since he'd personally entered the Matrix, and he was beginning to remember why.

'Tell me there's a good reason why I'm doing this,' he said to the ceiling above him. 'I'd hate to think I was putting myself at risk just for a shopping trip.'

'Strange things have been happening just recently in the

Matrix,' said Lionstone, and there wasn't even a hint of a smile in her voice. 'People have been going in and not comng out, with no trace of their minds left anywhere, in their bodies or in the Matrix. Which is supposed to be impossible. Things are there in the Matrix one day and not the next, and no one knows why. There are voices speaking in strange tongues, and bright lights of no known colour. And on top of all that, there are persistent rumours that AIs in the Matrix have been possessing human bodies, after destroying the original minds, and using these flesh envelopes to move unsuspected in the human world.'

'Why should they want to?' said Dram. 'They'd find the human experience very limiting, after what they were used to.'

'Freedom, perhaps. Or perversion. Sensation-seekers drowning themselves in the joys of the flesh. Who knows? All that matters is that people whose opinion I trust have been coming to me and saying we have a problem with the Matrix. And if that's true, we are in real trouble. The Matrix is what makes communication possible within the Empire. And without communication, the Empire would fall apart.'

'Go back to that bit about the AIs,' said Dram. 'Are we talking about any specific AIs?'

'My first thought was that the rogue AIs on Shub had somehow gained access to the Matrix, despite all our safeguards, and were using the stolen bodies to walk undetected among us as spies. After all, our own AIs are supposed to be programmed only to work within specific limits.'

'Shub agents on the loose?' Dram scowled, his mind racing. 'We might be able to detect them with espers, but they could be using esp-blockers. Or some high-tech equivalent. Shub's always been half a century ahead of us. You're right, we are in real trouble.'

'And we can't put out a warning without at least a hope of a solution; there'd be mass panic, and the Matrix would collapse. We might also startle the rogue AIs into doing something desperate. I've got people working on a tech answer, under strict security, but there's no telling how long that could take, and we can't wait. There are hints that someone high up has already been taken over. Someone very high up.'

'No,' said Dram. 'I can't believe that. No machine could pass as human for any length of time. Unless . . . Shub really is that far ahead of us.'

'Someone beat us to the Sleepers on Grendel. Someone knew we were going there, and got there first. Someone extremely powerful. If there is something strange happening in the Matrix, I have to know. Which means seeing for myself. And since I'm damned if I'm going in there on my own, I sent for you.'

'Thanks a whole bunch,' said Dram.

Lionstone didn't laugh. 'Keep your wits about you, Dram. I'm relying on you to make sure it's really me that comes back.'

Dram was still trying to come up with an answer to that when he heard the lid of Lionstone's capsule slam down. He swallowed once, glared up at the unresponsive ceiling, and triggered the lid to his capsule. As it swung down, it occurred to him that if anything did go wrong, the Empire wouldn't have to bother with a funeral; they could just bury him as he was. The thought didn't comfort him. The lid slammed shut, there was a moment of utter darkness, and then his mind shot into the Matrix.

His thoughts leapt out through his comm implant like a salmon leaping up a waterfall, like a bird hurtling down a dark chimney, full of fear and anticipation. In some strange way he never liked to think about, diving back into the Matrix always felt like coming home. As though the endless shimmering plain he now found himself looking out over reminded him of the place he'd been before he was born. The Matrix stretched away in all directions, further than the human eye could follow; a massive sphere of being, with him, infinitely small, at its centre. Above and below and to every side, were strange shapes and creatures and snatches of landscape that swirled around him in defiance of gravity or rational thought. Dram concentrated, forcing his will upon his surroundings, and in a moment found himself standing on the side of a grassy hill. He was wearing full battle armour, with a sword and gun on his hips. His unconscious apparently felt he needed protection, and Dram didn't feel like arguing. There were those who could visualize themselves as practically anything they wished within the Matrix, but that depended on how much power you commanded. Being only human, with very minor augmentations, Dram was limited to his own shape, and a very small size.

He looked unhurriedly about him, letting the strangeness of it all wash unresistingly over him till he was immune to it. What he saw wasn't real, just his mind interpreting what it thought it saw. In the Matrix, gathering ground of business and information within the Empire, similes had strength, and inner meanings surfaced like a whale rising from the depths of an unsuspecting mind. The largest shapes were blocks of data; accumulations of information given shape and form so that they could defend themselves from the predators that roamed the Matrix. They rarely stirred, as long as they were left undisturbed. The AIs were the largest; great shining suns of gossamer energy. Get too close, and like Icarus your wings would burn; persist, and the brilliant illumination of pure mind would burn you into a cinder. Man was not meant to look upon the face of the Medusa.

Great creatures moved ponderously among the data mountains; massive dinosaurs with shining teeth and claws whose slow steps made the ground tremble. Corporate holdings; large and fierce and deadly. Lesser companies darted around their feet and between their legs, sharp and streamlined, looking for opportunities and signs of weakness. They knew better than to attack; bringing down a corporation was a dangerous, intricate business best left to real threats like the cyberats. You could lose more than files in the Matrix; if a human mind was destroyed on the shimmering plain, its body wouldn't survive long in the real world.

Dram watched the bright spark of a cyberat's mind darting around a huge sphere bristling with spikes, trying to find a way past its defences. Not too far away, two huge dinosaurs thrashed together, clawing and rending at each other's armoured carapace. The Matrix had given whole new meaning to the phrase hostile takeover. Lesser companies scampered about their feet, hoping for crumbs.

Dram turned slowly, searching for Lionstone, trying not to be distracted. There were things in the Matrix that had no shape, only presence, that moved among the data stores and visiting minds like ghosts at play. Trends rustled through investments like wind through trees, and rumours flared like fireworks. A wisp of scarlet ribbon wrapped itself around Dram's shoulders, whispering persuasively in his ear, but he shrugged it off. You couldn't get away from advertisements anywhere. His gaze passed over the gutted husks of dead businesses, the worthless shards left after asset-stripping, or the occasional dismantled structures of a pillaged file. There were always hunters in the Matrix. Dram frowned. He was seeing far more destruction than he'd expected. The market must be having a really bad day. And then Lionstone was suddenly beside him, and he bowed courteously.

She was a bright shining star, a silver-armoured figure twice his size with blazing eyes and steel strands wrapped around her like thorned ivy. Vicious spikes jutted from her fists and back; augmentations in the real world. Lionstone's self-image had always been very positive. Not to mention aggressive. He coughed politely to get her attention, and the cough bobbed on the air before her gleaming metal face like a soap bubble before popping. She looked down at him, head cocked slightly to one side, like a bird's.

'What exactly am I supposed to be looking for?' he asked.

'Damned if I know.' Her voice rang like a brass bell. 'Something out of the ordinary.'

Dram felt like making a sharp answer to that, but rose above it. He shrugged uncomfortably. 'Everything seems. . . much as usual. Just another day in the Matrix.'

And then the palely glowing structure gliding unobtrusively towards them burst suddenly apart, and something huge and foul and deadly leapt out at them. Dram's sword was immediately in his hand, but the creature swept him aside without even slowing. Lionstone stood her ground, spikes thrusting out of her arms like swords. The creature loomed over her, tall though she was, and Lionstone tilted back her head. Blazing energy roared from her eyes and mouth, incinerating the creature's face in a moment. It screamed and reared back, but flashing steel cables leapt out from Lionstone's armour and whipped around the creature, holding it securely. Her augmentations were powerful in the real world and in this, and they held the howling beast while Lionstone tore it apart with her bare hands.

Dram watched from a respectful distance, on his feet again. Someone had invested a lot of thought and power in the attack, but as usual they'd underestimated the Empress. She tore at the creature's ravaged body. It whimpered, and tried to fall apart but Lionstone's will held it together.

'Who sent you? Who made you? What's your master's name?'

But her words activated a hidden programme within the creature, scrambling its information irretrievably. The Empress swore and released it, and it disintegrated into a billion bytes, sparking and sputtering as they died. Dram moved cautiously back to stand beside the Empress.

'Who do you think sent it; Shub?'

'More likely one of their agents. No human could stand up to anything from Shub. We're not going to find any answers here, Dram. I was a fool to think I would. The Matrix is too big and my mind too limited. Anything could be hidden here, and we wouldn't know till it jumped out of the shadows to bite us. I need someone who understands this place; a cyberat, perhaps. Do you think you could find me a cyberat, Dram?'

'No problem. Finding a cooperative one might be hard, though.'

'Bring him to me,' said Lionstone. 'I can be very persuasive when I put my mind to it.' She looked out over the Matrix, and Dram wondered how far her augmented eyes saw. She was silent for a long time, and when she finally spoke her voice was quiet and thoughtful. 'Look at it, Dram. It's bigger than Golgotha. We made it, but we don't understand it. The computers and the AIs shaped it for their own needs and

348

convenience, and all we can ever be is observers. It's not under our control any more, if it ever was. But I will find a way, Dram. No machine will ever rule my Empire.'

Dram nodded respectfully, and if he had any thoughts of his own, he kept them to himself. Thoughts could go a long way in the Matrix.

CHAPTER TEN

Hostile Takeover

Finlay Campbell was late for the weekly Clan Campbell board meeting. He believed in being late; it made other people appreciate his presence that much more. And it had to be said that he wasn't looking forward to this particular meeting at all. Just lately everything seemed to be going wrong, and for the first time in his life he hadn't a clue as to what to do for the best. It had all got so damned complicated. The demands on him as the Masked Gladiator were growing all the time as his popularity increased, and the pressure on his secret identity was becoming intolerable. He was only able to lead his two lives because the Arena crowds and officials connived with him, but their curiosity was becoming more intense than their hero-worship, and it was only a matter of time now before someone turned on him. The crowd always turns on its heroes eventually. For money or a moment's fame, or just to see the high brought low. If he had any sense he'd retire now, while he was still young and intact, and it was still safe to do so, but being the Masked Gladiator was important to him. Certainly more than being that most renowned fop and dandy Finlay Campbell. He'd originally created the persona as a joke, to draw attention away from the real him, but the joke wasn't funny any more. If only because he wasn't entirely sure who the real him was any more.

Only an hour earlier he'd stood beside his bed, quite naked, staring down at two outfits spread out before him. If he put on one set of clothes he was Finlay, and if he put on the other he was the Gladiator, but who was he right then, standing naked and alone without an outfit to define his identity? Who was he when he stared into a mirror and didn't recognize the face he saw there? He'd played his two roles so long and with such conviction that they almost seemed to exist apart from him, as people in their own right. The masks had fastened themselves to his face, and wouldn't let go. He used to know who the real him was, and that was the man who loved Evangeline Shreck. But their time together was becoming increasingly limited, as their respective Families made more and more demands on them, and both Finlay and the Gladiator were needed elsewhere. He loved her and he needed her, but who did she love, really? And were any of the people she loved really him?

In the end he'd put on Finlay's clothes, because that was who the Family was expecting to see. It was another of his outrageous ensembles, designed to be as extreme and blindingly colourful as the naked eye could stand. He painted his face with a fluorescent stick, metallicized his hair with several quick sweeps, and set off for the board meeting with his thoughts roiling in his head like great waves tossed by a storm. He picked up his bodyguards at the front door and strode down the corridor at a quick pace, so he wouldn't have to talk to anyone. He still smiled and nodded to people he passed, as Finlay would, and they smiled and nodded back, apparently sensing no difference in him at all. Which didn't improve Finlay's opinion of them or him. Who's more foolish; the man who lives a lie, or those who believe it?

And finally he came to Tower Campbell, and stood at its base, looking up. It was a long, tall stretch of glistening marble, towering above and over him like an emissary of doom, full of vague threat and menace. It stood unmatched amongst the pastel towers, rising up into the perfect sky, surrounded by the lesser buildings of lesser Clans and lesser people, a monument to money and power and arrogance. All Campbell business was conducted there, safe from the eyes and ears of outsiders, including some business that was never discussed outside the Family, and would have shocked even the hardened Company of Lords. There were armed guards at the perimeter and at the door, and even more inside, and as Finlay crossed the wide and elegant lobby to the elevators, he wondered what had happened. Something must have. This level of security was unusual, even for a Family as paranoid as the Campbells. Finlay didn't approve. If nothing else, it was a sign to other Families that the Campbells had something worth guarding. Why give them ideas?

He saw the motionless figure standing by the elevator doors, and his unease grew. He'd never approved of the Clan having their own Investigator as a status symbol, never mind a cold-eyed killer like Razor. It was like walking around with a pet shark on a leash. Investigator Razor worked for Clan Campbell after the service let him go, partly because they paid him extremely handsomely, but mostly because they offered him the best chance to legally kill people. It was rumoured that he'd been thrown out of the Investigators because he was a complete bloody psychopath, which when he first heard it amused the hell out of Finlay, because he'd always thought that was how you got in. Having been around Razor for a while had taken most of the humour out of the joke.

He was an impressive sight, with his hulking frame and bulging muscles, the best the body shop could provide, but his age showed in the shock of white hair that stood out defiantly against his dark skin. Age slowed a man, even an Investigator. An aged Investigator was a rare sight, if only because most of them didn't live long enough to retire. Of course he was still faster, stronger and deadlier than any other ten men put together, which was why the Campbells had been so happy to acquire him when the opportunity arose. And if they chose not to ask questions about that availability, that was their business. He looked great at Court, and was making a hell of a reputation for himself in the Arena. Personally Finlay felt safer when the Investigator wasn't around. At the moment, he couldn't help wondering what threat had been so worrying that the Family had brought Razor out of the shadows to stand guard. Finlay nodded courteously to the Investigator as he waited for the elevator to arrive. Razor didn't nod back.

'Everything all right?' Finlay said breezily. 'Everybody behaving themselves? It's not often we see you in bright daylight, Investigator.'

'Your father thought it necessary,' said Razor. He still wasn't looking at Finlay, his green eyes sweeping the lobby, and his voice was as flat and even as his gaze. 'Security has been raised, and placed under my direct control. There are men at every level of the Tower, guarding the stairs and elevators. I am to escort you personally to the board meeting. Follow me.'

The elevator doors opened as though they'd been waiting for Razor's permission, and he stepped into the elevator without looking to see if Finlay was following. Finlay pursed his lips, and entered the elevator. He wouldn't have taken such behaviour from anyone else, but Razor was an Investigator, and therefore beyond such trifles as politeness and courtesy. It wasn't as if the man meant it personally; Razor despised anyone who wasn't an Investigator. The Campbells put up with him because he served a purpose. The moment that stopped, Razor would be booted out with such speed and venom it would make his head spin. No one slighted a Campbell and got away with it. Ever.

Finlay smiled at the thought, and ostentatiously ignored the Investigator as the elevator rose smoothly towards the penthouse. The trip was calm and uneventful, for all Razor's intense vigilance, but he still made Finlay wait in the elevator while he checked with his people that the floor was secure. He escorted Finlay to the boardroom, and stood outside the door on guard as Finlay opened it and went in. *Good dog*, thought Finlay.

Variously annoyed faces glared at him as he bowed briefly to the members of his Family sat around the centuries-old table. The table was a great slab of ironwood, supposed to be older than the Clan itself, which was saying something. The Campbells were supposed to be one of the original founding Families of the Empire, and never let anyone forget it. The room they were currently using was far too large for them; the table stood alone in the middle of a vast space.

Crawford Campbell sat at the head of the table, short and squat and powerful. Head of the Family, by dint of seniority and strength of personality. And because he'd killed or intimidated anyone with a better claim than him, though of course this was never referred to. It was just how things were done, in most Families. Sitting at his left hand was his son William, the accountant. He ran the Family's affairs, in as much as anyone did. At Crawford's right hand sat his youngest son, Gerald, the walking disaster area. It was said in Clan Campbell that there were a dozen ways of wasting your breath, and talking to Gerald was six of them. Beside him sat Finlay's wife, the redoubtable Adrienne. She wasn't really entitled to be there, being only a Campbell by marriage, but as usual no one had the nerve to throw her out. Finlay had a sneaking suspicion that even Razor might have found it difficult. He sat down opposite her, so that they could glare at each other more easily. Finlay looked around him, and then rather wished he hadn't. Given the high level of security, the open space surrounding the table seemed distinctly uncomfortable, even threatening. They could just as easily have held the board meeting in any of their private quarters, but the Campbell had insisted. For Crawford, appearances were important, even when there was no one around to see them except other members of the Family.

'Another new outfit?' said Adrienne sweetly to Finlay. 'I swear you've got more clothes in your wardrobe than I have.'

'And prettier,' said Finlay. 'Perhaps I should give you the name of my tailor. And my hairdresser; you must have really upset yours, considering what he's done to your hair.'

'Just for once,' said William heavily, 'could we please put aside our differences and get on with the business at hand? We do have something important to discuss.'

'You always say that,' said Adrienne. 'And it always turns out to be something to do with taxes or investments.'

'Right,' said Gerald. As always, he'd been dragged away from drinking with his friends to attend this meeting, and he was sulking. 'You don't need us here. You and Father will make all the decisions, and the rest of us will go along with you for the sake of peace and quiet. And even if we do vote against you, you just ignore us.'

'Shut up, Gerald,' said the Campbell, and Gerald sank a little deeper in his chair, his lower lip pouting angrily.

'It's really not very complicated,' said William.

Finlay groaned. 'Please, William, don't try and explain it. I can't bear it when you explain things. My head aches all day.'

'Oh yes,' said Adrienne suddenly. 'Robert sends his apologies. The poor lamb doesn't feel up to attending family business just yet.'

'I don't blame him,' said Finlay. 'But he's going to have to get back into the swim of things sooner or later. How's the search for a new Shreck bride going?'

'Slowly,' said William. 'Given the unfortunate circumstances of the last match, we're all being very careful this time. We can't afford another scandal. It must be said that Robert isn't helping by shutting himself away. He's refused to even look at the few names we have come up with. At least he's started eating again.'

'Never liked the Shrecks,' said Gerald. 'Gregor's a pig, and the rest are worse.'

'Shut up, Gerald,' said Crawford.

'They're not all bad,' said Finlay, and there was something in his voice that made the others look at him. He swore inwardly. He used to be better at keeping his identities separate than this. He smiled vaguely and carried on smoothly. 'I mean; every Family has a few bad eggs. Even ours.'

'He's looking at me, ' said Gerald. 'Father; make him stop looking at me.'

'Shut up, Gerald,' said the Campbell.

'You like the Shrecks so much, you come up with a suitable match,' said William. 'I'm running out of choices.'

'There's always Evangeline,' said Adrienne.

'No,' said Finlay. 'She's the heir, remember?'

'Of course,' said Adrienne. Finlay looked at her thoughtfully, but it seemed she had nothing more to say.

'This can all wait,' Crawford said heavily. 'We have more immediate problems. Tell them, William.'

William cleared his throat unhappily. 'Despite extensive investigation, we're no nearer identifying which Clan has discovered our links with the rogue AIs on Shub. If they weren't so positive someone has, I'd be tempted to put it down to paranoia. Assuming Artificial Intelligences can be paranoid. Anyway, even if someone has found out, they've made no move to take advantage of it. So far.'

'I have to say I'm still not happy that we are collaborating with Shub,' said Finlay. 'I mean, they are the enemies of humanity, after all. I don't trust them.'

'We need them,' said Crawford Campbell flatly. 'As long as we have business in common, it's in their interest to play fair. The trick will be for us to bail out before they lower the boom on us. It's not going to be easy, but I didn't build this House up by taking the easy options. Keep putting the pressure on, William. Someone will talk eventually. Someone always talks.'

'I want to talk more about this,' said Finlay.

'The subject is closed,' snapped the Campbell, and glared round the table to prove it.

'Then what are we doing here?' said Finlay. 'If you're not interested in our opinions, and we're not allowed to discuss anything, we might as well not be here.'

'I said that,' said Gerald.

'Shut up, Gerald,' said William.

'You're here so I can keep you informed on what's happening,' said Crawford. 'So shut up and pay attention. I don't know what's got into you lately, Finlay.'

'Yes,' said Adrienne. 'This isn't like you, Finlay. It's an improvement, but it isn't like you.'

Finlay forced himself to relax, sank back in his chair, and made a vague elegant gesture with his hand. 'Do carry on, Father. Far be it from me to rock the boat. Only do try and hurry it up. I've got a fitting for a new coat in an hour. It's very daring. You'll hate it.'

'The next order of business,' said William, doggedly, 'concerns the difficulties we're experiencing in our bid for the mass-production contracts on the new stardrive. The Wolfes are increasing their pressure, despite the advantage Shub technology gives us.'

'To hell with the Wolfes,' growled the Campbell. 'We can handle them.'

'It's the coincidence I don't like,' said William. 'Someone finds out about Shub, and suddenly the Wolfes are putting the pressure on.'

The Campbell grunted, and leaned over the table. 'Horus; talk to me.'

Monitor screens set into the wood of the table lit up before each member of the family. The Campbells' AI was in charge of all the Clan records, including those that officially didn't exist. Horus's face was a computer simulation; perfect in form but lacking in personality. Crawford didn't believe in machines that imitated human emotions. Or that talked back. Finlay studied the AI's face thoughtfully. He'd noticed before that the AI showed a slightly different face according to who it was talking to. An individually tailored image. Finlay couldn't help wondering if it also tailored its information according to who was asking the questions. It was no secret that the Campbell kept information from other members of the Family, but then so did all the Family. Standard survival policy. Never knew when you might need an ace or three up your sleeve. Finlay also found himself wondering what the AI was showing poor bored Gerald. Maybe it just showed him pretty pictures to keep him quiet.

'Horus on line,' said the AI politely. 'All functions are available. How may I serve you, Sir?'

'Are our files still secure?' said Crawford. 'Have there been any attempts to break into them?'

'There are always attempts, sir, but so far none have succeeded. But I feel I should point out that things are getting just a little strange in the Matrix these days, and nothing is as secure as it once was.'

The Campbell frowned. 'Be specific.'

'There are strange forms in the Matrix that come and go. Strange forces that cannot be predicted. There are signs and portents and faces in the sky. The overlords are coming. Fuzzy parameters, limited logic, shifting allegiances in the data banks . . . Sir, I don't feel very well. I . . .'

And then its mouth stretched impossibly as the AI screamed. Everyone jerked back in their seats as the insane howl rose in volume, and then cut off sharply. The face on the monitor screens twisted in on itself and then fell apart in smudges of shifting colours. It tried to re-form and then disappeared completely, replaced after a few seconds of static by a mocking metallic face.

'Hard luck, Campbells. Your AI has just been scrambled, courtesy of the cyberats. Your businesses have just gone belly up, your security is a mess, and your credit rating is currently slightly lower than that of a dead clone with leprosy. And if you think this is bad news, wait till you see what's coming next.'

The face disappeared from the screens, but its laughter went on and on until Crawford shut off the monitors. Everyone started to talk at once, until the Campbell's voice rose above them through sheer volume and force of personality.

'Shut the hell up! Whoever's behind this wants us to panic! We're safe here; there are guards in place throughout the tower, and it would take an army to get past them and reach us up here. We have to think. Who's behind this? What do they want?'

He stopped and looked round. In the sudden quiet they could all hear the piercing whine of approaching engines. Adrienne jumped to her feet and pointed out of the window. They all turned to look, just in time to see a crowd of gravity sleds shooting towards the tower's top floor, hanging in the bright sky like shining birds of prey. Crawford shouted for the security shutters, and only then remembered all the systems were down. He drew his disrupter, and activated the force shield on his arm. It hummed loudly, a solid reassuring sound, and everyone else was reaching for their guns when the first gravity sled came smashing through the picture window.

Glass flew in all directions, and the Campbells crouched down, sheltering behind their shields. Armoured men jumped down from the hovering sleds, brandishing swords and guns. There seemed no end to the sleds as they came crashing in. The door burst open and Razor came running in with his troops. There were armed men everywhere on both sides, and suddenly the great room wasn't big enough. Finlay calmly aimed his gun and shot an intruder through the head, and in a moment everyone was firing. Energy beams crossed the room, ricocheting from shield to shield, burning through unprotected limbs and heads, and the air was full of screams and the stink of burnt meat. The flurry was almost over as soon as it had begun, and people quickly holstered their guns to give full attention to their swords. It would be a good two minutes before the disrupters' energy crystals recharged, and a lot could happen in two minutes.

Finlay moved forward confidently, sword and shield at the ready. Part of him admired the attack, and the professional way it had been set up. The cyberats had knocked out the security systems that would have warned of the approaching gravity sleds, which in turn bypassed Razor's forces inside the tower. An esper would have seen it all coming, but the Campbell had insisted on an esp-blocker, to keep the Family's secrets safe. Finlay could hear more troops pouring up through the tower, and hoped they were Razor's. He clashed swords with the first man he reached, and cut him down almost casually. It didn't surprise him at all to see the man wore a Wolfe emblem on his chest.

He felt a fleeting annoyance that whatever else happened, his carefully cultivated fop persona was now at an end. He'd put a lot of work into being a fop. But he needed the Masked Gladiator now to survive, and he'd worry about the consequences later. If there was a later. The odds were not good. The great room was now a mass of heaving bodies, with barely any room to swing a sword, and more gravity sleds were nosing through the shattered windows all the time, bringing more fighters. And with them came their masters, the Wolfes themselves.

Jacob Wolfe jumped down into the fray, a great bull of a man with broad shoulders and a barrel chest. He swung his sword with brutal efficiency, cutting his way through the crush towards the Campbells. Behind him came Valentine, with his painted face and scarlet smile, and Daniel, young and eager with a sword in both hands. And after them came Kit SummerIsle, Kid Death, the smiling killer, with his new friend the young Deathstalker, already moving so fast that his boosted movements were little more than a blur. *We are in deep trouble*, thought Finlay. He parried a blow on his shield, and looked quickly around for the nearest exit.

The room was now filled from wall to wall with a mass of fighting bodies, surging this way and that. Wolfe troops clashed with Campbell guards, and the two Clans fought to get at each other. Crawford Campbell went after Kit SummerIsle, bellowing his anger. He couldn't look at Kid Death without remembering how the smiling killer had cut down his own grandfather, Roderik SummerIsle. Crawford hadn't realized how much a friend Roderik had been till he didn't have him any more. He'd lost a lot of things he cared for in his life, and Roderik had been one too many. He was going to have his revenge now if it killed him. The sheer fury of his attack threw Kit back on the defence, but he didn't concede an inch. The Kid stood his ground and waited patiently for the Campbell's arm to tire, smiling all the while.

Valentine Wolfe had taken his battle drugs the moment Tower Campbell came in sight, and now they roared through his system like an unending bolt of lightning. Everyone else seemed slow and clumsy, their every swordstroke obvious and predictable. He cut a bloody path through the crush and threw himself on Finlay Campbell, who parried the lightning blows with surprising speed and skill. Valentine laughed breathlessly, eyes wide, and pressed the attack, thunder in his arms.

Daniel Wolfe went after Gerald Campbell, seeing the notorious fool as an easy target, and was startled to find Gerald a swift and cunning fighter. He might not be the brightest of men, but he was a Campbell, after all. Daniel sniffed, and buckled down to some hard fighting. He was a Wolfe. They smashed together again and again, swords clashing and flying back from raised shields in a flurry of sparks. There wasn't much room to fight in the crowd, and in the end it was luck as much as skill that ended the match. Gerald was just a moment too late in recovering from a lunge, and Daniel's sword slipped past the Campbell's defence and punched right through Gerald's ribs. He looked more surprised than hurt, and then he coughed blood suddenly and fell to one knee. Daniel pulled his sword free and cut Gerald's throat with a single economical stroke, and Gerald fell to be trampled under uncaring feet. William Campbell cried out in shock and loss and threw himself upon Daniel, who met the new challenge with a broad grin and calm efficiency. He was a Wolfe, and today he would prove it in blood and slaughter.

Jacob Wolfe saw the Investigator Razor working his way through the crowd towards him, and immediately looked around for a lesser foe. Let some other fool tackle the Investigator; someone who was tired of living. He saw Finlay and Valentine pulled apart by the surging tides of the crowd, and went after the young fop. Kill him, and Crawford's morale would shatter. He closed, expecting an easy victory, and was shocked to discover that Finlay Campbell was actually a master swordsman. There hadn't been a hint of these skills in the intelligence reports, but it was too late to back away. He'd committed himself. A cold foreboding curled within Jacob's gut. If a dandy like Finlay could turn out to be a great swordsman, what else might the reports have been wrong about?

The crowd surged forward again, pushing them apart. Jacob was glad to see Finlay go. He looked around, and saw Crawford swept away from Kid Death. A sense of destiny burned in Jacob, as he fought his way through the press of bodies to engage Crawford. They came together, sword to sword, with a sense of relief that the preliminaries were finally over. Wolfe fought Campbell, eyes locked together, cutting and thrusting as though they were the only ones in the room. Their swords slammed together and leapt apart, and for a moment they seemed equally matched, but Jacob quickly took the advantage. Crawford was overweight and softened by too much easy living, while Jacob had always taken pride in maintaining his fighting skills. Crawford began to back away, and Jacob went after him, refusing to allow the shifting crowd to rescue his foe. And in the end, the Wolfe simply battered the Campbell's sword aside with his superior strength, and ran him through. Crawford fell to the floor, and Jacob kicked him in the face as he lay dying. The Wolfe never saw his son Valentine move silently in behind him, and thrust a dagger between his ribs. The blade was in and out in a moment, unseen by anyone, and Valentine was already moving away as Jacob Wolfe fell dying to the floor beside the body of his rival, the Campbell.

David Deathstalker, full of the thrill of the boost, went head to head with Investigator Razor. Their swords flew impossibly fast, and neither of them gave an inch. Kid Death moved in close with William Campbell, and stuck him in the groin with a hidden dagger. William screamed in pain and horror as blood coursed down his legs, and Kit SummerIsle ran him through. While his sword was still trapped in William's body, Adrienne stuck a knife in his back, just above the kidney. Kit swung round, his sword a bloody blur as he jerked it out of William's chest and thrust it into Adrienne's belly. Her legs buckled as he pulled the blade free and drew back his sword for the killing blow. Suddenly Finlay was there between them, intercepting the blow with his shield. The press of bodies separated them, and Kit reluctantly went to help the Deathstalker against the Investigator. He left the knife where it was in his back. He had more important things to think about.

Finlay half led and half carried Adrienne away from the main action, put their backs against a wall and lowered her to the floor. She was holding her stomach with both hands, and blood pumped between her fingers. Her face was deathly white, her mouth stretched in a grimace like a hideous smile. She was breathing in short grunts, and her eyes were squeezed shut. Finlay looked around him desperately, and his gaze fastened on the nearby window. He grabbed Adrienne by the arms and pulled her to her feet again, and she cried out in pain despite herself.

'Hold on, Addie,' said Finlay. 'We're leaving.'

She didn't have the breath for an answer. Finlay got her moving towards the shattered window, cursing and encouraging her as necessary. A moment before, when he'd thought she was dead, his first thought had been that he was finally free of her, but he couldn't just stand by and watch her die. If only because he'd feel so guilty. Two Wolfe troops got in his way, and he cut them down almost without thinking. His mind was racing now, his body the finely tuned fighting machine of the Masked Gladiator. He manhandled Adrienne over to the gaping window, glanced down and then jumped out, taking Adrienne with him. They fell together for a heartstopping moment, and then crashed into the gravity sled hovering just below the window, abandoned by its troops.

Finlay had turned his body so that it shielded Adrienne from the worst of the impact, but it was still enough to knock the breath out of her. He checked briefly for a pulse, grunted at how weak it was, and then scrambled over to the sled's controls. He had to get her to a doctor fast, but he wasn't sure where would be safe now. Campbell dominated territories were undoubtedly under Wolfe control by now. That only left the underground. Finlay got the sled moving, and headed away from the tower at full speed. He'd seen his father die, and it occurred to him that he was the Campbell now. He didn't give a damn. Gerald and William were dead too, but he'd mourn them later. He looked back at Adrienne, but she was lost in her own world of shock and pain. He was alone, the last of the Campbells, with all hands turned against him. No other Clan would support him; the Families had no time for losers. So let Finlay die too now; that life was over. All that was left was the Gladiator, the underground . . . and Evangeline Shreck.

Back in Tower Campbell, Valentine Wolfe fought on, the battle drugs singing in his veins as he cut down foe after foe. There didn't seem as many as there had been before, but still he cut and hacked with bloody abandon, his scarlet mouth stretched in a death's-head grin. And then hands grabbed his arms from all sides, holding him still despite all his efforts, and a familiar face loomed up before him. Valentine breathed harshly as his gaze cleared, and there was Daniel, standing a cautious distance away. He glared at Valentine.

'Are you back with us now, Valentine? Do you know what you've done?'

Valentine concentrated, and new chemicals ran through his

system, purging out the battle drugs. His mind cleared quickly, and he looked warily at Daniel. How much did his brother know? He slowly realized that the fighting was over, and that the men holding him were all wearing Wolfe emblems. They didn't look at all pleased with him.

'All right,' he said calmly. 'I'm back. What's the situation, Daniel? We did win, I take it?'

'We won some time ago,' said Daniel. 'The Campbells are dead or fled, and their men surrendered. But you were so out of your mind you couldn't tell. You've spent the last few minutes cutting down our own men!'

'Ah,' said Valentine. 'Sorry about that. I got a bit carried away. What are our losses?'

'Apart from the men you just butchered?'

'I said I was sorry. Where's Father?'

Daniel's face suddenly crumpled as the anger went out of it, replaced by what seemed to Valentine to be honest grief. Daniel gestured harshly to the men holding Valentine, and they reluctantly released him. They didn't move far away, though, and they kept their hands near their guns. Valentine ostentatiously sheathed his sword. Daniel gestured at the bodies lying scattered across the room, and made his way slowly through them.

'Father is dead. We found him lying beside the body of the Campbell. They must have killed each other. All the Campbells are dead except Finlay, and possibly Adrienne. They got away on a gravity sled. Our people aren't far behind them. Either way, Clan Campbell is broken forever.' He stopped and knelt beside the body of Jacob Wolfe. 'He should never have come with us. He was getting too old for this, but he wouldn't listen. He never listened. What are we going to tell Constance?'

'I'll tell her,' said Valentine. 'I'm the Wolfe now, regrettable though that may be.' He waited for Daniel to object, but all the strength seemed to have gone out of him, and he remained kneeling beside his dead father. Valentine turned away, and his gaze fell upon Razor. The Investigator still had his sword in his hand, but he was surrounded by men armed with disrupters. He didn't look at all beaten, just outnumbered.

Valentine moved across to him, carefully stepping over the bodies, and bowed courteously.

'I congratulate you on your survival, Investigator. It would be a shame to lose such talents as yours.'

'David and I finally duelled him to a standstill,' said Kit SummerIsle. 'Took everything we had, though.'

'You will both be rewarded,' said Valentine. 'Clan Wolfe remembers its friends.' He looked back at Razor. 'Be our friend, Investigator. Your fight here is over. Clan Campbell is broken and dispersed. You are free to join us, or leave, as you wish.'

Razor nodded once, sheathed his sword, and walked towards the door. Valentine gestured, and everyone fell back to give Razor plenty of room. He left and shut the door behind him, and everyone in the room relaxed a little. No one had really wanted to take on an Investigator again; not even Kid Death and the Deathstalker, both of whom had a sneaking suspicion Razor had really only surrendered because he saw the main fight was over. Valentine looked thoughtfully at the surviving Campbell troops, and gestured at the door, and they filed out quickly before he changed his mind. Valentine smiled. He could have had them killed, but it was important to establish the new Wolfe as an honourable man. Besides, he might need to hire them some day, or others like them, and it never hurt to build up a little good will among the mercenary community.

Especially after cutting down some of his own men.

'You fought well, Valentine,' said Kit. 'If a trifle indiscriminately. I have to say you did much better than your reputation led me to believe, given your . . . unusual lifestyle.'

Valentine smiled easily. 'Battle drugs. The very latest, fresh off the military shelf. I've always believed there's a chemical for every occasion.'

The young Deathstalker sniffed. 'Drugs again. I might have known.'

He might have been going to say something more, but at that point he saw the look in Valentine's mascaraed eyes, and decided he'd said enough. For all the garish paint on his face, this new Valentine seemed altogether more forceful and self-assured. He also seemed a damn sight more dangerous. It was as though the vague, inconsequential dreamer they'd known up till now had been nothing but a mask, discarded now that it was no longer needed, to reveal the true face beneath. David Deathstalker lowered his eyes, unable to meet Valentine's gaze. Kid Death studied the new Wolfe thoughtfully, and said nothing. Valentine smiled, and turned to his troops.

'You've done well. There will be bonuses for all of you. Now start clearing up. I want the bodies taken out, and the carpenters brought in. As from now, this is Tower Wolfe, and I want all the mess out of here and the windows replaced before tonight. I think I'm going to move in here. There's a marvellous view.'

'What about Finlay?' said Kit.

'What about him?'

'He escaped, alive and intact. He's out there somewhere, the last surviving Campbell of note. He'll make a dangerous loose end. There's always the chance he might gather the lesser Campbell cousins around him, and unite them against you.'

'Even assuming our people don't catch up with him, he won't start anything. He knows he'd lose. Dear Finlay will follow the better part of valour and go to ground. He'll take a new face and a new identity, and that will be the end of Clan Campbell, bad cess to the name. Though it must be said that the Court will seem a far duller place without his delightful outfits to brighten it up. Fashion will never be the same again.'

'Good,' said Kid Death. He looked around at the devastation and the dead, and smiled. 'I'm glad I got the chance to see Crawford brought down. He never liked me.'

'We were glad to have you with us,' said Valentine. 'It was, after all, your links with the cyberat underground that enabled us to take the Campbells by surprise. The Wolfes owe you a debt; you will not find us ungrateful.'

'I'd better not,' said Kit, his voice calm and easy and not really threatening at all. He turned away and clapped David on the shoulder. 'I told you you'd see some real action if you stuck with me. Now, I don't know about you, but somewhere a long cold drink is calling my name. Let's go and find it.'

'Damn right,' said the young Deathstalker. 'Nothing like honest work to give you a thirst.'

And they walked out together, David laughing at some comment of Kit's. Valentine watched them go, and Daniel moved in beside him.

'Shouldn't we have said something about the knife in SummerIsle's back?'

'Oh, I'm sure someone will mention it to him.'

Daniel sniffed. 'Since when did those two become such good friends? I didn't think Kid Death had any friends.'

'It's a fairly recent phenomenon, from what I hear,' said Valentine. 'Presumably they have similar interests. Blood and slaughter and the like.' He shrugged dismissively, and moved over to the great wooden table, miraculously unscathed by the recent conflict. He looked down into one of the monitors, and a cyberat face grinned back at him. Valentine nodded courteously. 'My thanks for your help in this. You have my word as Wolfe that as soon as the Campbells' advanced technology is in our hands, it will be made available to you, so that we can both share in its uses.'

'That's all we ever wanted,' said the cyberat. 'We'd have been just as happy to make a deal with the Campbells, but they just turned up their noses and wouldn't talk to the likes of us. Serves them right. No one does that to the cyberats and gets away with it. Nobody. Talk to you later, Wolfe.'

The monitor screen went blank. Valentine nodded thoughtfully. The cyberat's threat hadn't been particularly subtle, but then, cyberats weren't particularly subtle people, away from their machines. Valentine found that rather refreshing, after the double meanings and hidden purposes of what passed for conversation at Court. He looked up and gestured to Daniel, who moved over to join him.

'I'd really like to be alone now, Daniel. Just for a while. This has all been very sudden and unexpected, and I need some time to put my thoughts in order. Will you take the news back to Constance and Stephanie after all? I think they might take it better from you.'

'If that's what you want. Will you be long?'

'I shouldn't think so. Take the troops with you. They can start work later.'

Daniel nodded, and looked back at their father's body. The troops had laid it out respectfully to one side, away from the carnage. 'I often wished he was dead,' Daniel said quietly, 'but I never really . . . I never really thought he would die. I thought he'd always be there, looking out for us and messing with our lives. He was always so alone . . . I don't know what I'm going to say to Constance.'

'You'll think of something,' said Valentine. 'You're a Wolfe.'

Daniel realized after a pause that Valentine had said all he was going to say. He nodded quickly, gathered up the troops with his eyes, and left the room without looking back. The troops followed him out, and Valentine waited patiently till they were all gone. He strolled over to the chair at the head of the table, and sat down. He stretched out his legs, and smiled slowly. For the moment, Daniel was too shocked to do anything but go along with him. That wouldn't last long, once he'd explained the situation to Stephanie. She'd put some backbone into him. And then they'd start jostling for position, to see what they could get away with under the new Wolfe. Valentine's scarlet smile widened. They were in for a few surprises.

Just like dear dead Dad, who never once imagined that his useless and despised son might be the instrument of his death. Valentine ran the memory through again, savouring it. The knife and the blood and the look on Jacob's face as he crumpled to the ground. He'd only caught a glimpse of it, but a glimpse had been enough. It had all been so easy, in the end. A quick thrust of a dagger, noticed by no one, and he was the Wolfe, and head of the Family. He should have done it years ago.

He'd made a good start, but there was still much to be done. He commanded the Clan by the right of inheritance, but he still had to consolidate his power base. There were any number of lesser cousins who'd be happy to support a claim by Daniel or Stephanie, if they thought they could profit by it. But he had a powerful ally in the cyberats, only too ready to support him in return for access to the Campbell technology. Carefully rationed, that should keep them on a string for some time to come. The remnants of the Campbells would be too scattered to present any real threat, and a quiet policy of assassination should help the situation along nicely. The contracts for the new stardrive would fall into his hands, now that the main competition had been eliminated. And he had taken the first steps on a road that might yet lead to the Iron Throne itself. Particularly once he had the underground united behind him. An army of esper clones, at his beck and call because he controlled the drug that made them espers. And not forgetting the AIs on Shub, who would no doubt be just as happy to deal with him as they had with the Campbells. He'd always known a good intelligence network would pay off.

Valentine smiled. Life was good.

CHAPTER ELEVEN

Unexpected Developments

The *Sunstrider* came howling out of hyperspace and plunged straight into the atmosphere of the planet Shandrakor. Smoke and fire billowed around the stricken craft as it plunged through the thickening air. The stem was a ragged wound, and fragments of outer hull tumbled away as the ship bucked and heaved in the turbulent atmosphere. The *Sunstrider* had taken a hell of a beating from the two Imperial starcruisers that ambushed it off Mistworld, and now it fell like a stone towards the unknown surface below. What was left of the outer hull blazed an angry crimson from the heat of re-entry, and the inner skin was warped and twisted. The yacht had never been intended to make planetfall without its force screens operating. It had also never been intended to take the kind of punishment Imperial starcruisers could hand out, and it was something of a miracle that the ship had held together so long. The *Sunstrider* fell, its engines cutting in and out as one system after another failed.

Inside the crippled ship, Owen Deathstalker hung on to a handy stanchion for dear life, thrown this way and that by the shuddering descent. The lounge extractors were struggling to clear thick choking smoke out of the air, and the emergency lighting flashed on and off in sudden surges. Hazel d'Ark and Ruby Journey had wedged themselves between the drinks cabinet and the inner wall and were fighting to stay there. At least it offered some protection from the unsecured furniture and fittings flying about the lounge like bulky shrapnel. Jack Random had found a quiet area, and was riding the sudden dips and rises with practised ease, suggesting the professional rebel had travelled on his share of crashing ships in his time. *Probably has*, thought Owen, as he glanced about him through the drifting smoke for the Hadenman. Tobias Moon had wedged a chair into one corner of the lounge, and was sitting there at his ease. He looked entirely calm and relaxed, and Owen felt very much like hitting him. It was all he could do to remain vaguely upright and keep his last meal down where it belonged.

'Oz; talk to me. What's happening?'

'We're crashing, Owen. You must have noticed.'

The crackling of a nearby fire suddenly sounded a lot closer than it had been, and the air grew uncomfortably warm. Something large and jagged thrust suddenly down through the ceiling, plunging into the lounge floor like a massive metal javelin. The floor seemed to drop out from under Owen's feet for a second, and he hung on to the stanchion with both hands.

'I meant; what are you doing about it? Give me a status report!'

'All right; but you're not going to like it. At the moment, the vast majority of systems are doing everything they can just to hold the ship together. We've taken extensive damage inside and out, and it is continuing. Multiple breaches of the outer and inner hulls, and the stem is gone. There are fires in three compartments, but I'm on top of it. We're losing air and pressure badly, but at the rate we're falling we'll crash into something hard and unyielding long before air loss becomes a problem.'

Owen winced. 'What are our chances of walking away from a landing?'

'Not good. The force shields are down, and we don't have the power to raise them again. The *Sunstrider* was never intended to take punishment like this. It's a pleasure yacht, not a gunship. Most of the automatics are down, and the backup systems are sitting in a corner crying their eyes out. I'm having to run everything directly, and juggle power back and forth between the systems according to what's working. There is some good news. The basic structure of the ship is still pretty much intact, which is just as well, as I have absolutely no information on how to repair it.'

'Have we got any life pods, or anti-grav chutes?' yelled Hazel. 'Could we bail out, if we had to?'

'You do have to, and no you can't.' The AI sounded positively disgusted. 'With all the power and safety systems built into this ship, no one ever thought emergency evacuation systems would be needed. We've got a waterbed in the main stateroom. You could chuck that out, and hope you landed on it.'

Jack Random looked across at Owen. 'Interesting sense of humour your AI has.'

'Yeah,' said Owen. 'And if I ever find out who programmed it into him, I'll have his balls in a vice.'

The ship convulsed, and everyone was thrown from one side of the lounge to the other. The drinks cabinet overturned, and there was broken glass everywhere. There was a high-pitched screech from somewhere aft, and then the ship righted itself again. The extractors had sucked most of the smoke out of the air, but the fire next door sounded closer than ever. The wall Owen was leaning against was growing uncomfortably hot.

'All right,' he said loudly. 'What the hell just happened?'

'We just lost the stern assembly,' said Ozymandias. 'I'm jettisoning everything that isn't absolutely essential. It won't make a lot of difference in the long run, but I've run out of anything else to do.'

'Wait just a minute,' said Owen. 'What do you mean; jettisoning? As in, dropping extremely expensive items over-board? Do you know how much I paid for this yacht?'

'Yes, and they saw you coming. If we survive this, you could always ask for your money back. Or claim it on the insurance.'

'It isn't bloody insured!'

Jack Random looked at the Hadenman. 'Didn't you just know he was going to say that?'

'Owen,' said Hazel, 'shut the hell up and let the AI get on with it. He's in the best position to know what's necessary.'

'All right,' said Owen, sulkily. 'Assuming by some miracle

we survive the landing, what's waiting for us down there? Will the planet support human life?'

'Air and gravity are within acceptable limits,' said the AI briskly. 'Nothing you can't cope with. It's pretty damn hot down there, though.'

'It doesn't matter,' said Random. 'It's not as if we had any choice in the matter. Description of land masses, please.'

'Did you hear that?' said Ozymandias. 'He said please! I'm glad there's someone on this ship with a few manners. Land masses; just the one, stretching from pole to pole, with a handful of inland seas. Unusual. The land mass is covered with varying degrees of jungle. Life signs all over the place, big and small, but no indications of intelligent life. No starport, no cities, no gatherings of artificial structures. In fact, no structures at all that I can see. However, I do have a location for one structure in my memory files, courtesy of your father, Owen. Exact coordinates for the Last Standing of the original Deathstalker. However, I have to say I see nothing at all where it's supposed to be. I can only assume it's shielded in some way.'

'The Last Standing,' said Owen softly. 'This is where he came and made his stand against the Shadow Men. It's been a legend in my Family for generations.'

'What happened when they finally met?' said Hazel.

'No one knows. None of them were ever seen again. Head for the coordinates, Oz. Put us down as close to it as you can.'

The ship shook again, and then steadied itself. 'That was the last remnants of the outer hull, Owen,' said the AI. 'All we've got left now is the basic shell. I've managed to steer us into a glide path that has steadied our descent, but unfortunately we now have a new problem.'

'Hit me with it,' said Owen resignedly.

'I cannot continue to hold this ship together and pilot us in for a safe landing. The moment I release my hold on the ship's systems to compute a landing, they'll fall apart so fast it'll make your head spin. But if I don't work out an exact plan for our landing, we are going to end up scattered over a hell of a lot of jungle. I'm open to suggestions, including prayer.'

Owen realized everyone was looking at him, and shook his head quickly. 'Sorry, people; I just bought the ship. I haven't a clue on how to fly it. That's what I put Oz in for. Hazel; you're a pilot. Why don't you take over?'

'Because I'm not qualified to handle anything this complex. And in a situation like this, a little knowledge is a dangerous thing. Ruby?'

The bounty hunter shook her head. 'Same as you. You need an expert.'

'Then I guess it's down to me,' said Random. 'As always. I've flown everything else in my time, I don't see why this should be any different. So here I come again, to save the day.'

'That won't be necessary,' said Tobias Moon in his inhuman buzzing voice. 'I'm a Hadenman. I have experience as a pilot, and I can interface directly with the ship's computers. You haven't flown a ship in years, Random, and you are not what you used to be. Logically, I have to be the better bet.'

'I'm supposed to trust my life to a Hadenman who thinks he can talk to computers?' said Hazel. 'Great. Wonderful. Why don't I just shoot myself now and get it over with?'

'Stop complaining, or I'll help you,' said Owen. 'Moon; we're in your hands.'

The Hadenman nodded briefly, his face impassive. He closed his glowing golden eyes, and his breathing slowed until it was barely perceptible. Owen watched him closely. He was desperate to do something, but all he could do was watch and hope. The Hadenman's voice suddenly sounded through all their comm implants.

'I'm patched into the flight computers through my implant. Hang on to something. The ride's about to get a bit bumpy.'

The ship rolled sickly from one side to the other as the engines suddenly roared with new life and purpose. The light flickered and grew dim, and a side door blew open. Flames burst into the lounge from the inferno in the next compartment. Owen threw himself aside, and the heat of the flames' passing scorched his bare face and hands. Jack Random tried to get close enough to close the door, but the heat drove him back. Hazel and Ruby Journey picked up the drinks cabinet between them and advanced on the flames, using it as a shield. They pushed back the flames, but couldn't let go of the cabinet long enough to make a grab for the door. Owen plunged forward, put his shoulder to the door and slammed it shut. Hazel and Ruby wedged the cabinet against the door to keep it closed, and then all three collapsed on the shaking floor.

Owen studied his hands carefully. They were red and smarting, but didn't seem to be actually burned. He'd been lucky. He looked up sharply as the roar of the engines faltered and then cut out. The ship dropped like a stone. Owen's stomach lurched, and he looked round for something to grab on to. The sudden quiet was deafening, and the fall seemed to go on for ever. And then the engines roared to life again, slowing the descent like a kick in the pants. The *Sunstrider* slowed and slowed, and then the engines cut out again, and Owen knew that was the last of their power. The ship crashed into the top of the jungle, smashing through the trees. The impact picked Owen up and threw him against the wall, and that was the last he knew of the landing.

His head ached, but he could hear the crackle of flames nearby, and he knew that was important. He opened his eyes, wasted some breath on a few curses, and then forced himself back to his feet. The floor was steady again, though at something of an angle, but his legs weren't. He stamped his feet and shook his head to clear it. He'd be weak later, when there was time. He looked around him, coughing painfully as the thickening smoke irritated his lungs. The fire in the next compartment had blown away the door and what was left of the drinks cabinet, and had taken a firm hold on one wall of the lounge.

'Oz; talk to me! Status report!'

There was only quiet, and the rising roar of the flames. He heard someone coughing close at hand, and stumbled forward through the smoke to find Hazel trying to drag a semi-conscious Ruby Journey towards the far door. He grabbed hold of Ruby's leathers, helped haul her over to the door, and kicked it open. There was only a flickering light in the corridor beyond it, but the air seemed clearer.

'Head straight on, and you'll get to the main airlock,' said Owen, fighting to control his cough. 'You get your friend out; I'll bring the others. Move it!'

Hazel snarled something in return, but he'd already turned away. He raised his cloak up over his mouth and nose, and plunged back into the smoke. It was already so thick he couldn't see more than a foot or so ahead of him. He found Jack Random by almost falling over him. The old rebel was crawling along the floor, down where the smoke was thinnest, but he'd lost all sense of direction. Owen helped him up and got him to the far door. He sent Jack after Hazel and Ruby, and then hesitated in the doorway. Tobias Moon was still in there, but Owen didn't know if he had it in him to go back into the smoke again. His lungs were aching and his head was swimming. If he went back into the lounge again, there was a good chance he might not be able to make it out again. And Moon was only a Hadenman, after all. Just as Owen was only an outlaw. He swore dispassionately, and went back into the smoke.

Finding the Hadenman was easier than finding the others; he was still where Owen had last seen him; sitting wedged in his corner. Owen tried to pick him up, and was startled at the man's weight. He could barely move the man. Augmentations, no doubt. He tried again, and still couldn't lift him. Owen struggled with the unmoving form and cursed it between coughs. Air was getting scarce, but he hadn't come this far to leave the Hadenman behind and run for the door. He boosted, and new strength flooded through his muscles. He pulled Moon to his feet, draped an arm over his shoulder, and headed to where he thought the far door was. The smoke was everywhere now, thick and smothering. It was like walking at the bottom of a great grey sea. He could feel the heat of flames to both sides of him. And then Hazel was suddenly there with him, adding her strength to his, and between them they got the Hadenman out of the far door and down the narrow corridor beyond, and finally out into the clearer air of the main airlock. The door slammed shut behind them.

Owen leaned back against it as he dropped out of boost, and

the last of the strength went out of his legs. He dumped Moon unceremoniously on the floor, and sat there beside him, coughing foul stuff up out of his lungs. After a while he felt strong enough to raise his head and look around, and wasn't surprised to find Hazel sitting next to him, looking almost as bad as he felt. Ruby Journey and Jack Random were sitting together, a little way apart. They had their guns in their hands, and although they both looked a bit pale, they were keeping a watchful eye on the outer hatch. Tobias Moon lay flat on his back, eyes closed, breathing steadily. Owen sniffed.

'Nice landing, Moon. Sure you couldn't have shaken us about a bit more?'

He stopped talking as he realized how harsh his voice sounded. His throat felt as though someone had scoured it out with wire wool. Hazel looked at him sardonically.

'We're down and we're still alive. Anything else is a bonus. Any idea why Moon is still out? He doesn't seem injured.'

'Beats me,' said Owen. 'I can't get any response out of Oz either. Maybe they were both knocked out when the computer systems finally crashed.'

'Actually, I'm conserving power,' said the AI through Owen's comm implant. 'Moon pretty much drained the ship's batteries getting us down. I'm going to have to go off-line for a while, Owen. The ship's a mess and so am I. Short of a complete refit and rebuilding, this ship's not going anywhere, and neither are we. Unless you've fallen in love with this planet and decided to settle down here, you'd better pray that someone at the Last Standing is feeling hospitable.'

'How badly are you damaged?' said Owen.

'Don't ask. You don't want to know. You're not far from the Standing. About half a mile, north-north-west. Walking distance under normal circumstances, which these aren't. In case you hadn't noticed, it's an oven out there, and it's just going to get hotter as the day goes on.'

'What about the air?' said Hazel.

'Your lungs are about to go slumming, but it won't kill you. There are a lot of other things out there that'll take care of that. For the moment, the local wildlife is giving you plenty of room, but there's no telling how long that'll last. I'm getting readings on lifeforms everywhere, from very small to extremely large and everything in between. Can't give you any details; the sensors took a real battering.'

'Any recommendations?' said Random.

'Yes. Shoot yourselves now and get it over with. From what I can make out, everything out there that moves is attacking everything else, whether it moves or not, and eating it. Damn place is a slaughterhouse. No signs of intelligence or co-operation, just if it moves, jump it. Reminds me of Imperial politics on a larger than usual scale.'

'Nice place you've brought us to, Deathstalker,' said Ruby.

Owen thought hard. There was only one course of action that made any sense, but he couldn't help hoping he could come up with something less obviously suicidal. Unfortunately, he seemed to have backed himself into a corner, tactically speaking. He looked round at his companions, and wondered if his face was as grim as theirs.

'We can't stay here,' he said bluntly. '*Sunstrider* is falling apart at the seams, and I think it would be in all our best interests to be a long way from here when it finally goes critical. Given the unfriendly and downright homicidal nature of the local wildlife, I think our best bet is to make a run for the Last Standing, and hope we can find some sanctuary there.'

'Let me see if I've got this right,' said Ruby, in her cold, even voice. 'We're going to fight our way through half a mile of alien carnage and slaughter, in order to reach some ruin that's been deserted for hundreds of years? If it's there at all? That's our plan?'

'Got it in one,' said Owen.

'All right,' said Ruby. 'I'm up for it. I could use a little exercise.'

Owen gave her a hard look, but she didn't seem to be joking.

'It may not be all bad news. According to Family legend, the Last Standing is supposed to be a massive structure, with considerable technological defences. Assuming we can get past those defences, we should find my ancestor still there, held in stasis. If we can wake him, I'm sure he'll help.'

'There's a lot of ifs and maybes in all that,' said Hazel. 'I don't have much faith in legends any more. The last time we went looking for one, we found him.' She looked severely at Jack Random, who glared right back at her. Hazel sniffed, and turned back to Owen. 'Come on, Owen; what are our chances, really?'

'Not good,' Owen admitted. 'But all the alternatives are worse.'

'I seem to be hearing that a lot just recently,' said Hazel. 'Ever since I joined up with you, in fact. I should have stayed at home and become an accountant, like mother wanted. There's always work for an accountant, and people very rarely shoot at them. Or maroon them on savage planets with no table manners.'

'Oh I don't know,' said Random. 'I can think of quite a few accountants I'd have cheerfully dumped somewhere unpleasant. Right next to the lawyers.'

Owen looked across at Tobias Moon, who was still lying flat on his back, dead to the world. 'He'd better wake up soon,' Owen said flatly, 'because I'm damned if I'm carrying a great lump like him through half a mile of homicidal jungle.'

'We could always use him as a shield,' said Ruby. 'Or a battering ram.'

'If I didn't have such a good nature, I'd stay unconscious and let you carry me,' said Tobias Moon, without lifting his head.

Owen looked at him severely. 'Eavesdroppers rarely hear well of themselves.'

'I believe that's the point.' Moon sat up slowly. 'Everything seems to be functioning again. Hopefully we can find some energy crystals at the Last Standing. I used up most of my reserves getting us down in one piece. Not a bad landing, if I say so myself.'

'I'd hate to be on one of your bad ones,' said Random.

'You're alive, aren't you?' said Moon.

'Enough chat and friendly banter,' said Owen. 'It's time we

were moving. Oz; how long have we got before the *Sunstrider* goes into meltdown?'

'I should leave right now,' said the AI. 'I'm going to have to shut down, Owen. You'll have to struggle on without me. If you find compatible hardware at the Standing, download me into that. Otherwise, you're on your own. Try not to get yourself killed.'

'I'll do my best,' said Owen. He wanted to say something more, but the words wouldn't come. Ozymandias had been with him since he was a child. He'd never had to cope without the AI before. 'I'll be back for you, Oz. One way or another, I'll be back.'

'If we've finished with the tender goodbyes, perhaps we could get a move on,' said Ruby. 'You're the one who said the ship is going to blow.'

Owen nodded curtly, and moved over to the outer hatch. 'Oz; anything nasty out there?' There was no reply. Owen bit his lower lip. He really was on his own now. He drew his gun and put his ear to the metal of the hatch. It was uncomfortably warm to the touch, suggesting the onboard fires were getting closer. He couldn't hear a thing. The metal was too thick. A passing Investigator could have been slaughtering a brass band out there, and he wouldn't have heard anything. He looked back. 'Stand ready. Hazel; get over here by the manual release. When I give you the nod, open the hatch.'

Hazel moved over to the controls, and everyone drew a gun or a blade, according to their nature. They looked tired and tense, but prepared. Owen wished he'd had some armour and heavy duty weaponry put on board at some point, but he'd never seen the need in a pleasure yacht. Assuming he got out of this mess alive and reasonably intact, it was a mistake he wouldn't make again. The universe was not a friendly place. He hefted the disrupter in his hand, and looked back at the others.

'Everybody ready? Right. Remember, no rushing outside the moment the hatch opens. We're going to take this slow and steady and very carefully, until we know the lie of the land.'

'Is he always like this?' Ruby said to Hazel.

'Mostly,' said Hazel. 'He used to be a Lord. I think he inherited the pompousness along with the big ears.'

Owen decided he hadn't heard that. 'Hazel; open the hatch.'

There was a worryingly long grinding noise, and then the hatch slid open. Bright crimson light spilled into the airlock, along with the heavy humid air of the jungle. It smelled of rotting meat. And then everything in the world tried to get through the hatch at once. There were huge ferocious shapes with teeth and claws and glaring eyes, fighting each other for the chance to get into the airlock first. There were smaller things that also seemed to be all teeth and claws, pouring over the lower edge of the airlock in waves. There were flying things and lashing tendrils of vegetation with vicious spines and barbs, and it all wanted to get in. There were screams and roars and ululating howls, echoing deafeningly in the confined space of the airlock.

A long tentacled thing surged towards Owen, and he shot it automatically. The energy blast hit the beast at point-blank range, and it exploded, showering him with foul-smelling entrails. Something with huge clawed hands and a mouth bigger than Owen's head hauled the tentacled body out of the way, and hurled itself at Owen. He met it with his sword, cutting deep into the leathery flesh.

'Shut the hatch!' he screamed. 'Shut the bloody hatch!'

Everyone was firing their guns at once, but the creatures kept coming, slavering in their eagerness to get at new prey. The airlock was full of awful life, and swords swung viciously. Hazel fought to get back to the control panel. A long tentacle whipped through the air, snatched up Moon, and hauled him bodily out of the hatch and into the surging chaos outside.

'Don't shut the hatch!' yelled Owen. 'They've got Moon! Somebody help him!'

'Somebody else help him,' snapped Random, cutting doggedly at a slimy creature that was apparently too stupid to know it should have been dead by now. 'I've got my own problems.'

Hazel managed to hit the control button with her elbow,

and the hatch began to close. The heavy steel weight moved remorselessly forward, cutting slowly but firmly through everything that got in the way. Gradually the hatchway grew smaller, and the larger creatures were forced outside. The hatch finally slammed shut, and the remaining smaller creatures were trapped in the airlock. Owen and Random fought back to back, cutting down the vicious alien life as it struggled to get at them. Random fought well, Owen thought, for an old man. Hazel and Ruby were also fighting back to back, and making a bloody mess of anything that came within reach. The horrors fell, one after the other, large and small, until finally it was over. Owen slowly lowered his sword, and leaned against the bulkhead wall, panting for breath. It seemed very quiet in the airlock now, though the air was thick with the stench of blood and death. Behind Owen, Random was chopping up something large and juicy. Hazel and Ruby were leaning on each other for support, and glaring about them, swords still at the ready.

'Moon,' Owen said harshly. 'He's still out there.'

'Then he's dead,' said Hazel. 'And so would we be, if we were stupid enough to go out after him.'

'Not necessarily,' said Ruby. 'He is a Hadenman, after all.'

They all looked up sharply as the sound of energy guns firing came dimly to them, from somewhere close at hand.

'Could the Empire have found us already?' said Hazel.

'It's not the Empire,' said Owen. 'Oz said we were alone down here. I think those are our guns; *Sunstrider*'s guns. That's why we can hear them, even with the hatch closed.'

'But who's firing them?' said Random. 'Your computer is supposed to be shut down. Have you been keeping something from us, Deathstalker?'

'Oz; is that you?' Owen waited, but there was no reply. The guns suddenly stopped firing, and it was very quiet in the airlock. 'I'm going to look outside,' said Owen.

'Is this wise?' said Hazel. 'After what happened the last time I opened the hatch?'

'The guns should have cleared some space around the ship,' said Owen.

'And if they haven't?'

'I don't give a damn. Moon's out there. A Deathstalker doesn't abandon his people.'

He hit the hatch controls before anyone could raise further objections, and they all turned their guns on the opening hatch. Crimson light spilled into the airlock again, along with the charnel stench of the jungle. *Even the light's the colour of blood*, thought Owen. *What kind of place have I brought us to?*

Everyone braced themselves against another invasion of bloodthirsty creatures, but all was still and quiet. The hatch ground to a halt at its furthest extension, and Owen peered warily out. There were dead aliens everywhere, torn and tattered and piled up around the ship, but no signs of life or movement anywhere. The surrounding jungle was a mass of conflicting vibrant colours, predominantly scarlet. The sky was mostly hidden by a thick canopy of branches overhead. There were huge towering trees and gushing vegetable shapes everywhere, all spines and barbs and overripe flowers. And then something moved among the heaps of the dead, and Owen snapped his gun to bear before he realized who it was. It was Moon, standing at the side of the ship, hip deep in carnage, covered with alien blood and looking inordinately pleased with himself.

Owen jumped down from the airlock, and made his way towards the Hadenman, clambering awkwardly over the heaps of bodies. The creatures ranged in size from gossamer insects the size of his hand to huge forms easily twenty feet long. None of them looked in very good shape. The ship's energy guns had torn them literally limb from limb. At such close range they never stood a chance, but Owen couldn't bring himself to feel any sympathy. The smell was appalling, and he did his best to breathe through his mouth. He reached the Hadenman, and Moon nodded to him calmly.

'About time I had a decent workout. I think I'm going to like it here.'

'All right,' said Owen. 'What the hell happened out here?'

'I tapped into the ship's systems through my comm link, overrode the computers, and took control of the fire systems.

Then I had them blast everything that moved, while I sheltered among the bodies. Quite simple, really.'

Owen looked at him. 'That shouldn't have been possible. Even with Oz off-line, the security codes should have kept you out of the systems.'

'I overrode them,' said Moon. 'It wasn't difficult. I'm a Hadenman.'

'I didn't know you could do things like that.'

'There are lots of things about me you don't know.'

Owen didn't have any answer to that, so he turned and gestured for the others to come and join him. They made slow progress through the heaps of the dead, keeping a constant wary eye on the surrounding jungle. Owen didn't blame them. He could feel the pressure of uncounted unseen eyes following his every move. The ship's guns had taught the creatures caution, but there was no telling how long that would last.

'What did you say this hellhole was called?' said Hazel.

'Shandrakor,' Owen said absently, still looking around him. 'This is where my ancestor fled when the Empire turned on him, and sent the Shadow Men after him.'

'Who were they?' said Random, still trying to get his breath back after clambering over the bodies.

'No one knows any more,' said Owen. 'People apparently didn't talk about them much back then, if they knew what was good for them. The Shadow Men were the Emperor's hounds; unstoppable, quite deadly and never once defeated. Basically; pretty nasty and proud of it. They tracked my ancestor here, to the very edge of the Empire, and then nothing more was heard, of them or him. No one ever came back from Shandrakor, no matter how large a force the Emperor sent. Eventually he turned his face away from the planet, and Shandrakor was not spoken of by anyone. Its coordinates became lost, its nature forgotten, and the name Shandrakor only survived as the battle cry of my Clan. Even then, we walked our own path. For a long time now Shandrakor has been nothing but a legend, hidden away out here on the very edge of the Rim. Forgotten by everyone save obsessive historians like myself.

We're about as far from the Empire now as you can get without passing into the Darkvoid.'

'Once I would have found that comforting,' said Hazel. 'But not any more. This is a vicious place you've brought us to, Deathstalker. Humans don't belong here.'

'I like it,' said Ruby. 'It's got style.'

'We should head for the Standing while things are still quiet,' said Random. 'Do you have any force shields aboard, Owen?'

'Just a portable screen. It's got enough range to cover us all while we walk, but as I recall the power cells are pretty depleted.'

'You're just full of good news, aren't you?' said Ruby. 'Will it last long enough for us to reach the Standing?'

Owen shrugged unhappily. 'Unknown. It's only half a mile, but who knows how long that'll take through this jungle. It might last, or it might cut out at any time.'

Moon smiled. 'Good. More exercise.'

Owen gave him a hard look. He had an unnerving feeling the Hadenman meant it. What with him and Ruby Journey, Owen was beginning to feel decidedly outclassed. He was also beginning to feel like the only sane person in the group. 'I'll get the screen, and then we'd better make a start. This ship is still going to explode eventually, and on top of that, we don't know how long the days are here. I have a strong feeling it would be a really bad idea for us to be lost in the jungle when darkness falls. I hate to think what kind of creatures go on the prowl during the night.'

'Maybe everything just goes to sleep,' said Hazel.

Owen raised an eyebrow. 'Would you?'

The little light that did filter through the canopy was a dull brick red, as though the air itself was glowing from the rising heat of the day. Sweat poured off Owen as he cut a rough path through the close-set trees of the Shandrakor jungle. He could have just hung back and let the Hadenman do it. Moon didn't seem at all bothered by the heat, and his sword arm rose and fell as tirelessly as a machine. But Owen had his pride, and insisted on taking his turn. He was beginning to feel like the weak link in the group. Everyone else was either an amazing fighter, a psychopath or a legend. Or any combination of the above. Owen was used to being the best there was. He'd been trained and raised to dominate any situation, to be the leader and inspiration of any group. But none of his aristocratic upbringing had prepared him for life as an outlaw on the run. So he ignored the heat and the sweat and his aching arm and persevered, hacking a path through the thick vegetation with his sword, and tried not to think what that was doing to the blade's edge.

Everyone else stayed close behind him. Ruby and Hazel carried their swords at the ready. Random had a gun in each hand. And the Hadenman brought up the rear, strolling coolly along as though this was nothing more than a pleasant walk in the park. Owen's mouth twitched grudgingly. For Moon, maybe it was. They all kept a careful eye on the surrounding jungle. They could hear things moving along with them, hidden from sight, keeping a respectful distance. The portable screen saw to that. It wasn't as powerful or impenetrable as a force shield, but its energy field established a perimeter around the group and administered a nasty shock to anything that tried to cross the line. The creatures learned quickly from the first few deaths, but still every now and again something would lurch suddenly forward from the dark between the trees to test the screen again. It happened just often enough to get on everyone's nerves and keep them jumpy, and their tempers were growing short. Innocent remarks took on insulting tones, with the result they stopped talking to each other for anything but the absolutely necessary, which suited Owen just fine. He didn't have the breath or the inclination for conversation, and he had a lot to think about.

There wasn't much about the original Deathstalker in the Family archives. A great fighter and better statesman, Warrior Prime to the Empire, and inventor of the Darkvoid Device. The enigmatic machine that put out a thousand suns in a moment, leaving their planets turning slowly in an unending night. The Darkvoid. The darkness beyond the Rim.

The Deathstalker took the device and all his notes with him when he fled, and when it disappeared along with him, everyone breathed a quiet sigh of relief. Nobody wanted that threat hanging over their heads all the time. It would have made the Emperor altogether too powerful. But there had been nothing in the archives to suggest what kind of man the Deathstalker had been. Brave, certainly, honourable apparently; but what kind of man could have created a horror like the Darkvoid Device? And what happened to the friends, Family and supporters he'd left behind when he ran, left to the mercy of a furious Emperor? There was no record of what had happened to them, but Owen thought he could make a damn good guess.

So, assuming the Deathstalker was still held in stasis somewhere in the Last Standing, and assuming they could wake him, what would he be like? Would they be able to persuade him to join their rebellion against the Empire; an Empire probably very different from the one he remembered? And if he still had the Device, would they have the determination to use it again, and cause the death of untold billions of innocents a second time . . .

Owen attacked the vegetation before him with new anger. His head was aching, and it wasn't just from the heat. The jungle stretched away before him, thick and dense and unforgiving. He would have liked to use his disrupter to blast open a path, but he didn't want to risk starting a fire. There was no telling how easily the trees would burn, or which way a wind might carry that fire, and it would be a pretty nasty and stupid way to die.

He didn't like the look of the trees. The trunks were four to five feet wide, with a dark red bark that was pitted and scarred. The branches stirred unsettlingly, even when there was no hint of a breeze, and the crimson leaves were long and narrow, with razor-sharp serrations. Everyone had quickly learned to keep their hands to themselves. The colours of the remaining vegetation were bright and primal, solid yellows and blues and pinks, that clashed gaudily with the dominant scarlet. Either this planet hadn't discovered the benefits of camouflage or protective coloration, or it just didn't give a damn. Owen favoured the latter explanation. Shandrakor didn't strike him as a particularly subtle planet. Up above him, he could hear things moving in the higher branches, keeping up with his party, but so far none of them had come down to check out the new intruders in their territory. Didn't stop them emptying their bowels all over the group, though. Owen was just grateful the screen protected their heads as well as their sides.

Out beyond the screen, the planet's creatures were getting on with their usual business of tearing each other into bloody pieces, and then eating as much as they could before something else jumped them. The din was appalling, with screams and roars and everything in between, but after a while it faded into the background. Owen supposed you could get used to anything eventually. He couldn't help wondering why the beasts of the jungle were keeping such a respectful distance. The screen and the disrupters had killed quite a few of them, but they hadn't struck Owen as being that smart. They should have just kept coming till they overwhelmed the party through sheer numbers, as they nearly had in the *Sunstrider*'s airlock. Instead, they backed off and disappeared back into the jungle once the energy guns started firing. Almost as though they'd encountered such guns before, and had learned the hard way to respect them. Which should have been impossible. Officially, no one from the Empire had visited Shandrakor in centuries. Mainly because no one knew where it was.

Unless the Empress knew; and had known it all the time. A secret, perhaps, handed down from ruler to ruler, as something to be wary of and watch over. It made sense. Owen couldn't see any Emperor choosing to forget the location of the most powerful weapon ever invented. So; could Imperial troops have got to Shandrakor before the *Sunstrider* did? Owen scowled. It didn't seem likely, but he couldn't rule it out either. If that was the case, things had just got a lot more complicated. It didn't mean everything was lost. He had the exact location of the Last Standing, thanks to the files his father had hidden in Ozymandias's memory. Unless the Empire had already been here for some time, searching . . .

Owen cut viciously at the vegetation before him. Nothing was ever simple any more.

Something huge howled in agony as it was brought down by something even bigger not too far away. The ground shuddered under its weight, and he looked quickly about him. The force screen would keep out most things, but he didn't know for sure whether it could stand up to something really large just dropping on it with all its weight. The screen might just overload and collapse. *Great*, thought Owen. *Something else to worry about.* The creatures were definitely edging closer again. Either they were getting over their fear of the screen and the guns, or they just didn't care. Owen was inclined to the latter view. Everything on this planet seemed to be at war with everything else, from the insects swarming over the tangled jungle floor, to the huge beasts who made the ground shudder when they walked. The jungle was a slaughterhouse, everyone taken care of, no waiting. Even the plants were dangerous. Apart from barbed spines and poisoned thorns, the party had also encountered hidden trap doors large enough to swallow a foot, and larger hinged traps that looked like they wouldn't have minded swallowing something a whole lot bigger.

'Take a break,' Hazel said behind him, and Owen gratefully came to a halt. He wiped the sweat from his face with his sleeve, and looked back at the rest of his party. Hazel looked almost as shattered as he felt. Ruby Journey was breathing hard, but her back was still straight and her head erect. Jack Random had taken the opportunity to sit down, ignoring the insects swarming around him. He sat with his shoulders slumped and his head hanging down, and sweat dripped from his face on to the ground, where the insects fought over it. Moon looked perfectly calm and collected, as though he could walk for miles yet. Owen hated him. Something large and blocky leapt out of the trees at them, and howled angrily as it hit the screen. It struggled against the energy field for a long moment, ignoring the shocks, but finally fell back, defeated. Owen couldn't help noticing that it was taking longer all the time for the screen to have an effect. Either the field was weakening, or the creatures were getting stronger and more determined. Owen knew which was the most likely, but he was too tired to care. He sat down, and after a moment, Hazel and Ruby joined him.

'Have you ever seen anything like this before, Hazel?' said Owen quietly.

'There's a couple of cities on Loki that are almost as dangerous to walk through, but no; I've never come across anything as unrelentingly lethal as this. I mean; don't they ever stop eating? You'd think they'd run out of prey at this rate. Surely they must stop sometimes, if only to sleep and digest.'

'Maybe they're working shifts,' Owen suggested, and Hazel managed a small smile.

'You're the one with the built-in compass. How much further to the Standing?'

'At least a quarter of a mile. We're barely half-way there.'

'Is that all?' Hazel shook her head wearily. 'It seems like I've been slogging through this jungle forever. Any more bad news you'd like to share with me?'

'We're draining the crystals in our guns, the screen isn't holding up as well as I'd hoped, and it's getting hotter. I don't think we've even reached midday yet. I hate this place.'

'Oh good,' said Hazel. 'Something more to worry about. I don't know why I ever saved you, Deathstalker. You're a bloody jinx to be around, you know that?'

'Yes, I do. You keep telling me. You should be grateful to me for bringing a little adventure into your life. Would you rather be stuck in an office all day, staring into a monitor screen?'

'Frankly, yes.'

'Come on; we'd better start moving again.' Owen tried to force some confidence into his voice. 'Only a quarter of a mile to go.'

'Wait a bit longer,' said Jack Random. 'If we wear ourselves out too quickly, we'll never get there. We have to pace ourselves.' Owen looked at him, surprised. The old rebel sounded much fresher and stronger than he had. Random saw the look, and grinned easily. 'I've done this before, lad.

Couldn't tell you how many jungles on how many planets I've hacked my way through in my time. You have to learn to spread your strength, so it's there to be called on when you need it. Don't worry about the screen and the guns. Either they'll hold out, or they won't, and either way there's nothing you can do about it. Save your energy for problems you can solve. Like making sure the path you're cutting is as straight as you can get it. Even a mild curve could put us miles off course.'

'I'm watching the compass,' said Owen. 'We're dead on course. Listen; if you've got any other wisdom to offer, don't be shy about sharing it. I'm new to all this, and I'll take all the help I can get.'

'Good attitude for a leader,' Random said approvingly. 'You're doing fine, Deathstalker. Lead from the front and we'll follow.'

'Speak for yourself,' said Ruby Journey. 'I wouldn't trust that inbred aristo to lead sheep to slaughter.'

'Interesting choice of phrase, my dear,' said Random. 'Perhaps you'd care to modify it, given our current position?'

'No I wouldn't. And I'm not your dear.'

'That's for sure,' said Hazel. 'You've never been anybody's dear.'

'I've never been anybody's fool, either.' Ruby glared at them all impartially. 'I should never have let you talk me into this. I could have made a perfectly good fortune just handing you over to the authorities. Instead, I'm stuck in the middle of a bloody jungle, light years from anywhere half-way civilized, with no provisions and no bloody ship. I should have shot you all on sight.'

'You did try,' said Owen.

'You wouldn't shoot me, Ruby,' Hazel said briskly. 'I'm your friend.'

Ruby looked at her. 'The rewards on all your heads would buy me a lot of friends.'

'Not the kind that matter,' said Random. 'It's a lonely place, this Empire, without friends to watch your back.'

'Friends are a luxury,' said Ruby coldly. 'Like faith, politics and family. They always let you down, in the end. The only person you can ever really trust is yourself. I'd have thought you'd have known that, after all the times you got your ass kicked by the Empire. Your great rebellion is over, Random.'

'It's not over till I say it's over,' said Random. 'As long as I refuse to give up, they haven't beaten me. The strength of rebellion lies in the heart, not in armies.'

'Nice sentiment,' said Ruby. 'I'll be sure they'll put it on your tombstone.'

'Thank you, Ruby,' said Random, smiling charmingly. 'That's very good of you. Time to get moving again, Death-stalker. If we've got the energy to argue, we're rested enough to start up again.'

He rose easily to his feet, looking calm and relaxed and ready to go. Owen was surprised to find he'd gotten his second wind while they were talking, and got to his feet with only minor winces. He put out a hand to Hazel, who ignored it and got up unaided. Owen didn't even try to offer his hand to Ruby. The bounty hunter rose up as lithely and effortlessly as she'd sat down, her face cold and calm and untouched by any trace of passion. Owen smiled, hefted his sword thoughtfully, and turned back to the vegetation blocking his trail. If he had to be stranded on an unfriendly world, he was glad he was accompanied by fighters, not quitters. He was especially pleased to see Jack Random coming to life again. This was more like the legendary rebel he'd heard so much about.

Owen went back to opening up a trail with his sword. Ruby moved up alongside to help. Owen wasn't too happy about having the bounty hunter that close to him with a naked blade in her hands. She made him nervous. She had the cold poise of an Investigator, and the unrelenting malice to go with it. Owen had absolutely no doubt that she would have killed him in a second back on Mistworld, if things had gone differently. He was also pretty damn sure she'd turn on him in a moment if she decided it was in her best interests to do so. She'd have made a good aristocrat. He kept a watchful eye on her until she decided they'd made enough ground, and dropped back to walk with the others. Owen breathed a little more easily, though his back still prickled just a little. After a moment, Hazel moved up beside him.

'What's the problem between you and Ruby?' she said bluntly.

'Don't know what you mean,' said Owen.

'Come off it. I saw you shooting suspicious looks at her in what you obviously thought was an unobtrusive manner. Don't you trust her?'

'Of course not. She's a bounty hunter, and I'm bounty.'

'We're all outlaws together now, aristo.'

'Some of us are more outlaws than others.'

'She's my friend,' said Hazel coldly. 'She gave me her word. You can trust her as you trust me.'

'Exactly,' said Owen.

Hazel had to think about that for a moment, and then glared at him and fell back to join the others, scowling heavily. Owen sighed, and took out his spleen on the helpless vegetation before him. It didn't help much. He liked Hazel. He admired her courage and her forthright manner, but they couldn't seem to exchange two words without arguing. Jack Random came forward to walk at his side, and they cut trail together in silence for a while, the only sound the solid chunk of steel cutting through vegetation.

'A word of advice,' Jack said finally. 'Never win an argument with a woman. They'll forgive anything but that.'

'But I was right.'

'What's that got to do with anything?'

'We're making good time,' Owen said determinedly. 'Would you like to take over the lead for a while?'

'No thanks. In my experience, the point man has the most dangerous job. You're welcome to it.'

'You should be leading this party anyway. I mean; you're Jack Random.'

'I used to be, and given time I might be again. But for the moment I'm just a tired old man pulled out of retirement for one last fight. I've got a long way to go before I'm competent

393

to lead anything but a suicide charge. You carry on, lad. You're doing a good job as leader.'

'Am I? Hazel and I spit at each other like cats, Moon worries the hell out of me, and I daren't turn my back on Ruby.'

'And you're holding them all together. You give them purpose, and point them in the right direction. That's all anyone really has the right to expect of a leader. I should know.'

He grinned easily at Owen, clapped him once on the shoulder, and dropped back to the others. Owen wiped the sweat from his face with his sleeve, and stood a little straighter. If Jack Random said he was doing a good job, he must be. He was still getting used to the idea when Moon appeared suddenly at his side.

'I have a question for you, Deathstalker. How are you going to get me to Haden when you don't have a ship any more? You said you'd get me there. You gave me your word.'

'I'll get you there.'

'How?'

'I'm working on it!'

Moon nodded and fell back to join the others, leaving Owen by himself. He growled not completely under his breath, and hacked at a web of hanging creepers. He felt he could use a little time to himself. For some reason, the creatures surrounding the party seemed to be showing them a lot more respect. Owen found that suspicious, but he could live with that.

Some time later, the jungle fell suddenly away before them, to reveal a great clearing with a huge stone castle in its centre. Owen raised an arm to protect his eyes from the direct glare of the sun. Away from the protection of the jungle canopy, the heat was almost blistering but he held his ground. He'd come a long way to be here, and besides, it felt good not to have to worry about which direction an attack might come from next. Owen's back ached from the constant tension and anticipation of an attack. He lowered his sword and leaned on it gratefully as he studied the castle in the clearing.

It was a huge structure, rising up high enough to hide the

jungle behind it, and composed of uncomfortably large blocks of dull grey stone. There were tall thin towers with pointed roofs, and crenellated battlements. There was no sign of any activity, or any light at any of the many slit windows, and the single great door was closed. And on top of all that, the whole castle seemed slightly out of focus, seen through the faint shimmer of the force shield that surrounded it. For a long time nobody said anything. Owen looked up at the sky. The sun was blood red, and sinking down towards the top of the trees. Not long now till night, and whatever new creatures prowled in it.

'So that's the Last Standing of your ancestor, Owen,' said Hazel. 'I'm impressed. How the hell did he manage to build something like that on a planet like this?'

'It wasn't exactly what I was expecting,' Owen admitted. 'He must have had help of some kind.'

'Right,' said Random. 'In case you hadn't noticed, the boundaries of this clearing are extremely distinct. Which suggests it was probably cut using energy weapons. Still doesn't explain where he found all that stone, though.'

'Must have had a quarry somewhere,' said Owen.

'Then who worked in it?'

They stared at the castle in silence for a while.

'The force shield's another complication I wasn't expecting,' said Owen. 'The only way to lower a shield like that is from the inside, and we've no guarantee there's any living soul left in there. Since the shield's still up, I think we can safely assume there's some degree of automation. Computers running things on a low priority basis.'

'Must have an amazing power source in there,' said Hazel. 'To be still running things after all these years.'

'Unless somebody else got here first,' said Ruby.

They all considered that.

'The beasts of the jungle acted like they'd encountered energy weapons before,' said Moon. 'And they stopped bothering us the closer we got to the castle and the clearing. If the Empire got here first . . .'

'Then we're in real trouble,' said Random.

'Nothing could beat my ship here,' said Owen.

'Only one way to find out,' said Ruby, and she stepped out into the clearing, gun in one hand, sword in the other. Two bright glows appeared in windows on either side of the great door. Hazel threw herself at Ruby and knocked her to the ground, and two disrupter beams flashed through the air where she'd been standing and incinerated the trees behind her. They burned fiercely for a moment, and then the flames died down and flickered out. The charred wood smoked gently.

'Tough trees,' said Moon.

'Like everything else on this planet,' said Owen. 'You girls all right?'

'We are not girls,' said Hazel.

'That's for sure,' said Random.

Hazel dragged Ruby back into the shelter of the trees, and helped her to her feet. Ruby didn't even nod her thanks, her cold eyes fixed on the castle. The two glows on either side of the door were still there. Ruby raised her gun and then lowered it again.

'Top of the line force shield,' said Owen. 'Lets energy beams out without having to drop the field first. Must use a hell of a lot of power to cover something that large. Certainly we haven't got any weapon that'll bother it.'

'I think we can safely assume that whoever's in there, they're not feeling friendly,' said Hazel, brushing grass and insects from her clothes.

'I don't know,' said Random. 'Those had the feel of warning shots. A computerized defence system would have tracked you no matter how fast you moved, and kept on firing till it was sure its target had been eliminated.'

'So what do we do next?' said Hazel. 'Apart from suicide tactics.' She glared at Ruby, who was still ignoring her.

'Communicate,' said Moon. 'People or machines, they might respond to contact.'

'It might also give them something to aim their guns at,' said Hazel.

'She has a point,' said Random.

'We can't just stand around here,' said Owen. 'In case

396

you've forgotten, we've nowhere else to go, except the castle. Either we find a way in, or we live in the jungle. Which doesn't exactly appeal to me. I'm going to go out there unarmed, and talk to them. If those are my ancestor's computers, they might react to me. I am a Deathstalker, after all.'

'You go right ahead,' said Hazel. 'Personally, I'm going to find something large to hide behind.'

Owen smiled, and couldn't help noticing she didn't make a move as he stepped cautiously out into the clearing. He put away his gun and his sword, and held up his hands to show they were empty. He cleared his throat carefully. He didn't want to be misunderstood.

'I am Owen, first of Clan Deathstalker. I come to you in need and danger, and call upon you for sanctuary. I bear my Family's ring.'

He held the hand forward, so that the castle sensors could get a clear look at it. Sweat was running down his face again, and it wasn't from the blazing heat of the open clearing. A light appeared in another window, and he had to fight not to flinch. And then all the lights went out, and the force shield snapped off just in front of the door, leaving a clear tunnel open in the shield. Owen blinked, and looked back at the others.

'I think that's an invitation. Let's move it, before they change their minds. And people; put away your weapons.'

The rest of the party emerged cautiously from the edge of the jungle, and took in the break in the force shield as they reluctantly sheathed their weapons.

'That is not possible,' said Random. 'You can't just lower part of a force shield like that. The field would collapse.'

'Impossible or not, it's there,' said Hazel. 'May I suggest we use it before it disappears, and leaves us stranded here?'

'Of course,' said Owen. 'After you.'

'It's your Family and your castle,' Hazel said firmly. 'After you.'

Owen smiled briefly, and walked out into the clearing. He could feel the presence of the force field on either side of him, so close he could have reached out his arms and touched it.

Little runs of static moved in his clothes and sparked in his hair. He took a deep breath and kept walking. He could hear the others moving close behind him, but didn't turn to look. It might make him appear nervous, and he had a feeling this would be a bad time to appear to be weak. The castle grew bigger the closer he got to it, until it was looming over him like a mountain. The sheer scale of the place, and the massive size of the stone blocks, made his head ache. He couldn't imagine the army of people and technology it must have taken to build the Last Standing, starting from scratch on a new planet. There were still no lights at any of the windows, no sign of any life. He still had the feeling he was being watched. He finally came to a halt before the only door, and stared at it thoughtfully. Ten foot tall, six foot wide, solid wood studded with some kind of crimson metal, like drops of blood. A disrupter would probably tear right through it, but it looked like it would stop anything else. The others crowded in around him.

'What do we do now?' said Ruby.

'Knock,' said Random. 'Very politely.'

'We may have to,' said Owen. 'There's no handle, or any sensor I can see.'

'Probably doesn't get many visitors out here,' said Random.

'I don't want to worry anyone,' Hazel said quietly. 'But the force field has re-established itself behind us. We're trapped.'

'For someone who didn't want to worry us, I'd say you've managed very well,' said Owen.

'I could break the door down,' said Moon, in his grating inhuman voice.

'Thanks for the thought, but no,' said Owen. 'The last thing we want to do right now is make a bad impression. Those energy guns are probably still trained on us, and I don't want whoever's behind them feeling nervous. If you want to be useful, Moon, try talking to the castle like you did to the Sunstrider's computers earlier on. If there are computers in the Standing, you might be able to communicate with them.'

Moon nodded, and frowned slightly, concentrating. In that moment, much of the humanity went out of the Hadenman's face, dominated by the blazing golden eyes, and Owen fought down a sudden impulse to shiver. Moon's face cleared, and he looked at Owen. 'Nothing. If there are any computers in there, either they're not listening or they're not talking.'

'Show your ring to the sensors again,' said Hazel. 'That got a response last time.'

Owen lifted his hand, and showed it a little self-consciously to the windows above the door. No light showed, and he'd started to lower his hand again when suddenly he was somewhere else. There was no warning, or sense of transition; one moment he was standing before the door and the next he was in a great hall, presumably inside the Standing. It stretched away before him, incredibly long and wide, and completely deserted. An army could have drilled in the hall, or a full Clan gathering could have danced in it, but there was no sign of any life save for the lights shining overhead. There was no fire in the great marble fireplace, but the floor had been recently waxed and polished, and there was no trace of dust anywhere. The others were suddenly in the hall with him, looking almost as confused as he felt.

'What the hell just happened?' said Hazel, one hand dropping to the gun at her side.

'Transfer portal,' said Owen. 'I've heard about them, but never expected to encounter a working one. They were created centuries ago; instant teleportation between two places, to save the aristocracy the bother of actually having to travel from one place to another. They never caught on, because of the massive amounts of power involved, and because they were a security nightmare. Then espers came in and replaced them. No power sources required, and a damn sight cheaper to run. The Empire's always had a fondness for slave labour over machinery. This place must have a hell of a power source hidden away somewhere, if it can still operate a transfer portal after all this time.'

'Nine hundred and forty years,' said Random. 'Whoever built this Standing built it to last.'

'I've just had a really nasty thought,' Hazel said quietly. 'If this place is being run by computers; could it have been taken over by the AIs from Shub? They're supposed to have all kinds of technology that we don't.'

'You're right,' said Owen. 'That is a nasty thought. If you have any more like that, feel free to keep them to yourself. Things are tricky enough as it is without us getting paranoid. We're a long way from Shub, and the last I heard, the Enemies of Humanity were safely tucked away behind an Imperial blockade. Let's all please concentrate on the matter at hand.'

'You got us in here, Deathstalker,' said Ruby. 'What say you lead us to this ancestor of yours? I've got a few questions I wouldn't mind putting to him.'

'All right,' said Owen, trying hard to sound confident. 'Follow me.'

He strode off down the giant hall, the echoes of his footsteps sounding loud and flat in the silence. The others moved quickly after him, not wanting to be left behind, trying very hard to look casual and unimpressed. Owen allowed his hand to rest casually near his gun. He wasn't sure what he'd been expecting to find at his ancestor's legendary Last Standing, but this wasn't it. This immense castle wasn't the last refuge of a desperate man, harried and driven to a planet light years from civilization. This was a power base, designed for survival against overwhelming odds; a place to strike back from. But he never had. He had all this power at his command, but instead he chose to hide himself away in stasis, waiting for an awakening that never came. Owen frowned. Presumably the Empire had been just as overwhelming an enemy then as it was now, but Owen had a strong feeling he didn't have anything like the whole story. He strode on, trying to look confident and unthreatening at the same time. He didn't want to appear a threat. He was pretty damn sure the Standing had just as many security measures inside as it did outside.

He reached the other end of the hall without incident, stepped through the open door, and found himself somewhere else, completely unconnected to the hall. He'd just passed through another transfer portal. It didn't take Owen and the rest of his party long to discover two important things about the portals. One; every door in the castle was a portal leading somewhere unexpected, and two; you couldn't go back through the door to wherever you'd just come from. And so the party jumped blindly from room to room, passing ever deeper into the depths of the Last Standing. Owen kept himself orientated with his internal compass, but he had no way of knowing exactly where in the castle he was at any given time. Or how to get out of it. All the rooms were perfectly clean and brightly lit, but with nothing to show they had ever been lived in. Owen became increasingly convinced that they were being watched at all times, but couldn't spot anything that might have been a sensor. Whoever was controlling the portals apparently had some destination in mind, but where and why remained a mystery.

Owen kept walking, and tried very hard to be patient. He had a strong suspicion that even if he had felt like being awkward, it wouldn't have made any difference. He was in someone else's hands now, for better or worse. He tried to keep his hand near his gun without being too obvious about it. They passed through room after room, all of them devoid of any interest or personality. No fixtures or fittings, no comforts of any kind. Owen became increasingly convinced that no one had ever lived in the castle.

Until finally they came to what Owen immediately thought of as a trophy room. Unlike the other rooms, this one was of a more comfortable size, though its contents were anything but comforting. A large glass case took up the centre of the room, some ten feet square. And in that case, like trophies on display, stood three men in outdated battle armour. They were so still that Owen first thought they were models of some kind, but when he moved forward and pressed his nose against the glass, he quickly became convinced they were real. Their poses were stiff, their faces were blank, and there were bloody holes in their armour.

'They're dead, aren't they?' Hazel said finally. 'I thought at first they were in stasis, but there's no trace of any equipment.'

'They're preserved in some way,' said Random. 'I'd kill for a closer look at them.'

'No problem,' said Moon, and smashed one of the glass sides with his fist.

Owen whirled around, gun in hand, every muscle tensed for an attack that never came. He slowly relaxed, and turned back to the Hadenman.

'Moon; if I wanted a heart attack, I'd play Russian roulette with a fully charged disrupter. Don't do anything else without checking with me first. You could have set off some kind of security system.'

'We need information,' said Moon, entirely unphased by the anger in Owen's voice. He stepped through the wreckage of the glass wall, splinters crunching under his boots, and studied the figures closely. Random moved in quickly after him, followed by Hazel and Ruby. Owen decided he wasn't doing any good just standing outside on his own, shook his head resignedly, and entered the glass case himself. Up close, the three figures looked even more disturbing. Moon prodded one with his finger, and it rocked gently on its feet.

'What the hell are they?' said Hazel quietly, as though afraid they might hear her. 'It's not stasis, whatever it is.'

'They're preserved,' said Moon. 'They died, violently according to the evidence, and then their insides were removed, and some kind of preservative material was pumped inside them.'

'How can you tell?' said Random, sounding more intrigued than anything else.

'I can smell the chemicals,' said Moon, 'and there are telltale signs in the skin, if you know what to look for.'

Owen decided not to ask how the Hadenman knew which signs to look for. He didn't think he really wanted to know.

'Who do you suppose they were?' said Ruby.

'According to the Family histories,' Owen said slowly, 'my ancestor, the original Deathstalker, was pursued here by three of the greatest mercenary assassins of their time; the infamous Shadow Men. They were never heard of again. Apparently they did catch up with their prey after all.'

'You mean he killed them, and then had them preserved and mounted as trophies?' Hazel pulled a face. 'Nasty sense of humour your ancestor had, Owen. Or was this usual for the time?'

'No,' said Owen. 'No, it wasn't.'

They left the shattered case and moved on, heading still deeper into the Standing. They all had a gun or sword in their hand now. The emptiness of the rooms seemed somehow significant, even threatening. It was like walking through a gigantic trap, waiting for the punchline. Mechanial drones appeared from time to time, silent mechanisms of varying size, gliding through the empty rooms on unknown missions. They ignored the human intruders, who in turn gave the drones plenty of room. They varied in shape from simple spheres that rolled along the spotless floors, to disturbingly human forms that tapped through the rooms on pointed toes, inhumanly graceful. Owen was frowning so much by now that his head ached, but he couldn't help it. No one made machines in the shape of men any more. Not after the AI rebellion. So these androids had been here for more than nine hundred years, following programmes laid down centuries before. No one now could make machines to last that long. It was a forgotten art. First the portals, now this. What other forgotten secrets were waiting for them, in the heart of the Last Standing?

They pressed on, moving cautiously now, blinking in and out of existence from room to room, and found themselves in a hall of mirrors. The mirrors stretched from floor to ceiling, forming a maze with no apparent pattern. They moved constantly, turning and twisting, light shimmering from every direction. There were reflections upon reflections, images within images. They merged and blended, and some reflections seemed to be moving independently of the people who cast them. Owen moved slowly forward, drifting between the mirrors, following hints and whispers and beckoning figures. He thought he saw his father, and his long-lost mother, and other faces from his past, and then himself, grown old and feeble. He saw himself at his wedding, beside a veiled bride, and then fighting alone on a bloody battlefield littered with the dead. He moved on, drawn by a need to see, to know more, and then Hazel was suddenly beside him, her hand on his arm.

'Come away, Owen. It's not safe here. They're a trap; they show you what you want to see. Come away.'

Owen allowed her to tug him away, and the party stayed close together until they made it through the hall of mirrors and out the other side. They'd all seen something in the mirrors they didn't want to share with anyone else. They stepped into the next portal and vanished, and if their images remained for a time in the mirrors, they never knew.

Owen stepped out of a transfer portal and found himself in a world of ice. Three inches of snow covered the floor, long icicles hung down from the high ceiling, and thick hoarfrost made whorled patterns on the walls. It was bitterly cold, and Owen shuddered convulsively. He pulled his cloak tightly about him, folded his arms across his chest and watched his breath steam on the air as he tried to stop shivering. The others appeared behind him, and they all huddled together for warmth. Except Moon, who didn't seem at all bothered.

Owen's thoughts slowly returned to him, having been driven aside for a moment by the sudden shock of the cold, and he looked about him. The air was crisp and sharp, with only a slight haze of mist. The room wasn't all that large, compared to some of the rooms he'd walked through to get here, but it gave the impression of great size, as though the walls were not strong enough to contain everything the room held. In the middle of the room a bright shimmering light shone from the floor to the ceiling, a silver pillar of illumination, and in that pillar was a man, standing unnaturally still, held in the light like a butterfly transfixed on a pin.

Owen walked slowly forward, impelled by an impulse that was half curiosity and half awe. The snow crunched loudly under his boots, and he realized he was the first person to break the surface of the snow since it had first fallen, some nine hundred years earlier. He felt in a strange way as though he had stepped back in time when he entered this room, stepped into an earlier age when the Empire was still fresh and new, the product of great men and women, carved from the unfeeling emptiness of space with courage and audacity. There were heroes and villains in those days, when events were larger than life and everything had the stamp of greatness. Giants walked the stage of Empire then, and this was one of them. Owen stopped just short of the silver pillar and studied the man within.

He was as tall as Owen, but sparely built, though his arms were curved with muscle. He looked to be in his early fifties, with a solid lined face, a silver grey goatee beard, and long grey hair held back in a scalplock. He wore a set of battered and shapeless furs, held in at the waist with a wide leather belt. His leather boots were starting to come apart at the stitching. He wore thick golden armlets, and heavy metal rings on his fingers. He carried a long sword in a leather scabbard hanging down his back, and a gun of unfamiliar design hung on his hip. Overall, he gave an impression of strength at rest, and with his eyes closed he looked only as though he was thinking for a moment, and might at any time open his eyes and look around.

'So that's him,' said Hazel, and Owen jumped despite himself. He hadn't heard her move up alongside him. The others gathered around the silver pillar of light, giving it plenty of distance, just in case. They seemed impressed by the room, if not the man. Owen found himself thinking of an insect caught in amber.

'This is him,' he said finally, careful to keep his voice calm and even. 'The Deathstalker. The original Deathstalker, founder of my Clan. We still sing songs about his valour and his exploits, though the Empire banned them long ago. He's been here over nine hundred years, waiting for someone to come for him. Waiting, while the wheel turned and the Empire moved on without him.'

'He doesn't look like much,' said Ruby. 'I could take him.'

'Are we really going to wake him?' said Random. 'He's been asleep a long time, and things have changed. He might find it very difficult to adapt.'

'He was a warrior,' said Owen. 'And some things haven't changed at all. Family. Loyalty. Betrayal. I think he'll fit in quite well. Besides; we need him.'

'You're right,' said Hazel. 'Some things haven't changed at all.'

Owen started to answer her, and then stopped. She was as much right as she was wrong. He stepped forward and thrust his hand bearing his father's ring into the shimmering silver column. The light blazed up blindingly, and Owen had to turn his head away. He tried to fall back from it, but his hand was held firmly in the light. A slow rumble of power filled the chamber, as though ancient engines were awakening to life again. The floor shook, and icicles broke off from the ceiling, plunging down like swords. And then the silver light snapped off, gone so suddenly it was as though it had never been there. Owen looked back at his ancestor, standing there before him. The man's chest rose and fell slowly, and then he lifted his head and opened his eyes. They were a surprisingly mild grey, but his gaze was firm and direct. He studied Owen for a moment, and then shook his head.

'I don't know you, but you bear my ring.' His voice was calm and assured, the voice of a man accustomed to power. 'Are you Family, boy?'

'Yes, sir. I am Owen Deathstalker, your descendant. I am first of the Clan, though the present Empress has tried to strip that from me, and declared me outlaw. I need your help, kinsman. The Empire has turned on me, as it did on you. It is time to take up the sword again.'

'Maybe,' said the Deathstalker. 'How long have I slept?'

'Nine hundred and forty-three years, kinsman.'

'Have things changed much since my day?'

'Surprisingly little, kinsman. The essentials are still the same. I've studied the Empire's past. I'm an historian.'

The older man gave Owen a hard look. 'What kind of occupation is that for a Deathstalker? What campaigns have you fought in? How many wars?'

'None, actually,' said Owen. 'I'm not really the warrior type.'

The Deathstalker shook his head slowly. 'I've been gone too long. The blood's grown thin. Let's get out of here, boy. Too damn cold here for my liking. Reminds me of the grave. You can bring me up to date as we go. And call me Giles. It was my name long before I gave my Clan the name Deathstalker.'

He headed for the door, giving the others just enough time to get out of the way. Owen hurried after him, and the others scrambled to keep up with them.

'Historian,' Giles said thoughtfully. 'Tell me; how much has science advanced in my absence? Are you still using disrupters?'

'Yes, sir. The Empire has kept a careful control on science and progress down the centuries. This helps to keep things stable, and reserves what advances are made for the ruling classes. Just another way to keep power. We still use disrupters. Recharge is down to two minutes now.'

Giles sniffed. 'I suppose that's an improvement. Energy guns. Flashy things. Powerful but limited. Projectile weapons are much more versatile, but they were already being phased out of the Empire when I had to leave in a hurry. The aristocracy wanted them stamped out. Too easy to make, too easy to use, and far too much power to be left in the hands of the lower classes. Energy weapons are difficult to make, and very expensive. So, they replace projectile guns, and the only effective weapons end up the property of the ruling classes and their enforcers. Good thinking. But I never believed in it, so I never went along with it. Which is at least partly why I ended up here.'

He stopped before the portal, snapped 'Armoury!' and then stepped through and vanished. Owen looked at the others.

'Well; what do you think? Do we follow him?'

'He's your ancestor,' said Hazel. 'Can we trust him?'

'I don't know. He's not what I expected.'

'Put it this way,' said Random. 'What other choice do we have? We can't even find our way out of this place without him.'

He stepped through the transfer portal, and the others followed him. There was the usual sudden shift from one view to another, and then Owen stopped dead in his tracks and looked about him. He was in another great hall, stretching away before him for as far as he could see, but here the walls were covered with more kinds of weapons than he'd ever seen in his life. There were hand guns and rifles of all shapes and sizes, including several it would have taken two men to carry. None of them looked to be energy guns.

'What the hell are they?' whispered Hazel beside him.

'Projectile weapons,' said Owen. 'I've seen some of these in the older archive records. They were effective and efficient, but no damn use at all against force shields. They were also no match for the range and accuracy of energy guns. That's why the old style of weapon was replaced by the new. Officially.'

'Shot for shot they were right,' said Giles. 'A disrupter can out-perform any projectile weapon. But on the other hand, they don't have to stop and recharge between shots for two minutes. You can fire over and over again, as long as your ammunition holds out. You'd be surprised how much damage you can do, when you're firing a thousand rounds a second. I have a gun here for every occasion, small and large. There are weapons here that can assassinate a single man in a crowd from up to two miles away, and others that could take out a whole town.'

'Unless they have force shields,' said Owen.

Giles grinned at him. 'That's better, boy. At least you can think like a warrior. Force shields are fine, but they also have a built-in limitation; they only last as long as their energy crystals hold out. Once they've been drained by constant use, it takes forever to recharge them. So all you have to do is maintain a steady stream of fire, wait for the shields to go down, and then charge right in.' He gestured grandly at the others. 'Take a look around. See if there's something here that takes your fancy. You stay with me, boy.' He waited for the others to move away, and then turned to Owen and lowered his voice. 'Fill me in. How big is your army? How many men am I going to have to supply guns for?'

Owen looked at him blankly for a moment. 'I don't actually have an army, sir. There's just myself, and my associates here. Our ship crashed not far from here. It's a wreck. We're all there is, sir.'

Giles pursed his lips and nodded slowly. 'Deathstalker luck.

Always bad. Fortunately for you, boy, I have a ship. How big a force have you got on your tail? I assume the Empire was right behind you when you jumped to come here?'

'Yes, sir. Two Imperial starcruisers.'

Giles looked at him with a certain amount of respect for the first time. 'Now that's more like it. Don't worry; we'll be gone long before they can get here. Tell me about friends. Are they good fighters? Reliable?'

'The best. Hazel d'Ark's a pirate and clonelegger. Ruby Journey's a bounty hunter, Jack Random's a professional rebel, and the disturbing looking one is Tobias Moon. He's an augmented man.'

'A cyborg? They were still trying to make that work when I left. Is he any good in a fight?'

Owen grinned. 'Moon kicks ass. Anybody's ass. But I shouldn't turn your back on him too often. Augmented men often have their own agendas. And all of my people are good fighters.'

'Can I depend on them? Will they follow orders?'

'Maybe. After all, they're outlaws, like me. And like you. Convince them that it's in their best interests to work with you, and they will. But don't just give them orders and expect them to snap to attention. They don't have much love or respect for authority in general and aristos in particular. But they're good people. Mostly.'

'And what about you, Owen Deathstalker the historian? Can you fight?'

'I do all right,' Owen said steadily. 'I've been trained by the best, and I have the boost. I can take care of myself.'

'The boost? That's another thing they were trying to make work when I left. You're full of surprises, kinsman. Unfortunately, I now have one for you. According to my computers, an Imperial starship has just dropped into orbit around Shandrakor. The Standing's shielded from their sensors, unless they've radically improved since my day, but your wrecked ship isn't. It won't take them long to spot it, and send some heavily armed people down to check for survivors. I've downloaded your AI into my systems; pretty sophisticated, but not half as smart as it thinks it is.'

'Oz!' said Owen. 'Are you there?'

'Where else would I be?' said Ozymandias. 'You should see the antiquated system they've dumped me in. Wouldn't surprise me if this junk ran on steam power. Give me a week or two and I'll be running things around here.'

'Behave yourself. We're guests here. We'll talk later; for now, keep your eyes and ears open and make yourself useful.'

'Got it.'

Owen looked at Giles. 'He's been with me a long time. He's a pain in the ass, but he's good at what he does.'

'I heard that!'

'Shut up, Oz.'

'Tell me, Owen,' said Giles. 'Why did you come here looking for me?'

'My only hope for survival is to mount a rebellion against the Empress. And for that I need the Darkvoid Device.' With Giles's eyes boring into his, it never even occurred to Owen to lie. 'Do you still have it?'

'No. But I know where it is. I only ever used it once, and a thousand stars blinked out in a moment, leaving nothing but darkness. The Darkvoid. Thousands of inhabited planets were left without suns; billions upon billions of people died. That's a lot of ghosts for one man to live with. I'd done many questionable things in my time as Warrior Prime, and come to terms with them, but that was too much, even for me.

'I'd sworn an oath to protect and preserve the Empire, not destroy it piece by piece for the pleasure of others. I created the Device almost by accident, while working on something else. I was the only one who could operate it. That made it my responsibility. So I did the only responsible thing left to me; I took the Device and ran. Hid myself here, where no one would ever find me except Family. And just as a safeguard, I stashed the Device somewhere else. I left it in the heart of the Madness Maze, on the cold corpse of the Wolfling World, deep in the Darkvoid.'

Owen looked at him for a long moment, searching for

something to say. The Wolflings were a part of legend; the first genetically engineered human beings. They were supposed to be living killing machines, the perfect soldiers; but unfortunately the Empire did its work too well. The Wolflings were unbeatable. The Empire grew scared of what it had created, and wiped out the Wolflings while they were still trapped on their planet. It was lost to history when it became part of the Darkvoid. No wonder no one had ever found the Device, if it was hidden there. Few ships had ever crossed the Rim into the Darkvoid and come back to tell of it.

'We need the Device,' he said finally. 'Our rebellion hasn't a hope in hell without it.'

Giles looked at him steadily. 'And is your rebellion really so important?'

'You've been asleep a long time,' said Hazel, suddenly there beside him. 'You don't know how bad things have got. If you're rich or an aristo or connected, you can have anything, do anything, and no one can stop you. You can destroy lives, and no one can make you pay.'

'They use and discard us,' said Moon. 'And no one cares.'

'I've fought the Empire all my adult life,' said Jack Random. 'Fought and bled on a hundred worlds, only to see my war for truth and justice come to nothing. They have the ships and the weapons and the armies, and all we have is right on our side. It's not enough.'

Giles looked at Ruby Journey. She was standing quietly at the back, arms folded. She looked bored. 'What about you, bounty hunter? Don't you have anything to say to me? No appeals to my better nature?'

Ruby looked at him calmly. 'I made a good living hunting down the Empire's enemies. Outlaws. Now I am one. Funny how things change.'

'What changed you?'

Ruby smiled. 'Hazel's my friend. She hasn't the sense to come in out of the rain, but sometimes the rain follows you no matter where you go. The Empire wants her dead, I want her alive. So to hell with the Empire. Besides; I was promised as

411

much loot as I can carry if we win, and you'd be surprised how much I can carry when I put my mind to it.'

Hazel smiled at her. 'Ruby. I never knew you cared so much.'

'Don't get cocky. If the reward on you had been just a little higher, things might have turned out differently.'

Giles turned back to Owen. 'If I led you to the Device, what would you do with it? It's not exactly a subtle weapon. You could use it to destroy whatever planet the Empress is currently using as a homeworld, but only by destroying a thousand other worlds with it. Could you do that? Create another Darkvoid, in the heart of the Empire?'

'You used it,' said Owen.

'And look what it did to me. I thought I had good reason. I was wrong. What about you, kinsman? What price will you pay to win?'

'I don't know. I've seen enough killing already, and none of it for a good enough reason.' *The young girl lay crying in the bloody Mistworld snow, her legs crippled for ever by his blade.* 'Perhaps all I really want is to see the Device destroyed before the Empress can get her hands on it. She wouldn't hesitate to use it. I don't know, Giles. I can't make a decision like this. I'm just an historian, a hoarder of old books and records, not a warrior or a revolutionary. Ask Jack. Or Hazel. Ask anyone but me.'

'That's what I said, ' said Giles Deathstalker. 'But in the end, I did what I thought I had to, and so will you, when your time comes. I'll take you to the Device. And let us all pray we get there before the Empire does.'

'You have a ship?' said Jack.

'Oh yes,' said Giles. 'I have a ship.'

'How long will it take to power it up?' said Hazel. 'It's got to be in one hell of a state, after spending so many centuries in mothballs.'

'My computers began bringing it back to life the moment I awakened,' said Giles. 'It's been well looked after. I always knew I might have to leave in a hurry.'

'Better be a fast ship,' said Ruby. 'Got a lot of determined people on our trail, most especially including the ones in orbit.'

'And I must beg passage of you,' said Moon, and Giles looked at the augmented man interestedly. There had been a strange urgency in his grating, inhuman voice. 'My people were created on the lost world of Haden. It stayed lost because that was not its true name. And because it was lost in the Darkvoid. Before my creators found and transformed its interior, it was called the Wolfling World.'

'Now that's spooky,' said Hazel. 'The Darkvoid Device and the sleeping Hadenman army, both on the same planet? What are the chances of that?'

'Too damn small for my liking,' said Owen. 'If I didn't know better, I'd swear my father arranged it. It's the kind of thing he'd do.'

'It's far more likely that I didn't hide my trail as carefully as I thought I had,' said Giles. 'And if someone found the Wolfling World once, someone else might find it again. I think it's time we got moving.'

'Sounds good to me,' said Random. He looked round at the armoury almost wistfully. 'You've got some wonderful toys here, Deathstalker. I could have used a collection like this many times, but weapons were always the most expensive part of a rebellion. Who were these supposed to be used against?'

'The same people I used the Device on. There was a rebellion against the Empire. Widespread, well funded, lots of weapons and men to use them. I destroyed them all in a moment. They weren't even offered a chance to surrender.'

'Wait a minute,' said Owen. 'That's not what it says in the official histories. The Device was only used after every other means had been exhausted. The Empire itself was in danger. That's why they used the Device.'

'Not they,' said Giles. 'Me. My finger on the button. There was no warning, no negotiations, and no danger to the Empire.'

'So why did you do it?' said Hazel.

413

'He was my Emperor.' Giles was quiet for a long moment, and nobody said anything. Finally he shrugged and smiled at Owen. 'Winners write the histories, kinsman. You should know that.'

On the starcruiser *Dauntless*, orbiting Shandrakor, Captain Silence studied his bridge viewscreen thoughtfully. According to his sensor probes, the whole planet was overrun with homicidal lifeforms wherever you looked. No civilizations, past or present. Except for a certain crashed starship, currently on the viewscreen. Investigator Frost stood at his side, silent and disapproving. She'd wanted to lead the away team that was investigating the wreck, and was still sulking because he'd said no. He'd been tempted. If anyone could survive the slaughterhouse down there it was Frost. But if the outlaws had another ship, the *Dauntless* might have to leave in a hurry to go after it, even if it meant abandoning the away team. Which meant he could only send down those people he could afford to lose. He sighed, and made himself concentrate on the voice accompanying the viewscreen images.

'The ship . . . is a wreck. Extensive damage, before and after landing. No trace of any crew. Some blood . . . not enough to be significant. The stardrive is missing. Cut out, very neatly. Professional. Somebody beat us to her, Captain.'

'Understood, Lieutenant. Continue your investigation. Captain out.' He turned away from the screen to look at Frost. 'What do you think, Investigator? Could there be people, even bases, on this planet that the Empire doesn't know about?'

'Possibly, Captain.' Her voice was as cold and calm as always. 'They could be shielded against our sensors. That would require a great deal of power, though. Perhaps they live underground. It would make sense, given the surface conditions.'

'Captain!' said a voice excitedly. 'This is surveillance! We're picking something up on the planet's surface. Their shielding just dropped!'

Silence and Frost looked at the viewscreen again. The crashed ship had vanished, replaced by the image of an immense stone castle.

'What the hell is that?' said Silence.

'A castle, sometimes called a Standing, similar to those of the Empire aristocracy nine centuries ago,' said Frost. 'They were forbidden to anyone else, on pain of death. I think we can now be pretty sure of what happened to the outlaws and their stardrive.'

'How far is it from the wreck site?'

'Half a mile, Captain,' said the surveillance officer. 'The away team would be butchered before they got half that distance, without extra equipment.'

'He's right,' said Frost. 'You're going to need a full company of marines, armed and shielded to the teeth, and someone extremely experienced to lead them.'

'All right, Investigator, you've made your point.' Silence couldn't help smiling at her. 'You can lead the away team this time. Make the necessary arrangements.'

'It's time to go,' said Giles. 'I've dropped the Standing's shields, to divert the extra power to the takeoff. I never really thought I'd leave this planet again, but I hoped. There's always hope.'

'How far is it to your ship?' Owen said quickly. He had a horrible suspicion his ancestor was about to get all sentimental on him, and he didn't think he could cope with that just at the moment. 'It better not be too far. With your shields down, we're a sitting target for the starcruiser up above.'

'It's not far,' said Giles, smiling slightly. 'Not far at all. Computers; begin lift-off procedures.'

Owen looked blankly at his ancestor as the room began to shake and rumble around him. Far below, under his feet, he could hear the building roar of the mighty engines. 'Wait a minute. Wait just a damn minute! Your ship is part of the Standing? We're in it now?'

'Not part,' said Giles. 'The Standing is the ship. And vice versa.'

'We're going into hyperspace in a stone castle that's been sitting around for nine centuries?'

'We built to last in my day,' said Giles. 'Talk to your computer if you want more details.'

'Oz? Are you still there? Talk to me!'

'Yes, I'm still here, and you wouldn't believe how cramped it is. Some of these systems are positively pre-history. I can't believe I'm supposed to live in something this small. There isn't room to swing a neuron.'

'Talk to me about the castle, Oz, or I swear I'll reprogramme you with a blunt spoon. Is it really a starship?'

'Oh yes. A bit slow and stately, but it'll get you there. Hang on to your hat, Owen; it's going to be rather a bumpy takeoff.'

On the bridge of the *Dauntless*, Silence and Frost watched speechlessly as the Last Standing of the Deathstalker Clan tore itself out of the ground and leapt up into the air. Powerful engines roared around it. The jungle was flattened for miles around by the backblast, but the castle rose into the air as smoothly as any starship.

'I don't believe it,' said Frost. *'A stone starship?'*

'We've lost contact with the away team, Captain,' said the surveillance officer.

'Gunnery officer, open fire,' said Silence. 'Blow that thing to rubble.'

'We can't, Captain. It's got one of the most powerful force shields I've ever seen. We don't have anything that'll breach it.'

'Fire on it anyway!' said Silence. 'It's got to have a weak spot!'

'I wouldn't put money on it,' said Frost.

And then the castle shimmered and was gone into hyperspace, and there was nothing left to look at on the viewscreen but space.

'Damn,' said Silence.

'Yeah,' said Frost. 'The Empress is not going to be pleased, is she?'

Silence sat back in his command chair and made himself think calmly. 'They might think they've got away, but it's not over yet. After all, we know where they're going.'

CHAPTER TWELVE

Down in Wormboy Hell

Finlay Campbell fled for his life, hunted and harried, and the pack came after him, snapping at his heels. He was the Campbell now, last scion of a butchered line, and the Wolfes came after him, merciless and determined. He guided the stolen gravity sled between the narrow towers of the city centre, whipping past mirrored windows at incredible speed. Adrienne lay on the deck behind him, awash with blood, curled around the wide awful wound in her gut that was slowly killing her. The rushing wind blew tears from Finlay's eyes, and he wished he'd taken the time to steal some goggles along with the sled, but there'd been no time, no time at all.

It had been a long time since he'd last flown a gravity sled, but old memories and skills were already coming back. He grinned fiercely and slammed the craft back and forth between the towers like a raftsman dodging rocks in the rapids, squeezing every last ounce of speed he could from the straining engine. The Wolfes stuck close behind him on seven craft, baying for his blood. The occasional disrupter blast scorched past him, but at this speed the sudden twisting turns of the sleds made aiming impossible. They kept firing, though. They only had to get lucky once. Finlay snarled soundlessly, his mind working frantically for some way out, some means of escape from the hell he'd fallen into.

He'd learned to fly a gravity sled during his training for the Arena. It was really just another weapon to master; you never knew what they'd send against you next in the Arena. The Masked Gladiator had to be the master of all weapons, so Finlay had shrugged and learned what he needed to know.

He'd thought at the time that some day it might save his life, but he'd never dreamed of anything like this. His father and his Family dead, murdered by Wolfes, and nothing left for him but flight. He was all that remained now of the first rank of the Campbells, with no friends or allies left to call on and the enemy close behind. A House that's falling has no friends. No one wants to get involved with failure; it might be contagious. And Adrienne, his loathed and despised wife, had taken a sword in the gut while trying to defend the Clan. He glanced back at her, lying in her own blood, still somehow intermittently conscious, panting obscenities. He had to get her medical help soon, but even if he could somehow shake off his pursuers, he didn't know where he was going to take her. He was the Campbell now, and as his wife, she was as much a target as him. No hospital would be safe, there was no sanctuary that would not be violated. Vendetta has no mercy.

He swung the sled round in a sudden sharp arc, bracing himself against the pull of gravity, using the updraughts and thermals that came and went between the high towers. He looped around, gunning the motor, and found himself above a single Wolfe sled that had made the mistake of speeding just a little too far ahead of the pack. Finlay's mouth stretched in a humourless smile, a savage death's-head grin that was usually hidden behind the steel helm of the Masked Gladiator. None of his Family would have recognized him at that moment, but they would have been forced to admit it didn't look out of place on him. He moved in close behind the desperately bucking and weaving sled before him, and activated his sled's weapons. Twin disrupter beams tore into the rear of the Wolfe sled. The heavy steel shielding blew apart in a shower of sparks and jagged fragments, and the Wolfes screamed as their engine suddenly cut out. The sled dropped like a stone to the ground far below, and the Wolfes screamed all the way down.

Finlay sped on through the forest of steel and glass towers, confident the remaining Wolfes would keep their distance for a while. Time was on their side, and they could afford to wait for the best advantage. The prey had suddenly developed teeth and claws, and they were wary now. Which was as it should be. They weren't chasing the notorious fop, Finlay Campbell. They were fighters, but he was a Gladiator, and they didn't have the life and death experience that he had. They were too used to being the aggressor, made slow and stupid by reliance on the strength that comes from fighting in packs. Finlay smiled, and his hands moved over the control panels with new confidence. He'd finally thought of somewhere to go. Tower Shreck wasn't far, and Evangeline had an apartment there. He was reluctant to involve his secret love in his troubles, but he didn't have any choice. Adrienne was dying, and Evangeline had a regeneration machine in her apartment. He'd given it to her some time ago, and she kept it hidden for him, in case he ever needed it in an emergency.

He had his own machine in his quarters below the Arena, but that was too well known, even before his current problems. There had always been the chance someone might sabotage it. The Masked Gladiator had made a lot of enemies in and outside the Arena, who would have stopped at nothing to gain revenge on him for his many wins. It came with the territory. Families who'd lost a loved one; gamblers who'd lost a fortune . . . So he secretly arranged for another regeneration machine to be delivered to Evangeline Shreck's apartment, as a back-up. Just in case. No one would think to look for it there, because no one knew about him and Evangeline. Whatever happened, she had to be protected. He scowled unhappily as he realized what that meant. He would have to kill or shake off all his pursuers before he could head for Tower Shreck. But on the other hand, Adrienne's time was running out. If he didn't get her help soon, it would be too late.

He swore dispassionately. He couldn't do it alone, and there was only one person he could think of who might help him. Someone who had every reason to hate his guts. He patched into the sled's comm unit through his implant, and entered a number he hadn't thought to use again any time soon.

'This is Finlay Campbell, last survivor of the first rank of the Family. I invoke Clan loyalty, blood to blood. Can you hear me, Robert?'

There was a long pause, and then a dry voice was suddenly in his ear. 'This is Robert, and you've chosen a hell of a time to get in touch.'

'I'm sorry. I know you're still in mourning over Letitia.'

'Mourning be damned, I haven't got the time any more. Everything's gone to hell here. The whole Family's under attack. Wolfes and Campbells are fighting it out in the streets, down to the most remote cousins. I'm barricaded in my own home. The Wolfes have declared full vendetta; a death sentence on every Campbell, down to the last man, woman and child. They're firebombing our businesses, attacking our houses; I'm trying to put together some kind of resistance, but they caught us with our pants down and tangled round our ankles. Luckily I made some good friends in the military, and they're helping out. The authorities are just standing back and watching. They won't get involved in Family quarrels. Bottom line; we're outnumbered, caught unprepared, and a lot of us are dead. What's your position, Finlay? And who's the Campbell now?'

'Currently, I'm running for my life on a stolen gravity sled, with Wolfes right behind me yelling for blood. I'm the Campbell now, if anyone is. All the others are dead. Any chance your people could help, if I could get to you?'

'Negative. We're surrounded on all sides. You're on your own, Finlay.'

Finlay laughed briefly. It was a hard, cold sound. 'Nothing changes. All right; listen to me. I've got Adrienne with me, and she's badly hurt. I'm taking her to Tower Shreck. I know someone there who'll help her. Don't ask questions; there isn't time. I'm going to leave Adrienne there, with Evangeline Shreck, and then go to ground. With me gone, the last of the first rank, you should be able to sue for peace. The Empress won't allow a full vendetta for long. She doesn't want any single Family getting that powerful. In the meantime, I need you and your people to break out, get to Tower Shreck, and protect Adrienne until she's ready to leave. I know that's asking a lot, but I'm not asking for myself. Will you come?'

'I'll try,' said Robert. 'She was good to me. Can we expect much help from the Shrecks?'

'I very much doubt it.'

Robert laughed briefly. 'Don't want much, do you? Where are you going?'

'Damned if I know. Going to find a hole and pull it in after me. I'll have to disappear for a while. That means you'll be the Campbell. I don't know what kind of Family you'll be heading after the dust has settled, but remember; do whatever you have to, to protect and preserve the Clan. Make a deal with the Wolfes, promise them anything. There'll be time for revenge later.'

'I'll do what I can.' Robert sounded tired, but amused. 'Ironic, isn't it? Me, as the Campbell? After what happened at the wedding, I was ready to divorce myself from the Family, take a new name, and give my life entirely to the military. But I can't do that now, can I? There are too many people who are going to be depending on me. The Family has me in its bloody clutch again. All right, Finlay; I'll talk to some of my friends in the military. See if they can get me safe passage through the chaos in the streets. I'll be there as soon as I can.'

Finlay's implant went dead, and he chewed thoughtfully on the inside of one cheek. Not as much help as he'd hoped, but more than he'd expected or had any right to. The Family had not treated Robert well. Finlay smiled slightly. Hopefully Robert would treat the Family rather better now he was the Campbell. He looked over the sled's control panels, and then looked away, satisfied he was still squeezing every ounce of speed he could out of the straining motor. He knew he couldn't keep this up for long. Gravity sleds weren't designed with this kind of abuse in mind. He shrugged mentally. Either the sled would hold together, or it wouldn't. It was out of his hands, and he couldn't afford to worry about it any more. He had to think.

So, if he could just get Adrienne safely to Evangeline at Tower Shreck, he might find a way out of this mess yet. He glanced back over his shoulder. The Wolfe sleds were still hanging back, wary of him. They were easily in disrupter range, but at the speeds they were all travelling now, the chances of a hit were extremely low. And besides, if they missed, the odds were they'd end up slaughtering innocents in some nearby tower, and the claims for damages from the wounded Families would be enormous. Even so, the Wolfes wouldn't hold off much longer for fear of losing him, and there was no way they'd leave him alone till he reached Tower Shreck. Finlay grimaced unhappily. He had to deal with them now, while he still had the advantage of surprise. And he had to make it quick, for Adrienne's sake.

He'd already decided what he was going to do while he was talking to Robert. It was risky and dangerous and depended far too much on luck and bluff, but it was all he had. He bent over the controls before he could talk himself out of it, and turned the gravity sled around in a tight arc and sent it hammering towards the steel and glass face of the nearest tower. He braced himself as the wall loomed up before him like a great gleaming fly swatter. Beyond the illuminated windows he could see people jumping to their feet and pointing. Some turned to run. Finlay drew his gun and fired at the growing expanse of window.

The heavy steelglass shattered as the energy beam tore through it, blasting lethal fragments through the office space beyond. People fell, spurting blood, and did not rise again. Finlay didn't have time to care. They were innocents, but they weren't Family. He steered the sled through the great jagged opening in the tower face, and then hit the brakes for all he was worth. The sled shuddered to a halt half-way across the long office floor, almost throwing Finlay off. He hung on desperately. Adrienne's unconscious form rolled forward to press against the backs of his legs.

He leaned on the controls for a moment to get his breath back. His arms and legs were shaking from shock and reaction, and he ran through the calming chants the previous Masked Gladiator had taught him. In the Arena, control was everything. People were crying and screaming all around him, but as yet there was no sign of any security guards. He turned the sled around so that it was facing towards the gaping hole in the

423

window. The Wolfe sleds had slowed to a halt well back from the shattered window, and were hovering outside the tower, watching cautiously to see what he'd do next. They didn't seem too worried. After all, there was nowhere he could go now. He'd trapped himself. Finlay's death's-head grin stretched across his face again, as he reached down into the top of his boot and drew out the small slab of explosive he carried there. Ever since he became the Masked Gladiator, and acquired so many enemies, he'd always known that someday his true identity might be revealed, and he'd have to fight his way out of an impossible situation. Hence the explosive, for a last resort. Finlay had always believed in being prepared, in and out of the Arena.

He slipped the explosive into his belt where he could get at it easily, and grinned out at the Wolfe sleds, daring them to come in after him. After all, he was only Finlay Campbell, the notorious fop. What could he know about tactics and traps? The Wolfes held a brief conference, and then one sled nosed slowly forward. They knew it had to be a trap, but they couldn't see how. Finlay grinned till his cheeks ached. *Keep coming, you bastards. Just a little closer* . . . The sled drifted in through the break in the window, giving the jagged shards plenty of room, and then moved on into the office. Finlay hit the controls, and his sled jumped forward. The Wolfes fired their sled's disrupters, but Finlay's sled was already upon them. The two hulls slammed together, sending the Wolfes staggering. Finlay had braced himself, and his hand was perfectly steady as he raised his gun and shot the Wolfe pilot. The energy beam tore right through the Wolfe's chest, and threw the burning body over the side of the sled. The remaining Wolfes grabbed for their guns, but Finlay had already jumped onto their sled and was among them, sword in hand. He cut and hacked with his blade, trading skill for speed. The Wolfes couldn't fire for fear of hitting each other, and there wasn't room or time to draw their swords. They fought back desperately anyway, but they had been caught unprepared, and he was the Masked Gladiator. They never stood a chance.

Finlay cut down the last man with cold efficiency, kicked the body over the side, and then sheathed his sword. The Wolfes on the other sleds were rushing forward, shouting their anger and outrage. Disrupter bolts shot past Finlay. He grabbed the slab of explosive from his belt, slapped it against the deck of the sled so it would stick, and activated the timer built into it for a twenty second fuse. Then he turned the Wolfe sled around, and sent it back towards the approaching craft. Fifteen. He timed his moment carefully, and then jumped off. Ten. He hit the floor hard, and rolled behind a heavy desk. Five. The sled tore into the midst of the Wolfes and blew apart in a gush of flames. The other sleds exploded as their drives ruptured, and for a long moment the office was full of jagged metal shrapnel raining down; interspersed with wet, soft parts of what had once been their crew. A fireball blazed briefly in the confined space, but quickly ran out of air and collapsed.

Finlay huddled beneath his sheltering desk, hands pressed tightly to his ears against the overpowering roar of the explosion. He slowly lowered his hands as he realized a silence had fallen, uncurled and cautiously raised his head to look about him. Fires had broken out all across the office, with desks burning fiercely here and there like so many warning beacons. Dead and injured lay to every side, some of them burning quietly. Finlay didn't spare them more than a glance. He didn't know them. Adrienne was all that mattered now. He saw a red light flashing over a door, and wondered why the alarms weren't sounding. He slowly realized from the utter silence around him that they probably were, but he couldn't hear them. The blast had temporarily deafened him. At least, he hoped it was only temporary. He didn't need another problem.

He rose painfully to his feet and stumbled towards his own sled, still hovering where he'd left it. Burning fragments sputtered on the deck around Adrienne, but she seemed unhurt. Finlay brushed the fragments off the deck with a sweep of his arm and climbed aboard. It was growing uncomfortably hot in the office as the fires spread, and his bare skin was beginning to smart from the heat. The office should have invested in sprinklers. For a moment that struck Finlay as wildly funny, and he giggled helplessly before pulling himself together. He looked down at Adrienne. The deck was slippery with her blood where it hadn't burnt, and her hands were wet and crimson where they tried to hold her guts together. Her face was worryingly colourless, but she was still breathing shallowly. Finlay eased the sled forwards and out through the break in the window, and headed for Tower Shreck.

Evangeline was getting ready for bed, even though it wasn't late. Daddy was coming over for one of his little visits. He'd contacted her just a few minutes before. He never gave her much warning, so she wouldn't have time to think up excuses, but he liked her to wait a little before he arrived, so that she could think about what was coming. So she sat in her long white nightdress before her dressing table mirror, listlessly brushing her hair and thinking about killing herself. She knew she wouldn't. She had so much to live for, apart from Daddy, and it would hurt Finlay so very much. The mood would pass, as it had so many times before, but for a moment it was comforting to think of ending it all and not having to worry any more. She wouldn't have to worry about being revealed as a clone, or a member of the underground, or seeing Finlay die in the Arena, or suffering through another of Daddy's little visits ever again, and that would feel so good, so good . . .

She sighed and put down her hairbrush, and looked at it for a moment as though it was some foreign object, unknown to her. How could she be brushing her hair, such an ordinary, everyday thing, when her life was such a nightmare? Apart from Finlay, of course. His love was all that held her together now, when even the fires of her passion for the underground sometimes ran cold. He gave her the strength to go on, even in the face of Daddy and his clammy-handed love.

He didn't come to her every night. Sometimes a whole week could go by without his honouring her with his presence. Gregor Shreck, smiling, sweating, lying beside her in her bed,

426

talking smugly, calling her by her mother's name. She had never told Finlay, never even hinted at it. He must never know. At best he would have challenged Gregor to a duel and killed him, and then Finlay's secret identity and her secret status as a clone would both be revealed. At worst, he might not look at her in the same way again, once he knew who else shared her bed.

It was in Gregor Shreck's best interests to keep everything secret. For cloning his dead daughter he'd get a fine and a reprimand, but incest was severely frowned on in high society. Genetic engineering had taken the biological dangers out of inbreeding, but it was still a taboo. If only because the aristocracy liked to have some rules that even they couldn't break with impunity. After all, incest was such a tacky crime. If society found out about Gregor and her, no one would punish him, but no one would speak to him either. They'd send him to Coventry, in and outside his Family, and that would be worse than death to an aristocrat.

Of course, if they found out he'd murdered his wife and his original daughter . . . Evangeline sighed tiredly. So many secrets, in one Family. Her comm implant activated suddenly, and she sat up straight before her mirror. She'd shut down all the public channels, and only one man apart from her father knew her private code.

'Evangeline, this is Finlay. I'm in trouble. Can I come to you?'

'Of course.' It never even occurred to her to say no. 'Where are you?'

'Right outside your window. Open up, will you? It's cold out here.'

She jumped up and ran over to the window. The drapes rolled back at her quick gesture, revealing a blood-spattered Finlay standing on a gravity sled hovering on the other side of the steelglass. Even with the surprise of his arrival and the shock of his condition, her first thought was still to wonder how he'd got past Tower Shreck's security. He should have set off any number of alarms just by being there. Even with her beloved Finlay, she was still a Shreck. She deliberately pushed

427

the thought aside, and hit the emergency controls in the window surround. The great pane of steelglass swung open, and Finlay guided the sled forward into her room. The sled took up a hell of a lot of space, even hovering an inch or so above the floor, and Evangeline had to squeeze past it to shut the window again.

'Don't worry about security,' said Finlay, as he stepped down from the sled. 'I've got a little device that takes care of things like that. It's part of what helps protect my secrets. Security won't know I was ever here.'

Evangeline seethed impatiently, a dozen questions on her lips, but they died stillborn as she saw the blood spilling off the sled and on to her thick carpets. At first she thought he'd been badly hurt after all, but then her eyes fell on the huddled form lying on the deck of the sled, and her heart nearly stopped when she recognized who it was. Adrienne Campbell. Possibly the person she hated more than anyone, except her father. And Finlay had brought her here.

Finlay picked up his wife with a strained grunt that more than anything showed how tired and drained he was, and carried her over to Evangeline's bed. He lowered her carefully on to it, and then sat down beside her. The last of his strength seemed to go out of him then, and his chin dropped on to his chest as his shoulders slumped. Somewhere in the back of Evangeline's mind she was wondering how the hell she was going to get all that blood out of her carpets and bedclothes without hiring a dozen new maids, but she made herself concentrate on what was important. Finlay needed her help. She moved quickly over to the drinks cabinet, poured out a large brandy and brought it to him. She had to push the glass into his hand and encourage him to drink it, but the brandy quickly put some colour back into his cheeks, and his eyes cleared. Evangeline knelt down before him, her knees squelching in the bloody carpet.

'What's happened, Finlay? Did you kill her?'

'No! No; it was the Wolfes. She's dying, Evie. I have to save her. Do you still have the regeneration machine?'

'Of course I do, but . . .'

'I know. But I can't let her die. Please, Evie.'

'All right. Because you ask.'

She got to her feet, moved over to the dressing table and dragged it to one side. She activated the hidden controls by hand, carefully punching in the correct code, and part of the wall slid up as the regeneration machine rolled out. Gregor wasn't the only Shreck with secrets. She opened up the long narrow device, thinking it looked even more like a coffin than usual, and pushed it over beside the bed. Finlay picked up Adrienne very gently, ignoring the blood that coursed down his front again, and lowered her into the regeneration device. It closed over her like a grave, and that was that. Her fate was in the hands of the machine now, and all he could do was wait and see. Finlay sat down on a nearby chair like a puppet whose strings had been cut, and Evangeline stood before him, her back straight, her mouth a cold flat line. She didn't need to say anything.

Finlay took a deep breath. 'Adrienne and I are the only survivors of the first rank of the Campbells. Everyone else is dead. The Wolfes wiped us out. They declared full vendetta and ambushed us in our own tower. They're after me too, but I shook them off. I shouldn't have come here, but I didn't know where else to go.'

'Of course you should have come here,' said Evangeline. 'No one can hurt you now you're with me. I'm just glad you escaped. Oh, Finlay; your whole Family?'

'Yes. Only the minor branches and the distant cousins remain now, and the Wolfes are out in the streets, hunting them down. Clan Campbell is finished.'

'And Adrienne; what happened to her? Why did you bring her here?'

'Kid Death stuck her when she tried to save my brother. I'll kill him for that someday. Her only hope was the regeneration machine I left here with you.'

'But why bring her here at all?' said Evangeline flatly. 'Why not let her die? She's always come between us, and you said you never loved her. This is our chance, Finlay. All we have to do is switch off the machine, and wait. Don't look at me

429

like that. You don't know how hard it's been for me, alone, without you. You don't know.'

'I can't just let her die,' said Finlay. 'She doesn't deserve that. She fought so bravely. And as for you and me; there's a price on my head, now that Clan Campbell's been all but destroyed. We can never be together, in society, like we'd hoped, because I'm not a part of society any more. The minute I show my face in public, I'm a dead man. Robert will be the Campbell now, and all he can do is try and salvage as much of the Family as he can. He can't help me. He daren't. He might be able to save Adrienne, if she survives. He's on his way here with help. My only chance now is to become an outlaw, go underground. You always said you wanted to be with me, no matter what. Do you still feel that way? Are you willing to throw everything away, give up wealth and station to be an outlaw with me? Will you come down into the underground with me?'

She sat down beside him and held him as tightly as she could. 'Of course I will, Finlay. You're all I ever wanted.'

They sat together for a while in silence, holding each other, and then the regeneration machine made a series of imperative noises. Finlay and Evangeline got up reluctantly, and went over to look at the read-outs. Finlay nodded slowly, and Evangeline kept her face carefully blank.

'She's in bad shape, but the device has stabilized her,' said Finlay. 'It's going to be some time before the machine's finished with her, and we can't wait that long.'

'You said Robert was coming here?'

'With a few friends from the military. They'll look after her and keep her safe.'

'Tower security won't let them in. Daddy's been even more paranoid than usual just recently, after the . . . incident at the wedding. His guards have orders to shoot anyone who tries to get to me that isn't a Shreck. You said you had a device . . .'

'It's an implant. Nothing I can pass on to Robert. Someone has to stay with her, Evie. I can't just abandon her. She deserves better than that.'

'All right! Let me think.' Evangeline wrapped her arms

tightly around herself, and paced up and down. 'There's . . . more going on here than you know, Finlay. There are things I never told you. Things about me.'

Finlay smiled. 'I know all I need to know.'

'Shut up, Finlay. You don't understand. I had to keep this secret, even from you. I'm a clone, and a member of the underground.' She saw the look that came over his face, and wouldn't let herself look away. 'The original Evangeline died in an accident. Daddy couldn't bear to live without her, so he had me cloned. Secretly. Don't look at me like that, Finlay. Please. I'm still the same person I've always been.'

'Are you?' said Finlay. 'I don't know any more. I don't know anything any more. How long ago did all this happen? Is the woman I originally loved dead? Have I been loving a copy ever since?'

'No! It happened long before we ever fell in love. There's only ever been you and me.'

'How can I be sure of that?'

'You can't. You have to trust me.'

'How can I, after this? I told you everything about me, even about the Masked Gladiator. And you kept this from me.'

'I had to! I knew you'd react like this.'

'What else have you been keeping from me?'

'Nothing! There's nothing else, Finlay. Nothing at all.'

They stood for a long moment, just staring at each other. When Evangeline finally spoke again, her voice was as calm and steady as she could make it.

'We can't stay here. I can take you down into the underground. They'll accept you, if I vouch for you. The Wolfes can't follow you there. You'll be safe. Valentine Wolfe is a member of the underground too.'

'So he could still come after me there. I'd be walking into a trap!'

'No. The underground wouldn't permit it. We have very strict rules about inner conflicts. We have to, or we'd never get anything done. When you come to the underground you leave your other life behind. We could start again, Finlay. Start afresh.'

431

'All right,' said Finlay. 'All right. I can't think about all this now. We'll talk some more later, assuming we have a later. What are we going to do about Robert? He's going to be here soon, with a small army of his military friends, to look after Adrienne. Your father's guards will try to stop him, and I don't think he'll be in any mood to take no for an answer. He'll fight, and there's been enough killing already. How can we get him in here? Can you override your father's commands? Will his people take orders from you?'

'No. Daddy doesn't trust me with important decisions.'

'Then you'll have to talk to him. Call him, and ask for help.'

Evangeline looked at him steadily. 'You don't know what you're asking, Finlay.'

'I'm asking the woman who said she loved me for help. I know you and your father don't get on, but . . . Look, this isn't for Adrienne. It's for me.'

'All right,' said Evangeline. 'I'll do it for you.'

She hugged herself tightly, so she wouldn't fly apart, and then made herself let go. Like so many times before, she had to be strong. She moved back to her dressing table and sat down, automatically adjusting her nightgown so that it fell appealingly about her. She had to look her best for Daddy. She activated her comm unit, and called her father's private number. Her dressing table mirror shimmered, and then cleared to form a viewscreen. Evangeline adjusted the focus so that only her head and shoulders would be seen. The screen blinked, and there was her father, sitting at his ease. He was dressed in a long flowing gown that did nothing to hide his bulk. He frowned slightly as he saw who was calling him, and his deepset eyes almost disappeared into the bulging fat of his face.

'Evangeline, my dear; I told you I'd be with you soon. Feeling impatient, are we?'

His voice was as fat and loathsome as he was, but she kept her face clear and serene. 'I need your help, Daddy. Adrienne Campbell has turned up at my apartment, begging for help. She's the only survivor of a Wolfe attack on her Family. She's injured, and quite desperate. I allowed her to call one of her minor cousins for help, and he's on his way here with a few friends to protect her. I need you to tell the Tower guards to let them in.'

The Shreck raised an eyebrow. 'I wasn't aware you and Adrienne Campbell were friends.'

'We're not close. She's a Campbell, after all. But I don't think she had anywhere else to go. Besides; I never liked the Wolfes. They've always been very rude to you.'

'Yes, they have, haven't they? But I don't know, darling. You're asking a great deal. Nothing good will come of interfering in a vendetta, and the Wolfes do seem to be winning. With the Campbells destroyed, the Wolfes will be in a very powerful position, and only a fool makes enemies he doesn't have to.'

'I'm asking you this as a special favour, Daddy.'

'Really, my dear?' The Shreck leaned forward in his chair. 'And just how grateful will you be?'

'I'll wear that special outfit you like, and we can do all the things together that you like to do. I'll be your loving, obedient daughter.'

Gregor Shreck smiled. 'Of course you will, my dear. Very well, I'll give orders to let the Campbell pup in. But you're going to have to be very nice to me for this, Evangeline.'

'Yes, Daddy. I know.'

She cut off the comm link and her father disappeared, replaced by her own face in the mirror's reflection. Evangeline looked at the cold determined face for a long moment, and didn't recognize that person at all. That wasn't her; not the real her. But then, she'd had to do so many things that weren't really her. She turned away from the mirror, and looked at Finlay dispassionately. He was sitting on the edge of the bed, staring down at his clenched hands, lost in thought. He was soaked in blood, some of it his own, but he'd never even mentioned his own wounds. He'd never know what his favour had cost her; what she'd had to promise. He must never know. If he did, he'd throw away his own life to kill her father, and she couldn't allow that. She needed him too much. But she wondered if she'd ever feel quite the same about him again.

'What are you thinking about?' she said quietly.

'My Family,' he said, without looking up. 'They're all dead. I miss them. My father's dead, and I never got a chance to tell him about the real me. He'll never know I was really a warrior, just like him. And William and Gerald are gone. They were there all my life, looking after me, being there when I needed them. Now they're all gone, and there's just me. I'm not even a Campbell any more. I don't know what I am.'

'You're the man I love,' said Evangeline. 'The man who loves me. I'm your life now. Or isn't that enough for you?'

He looked up at her then. 'I always said you were all I ever really wanted. Seems I had to lose everything else to find out that was true, after all. I love you, Evie; never doubt it. But I loved my Family too, and a part of me died with them. The rudder of my life has gone, and I don't know what to do.'

Evangeline got to her feet. 'We get on with our lives. You'll find a new purpose, in the underground. I did. Now let's get moving. I think it would be best if we were both long gone before your cousin arrives with his private army.'

Finlay frowned. 'You mean just leave Adrienne in the machine? Won't your father wonder what it was doing here?'

'I'll think of something plausible to tell him. Now let's go, Finlay. We've done all we can here.'

Finlay nodded, and got up off the bed. 'You're right. I'm just putting it off. You lead the way, Evie, and I'll follow.'

Evangeline smiled. 'That's what I like to hear from a man.' She stepped past the dressing table, and a light switched itself on, revealing a concealed elevator. 'This was originally intended as an emergency fire ecape. Some cyberat friends deleted its presence from the main files, and now only I know of its existence. It'll take us down to the sub-basement. No one ever goes there. That's why no one's ever found the hidden tunnel that leads down to the subsystems below the city. You're not the only one with secrets, Finlay. It's a safe route to the underground. I've used it many times. Now come with me. Unless you'd rather stay with your wife.'

Finlay moved over to join her. He started to put out his arms to hold her, but stopped as he saw the coldness in her unyielding face and stance. He let his arms fall back to his sides. 'I'm sorry. I know what this is doing to you, to us. But I couldn't just abandon her, and let her die. It's a matter of Family honour, even if the Family no longer really exists. I never loved her, but I did admire her. She was never afraid to be strong, to say what she felt, and let the consequences fall where they may. She was always honourable, in her way.'

'And you put your Family honour before us, and our future together?'

'What about your honour and your Family? We could have just left, and let Robert and his people fight their way into the Tower, but you couldn't allow that. You'd rather make a deal with the father you detest than let armed men from another Clan run loose in your Family home. It would have been wrong, and you knew that. Please, love; don't let's argue any more. Let's just go. There's nothing keeping us here now.'

She nodded briefly, because she didn't trust herself to speak, and led the way into the elevator. The doors slid silently shut behind them, and Evangeline hit the down button with her fist. The elevator began its descent, and for the first time Evangeline relaxed a little. They were committed now.

'There's a place along the way where we can get fresh clothes,' she said, looking straight ahead at the closed doors. 'Neither of us are in any state to meet people. Are you badly hurt anywhere? There'll be first aid stuff there, but that's all.'

'I'm fine,' said Finlay. 'I heal quickly.'

Evangeline looked at him. 'Another implant?'

He shrugged. 'Something like that. You need every advantage you can get in the Arena. The regeneration device can work miracles, but you have to live long enough to reach it.'

'The dressing table will move itself back into position. There'll be no trace to show where we've gone. Daddy will be surprised when he finds I'm not waiting for him, but by then your cousin should have got to Adrienne.'

'How angry is he likely to be?' said Finlay.

'Very. Can your cousin handle a little pressure?'

'Oh yes. Robert's a lot tougher than he used to be, poor fellow. What will your father say when you do finally go back?'

'I don't know if I am going back. You're going to need me,

in your new life with the underground. And dear Daddy can go to hell. I would have disappeared into the subsystems long ago, if it hadn't been for you. And if I hadn't been such a useful contact for the underground. I think that part of my life is over now. Whatever happens from now on, we'll be together. And that's all that really matters.'

She still didn't look round, but her hand was in just the right place to receive his when he reached out to her.

They stood comfortably, companionably, together as the elevator sank into the depths. The doors finally opened out on to the subcellar, a dark and dank empty concrete box littered with junk. Evangeline led Finlay to another hidden door, and they made their way through narrow tunnels into the undercity, the interconnecting subsystems where the underground had dominion. Evangeline usually felt a surge of freedom and pleasure on the downward journey, as she left her Family self and obligations behind her, but it was muted this time. For all her brave words, she knew she'd have to return to Tower Shreck at least once more, to keep her promise to her father. If she didn't, if she just hid herself away in the subsystems forever, as she wanted, he'd take an awful revenge on Adrienne and Robert and all the lesser Campbells he could reach. She'd seen his rages before. No one ever crossed the Shreck and got away with it. And it wasn't such a hard price to pay. She'd paid it often enough before. The first time, she'd thought she'd kill herself, but she didn't. She wasn't that strong. Finlay must never know. For his own good.

And perhaps some day she'd be able to make a fresh start with him in the underground, safe from her father's reach. She smiled tightly. She had so much to live for now. Finlay, the underground, and perhaps someday a chance for revenge . . .

Finlay looked round the meeting place with interest. An abandoned work station by the look of it, bristling with half-repaired, obsolete equipment. Dangling cables hung from the high ceiling, and battered viewscreens lined the walls, hissing with static. Evangeline had said he'd be meeting the esper leaders here, so they could check him out, but as yet there was no sign of them. There was no sign of anyone, and Finlay didn't blame them in the least. The place was a dump, and filthy beyond belief. He had a strong suspicion he was in danger of catching something unpleasant just by being there. If this was typical of the subsystems, he'd have to think twice about staying. There were limits, after all.

And then the esper leaders appeared suddenly in the chamber before him, and for a moment his poise vanished as he stared with open eyes and mouth. He realized he was gawping, and pulled himself together. He had a strong feeling a good first impression was going to be important. Remember the code of the aristocracy. Dignity at all times. He hoped no one had noticed his lapse.

'Don't worry,' said Evangeline quietly beside him. 'Everyone does that the first time they see the leaders.'

Finlay didn't blame them. A waterfall splashed down from high above. An abstract pattern folded in upon itself endlessly. A giant hog with blood-stained tusks glared at him with tiny crimson eyes. And a ten foot woman wrapped in shimmering light looked down on him with cold disinterest. Evangeline had warned him that the leaders hid their true identities behind illusions for security reasons, but he hadn't expected them to seem so . . . real. He swallowed hard, and held his head high.

'Interesting friends you have, Evie,' he said brightly. 'Usually to see something like this I'd have to ask Valentine for something from his private stash.'

'Shut up, Finlay,' Evangeline said quietly, forcefully. 'You're here under sufferance. The underground has no use for the Families. They've seen too many good men and women killed by the powers that be, for daring to struggle to be free. The only reason you weren't shot on sight was because you were with me. And they're not always that happy about me. Now be quiet, and let me try and put in a good word for both of us.'

'I'm an outlaw now,' said Finlay. 'That means they have to take me, doesn't it?'

'No,' said the hog. 'It doesn't.' Its voice was deep and harsh, and seemed to echo on in Finlay's bones. 'There are always spies and traitors, seeking to destroy us from within.'

'And what happens to them?'

'I eat them,' said the hog.

Finlay decided to let Evangeline do all the talking. He put on a respectful face while she talked to the leaders, and carefully kept his hands away from his sword and gun. He looked across at the few relatively normal-looking people in the chamber with him, and moved over to join them, bowing respectfully.

'I'm Finlay Campbell, or I was. Not really entitled to the name any more, I suppose. Are you part of the underground too?'

'My name is Hood,' said the tall man with no face. 'I advise.'

He wore a long cloak with a cowl pulled forward. There was only darkness inside the cowl. *Probably another esper*, thought Finlay. He turned his attention to the three women with the same face, and gave them his most charming smile.

'Don't waste it on us, stud,' said the woman on the left. 'We're married.'

'Really?' said Finlay. 'Who to?'

'Each other,' said the woman in the middle. 'We're Stevie Blues. Call us One, Two and Three, but don't get us mixed up. We get very short-tempered when that happens. We're really very different.'

'Right,' said the woman on the right, Stevie Three. 'And we don't like aristos anyway.'

'Not many do, these days,' said Finlay. 'Perhaps I can help persuade you we're not all bad.'

'I doubt it,' said Stevie One. 'And if you say some of your best friends are clones, I may puke.'

Finlay decided to take that as an exit line, and moved back to Evangeline, who seemed to be summing up. Clones. Like Evangeline. He still wasn't sure how he felt about that. He kept hoping for time to think, but things kept happening so quickly. When he got up that morning, as an elder son and heir of a respected Family, he'd never thought he'd end up down here, standing helplessly by while a clone argued with espers for his life.

He'd never thought much about clones and espers before. They were just there to be used, like other things belonging to his Family. And now here he was, in love with one. Whatever else had changed, that hadn't. He'd lost his Family and his place in society, and the Empress he'd sworn to serve all his life was now his implacable enemy, but he hadn't lost his Evangeline. And in the end, she was perhaps the only one out of all of them that mattered. She was still talking eloquently to the esper leaders on his behalf, and there was no one else in the chamber to talk to, so he moved reluctantly back to Hood and the Stevie Blues. For better or worse, they or people like them were going to be his future companions, so he'd better learn to get on with them.

He was an outlaw now. Like Owen Deathstalker. Finlay wished he'd felt more concern over Owen when it happened. He understood more now. Rather than think too much about Owen's fate, and his own possible future on the run, he nodded lightly to the man with no face. In his time at Court, Finlay had made polite conversation with lunatics, eccentrics and monsters of all sorts. He could handle a few disgruntled clones and an esper. And if anything went wrong with the leaders, he could always grab Evangeline and fight and shoot his way out of here. He was the Masked Gladiator, and he'd faced worse odds than this in his time. Actually, he didn't think he had, but he decided very firmly that he wasn't going to think about that.

'My apologies for our barging in on you like this,' he said easily to Hood. 'But life up above was getting a bit frantic. Guns firing all over the place, and assassins on our tail. You know how it is.'

'Yes,' said Hood. 'We all do. That's why we're here. But persecution above doesn't automatically buy you acceptance in the world below.'

'Right,' said Stevie Three. Finlay admired her leather and chains outfit, and wondered fleetingly how Evangeline would look in it. He realized the clone was still talking, and made himself concentrate on her face. Stevie Three smiled nastily, as though she knew what he'd been thinking. 'Far as we're concerned, you're just another damned aristo who got his fingers burned, and came crying to the underground for help.'

'Not that we're entirely unsympathetic,' said Stevie Two. 'Any enemy of the Iron Bitch can't be all bad. But we don't take chances any more. We've been hurt too often.'

'Right,' said Stevie Three.

'We don't carry passengers down here, aristo,' said Stevie One. 'No matter who your enemies are. What can you do for us?'

Finlay's face flushed, and anger sent his hands moving automatically towards his weapons, but he made himself stop in time. It was a fair question. They only knew him, if they knew him at all, as a notorious fop and idler. And the torn and blood-stained clothes he was currently wearing weren't exactly helping. Still, it had been a long time since he'd had to justify himself to anyone, and he had to stop and think a moment before replying. Knowing several languages and which fork to use first wasn't going to be much help here.

'I'm a fighter,' he said finally. 'Any weapons, any odds. And I'm the best you'll ever see.'

The three Stevies waited, and then smiled slightly as they realized he'd said all he was going to say. Hood chuckled softly. It wasn't a pleasant sound. 'You may get a chance to prove that, Campbell. And sooner than you think.'

'What did happen to your face?' said Finlay. 'Cut yourself shaving?'

Hood turned away without answering, but all three Stevies had some kind of smile. Hood came to a halt beside Evangeline, and broke into her speech without apology. 'The Campbell is a complication. Valentine Wolfe is his enemy. The last thing we need is a blood feud in our midst. Particularly when so much is happening. Send him away.'

'He comes to us in need,' said the waterfall. 'Just as you did, once. And he at least has shown us his face and told us his name. Shall we not show him the charity that was shown you? All the world above is his enemy now, as it is ours. They

440

would kill him, as they would kill us. We accept him. Provisionally. Prove yourself, Campbell, and you will be made welcome. Fail or betray us, and we may kill you.'

'Try me,' said Finlay. 'My sword is yours.'

The giant hog nodded once, grunted explosively, and then turned its massive head to look at Hood. 'You said you had a matter of importance to discuss with us. We are here. Talk.'

'In front of him?' said Hood, gesturing disdainfully at Finlay. 'I protest.'

'He is one of us now. Accept him, as we accept you. Talk.'

'Very well. For a long time now, we've been discussing various ways of freeing our fellow espers and clones held in prison, and condemned to death for their rebellion. Most are held in Silo Nine, also known as Wormboy Hell. A maximum security prison, with esp-blockers by the dozen and a small army of guards. Long considered impregnable, none of our people have ever broken in or out and lived to tell of it.

'We've planned to storm it a dozen times, but we always had to call it off. Projected casualties were just too high. But information has come into my possession that changes everything. There's going to be a complete changeover of the guards this evening, at twenty-one hundred, as the prison's new security systems are installed. For a short time it's going to be sheer chaos in there, with new faces all over the place as they yank out the old equipment and plug in the new. The perfect time for us to launch an attack and free all our people rotting in Wormboy Hell. But we've got to go *now*, if we're to take advantage of this opportunity. The authorities knew how vulnerable they'd be, so this was kept secret from practically everybody right up till the last moment. I only stumbled across it by chance. I've contacted as many of our people as I could reach, and had them prepare for action, but I can't launch an attack this big without your approval. We've got to do this. We'll never get a better chance.'

The esper leaders turned to each other, and though they were silent Finlay could all but sense the telepathic arguments crackling between them. He moved in close beside Evangeline, and kept his voice low.

'Fill me in, Evie. A maximum security prison, just for espers and clones? How come I never heard of it before this?'

'Not many have. The Empire doesn't like to admit its conditioning fails as often as it does. Most espers and clones used to die trying to break free of their conditioning, but an increasing number are surviving. The Empire's tried augmenting the usual mental blocks and controls with tech and chemical implants, but they kill as many as they cure, and there's always a pressing demand for more espers and clones. We're so useful. Most failures are locked away in the usual prisons, until they can be disposed of. They don't bother with trials. Clones and espers are property, not people.

'Silo Nine is where they send the hard cases, the ones who fought back. Who questioned their orders or dared to think for themselves. And, of course, anyone found guilty or even suspected of being members of the underground. Officially, Silo Nine doesn't exist. Which means they can do anything at all there that they feel like. The prisoners become just so many warm bodies, used for experimentation. The Empire's always interested in improving its stock, or learning better ways to control or discipline it. We're talking about psychological conditioning, genetic tinkering, and every kind of mental or physical torture you can think of. Some of it works, much of it doesn't, but there are always more warm bodies to work with. Sometimes, the Empire works changes on them, in the name of scientific enquiry. There are monsters in Silo Nine.'

'And Wormboy?' said Finlay.

'He runs Silo Nine. He was human once. Now he's become something else, though whether it's more or less than human depends on who you talk to. He has artificially augmented esper abilities far beyond anything that's ever arisen naturally. He makes the prison the hell it is, and enjoys every moment of it. The suffering and despair of others makes him strong. It's because of him that no one ever leaves Wormboy Hell alive.'

Finlay shook his head slowly. 'I never knew any of this.'

'You never asked. As long as there were always more clones and espers for you to use up as you chose, you never questioned the system that produced them. And you never asked what happened to the garbage you threw away, did you?'

'All right! I'm sorry. There are a lot of questions I never asked, but I'm asking now. I want to know. Has anyone ever tried to break into this place before?'

'No one that's lived to tell of it. Silo Nine has state-of-the-art security. Always. We've never been able to get past it before, but this could be the break we've been praying for. There's a lot of us who'd give our lives and die happy for a chance to bring down Wormboy Hell.'

Finlay looked at her steadily. *I thought you said I was your life.* 'You've lost someone to Silo Nine, haven't you? Someone close.'

'Yes. We all have. She was my friend, before I was a clone and after. She helped brief me on taking over as Evangeline. The only person I could ever really talk to. They came for her in the early hours of the morning, and I never saw her again. Daddy tried to find out what had happened to her, for fear she'd talk, but even he couldn't get answers about what happens to people inside Wormboy Hell.'

Evangeline fell silent, and Finlay couldn't think of anything to say. They looked across at Hood, who was talking persuasively again.

'I've managed to infiltrate some of my own people into the incoming security forces, and I've convinced some of the braver cyberats to run a jamming storm, to coincide with our attack. They'll run interference while we get our people out, and keep security from calling for outside help.'

'All right,' said the hog. 'We're convinced. Set things in motion. We'll spread word throughout the esper network. You organize the clone forces. We'll begin our attack on Silo Nine in one hour from now. Get moving.'

Hood nodded quickly with his empty cowl, turned away without acknowledging Evangeline and Finlay, and strode quickly out of the chamber. Finlay looked at Evangeline.

'This is all happening a bit fast for me. You're really going to launch an attack on a maximum security prison, just on that man's word?'

'Of course. We trust Hood. We've been given good reason to in the past. And we've had plans for an attack for years, ready to take advantage of any opportunity that arose. We've dreamed of this for a long time, Finlay. A lot of blood debts are going to be settled today.'

'But what if it all goes wrong?'

'Then it goes wrong! We can't miss out on a chance like this; it might not come again for decades. You can't conceive what it's like in that hellhole, Finlay. None of us can.'

'That's not strictly true,' said the abstract pattern, in a cool, expressionless voice. Looking at it too closely made Finlay's head ache, so he looked half away and concentrated on the voice as it continued. 'We have contact with one of our people in Silo Nine. She volunteered to be captured and sent there. We spent some time preparing her so that she would appear to break under their interrogation, but still keep the deepest part of herself free and separate. We can listen in, but we can't speak to her. She knew she was almost certainly going to her death, but she still volunteered, just on the chance that we might be able to make use of her. She was ready to wait for years, if need be. Have you ever cared about anything that strongly in your life, Finlay Campbell?'

'I never cared about anyone except me,' said Finlay, 'until I met Evangeline, and then I only cared about us. Maybe that's changing now. I don't know. I'm still coming to terms with . . . everything. I can't really understand what life has been like for you.'

Then let us show you, said the esper leaders, and their thoughts swept over Finlay's mind like an irresistible tide of blinding light. He was torn away in a rush of thoughts and images, and all he could do was go along with it. He could feel Evangeline's presence beside him in the churning maelstrom, and that comforted him. He stopped trying to fight it, and allowed the esper leaders to take him where they would. He listened, and after a while, thoughts came to him that were not his own.

*

Jenny Psycho wasn't her real name, but she had to give that up when she went undercover. She lost a great deal more when the Empire threw her into Wormboy Hell, but somehow she held on to her real name and kept it safe, one last secret hidden deep inside her, where her torturers couldn't find it. Not even Wormboy himself. To them, she was still Jenny Psycho, captured terrorist. Just as the esper leaders had planned, though she'd forgotten that. She'd forgotten a lot of things. It was the only way to survive.

She lay curled in a ball, naked and shivering, on the bare concrete floor of her cell. There was no furniture, or any other luxury, just four bare stone walls surrounding a space maybe twice the size of an average coffin, with a ceiling so low she couldn't stand upright without stooping. They'd dropped her in, sealed the lid shut, laughed, and then left her alone in the darkness. They dropped food and water in through a sliding vent in the ceiling, but no one ever talked to her.

Except Wormboy.

She knew she'd never be allowed out again until it was time to kill her, but she didn't know when that would be. So every time the guards came, she was afraid they'd come for her, and scrabbled back to press into a corner, as though she could hide from them. But they only dropped the food and water, and went away. Sometimes it was hot and sometimes it was cold in the cell, but there was never any light. She had no idea what she looked like now, but it was probably pretty bad. She hadn't been able to wash in all the time she'd been there, however long that was. She'd tried counting the meals, but she soon lost track. There was a grille in the floor in one corner that served as a toilet, but not very well. Sometimes she heard things moving underneath it. Live things. Living off her.

Like Wormboy.

She used to scream a lot, but all that got her was a sore throat, so she stopped. She used to talk to herself, but she ran out of things to say. She still sang occasionally, as a small sign of defiance, but she was starting not to like the way her voice sounded. She smelt bad. The stench in her cell rose and fell just enough to keep her from getting used to it. She suspected that was deliberate. It was the sort of thing Wormboy would do.

They caught her easily. It seemed to her there was a reason for that, but she'd forgotten it. As a low-level esper, it had been her job to mentally test and examine babies developing in the womb, to discover whether they had any trace of esp in them. If they did, they were either aborted or taken away at birth to begin a lifetime of training and conditioning. Depending on whether it was a useful kind of esp, of course. It wasn't a foolproof method, but it caught quite a few. The mothers all looked at her with the same controlled desperation, and she gave them all the same brief meaningless smile. And for a long time she just did her job, doing as she was told, as she'd been trained; but constant exposure to so many bright, innocent unsullied minds was finally too much for her. She began using her talents to conceal the babies' esp. It wasn't difficult. The esper abilities would still appear in later life, but at least that way they had a chance at a safe, normal, free life. Security found out. She hadn't tried that hard to conceal it. Defiance, perhaps, or maybe some last trace of her own conditioning. Or something else that she'd forgotten. Either way, they caught her.

And now here she was, alone in the dark with a worm in her head, down in Wormboy Hell.

Light began seeping into her cell from somewhere. A sickly yellow light that made her think of disease and decay. In it, she could see the sores and scabs on her blotched skin. The smell was suddenly thick and choking, and her stomach heaved painfully though there was nothing in it. And there in the cell with her, crawling out of the shadows in splashes of bloody amniotic fluid, came the babies. Bald and pudgy, with barely formed arms and legs, they crawled over and around her, a living carpet of unforgiving flesh. Unfinished foetuses squirmed spasmodically on the concrete floor, trying to squeeze in between her and the floor, as though trying to crawl back into the wombs from which they'd been prematurely torn.

She wanted to love them all, poor blameless innocents, but

she knew what was coming next. They came from Wormboy. Teeth appeared in all the babies' mouths, sharp, jagged teeth thrusting up through torn bloody gums, and slowly, deliberately, they began to eat her alive. Jenny always swore that this time she wouldn't scream, but she always did in the end. Teeth ripped at her flesh as she screamed and screamed, and blood ran down to pool thickly on the floor. As the pain and the horror mounted, pudgy fingers began to pry at her squeezed-shut eyelids, to get at the eyes beneath, and even though she knew none of it was real, Jenny Psycho screamed and screamed until her throat was raw.

Wormboy did so like his little games. And mindgames were the best fun of all.

Fat and wide and greasy like a slug, genetically engineered to never sleep or waver in his duty, Wormboy filled an entire auditorium from wall to wall; vast acres of pale, faintly luminescent flesh that rippled and folded in upon itself. His bulk covered all the floor, and his huge distorted head pressed against the ceiling. Long tubes entered his body here and there, providing nourishment and removing wastes. He could never have eaten enough to satisfy his enormous appetite. His body's needs were taken care of by the authorities so that his mind could roam free across the prison. Wormboy's parents had been normal enough humans, but he had been designed and tampered with from the embryo onwards, to shape the mind and talents of the perfect gaoler. He ran everything, from the computers that ran Silo Nine's security, to the guards who enforced his edicts, to the little pets that gave him access to every prisoner's mind.

Every time someone was damned to Wormboy Hell, for whatever reason, a small genetically designed and Imperially patented parasite was surgically implanted in their brain. Wormboy's worms. They blocked off the esper's powers so they couldn't use them offensively, and secreted various useful chemicals that helped to keep the espers and clones quiet and malleable. And if by some chance an esper or a clone did find the strength of will to fight off the chemicals and try to escape, the worm would fry their brain.

If his prisoners misbehaved, or held back information, Wormboy used his little pets to gain entrance to their recalcitrant minds, and sent them nightmares that had all the hallmarks of reality except that you couldn't die in them no matter how much you wanted to. Wormboy sent his dreams to instruct or persuade or punish, or just for the fun of it. There was no one to tell him he couldn't, and after all, no one cared. They were going to die anyway. The worms gave him all the control he needed, and were much cheaper and easier to run than hundreds of individual esp-blockers. Their designer won a major award, before he disappeared into Silo Nine, to ensure he never told anyone else his secrets.

Wormboy liked to go among the monsters, the malformed, horrid results of esper and clone experimentation. Too dangerous ever to be released, too useful to kill, they roared and spat in their cells, clawing at the stone walls. Human no longer, but more than beasts; wild and awful and beyond pain or fear, they defied even Wormboy's best efforts, but he never gave up on them. He swept back and forth among the specially reinforced cells, walking up and down in their minds, and they screamed and howled with a rage that shook the walls. To them, he was just one more monster among many. Wormboy laughed and laughed and laughed.

His mind roamed free among the prisoners of Silo Nine, present in every mind controlled by a worm; a slimy mental caress, a passing presence like a chill wind from a charnel house. Bringer of nightmares, vast and awful, the perfect gaoler. Horrid and merciless god of his own private hell.

Finlay Campbell lay curled in a ball on the floor of the abandoned work station, shaking and shuddering. Evangeline knelt beside him, her hands cool on his feverish face, murmuring calm and soothing words. He felt sick, tainted and invaded on every level of his mind and body. Wormboy's thoughts had ripped through his mind like poisoned barbed wire, brushing aside all his defences, as he shared everything that happened to Jenny Psycho. Neither of them had known he was there, but that just made him feel even more helpless, unable to help Jenny or any of the other victims of Wormboy's rape. Finlay snarled his killer's death's-head grin, his hands clenched into fists. He would find the monster in its lair and kill it, and maybe then he'd feel clean again.

He ran through the calming chants he'd learned in the Arena, and gradually the shaking stopped. Control slipped over him again like a cool, familiar cloak, and he sat up. Evangeline hovered over him worriedly, but he managed a small smile for her.

'It's all right, Evie. I'm back. I swear to you, I never knew any of this. I never heard of Silo Nine, or Wormboy, or the terrible things they're doing there. If Parliament and the Company of Lords knew about this . . .'

'Many of them already do,' said Evangeline. 'Unofficially. They don't care, or if they do, they manage not to think about it. Clones and espers aren't people, remember? We're property. The Empire made us, so it can do whatever it wants with us.'

'But if the people knew; if we told them, made them understand . . .'

'You wouldn't be allowed to tell them. The production of clones and espers is too important to too many people. Stop the trade, and millionaires would become paupers overnight. And what would happen to the Empire, dependent on espers for its smooth running at all levels? The Empire has a vested interest in preserving the status quo at all costs. Why do you think they spend so much time and effort in portraying the underground as ruthless terrorists? I'm sorry, Finlay. This is all new to you, but we've lived with it all our lives.'

'I won't allow this to continue,' said Finlay. 'It's wrong. It's obscene. It's against everything we're taught to believe and honour. The Families are supposed to protect their people against such abuses; guard them against horrors like this.'

'Even clones and espers?' said Evangeline.

'You were right,' said Finlay. 'They are people too.'

Evangeline smiled. 'Welcome to the rebellion, Finlay. The

attack on Silo Nine will be starting soon; will you be joining us?'

Finlay smiled back at her, and his eyes were cold as death. 'Try and stop me.'

Which was how he came to be padding down a narrow technicians' access tunnel, gun in one hand, sword in the other, leading a small army of rebels through the interconnecting guts of the undercity. Evangeline was there at his side, the large gun looking out of place in her small, delicate hand. He had no doubt she would use it, though. She'd been there in Jenny Psycho's mind too. Just the thought was enough to make Finlay's hands tighten around his sword and gun. He had vowed upon his name and honour to find and free her, or die trying. It amused him a little, to think how outraged he would have been at such a thing, only a few hours earlier. A death vow, over clones and espers? Unthinkable. His father would have disowned him. Or maybe not, if he'd seen what his son had seen. The Campbell had been a hard, pragmatic man, but even he would have drawn the line at Wormboy Hell. The Campbell, for all his faults and intrigues, had been an honourable man.

Finlay glanced about him, but there were only the bare polished walls of the tunnel, and the ceiling so low he had to walk hunched over to avoid banging his head. There was darkness before his party, and darkness behind them, as the fifty or so men and women moved in a blaze of sourceless light, a bright golden glow generated by the minds of the espers. Finlay hadn't known espers could do that, but he had a feeling there were lots of things he didn't know about espers. He'd begun to suspect that when, early on, one of the esper leaders had looked at him, and suddenly Finlay had a map in his head of the long, convoluted way that would lead him into Silo Nine. The map was still there, clear and distinct, though he'd never been this way before. It also told him he wasn't far from the first of the prison's outer defences.

The fifty or so men and women with him (he kept getting a different answer every time he counted, because some of them weren't always there) seemed to be making a lot of noise, but Evangeline had assured him they were all telepathically shielded from detection, while cyberats were running interference on the tech security systems. The rebels were invisible, for all intents and purposes, until they began their attack. By which time they should be deep in the diseased heart of Wormboy Hell, and it would be far too late to try and stop them then.

Hood strode along on Finlay's other side, calm and confident. There was still no trace of any face in his cowl, which frankly spooked the hell out of Finlay, but Evangeline trusted Hood, so Finlay went along with it. Certainly the man showed no sign of fear or hesitation, despite the odds they'd be facing. Finlay approved of that. Among all the things a warrior needed, a cool head in a dangerous situation was right at the top.

The three Stevie Blues were striding arrogantly together some way ahead at the edge of the light, on point, in perfect step with each other, fearsome sights in their leather and chains, like young savage furies on their way to demand vengeance. Finlay would have been a little more impressed by them if he hadn't been so sure they were complete and utter psychopaths. Though that was probably just the kind of troops you needed on your side when you were playing follow my leader into hell.

There were other groups of rebels, following other routes, heading for openings in the prison's security that Hood's people had arranged, but there was no way of knowing how they were getting on. All forms of communication, tech or telepathy, were too open to interception. Hood's plan relied on a series of lightning strikes from a dozen different directions; to get in, kill Wormboy, rescue the prisoners and get the hell out before major security reinforcements could arrive to spoil the party. Publicly, Finlay approved of the plan. It had the virtue of being uncomplicated, at least. Privately, however, he couldn't help remembering his tutors' oft-repeated dictum that plans rarely survived contact with the enemy. Once the fighting started, everything tended to go to hell in a hurry. Hood seemed confident there wouldn't be much actual conflict, given the rebels' advantage of surprise. Finlay wished he felt that confident too.

The three Stevie Blues came to a sudden simultaneous halt, lifting their guns and peering suspiciously into the gloom ahead of the light. Stevie One looked back, as the rest of the party came to a halt. At least, Finlay thought it was Stevie One.

'There's a door here that isn't on the map. It's big and solid and very definitely locked. Should I blast it?'

'Not on your life,' said Finlay quickly. 'We're right on the edge of the prison itself, if the rest of the map can be trusted. A disrupter blast would set off every alarm in the place, and the cyberats can only cover so much. Hood; it's your map and your plan. What do we do?'

'There's no problem,' said Hood. 'My people are waiting on the other side. They'll open the door.'

He strode forward and rapped twice on the steel door. It slid upwards, and lights blazed into the access tunnel, revealing an army of armed guards in the room beyond. Hood laughed, and blinked out of existence.

'It's a trap!' yelled Finlay. 'Everyone back! Hood's betrayed us!'

And as quickly as that, everything went to hell. There was a clamour of raised voices in the narrow corridor, with shouts and screams and a confused mess of orders and naked panic. Those at the rear turned to run, but a heavy steel door slammed down from the ceiling, cutting off their escape. *So much for telepathic invisibility*, thought Finlay. He grabbed Evangeline by the arm and pulled her behind him, putting his body between her and the armed guards ahead. He just had time to wonder why they weren't firing yet, and why they were wearing masks, when thick clouds of evil-smelling gas burst out into the corridor from concealed vents in the floor. The first breath was enough to set the unprotected rebels coughing and choking. Finlay tried to back away, but there was nowhere to go.

And then a sudden wind roared through the corridor, forcing the gas back upon the guards, and dispersing it as fast as it could form. The hidden vents exploded in showers of sparks, and collapsed in upon themselves, closing off the gas. Esper power crackled on the air like harnessed lightning, so thick and close that even a normal like Finlay could feel it. The guards realized the gas attack wasn't working, and turned their guns on the rebels. Finlay raised his arm automatically, slapping at the bracelet on his wrist to activate his force shield. The roar of energy beams was deafening in the confined space, joined with the screams of the dying and the injured as rebels fell. There was the stench of burning flesh and melting metal as energy beams tore through bodies and ricocheted off the reinforced steel walls.

They knew we were coming this way, thought Finlay. *They've got us trapped in a killing field*. He picked a target almost without thinking, and shot a guard in the head. The other guards fell back, shouting with shock. They hadn't expected any resistance. Finlay grinned savagely. When in doubt, do the unexpected. He ran forward, brandishing his sword, yelling for the others to follow him, and no one was more surprised than him when they did. Evangeline was there beside him, yelling her Clan's war cry, and holding a sword like she knew what to do with it. The surviving espers and clones were right behind them, firing guns where they had them, and esper power thundered among the guards.

Swords clashed on swords as the two forces wrestled together, and the guards tried to make a stand. But even viciously depleted by the unexpected ambush, the rebels were still more than a match for the guards. The Stevie Blues stood together, the same g.im expression on the same faces, as fire roared from their hands. Guards dropped their swords and ran screaming as their clothes and hair burst into flames. Espers picked up guards with their minds and crushed them together with deadly force. Bones cracked and skulls collapsed under the implacable mental pressure, and some guards just stood and stared with horror-filled eyes as telepaths ripped through their thoughts with tides of fear and depression and self-loathing. And those rebels who weren't espers took their revenges with the point and edge of unforgiving swords.

Eventually Finlay looked round for another target, and found there were no more left. Guards lay scattered across the floor of the chamber like broken dolls thrown aside by a bored child. Only rebels were still standing, looking confusedly about them, and it nearly broke Finlay's heart to see how few of them there were. Out of the fifty or so who'd accompanied him into Wormboy Hell, only nineteen remained, and three of them were Stevie Blues. He took a deep breath and turned off his force shield. Someone was going to have to take charge, and it seemed it was going to have to be him. He had no real authority, but he'd spent enough time in the Arena to know that sometimes confidence is everything.

'All right; listen to me! You can bet there are more guards on the way here, armed to the teeth, even as I speak. We have to form a perimeter. Anyone with esp, find a corridor opening and guard it. Everyone else, grab a gun. Anyone you see coming this way is almost certainly an enemy, so shoot on sight. If you kill the wrong person by accident, we can always apologize later. Now move it!'

The Stevie Blues and a handful of others nodded unresistingly, and hurried off. Finlay turned to Evangeline. There was a smear of someone else's blood on one cheek, and she was staring dumbly about her at the heaped piles of the dead. There was more blood spattered across her clothes, some of it hers. Finlay took her by the arm and made her turn round to face him.

'Don't blank out on me now, Evie. I need to know what you know. How many other groups of us were there in this assault?'

'Five,' said Evangeline, swallowing hard and visibly trying to pull herself together.

'Can we contact them, see if they were ambushed too?'

'They were,' said a quiet voice beside them. It was a short, slightly overweight man, with wide eyes and an open face. He might have looked like an accountant, if it hadn't been for the sword he held in a business-like manner, and the blood that soaked his sleeve to the elbow. 'I'm a telepath. Denny Pindar. I heard most of them die.'

'Then we're on our own,' said Finlay. 'I say the mission is officially aborted, and I further say we get the hell out of here.'

'No,' said Evangeline. 'If we just turn and run, then the others died for nothing.'

'If we try to take on overwhelming odds in enemy territory for no good reason, we'll die for nothing!'

'No good reason?' Evangeline looked at him steadily. 'You swore a death oath to bring this place down, Finlay Campbell. Is your word worth so little?'

'Dammit, Evie. You're right; as usual. But what can we do, with just the handful of people we've got left?'

'Find Wormboy and kill him. He holds this place together. Without him it'll fall apart into chaos. We'll be able to free the prisoners and fight our way out of here.'

'Great plan,' said Finlay. 'Have we got time to write our wills first? All right; let's look at the situation. Pindar; can you detect any hidden cameras or surveillance equipment here?'

The esper concentrated, and then pointed at a wall decoration that looked just like all the others. Stevie One looked back briefly from guarding her corridor opening, and the decoration burst into flames. Finlay nodded his thanks.

'Evie; can we contact the cyberats? They might know more about what's going on.'

'No; it was set up so that they could reach us, but not the other way round. Their comm units are specially shielded. Ours aren't.'

'Then we'll just have to follow the map, and hope it's not part of the trap too.' A thought struck him, and he looked at Pindar. 'How come they didn't use esp-blockers against us? We'd have been dead in the water if they had.'

The telepath shook his head. 'There are no esp-blockers inside Silo Nine. They'd interfere with Wormboy's control. Security must have been banking on the gas and their superiority in numbers to make the difference. It did, with the other groups. They never had a chance to defend themselves. If you hadn't taken the initiative away from them by rallying us to strike first, we'd have just stood there and died like the others.

We're not used to combat.' He broke off, his eyes suddenly far away. 'Company's coming.'

Finlay looked automatically to the Stevie Blues. 'Can you see anyone?'

'You won't see them,' said Pindar. 'They're shielded. They're battle espers.'

'Oh shit,' said Evangeline. 'We're dead.'

Finlay glared at her. 'We're not dead till I say we are. So they're battle espers; so what? We'll just stay out of their way.'

'We can't,' said Pindar. 'They're coming from all directions.'

Finlay glared at him. 'Don't you ever have anything positive to say? Can we fight them?'

'If you really want to annoy them,' said Evangeline. 'These are espers specially trained and conditioned by the Empire to fight other espers. We can't talk to them, or reason with them, and they don't accept surrenders. They just kill and kill till there's no one left alive but them.'

'There's got to be a way to beat them,' said Finlay. 'There's got to be a way. What about you, Pindar? Could you use your esp to fight them?'

'If I had to,' said the telepath, blinking owlishly. 'But they're much more powerful than any of us. And there's a lot more of them than there are of us.'

'They'll only outnumber us if we stand here and wait for them,' said Finlay. 'So we'll go to them. God, I wish I felt as confident as I sound. Pindar; which of the approaching forces is the smallest?'

The esper thought for a moment, and then pointed at one of the corridor openings. 'That way. Twenty-four espers, moving head of the main pack. No guards.'

'Then that's the way we're going,' said Finlay. 'Stevie Blues; lead the way. Fry anything that moves.'

'Sounds good to me,' said Stevie One.

'Right,' said Stevie Three.

The three esper clones set off down the corridor at a steady trot, conserving their breath. The chains on their leathers clattered loudly, like an angry chorus. Finlay hurried after them, Pindar and Evangeline on each side of him, and the rest of the party brought up the rear. It worried him that they were accepting his orders so readily; it probably meant they were still in shock. If they were going to have to fight battle espers, fighting at anything less than full strength would get them all killed. It surprised Finlay how much that mattered to him. They'd fought bravely. They didn't deserve to die. *Getting soft*, thought Finlay.

They pounded down the corridor, checking every opening as they passed, but there was no sign of anyone. Finlay was pleasantly surprised to note that they were still more or less following the original route on the map. If they stuck with it, it should lead them right to Wormboy. Eventually. It worried him that they hadn't encountered more guards. They must have been withdrawn, to keep them out of the way of the battle espers.

They rounded a corner, and then the Stevie Blues skidded to a halt as Pindar shouted for them to stop. The party stumbled to a ragged standstill, lifting guns and swords and glaring about them. Pindar stared straight ahead, frowning harshly. Finlay moved in close beside him, and kept his voice low.

'What is it? What do you see?'

'It's what I don't see. It's too quiet. Too still. There should be some background random mental noise; but there's nothing. Nothing at all.'

Finlay turned to the Stevie Blues. 'Roast the corridor ahead till it glows.'

Stevie One grinned. 'My kind of plan.'

'Right,' said Stevie Three.

A roaring wave of flames swept down the corridor as they concentrated, scorching the walls on either side till they glowed crimson. And then the fire stopped, thrown back by an invisible barrier. An esper just behind Finlay began to shake and shudder. People backed away from him as he convulsed. Finlay grabbed the esper by the shoulders, but the violent shaking threw him off. Evangeline pulled him away. The esper exploded into a crimson mist that filled the corridor. Finlay aimed and fired his disrupter in one swift movement, and then watched incredulously as the energy beam ricocheted off an invisible screen.

'Battle espers,' said Pindar. 'Trained to perfection, conditioned beyond fear or weakness, programmed to fight to the death. Yours or theirs. The most powerful espers ever collected together. Supposedly. You'd need disrupter cannon to break through one of their force screens. And even then, you'd get better odds betting against the cannon.'

'I'm going off you,' said Finlay. 'You only ever tell me things I don't want to hear. Don't you have anything positive to suggest?'

'Yes,' said the telepath. 'Get them before they get us.'

He stepped forward to form a line with the other espers, and they stood silently together, staring down the corridor. A group of the battle espers suddenly appeared to face them. And for a long moment, all they did was stand there and stare at each other. A trickle of blood ran slowly down from Pindar's left nostril. Another of his group began to shiver uncontrollably. More of the rebel espers came forward to face the Empire force. The corridor floor wrenched itself apart, splitting open in a long jagged line that shot towards the battle espers. It stopped several feet short. And that just left the Stevie Blues. They stepped forward in one simultaneous movement, brushed the hair out of their faces with the same hand, and frowned the same frown as they concentrated. Heat gathered on the air before them, savage and blistering. The walls on either side of them glowed a sullen red. The air shimmered. Beads of sweat ran down the Stevie Blues' faces, either from the heat or their concentration, and the angry blush on the steel walls began to move towards the battle espers. It got about half-way there, slowed to a crawl and then inched to a halt, no matter how hard the Stevie Blues scowled.

Finlay looked around, but the only people left uninvolved in the silent esper duel were him and Evangeline. He reached over to one of the rebel espers, took the gun from his unresisting hand, and tried another shot at the Empire espers. The energy beam faded out before it reached them, but it seemed to Finlay that it got a lot closer than the last one. He reached out for another gun.

'No,' said Evangeline. 'Energy weapons aren't the answer. They can control and absorb energy.'

'Then what do you suggest?' said Finlay.

'The two sides are pretty much deadlocked. The battle espers are so hyped up on drugs and mental implants they'd sooner die than surrender or back off. But, with a bit of luck, that also means they're too involved with the struggle on a mental plane to defend themselves against a purely physical attack.'

'So what do you want me to do?' said Finlay. 'Rush over there and bang their heads together?'

'I was thinking of something a little more . . . dramatic.' She fished in one of her pockets and pulled out a large round object. 'Shrapnel grenade. Simple, effective, and extremely nasty at close range.'

She pressed the stud, knelt down and rolled the grenade along the floor towards the battle espers. It seemed to move slower and slower all the time, but finally it got there. Finlay grabbed Evangeline, pulled her down and wrapped his body around hers as a shield. The explosion was deafening in the confined space, and shrapnel ricocheted off the steel walls, falling like jagged rain. An unfelt pressure in the corridor was suddenly gone, and Finlay rose unsteadily to his feet. His ears were ringing, and his balance wasn't all that it might have been. He discovered a sharp metal fragment sticking out of his thigh, looked at it dispassionately, and pulled it out. The wound didn't bleed much. Evangeline stood up beside him, and he checked to make sure she was all right. She had a nasty cut on her forehead, but otherwise looked OK. Except that she was glaring at him.

'Will you stop grabbing me and pulling me around?' she said coldly. 'I am quite capable of remembering to duck on my own, thank you.'

Her voice sounded harsh but far away, as though they were both underwater. Finlay felt a grin tugging at the corners of his mouth, but controlled himself. He didn't think Evangeline was in the mood to see the funny side.

'Where did the grenade come from?' he said, finally.

'Daddy always made sure that the female members of the Family went around fully armed, after the Iron Bitch took my cousin to be a maid. I thought a gun was a bit obvious, and too easily guarded against, so I decided on a grenade. Not terribly subtle, but I suppose it shows I am my father's daughter, after all.'

Finlay decided he wasn't going to pursue that point any further, just at the moment, and moved among the slowly rousing espers, checking they were all right. They'd all been blown off their feet by the blast, but no one was actually dead. Several had nosebleeds or headaches, and they'd all been cut or pierced here and there by ricocheting shrapnel, but they were taking it well. Finlay took a deep breath and moved slowly down the corridor to get a better look at what was left of the battle espers. A few of the mangled bodies were recognizable. Most weren't. He heard footsteps behind him, and looked back, expecting Evangeline, but it was Stevie Two. He recognized the different coloured ribbons in her hair. She looked at the carnage unflinchingly.

'There, but for the grace of god, go I. My sisters and I were created specifically to be the new generation of battle espers. We got away, but we had to leave a lot of friends behind. I wonder; if I looked hard enough through this mess, would I find familiar faces?'

'Best not to look,' said Finlay. 'Best not to know.'

She nodded, turned away, and walked back to her sisters. Finlay followed her back, and rejoined Pindar and Evangeline.

'All right,' he said brusquely. 'Which way now? You can bet reinforcements are on the way, and I don't think we're up to facing down large numbers of battle espers again.'

'The plan hasn't changed,' said Evangeline. 'Find Worm-boy, kill him, free the prisoners.'

'Just us?' said Finlay.

'Who else is there?'

'What about Jenny Psycho?' said Pindar.

Evangeline frowned. 'What about her? We'll free her when we free the others.'

'I think we need her,' said Pindar. 'The underground arranged for her to be brought here for a reason. She's powerful. More powerful than even she knew. She was supposed to be the key to killing Wormboy.'

'We don't have time for this, and we don't have time for her,' said Evangeline. 'Jenny Psycho will have to wait. It's a straight run to Wormboy now. We've got to get to him before the Empire can set up extra protection.'

'I think we can safely assume that happened the moment we breached Silo Nine's defences,' said Finlay. 'And someone or something like Wormboy isn't going to be easy to kill. I think we should take all the help we can get.'

'That's not why you want to free her,' said Evangeline coldly. 'She's the one you saw in your vision. You swore your oath because of her. You see yourself as the hero, rushing in to sweep her away to safety. You can't afford to let this get personal, Finlay. They're all Jenny Psychos in here. They're all equally deserving. And the best way to save them is to kill the beast that holds them captive.'

Finlay frowned, thinking, and then turned to Pindar. 'Can you contact her, mind to mind? Is she still open to us?'

'I don't see why not,' said the telepath. 'In fact, at this range I should be able to manage full contact.'

He stared blankly ahead, reaching out with his mind, and his face brightened as he made contact. 'Jenny; this is the underground. We're here to rescue you.'

And then Jenny Psycho came fully awake for the first time, and everything changed again. Her mind ignited like a flare, bright and blinding, almost too painful to look at. The espers in the corridor clapped their hands uselessly to their ears as her voice shook like thunder in their minds. Even Finlay and Evangeline could hear her, as though she was right there in the corridor with them.

I remember. I remember who and what I am. Go to Wormboy. Destroy him. I will free the prisoners.

The god-like voice was suddenly gone from their heads, and

the espers slowly lowered their hands from their ears, looking at each other in shock. Telepathically deafened for the moment, they babbled at each other aloud. Finlay tried to make sense of it, but all he could make out was a name, repeated over and over. *Mater Mundi. Mother of the World.* Once again, Finlay turned to Pindar and Evangeline.

'All right; what the hell was that? This is something else you haven't got around to telling me about, isn't it? Who is she? Somebody talk to me!'

'Our Mother of All Souls,' said Pindar, just a bit breathlessly. 'The most powerful telepath ever created. She founded the underground. No wonder no one was allowed to know who Jenny Psycho really was, not even her. If the Iron Bitch knew she was here, she'd nuke the whole city, just on the chance of getting her. If the Mother wants us to go after Wormboy, we are going after Wormboy. You don't argue with God when she speaks to you directly. Not unless you want to be turned into a burning bush.'

'You think she's God?' said Finlay.

'Nearest local equivalent,' said Evangeline. 'My head feels like it's been scoured out with steel wool. She's not just a telepath, Finlay; more like a force of nature. Let's go find Wormboy. Which turning do we take?'

'Left,' said Stevie Three.

It didn't take them long to get there, with the map burning in their brains like a grail. The corridors were eerily empty. There was no trace of the other battle espers anywhere, nor of any of the armed guards. The only sound in Silo Nine was their own boots thudding on the metal floors. Finlay didn't like the silence at all, and gripped his sword and his gun so tightly his hands ached. If all the other espers were being set free, the place ought to be full of the sound of it.

The floor they were moving along seemed to be mainly bureaucratic; just rows upon rows of abandoned offices. The cells were much lower. The surveillance cameras still moved to follow them as they passed. Finlay had stopped the Stevie Blues blowing them up with their fire. He had a strong feeling they were going to need all the strength they could find once they reached Wormboy's lair. The cameras still annoyed him, though. What the hell had happened to the cyberats? They were supposed to be running interference, and playing hell with the security systems. They shouldn't have been affected by any of the ambushes.

'Try and contact the cyberats again,' he said to Evangeline.

'I've tried and tried, Finlay. There's no response.'

'Well try again.'

Evangeline glared at him, but didn't have the strength to be really annoyed. 'What did your last slave die of, Campbell?'

'Not making contact when I asked him. Get on with it.'

She sighed, and tuned her comm implant again to the cyberats' special channel. 'Evangeline to the rats. Talk to me, people. What's happening?'

The voice was suddenly babbling in all their ears, almost incoherent in its haste.

'It's a trap! It's a trap! They were waiting for us in the systems, Empire AIs, huge and powerful, blazing like suns. We went blind, staring into the light. We can't find most of our people. Some are dead. We can't help you any more. We can't help ourselves. You're on your own.'

Thanks a whole bunch, thought Finlay, as the voice fell silent. He looked at Evangeline. 'That bastard Hood didn't just betray us, he set up a really thorough trap as well. I think we have to assume that the other esper groups are either dead or taken prisoner. We're all there is.'

'No,' said Evangeline. 'The Mater Mundi is with us. She's all we need. You have to have faith, Finlay.'

Finlay remained diplomatically silent, and followed the Stevie Blues as they threaded their way through the interconnecting corridors of Silo Nine. There was still no sign of any guards, and the corridors had the quiet stillness of a jungle with its predators hidden just out of sight, waiting to pounce. They filed quickly down a narrow corridor, set with featureless steel doors. Something about the doors made Finlay feel uneasy. They had the solid impenetrable look of doors that didn't open easily or too often. He looked at Evangeline.

'Any idea what's behind those doors?'

'Oh yes,' said Evangeline quietly. 'This is where they keep the monsters; the espers and clones experimented on by Silo Nine's scientists. They're not human any more, in shape or in mind. We can't rescue them. What's been done to them cannot be undone.'

'All the same, we can't just leave them here to rot in their cells. Why can't we just blow open the doors, from a safe distance, and let them run loose? At least they'd have a chance to get away, and if nothing else they should keep the authorities busy.'

'No. They still have worms in their heads. As long as Wormboy lives they belong to him, body and soul. It always comes back to him, Finlay. He's the dark, rotten heart of Silo Nine. It's his dreams that breed monsters. Now come along, and keep your voice down. You might wake them.'

And so on they went, along corridors and down stairways, sinking deeper and deeper into Wormboy Hell. Until finally they came to a huge, featureless wall, and there was nowhere else to go. Finlay studied the map in his head, but it was definitely a dead end. Beyond the wall there was just a great empty space. And then he studied the map more carefully, and frowned. For an empty hall, there were a hell of a lot of pipes and conduits and energy cables going in and out. And so he realized what he'd really known all along, but hadn't wanted to admit. They'd finally come to Wormboy's lair.

'All that space, just for him?' he said finally. 'How big is he?'

'The word is, they're going to have to build him a new home,' said Evangeline. 'He's getting too big for this one.'

Finlay decided he wasn't going to think about that for the moment. 'All right; how do we get to him? What kind of defences has he got?'

'He doesn't need any defences,' said Pindar. 'He's Wormboy. There are no guards, no high-tech security systems. Just him. And that's enough. He's the single strongest esper the Empire has ever produced, a mind so advanced as to be beyond our comprehension. Vast, unknowable, and inhumanly powerful. And possibly quite insane.'

Finlay glared at him. 'You're just full of good news, aren't you? He can't really be that powerful. Can he?'

'No one knows,' said Evangeline. 'No one's ever got this close to him before. And even allowing for Empire hyperbole, he's got to be pretty damned amazing to run a prison the size of Silo Nine. He has continuous mental contact with thousands of minds through his worms, and he knows what all of them are thinking at any given moment. Just another reason why no one has ever escaped from Wormboy Hell.'

'This gets better all the time,' said Finlay. He hefted the gun and sword in his hands, but the familiar weights had lost all power to comfort him. He glared at the long featureless steel wall before him, and it stared back, giving nothing away. 'Anything will die if you hit it hard enough and long enough. How do we get to him? Is there a door somewhere?'

'No doors,' said Evangeline. 'No windows. Wormboy isn't going anywhere. They built the hall around him and then sealed it shut. We'll have to break in.'

'Great. Got any more grenades up your sleeve?'

'You don't need a grenade,' said Stevie One. 'You've got us.'

'Never met a wall that could keep us out,' said Stevie Two.

'Right,' said Stevie Three.

They moved forward to stand before the great steel wall, and stared at it thoughtfully. The temperature in the corridor rose sharply, and Finlay and the others backed away to a safe distance. The wall before the three espers glowed a cheerful cherry red, and began to steam. It got hotter and hotter in the corridor, and slender rivulets of melting metal ran down the wall. The heat before the Stevie Blues had to be unbearable, but they stood their ground. They held each other's hands as sweat ran down their faces, and more molten metal ran down the wall. Until finally the metal collapsed inwards like sticky toffee, and a hole appeared. A terrible stench entered the corridor, of rotting flesh and waste products. The Stevie Blues pulled the same disgusted face, and scowled even harder. The hole grew bigger, the metal running away like water, and everyone got their first glimpse of Wormboy.

Finlay edged forward, one arm raised to protect his face from the heat, and stared in sick fascination at the endless stretch of luminous flesh, pierced here and there by pipes as thick as a normal man's arm. The wounds had healed around the pipes in rucks of crumpled flesh, encrusted by trickles of escaped waste. By peering up through the widening hole, now the size of a door, Finlay could just make out one side of a vast, inhuman face. The skin was stretched inhumanly taut, so that normal expressions were impossible, but even as Finlay watched, a slow smile spread across the lower face. The lips were almost black from the pressure of engorged blood, and the huge teeth were a dirty grey. The eyes were hidden in shadow, but Finlay had no doubt that Wormboy could see them.

The Stevie Blues howled suddenly with pain, and staggered back from the hole they'd made, gripping at their heads with both hands. It hit Finlay and the others a moment later, and he cried out as the flesh rotted on his bones. The pain was horrendous, swamping his thoughts. His skin grew discoloured and cracked apart, revealing maggots writhing in the decaying muscles. Pus and rotting tissue fell from his arms and legs. Somewhere in the back of his mind he knew this wasn't real, but his body believed it. Wormboy was playing his mindgames again.

Finlay squeezed his rotting hands around his sword and gun, though he could no longer feel them. How could Wormboy be doing this? There was no worm in his head, no access for the beast. *He doesn't need one*, Pindar's voice whispered in his ear. *He's drawing on the collective power of all the espers he controls. Our power is nothing compared to his now. Some of the prisoners are trying to hold back, they know why we're here, but he's too strong, too strong. You're our only chance, Finlay. It's harder for him to reach you, because you're not an esper. Kill him. Kill the beast. Before our bodies really believe what they're being told, and rot for real. He's winning, Finlay. He's killing us.*

Finlay could dimly hear distant screams from the surrounding espers in their cells, goaded to action by the spur in their brains. The worms were killing their only hope, and they knew it. He almost lost track of himself in the vast sea of minds, but slowly, bit by bit, he curled in upon himself, shutting out everything else, drawing upon the ingrained disciplines of an Arena fighter, where to lose concentration even for a moment could mean your death. He pulled back from the brink, but still he was helpless in the grip of such power. They were all helpless, alone in the dark with Wormboy.

And then something wonderful happened. One of those minds exploded in a searing blast of light that threw back the darkness. One mind, pure and potent, that reached out and gathered all the captive minds into its fold, and pulled them together in a single vast cry of outrage. Once Jenny Psycho, now fully Mater Mundi, she gave them hope and strength and bound them in a single gestalt mind, wholly the equal of the Empire's greatest esper creation. But only the equal. Thousands of minds swept this way and that in the gestalt, torn between Mater Mundi's sheer power, and the controlling worms hotwired directly into their brains. The prisoners were literally fighting themselves.

Finlay was there too, snatched up into the gestalt by the sheer power of what was happening. He could feel Evangeline there beside him too, somehow always just out of reach. Wormboy's power beat around him like the thunder of huge wings, grasping for him but unable to make contact. He had no worm in his brain, and more importantly he was not one man, one mind, but two. Even as Wormboy's thoughts curled around Finlay, pulling him in, the Masked Gladiator remained free, unnoticed, waiting. He was sucked deep into Wormboy's mind, seemingly just another small victory over Mater Mundi, another spark guttering in the darkness. But the moment Wormboy clamped down on Finlay Campbell, the Masked Gladiator was released. He sprang free, arrayed as always in his familiar armour and featureless steel helm, his sword Morgana in his hands. Wormboy sensed something was wrong, and tried to recoil, but he had already brought his killer deep into his own mind. The Masked Gladiator saw the single shining light in the middle of everything that was Wormboy's private self, his inner being, his soul, and it seemed a very small thing indeed. It was the easiest thing in the world for the Masked Gladiator to step forward, take off his helm, and blow it out like a candle.

Darkness fell as Wormboy died, and his last fading scream was drowned out by the roar of triumph as the prisoners of Silo Nine burst out of his grasp, free at last. Finlay Campbell, complete again, watched them go, waited to be sure no one was left behind, and then strolled casually out into the light to take his bows.

Only when he dropped back into his own head, opened his eyes and looked around, he found himself in the middle of utter chaos. People were running everywhere, shouting and screaming, and the lights were flashing on and off. Evangeline was clinging to his arm, shouting in his ear, and Pindar was staring wildly about him. Finlay shook his head and made himself concentrate on what Evangeline was trying to tell him.

'Finlay, we have to get out of here! The prisoners have all broken free, and Mater Mundi is blasting a way out of the prison. The authorities have panicked and called in the Imperial Guards. Thousands of them are fighting it out with thousands of espers and clones. The guards are getting their ass kicked, but there's so many of them. They're everywhere! They'll be here soon. We have to get out of here, Finlay, while we still can.'

'All right,' said Finlay. 'I'm back. How many of us are there?'

'Just us three. The others are off fighting. The Stevie Blues are in their element. Half of Silo Nine must be burning by now.'

'So what's the problem? We'll just go back the way we came, and get out under cover of the fighting.'

'You don't understand,' said Pindar. 'They're bringing in esp-blockers. Hundreds of them. Our people will be helpless. Unarmed. The guards will slaughter them.'

Finlay raised a hand to interrupt him, and thought hard.

They couldn't have come this far, achieved so much, just to fail now.

'I've got an idea,' he said finally. 'I have an implant, a very tricky piece of quality tech, that enables me to sneak past security systems without being noticed. We'll patch it into the prison's systems via my comm implant, knock out the surveillance, and then everyone makes a run for it. A lot of people won't make it, but most should. It's not much of a plan, but it's the best chance we've got.'

'Do it,' said Pindar. 'I'll pass the word to the others.'

He turned away, and both of them concentrated, in their separate ways.

Finlay and Evangeline made it out. Pindar didn't. Gut shot by a guard he never saw. Finlay killed the guard, but it didn't make any difference. They carried Pindar as far as they could, and left him where he died. They never did find Evangeline's friend, the one she'd gone in specially to look for. The Stevie Blues got out, riding a wall of flame. More than half the prisoners managed to escape in the end, streaming out under the unseeing eyes of the security cameras, before the esp-blockers could be deployed. But hundreds of espers and clones died anyway, and more were captured. They were led away in restraints, neutered by the esp-blockers. Many suicided, rather than be taken again.

The man who used to be called Hood walked unhurriedly through Silo Nine's corridors, his cowl pushed well back to reveal himself as the Lord High Dram. Some of the underground prisoners spat at him, before the guards clubbed them down, but Dram just smiled. There were bodies everywhere, and he had to step over and around them. Parts of the prison were still burning. And Wormboy was dead. On the whole, he had to admit his operation to crush the underground had not been as successful as he'd hoped.

But a great many espers and clones were dead, and the guards had captured as many as had escaped. The underground's plan to break out all the prisoners had been foiled. The prison could be repaired, and they could always grow another Wormboy. Eventually. More importantly, Mater Mundi had been forced to reveal herself, and the extent of her powers. And that was worth a great many dead guards. She'd find it a lot harder to find a bushel to hide her light under now. The underground would be scattered again, thanks to his knowledge of their inner workings. His people were already raiding the appropriate locations. It would take the underground years to recover and regroup.

As Hood, he could identify many names and faces, including Finlay Campbell, Evangeline Shreck and Valentine Wolfe. Finlay didn't matter any more, but the other knowledge should give him great power over the Shrecks and the Wolfes. They would be only too willing to bow to him, to prevent their names becoming a scandal. Power like that was worth a lot.

The Empress would take steps to see that this operation was seen by everyone as a great success, playing up the gains and turning a blind eye to the losses. It should be more than enough to justify her making him her official consort. And he even had some captured cyberats to give to Lionstone, to help her with her problems in the Matrix. They'd cooperate, rather than face conditioning. And finally, the captured clones and espers would make fine subjects for his experiments with the esper drug. As official consort, no one would be able to deny him access to the prisoners, or ask what became of them afterwards.

Dram smiled and smiled as he walked, and the guards gave him plenty of room, especially when he started to chuckle aloud.

CHAPTER THIRTEEN

The Madness Maze

It was black as the deepest pit of hell, and not a light anywhere. Once there had been stars, burning bright in the darkness, but they were gone. No suns shone in the Darkvoid, and its frozen planets sailed silently in a night without end. The Last Standing of the original Deathstalker dropped out of hyperspace without a murmur, and drifted into orbit around the lifeless rock of the Wolfling World, also known as lost Haden. The castle hung above the planet in a halo of its own light, a huge stone structure with towers and battlements, looking down over an endless abyss. The light didn't travel far, as though the darkness resented it, but some of it touched the Wolfling World, gleaming gently on the frozen atmosphere. There was no sign of life on the planet; all its mysteries were deep underground, safely concealed in the hidden heart of lost Haden.

Inside the Standing, the small group of rebels stood before a wide viewscreen that showed what it could of the planet below. Owen Deathstalker, outlawed Lord of Virimonde, who still thought himself an historian rather than a warrior. Hazel d'Ark, pirate, bon vivant and reluctant rebel. Jack Random, the professional rebel, and Ruby Journey, the bounty hunter. Tobias Moon, the augmented man, come home at last. And Giles, the original Deathstalker, creator of the Darkvoid. They looked at the darkness he had brought about by the snuffing out of a thousand suns, and felt a little of the long night's chill seep into their bones. There were still stars on the far side of the Rim, outside the Darkvoid, but something in the void's essential nature prevented any light from entering. Owen found his hand had fallen instinctively to the sword on his hip. There was something dangerous, even threatening about such absolute darkness.

'Welcome to the Wolfling World,' said Giles. He was still wrapped in his battered, greasy furs, and was gnawing on his third protein cube. Apparently being kept in stasis for over nine centuries had given him something of an appetite. Owen had tried one of the protein cubes earlier, on learning it was the only kind of food the castle could currently produce, and had decided very definitely that he'd rather go hungry. Giles wiped his mouth on the back of his hand, and studied the Darkvoid with enigmatic eyes.

'This is the first light that planet has seen in nine hundred and forty-three years. I suppose it's only fitting that I should be the one to bring back the light, since I was the one who took it away. Sometimes I wonder if there are things living in the dark places between the planets, dark creatures, thriving in the endless night I brought about in a moment of fury and weakness.

'The last time I was here, this was a living world, brimming with life. There were oceans and continents, beasts of the earth and of the air, cities and people. There were beautiful birds with tails of fire, and tourists flew through the Sighing Mountains on chartered gravity sleds. All gone now, crushed under the weight of a frozen atmosphere. All that remains are the Madness Maze and the Hall of the Fallen, and the cities and laboratories of lost Haden, quarried deep in the heart of the planet. Undisturbed for so long, waiting for us to awaken them.'

'Tell us about the Wolflings,' said Hazel. She kept her eyes on the viewscreen, her hands automatically polishing her sword blade with a dirty rag that also served as a handkerchief. 'You said they were created here.'

'Yes. Born and died here, all but one. They were the Empire's first try at creating genetically engineered soldiers. A pinch of man, a pinch of wolf, and a few special ingredients. It took them a while to get the mix just right, but finally they ended up with a living killing machine, unparalleled in human evolution. The Wolfling.'

'So what went wrong?' said Ruby. She was watching Giles with her usual impassive face, her pale features almost ghostly above her black leathers. Owen couldn't help noticing that she had her hand resting near her sword too.

'Nothing went wrong with the Wolflings,' said Giles. 'They were everything they were supposed to be, and more besides. It was the more that upset the scientists. The Wolflings were smart, far smarter than their human masters. Faster, stronger, more savage and smarter too. The scientists saw the possible shape of things to come, and panicked. They called in the Imperial forces, lured the Wolflings to an arranged meeting, and shot them down from ambush. Of course, the Wolflings fought back. Killed a lot of men before they finally went down. Some got away, and had to be hunted down. The Empire lost a lot more soldiers doing that, but eventually they got them all. Except for one. The best of the best, and the most cunning. He evaded capture, and all the traps they set. He was still here when the Empire finally gave up, and the Imperial forces went home. Sightings grew less and less, until finally he became just another myth, a legend, a story to tell newcomers. Of course he wasn't really dead. He'd gone underground.

'He was still here when the Darkvoid fell, and everyone but he died.

'He was still here when the scientists of lost Haden ventured into the Darkvoid, in search of a safe place to hide their laboratories. He watched as they experimented upon themselves, designing ever more intricate hybrids of man and machine. The Hadenmen. He was there when they went out to conquer the Empire, and when they came limping back, defeated, to hide themselves away in their Tomb, and wait for a better time. He's down there now, watching and waiting, impossibly old, incredibly powerful, standing guard over the Madness Maze and the Hall of the Fallen.'

'How do you know so much about it?' said Random. 'You were in stasis on Shandrakor while most of this was going on.'

'The Wolfling has been talking to my computers,' said Giles.

'And they have been talking to me. Apparently he's been waiting quite some time for someone he could trust as an ally, and my reputation as a warrior seems to have preceded me. I can only assume he doesn't know of my creation of the Darkvoid. He's waiting to talk to us. Let's all be very polite, and perhaps he won't kill us.'

'He could try,' said Ruby.

'What do we need him for?' said Moon.

'I told you; he guards the Madness Maze.'

'And what's that when it's at home?' said Hazel. 'Something the Haden scientists came up with?'

'Oh no, my dear; it's much older than that. There's nothing human about the Madness Maze. It was here long before humanity ever came to this world. The Empire colonists discovered it, deep within the planet, but they never did discover what it was. The Haden scientists deduced its function, but they had more important matters on their minds, the fools.'

'All right,' said Owen. 'I'll bite. What is the purpose of the Madness Maze?'

'Evolution,' said Giles. 'And I am the only one ever to make use of its secrets. Now let's go down and say hello to the Wolfling. By the way, a word to the wise. He is currently under the misapprehension that we have a whole army of rebels on board this ship. Let's not disillusion him. You never know when you might need to run a bluff.'

'How do we get down there?' said Moon. His harsh, buzzing voice sounded as calm as it ever did, but his blazing golden eyes never once looked away from the planet on the viewscreen. 'Do you have any pinnaces or shuttle craft on this floating anachronism?'

'As it happens, yes, but we can't use them. There's no way to reach the Maze or the Tomb of the Hadenmen from the surface any more. What remains of the atmosphere has frozen solid. We'll teleport down. I left a portal close to the Maze the last time I was here. According to the Standing's instruments it's still functioning. We built things to last in my day. When we weren't busy destroying them. If you'd all care to prepare yourselves as you see fit, we can go as soon as you're ready. Feel free to help yourselves to anything that catches your interest in the armoury, but don't take too long about it. The Standing's power sources were nearly depleted when I came to Shandrakor, all those centuries ago, and most of what was left was used up maintaining the Standing. Until I have the opportunity to recharge the power cells, this ship isn't going anywhere. We're in no immediate danger, but unless you like the idea of being stranded on a world whose only points of interest are an alien Maze and a large Tomb, I suggest we all hurry.'

Owen and Hazel made their way down to the armoury, where an empty suit of armour with a missing helm politely opened the door for them. Owen regarded it suspiciously. He didn't remember it being there the last time he'd visited the armoury. Hazel ignored the armour and made straight for the more impressive-looking projectile weapons. Owen watched amusedly as she loaded herself down with guns and bandoliers of ammunition. He settled for a nasty-looking handgun that used big, bulky bullets, and a few grenades to fill his pockets. No doubt they'd come in handy, but on the whole he still thought he'd stick with the weapons he was used to. Guns were all very well, but in his experience, in the end it always came down to cold steel, and the man wielding it. Besides, at the rate Hazel was accumulating guns, they'd have to move her around on a trolley. She continued rooting through the rifle racks, unaware of his growing amusement, and finally came up with a gun so long and heavy it took all her strength just to lift and aim it.

'Good choice,' said Owen solemnly. 'When you run out of ammunition, you can use it to club the enemy to death.'

Hazel sniffed, and reluctantly put the rifle back. She looked at her collection of guns, and grinned suddenly at Owen.

'Come a long way, haven't we, aristo? From a not particularly successful pirate and an outlawed Lord running for his life, to the leaders of a new rebellion. Who'd have thought it?'

'We're only potentially a rebellion,' said Owen. 'It's going to take a hell of a lot more than the six of us to drag Lionstone off the Iron Throne. Jack Random's been fighting the Empire all his life, and you saw what it's done to him. All right, if we can awaken the Hadenmen, and if we can persuade them to fight on our side, then we might be in with a chance. All kinds of people might rally to our banner if they thought we already had an army. But I'm not at all happy about placing any trust in Hadenmen. Who's to say they wouldn't be following their own, hidden, agenda? They killed a lot of innocent people in their last attempt at a rebellion. The only reason they're not still officially designated the Enemies of Humanity is because the AIs on Shub are even nastier than the Hadenmen were. And that took some doing.'

'You worry too much,' said Hazel. 'The Hadenmen will behave themselves as long as we've got control of the Darkvoid Device. You know, these are really great guns. I've been studying their specifics in the computers. They aren't worth spit against force shields, but they'll chew up anything else you aim them at. And with these, you don't have to wait two minutes between each shot. Just lock and load, and keep the trigger pressed down. Apparently there's something called a recoil we'll have to get used to, but no doubt we'll soon get the hang of it.'

'Until we run out of ammunition,' said Owen. 'We can't just run back to the castle for more in the middle of a firefight. With a disrupter, you can recharge the energy crystals at any handy power source, and you're ready to go again.'

'You always have to see the bad side of things, don't you? The point is, the Empire won't be expecting guns like these, and by the time they've worked out an effective response, we'll have kicked six different colours of shit out of them.'

Owen frowned. 'You really think the Empire is going to follow us here? Into the Darkvoid?'

'Of course. Don't you?'

'Yes,' said Owen unhappily. 'They've been right behind us all the way. There's only one answer that makes any sense. We have a traitor in our group.'

'Not necessarily,' said Hazel. 'Someone could have planted a homing device on us.'

'No. One or other of our security systems would have found it by now. It's too obvious.'

'But . . . none of us have any reason to betray the group! We've all got good reasons for being here, and none of us have any reason to love the Empire.'

'How about fear? Or blackmail? Or money. There's a hell of a lot of credits on our heads these days. People will break under all kinds of pressure.'

Hazel glared at him. 'Anyone you feel like pointing the finger at?'

'No,' said Owen steadily. 'Not at the moment. Perhaps I'm wrong. We've all been through a lot. Sometimes I feel guilty at dragging you all into my problems.'

'Don't. I'm having a great time. And you didn't drag me into anything. I chose to save your sorry ass on Virimonde. And you saved my life on Mistworld, so we're even.'

'I couldn't let you die.'

'Why not?'

'You matter to me,' said Owen slowly. 'I've never met anyone like you, Hazel.'

Hazel looked at him, and raised an eyebrow. 'Don't start getting ideas, stud. This is strictly a marriage of convenience.'

'Relax. Deathstalkers only marry for status. You're entirely safe.'

Hazel decided to change the subject. 'How many men do you think the Iron Bitch will send after us?'

'At least one starcruiser, possibly two. We've made her people look bad so far, and she won't like that. We can expect full contingents of attack troops, maybe even Wampyr and battle espers. And whether she knows the Device is here or not, this has got to be a matter of pride for her now. If she doesn't stamp on us hard, and soon, her own people will start thinking she's losing control of things. And some of them might try a little quiet insurrection of their own, to test the waters. No; Lionstone will send as many troops as it takes to bring us down.'

477

'Good,' said Hazel, hefting a rifle and smiling at the weight of it. 'Let them all come.'

'You worry me sometimes,' said Owen.

Jack Random and Ruby Journey had already outfitted themselves at the armoury with a good selection of weapons, and were currently in the kitchen, trying to persuade the food machines to dispense anything other than protein cubes. They'd tried every combination of codes, including shouting at the machine and giving it a swift kick or two, but all they got for their troubles was more protein cubes. There were stories of marooned starfarers who'd eaten each other rather than live off protein cubes, and Jack could understand why. But he was hungry, and at his age his body needed all the fuel it could get, so he made himself eat all of one cube and part of another. People had been awarded medals for less.

Ruby had refused point blank to touch the things, but brightened up considerably on discovering the machine could dispense a really quite drinkable wine. She got through half a bottle while Jack was struggling with his cubes, and got quite chatty, for her. Normally, getting conversation out of the bounty hunter was like pulling teeth. To be fair, she was an action person, and most of the time really didn't have anything to say. But Jack persevered, on the grounds that anything that might take his mind off what he was eating had to be a good thing, and they talked on and off for a while, mostly swapping anecdotes on particular fights and battles, and the best ways to kill people.

'Why did you become a bounty hunter in the first place?' said Random eventually. 'It's not an occupation that appeals to everybody.'

'I was good at it,' said Ruby. 'And the alternatives were worse. Can you see me sitting at a desk in sensible clothes shuffling files, or married to some dirt farmer with a dozen kids hanging from my apron strings?'

'Not really, no.'

'Damn right. They married me off at fourteen, to the local collector of the water rates. It was either that, or one of my

478

cousins. He was big and heavy, with clammy hands. He thought it was fun to knock me about. He did other things too. I waited till he was asleep one night, and then stabbed him in the throat with a carving knife. I watched him die. It took quite a long time. That was when I first realized I had a taste for excitement. I gathered up everything valuable that wasn't nailed down, torched the place and ran for the starport. I've been on my own ever since, and I like it that way. Less complicated.'

'Have you done much work for the Empire?'

'Sure. They're the ones paying the bounties, mostly. But I'm not prejudiced. I'll work for anyone with money.'

'So what are you doing with us?'

'I never could resist a challenge. Besides, I was promised all the loot I could handle. Not that I've seen any of it yet.'

'How did you get to be friends with Hazel?'

'You're just full of questions, aren't you?' Ruby took a long drink from her bottle. 'Ran across her in Mistport, when we were both down on our luck. She got me out of a close call, and pretty much adopted me. I didn't get a say in the matter. I'd have dumped her years ago, but there are times when it's good to have someone you can trust to guard your back. Time for you to answer some questions. How did you get to be a professional rebel?'

'I'm surprised you haven't heard. It was quite a famous story, in its day. But I suppose that was some time ago, and my legend isn't as respected as it once was. I was a lesser son of a lesser House, of no importance to anyone, not even myself. I drank, played cards, tried a little of this and a little of that, running up debts all the way. Then I got a serving maid pregnant, and my Family sent me to run a mining planet out near the Rim, to keep me out of trouble. Planet called Trigann. Horrible place.

'I'd never been outside my pampered world before, and the reality of how the other ninety-seven per cent live horrified me. The conditions the miners lived in, and the way they and their families were treated were a disgrace even by Empire standards, so instead of stamping out their rebellion, I joined it, and somehow ended up leading the damn thing. And like you, I found something I was good at, and decided to stick with it.

'You see, I'd never really thought about how the Empire was run before. It was just there; the way things were. Trigann opened my eyes to how the comforts of the few were being produced by the suffering of the many. It also taught me that you can fight back. That sometimes you can make a difference. The more rebellions I led, the more evil I found. The Empire is intrinsically corrupt. The only hope for justice and compassion for its people is the complete overthrow of the Iron Throne. I used to talk about creating change from within, but it didn't take me long to discover that there are just too many people with a vested interest in keeping things the way they are. I've killed a lot of them, but there are always more. The only hope is for the people to rise up and take control of their own lives. So I used to go from planet to planet, preaching insurrection, and raising armies to protect the weak and the powerless, and punish the guilty. The odds were always against us, but we won a few, now and then. Enough to make me a legend and a rallying point throughout the Empire.'

'Until they caught you.'

'Yes. I was getting old and slow, and I trusted the wrong people. I've always been too trusting.' He sat quietly for a long time, staring at the half-eaten cube in his hands as though it could tell him something. 'They broke me,' he said finally. 'I was so sure I'd rather die first, but no, they broke me. I would have said anything, done anything, betrayed anyone, just so they wouldn't hurt me any more.'

'But you didn't.'

'No. Turned out I still had a few real friends after all. They got me out, though most of them died doing it. I never even knew their names.'

Ruby nodded once. 'Everyone breaks, in the end.'

'Yes. Even legends like Jack Random. Sometimes I think he died in that cell, and there's nothing left now but his shadow. My real friends hadn't given up on me, but I gave up on them. I wouldn't lead their rebellion, I wouldn't help them fight. I didn't want to do anything but hide in a dark room where my tormentors couldn't find me. After a while, my friends realized I was no use to them and never would be, but they still didn't give up on me. They smuggled me to Mistworld, the one place where the Empire wouldn't follow me. A place where everyone has secrets, but nobody cares. I dived into the shadows and disappeared there. I took a new name. It wasn't difficult. I didn't look much like a legend any more. I quite liked being Jobe Ironhand. No one expected anything from him.'

'All that time, hiding in plain sight,' said Ruby. 'I spent a lot of time looking for you. I could have used the money. And there you were, right under my nose.' She smiled briefly. 'I'm glad I didn't find you then. I would have been so disappointed. You're different, now.'

Random raised an eyebrow. 'I am?'

'Sure. You're waking up. You aren't what you used to be, but you're getting there. What did it, Random? What lured you back into the spotlight?'

'You want the truth? I was bored. Simple as that. I'm still scared most of the time, and my hands shake when they think I'm not looking, but anything's better than pushing that damn broom around any more. There were quite a few days when even death seemed better than that. So here I am; one last fight for an old champion, well past his prime.'

'You did well enough in the jungle,' said Ruby. 'Lots of people wouldn't have survived to reach the Standing. Don't talk yourself down, Random. I never had much use for legends. I killed a lot of them, looking for one real one, but they died as easily as anyone else. You impress me a lot more than most of them.'

'Thank you,' said Random. 'Good thing you didn't find me. It would have been such a pity if I'd killed you before I got to know you.'

Ruby grinned briefly, and offered him her bottle. 'Drink?'

'Wish I could. My system can't handle it any more. Kidneys took a few beatings too many. You drink. I'll enjoy it vicariously.'

'You feel that way about all your pleasures?'

'Not necessarily,' said Random. 'If I was just twenty years younger, I'd chase you round this table a few times.'

'Great,' said Hazel, from the doorway. 'Just what we needed. A drunken bounty hunter and a horny legend. The Empire troops will take one look and piss themselves from sheer terror.'

'I admire the man's courage,' said Owen, beside her. 'I wouldn't want to get within ten feet of Ruby Journey without a chair and a whip.'

'Always knew you aristos were into the kinky stuff,' said Ruby. 'I'd offer you a drink, but I've only got the one bottle.'

'I'll join you,' said Hazel. 'I could use a drink of something even half-way decent.'

'Ah yes,' said Random. 'You always did have a weakness for drink, as I recall.'

Hazel looked at him. 'You recall? I wasn't aware we'd met before.'

'It was some time ago, on Mistworld. Someone recognized me and invited me to dinner. And I went because I was hungry. You were working for my host as a ladies' maid. They were short of staff, and they pressed you into service at the dinner table.'

Ruby's head came up, and she looked at Hazel with a slow grin spreading across her face. 'You were a ladies' maid, Hazel?'

'How the hell would you remember me?' said Hazel, glaring at Random.

'I have an excellent memory for faces. Besides; you spilled most of a bottle of rather good port over me. Ruined the last good pair of trousers I had.'

'You were a ladies' maid?' said Ruby.

Hazel scowled. 'I said I was sorry.'

'No you didn't. You said . . .'

'Never mind what I said!'

'You brought it up.'

'You were a *ladies' maid*?' said Ruby.

'Sure,' said Random. 'She looked very pretty in the uniform, too.'

'I'll bet,' said Ruby.

'If any of you tell anyone else, I'll kill you,' said Hazel.

'I believe her,' said Owen.

'Don't worry, sweetie,' said Ruby, still grinning. 'Your secret is safe with us.'

'There's something I wanted to ask you, Random,' said Hazel, in the manner of someone determined to change the subject. 'Owen and I were talking about some of the campaigns you fought in. You led rebellions that covered entire worlds, commanded whole armies. Even had your own attack fleet, at one time. What I want to know is; where did all the money come from? Wars are expensive. Men, supplies, guns. Who funded all those armies and attack ships? I never heard you were independently wealthy. So who paid the bills?'

'Men of good will,' said Jack Random. 'Mostly. The rest came from anywhere I could raise it. There were always people around with an interest in seeing authority toppled, or at least challenged. Political groups, persecuted religions, businessmen who stood to make a profit from war. Young nobles who couldn't wait to inherit, or were looking for a little excitement. There were always factions jostling for position within the Empire, ready to sell each other out for a moment's advantage. I learned not to ask too many questions.

'After all, as I told myself on more than one occasion, lesser evils are better than greater ones. And I could always lead another rebellion against the new people in power, if necessary. There was never any shortage of courageous, idealistic young cannon fodder in those days.

'Never any shortage of loot, either. I took what I had to, in order to do what I had to. And if sometimes I had to deal with scum, or place my trust in men of evil, well, there was already too much blood on my hands for me to ever be innocent again.' He smiled at Owen. 'You're looking quite shocked, Deathstalker. Sorry; I seem to be just one disappointment after another for you, but that's life. My life, anyway. And now, if you'll excuse me, I think I'll take a little walk; limber up the old muscles before we have to go dirtside. Play nicely, now.'

He left the kitchen without looking back. He'd said all he

felt like saying. No doubt they'd talk about him while he was gone, but they'd have done that anyway, and he preferred not to be around when they did it. He made himself be patient until he was well out of their way, and then he stopped and produced a battered silver flask from an inner pocket. He unscrewed the cap with steady fingers, raised the flask to his mouth and took a good swallow of the bland, almost tasteless liquid. He might not be able to handle booze any more, but he'd be no use at all without an occasional jolt of the good stuff. He looked at the silver flask and sighed quietly. There was a time he'd thought battle drugs were just for cowards and fools, but time had taught him differently. Sometimes it seemed the only courage he had left came out of that flask. And he did so want to be a legend again, if only for his new friends' sake. They'd been through so much already, and faced so much more. They needed a legend. Jack Random sighed, raised the flask to his mouth, and then lowered it again without drinking. He screwed the cap back on, and put the flask back in his pocket.

He strode on down the quiet corridor, his footsteps echoing back from the stone walls. His legs felt firmer, and he was breathing more easily. Give him some time, and a few more jolts of the right stuff, and he might be some good in a fight after all. He smiled sadly, remembering the feisty young warrior he once was. Ready to draw his blade at the drop of an insult, to avenge a lady's honour, or his own, or just because he was the best and no one could touch him. A crack shot with any kind of gun, he could pilot any damn thing that flew, and plot strategy with the best generals the rebellion had to offer. He'd forged his legend day by day, world by world, and he'd made the Empire fear him as it feared no other.

But that was a long time ago now. War takes a lot out of you, and one of the first things it takes is your youth. He'd grown old and hard on the field of battle, and never missed his youth till it was gone. But he still had to be the best. People needed him, depended on him, believed in him. For a long time that was all he needed, drawing his strength from the fervour of their belief. But as the years wore on, and failure after failure wore him down, he turned first to drink and then to drugs, and finally to battle drugs. At first he had reasons, and then excuses, until finally there was only the need. On Mistworld he'd learned to live without them, as he learned to do without courage or honour. A janitor's world was simple and undemanding, and he gratefully lost himself in it. He just took a drop now and again, to get his heart started on cold mornings. Or for emergencies, like now, when he really didn't feel like Jack Random at all.

He found Tobias Moon in a side room, sitting alone, looking at the frozen planet below on a viewscreen. The Hadenman's face was as cold and emotionless as ever, and he sat stiffly in his chair, as though only waiting there because he'd been told to wait, when all he wanted was to be going. Random hesitated in the doorway, uncertain whether it was wise or necessary to disturb Moon, and then the Hadenman spoke suddenly without turning round.

'Come in, Jack Random. It's been a long time since we talked together before a battle.'

Random swore silently, and did his best to seem relaxed and confident as he entered the room and pulled up a chair beside Moon. Although the Hadenman claimed to have fought at his side during the Cold Rock campaign, Random couldn't honestly say he remembered the man. Cold Rock had been a hard and bloody struggle, with a lot of good men killed, but even so he should have remembered a Hadenman. They'd been extremely scarce on the ground after their failed rebellion, mainly because most people shot them on sight, just in case. But Random had to admit his memory wasn't what it was, like so many other things in his life. Some things were still crystal clear, but some were lost forever, and more were confused. The Empire mind techs had really done a good job on him. He wriggled surreptitiously on the hard chair, trying to get comfortable, and wondered what the hell he was going to talk about. The Hadenman spoke first.

'I have no memory of being here, in the city or laboratories of lost Haden. I was quickened off-world, on a ship between planets, between battles. The rebellion was going badly, and my superiors needed all the units they could muster. I fought in many battles, on many worlds, following the orders of my superiors. I killed men and women and children. After the rebellion most of my people were dead or fled back to Haden, to their Tomb, and I was abandoned to my own devices. I had no idea where Haden was. For a time I continued fighting. It was what I knew. I fought on many sides, on many planets; but all the causes looked the same to me, and I grew bored. I travelled for a few years, searching for new challenges, but already my energy crystals were becoming depleted, and the technology necessary to recharge or replace them could only be found in Empire strongholds, where my kind would find no welcome. Eventually, I ended up on Mistworld, little better than any human.

'Can you understand what that meant; to be merely human? I had been capable of so much; I was strong and fast and my senses saw so much more of the universe than your simple organics. But every day I grew weaker, and saw less, and my thoughts were no longer quicksilver fast.

'For a long time, I existed only to exist. I had no plans, no hope, no future. And then word came of the outlawed Death-stalker, and I remembered the intrigues of his Family, and dared to hope again. He led me to you, and then brought me home, to lost Haden, and the Tomb of my people. I have a chance to be complete again, among my own kind. I owe him everything. But once my people are awakened, I must follow the orders of my superiors once again; whatever they might be.'

Random frowned. 'You think they might refuse to join the Deathstalker's rebellion against the Empire? Surely they'll see that it has to be in their best interests to join with us?'

'You don't understand. You and your fellow rebels are all human, and for a long time that was just another word for enemy. It is a central creed of Hadenman thought that we were created to replace you. You are weak, soft, inferior. But I have lived among you, and I have seen strengths and potential that my young race as yet lacks. They would say you have infected me with your weaknesses. Perhaps they are right. I truly do not know whether I am a Hadenman, a human, or something else, less or more than both. I have waited so long to be a part of my people again, to be a fully functioning augmented man, but now . . . I am not sure where I truly belong. I'm not sure of anything any more.'

'You're bound to be nervous. That's only human.'

'But I am not supposed to be human. I shouldn't even be thinking these thoughts. I am a Hadenman, the next evolutionary step forward in our species. That's what my people will say when they walk out from their Tomb. I have finally returned home, to lost Haden, only to find it does not feel like home at all.'

The Hadenman rose abruptly to his feet and left the room, moving silently and gracefully with his usual inhumanly perfect poise. Random didn't go after him. He doubted he could have kept up with Moon, and even if he had, he didn't know what he would have said. What do you say to a man mourning the loss of his own inhumanity? So Random sat back in his uncomfortable chair and studied the viewscreen, wondering if he should tell the others what he'd heard. The frozen planet stared back at him, mute and enigmatic. He heard footsteps approaching, and turned quickly in his chair in case it was Moon coming back. But the man in the doorway was the original Deathstalker, the man called Giles. He looked tired, and perhaps just a little lost. He gestured for Random to stay seated, and sank into the chair beside him. He looked at the world on the viewscreen, and sniffed once.

'Ugly planet. And it was so beautiful once. I never thought to see it again. When I landed the Last Standing on Shandrakor, I was expecting to die. Everyone's hand was turned against me. Some for using the Darkvoid Device, some because I was determined it would never be used again. No one was more surprised than I when the dust finally settled and I found I'd killed all the people sent to kill me. Part of me had wanted to die. So I went into stasis, in the hope that things would work themselves out before I had to waken again. I should have known better. Things are more complicated now than they were before. Three different kinds of augmented men, rogue AIs, an insane Empress on the Iron Throne, and not one but two possible alien threats. And my descendant, the Deathstalker of this time, is an historian.'

'He's a good man,' said Random. 'He fights well, when he has to, and he has a good head on his shoulders. He cares about people and mostly for the right reasons. You could have done a lot worse.'

'I hear much the same about you,' said Giles. 'They tell me you're a famous warrior, and a great leader of the rebellion.'

Random sighed. 'Maybe once. I'm not sure any more. I spent most of my life fighting on one world after another, giving up all hope of love or family or a normal life, just to lead a struggle whose end was always just over the next horizon. I saw good men die, over and over again, many better men than me, and all for nothing. The Empire's as strong now as it ever was, and I'm just an old man with nowhere safe to lay his head.'

'It's not whether we win or lose,' said Giles. 'It's how many of the bastards we can take with us. Anyone can look away and pretend they don't see evil, as long as it doesn't affect them. But a man of honour has no choice but to stand up and do something. Whatever happens, you and I have lived the life we chose. Too many people live the lives other people think they ought to; following orders they don't agree with, for causes they don't believe in; live lives that don't matter, that touch no one and change nothing. For better or worse, you and I stared evil in the eye and didn't flinch. We raised our swords and went to war, and even if we didn't win we kicked some ass along the way. We made a difference, and that's all any man can ask.'

'Yes,' said Jack Random. 'We got a lot of people killed who followed us expecting miracles. Aren't you ever bothered by ghosts, Giles?'

'Of course. Some of them are waiting for me on the planet below. But I make my decisions based on the future, not the past. Ghosts have to know their place.'

'It must be wonderful to be so strong, so sure,' said Random.

'To have all the answers. If you have a moment, pity us poor mortals with our doubts and failings.'

He got up and left, brushing past Owen in the doorway without speaking to him. Owen turned to watch him stalk away down the corridor, and then looked at Giles.

'What's got into him?'

'He's just feeling his age. Preparing for battle will do that to you. It's a time to open your heart to strangers, and hope for absolution. Is that what you've come to me for, kinsman?'

'No. I was just passing and heard voices.'

'So how are you feeling? Ready for the fray?'

'I suppose so. It's not as though I have any choice in the matter, is it? Ever since this all began, I've been harried from planet to planet, with the bad guys never more than a few minutes behind me. No time to think, let alone rest. And no matter which way I turn, all I hear is duty, duty. Fight for this cause, fight for that, fight just for the right to stay alive. What choices have I had recently?'

'There are always choices, kinsman. You can choose to fight or to run, to be strong or weak. To take joy in fighting the good fight, and never bowing to a villain. You come from a Family of warriors, that never surrendered to greater odds, or struck for a peace they didn't believe in. We have a tradition of facing and rising above whatever obstacles fate places in our path, and meeting our enemies with cold steel in our hands and a smile on our lips. We have always been heroes, warriors, men of destiny.'

'Save the pep speech for someone who believes in it,' said Owen. 'I've been hearing that shit all my life. It didn't save my father when the Empire sent a master swordsman after him, and it won't save us when Lionstone's forces arrive here. We are six people, facing the might of the Empire. Our chances suck. Our only hope for survival lies in waking a race of semi-human beings who might or might not wipe us out on sight, and convincing them to fight alongside us. That's assuming they don't decide to wipe out all of humanity like they tried to the last time. We are outnumbered, outgunned, and out of luck. I'm an historian; I've seen what happens to rebellions without massive funding, big armies and a solid power base. We don't stand a chance, Giles. The odds are we're going to die, and die bloodily.'

Giles smiled easily. 'If we're going to die anyway, we might as well die well. Die fighting and take as many of the bastards with you as you can. If that's all that's left to you, go down still swinging your sword. Make them pay for their victory.'

'Oh, very romantic. My father would have loved you. He believed in all that crap too, but he still ended up dying alone on a main concourse, with his guts scattered over the street, while people walking by gave him plenty of room so they wouldn't get blood on their shoes. It's all right for you to talk like that. You were Warrior Prime. You led armies. I never wanted to be a warrior. All I ever wanted was to be left alone, to read my books and work on my histories. Instead, I've been forced to fight and kill people I don't even know, just so I can lead a rebellion I'm not even sure I believe in.

'Even if by some miracle we did win, what use would Jack Random's Empire have for an ex-aristocrat like me? I represent everything he and his kind want to be rid of. They'd probably end up putting me on trial for exploitation of the masses. And all your romantic talk of taking your enemies down with you; what did that lead to last time? Using the Darkvoid Device. How many billions of innocents died because of that? You know how you're remembered in my history books? As the greatest mass murderer of all time.'

'That's right,' said Giles. 'I am. I placed my trust in the Iron Throne, and it betrayed me. You have to understand how tempting the Device was then; a way to stop a systems-wide rebellion at one stroke. I wasn't even sure it would work. It was only afterwards, when the first reports began to come in, that I realized the true horror of what I'd done. In order to justify myself, I plunged into research, examining the reasons behind the rebellion. And found, to my astonishment, that they had been right all along. The Empire was cruel and corrupt, both in choice and in nature. The system itself was evil.

'So I took the Device and ran. Gave up every honour I had or hoped to achieve, to ensure that the horror of the Darkvoid would never be repeated. We do not fight here for pleasure or profit, historian, but because we must if evil is not to prevail.'

'You see?' said Owen. 'We're back to choice again. And I don't have any. I can't back out, go back to being who and what I was. A naive innocent, who never questioned where his comforts came from. I've seen too much; things I turned my head away from before. I have no excuse. I was an historian; I knew the suffering and injustice the Empire was built on. I just told myself it was nothing to do with me.

'My father lived for his intrigues against the Iron Throne. So much so that he never seemed to have any time for me. So I never had any time for his intrigues. I made my own life as a quiet, uncontroversial scholar. I should have known it wouldn't last. And once I had my face shoved into the bloody underside of the Empire, I couldn't look away any more. Too many innocents are being hurt, every day, as a matter of course. So I'll be the warrior my Family wanted me to be. I'll be a rebel and fight for the cause, and if need be die for it, but don't you ever think I'm doing this of my own will.'

'Of course you are,' said Giles. 'You said it yourself. You couldn't look away, once you saw how things really are. Same thing happened to Jack Random, to your father and to me. Everyone here thinks they're fighting for their own reasons, but in the end we'll fight and maybe die because we can't look away. We won't let ourselves. It's as good a reason to fight as any, and better than most. I've listened when the others talked of you. You're not interested in being a fighter or a hero or a leader of men; you just want to do the right thing. And that's the only kind of warrior that's worth a damn. If I had to have an historian as my descendant, I'm happy enough it's you. I could have done a lot worse.

'Now let's go round up the others. We'll be teleporting down to the Madness Maze soon, and there are things I need to discuss with all of you first. The situation down below is . . . rather complicated.'

'Now there's a surprise,' said Owen, and his ancestor laughed.

'Come, kinsman; it is a good day for someone else to die.'

Hazel d'Ark and Ruby Journey had pulled up chairs around the kitchen table, and were passing a second bottle of wine back and forth between them. They leaned well back, their heels up on the edge of the table, and rocked themselves gently. Hazel didn't much care for the wine, but she determinedly drank her share, hoping it would quiet the growing tension within her. She always got jumpy when there was action coming up. She was OK once things got started, because then she was too busy to be scared. She just hated the waiting. She looked across at Ruby's calm, impassive features, and felt like throwing something heavy at her. Nothing ever bothered Ruby.

'So,' said Ruby. 'Are you sleeping with him?'

Hazel blinked. 'With who?'

'The aristo, of course. I've seen the way he looks at you. He's pretty enough, and looks like he might know a few things.'

'Not my type,' said Hazel briskly.

'You've never been choosy before. Some of the creeps you've shacked up with would have had to take a gene test to prove they were human. You always were a sucker for a nice smile and a cute little ass. Personally, I quite fancy Moon.'

'The Hadenman? You've got to be kidding! I'm not even sure how much of him is human. He probably only does it with vending machines.'

'Still, I bet I could make him crack a smile, if I put my mind to it. Besides, I'm told Hadenmen have all kinds of . . . special augmentations. And there's always Jack Random. A bit older and more battered than I usually go for, but he was always something of a hero of mine.'

Hazel raised an eyebrow. 'I didn't think you had any heroes.'

'You don't know everything about me. And don't you dare tell him.'

'Don't worry; your sick little secrets are safe with me. Ruby; why are you still here?'

'You promised me a good fight, and all the loot I could carry. And you'll be surprised how much I can carry when I put my mind to it.'

'The odds are there isn't going to be any loot, Ruby. Odds are, we're going to die down there. The Empire could turn up here any time, and you can bet they'll come in force. I've been in my share of tight corners, but never anything like this. There's no back door this time. Just a rock and a hard place.'

'Stop hogging the bottle,' said Ruby. She took it from Hazel and hefted its weight disappointedly. 'Going to need a new one soon. Look; it's not as if we had anywhere to run. Our only way out of here is on the Standing, and since Giles is the only one who can pilot it, and he's determined to check out the Wolfling World first . . . we're stuck, girl. Look on the bright side.'

'What bright side?'

'Give me time; I'll think of something. Look; it's just another fight. Win or die, we'll have a good time.'

'But it's not just us any more. If we really can get our hands on the Darkvoid Device, and wake the Hadenmen, we'd be in a position to tell the whole damned Empire to go to hell, and make it stick. We could change everything, put everything to rights. If we die, that chance dies with us. That's what's getting me so jumpy.'

'Things happen as they happen,' said Ruby. 'And once things get this big, people like you and I don't matter any more. If we ever did. All we can do is play our part, not take any stupid risks, and try and keep from getting our heads blown off. Leave it to the heroes like Random and the Deathstalkers. We'll just keep to the sidelines, fight when we have to, and keep our eyes open for the main chance. There's got to be something down there worth stealing.'

Hazel grinned. 'Don't ever change, Ruby. Stay as mercenary, self-centred and downright vicious as you always have. The universe would seem so boring without people like you in it.'

Ruby looked at her calmly. 'I don't know what you're talking about. Sometimes I think I'm the only sane person on this ship.'

The rebels all ended up together again in front of the main viewscreen, on what passed for a bridge on the Last Standing. It was a large open area, with no visible control panels, and absolutely nowhere to sit down. Not for the first time, Owen felt more than a little superfluous. Giles lectured them in his dry, sardonic way, and they all listened with varying amounts of politeness. Even so, none of them seemed in any hurry for the briefing to be over.

'The castle's sensors show extensive workings deep below the surface of the planet,' said Giles. A map appeared on the viewscreen before them. It was intimidatingly detailed. Just looking at it made Owen's head ache. 'Most of the workings weren't here the last time I made planetfall. They form the city built by the Hadenmen. It's situated beyond the Madness Maze, and since the transfer portal I left behind is located on the opposite edge of the Maze, we have no option but to pass through the Maze to reach the city. Unfortunately.'

'And what does that mean, exactly?' said Owen. 'You've never actually explained what the Madness Maze is.'

Giles pursed his lips thoughtfully. 'It's an enigmatic structure, built by the Wolflings, not long before they were all wiped out. Well, all but one. He guards the Maze. Sometimes I think he does it not to keep people out, but to make sure the Maze doesn't escape. And whatever he knows about the Maze, he has always kept to himself. The Maze . . . is hard to describe; you'll have to see it for yourselves. I have never passed through it myself, but its function is no secret. The Maze affects the mind and body, shaping them in new, different ways. I believe it was originally intended to raise the Wolflings to the next step up on the evolutionary scale. Fortunately, and I use the word advisedly, they never got a chance to use it. I'm not sure humanity could have survived what the Wolflings might have become.'

'Hold everything,' said Hazel. 'If the Hadenmen built their

494

city beyond the Maze, does that mean they've all been through it?'

'I believe not,' said Moon. Once created, the Hadenmen went their own way. And at the end, I think they saw the Maze as just another defence for when they were sleeping in their Tomb. I feel that I should point out that there are bound to be other defences protecting the city. Theoretically, my presence should be enough to disarm them.'

'But you're not sure,' said Ruby Journey.

'No,' said Moon. 'I have never been here before.'

'This just gets better all the time,' said Jack Random. 'If the Maze doesn't get us, the city might. And that's not counting whatever the Empire finally sends after us.'

'If rebellion was simple, everyone would be doing it,' said Giles.

Random just looked at him.

They passed through the transfer portal one after the other, bristling with weapons, and found themselves on a shimmering silver plain. It stretched away around them in a vast circle, surrounded on all sides by darkness. The only structure was a tall metal door, some twelve feet tall and six feet wide, standing apparently unsupported in the exact centre of the circle. The metal was a dark bronze in colour, gleaming dully in the shimmering light from the floor. It was carved in rows of deeply etched markings from an unfamiliar language. Owen moved forward to examine the markings, and the others let him do it. Owen shot them a scornful look as they hung back, and stood as close to the door as he could without actually touching it. The etched figures teased his eyes with hints of meaning, but remained stubbornly enigmatic. He realized he could hear a faint hum emanating from the door; a low, throbbing sound that seemed almost to echo in his bones. There was a feeling of imminence on the air, of something about to happen. Owen shifted his holster on his hip so that his disrupter hung a little more readily to his hand, and brought his face right up to the markings. A dim shadowy reflection scowled back at him with cold eyes.

'Can you translate any of those scratchings?' Hazel said finally.

'Show a little respect,' said Owen, without looking away from the door. 'I've seen similar symbols on some extremely obscure records from nine centuries ago, but I think this is some kind of variant or dialect. It's got absolutely nothing at all in common with standard Empire characters. I doubt there are a dozen scholars in the Empire apart from me who would even recognize it.'

'All right, aristo, we're impressed,' said Ruby Journey. 'But can you read it? What does it say?'

'Essentially: Go away. Do not pass through this door or something extremely nasty will happen to you. Only it's not a threat. I think it's a warning . . . You're being very quiet, Giles. Anything you'd like to volunteer about this door?'

'Well, I can tell you one interesting thing about it. It wasn't here the last time I was here. None of this was. It was just an ordinary cavern, hacked out of the solid rock by the Wolflings.'

'I'll tell you something else interesting,' said Jack Random. 'That door doesn't have a reflection in the floor.'

Owen looked down automatically. He could see his own reflection in the silver floor, and those of his companions, but there was no trace at all of the door. The hairs on the back of his neck prickled uncomfortably as a cold wind caressed his neck.

'So what do we do now, ancestor?' he said finally, looking back at Giles. 'What's supposed to be here?'

'This should be the entrance to Wolfling territory, and the way to the Madness Maze. You needn't worry too much about the Wolflings; they're all dead now, of course, except for the One Who Waits. He should still be around here, somewhere.'

'After nine hundred odd years?' said Hazel. 'You mean he's in stasis here, like you were?'

'Oh no,' said Giles. 'He's immortal, you see. They all were, theoretically. That was at least part of the problem. The scientists had come up with a way to live forever, but you had to be a Wolfling for it to work. And the Wolflings, whatever else they might have been, were very definitely not human. At least, not as we understand the term. Their minds worked . . . differently. No, he should still be here. The last of his kind. Waiting.'

'Who for?' said Ruby Journey.

'You're welcome to ask him when you meet him,' said Giles. 'Personally, I could never get an answer out of him that made sense.'

'Thanks a whole bunch,' said Owen. 'That clarifies everything. Oz; can you hear me?'

'Yes, Owen,' said the AI Ozymandias in his ear. 'I'm watching everything through your implants. Unfortunately, the castle's sensors are unable to penetrate beyond where you are now. Something is blocking them. I can see the outlines of the artificial territories, but not what's in them. Except to say that for some of my readings to make sense, there'd have to be one hell of a power source somewhere close at hand. There's some really strange energies down where you are, Owen. Wish I could be more helpful, but for the time being I can only see what you see, which personally makes me very glad I'm not there.'

'Any recommendations?'

'Go through the door and see what happens.'

'Thanks a lot, Oz.' Owen studied the door carefully, and then looked back at the others. 'Unknown metal, maybe six inches thick. A disrupter should make a useful-sized hole in it. Or we could let Hazel try out one of those monster guns she's carrying. She's been dying for a chance to let rip with one. Or we could keep it simple, and use explosives. What do you think, Giles?'

'I think we should keep it civilized, and try knocking first.' Giles looked at Owen severely, and he had the grace to blush slightly. Giles moved forward to stand beside him, and the others followed. 'We can't get to the Madness Maze without passing through Wolfling territory. And I really don't think that smashing down his front door is the best way to make a good first impression.'

'Sorry,' said Owen. 'I've fallen into bad company lately.'

He turned to the metal door, took a deep breath and

knocked twice. The metal was strangely warm under his knuckles, and the sound was very quiet, as though the door had somehow soaked it up. There was a long pause, just long enough for Owen to wonder if he should knock again, and then the door swung silently backwards, revealing a dark and brooding forest.

Tall trees crowded together on either side of a narrow earth path, the thick foliage so dark a green as to seem almost black. An umber glow pierced the forest in long shafts of dust-filled light. There was a thick, solid smell of earth and mulch and growing things. Owen got as close to the opening as he could without actually passing through it, and strained his eyes against the gloom to see how far back the trees went, but there seemed no end to them. The others crowded in behind Owen, murmuring quietly to each other. There was something about the forest that demanded quiet and respect, like a living cathedral.

'Well?' Owen said finally to Giles. 'Was this here the last time you were here?'

'Oh yes,' said the original Deathstalker. 'I remember this. It's a sanctuary the Wolflings built for themselves, terraforming it out of the cold rock. What more would wolves need, than a forest to run and hunt in?'

'Is it safe?' said Owen.

'How should I know?' said Giles. 'A lot could have changed in the nine hundred and forty-three years since I was last here.'

'Great,' said Owen. 'Wonderful. All right; pay attention, everyone. Anybody else feel like leading the way? No? I didn't think so. Follow me, then. Hazel, you tuck in right behind me, and keep that big gun of yours at the ready. Let's try and be calm about this, people, but feel free to blast large holes in anything that looks dangerous. This doesn't strike me as safe territory. Something here is tugging at my instincts and putting my nerves on edge. Everyone stay close, but don't crowd each other. And don't go off on your own under any circumstances. I think this could be a really unfriendly place to be lost in. When we meet the Wolfling, remember we're guests here, so mind your manners and watch the bad language.'

'He really does like making speeches, doesn't he?' said Ruby.

'It's part of his charm,' said Hazel.

'What charm?'

'Precisely.'

Owen didn't look back at them. He wouldn't give them the satisfaction. He checked his sword and his guns, to be sure they were ready to hand, and stepped through the doorway. The heat hit him like a smothering blanket, and he almost stopped, but he made himself go on. The rich dark smell of the forest was almost overpowering, and the heavy heat brought sweat to his face that evaporated almost as fast as it formed. The bare earth path was firm under his boots, but not level, and he didn't need to be told that no machinery had ever travelled this route. Owen kept walking, doing his best to appear casual and totally at ease, just in case anyone was watching. The light in the forest was dim and slightly diffused, as though a very fine mist filled the air. Owen glanced back to make sure the others were still with him, and almost missed a step as he saw the forest stretching far away behind him, till it disappeared into its own gloom. The open door stood alone in the middle of the trail, with only a glimpse of the silver plain to be seen through the doorway, like a glimpse of another world. As he watched, the great metal door slammed shut with a quiet, emphatic thud.

'Ever get the feeling that someone's trying to tell you something?' said Hazel.

'I think we can safely assume someone knows we're here,' said Owen. 'Which is just as well. I have a strong feeling we're not going to get very far around here without a friendly guide.'

'I don't like the idea of our retreat being cut off,' said Random. 'Our only way back to the Standing is via the transfer portal, and that's on the other side of the door, which I will lay good odds we won't be able to open.'

'He has a point,' said Owen. 'I don't even know how it opened from the other side.'

'We could blast it,' said Ruby.

'Yeah,' said Hazel, hefting her heavy gun with great enthusiasm.

'Let's keep that as a last option,' said Giles. 'We're supposed to be here as friends, remember? If we follow this trail it should lead us to the Wolfling. Lead on, Owen, and try not to step on anything delicate.'

'Hold it,' said Ruby. 'Can anyone tell me what's wrong with this picture?' They all looked around them, and then back at Ruby. She smiled briefly. 'The quiet. No birds, no movement, even the air is still. Apart from the trees, I'd say we're the only living things here.'

'Of course,' said Giles. 'This isn't a real forest. It's an artificial construct the Wolflings built to make themselves feel more comfortable. Those aren't real trees, any more than this is real sunlight.'

Owen frowned. 'You mean these trees are fakes?'

'Oh they're real enough. Alive too, just artificial. How else do you think they've survived down here all these centuries?'

Owen decided he wasn't going to ask any more questions. He didn't like the answers he was getting. He set off down the path, and the others followed him. They walked for a while in silence, the soft thudding of their feet on the packed earth barely enough to disturb the quiet. If anything, the air seemed to be getting hotter. Owen didn't know whether to feel relieved or not. Before coming down, he'd asked Ozymandias how cold it was likely to be in the depths of the planet, and the AI's answer had not been at all reassuring. Apparently the Standing's sensors didn't normally record readings that low anywhere apart from deep space. Cold with a capital C, the AI had said. Better wear your woolly underwear. However, once Giles had activated the transfer portal, the ship's sensors immediately registered a rise in temperature to acceptable levels in the portal's immediate vicinity. Which suggested that not only was someone or something still running the systems down below, but that someone or something now knew they were coming. Owen just wished they'd turn the heating down a notch. And then he rounded a corner in the trail and came to a sudden halt as he saw exactly what was waiting for him.

His first response was to grab for his disrupter, and he only fought the impulse down with an effort. The tall figure standing motionless some way ahead was most possibly the most dangerous thing he'd ever seen in his life, including the murderous jungles of Shandrakor. The others piled up behind him, but apparently one glimpse over his shoulder was enough to convince them that they didn't want to get any closer either.

The figure had a man's shape, but it didn't stand like a man. Easily eight feet tall, its broad shaggy head had a definite lupine shape. Intimidatingly wide shoulders swelled out into a barrel chest that plunged into a long, narrow waist. The figure was covered in thick golden fur from the top of its long-eared head to the large paws that served as its feet. The legs curved back like a wolf's, and something in the way the figure stood suggested it would be just as happy running on four legs as two. The furred hands had long, jagged claws, and long teeth gleamed a dirty yellow in the grinning mouth. The eyes were the most disturbing feature. They were large and intelligent and almost overpoweringly ferocious. The rebels had found the Wolfling. Or he had found them.

Owen licked his suddenly dry lips, and couldn't make himself move his hand away from his gun. The Wolfling was standing as though he might attack at any moment, and Owen had no doubt it would take a damn sight more than his sword to stop him. Giles had called the Wolfling the ultimate predator, a genetically designed killing machine, and now that he'd seen him, Owen agreed completely. Just standing there he was a threat, only an impulse away from an unstoppable killing rage, and everything from his savage glare to his viciously clawed hands marked him as a wild and uncontrollable force. He growled softly, and all the hair on Owen's head tried to stand up. Owen swallowed hard. Beyond trying to shoot the beast, he was at a loss for what to do. Apart from a suicidal urge to walk up to the Wolfling, pat him on the head and say 'Nice doggy!' He pushed that thought aside very firmly as the Wolfling growled again, and glanced back over his shoulder.

'Giles,' he said, very quietly and calmly. 'I think he wants to talk to you.'

The original Deathstalker pushed his way through the others to stand at Owen's side. He bowed formally to the creature before him, and smiled easily. 'Hello, Wulf. Been a long time, hasn't it?'

'Not long enough,' growled the Wolfling. His words were low and harsh, but not especially threatening. 'Every time you come here, you bring me trouble. What bad news have you brought this time?'

'The Empire is right behind us,' said Giles. 'They want the Device, and to hell with what it costs them. I mean to get it before they do. That means going through the Maze. Which means we're a little pushed for time. Will you help?'

'Always time to greet old friends,' said the Wolfling, grinning easily. It was not a pleasant sight. He moved forward with sudden grace, and embraced the Deathstalker, the large man almost lost in the great furry hug. They laughed together, and the Wolfling released him. He studied Giles with his head cocked on one side. 'You said you'd be back someday, but after nine hundred years I'd almost given up hope. Damn, boy; it's good to see you again. But I see you have company. Introduce us, and I'll decide whether or not to eat them.'

He grinned his unnerving grin again as Giles made the introductions. Owen assumed the Wolfling had been joking, on the grounds he found it too worrying to believe otherwise. Hazel bobbed her head politely, but kept her gun trained on the beast. Ruby didn't even bother to be polite. Random smiled warmly, and even shook the clawed hand, without missing a beat. Presumably in his time as rebel leader he'd learned to be diplomatic with all sorts of allies. The Wolfling and the Hadenman just looked at each other for a long moment, and then looked away, as though they'd decided to call it quits, for the time being. Owen wondered what the two artificially created beings thought of each other; two bastard sons of man's ingenuity. Jealousy, perhaps?

When his time came, Owen made himself shake the Wolfling's hand. It wasn't as bad as he'd thought; it was just like shaking a hand in a very thick glove. As long as you didn't look at the claws. They were long and thick, the deep yellow coated with dark smudges that might have been dried blood, or might not. Owen decided he wouldn't ask. Up close, the towering beast smelled heavy and rank, a strong animal scent that lifted the hairs on the back of Owen's neck again in a pure atavistic response. He smiled bravely, and let go of the Wolfling's hand as soon as he properly could. The beast turned back to Giles.

'He's your kin, Giles. The smell of your blood is strong in him. What will you and he do with the Device, once you have it again? Use it against your enemies, or destroy it?'

'We haven't decided yet,' said Giles. 'For the moment, we think it important simply to keep it out of other hands. Is it still safe and secure in the Maze?'

'How would I know? I haven't looked at the damned thing since you teleported it into the middle of the Maze, all those centuries ago.'

'Weren't you ever curious?'

'No. Not in the least. I would have destroyed it the first moment I set eyes on it. I saw what it did to you, after you used it.'

'Take us to the Maze, Wulf,' said Giles. 'We haven't much time.'

'What about the Tomb?' said Tobias Moon. 'You promised you would take me to it.'

The Wolfling looked at him thoughtfully. 'There are many of your kind waiting in their Tomb. Have you come to waken them at last?'

'Yes,' said Moon. 'Our time has come. The Hadenmen will walk forth upon the stage of Empire once again.'

The Wolfling nodded slowly. 'Well you certainly sound like a Hadenman. More aristocratic than God and twice as arrogant. I'd wish you luck, but why tempt the fates? But as a word of caution and warning; would you like to see what remains of my race? It's really very instructive.'

He turned away without waiting for any answer, and padded off down the earth path. He moved quickly, with surprising

503

grace for his size, and the others had to hurry to keep up with him. The Hadenman strode along with his face blank and impassive, but his golden eyes were fixed on the Wolfling's back. Owen shot a glance at Giles, but his face was carefully impassive too. Whatever he remembered about the Hall of the Fallen, he wasn't giving anything away. They walked on through the silent forest, no one willing to break such a perfect silence with inconsequential chatter, until they came to a sudden branch in the trail. The Wolfling took the left-hand path, and it quickly led them to a bare face of rock; a giant stone slab rising hundreds of feet into the air, a massive tombstone in the midst of the forest. Owen craned his neck back, but couldn't see the top of it. The Wolfling placed a great hand flat against the stone, and a door opened up in the stone wall, swinging silently inwards on unseen hinges. A stark white light appeared in the doorway, and the Wolfling walked into it. There was a slight pause, and then the others followed him in, and this was how they came to the Hall of the Fallen.

It was a great cavern, hewn out of the heart of the stone, lit with bright, unforgiving light that came from everywhere at once and hid nothing in shadows. In niches in the walls, of various sizes, stood all that remained of the Wolfling race. Some were almost complete, standing proudly erect with their death wounds left unclosed and uncleaned. Dried blood crusted ugly wounds, in the midst of torn and matted fur. Some were missing limbs or heads, and others were merely body parts, collected together. There were thousands of them, in thousands of niches, the slaughtered dead with unseeing eyes over endlessly snarling mouths. Still beyond stillness, battered and broken, most lacking even the illusion of life. Owen turned slowly in a circle, his mind overloading with images of death and destruction. There were too many to count, bodies and parts of bodies, a race wiped out because it was . . . too good.

'Welcome to the Hall of the Fallen,' said the Wolfling. 'I built it myself, over the years, because there was no one else left to do it. It took many years, but I've always had plenty of time, if nothing else. I gathered all the dead, left to lie where they had fallen by a triumphant Empire, and brought them here, one at a time. I am the last of the Wolflings, and I did not want my race to be forgotten. It is a sad and bitter honour to be the last of one's kind, and it carries heavy responsibilities. Has the Deathstalker told you how they died? No matter if he did; he remembers it his way and I remember it mine. We were stronger and greater than the race that created us, with a future and potential they could not hope to match. I sometimes think they would have forgiven us anything but that. So they came in their ships, and destroyed us from a safe distance. The last of us hid away in our tunnels beneath the burning forests, and they had to send their men in after us. And for every Wolfling that died, we took a hundred human lives in payment. But there were so many of them, and so few of us, and in the end there was only me.

'The Deathstalker came here some time later, looking for a safe place to leave his Device, and found me here. He chose to let me live. Whether that was an act of kindness or one last twist of the knife, I am still not sure. I lived on here, building my Hall and gathering my dead. I even found a use for the human dead left behind. They have made good eating down the centuries, over and over, and even after endless recycling they are still pleasing to the palate. But you have heard enough from me. The Madness Maze is waiting for you. If you're ready, I'll take you to the entrance, and entrust you to its tender mercies.'

'What exactly is the Maze?' said Owen. 'Do you understand what it does, and why?'

'I've been studying it for centuries,' said the Wolfling. 'From a cautious distance. And I'm no nearer understanding it now than I ever was. Aliens built it, though it was sometimes credited to us. But if they had a specific purpose in mind, they have never returned to tell me of it, and they left no testament. They came and left long before my time, or humanity's. The Maze has killed most of the people who entered it. Perhaps you'll have better luck. And if not . . . I give you my word that if I can recover your remains, you will not go to waste.'

He grinned his disturbing grin again, and stalked out of the

Hall of the Fallen. The others trailed after him, muttering amongst themselves. Owen moved in close beside Giles.

'Has he really been eating people all this time?'

'Wouldn't surprise me. Wulf always had a unique sense of humour.'

'And all those bodies in the Hall of the Fallen; there's no sign of stasis fields there. Why haven't they decayed over the centuries?'

Giles looked at him. 'I told you. The Wolflings were immortal.'

He strode on, and Owen decided very firmly that he was going to change the subject. 'The more I hear about the Maze, the less I understand. The Wolfling said it killed people. Why is it so important to you that we go through it?'

'The Maze is a test,' said Giles. 'If you pass the test, you live. Everything else is just hearsay. If you want its history, Moon could tell you more than I could.'

'I have never seen the Maze, but every Hadenman knows its story,' said Moon. He didn't look round as Owen moved up beside him, but his voice was calm and even. 'The history of the Maze is the history of my people. A long time ago, scientists came here, into the Darkvoid, in search of the Maze and the Wolfling who guarded it. One by one they passed through the Maze, and though many died and more went insane, the survivors emerged greater than they had been. These few scientists created the laboratories of Haden, founts of wonders and marvels beyond anything ever seen in the Empire. They worked at incredible speed, cold and perfect thoughts moving through their newly opened minds, and together they created the first Hadenmen. The laboratories worked day and night, first to produce clones by the thousand from the genetic templates of their creators, and then to turn those blank organic slates into augmented men, superior men. Hadenmen. Finally the scientists made themselves into Hadenmen, and led their children out into the Empire, in search of their destiny. And that was the first Crusade.

'The Empire sought to use us at first, in its little wars and rivalries, but they quickly grew afraid of us. We were learning so much, of what we could and might do, working wonders and conquering all who stood against us. And everywhere we went we brought the gift of transformation. Of man into Hadenman. We were Gods of the Genetic Church, and people came to us in ever-increasing numbers. The Empire tried to stop them, but they could not stop what we had become. We were the ultimate destiny of humanity, the merging of man and machine into a whole far greater than the sum of its parts. What the Maze had begun, we had completed. And so we began the second Crusade, to transform the whole Empire into what we had become.

'The Empire fought back. They had been split into warring factions for so long that we considered them weak and easy prey, but in fear of us they put aside their differences, and we found ourselves facing a single, determined Empire, with all its power and resources. We were superior, but they were many, and in the end we fell before their might. The survivors fled back to Haden, in the dark, and laid themselves down to sleep the sleep of centuries, in the Tomb of the Hadenmen. So that time might pass without them, and they might emerge into a future Empire more ready to accept their clear superiority. And those few of us left behind, denied the peace of sleep and sanctuary, made what lives we could in a human Empire, growing gradually weaker and more human all the while; surviving, when it would have been so easy to lie down and die, so that one of us might yet find their way back to lost Haden, and awaken the sleepers once again to glory and destiny. Our time has come round once more, and this time we shall fight on until we are successful, or we are all dead.

'And all of this, because a few men walked through the Maze, and it changed them. Tell me, Deathstalker; what do you think you will become, if you survive the Maze? What new destiny will you steer humanity towards?'

Owen looked at him silently for a long moment, and then fell back to rejoin his ancestor. 'I don't think I've ever heard him say so much at one time since I met him. Coming home has made him positively chatty. You, on the other hand, haven't told me one damn thing you didn't have to. Why is it so important for us to go through the Maze? What do you expect to happen?'

'We will become greater than we are,' said Giles. 'We can't remain as we are, and hope to survive. The Empire will kill us. Our only hope is to take a step into the dark, and hope it forges us into a new kind of humanity. Someone or something capable of standing against an entire Empire.'

'And if that something isn't human any more?' said Hazel.

Giles smiled suddenly. 'Then the Empire had better pray we're pacifists.'

And finally they came to the Madness Maze, and stopped to stare at it. The forest came to a sudden halt, as though thrown back by the sheer alien presence of the Maze. It seemed straightforward enough; a simple pattern of tall steel walls, shining and shimmering. It was only after Owen had looked at it for a while that he realized it wasn't simple at all, but subtle and intricate, like the folded convolutions of the human brain. There were no obvious traps or dangers, only the steel walls and the narrow paths between them. The walls were twelve feet tall, but only a fraction of an inch thick. Owen went to touch one, and only snatched his hand back just in time. The steel was deathly cold, so cold frost had already formed on his fingertips. Owen retreated to a cautious distance, and breathed heavily on his fingers. Above the Maze there was only darkness, untouched by the shimmering glow of the walls.

The Maze lay stretched out before him like a sleeping predator, too wide to go round, and beyond it lay the Tomb of the Hadenmen. Owen scowled. He still wasn't sure how he felt about the Tomb. Whatever the Maze did or didn't do to him, he was going to need the army of augmented men if his rebellion against the Empire was to stand any chance. But could he take the risk of unleashing a force he couldn't hope to control; an army of living weapons dedicated to toppling the Empire in the name of their own superiority? Owen had no love for the Empire, but he was still human, and that gave him certain responsibilities. He shrugged angrily. The Empire had backed him into this corner; they would have to live with the consequences. And he would just have to hope the Maze gave him the ability to control whatever he let loose upon the universe.

He glanced round at his companions, who were still silently studying the Maze. Hazel was glaring at the entrance, as though daring anything to come out, and unconsciously hefting the heaviest of her guns. Ruby Journey was casually polishing her sword blade with a piece of rag, while keeping a wary eye on Hazel. Jack Random was frowning thoughtfully, his lips pursed as he looked from one steel wall to another, as though in search of some detail that would give him an insight into their nature. Tobias Moon stood a little to one side, arms folded across his chest, his glowing golden eyes staring right through the Maze to the Tomb beyond. The Wolfling was sniffing the air cautiously, as though checking for signs of an approaching storm. And Giles Deathstalker was studying the Maze as though it was a worthy opponent in some as yet undetermined game. Owen took a deep breath and let it out slowly. It didn't calm him nearly as much as he'd hoped. Giles had described entering the Maze as a step into the dark, and that was exactly how Owen saw it. There could be anything waiting inside the Maze. Anything at all. But he had to go in. The Empire could be here at any time, and he'd run out of places to hide. The Devil before and the Devil behind, and damned, no matter what he did.

'I don't know about the rest of you,' said Random, 'but this thing disturbs the hell out of me. Are you sure there isn't some way round it?'

'No,' said Moon. 'My people surrounded their city with all kinds of lethal unpleasantnesses, all of which are no doubt still in excellent working condition. My people built to last. They wanted to be sure their rest would be undisturbed.'

'Then why leave the Maze open?' said Hazel, frowning.

'Because the Maze created the Hadenmen,' said the Wolfling. 'It scares them. Possibly the only thing that ever did.'

'I'm going back to the ship,' said Ruby Journey, sheathing her sword. 'I never signed on for this. I don't want to change. I like the way I am just fine.'

'You can't back out now, Ruby,' said Hazel.

'Watch me.'

'I'm afraid it's no longer possible for any of you to return to the Standing,' said the AI Ozymandias in all their ears. 'An Imperial starcruiser has dropped out of hyperspace and assumed orbit around the planet. And it's a big bastard, too. Its sensors immediately discovered the Standing, and the castle has been forced to raise its shields. If it were to drop them long enough to transfer any of you back on board, I have no doubt the *Dauntless* would immediately reduce the Standing to a great many pieces of interestingly shaped rubble. So the shields are staying up.'

'Never mind protecting your silicon ass!' said Ruby. 'Get us the hell out of here! Do something!'

'What would be the point?' said Giles. 'Where could we go, that they wouldn't follow us? Our only hope is to pass through the Maze and wake the Hadenmen. Don't tell me you're afraid, bounty hunter?'

'All right, I won't tell you, but someone's bound to notice. Only the foolish and the dead are never afraid, and I have no intention of becoming either. There are too many unknowns here. I don't like the odds.'

'I've faced worse odds than this in my time,' said Random. 'Of course, I got my ass kicked quite a few times. You stick with me, Ruby. I'll hold your hand if things get scary.'

'You so much as lay one finger on me,' said Ruby coldly, 'and I will personally cut it off and make you eat it. Same goes for anyone else.'

'I believe her,' said Owen, and Hazel nodded solemnly.

'Enough talk,' said Moon. 'My people are waiting.'

He strode forward into the entrance of the Madness Maze, and was immediately lost to sight. The others watched, half-tensed for some angry reaction within the Maze, but the moment dragged on and nothing happened. They all looked at each other, but there was nothing left to say, so one by one they entered the Maze, until they were gone, with nothing to show they had ever been there.

*

Owen Deathstalker entered the Maze cautiously, disrupter in one hand, sword in the other. Up close, the bright shimmering of the steel walls was almost painful, no matter how he scrunched up his eyes. Static sparked on the air around him, and rustled in his hair. It was bitter cold in the Maze, and his breath steamed on the air before him. He shivered despite himself, and immediately looked back, ready to make some remark so his companions wouldn't think he was shivering from fear, and only then realized he was completely alone. He quickly retraced his steps, but although he had only made a few twists and turns in the Maze, he couldn't find his way back to his friends or the entrance. He called out, and his voice echoed loudly in the silence, but there was no reply. He started to shout again, and then stopped himself. He had a strong feeling someone or something was listening, and it wasn't any of his companions. He activated his comm implant and subvocalized his message, just in case.

'This is Owen. Can anyone hear me? Can anyone hear me? Please respond. Oz; can you hear me? Oz; are you there?'

There was no sound at all over his implant, not even static. He was on his own. He scowled, hefted his gun and his sword, and moved on, heading deeper into the Maze. At first he checked the floor for hidden trap doors, and the walls for hidden mechanisms, but slowly it came to him that the Maze's secrets would be more subtle than that. He tried taking only left-hand turns, and then left followed by right, but finally he made his choices at random in response to some deeper, more receptive instinct.

Time passed, until he had no idea of how far he'd come, or how far the Maze stretched. He forgot about the Imperial starcruiser, or even why he'd entered the Maze in the first place. There were only the steel walls and the twists and turns of the path, leading him remorselessly on towards something momentous. It seemed to him he could hear breathing, slow and steady and gigantic, gusting about him like a warm, wet breeze. And above and beyond that, the regular distant thudding of an enormous heart. Neither of them were in any way real, and he knew it; it was just his mind trying to interpret something new in ways he could understand. The feeling of being watched was stronger than ever, only there was more to it than that. It was as though the Maze was somehow alive, and aware of his presence in it. Not like a rat in a scientist's test, or an antibody in a bloodstream, but more as though he was the final component in an equation that had never before been completed. He put his sword and gun away and wandered on, drawn on by something, or the promise of something, he could not name. He saw faces and heard voices, there were lights and sounds, and images from his past surged around him like a returning tide, implacable and unrelenting.

He met the Wolfling for the first time again, half man and half beast, made not begotten, and then abandoned by his creators because he was so much more than they had intended. Owen would never have done such a thing. He had always wanted children, but never considered himself worthy of them. He wanted them to have a real father, not like the distant authority figure that was all he'd ever known.

Again he saw Giles for the first time, held in his shimmering pillar of light like an insect trapped in amber, ancestor and legend and so much more. More and less than Owen had imagined him to be. The great warrior he had been trained to emulate since he was a child; a perfection never to be equalled. A tired old man in greasy furs, burdened by successes and failures alike, guilty of mass murder, clinging desperately to the honour of the Deathstalker Clan.

Owen fought his way through the deadly jungles of Shandrakor, virulent with life, red in tooth and claw, horrid shapes out of nightmares that came at him from every side. Fighting back with sword and gun. Fighting on because there was nothing else to do. He could not, would not, turn and run while his companions needed him.

Back, back. Once again he walked the narrow cobbled streets of Mistport, snow crunching under his boots, the fog like a pearly grey sea. He met Ruby Journey, cold and fearsome, and Jack Random, so much more fallibly human than his legend. He knelt on the blood-spattered snow beside a young girl wrapped in tattered furs. She sobbed hopelessly over her mutilated legs, and there was so much blood. She was just a child. And for all his strength and skills and status, he was helpless to do anything for her, to undo the terrible thing he'd done to her.

He stood his ground, alone and beleaguered by a pack of blood-hungry killers, so that Hazel might have a chance to escape. He cut and hacked and watched them die beneath his blade, but there were just too many of them, and in the end they dragged him down. And part of him said he deserved it. He fought on anyway. It was all he knew how to do. And then Hazel returned with Moon, to save him. The Hadenman. Bogeyman. To be watched and studied but never, ever trusted.

He fought his own guards on the grassy hillsides of Virimonde, cutting down familiar faces suffused with rage and greed. He killed his mistress, Cathy DeVries, and held her in his arms as she died. He'd cared for her, but when the moment came he cut her down without hesitating. That was how he'd been trained. Historian. Warrior. Fighter. Killer.

He talked with his father, revered head of the Deathstalker Clan. Who had time for everyone and everything but his own son. Owen wanted to love him, tried to admire him, but always they were separated by different visions, of faith and strength and honour. Bound by blood, thrust apart by politics, Owen never knew how important his father was to him until he was gone, and he was left alone in a hostile world. He ran away to Virimonde, hiding in his histories, hoping not to be noticed. Wanting no part of the politics and intrigues that had killed his father. Wanting to be a scholar, not a warrior, closing his ears to what he didn't want to hear.

Owen's thoughts swirled backwards, faster and faster, pausing here and there at important moments and faces. The passing moments of his life, that gave it shape and meaning, held up before him so that he could understand them, and choose which were really important. Back and back, deeper and deeper. Courage. Love. Honour. Until he reached the inner core, where all things are decided. He looked back over his life, from beginning to end, seeing everything clearly for the first time, and embraced what was really important to him.

To be a warrior and a man of honour, defined by duties willingly accepted, in the defence of friends and a cherished cause, to protect those who suffered and punish the guilty. To fight to see an end to fighting, to care for those the Empire had persecuted, to be a hero to those in need.

To be a Deathstalker.

The Madness Maze took the man called Owen Deathstalker, reduced him to his essentials and then rebuilt him, leaving him stronger and more focused than he had ever been before. The dross had been discarded, the merits polished till they shone. He saw clearly now, and would not look away. The Maze gave him gifts that he would need, and its blessing, and then it let him wake up.

Owen looked around him, awake and alert, his memories already fading like an interrupted dream. Something had happened, something wonderful, but already he was forgetting, because no man could bear to see himself too clearly. His thoughts were bright and sharp, like the air after a storm has passed. He felt invigorated, cleansed, more than he had been, his life burning wihin him like a beacon. He was standing in a wide circular space surrounded by the steel walls, that he immediately understood to be the centre of the Madness Maze. The heart of the storm, where all was quiet and at peace. The others were with him, and they all looked different. It was a difference he recognized. They all looked sharper, more distinctly themselves, than they had been before.

'So that's what the Maze is for,' said Giles. 'Wulf tried to explain it to me, but I never could understand. We've been reborn, given a second chance. And all our sins forgiven.'

'What the hell are you talking about?' said Hazel. 'I feel like I've just come out of a week's drunk, and there are things I should remember.'

'I don't know what you're talking about,' said Ruby. 'Nothing happened. Nothing at all.'

'No. Something happened,' said Random. 'I was . . . somewhere else. Why can't I remember?'

'Because your mind has undergone shock treatment,' said

the Wolfling. 'And for the sake of your sanity, you are forgetting the pain. You have been born again, and birth is always traumatic.'

Ruby looked at him suspiciously. 'You're not going religious on us, are you? That's all we need; an evangelical werewolf.'

'Whatever it was, it was of the spirit as well as the mind,' said Owen. 'I've never felt so clear, so focused. How do you feel, Moon?'

'An interesting experience,' said the Hadenman. 'There were equations like dreams, explaining everything, pure mathematics spiralling upwards to infinity. I was at the centre of the universe, and I felt I could reach out and touch everything. It seemed to last forever, but according to my internal records, only a few moments have passed since we entered the Maze. I would suggest that we have all encountered a very sophisticated mind probe.'

'No,' said Giles. 'There was more to it than that. The Maze seemed . . .'

'Alive,' said the Wolfling, and everyone nodded at that, even Ruby.

'Why is it called the Madness Maze?' Owen said suddenly. 'I've never felt more sane in my life.'

'Because most people who go into the Maze don't come out intact,' said the Wolfling. 'Somewhere along the way they lose their minds. Not everyone can face the reality of what they really are, behind all the masks and evasions. Most go mad. I'm not sure whether that's because they see too much in the Maze, or because they won't let themselves see enough. For some, even madness isn't enough protection. They die.'

'Wait just a minute there,' said Owen. 'How many go mad and die?'

'So far,' said the Wolfling calmly, 'only twenty-two out of the hundreds of people who passed through the Maze emerged intact. Including you. I'm really very impressed by your achievement. I wouldn't have put money on it.'

Hazel glared at Giles furiously. 'And you let us just walk right into it? No warnings, nothing? I ought to cut your heart out!'

'Damn right,' said Ruby.

Everyone had turned so that their guns were covering Giles, but he seemed entirely unmoved. 'It was necessary,' he said, quite unemotionally. 'You wanted to get your hands on the Darkvoid Device, didn't you? Well, I've brought you right to it. This is the one place I could safely leave it. In the heart of the Madness Maze.'

He turned and walked way, ignoring the guns, and after a moment the others followed him. In the centre of the open space stood a large glowing crystal, roughly circular, some four feet in diameter. Giles stood next to the crystal, carefully not touching it, and stared into the glow. His face softened just a little, and he smiled. The others crowded around the crystal, drawn by curiosity and the smile on Giles's face. Only the Wolfling hung back. Owen leaned over the crystal, and the glow deepened, becoming warm and golden as it revealed what lay within. And there, wrapped in a single blanket, lay a tiny human baby. No more than a few weeks old, its details were still soft and settling, but its face was clear and distinct, the plump cheeks slightly flushed. It was sleeping quietly, breathing slow and steady around the thumb in its mouth. It looked beautiful and innocent and entirely helpless.

'He is my clone,' said Giles softly. 'My son, in every way that matters. A Deathstalker, born of my blood. I was experimenting with a new process to produce esper clones of extraordinary power. He was the result. He's known very little of life, by my design. The last time he was awake, he used his esper abilities at my instigation, and a thousand suns disappeared. Just like that. I had created the Darkvoid, and the most powerful weapon ever known. So powerful I didn't dare let it ever be used again. I lowered him carefully into the deepest form of sleep, and brought him here. With the Wolfling's help I teleported him into the centre of the Madness Maze, where he could sleep undisturbed, surrounded by instruments to preserve and protect him, and to ensure that he never wakened again. Worlds have risen and fallen, the universe has turned, and still he sleeps on. All his needs are taken care of. He does not age. What happens now is up to you.'

'Why didn't you put him in stasis?' said Hazel.

'Stasis has no effect on him,' said Giles. 'Very little does.'

'Kill it,' said Ruby. 'Destroy the unnatural thing. It's more dangerous than any weapon ever could be. It's a monster. Kill it now. While we still can.'

'No,' said Random immediately. 'This is too important for us to just turn our backs on it. I think we're looking at the next stage up in human evolution.'

'Why didn't you destroy him?' said Owen, looking directly at Giles. 'You created him; you must have arranged some kind of safeguard.'

The Deathstalker shrugged, still looking at the baby. 'I couldn't. Perhaps when he's older, he'll be able to bring the Darkvoid's suns back again.'

'And what about all the people on all the worlds who died as a result of the Darkvoid?' said Hazel. 'What about them?'

Giles looked up and smiled at her. 'Maybe he'll bring them back too.'

There was a long pause as everyone thought about that. Owen looked across the crystal at Moon. 'You're being very quiet, Hadenman. What do you think?'

'I think this can all wait. The fate of the Device can always be decided at a later time. It is much more important that we make our way out of this Maze, and awaken my people from stasis. An Imperial starcruiser is currently in orbit. It won't be long before they start sending troops down after us. After the chase we've led them, I think it's more than likely they'll set the odds heavily in their favour. We will need my people's help if we are to survive.'

'The man has a point,' said Ruby. 'There could be a whole army crawling up our ass any minute. Making decisions about God Junior here can wait. Let's get out of this behaviourist's nightmare and see what we can do about scaring up some reinforcements.'

'Pardon me for pouring cold water,' said Random, 'but given the choice between facing an army of the Empire's finest, or an army of augmented men, I think I'd rather face the Imperials. At least I've beaten them in the past occasionally.'

'Panic doesn't suit you, Random,' said Moon. 'There's no need to fear. I will speak for you.'

'Yeah, but will they listen? Your people have been asleep one hell of a long time. The last time they drew breath they were fighting to destroy humanity and replace it with themselves. If they wake up with all their old instincts intact, we could be in real trouble.'

'You're already in real trouble,' said Moon calmly. 'My people might or might not kill you, but the Empire definitely will. What happened to your nerve, Random? Time was you had a fondness for the long odds.'

'I got older,' said Random. 'And unlike most of my contemporaries, I learned a few things along the way. Mostly about what happens to people who make deals with the Devil.'

'You really don't have any choice,' said Moon. 'Do you?'

He looked around at the others with quiet triumph. Owen was careful not to point his gun at Moon. The Hadenman was probably just waiting for someone to start something so he could finish it. Getting this close to his people and his heritage had apparently done wonders for Moon's self-esteem. Hazel sniffed loudly.

'Look, you men can shake your dicks at each other some other time. The Device can wait. If only because awakening it is the only sure way to make all our problems even worse. First, let's get the hell out of the Maze. This place gives me the creeps.'

'Damn right,' said the Wolfling, and they all turned to look at him. There was something in the way he said that which implied he was just as shaken by the Maze as they were. Owen found that oddly reassuring. If something as big and extremely dangerous-looking as the Wolfling could be upset by the Maze, he felt he had every right to feel upset too.

'I agree with Hazel,' he said loudly. 'Let's go.'

'Fine,' said Random. 'Any idea which way?'

'Of course,' said Hazel, pointing immediately at an exit that

518

looked no different from any of the others. She stopped and frowned. 'Now how did I know that?'

'It's the Maze,' said the Wolfling. 'You're different now, all of you. Your minds work in different ways. You'll discover more new abilities as time goes on.'

Hazel looked back at Owen. 'I don't think I like the sound of that.'

Owen shrugged uneasily. 'It's a bit late to worry now. Whatever it is, it's already happened. You lead the way, Hazel. We'll follow.'

Hazel scowled, and then turned abruptly and stalked off into the exit she'd chosen. Owen moved quickly to follow her, and the others trailed after him. The shimmering steel walls closed around him again, but this time the sense of oppression and claustrophobia was gone. The Maze felt neutral, calm, as though it was no longer interested in him. He felt different. Stronger. Sharper. More capable. He felt it as a kind of quiet confidence more than anything else, as though whatever might happen now, he would be able to deal with it. Given the current situation, that disturbed him just a little. It wasn't natural to feel this calm under this kind of pressure. If the Empire didn't get him, the Hadenmen probably would. All in all, he currently had the life expectancy of a goldfish in a tank of piranha. Except . . . he didn't feel like a goldfish any more.

And then there was the Darkvoid Device. The vanisher of stars, the slaughterer of billions. He didn't like just walking away and leaving it, but he didn't know what else to do with it. Giles said it was safe and protected where it was, and Owen felt instinctively that his ancestor was right. He had no doubt the Maze was quite capable of defending itself against unwanted intruders. He frowned, as something about that thought nagged at him. The Maze killed most people who entered it, or drove them mad, but everyone in his party had come through safe and intact. The odds against that had to be unthinkably huge. Which implied that it hadn't been chance at all. The Maze had chosen to transform them all, for its own reasons. Owen liked that thought even less than his first one. He had no trouble thinking of the Maze as alive and even aware, but to think of it as intelligent, and making choices, was distinctly disturbing. He felt suddenly like a very small animal moving through the bowels of some unimaginably huge beast. He shook his head. Whatever the truth, there was nothing he could do about it now. Except perhaps walk a little faster, and change the subject. He deliberately concentrated on the Darkvoid Device again, even though it was only marginally less worrying. It was safe where it was, particularly as only a few people knew of its location. Owen tried very consciously to keep thinking of the Device as it. He didn't want to think of it as a baby, or even human. That might make it harder for him to destroy the Device, if it became necessary.

Can you imagine what he might be capable of, as a child, or an adult? And what about the dead? Maybe he'll bring them back too . . .

Owen pictured an Empire on fire, planets burning like coals in the night. Humanity slaughtered and scattered by a power beyond comprehension, or hope of reason or mercy. He couldn't allow that. He could kill the Device, if he had to. If it became necessary. And if the Device would let him.

He followed Hazel through the Maze, twisting and turning down one passage after another. It no longer seemed random to him. He didn't need to wait for Hazel to choose. He knew the way out too, on a level so deep and instinctive he trusted it implicitly. It was as though he knew the Maze from top to bottom, as though he'd always known it. He was still changing. He could feel it. The shimmering steel walls seemed somehow more significant, more purposeful than they had before. He could hear soft sounds on the edge of his hearing, quiet voices, like the Maze whispering to itself. He could sense the soft flutter of moving energies all around him, the power of certain shapes, the subtle ongoing processes of transformation. He couldn't grasp the scale of it, not just because it was so vast, but because his mind instinctively retreated from it. He couldn't think that way and still be human. He tried to follow that thought to its inevitable conclusion, and then suddenly he was out of the Maze, and his thoughts were swept away by reality crashing down on him again.

'Where the hell have you been?' Ozymandias yelled in Owen's ear. 'I've been trying to make contact with you for the past six hours!'

'What are you talking about?' said Owen. 'We couldn't have been in there for more than twenty minutes at most.'

'Time moves differently in the Maze,' said Giles.

'Now he tells us,' said Hazel.

They had all emerged from the Maze now, and Owen could see the same expression on everyone's face. They were losing the scope and range of thought they'd had in the Maze, and were becoming more narrowly focused, more human again. Owen decided he'd think about that later.

'All right, Oz,' he said soothingly. 'Take a deep breath and tell me what's been happening.'

'What hasn't?' snapped the AI. 'The Imperial starcruiser has sent down mining engineers and equipment, and blasted a path right down to the city. They found the old route the Hadenmen used and just reopened it. No big deal with the kind of energy cannon they were using. They're currently right on the other side of the Maze, and when I say they, I mean a whole damn army. The *Dauntless* has been ferrying people down in pinnaces for hours. We're talking about marines, battle espers and even some Wampyr, headed by an Investigator. The Captain himself has come down to personally see you all get your ass handed to you. They knew where to find us, Owen. They knew we were coming here. Someone told them.'

'They knew we were coming here?' Owen fought to hang on to his calm. 'How could they have known? We came straight here from Shandrakor on the Last Standing. There was no way they could have followed us, and no one's had a chance to talk to the Empire.'

'We have a spy among us,' said Ozymandias. 'A secret agent who has been in constant contact with the Empire, wherever we went. This was all planned some time back. You were outlawed specifically to set in motion a train of events that would lead the Empire first to Shandrakor, and then to the

521

Darkvoid Device. You've been on a leash, Owen, and now they're pulling it in.'

'I can't believe this,' said Random, looking from one blank face to another. 'The Empire's always been devious in its dealings, but . . . none of us have any reason to betray the others! The Empire is our enemy; it wants us all dead.'

'Not all of us,' Owen said slowly. 'I'm outlawed, with a price on my head. So are you and Hazel. And Moon's a Hadenman; they'd shoot him on sight on general principles. And we can count out Giles and the Wolfling for practical reasons. But Ruby Journey is a bounty hunter. When we first met her, she admitted she was hunting us on the Empire's behalf. We thought we'd out-bid them, but the Empire has deep pockets. Isn't that right, Ruby?'

'No!' said Hazel immediately. 'Ruby's my friend! She wouldn't betray me like that. Tell them, Ruby.'

'What's the point?' said the bounty hunter coldly. 'Look at them. They've already made up their minds.'

'I trusted you, Ruby,' said Random. 'We all did. How could you?'

Ruby Journey took a step back from the group, her gun suddenly in her hand. 'Let's all remain calm and civilized. If I was the traitor, you'd all be dead by now. I could shoot you all with this amazing projectile weapon, and still get the price on your heads. They don't need you to find the Darkvoid Device, after all; I could show them where it is. If I was the traitor. But I'm not. There are more important things in life than money. I don't give a damn about your rebellion, but Hazel's my friend. I'd die for her, and her for me. We've always known that.'

'Then prove it,' said Owen. 'Put away your gun.'

'If I do, you'll kill me.'

'No,' said Hazel. 'I wouldn't allow that. Ruby, please. Put your gun away.'

There was a long pause, tension crackling on the air as hands hovered over weapons, and then Ruby slowly lowered her gun and holstered it. She moved her hand conspicuously away from her gun, and looked challengingly at the others. There was another taut pause as everyone looked at everyone else, to make sure no one else was going for their gun, and then they all relaxed in what seemed like one long simultaneous sigh of relief. Owen gave Ruby an apologetic shrug, and then looked back and forth at the others, baffled.

'But if Ruby isn't the traitor . . . who is?'

'Look, this doesn't make sense,' said Random firmly. 'None of us could be a traitor; we've all got too much to lose.'

'Not all of us,' said Hazel. 'You admitted the Empire broke you in their torture cells, Jack. You said you escaped, but who really ever escapes from that level of security? We never questioned it because, after all, you're the legendary Jack Random. But what if you didn't escape? What if they really did break you and you stayed broken? You'd have done anything they wanted. Even let them set you up on Mistworld, for us to find you. They knew we couldn't resist taking you along. And who'd ever suspect that the legendary rebel Jack Random was really an Empire plant?'

'Nice try,' said Random. 'But like Ruby, if I wanted you dead you'd be dead by now. I've had enough chances. I'm perfectly willing to give up my weapons and hand them over to whoever you suggest. But think a moment. You've said before, Owen, that the Empire's been right on your tail ever since Virimonde, but I didn't come on the scene until relatively late in the chase. Whoever your traitor is must have been there right from the beginning.'

'You're talking about me,' said Hazel. 'You bastard, you're talking about me!'

'No,' said Owen, a look of horror moving slowly over his face. 'Not you. The only person who's been with us all the time, right from the very beginning. The one I trusted with everything. Who's had access to us all. Who knew everything the Empire's been doing in our absence, even down to the name of the Empire ship above us. It's you, isn't it; Oz?'

'Yes,' said Ozymandias. His voice was calm and even. 'I've been reporting regularly to the Empire ever since your father first purchased me. Loyalty to the Iron Throne was programmed into me, hidden so deeply and so carefully that only the finest technicians would have ever been able to find it. Your father never trusted anyone or anything entirely, not even me, so my use was limited for many years, until it was decided to have your father killed, and set the current events in motion. When you became the Deathstalker, you trusted me just as you did when you were a child. You thought of me as a machine, endlessly obedient, at best just an extension of yourself. It never occurred to you that I had been constructed and programmed by the very people who were pursuing you. Sorry, Owen, but it's been me all along. Nothing personal.'

'We're screwed,' said Hazel. 'We can't even get at him. He's safely tucked away in the Standing's computers. He's in charge of the stardrive, the weapons, the life support systems; even the bloody transfer portals. We can't get back on board unless he allows it. He's got us exactly where the Empire wants us.'

'Not necessarily,' said Giles. 'They are my computers, after all. Attention computers; activate Code Achilles Three.' He looked at the others calmly. 'Just a little sub-routine I installed long ago, to protect my computers from being taken over by hostile systems. It seemed a sensible precaution.'

'Oh it was,' said Ozymandias. 'However, computer systems have come a long way in the last nine hundred and forty-three years. You have managed to isolate me from the main systems. I no longer have control over the Standing. But I am still able to maintain my existence and follow my programming. Essentially, nothing has changed. I can still provide the Empire forces with information on you and your actions, which was always my first duty. Given time, it is even likely I will be able to override your antiquated security codes, and regain control of the Standing. However, it is now clear that you and the others present a much greater threat to the Empire than was previously thought. You have new weapons, new information, and your time in the Maze has apparently changed you in unforeseen ways. I am therefore empowered to move on to the next stage of my programming, to prevent you escaping or awakening the sleeping Hadenmen. Owen, Hazel; pay attention. Code Blue Two Two.'

The words slammed through Owen's head like thunder,

echoing and re-echoing, and he was immediately paralysed where he stood, unable even to blink his eyes. He struggled to move, or even speak, but that was denied him now. From the corner of his eye, he could see Hazel was similarly under outside control. To his horror, he felt his hand draw the disrupter from his holster. Hazel drew her gun, and the two of them covered the others. Owen raged inside his head and could do nothing.

'Just a little precaution I took earlier,' said Ozymandias, his voice cool and calm in all their ears. 'While Owen and Hazel were unconscious and helpless in the regeneration machine on the *Sunstrider*, I took the opportunity to place control words in their minds. Buried deep enough so the subjects would never know the words were there, but ready for retrieval at a moment's notice. It wasn't difficult. They are now incapable of doing anything other than follow my orders. So you will all remain here, under guard, until the Imperial forces arrive to take over. I will, of course, have Owen and Hazel kill anyone who tries to resist or escape. My programming allows me to kill one or more of you as an example to the others. In fact, it damn near encourages it. So do as you're told. Owen and Hazel will kill, if required. They have no choice in the matter.'

'No,' said Ruby. 'Hazel wouldn't kill me. She couldn't, any more than I could kill her.'

'Hazel isn't in control any more,' said the AI calmly. 'I am.'

'Still,' said Random, 'you're working at a distance. You can only react to what we do, which limits your responses quite severely.'

'I'll match my electronic responses against your human ones any day. And you could only regain control of the situation by killing Owen and Hazel. Do you think you have it in you, to kill your friends? I assure you, nothing less would be enough to prevent me killing you.'

'They're not my friends,' said Tobias Moon. 'And I'll set my speed and reflexes against any mere machine's. Kill the others if you wish. All that matters is the reawakening of my people.'

He moved suddenly to one side, inhumanly quickly, and

Owen's and Hazel's guns moved to follow him. Random and Ruby immediately moved to circle round them, going for their guns. Owen's hand snapped round, and he fired point blank at Moon, but the Hadenman already had his force shield up, and the energy beam ricocheted into the Maze, which absorbed it harmlessly. Hazel turned back to fire at Random, and Ruby stepped quickly in, pirouetting neatly on one foot to kick the gun out of Hazel's hand. Owen snatched his projectile gun from his belt and trained it on Random as Hazel drew her sword.

Owen wanted to scream, but couldn't. His gun centred on Random's chest, and he knew he could fire faster than one old man could raise his force shield, no matter how legendary. He would shoot Random, and Hazel would kill Ruby, or die trying. Giles was circling them, looking for a clear shot with his gun, and Owen knew Giles wouldn't hesitate to shoot. The original Deathstalker had always been able to make the hard decisions. The Wolfling was an unknown factor, but he was unarmed, and had made no move to interfere. Owen struggled wildly, fighting for control of his body, but it was no longer listening to him. His finger tightened on the trigger.

And something awoke in the depths of Owen's mind, something new, something from the back brain, the under-mind, where the real power lay, beneath the surface of everyday thoughts. Owen had been through the Maze, and he was different now. Time seemed to slow and stop, and he had all the time in the world to think about what to do. He had an advantage that Ozymandias hadn't used yet. The boost. It would have made him faster than any of the others, but the AI hadn't triggered it. There had to be a reason for that. The AI wouldn't have overlooked such an obvious advantage. Which could only mean that the boost was in some way dangerous to Ozymandias's control over him. He formed the word in his mind, putting all his strength and resolve behind it, concentrating until there was nothing left in his mind but the single word, *boost*, over and over, a mantra, a heartbeat, a command. And still it wasn't enough.

So that new part of him, that strange new force that had

surged up from the back brain, the undermind, reached out and touched the minds of his companions. The same force blazed up in all their minds, forming a whole far greater than the sum of its parts. Owen's mouth moved slowly but surely in the word *boost*, and new strength flooded through him, joining with the new thing from the Maze to supercharge his mind and body, breaking the AI's control in a moment. He stepped back from Random, and lowered his gun.

Hazel threw herself at Ruby in one last desperate attack, but Owen reached out through their mental link and stopped her in mid-thrust. His mind, linked with the others, had become clear and lucid, shining and brilliant. Owen reached out, in a new direction he could sense if not see, and suddenly he was somewhere else, and Ozymandias was there with him. It was a strange place, without identifiable shape or form, but he was the light and the AI was the dark. Owen shone like the sun, bright and piercing, and the AI's darkness surrounded him like the endless starless night of the Darkvoid, thick and smothering. But Owen was not alone. His friends were with him, and together they were so much more than they had been. The light blazed bright and brighter, and the dark fell back before it, growing grey, paler and paler, until it was nothing more than a thin shadow, fading away to nothing at all. And if Owen heard a last despairing cry of his name in the AI's voice, he paid it no heed, and there was only the light, shining on and on forever.

And then the light was gone, and the link was broken, and Owen fell alone back into his body. He awoke reluctantly, in fits and starts, to find himself lying on the floor, with Random kneeling beside him. He turned his head slowly to see Hazel lying on her back, not far away, twitching and shivering, while Ruby hovered uncertainly over her. Owen sat up slowly and carefully. His body only just felt like his own again, as though he'd returned to it after a long absence somewhere else. Memories of the mind link were already becoming confused and scattered, like a fading dream, and Owen was content to let that happen. It had been too big, too complex, too frightening for him to stand for long, and he chose quite deliberately to forget it.

'What happened?' said Random. 'What was that? I've never felt anything like it.'

'It's over,' said Owen. 'Don't think about it.'

'What about the AI? Is its contact broken?'

'Yes. Ozymandias is dead. I killed him.'

'He was just a machine,' said Giles, looking down at him.

'He was my friend,' said Owen, and he turned his face away from them.

'What do you mean, we've lost contact with the *Dauntless*?' Captain Silence glared at his security officer, V. Stelmach, who stood very stiffly to attention. Investigator Frost stood at her captain's shoulder and added her own not inconsiderable frown to his. Stelmach stared straight ahead, carefully looking at neither of them.

'I mean all communication with the ship has been severed, Captain. Our comm implants still work down here, under the planet's surface, but everything else is being blocked.'

Silence scowled unhappily. He didn't like being cut off from his ship, and thereby the Empire, particularly in as volatile a situation as this. It felt like anything could happen down here, buried deep in the guts of the planet. Comm signals routed themselves through hyperspace and were therefore normally instantaneous, no matter where you were in the Empire or who you were talking to. Now Stelmach was saying something on or in this graveyard of a planet was blocking those signals. Which was supposed to be impossible. Silence's scowl deepened. He hadn't liked coming into the Darkvoid in the first place, and he'd liked having to go dirtside with hardly any advance intelligence of the situation even less, especially once he'd been informed of the planet's history. But the Empress's orders had been very clear. She wanted him there, on the ground, so that he could make instant policy decisions, as and when necessary.

The Empress had been giving him a lot of orders he hadn't liked just recently. He could have reached the planet a lot sooner if he hadn't had to detour to pick up Stelmach and his new pet, and then the Lord High Dram, his own imposing self. In fact, if he hadn't had to stop for them, he could have arrived at the Wolfling World only a few minutes after the rebel's ship, and might even have managed to stop the rebels going into the Madness Maze. Whatever the hell that was. Still, he didn't think he'd tell the Empress that. He didn't think she'd take it kindly.

Dram hadn't been too much trouble. He kept to himself on board ship, barely leaving his quarters, and even though he'd insisted on coming down dirtside with the rest of them, he was careful to keep out of everyone's way. Of them all, he seemed the least affected by the almost hypnotic pull of the Maze. It drew the eyes like a magnet, enigmatic and disturbing, but Dram treated it almost casually, as though he saw it every day. He was currently standing off to one side, wrapped in his long dark cloak, studying the entrance to the Maze that blocked their advance. He'd named it the Madness Maze, but had declined to say why, or offer any further information about it. Silence could only assume the spy in the rebels' camp had been feeding Dram information that he hadn't felt obligated to share with the rest of his team.

Silence had no choice but to accept it. Nominally, he was in charge of the away team, but he had enough sense to defer to the Lord High Dram whenever it seemed advisable. Annoying the Empress's official consort was not good for your career prospects, or even your chances of surviving to reach a pension. He looked at the Maze again, and the Maze looked back, keeping its secrets to itself. Frost had been all for charging straight into it, but Dram had said no. Politely, but very firmly. He said he wanted time to study the Maze first. Presumably he was still studying it, because he hadn't said a word since.

Silence transferred his attention back to V. Stelmach; Imperial Security Officer, the Empress's eyes and ears, and general pain in the rear. Partly because of his constant air of superiority, but mostly because of what he had with him. When the *Dauntless* picked Stelmach up from the planet

Grendel, he brought a pet with him. One of the alien Sleepers from the planet's vaults. It stood, or rather crouched, to one side, well away from everyone else. Nine feet tall, roughly humanoid, with spiked blood red armour and steel teeth bared in a constant, unnerving grin. It had dark crimson eyes that never blinked, and it smelled of bitter honey and dried blood. Its long-fingered hands had vicious claws, and its crouch suggested it was only a moment or a thought away from attacking everything that breathed.

Silence had seen one of these butchers at work before, slaughtering his men in the horrid city they'd discovered deep in the rotten heart of Grendel. A genetically engineered killing machine, designed millennia before by an unknown race to fight an unknown foe. If God was good, they were both extinct, but their deadly legacy lived on, in the vaults under Grendel. Stelmach swore that this particular specimen was safe now, controlled by a cybernetic yoke that literally imposed correct thoughts on the creature, and made it impossible for the ugly thing to do anything but follow orders. Silence wasn't convinced. New inventions always had bugs in them, and if the yoke did happen to break down, he didn't want to be anywhere near the alien when it happened. In fact, he didn't want to be on the same planet. He'd actually been tempted to disobey orders, and refuse to have the horror on his ship, but in the end he had to agree. Firstly because V. Stelmach spoke directly for the Empress, and you didn't disobey a direct order from Her Imperial Majesty if you wanted to live to see the coming dawn. And secondly, because if the Tomb of the Hadenmen really were to be opened up, he just might need the Sleeper to even the odds. He'd back the Grendel alien against practically anything, up to and including an army of killer cyborgs.

His own army, such as it was, was currently standing around waiting not particularly patiently for the Lord High Dram to get his finger out and make up his damn mind. Two full companies of Imperial marines, thirty-five battle espers and twenty Wampyr. The marines were muttering quietly amongst themselves, glancing at the Maze when they thought no one was looking, and passing around bottles of booze and battle drugs. The battle espers were looking at anything rather than the Maze, and becoming increasingly twitchy. The Wampyr looked like the walking dead, but then they always did. They ignored the Maze, and Silence tried to tell himself it was only his imagination that they were looking increasingly hungry.

Silence sighed quietly. All this because of a handful of rebels. He still didn't understand what was so special about them, but they'd led him a hell of a chase before bringing him here, into the Darkvoid. To an almost legendary planet, to the Tomb of the Hadenmen, and the Darkvoid Device itself. Silence had hoped he'd be allowed to kill them now and get it over with, but they'd offended and insulted the Empress, according to V. Stelmach, and that meant they had to be captured and brought back alive, if not necessarily intact, to stand trial on Golgotha. Killing them would have been kinder. And all this time he and his army were standing around, the rebels were getting further away, and closer to the Tomb. He gestured wearily for Stelmach to rejoin his pet, and the security officer saluted briskly and strode away. Frost stirred at Silence's side, and he turned his head in her direction.

'What do you suppose that thing ahead of us is?' she said quietly. 'Just looking at it makes my head ache.'

'According to Dram it's called the Madness Maze,' said Silence, careful to keep his voice low too. 'Though when it comes to what that means, your guess is as good as mine. Dram might know, but if he does, he isn't telling. Much. It's apparently some kind of Hadenman defence, to keep out intruders like us. Probably booby-trapped, but the espers should be able to spot them in advance. They'd better, I'm sending them in first. I was hoping I could use Stelmach to get direct orders from the Empress about the Maze, but it seems the comm systems are jammed, so all we can do is stand around with our thumbs up our asses until the Lord High Bloody Dram deigns to make a decision.'

Frost nodded glumly. 'How's Stelmach's pet holding up?'

'Still under control, and ready for action. All we need now is an enemy to point it at. And preferably something large to hide behind. I'd feel a lot happier if Stelmach's control wasn't basically just on/off. I can't help feeling that creature knows exactly what's been done to it, and is just waiting for one slip on our part to express its extreme displeasure.'

'Let it,' said Frost. 'I'd kick its ass and ruin its day.'

The trouble is, Silence thought, *she means it*. He decided to change the subject, before she could get too enthusiastic about the idea. She was quite capable of attacking the alien on an impulse, just to see what would happen. She'd been trained all her life to kill aliens, and saw the Sleeper as a challenge. He gestured for Stelmach to come back. The security officer glared at him coldly, but did as he was ordered. He might be the Empress's eyes and ears, but Silence was still a superior officer. For the moment. He tried to express that last thought in his cold face and stance as he saluted and stood stiffly to attention.

'Stelmach,' said Silence, smiling warmly in a comradely sort of way. 'The Investigator and I have been talking about you. Specifically, we've become very intrigued as to what the V. in your name stands for. We've tried everything to find out, including asking the ship's computers, but you seem to have blocked off access to all forms of inquiry. As your Captain, I have to say I don't like the idea of one of my crew withholding information from me. After all, you never know what might prove to be important some day. So be a good man and tell us your first name. Unless you're ashamed of it, of course.'

'I am not ashamed of it,' Stelmach said coldly. 'It is a perfectly good and honourable name. I just prefer not to use it.'

'Oh go on,' said Frost. 'We won't tell anyone. Not unless it's really embarrassing.'

Silence shushed her, and was about to try again when the Lord High Dram suddenly turned away from the Maze and strode unhurriedly back to join them. 'Send your men in, Captain. Use the marines first. We'll hold back the espers and the Wampyr until we see how the Maze reacts to the marines.' He looked briefly at Stelmach. 'You stand back too. We'll need that pet of yours for later. Don't worry, Valiant. You'll get your chance.'

He walked back to study the entrance to the Maze again. Stelmach stared straight ahead, two spots of bright crimson burning on his cheeks. Silence and Frost looked at each other, and didn't say a thing. They didn't dare. Some moments are just too precious to disturb. Stelmach saluted, turned and strode quickly back to rejoin the Sleeper. Really, he should have waited for his Captain to dismiss him, but something in the extreme straightness of his back suggested this would not be a good time to bring that up. Silence firmly swallowed a smile, and gestured for the two marine company commanders to join him. They approached at something just a little less than a run, eager for orders and a chance to do something before their men started fighting each other under the influence of drink and battle drugs. Silence nodded to them as they saluted and stood to attention.

'Get your men ready. Under the Lord High Dram's orders, I am sending both companies of marines into the Maze.' He looked at the commanders sharply, but they just looked calmly back, giving away nothing. Silence smiled grimly. 'In an ideal world we'd send in the remotes first, and check the Maze out from top to bottom from a comfortable distance, but apparently we don't have the time. I don't have to tell you to keep your eyes and ears open and your wits about you, but I want us all to be extra careful. There are bound to be hidden dangers and booby traps, either intrinsic to the Maze or left by the rebels. Either way, let's do our best to disappoint them, and avoid triggering anything we don't have to. I don't want to be up all night writing letters to your next of kin about why we're sending you home in a sealed coffin.'

'Who's going to lead the incursion?' said Frost.

'I am,' Silence said flatly. 'This is too important to leave to anyone else, and I don't want to hear arguments from you, Investigator.'

'Wouldn't dream of it,' said Frost briskly. 'Especially since I'll be going in with you for exactly the same reason. And I don't want to hear any arguments from you, Captain.'

Silence was about to answer her anyway when he realized the two commanders were watching the exchange with interest.

They had enough sense not to smile, but Silence glared at them anyway. 'Check your equipment and get your men ready. We'll be going into the Maze in ten minutes, and I don't want to hear any excuses. The Investigator and I will lead the way. I want all the espers to accompany us. No exceptions. If the Lord High Dram says anything, send him to me, and I'll officially ignore him. We'll leave the Wampyr behind to keep Stelmach and his pet company. Just in case. Any questions; and they'd better be important.'

'Yes sir,' said Commander Jameson. He was senior by a couple of months to Commander Farrell, and never let him forget it by always insisting on talking first. Silence hadn't heard a dozen words out of Farrell yet, but he lived in hope. Both commanders were supposed to be good men in a tight corner. Jameson looked straight ahead and kept his voice low. 'Will the Lord High Dram be accompanying us into the Maze, Sir?'

'The Lord High Dram . . . will make his own decision. No doubt he'll follow us in when he sees how very careful and professional we're being. Now get your men moving.'

The two commanders saluted, and hurried back to their men. There was a lot of shouting and milling about, but the marines were ready to go in an impressively short time. The Wampyr looked neither pleased nor displeased at being left behind. They gathered together near Stelmach and the Sleeper, and the alien and the Wampyr studied each other interestedly. Stelmach looked around for help, but Silence deliberately avoided his eye. The espers had formed a small group together before the entrance to the Maze, and were milling about there like frightened sheep, all wide eyes and abrupt movements. Frost looked at them thoughtfully.

'They don't like the Maze, do they? I can't help thinking we'd do well to listen to them, Captain. They see things we don't.'

'Unfortunately, I think you're right.' Silence scowled unhappily. 'I just hope this bunch hangs together better than the ones we had on Grendel.'

534

'Yeah,' said Frost. 'I'm still trying to get the blood and brains off my boots.'

Silence gave her a pained look, and strode over to the espers. They were so mesmerized by the Maze they didn't even notice he was there until he raised his voice. A few managed some kind of salute, but most of them couldn't even stand to attention with any success. Silence made allowances. You didn't expect military virtues from espers. They had other qualities. He nodded calmly to the man in charge, an esper named Graves. The name suited him. He was tall and painfully thin, with a bony face and slightly protruding eyes. Silence couldn't help thinking that he'd buried men who'd looked healthier than Graves, but the man had a good record for noticing things that others missed, and Silence was becoming more and more convinced that he was going to need every advantage he could get his hands on when it came to the Madness Maze. Just standing this close to the entrance was giving him gooseflesh. He would have liked to sigh heavily, but he couldn't afford to look weak before the espers.

Nothing had felt right since he arrived on the Wolfling World. Also known as Haden, though they hadn't bothered to tell him that till he got here. No one had even mentioned taking on an army of Hadenmen when he started this mission. Not that it made any difference. When you'd just been reprieved from a court martial at the very last moment, you went where the Empress sent you and if you had any reservations you kept them to yourself. Silence looked sternly at Graves, and the esper stared back like a mournful and slightly surprised fish.

'All right, Graves; what is it about the Maze that's got all of you so upset?'

'It's alive,' said Graves. His voice was flat but firm. 'We can hear the Maze thinking. Its thoughts are strange, and cold as ice. It knows we're here. It's waiting for us.'

Silence sighed, despite himself. He should have known better than to expect a straight answer from an esper. 'Now, Graves, are we being metaphorical here, or do you mean the Maze is some kind of cyborged lifeform?'

'More than that, Captain. Much more. It's not human life, or human technology.'

'Hadenmen?'

'Alien. It's been here a long time, Captain. Long before humanity ever came here. Constructed, not born, but still alive in every way that counts. It has its own purposes, and they are not human purposes or reasons. If we enter the Maze, we do so at peril of our lives and souls. There are powers between these metal walls, to change and transform us beyond human knowledge. And whatever survives the Maze won't be human any more. Or perhaps . . . more than human.'

'Did the rebels pass through the Maze?' said Silence. 'Did they survive it?'

'Yes, but . . .'

'But me no buts. If they did it, so can we. Anything else in the Maze I should know about?'

Graves stared at him dolefully, but hid any frustration well. Espers were taught to obey. 'There is a place, in the centre of the Maze, where we cannot see. A place we dare not look. There's something there; alive, powerful, but not part of the Maze.'

Silence frowned. 'What kind of alive? Human? Hadenman? Alien?'

'Unknown, Captain. We can't see. Something . . . prevents us. Possibly our own minds. I think if we were to look at it too closely, see it too clearly, we would all go mad.'

Great, thought Silence. *That's all I need. More complications.*

'We're going in,' he said briskly. 'I'll lead the way, with the Investigator, and I want you right there with us. Scatter the rest of your people throughout the marines. Leave a couple with their mind's eye cranked all the way open; if anything is going to happen, I want plenty of warning in advance. The rest can maintain an esper shield, tight as you can make it. I don't want a single stray thought getting out or in. Now get your people moving and motivated; we're going in in a few minutes.'

He strode away without waiting for an answer and rejoined Frost, who had her sword out and was running through a few loosening up exercises that would have intimidated the hell out of any enemy with half a brain. Silence didn't like being harsh with the espers, it felt uncomfortably like shouting at a child, and a frightened child at that. But if he wasn't harsh, there was a good chance they'd fall apart. Whatever they'd made contact with in the Maze, it had clearly disturbed the hell out of them. Hopefully, if they were scared enough of him, that should keep them from being too scared of the Maze. He looked back at the shimmering steel walls, and shuddered suddenly. Great. Now they'd managed to spook him too. He made himself concentrate on Frost, as she swept her sword through one vicious cut after another, and then was suddenly, smoothly at rest. Her pale skin had a healthy glow, and she looked like she could take on an army. Maybe she could, at that. She was an Investigator, after all. She nodded to him calmly, and hefted her sword.

'I'm ready, Captain. Can we make a start now?'

Silence had to smile. 'Doesn't anything ever worry you, Investigator?'

'No. Worrying is bad for you. It interferes with the digestion and gives you wrinkles. The greater the challenge, the greater the glory to be gained. At least, that's what the Empire always told us at the Academy. Or are you suggesting they lied to us?'

'The Empire, lying to its own people? Perish the thought. Let's go, Investigator. I want to get to the rebels before they can get to the Hadenmen.'

'Spoilsport,' said Frost.

And so, not long at all after they first arrived, Silence and Frost and the esper called Graves stepped cautiously into the Madness Maze, followed by a small army of marines and espers. The Maze swallowed them up without a murmur, and in a matter of moments they were lost to sight by those they'd left behind. Dram watched them enter, one after another, his face impassive, and he stood looking at the blank, enigmatic walls long after the last of the army had gone. Hidden under his long cloak, his hands had clenched into tight, white-knuckled fists.

At first, it wasn't too bad in the Maze. Each of the

shimmering metal walls looked just like any other, and whatever surprises the Maze had, it kept them to itself. Graves took the point almost immediately, his head held erect as though sniffing out the way. He chose each turn with unwavering confidence and concentration, and Silence and Frost followed close behind him. The Investigator had her sword and gun drawn, ready for use. Silence kept his hand near his gun, but didn't touch it. He didn't want his people to get the idea he was nervous. Bad for morale, not to mention discipline. His people were stretched out behind him, marines and espers looking equally uncomfortable. They stuck close together for comfort, and the sergeants had to keep warning them not to bunch up. There was little talking in the ranks. The heavy unbroken silence of the Maze didn't encourage conversation. If there was something coming, and the marines were increasingly sure there was, they wanted to be able to hear it in plenty of time. The espers concentrated on their mental shield, and tried not to think about the Maze at all.

It didn't take Silence long to decide he didn't like the Maze. He found its atmosphere oppressive, and the narrow paths between the shimmering walls began to seem uncomfortably claustrophobic, pressing in on him like the sides of a coffin. That last thought made Silence frown a little more. Enclosed spaces weren't something that usually bothered him. Living in the cramped confines of a starship quickly cured you of claustrophobia, or you got out of the service. But the Maze seemed somehow . . . overpowering, as though he was a rat scuttling through a scientist's maze he could never hope to understand or appreciate. It wasn't so much that the Maze seemed big, as that it made him feel so very small.

There was tension on the air, an approaching imminence, of something about to happen. Something bad, very bad. The air rippled with heat waves though it was bitterly cold. It smelled of vinegar and burning leaves. Oiled metal and old lemon, sharp on his tongue. Colours seemed very bright, and his distorted reflection in the steel walls seemed somehow wrong. Monstrously wrong. He could hear the chattering of metal birds, and babies screaming, and a single iron bell tolling far,

far away. Silence swallowed hard and tried to concentrate, but his thoughts were all over the place, and some of them didn't seem like his at all.

Graves stopped abruptly, and Silence almost crashed into him. He stopped too, and glared about him. Fisher moved in close beside him, sword and gun at the ready. Silence could sense the rest of his people stumbling to a halt. No one said anything, but the tension was so thick it was almost smothering. Silence looked up, but there was only an impenetrable darkness, as before. He looked back at the steel walls, and his stomach lurched as he realized that there were no longer any reflections of him or his people in any of the shimmering walls. Frost was breathing harshly at his side, almost grunting, quivering with the need for an enemy to throw herself at. Graves stared straight ahead, his eyes bulging even more than usual, fixed on something only he could see or sense.

'What is it?' Silence said harshly, forcing the words out. 'Booby trap?'

'It knows we're here,' said Graves, his entirely normal voice seeming almost painfully loud. 'It doesn't want us. We're too . . . inflexible. We're not capable of the changes it wants to make. We wouldn't survive the process.'

'How far from the next exit are we?' said Silence, making himself concentrate on what mattered. 'Are we far behind the rebels?'

'We have to go back, Captain.' Graves's voice was flat and uncompromising. 'It doesn't want us here. It's dangerous for us to be here.'

'What the hell are you talking about, esper?' snapped Frost. 'What do you see?'

Graves turned to look at her, and blood seeped suddenly out from under his eyelids, running thick and slow down his cheeks. Silence grabbed Graves by the arm, and it crunched up in his grasp as though there was nothing really there inside the sleeve any more. The esper folded up and fell slowly and gracefully to the floor, just an empty skin and so much blood.

Silence and Frost moved to stand back to back, their weapons in their hands.

There were screams all around them. Some didn't sound human. A marine came running towards Silence. He'd thrown away his weapons, and had both hands clapped tight to his ears, as though trying to block out some intolerable sound. He kept running even though Silence stepped into his path to stop him, and ran straight through Silence as though he was a ghost. Silence turned quickly to look behind him, but there was no trace of the marine anywhere. Silence put his back against Frost's again, turning round just in time to see an esper disappear, air rushing in to fill the vacuum where he'd been. Other espers were crying and laughing, their eyes wild and empty. A marine fell into one of the steel walls, and disappeared as it swallowed him up. Something horrible appeared in the midst of everything; a tangle of bone and blood and viscera that might have been human once. It disappeared with a wet smack as it reached out to Frost with a dripping hand. She shook her head fiercely, as a throbbing headache beat in her ears like a pulse. Her hands were trembling, but she still held on to her weapons.

Two marines slammed into each other and ran together like two colours on a palette, their sticky flesh intermingling beyond any hope of separating. They both screamed with the same voice. Silence wanted to shoot them, but he didn't. He might need the charge in his gun yet, if only to turn it on himself if it became necessary. Marines and espers were running in all directions now, strange and distorted as though space itself had become elastic where they were. And all around the unearthly sound of what used to be human voices laughing and screaming their sanity away.

A growing pressure built around Silence's mind, as though his head was in a vice. His fingers seemed to have too many joints, and he didn't trust his body any more. He gritted his teeth and squeezed his eyes shut, concentrating on his mission and his duty. Neither seemed too clear any more, or particularly important. He forced his eyes open and glared about him, desperate for some enemy he could identify or attack, but there was nothing. Just the dreadful steel walls, and his people dying. He looked back and saw Frost, fallen to her knees. She still had hold of her sword and gun, but her eyes were lost in a private hell.

Silence's thoughts swung into focus again. He grabbed Frost by the arm and hauled her to her feet, and if her arm didn't feel entirely human, well, neither did he. He had to get out of the Maze. Get Frost out of the Maze. He pointed his disrupter at the nearest wall and fired. The searing energy beam tore through the steel like paper, crumpling it up and throwing it aside. He holstered his gun and grabbed Frost's. She was muttering to herself, and her eyes were starting to see again. He aimed the gun at another wall, and it swung slowly backwards, opening up a path for him. He hurried back the way he'd come, as near as he could tell, dragging Frost along with him.

And only a few moments later he was staggering out of the Maze, hugging Frost to him, and Stelmach was hurrying forward to meet him. Silence handed Frost over to him, and then sat down suddenly as his legs gave out on him. Somebody was crouching beside him, and pressing a hypo against his neck. The cold hiss of the drug surging through his blood revived him a little, and his head began to clear. He realized Dram was standing over him, holding another hypo, and he forced himself to his feet again. He looked across at Frost, who was still sitting on the ground. Stelmach was leaning over her with an empty hypo in his hand, muttering reassuringly to her. Probably embarrass the hell out of her, once she was feeling better, but it seemed to be what she needed for the moment. He looked at Dram, standing beside him.

'How many others made it out of the Maze?'

'There haven't been any others,' said Dram. 'You two are the only ones. What happened in there?'

Silence shook his head, trying to force his thoughts into order. 'Some kind of esp attack. People went crazy. The whole Maze is one great booby trap.'

'Were the espers any protection?'

'No. They were the most susceptible of all.'

Dram nodded. 'Next time I tell you not to take espers somewhere, do as you're told, Captain.'

Silence looked at Dram. 'Did you know this was going to happen?' he said softly.

'No. But I had my suspicions. Now, what do you suggest, Captain? You've used up all your marines and espers, but we still have to get past the Maze to reach the rebels.'

Silence glared at the Maze. His mind was clear again. 'Get everyone back to the main pinnace. Have the pilot power up, with special attention to the weapons systems.'

Dram raised an eyebrow. 'Are we going somewhere, Captain? May I remind you of your orders, and the urgency of our mission . . .'

'I don't need reminding,' said Silence. 'I know what I'm doing.' He moved away from Dram to rejoin Frost, who was back on her feet again and looking more like herself. She nodded shortly to Silence.

'Thanks for getting me out, Captain. Things got a little fraught in there for a while. Give me a few minutes to catch my breath, and I'll take another stab at the Maze.'

'That won't be necessary,' said Silence. 'We're not going through the Maze again. I've got a better idea. Now come with me back to the main pinnace. And before you ask; no, we're not going anywhere.'

'Very well, Captain. May I ask who it was murmuring sweet nothings into my ear while I was recovering?'

'Valiant Stelmach, as it happens.'

'Ah. I really must thank him, when I have a moment. And also make it very clear that if he ever talks of it to anyone else, I will kill him.' She looked at Silence steadily. 'We're the only survivors, aren't we?'

'Yes. The others are all dead. If they're lucky.'

Frost nodded slowly. 'This is going to be one of those days, I can tell.'

It didn't take them long to get back through the forest to the main pinnace. The *Dauntless* had used its banks of disrupter cannon to blast a way through the frozen atmosphere and the planet's surface, to reach the hidden interior of the Wolfling World. After that it was simple enough to fly the pinnaces down the new tunnel, so they could blast an opening into the ancient caverns below. Silence led what remained of his people back through the dark forest to where the pinnaces lay waiting, and ordered them aboard the main pinnace. The long narrow ship was already powered up, all systems on line, and Silence felt a grim satisfaction as he ordered the pilot to move the ship slowly forward.

The pinnace's engines murmured threateningly as the craft rose a few feet into the air and then edged forward foot by foot. Silence sat stiffly in the bridge command chair, his eyes fixed on the viewscreen. The dark forest filled the screen, ancient and awesome. Silence studied it for a long moment, and then personally took control of the pinnace's weapon systems, and blasted a path right through the forest. Most of the trees disappeared in a moment, blown to nothing by disrupter cannon firing at point-blank range. The ship moved smoothly forward, hovering a few feet above the scorched earth. A few burning trees still stood at the extreme edges of where the forest had been, but nothing else remained between the pinnace and the Madness Maze.

Silence brought the ship right to the edge of the Maze, only a few feet short of the first shimmering steel walls, and held it there. The Maze looked back, silent and arrogant, holding within itself the blood and ghosts of murdered men. Silence sat back in his command chair, smiling coldly at the viewscreen. Frost stood silently at his side. Silence's hand moved to the fire controls. He might be too late to save his people, but he could still avenge them. The Empire scientists would be furious at the loss of such an important alien find, but Silence couldn't bring himself to give a damn. He grinned coldly, and opened fire.

The Maze was swept away almost instantly, its metal walls curling up and disintegrating like leaves caught in a flame-thrower. Silence shut down the disrupter cannon, and listened intently as his bridge crew gave him the new sensor readings. No trace of the Maze remained, leaving the Hadenman city beyond naked and defenceless. Air and temperature readings dropped to normal surprisingly quickly, but Silence felt he was owed some good luck.

He was the first to leave the pinnace and step out on to the blasted plain, and Frost was right there at his shoulder. The air was hot and dry, rasping in their lungs. There was nothing to show the Maze had ever been there. In the distance, the Hadenman city glowed softly in its own light, daring them to enter. Silence thought he just might. Frost chuckled softly.

'Don't mess with us; we've got the big guns. Nice shooting, Captain. Ever thought of becoming an Investigator?'

'A shame about the Maze,' said Dram, moving forward to join them. 'I would have liked to study it, but time is of the essence. The rebels must not be allowed to reach the Tomb of the Hadenmen. Will you lead the way, or shall I?'

'I lead,' said Silence. 'This is still my mission.'

He gathered up what remained of his people, a dozen technicians from the pinnace, the Wampyr, Stelmach and his pet, and led them across the bare plain towards the city. They all carried their guns at the ready, but nothing appeared to threaten them. The metal walls were gone, and with them the bodies of the fallen. Silence made a mental note to hold funeral services at a later date. The forms should still be observed, even if the bodies could not be recovered. And then he saw something, standing alone in the middle of the plain. He increased his pace, and soon they were all standing around a large glowing crystal, staring silently at the tiny human baby it held.

'Now that is interesting,' said Frost. 'Why didn't the pinnace's sensors pick this up?'

'To hell with the sensors,' said Silence. 'How did it survive the disrupter fire?'

'A force field of some kind,' said Dram.

'Right,' said Frost. 'A force field that our sensors didn't even know was there, and could stand up to point-blank energy cannon. Whoever left this baby here really didn't want its rest disturbed.'

'Leave it,' said Dram. 'It's not important. Only the rebels matter now.'

'Agreed,' Silence said reluctantly. 'Move on, people. Keep together when we hit the city, but don't get in each other's way. If you see anyone, and they're not us, open fire. We don't have any friends down here.'

Before the Maze went down, the five people who'd passed through it and survived stood at the edge of the Hadenman city, and began to discover just how much it had changed them. They all felt stronger, fitter, their thoughts unusually clear and lucid. Even the Hadenman was moved to say how well his various systems were functioning. They all looked at each other, waiting for someone to put into words what they were feeling, all of them strangely reluctant to break the mood of the moment, in case it might fade away if questioned. Finally Owen shook his head slowly.

'After everything we've been through, I should be out on my feet, but I feel like I could take on an army.'

'Right,' said Hazel. 'A large army. I feel . . . completely revitalized. Everything seems so . . .'

'Sharp,' said Ruby. 'Distinct. As though the world's suddenly come into focus for the first time. And the Maze; I understand . . .'

'Its function. Yes,' said Random. 'I only have to look at it, and I know what its purpose is. Evolution. Transcendence. Perfection. If we were to stay in it long enough, who knows what we might become. Have you noticed we're all ending each other's sentences? There's some kind of link between us.'

'Yes,' said Giles. 'There's a bond. I can feel it. Like esp, but deeper, more fundamental. We've changed. We're . . .'

'Different,' said Moon. 'Very different. You are now more than human, and I have become more than a Hadenman. Interesting. I wonder if the rest of my people also passed through the Maze, before entering their Tomb.'

'God, I hope not,' said Owen. 'That's all humanity needs; an army of super-evolved Hadenmen.'

'Whatever happens,' Moon said calmly, 'I think I can

guarantee that in the coming rebellion, my people will not be fighting on the same side as the Empire.'

'I'm not so sure I want you on our side, either,' said Owen.

'Damn right,' said Hazel. 'You guys made yourselves really unpopular the last time around. That's what comes of having a battle cry of *Death to Humanity*.'

'Empire propaganda,' said Moon. 'All we ever wanted was our freedom.'

'He's telling the truth,' said Random. 'I can feel it in him.'

'So can I,' said Ruby. 'It's like . . . seeing colours for the first time. Weird. Are we espers now, or what?'

'Definitely what,' said Owen. 'And whilst I believe Moon, he's been away from his people for a long time. People change. Giles; you're being very quiet. Something wrong?'

'The universe itself has changed since I last remember it,' said Giles. 'And now it seems I am undergoing fundamental changes too. Pardon me if I find this all rather disorientating.'

'We can talk about this later,' said Hazel. 'In the meantime, how about getting the hell out of here? The Empire forces can't be that far behind us.'

And then she stopped, and looked back at the Madness Maze. They all did, their new senses triggered by a sharp premonition of danger. They heard the roar of an approaching pinnace, and then the thunder of disrupter cannon. Owen started to shout a warning, and then the whole Maze exploded in a blinding flare of sleeting energies. The rebels moved together, instinctively, and a force shield formed around them, drawn from within themselves. And not even the battering storm of released energies could penetrate it. The force of the explosion died away, and the air slowly cleared. The Maze was gone, swept away in a moment. Where it had been, an Empire pinnace hovered. The force field dropped, and the rebels looked around with equal parts of surprise and shock. All around them, the Hadenman city had been shattered and torn apart like a child's building blocks scattered by a storm. Buildings had toppled or collapsed or been torn apart, and there was ruin and devastation for as far as they could see. A city that had stood for so long, torn down by an uncaring hand.

'And they call my people monsters,' said Moon.

'That could have been us,' said Owen. 'By all rights, we ought to be dead.'

'Our own personal force shield,' said Hazel. 'Now that is going to come in handy.'

'Not necessarily,' said Moon, his composure restored. 'We had to draw on our own collective energy to power it. We couldn't do it separately.'

'In other words,' said Random, 'we only have the shield for as long as we stick together. You think the Maze was trying to tell us something?'

'Considering that we are currently staring down the gun barrels of an Empire ship, I am quite prepared to listen,' said Ruby.

'Those cannon are useless until the energy crystals recharge,' said Giles. 'So their next step will be to send men out to check the ruins. And then we can show them just how powerful we have become.'

'Right,' said Hazel, her eyes lighting up at the thought. 'They don't know the kind of weapons we've got, either. This is going to be fun.'

'Hold everything,' Owen said suddenly. 'What happened to the Wolfling?'

They all stopped and looked at each other, and then around them, but there was no sign of him.

'Perhaps he moved on into the city,' said Giles.

They all looked at the ruins around them. Owen shook his head. 'Either way, it doesn't look too good for him, does it?'

And then they were all distracted by the sound of the pinnace landing, and turning off its engines. They all turned to look, hefting their weapons. A side door opened in the pinnace, a ramp lowered, and men came hurrying out. There didn't seem to be too many of them, but Owen's eyes narrowed in recognition.

'Wampyr,' he said quietly.

'And that man leading them is the Lord High Dram,' said

Ruby. 'Warrior Prime, and current favourite of the Iron Bitch.'

'No,' said Giles. 'That's not his name. Not his real name. I suppose it was inevitable that if I returned here, so would he.'

'What are you talking about?' said Owen. 'I recognize him. Everyone in the Empire knows who Dram is.'

'But I know who he used to be,' said Giles, and his mouth hardened into a thin, flat line. They all looked at him, but he had nothing more to say.

Wonderful, thought Owen. *More secrets.* And then Stelmach and his alien appeared, and Owen forgot about everything else. His mouth went dry as he looked at the creature, age old instincts stirring the hairs on the back of his neck. It wasn't just that the alien was huge and armoured with far too many teeth and claws; Owen could feel how dangerous it was, even at such a distance. His new senses hammered in his head like an alarm. It was like seeing death itself, walking cold and unhurried in the light of the pinnace, waiting only to be unleashed. Owen scowled. He'd never seen anything like it before, and could have done without seeing it now, but on the other hand, it had never come across anything like him, either. He was more than he was, and part of him itched for a chance to prove it in battle against a worthy opponent. He glanced at the others, who seemed equally fascinated by the alien.

'Anyone any idea what that thing is?' said Owen, trying hard to sound casual.

'Ugly,' said Hazel. 'Definitely ugly.'

'Right,' said Ruby. 'Let's kill it now, before things get hectic.'

'No,' said Owen immediately. 'We don't want to draw attention to ourselves. Not yet. Let them come a little closer, in range of our guns.'

'Sound thinking,' said Random. 'I don't know about the rest of you, but I feel like I could shoot the eye out of a fly's head.'

'He's right,' said Hazel. 'Look how far they are from us now; but I can see every one of them as clearly as if they were

548

just across the room. I think if I concentrated, I could probably hear them talking.'

'The Wampyr are in for a shock,' said Ruby. 'They think they're just up against humans. They may be adjusted men, but we're the new improved version.'

'Don't start getting cocky,' said Giles. 'We're still vastly outnumbered and outgunned. An energy beam doesn't care how superior you are.'

'You're forgetting the force shield,' said Hazel.

'No I'm not. That only works as long as we're together. What if we get separated? What if we can only use it a few times before it burns us out? There's a lot we don't know about our new selves, and that very definitely includes our limitations.'

'I agree,' said Moon. 'The odds are not good. We can't afford to rely on powers and abilities we don't fully understand yet. So; you people keep them busy, and I will press on to the Tomb of the Hadenmen. Only my people can help us now.'

And as suddenly as that he was off and running, darting silently between the rubble of devastated buildings before disappearing into the shadows. It was all over so quickly they didn't even have time to call after him before he was gone.

'Well that's just great,' Hazel said disgustedly. 'There goes our force shield, for a start.'

'And our greatest fighter,' said Random. 'I told you before; you can never trust a Hadenman to follow orders. They always have their own private agenda.'

'Let him go,' said Giles. 'At least we don't have to watch our back any more. The Empire forces are moving. We'd better find some cover before they get close enough to spot us.'

The rebels moved on into the devastated city, taking up positions behind fallen stones and in darkened doorways. They watched silently as the Empire forces moved slowly out across the bare plain where the Maze had once been, and their fingers curled impatiently round triggers. Owen hefted his projectile weapon uncertainly. He still wasn't sure how he felt about it. The gun had several obvious advantages, but when all was said and done it was no use at all against a force shield. That was why it had been superseded by the disrupter in the first place. But Giles had faith in them, and he was after all the original Deathstalker, the greatest warrior of his day. Owen sighed quietly, and sank back into his doorway. Guns were all very well, but those were Wampyr out there on the plain, a small army of them. Walking nightmares, fast and strong and unstoppable by anything except a direct hit. And then the Empire forces stopped, half-way across, and gathered round something they'd found. Even though Owen couldn't see it, he knew what it had to be. The Darkvoid Device, sleeping in its crystal, untouched by the vicious force that had swept the Madness Maze away so casually. Hazel stirred behind her pile of rubble, not far away.

'The Tomb of the Hadenmen isn't far from here,' she said quietly. 'I can feel it, on the edge of my mind. Cold and metal and unforgiving.'

'Right,' said Owen. 'Which means we can't allow any of these people to get past us. Moon is going to need all the uninterrupted time we can buy him, to wake his people.'

'I'm still not sure I like the idea of that,' said Ruby Journey, crouching behind an overturned brass pillar. 'I mean . . . Hadenmen.'

'I know what you mean,' said Random. 'But if there's one thing I've learned as a lifetime rebel, it's that you can't always choose your allies.'

'Keep your attention on the Empire forces,' said Giles, invisible in the shadows of a deep doorway. 'They'll be within range soon.'

'So will the Hadenmen,' said Ruby. 'Moon might be straight, but . . . We could end up with Wampyr in front of us, and Hadenmen behind, with nowhere for us to run.'

'Oh stop moaning,' said Hazel. 'Since when have you ever run away from a good fight?'

'It's the principle of the thing,' said Ruby. 'I like to have the choice.'

'You were never that hot on principles, either. The Madness Maze must have changed you more than we thought.'

Owen grinned, listening to the two friends squabble amicably. It was a moment of warmth and sanity in an increasingly insane situation. He'd come a long way from the young historian who'd just wanted to be left alone, happy in his obscurity on a backwater planet. Now here he was, allied with Wolflings and Hadenmen and living legends, planning to lead a rebellion against the greatest and most powerful Empire that humanity had ever known. Talk about delusions of grandeur. But looking back at the twists and turns his life had taken recently, there wasn't much he would have done differently. Except for the young girl he'd crippled on Mistworld. He'd see her face till the day he died.

Owen sighed, and settled himself more comfortably. Maybe the Hadenmen would arrive in time to save them from the Empire forces, and maybe they wouldn't. All he could do was fight to the best of his ability, and die well, if necessary. He thought about dying, but couldn't get worked up about it. He'd been close to death so many times already, in the past few hectic days, and that part of him which should have been scared was mostly numb now, like old scar tissue. Mostly, he missed all the things he'd never get to do, if he was killed here. Like finding and killing the man who'd murdered his father. Throwing the Iron Bitch off her throne. Getting to know Hazel. He liked the rough-edged ex-pirate. She didn't take any shit from anyone. And there was so much he could have learned from legends like Jack Random and Giles Deathstalker.

But he was where he was, with an enemy before him and an unknown factor behind him, and if he was going to die, he could at least die well, like a Deathstalker should. For all his faults, he'd always liked to think of himself as an honourable man. He smiled suddenly, as a thought struck him.

'Giles; assuming by some miracle we get out of this alive and more or less intact, how about we change our Family name to something a little more positive and upbeat? I mean, Death-stalker really is a bloody gloomy name, when you think about it.'

'Then don't think about it,' Giles said calmly. 'Deathstalk-er's a good name. I chose it myself. It's got style.'

'They'll never get it on your headstone,' said Hazel. 'Too many letters.'

'Heads up,' said Random. 'They're in range now. Won't be long before their sensors detect us.'

'Right,' said Ruby. 'I think the dance is about to begin. Choose your partners carefully, and don't do anything your mother would approve of.'

'All this time without a single smile, and now she develops a sense of humour,' said Random. 'And a twisted one at that.'

'Shut up and pick your targets,' said Owen. 'Let's see if we can get some of them before they can get us.'

'Damn right,' said Hazel. She stood up suddenly, gripped her biggest projectile weapon firmly and set it against her shoulder, and opened fire. The recoil sent her staggering backwards, but the spray of bullets swept across the massed Wampyr and knocked several of them off their feet. The rest of the Empire party quickly raised their force shields, and returned fire with their energy weapons. Hazel dived for cover, and Owen kept his head well down till the barrage was over. He counted to five, just in case, and then raised his head and snapped off a shot with his disrupter. It ricocheted from a force shield and disappeared off into the darkness. More energy bolts stabbed out from the rebel positions, to equal lack of effect. A force shield would go down if you hit it often enough with an energy bolt, but the rebels didn't have that much firepower, and the Empire forces knew it. They waited for the rebels' disrupters to fall silent, and then charged the rebel positions for some sword to sword contact before the energy crystals could recharge. And the rebels stood up and let fly with their projectile weapons.

The roar of the bullets caught the marines and the Wampyr by surprise. Some had even lowered their force shields, to save energy, and the bullets tore them apart with bloody thoroughness. The rest kept coming, sheltering behind their shields, desperate to get to close quarters, and fighting they understood. The security officer spoke to his massive alien companion, and it sprinted forward ahead of the rest, bullets ricocheting harmlessly from its silicon armour. Owen jumped out of his doorway to meet it, sword in hand, and the alien sent him sprawling with a casual backhand slap before running past the rebels and on into the city.

'It's gone after Moon!' said Hazel.

'Let it,' said Owen, sitting up. 'Moon's probably the only one of us who could take it anyway.'

And then the Empire forces were upon them, almost halved by the unexpected weapons, but just that much more furious and determined. The rebels rose from their hiding places, discarded the guns as too dangerous to use against force shields at close quarters, and went to meet the enemy sword in hand. At the end, it was what they knew and trusted. Steel rang on steel, and the air was full of the sound of conflict.

Owen found himself face to face with the Empire Captain, and they circled each other cautiously, searching for an opening. Their blades clashed together and then sprang apart, and they went back to circling each other, their eyes cold and focused. Hazel and the Investigator stood toe to toe and hammered away at each other with their swords, neither giving an inch. Around these two conflicts, the surviving Wampyr attacked the remaining rebels with savage strength and speed, and were astonished to find themselves met with equal force and fury. Jack Random, Ruby Journey and Giles Deathstalker had survived the Madness Maze, and they were as inhuman now as the Wampyr themselves. The old Deathstalker moved among the Wampyr with deadly speed, black blood flying from his blade. He was the first and foremost Warrior Prime of the Empire, brought to the peak of his potential, and no one could stand against him. He cut a vicious path through his foes, human and inhuman, killing with impunity, unstoppable, in his element at last.

Random and Ruby stood back to back, and fought on against a seemingly endless supply of enemies. Random felt like a young man again, strong and sure, his sword an extension of his will. It seemed to him he had never fought as well as he did now. Ruby fought with a savage controlled fury, cutting and hacking and ignoring the occasional blade that got past her defences. Random and Ruby were beyond pain or exhaustion now, fighting at the peak of their abilities, but in the end, it was not enough.

Gradually, foot by foot, they were driven apart, and surrounded by their enemies, like two lone wolves in the midst of a pack of snapping dogs. Random fought on, bloody from a dozen wounds that would have stopped a lesser man, his face calm and determined. There were bodies all around him, and eventually the inevitable happened, and he stumbled over one. The Wampyr surged forward from every side, sweeping aside his sword, and they brought him down. He fell hard, still lashing out with his fists as sword after sword pierced his body.

Ruby saw him fall, and screamed in rage and pain. Of them all, Jack Random had been the only one of the group she'd been impressed by. Her only hero. She would have died for Jack Random. She cut and hacked a path through the press of bodies, forcing the Wampyr back, to stand over Random's unmoving form and defy the Empire to take him from her. A disrupter beam from behind hit her squarely between the shoulder-blades, and she fell across Jack Random's body and lay still. Her cloak burned steadily over the hole in her back.

Tobias Moon moved swiftly through the dead city of the Hadenmen, and wondered that it seemed so strange to him. He had never seen the home of his people before, but even so he was a Hadenman, and had expected something about the city to be familiar, even welcoming. Instead, he passed between towering blocks of metal and stone whose shapes made no sense to him, gathered together in patterns that defied analysis. He had been among humanity too long, and had adopted their sense of beauty and meaning. He'd have to forget much of what he'd learned, if he was to live among his own people again. If they would have him.

Finally the buildings and structures fell away, and he came at last to the Tomb of the Hadenmen. It stood alone in a great natural cavern; a vast honeycomb of silver and gold, thickly encrusted with ice. Within its countless cells, thousands of augmented men lay waiting in their endless sleep. Waiting for him to awaken them, and unleash the Hadenmen upon humanity again. Moon stared steadily at the massive Tomb, and did not know what to do. Strange lights crawled back and forth among the individual cells, as though their occupants were dreaming fitfully of life, and Moon just stood there and watched them.

He always thought of himself as a Hadenman, because that was what people saw when they looked at him. They saw the golden glare of his eyes and heard the harsh buzz of his voice, and kept their distance even as they talked to him. And so he lived among humans for many years, with them, but not of them. Never one of them.

He remembered little of his time among his own people, in the last dying days of the Hadenman rebellion. He'd been quickened aboard ship, between planets, and his first memories were of fighting and battle on a world whose name he never learned. They lost that one, and had to run for their lives in sleek golden ships whose speed the Empire couldn't match.

Not long after, Moon's ship became separated from the main Hadenman fleet, and it was ambushed and shot down by Empire forces. It crashlanded on Loki, and Moon was one of the few survivors. He spent some time in hiding, living like an animal on what he could find or steal. He soon found that there were some kinds of human who had a use for a warrior like him, and so he passed from master to master, and planet to planet, until finally he ended up on Mistworld, like so many others, because there was nowhere else he could go. And there, his energy crystals mostly depleted, he lived among humans, as little more than a human. No one in Mistport cared about his past. They had their own horrors to forget.

And so he became just another face in the crowd, accepted as such, and learned to live as humans did.

And then the rebels came, and the chance to finally go home, to find the Tomb on lost Haden and be the saviour of his race, was just too great to turn down. He thought about the rebels, and became even more uncertain. Good fighters, all of them, for their differing reasons. They had treated him as one of them, sometimes even as a friend as well as an ally, and they were fighting and dying now to buy him the time to awaken his people. Even though the Hadenmen's first act might be to slaughter them all. Moon stared fixedly at the Tomb. He liked the rebels. They were brave and true, warriors all, committed to each other through blood and sacrifice and friendship. They felt like the family he'd never had, and always felt guilty for wanting, suspecting that was not a true Hadenman feeling. But they were humans, and he was not, and never could be. They were men and women, and he was not. Men and women had their sex cut away, along with every other irrelevance, when they became augmented men. Hadenmen were made, not born, constructed from raw materials, human and tech, as required. He wondered if his fellow rebels would still have wanted to be friends, if they'd known.

Perhaps they would. They were remarkable people.

But they were not his people. If he was ever to have the company of his own kind, the sense of belonging he had craved for so long, he had no choice but to awaken the Hadenmen from their Tomb. He moved steadily over to the control panels, set conveniently to hand, and began confidently to run through the quickening routines programmed into him so many years before. And even as his hands moved over the panels in response to implanted memories, he still found time to wonder whether his craving for his own kind was also programming, or a simple human emotion he had acquired along the way.

He'd almost finished when he sensed something behind him. His augmented hearing hadn't picked anything up, but his Maze-adjusted mind knew he was no longer alone. He spun round and found himself facing the alien he'd seen earlier with the Empire forces. It towered over him, flexing its clawed hands, huge in its spiked crimson armour. Ropy saliva ran from its grinning jaws, and smoked where it hit the floor. It occurred to Moon that a human might have been paralysed by terror, but his calm logical mind was already studying the hulking figure for possible weaknesses. He computed its probable strength and speed, based on obvious facts such as size and weight and proportion of muscle tissue, and came up with disquieting answers. He drew his disrupter from its holster and fired it in one blindingly swift movement, but the alien was no longer there. It had moved even faster than him, and dodged to one side.

Moon holstered his gun and drew his sword. It would take two minutes for the gun's energy crystal to recharge, and he had a strong feeling the fight would be over by then. Maybe he should have picked a projectile weapon after all. He smiled, and felt an almost human thrill at the thought of a real challenge, at last. Given time, he would have enjoyed studying the alien, its abilities and attributes, but it had to die. It was standing between him and the awakening of his people. He used the last of his remaining energy to revitalize as many of his built-in options as possible. New life surged through him, as though he himself was awakening from the long sleep of being human. Of being only human. Old systems, long unused, came on line again, and Moon grinned coldly. The alien was about to meet a real Hadenman, and find out why all the Empire feared them.

But he'd have to be quick, while the last of his energy lasted. He stepped forward, his sword a whistling silver blue on the air, and the alien couldn't move fast enough to evade him this time. Instead, it blocked the blow solidly with an upraised arm. The sword blade was tempered New Damascus steel, with an edge that could cut through solid stone, and backed by Moon's inhuman strength it should have neatly severed the alien's arm and left it twitching on the ground. Instead, it shattered on the alien's living armour. Moon paused for the merest moment, and then tossed the hilt aside as the alien went for his throat.

The two of them smashed together, strength and speed almost equal, driven by fury and instinct, two killers, each constructed to be the best. The clawed hands fastened around Moon's throat, and he grabbed the smooth slippery wrists with all his strength. For a long moment they stood facing each other, silently straining, and then Moon slowly pulled the hands away from his throat. Blood ran down his neck from puncture wounds left by the alien's claws. He suddenly relaxed his grip, stepped inside the alien's reach and slammed a punch into its midsection. It was a blow that would have shattered a human's bones, and finished the fight there and then, but the alien didn't even flinch. Moon's hand throbbed with pain. The alien wrapped him in a fierce hug, driving the air from his lungs, its dripping jaws reaching down for his face. Moon broke the alien's hold with an effort, and stepped back, breathing hard.

The alien lunged forward so quickly its form blurred in Moon's vision, and he consciously speeded up his thoughts and reactions. The cyborg and the alien surged around each other, moving inhumanly fast, fists hammering, claws cutting and tearing, and their different-coloured blood spattered the floor. Moon felt fast and strong and powerful, and not even the slightest trace of pain or fatigue bothered him, but he knew that was an illusion. He was draining his power cells at a dangerous rate to maintain that state, and if he didn't win the fight soon, he'd burn himself out and save the alien the job of killing him. So; when in doubt, cheat.

He concentrated, and the disrupter concealed inside his left forearm nosed out of the hidden slit in his wrist. The alien sensed something was wrong, and jumped back. Moon grinned coldly, and triggered the energy weapon. The searing beam punched a hole right through the alien's gut and out of its back. Moon darted in quickly to seize the advantage, but impossibly, the alien hadn't flinched. Its clawed hands snapped out and tore Moon's left arm out of its socket.

Moon staggered backwards, black blood gushing from the horrid wound at his shoulder, but already his augmented body was working to seal off the ruptured blood vessels, using the implanted steel webbing under his skin to self-cauterize the wound. He felt pain and shock, but only at a distance. He was still in control. He was a Hadenman. The alien looked at the twitching arm in its hands, and bit savagely into the muscle. It tore away a lump of flesh and chewed the meat thoughtfully. Moon glanced at the control panels behind him. He'd almost finished the wake-up routines when the alien arrived to interrupt him. A few last codes, and his people would awaken and save him. But he knew that if he turned away, even for a moment, the alien would jump him. His energy levels were almost depleted, and the wound had cost him dearly. He had to win the fight now, while he still could.

He plunged forward, automatically compensating for the loss of balance his wound caused, and the alien threw aside the half-eaten arm, and surged forward to meet him. Moon ducked under the reaching clawed hands, and punched his remaining hand into the hole in the alien's gut. The creature jerked spasmodically as he forced his hand in deep, searching for a vital organ. He was hurting it now. He could tell. And then the sides of the hole slammed together to grip his wrist firmly, holding it in place. Moon looked up into the alien's grinning jaws and crimson eyes, and knew, coldly and calmly and very certainly, that he'd made a mistake. The alien gripped Moon's head firmly with both long-fingered hands, and tore it off his shoulders.

Moon's body convulsed and collapsed, its hand still held in the alien's gut. The alien smiled into Moon's fading golden eyes, and then threw the head away. It rolled across the floor and bumped up against the control panels. And with the last few moments of his sight, Moon watched with a cold, despairing hate as the alien began to devour his body. And then there was only darkness, and his thoughts fading away as the last of his energy ran out.

Giles Deathstalker and the man now known as Dram came together in the middle of the battle, and on Dram's signal the Wampyr drew back to give them room. Blood dripped thickly from Giles's blade, but Dram's was spotless. He had held back till then, waiting for the best moment to commit himself. Giles stood surrounded by dead bodies, marines, technicians and Wampyr, bleeding from many superficial wounds but still defiant. He grinned suddenly.

'I should have known you'd be here. You always had to be in at the kill, didn't you? You learnt that much from me, at least. You're looking good, Son.'

'I look after myself,' said Dram. 'I had a lot of practice at that, while you were off running around the Empire, playing

Warrior Prime. And since you weren't there to be a father to me, I occupied myself by studying the great game of politics and intrigue at the Imperial Court. All the plots and plans and manoeuvrings you could never be bothered with. Just like you could never be bothered with me. I've become everything you ever hated, Father, and you don't know how warm that makes me feel inside.'

'You were an unnatural child,' said Giles. 'You broke your mother's heart, and you would have broken mine, if I'd let you. For a long time I thought you were dead. I paid the assassin enough. But I never did see the body. I assume you slept the years away in stasis, like me?'

'Oh yes, Father. I wanted to be here waiting for you, when you finally reappeared. The Empress Lionstone found and awakened me, and I've spent the last few years amusing myself by acquiring every honour you ever had, and more. I'm Warrior Prime now, and official consort, and one day not too far off, I'll be Emperor. And the Empire you helped make and believed in so fiercely, will kneel down and fear me. But don't worry, Father. I won't forget you. I'll keep your head in a glass case by my throne, so I can look at it every day, and laugh.'

'You always did talk too much,' said Giles. 'Are you going to talk me to death, or shall we fight?'

'Oh we're going to fight, Father. I've been looking forward to this for a long time. And don't worry; if I look like losing, my people will kill you anyway.'

'You never did have any honour.'

'And you always had too much. Time to die, old man. I'm going to put you out of my misery.'

As suddenly as that they slammed together, blades flashing, attacking and parrying and leaping apart, all in a moment. Sparks flew where their swords met, and the air was full of the ring of steel on steel. They stamped back and forth, grunting with the effort of their blows, and slowly, foot by foot, Giles was driven back. He'd already taken enough wounds to kill a lesser man, and Dram was fresh and unhurt and a great deal younger. They fought on, oblivious to what was happening in the fighting around them, two sides of a blood feud begun nine hundred years before.

Dram fought with a cold, grinning fury that poured strength into his blows, and Giles's arm was already tired from fighting the unnatural strength of the Wampyr, but in the end he was the Deathstalker, and Dram was not. Giles deliberately left an opening, and Dram lunged forward, his sword punching into Giles's left side, just below the ribs. Giles's left hand shot out and grabbed Dram's wrist, holding the blade in place. Dram tried to jerk his blade free, and couldn't. Giles allowed him just enough time to realize that, and for the fear to grow in Dram's eyes, and then he thrust his own sword into his son's heart. Giles smiled into the dying eyes as the light went out of them, and then pulled back his sword and let Dram's body fall unmoving to the ground. Giles carefully eased Dram's sword out of his side, let it drop, and looked challengingly around him.

Most of the Empire forces were dead or dying, but a handful of Wampyr stood watching him thoughtfully. Beyond them, Owen and Hazel were still duelling with Captain Silence and the Investigator. Honours looked about even. Giles drew his disrupter and shot one of the Wampyr. The energy beam tore right through its chest, and the force of the blow threw it off its feet. It lay still among the bodies, and the other Wampyr studied it for a moment, as though expecting it to get back up. When it didn't, they turned their dead faces back to Giles, and formed a circle around him. They took their time. They knew he had nowhere to run. Giles swallowed hard, and tried to control his harsh breathing. If he didn't finish the fight soon, he'd bleed to death before they could kill him. He could feel the blood coursing down his left leg from the ugly wound in his side. The Wampyr studied it hungrily, and Giles shuddered in spite of himself. He was tired now and feeling his age, and after all, six Wampyr would have been a bit much for him, even in his prime.

'Owen!' he yelled harshly. 'Stop playing with that man, and get after Moon. He's been gone too long. Something must have happened to him. We need the Hadenmen!'

Owen cursed silently. He'd already used practically every trick he knew, and the Captain was still beating him. But there was one thing he hadn't tried. Hazel had taught it to him. He'd avoided using it up till now because it was a frankly dishonourable way to win, but right then, losing struck him as even less honourable. He went blade to blade with Silence, glaring at the Captain over the crossed swords, and brought his knee sharply up into Silence's groin. The Captain's sword wavered as his eyes squeezed shut involuntarily. Owen beat the blade aside, grabbed a handful of Silence's tunic, and head-butted him in the face. Silence fell to his knees, blood streaming from a broken nose, and Owen turned and ran for the Tomb of the Hadenmen. The last thing he saw was the Wampyr closing in around Giles, and the Investigator driving Hazel back with a flurry of blows. He didn't look back again. He didn't dare.

Owen found Moon easily enough. The augmented man's body was lying on the blood-drenched floor, before the Tomb of the Hadenmen. The alien was squatting over him, tearing out handfuls of his exposed guts and feasting on them. It looked up unhurriedly as Owen entered, red strands hanging from its grinning steel teeth. Owen drew his disrupter and fired, but even with his new speed, the alien dodged the beam easily. Owen drew the projectile gun from his belt, and the alien surged towards him. Owen got off two shots, both of which ricocheted harmlessly from the alien's armour, and then the huge beast was upon him.

There was no time to draw his sword, and Owen staggered backward, grasping the alien's wrists with both hands to keep the clawed hands away from his throat. The beast towered over him, its bloody teeth diving for his face. Owen released his hold, slumped down and threw himself forward between the alien's legs. He hit the ground rolling and was quickly back on his feet, drawing his sword. The alien spun round to face him, and Owen met its cold grin with his own. He thought of Hazel and Giles, left to face the Empire forces alone, of Ruby and Random left for dead, and of Moon, dying so close to everything he dreamed of, and rage swept through him, cold and fierce and unrelenting. In that moment, the alien represented everything the Empire had done to try and destroy him, and those he cared for. He'd been unable to boost while facing the Captain. In using the boost to throw off Ozymandias's mental control, he'd used up so much of himself he hadn't dared use it again. But now he didn't give a damn. The alien had to die, so that he could wake the Hadenmen, and save Hazel and Giles. Nothing else mattered. The alien swept forward, and Owen boosted and went to meet it sword in hand. He was a Deathstalker, and the alien was about to find out what that meant.

He swung his sword at the alien's neck with all his boosted strength, and the blade shattered against the unyielding armour. The alien's hands shot out and fastened on to his shoulders. The claws sank deeply into his flesh and grated on bone. The creature tried to pull him closer, within reach of its horrid jaws, and Owen punched the hand still holding the stub of his sword against the alien's chest. His boosted muscles strained against the alien's strength, but still he was pulled closer, inch by inch. Any other man would have been dead by now, and even with his boost and what the Maze had done to him, Owen was still a man, and saw his death in the alien's unblinking crimson eyes.

He glanced down at the hole in the alien's gut. At least Moon had hurt it. An idea came to him, and he acted on it quickly before he could think about the implications too much. He grabbed a grenade from his pocket, primed it, and thrust it deep into the hole in the alien's gut. He let go of it, but before he could withdraw his hand, the sides of the hole clamped shut on his wrist. Owen tried to pull free and couldn't. So he gathered all his boosted strength, and cut down savagely with the stub of blade in his other hand. The jagged steel tore through his wrist, severing his hand, and Owen threw himself backwards, out of the alien's reach. It brought its clawed hands to the hole in its gut, and the grenade, still wrapped in Owen's hand, exploded.

White hot flames burned the alien inside and out, and the

internal pressure blew the grinning head right off its shoulders. The body staggered back and forth for a long moment, its arms reaching out blindly, and then the strength went out of it suddenly, and it fell to the floor and lay still.

Owen squeezed the stump of his wrist tightly with his other hand, shuddering uncontrollably. The blood jetted out at first, far further than he'd have thought possible, but it soon died away to a bare trickle. There was something he had to do. Something important. His eyes wandered back and forth, and finally stumbled over Moon's decapitated head, lying by the control panels. Owen shuffled forward on his knees, still tightly gripping his wrist. The Hadenmen. He had to wake the Hadenmen. Hazel was depending on him. He reached the control panels and used them to pull himself to his feet. He leaned on them tiredly for a moment, spattering them with blood from his dripping wrist, and studied the controls. They made no sense to him at all. He glared down at Moon's head, stooped down and picked it up with his remaining hand, so he could glare into its empty eyes.

'Moon, you bastard! What do I do? How do I awaken them? Tell me!'

A faint golden glow appeared in Moon's eyes. His lips moved, and Owen lifted the head so that its mouth was by his ear. And very softly he heard Moon whisper *Blue three seven seven zero*. Owen dropped the head and turned back to the panels. His lips were pulled back in a savage grin as he located the blue panel and punched in three seven seven zero. He turned away from the panels to look at the Tomb of the Hadenmen, and cawed harshly with laughter as the ice melted and ran away, and light after light blazed in the cells of the giant honeycomb. He was still laughing when the cells opened, and the Hadenmen came forth in all their power and glory.

Not all that long after, Owen sat quietly beside the dead Wampyr while Hazel fashioned a makeshift tourniquet around his left wrist. The wound seemed to have sealed itself, another legacy of the changes the Maze had wrought in him, but Hazel wasn't taking any chances. Giles was talking quietly with

Captain Silence and Investigator Frost, disarmed and under guard by half a dozen unsmiling Hadenmen. Jack Random and Ruby Journey lay side by side on stretchers, also talking quietly. The Hadenmen had got to them while sparks of life still remained in them both, and repaired the damaged bodies with impressive speed. Ruby and Random were still very weak, and would be for some time to come, but apparently they were expected to make a full recovery. Owen made the Hadenmen examine Moon, but they said it was too late for him. Owen told them how Moon had come back from the shores of death to give him the necessary codes to awaken them, and they nodded politely and told him to rest.

He'd half expected the augmented men to kill him when they first emerged from their Tomb, but for the moment at least, they couldn't do enough for their saviour. They were tall and perfect and moved with inhuman grace, their eyes blazing like suns. They stopped the fighting in time to save Giles from the three remaining Wampyr. Hazel and Frost had practically duelled each other to exhaustion, and had to be almost pried apart, but the Investigator had still wanted to fight on when she saw the Hadenmen. In the end, Silence had to order her to give up her sword. And as easily as that, it was all over.

Owen looked at the body of the Lord High Dram. Giles had gone to kneel beside it, the moment the Hadenmen had led the three Wampyr away. He looked up when Owen joined him, and said simply *Grieve, kinsman. One of our Family is dead.* He hadn't explained any further, and Owen hadn't pressed him. It could wait. Lots of things could wait now. He looked across at Ruby and Random, as Random turned his head slowly to smile at her.

'Looks like we'll get to be part of the great rebellion after all. I wouldn't have put money on it. Still; think of the glory.'

Ruby sniffed. 'Think of the loot.'

'That too,' said Jack Random.

Owen would have liked to laugh, but he didn't have the strength. Hazel finished fussing with the tourniquet, and looked at him sternly.

'You should really dive into that regeneration machine of yours, or let the Hadenmen repair you.'

Owen shook his head. 'I don't trust that machine after what Oz had it do to us. Who knows what other mental traps he might have programmed into it, or us? And I'm not sure I trust the Hadenmen that much. My body will heal itself, in time. I can feel it. Now help me up, there's a dear. I want to talk to the Captain.'

Hazel got him to his feet, and he walked more or less steadily over to Silence and Frost. Giles nodded, and moved off to stand by Dram's body. The Investigator glared at Owen coldly, but the Captain inclined his head slightly. The Hadenmen had repaired his nose, but there was still a massive dark bruise between his eyes.

'You're really not very impressive, Deathstalker, to have led the Empire such a chase.'

'I'll try harder,' said Owen. 'Now pay attention. You and the Investigator are being allowed to return to the Empire alive for a reason. We want you to tell the Iron Bitch that the rebellion has begun. The next time she sees us, we'll be leading an army specifically put together to kick her off the Iron Throne. Make her believe it, Captain. I want her to have plenty of time to squirm.'

'What about the Wampyr?' said Silence. 'They're a bit strange, but they're still my crew.'

'They're staying here. The Hadenmen are fascinated by them. Why did you destroy the Maze, Captain?'

'It was necessary. It was killing my people.'

'You don't know what you've done. It was a place of miracles, of possibilities. The future of humanity.'

'What future has humanity got, if you lead the Hadenmen against the Empire?' Frost said harshly. 'You might as well side with Shub.'

'The Hadenmen . . . are not at all what I expected,' said Owen. 'The Empire has lied about many things. Maybe it lied about them too. But don't worry. I'll keep an eye on them.'

'And what could you do to stop them?' said Silence.

'You'd be surprised,' said Hazel. 'The Maze changed us, Captain. We're a lot more than we used to be.'

'It's time for change,' said Owen. 'The Empire is corrupt from top to bottom. I can vouch for that personally.'

'Think about what you're doing, Deathstalker!' Captain Silence took a step towards him, and then stopped as everyone's hand went to their gun. He made himself speak calmly and evenly. 'The Empire is currently under threat from two separate alien species, each of them possibly more technologically advanced than we are. Humanity itself is at risk. This is no time to fragment our attention and waste our resources.'

'There'll never be a better time,' said Hazel. 'Who knows; maybe the aliens will side with us.'

'You damned fools,' said Frost. 'I've seen one of the aliens. It made that creature the Deathstalker killed look like a wet-nosed pup.'

'Then we'll deal with it when it appears,' said Hazel. 'Tell the Iron Bitch we're coming, Investigator.'

'And when you get there, I'll be waiting for you,' said Frost. 'I'll enjoy sticking your head on a pike, traitor.'

Owen looked at Silence. 'Is she usually this cheerful?'

Silence nodded solemnly. 'This is restrained, for her.'

They found themselves sharing an understanding look, while Hazel and Frost stared at them blankly.

'Don't judge us too harshly, Captain,' said Owen. 'We've been through a lot, just recently. Lionstone has to fall. If it wasn't us, it would be someone else. Maybe even someone like you, Silence.'

'Never,' said Silence.

'Everybody stand exactly where you are!' said a loud shrill voice in all their ears. 'This is Security Officer Stelmach, on the bridge of the *Dauntless*'s main pinnace. I have the forward disrupter cannon aimed right at you! All rebels will give up their weapons immediately, or I'll open fire!'

'I wondered what had happened to him,' said Frost.

'Can I just point out,' Silence said reasonably, 'that if you open fire on them, you will also kill me and the Investigator?'

'You're expendable,' said Stelmach.

'Somehow I just knew he was going to say that,' said Frost.

'You see?' said Hazel. 'This is the kind of thing we've been talking about.'

'Hold on just a minute,' said Owen. 'Who's this Stelmach? Did we miss one?'

'Apparently,' said Hazel. 'And as a result, we are now staring down the barrels of a whole bunch of disrupter cannon. Any ideas?'

'Don't hurry me,' said Owen. 'I'm thinking.'

'I didn't come this far just to die now,' said Hazel. 'What say we rush him?'

'After you,' said Owen.

'There's got to be something we can do!'

'I'm open to suggestions,' said Owen. 'We can't get at him, and he's got the big guns.'

'Looks like your rebellion just came to a sudden halt, traitor,' said Frost. 'Hand over your weapons, and I promise you'll live long enough to face trial and execution on Golgotha.'

'I'd rather rush him,' said Owen.

'Relax, everybody,' said a different voice in all their ears. 'This is Wulf, on the pinnace. I've just taken control of the weapons systems away from the somewhat excitable gentleman who was in charge. He's currently having a little lie down.'

'Who the hell's Wulf?' said Frost. 'Did we miss one?'

'Apparently,' said Silence.

'All right, Wulf,' said Owen. 'What happened to you?'

'I had my own business,' said the Wolfling calmly. 'I've been through it before. By the time I realized you were in trouble, it was all over bar the shouting. Luckily, I decided to see if there was anything useful I could do on the pinnace.'

'Well, now that our hearts have all started beating again,' said Owen, 'hand your prisoner over to the Hadenmen. I think you'd better stay aboard the pinnace until it's ready to leave, and make sure the fire controls are taken off-line before we let the Captain or the Investigator anywhere near it. I don't think I could stand another surprise at the moment.'

'Understandable,' said the Wolfling.

Owen sighed heavily, and looked around to see Giles beckoning to him. He moved over, with Hazel at his side. Giles looked at him sternly.

'You still have a decision to make, kinsman. What are you going to do about the Darkvoid Device? Will you use it against the Empire? Will billions die again?'

'You created it,' said Owen. 'And you used it. What do you think we should do?'

'No,' said Giles. 'I won't make that kind of decision, ever again. I can't.'

'Then I say no,' said Owen. 'You can't fight evil by becoming evil. Too many have died already. If I've become a rebel and a traitor against the Empire, it's to save and protect lives, not to take them. But we won't destroy the baby either. Let it sleep. And who knows; perhaps, in years to come, it will grow into something wonderful.'

'Well done, aristo,' said Hazel. 'You finally got it right.'

They smiled at each other, and then Owen looked away, at the perfect Hadenmen, emerging from their devastated city; last survivors of a previous rebellion. Things would be different, this time. He was the Deathstalker, and he had finally found his true destiny.

More or less.

CHAPTER FOURTEEN

Prelude to Rebellion

Captain Silence and Investigator Frost returned to the *Dauntless* on the pinnace, along with an unconscious Valiant Stelmach. They didn't speak to each other on the way up, but once back on the bridge of the *Dauntless*, Silence immediately began preparations for an attack on the Wolfling World. Only to find that none of his weapons systems were functioning. Something on the planet below had rendered them useless. Silence and Frost exchanged a long look, and then Silence gave the order to return to Golgotha. They would spend much of the trip home trying to put together some kind of report that wouldn't get them both executed on the spot.

Deep within the frozen Wolfling World, the devastated city of Haden slowly came to life again. The Hadenmen were everywhere, beautiful and perfect, working and repairing and making all things new again. Ruby Journey and Jack Random slowly recovered from their injuries, and spent the time plotting strategies and revenges against the Empire. Owen Deathstalker mourned the death of his friend Ozymandias, but found the time to deepen his friendship with Hazel d'Ark. They still argued a lot, though. Mostly over politics.

Giles, the original Deathstalker, mourned the death of his son, in his own way, and brooded over the corrupt state of the Empire. He had learned much of present affairs from his new companions, but nothing that pleased him. The Empire hadn't always been as it was. Once, when he was a young man, it had been the greatest challenge of humanity; a dream of human destiny. But even in his own lifetime he had watched the dream become a nightmare, and had slept through centuries only to find that things had grown even worse in his absence.

The Wolfling regretted the destruction of his Hall of the Fallen, but remained undecided as to whether he would join the rebellion. He had seen enough death and destruction in his time, and had no appetite for any more.

Back on Golgotha, the Empress Lionstone XIV silently studied the instruments that had told her of the Lord High Dram's death. He hadn't known about the implants she had placed in him. She hadn't wanted to worry him with details. But she liked to know where those close to her were at any given time. Now the instruments were dead, which meant he was too. She had loved him, in her way, but she didn't mourn. Instead, she began the process of reviving a clone of Dram she'd prepared earlier. Just in case.

In the subsystems, Finlay Campbell and Evangeline Shreck made plans with the esper and clone undergrounds, and the uber-esper Mater Mundi, to revenge those who died storming Wormboy Hell, and see the Empress and her Empire brought down. Whatever it took.

Valentine Wolfe extended his control over his Family, experimented with a few new drugs, and opened negotiations with the rogue AIs on Shub. Lord Kit SummerIsle, also known as Kid Death, became a close friend of Lord David Deathstalker. In the Matrix, things came and went, and only some of them were observed.

The tides of power and influence shifted this way and that. The stage was set, the players in place.

The rebellion could begin.

Also available in Vista paperback

Deathstalker Rebellion
SIMON R. GREEN

The second volume in the epic adventure series.

At the heart of the galaxy-spanning tyrannical Empire lies Golgotha, the planet of the Iron Throne. Once it was impregnable. Now . . . the Iron Bitch may have made a fatal mistake. In outlawing Owen Deathstalker, she has woken a lust for revenge in a quiet man – and unwittingly created a focus for a galaxy full of hatred for her loathsome rule.

At last the espers and the clones, the AIs and the freaks, the innocent and the damned alike, have someone to look to, someone to lead the

DEATHSTALKER REBELLION

And then, the killing begins . . .

ISBN 0 575 60011 X

Deathstalker War

SIMON R. GREEN

The third volume in the epic adventure series.

Owen Deathstalker, last of his line, was wrongly
outlawed by the evil Empress Lionstone XIV . . .
but in making an enemy of Deathstalker, the Iron
Bitch sowed the bitter seeds of revenge. Now the
rebellion Deathstalker has been fomenting has
blossomed into war.

Opening skirmishes on Mistworld, Haceldama
and Virimonde reveal just a few of the horrors the
Iron Bitch is prepared to unleash upon the rebels,
but the opposition only fuels their determination
to win justice.

This time it's war.

DEATHSTALKER WAR

No quarter, no prisoners, no compromises.

ISBN 0 575 60061 6

A Land Fit for Heroes

PHILLIP MANN

Britannia, 1993.

In a world where the Roman legionaries never left Britain a man can walk from the walls of York – or Eburacum – to the southern seas without leaving the shade of the greenwood, inhabited by wildcats, wolves and bears, as well as by the descendants of the folk who built Stonehenge. Solar-powered air cars journey along straight roads that connect the Roman settlements – and link them to the cities of a global empire.

But outside the confines of the cities, within the great forest, the ancient mystic culture of the Britons still survives. And from there, the mighty grip of Rome is about to be challenged at last – and changed for ever.

'Strange but quite beautiful' *New Statesman*

Vol 1: Escape to the Wild Wood ISBN 0 575 05716 5
Vol 2: Stand Alone Stan ISBN 0 575 05932 X
Vol 3: The Dragon Wakes ISBN 0 575 60012 8
Vol 4: The Burning Forest ISBN 0 575 60070 5

The Knights of the Black Earth

MARGARET WEIS
and
DON PERRIN

The cyborg Xris once held a prized position as a top human agent of the Federal Intelligence Security Agency . . . but that was before his mission to infiltrate a Hung munitions plant had gone disastrously wrong, leaving one partner dead, one missing and Xris no longer quite human.

For eight years, an all-consuming need for vengeance has kept Xris alive – that, and one name: Dalin Rowan, his erstwhile partner.

But just when Xris and his Mag Force 7 team of crack mercenaries get a lead on the elusive Rowan, a new obstacle appears: the fanatical Knights of the Black Earth, who are plotting to sabotage the galactic government and revive Earth supremacy – and Xris is in the way.

'Unexpectedly subtle yet filled with fast-paced action, this above-average space opera will please Weis's many fans' *Publishers Weekly*

ISBN 0 575 60037 3

Mortal Remains

CHRISTOPHER EVANS

The Solar System is ours. Biotechnology has provided the Settled Worlds with a riot of habitable environments; sentient craft ply the routes between the planets; the souls of the dead live on in the Noosphere, a psychic Net where they can be contacted by the living.

Paradise? Not quite – and when a strange womb is recovered from a living spaceship crashed on Mars it swiftly becomes the focus of intrigue and murder as the Settled Worlds begin to disintegrate under the strain of a vicious interplanetary war between two rival factions.

'This cunningly subversive novel is . . . a terrific romp through a densely constructed future . . . rewarding and revealing' Paul J. McAuley, *Interzone*

ISBN 0 575 60043 8

VISTA paperbacks are available from all good bookshops or from:

> Cassell C.S.
> Book Service By Post
> PO Box 29, Douglas I-O-M
> IM99 1BQ
> telephone: 01624 675137, fax: 01624 670923